❧ PART ONE ❧
BLOOD UNION
BLOOD GRACE BOOK V

VELA ROTH

Meigan,

Enjoy your travels
with the Hesperines!

Vela Roth

8/22

FIVE THORNS PRESS

ISBN 978-1-957040-12-7 (Ebook)
ISBN 978-1-957040-16-5 (Paperback)
ISBN 978-1-957040-17-2 (Hardcover)

Edited by Brittany Cicirello, Suncroft Editing

Cover art by Patcas Illustration
www.instagram.com/patcas_illustration

Book design by Vela Roth

Map by Vela Roth using Inkarnate
inkarnate.com

Published by Five Thorns Press
www.fivethorns.com

Visit www.velaroth.com

CONTENTS

For the coven.
I thought this would be the first book I wrote alone.
Instead, it was the first book I wrote with you.
Thank you for being my author family.

CONTENT NOTE

BLOOD UNION Part One portrays a character healing from her father's emotional abuse. She confronts painful emotions and memories, including a traumatic flashback in "Friends in High Places" (69 Days Until Notian Spring Equinox).

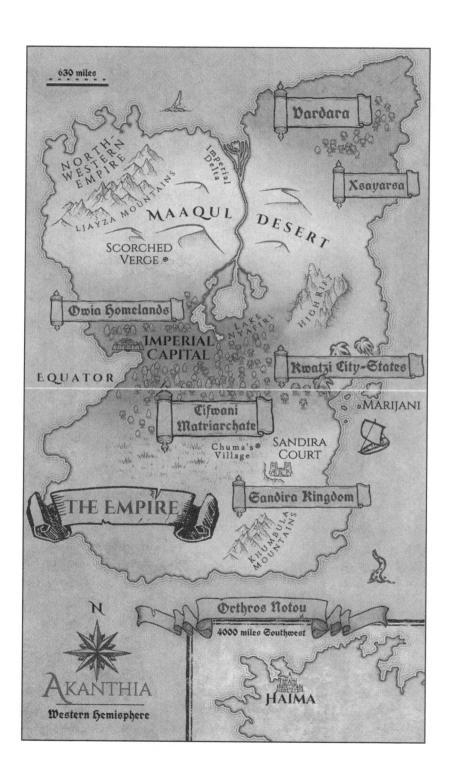

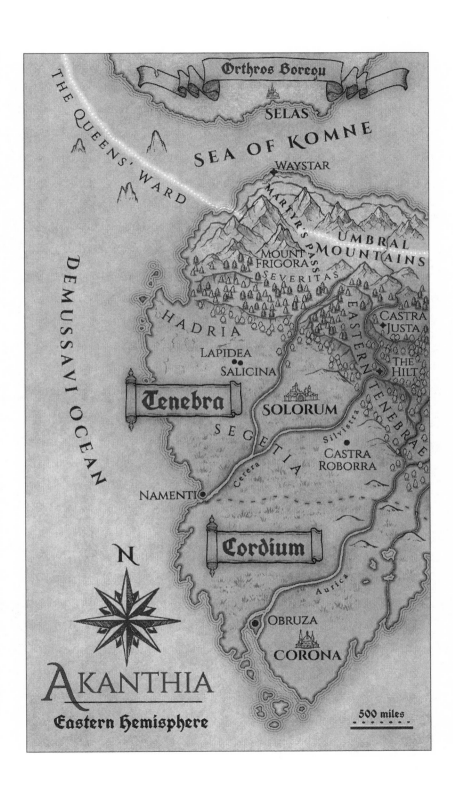

⚜42⚜

nights until

BOREIAN SPRING EQUINOX

12th Night of the Month of Khariton
1,596th Year In Sanctuary (IS)

READY OR NOT

THESE WERE THE LAST hours Cassia would ever spend as a mortal. She had survived the twenty-two years of her human existence. Tonight it would end, and her life would begin.

Before this night was through, she would have fangs, magic...immortality. She would be a Hesperine.

At last. Her Gift Night had arrived.

"Your heart is pounding." Lio touched a hand to her chest.

She looked up at his handsome, beloved face. He was at her side, just like every night since she had come here to Orthros, leaving her old life in Tenebra behind. He would be at her side every night from now on. Forever. "I almost can't believe it. We made it this far. It's finally happening."

The front doors of House Komnena stood open before them, waiting for Cassia to make her grand entrance to her Gift Night celebration. Spell light and familiar voices, happy music and the aromas of her favorite foods spilled out into the night. The grand white marble edifice of Lio's bloodline was filled with guests.

Her home, her bloodline, her family and friends. All gathered here tonight for *her*.

Lio leaned down and gave her a tender kiss on her lips. She sensed his veil spell close and reassuring around them. She knew his concealing magic was the only reason no one spotted them and pulled them into the celebration.

Lio ran his hand up and down her back in soothing strokes. "We don't have to go in until you're sure."

"Of course I'm sure." She swallowed.

Her hound stood near, concerned and attentive. Knight's shaggy fur would soon be all over her and Lio's formal silk robes, but the shedding was just more evidence of his comforting presence.

"Is there anything else you wish to do first?" Lio asked.

"I've had weeks to prepare. And if we wait any later in the season, there won't be enough time for my seclusion before we leave for Orthros Notou on Migration Night."

She glanced up at the bright stars overhead. Orthros's astrologers assured her that tonight's celestial portents were auspicious for a Gifting. Even the martyrs' constellations agreed that she was ready. So why were her palms sweating in her silk gloves?

"Come." She took Lio's hand. "Everyone is waiting for us."

He tugged her closer. "The entire world can wait for as long as you need. This is your Gifting. This night is for you. You don't have to take a single step until you are certain and comfortable."

He adjusted her cloak and kept holding her. The garment might be enchanted to protect mortals from the cold of Orthros, but Lio's embrace was her true warmth. She knew he would stand there with her in the polar night for however long it took her to feel ready.

She leaned into him. "I love you."

"And I love you, my rose."

"It has to be tonight, Lio. I can't wait any longer to begin our new life. And this is *the* night. The night we met. One year ago, I first saw you by moonlight in the woods, at the Font of the Changing Queen."

"And you faced me so fearlessly." He caressed her cheek, his gaze full of emotion and memories. "I can scarcely believe it's only been a year. It took you so little time to completely change my eternity."

Eternity. Her heart fluttered again, and she ran her hands over his chest. "Lio. Tonight. I'll finally get to taste…your blood…you." The thought of it made her throb much lower than her heart.

A huge grin spread over his face, showing her the full length of his fangs. "Patience, my hungry Grace."

"Being your Grace offers many magical benefits, but patience is not one of them." The now-familiar Craving stirred in her, the proof of their Grace bond. It still amazed her that even as a human, she could feel their addiction to each other. He kept her sated with pleasure, but soon she would know the satisfaction of both his body and his blood.

"You need all your strength for tonight," she said. "I still think you should have had breakfast."

"I'm still satisfied from dinner." His smile reminded her of how good last night had been. "Weeks of drinking your blood has fully restored my health and made my Craving for you much easier to bear."

She tucked a strand of his black hair behind his ear, observing the healthy flush upon his pale, nocturnal complexion. Under the trimmed lines of his light beard, his face was no longer gaunt, and muscle now strengthened his lean frame. "I suppose I must take you at your word."

"My parents will give me the Ritual Drink tonight before we begin, so their power will be potent in my veins—for you and me."

"You truly don't need to feast on me before we start?"

"No, Cassia." His voice was a low purr. "The next time I feast on you, you will be feasting on me as well."

It was difficult to imagine any pleasure greater than what he had given her mortal body. But what they would do tonight, once her body was powerful like his, would be far better. "I can't wait to experience the Feast."

"Neither can I. Cup and thorns. At last, I'll feel your bite." He reached for her with his mind magic. The thelemancy that gave him the power to control a person's Will now touched Cassia's thoughts with the utmost gentleness.

At the intimate caress of his magic inside her mind, she bit back an indecent moan. Starting tonight, their bond would be even closer than it was in moments like this. She would hear his thoughts even when he didn't use his magic, and she would sense his emotions, as he did hers. "Finally, we'll get to experience Grace Union all the time."

"I can't wait to show you," he said.

She studied the gleam of anticipation in his dark blue eyes. His body felt strong and relaxed against her. He took his duties to heart, and Gifting her was one of the greatest responsibilities he would ever undertake. But there was no sign he harbored any self-doubt in this case. "You feel ready."

He looked into her eyes, his own full of love. "Everything will go beautifully for you tonight. I will make sure of that."

She stood there in his embrace a moment longer.

"And you, my rose?" He held her gaze. "Are you ready?"

For weeks now, her determination to become a Hesperine had been so much more powerful than her fears. But there were still moments when she dreaded the transformation itself. Moments like now.

She didn't bother putting on a brave face, for he saw through all her masks, and they weren't necessary with him. They were part of her old life in Tenebra. Here in Orthros, she could be honest about who she loved, what she wanted—and what she feared. "My Gifting won't be easy."

"I will be with you every step of the way."

"We fought so hard so I can leave my past behind. But tonight it will come back to haunt us as I relive my memories during the transformation."

"Sometimes the only way to banish a specter is to face it. We will do it together, as we have before."

She would never forget when she had first told Lio her worst memories of her sister's death. She had never shared her grief for Solia with anyone until that night. He had held her for the first time and given her the gift of empathy. Little had she known that night would lead to this one, when he would hold her and give her the Gift.

"You've helped me with the wounds I've suffered. But now we must confront the wounds I've dealt. I committed so many callous deeds without a thought. Now that I've changed, I can scarcely bear to think of what I did then. I can only imagine how much worse I'll feel about my actions as the Gifting brings me into Blood Union and makes me empathize with the people I once hurt."

There was no fear in his eyes, only reassurance. "You chose your side a long time ago, Cassia. Hespera knows you are her own. Remember that she is not only the Goddess of night, but also Mercy and Sanctuary. She will guide you through your Gifting with compassion and keep you safe."

Cassia drew in a deep breath. She had many guides on her path tonight. The Goddess who had created Hesperines, her friends and family waiting inside, and most of all, the partner holding her in his arms.

She was no longer alone. These people knew her, understood her. Loved her.

And they all had faith in her redemption. She must try not to think about those who didn't survive their transformations. Surely she wouldn't be one of the few who were tortured to death by their own consciences during the empathic visions the Gifting induced.

Lio looked into her eyes, and she knew he was alert to all her emotions that he could sense in their Blood Union. "I arranged a final consultation for you with a knowledgeable special adviser on the Gifting. She can help you be absolutely certain you are ready for tonight."

"Oh. That will surely help. Thank you."

Lio lifted a hand and beckoned to someone in the crowd inside. He must have adjusted his veil spell so only that person saw them. Cassia stood with him and waited expectantly.

A moment later, in the high double doorway, there appeared a small figure in purple formal silks. She descended the front steps with great dignity, escorted by two gangly goat kids. Cassia grinned at Lio's little sister.

The closer Zoe came, the faster her steps became, until she raced forward and threw her arms around Cassia. "Happy Gift Night, Grace-sister!"

Cassia hugged the suckling to her. "Thank you, Zoe. I'm so excited."

"And nervous." Zoe's Hesperine intuition about others' emotions was already strong, although she had undergone her own Gifting as a seven-year-old child mere months ago. "I'm here to help you make sure you're ready."

Cassia reached for Lio's hand again and gave him a grateful squeeze. Together, they all sat down on the broad front steps, where warmth spells emanated up from the foundation of the house. Zoe and Lio settled Cassia between them. The fragrance of roses surrounded them, wafting from the wreaths of white blooms on the wrought iron doors.

Zoe tucked her brown-and-white goat, Rainbow Aurora, under one arm. Her black-and-white goat, Midnight Moonbeam, jumped onto Cassia's lap. The kids seemed to get bigger all the time, but the miniature breed would always be easy for Zoe to manage, even when her two caprine familiars were fully grown. Cassia took comfort in stroking the little goat's hide. Knight stretched out on the lower steps, covering her feet with his warm, furry belly.

"I'm so glad for your advice," Cassia told Zoe. "Your Gifting was only last year, so you're an expert."

"It's the only thing I know more about than Lio does!"

Lio laughed. "It's true that as a bloodborn, I'm not much help, since Papa gave Mama the Gift while she was pregnant with me. But one night, Zoe, you'll be an expert on many things I don't understand. You're so smart, and such a fast learner."

Zoe blushed at the praise from the elder brother she adored. "When I get my magic and decide on my craft and service, I'll study hard, just like you."

"You're a very good student—and teacher."

Zoe sat up straighter and began to count off items on her fingers. "First of all, Cassia, you went to see the healers, right?"

Cassia nodded. "The physicians say I'm strong enough to undergo the transformation. I have…leftover effects…from an illness when I was fourteen, but it won't matter after I become a Hesperine."

Lio voiced none of his dire thoughts in front of Zoe, but Cassia knew he was still angry about the poor care she had received as King Lucis of Tenebra's inconvenient bastard daughter. That fever eight years ago had nearly killed her.

It had been one of the many brushes with death that might have prevented her from making it to her Gift Night. But she had escaped with her life.

Zoe counted off another finger. "You went to affinity readings with all the circles to see if you have any magic already, so you can be ready in case your powers flare up in the middle of the Gifting."

Cassia sighed. "Some of the magic circles even read me twice. Nothing."

"We will discover your mysterious abilities yet," Lio said, as he had so often over the past weeks. "There is no doubt you have magic. It's not unusual for an affinity to remain dormant until a catalyst awakens it. Whatever power you possess will become clear once you are Hesperine."

"Whether I have an affinity or not, I'll have Hesperine blood magic after my Gifting."

"And *your* magic," he insisted.

The months she had known Lio had overcome a lifetime of expecting the worst. Now she couldn't seem to stop getting her hopes up. "Perhaps I have garden magic after all, and it will take blood to awaken it."

"Just like our roses," Lio reminded her. "Even back in Tenebra at the abandoned shrine of Hespera where we fell in love, our blood brought the Goddess's sacred flowers back to life."

"And the seeds I salvaged from them proved viable."

"More than viable. Potent. The rose vines they've produced are maturing at a rate no gardener could achieve without magic."

"The roses' innate magic might not be the only reason," Cassia allowed. "Maybe it is me."

"Of course it's you," Zoe said, as if it were obvious. "You're the Brave Gardener."

Lio had indeed given Cassia a magical epithet in the bedtime stories he told his little sister. "Thank you, Zoe flower."

"Ready for the next question?"

"Yes."

"Do you feel better about your past?" Zoe looked up at her, brown eyes big and earnest. "You've spent lots of time with Mama, talking about it so it won't be as scary."

"Our conversations have helped me so much. She's a very reassuring person, and not only because she's a mind healer."

Zoe nodded. "The more I talk to Mama about Tenebra, the fewer nightmares I have."

Cassia stroked Zoe's long hair, which shone, uncovered, the color of creamed coffee. Zoe had suffered more in her short years as a human than any child ever should. At least Solia had been with Cassia until her seventh year. No elder sister had shielded Zoe from the ugliest parts of life. Until now.

Zoe reached out to run her little hand through Knight's thick fur. "I'll take good care of Knight for you while you're busy with your Gifting. Don't worry about him at all."

"I'm so glad you and Knight are such good friends. Usually liege-hounds can't bear to spend this much time away from the person they're bonded to. But he enjoys his time with you, even when I'm not near him. I don't think he would be able to get through this without you."

Lio must have sensed Cassia's pang of worry. "Knight has adjusted to our family beautifully. He is learning to be more of a companion than a bodyguard—a change in circumstances he richly deserves. What you've accomplished with him is unprecedented in the history of liegehounds."

"It wasn't hard." She took his furry head in both her hands, rubbing his ears. "I just asked him."

Now she must ask him to tolerate weeks away from her while she adjusted to her new nature. She would ask him to love her, even after she was a Hesperine.

She didn't fully understand the ancient magic that had played a role in liegehounds' breeding and training. But she knew it had shaped them for two purposes: to protect humans and destroy Hesperines.

Knight lived to guard her and was bound to her until death. Would the end of her mortal existence change that? Could Hesperine blood magic sever that tie?

Lio scratched the patch of blood-colored fur under Knight's chin and raised an eyebrow at Cassia. His gesture reminded her that Knight would once have eaten his fingers for dinner rather than sit here wagging his tail in contentment. "He will do anything for you."

"I wish you didn't have to spend so much time away from everyone." Zoe sounded anxious. "I didn't have to do that."

"The Gifting is easier for sucklings," Lio reminded her. "Cassia will need to remain in seclusion until she masters her new power."

"I still don't understand why we can't all help her tonight. You stayed with me during my Gifting while I drank Mama and Papa's blood and turned into a Hesperine."

How fortunate Zoe was that Hesperines had adopted her at a young age. In their innocence, children were spared a harrowing transformation, and their power awoke gradually as they grew at the slow pace of new immortals.

But Cassia would never regret that she would undergo the transformation as an adult. She wouldn't want anyone but Lio to turn her into a Hesperine. She wouldn't merely drink her Gifter's blood. She would feast on her Grace's blood and body, transforming while they made love. She wanted that for her and Lio. She would risk the danger for them to experience that ecstasy.

She would remain focused on that. Every time the fear threatened, she would fill her mind with thoughts of the life-altering pleasure she would experience as Lio loved her into immortality.

He gave her a suggestive wink while Zoe was looking at Knight. "The Gifting is a little different when two Graces are involved. I must Gift Cassia all on my own."

"You and Knight and the goats will have so much fun," Cassia reassured Zoe. "You won't have time to miss me. And if you do, just remember I'm nearby in Lio's residence, right here on the grounds of House Komnena, even though we can't see each other."

Zoe sat up straighter and nodded, clearly gathering her courage.

Cassia hated to put her through any separation when the losses the child had suffered in Tenebra still haunted her. "We'll be apart for just a little while so we can be together forever."

That made Zoe smile. She folded her hands. "There's one more question. It's not important for you, but I'm supposed to ask."

"What question is that, Grace-sister?"

"Well, before the Gifting, everyone is supposed to apologize to anyone for anything they've done wrong. But you're the Brave Gardener. You saved me and all the other sucklings. You've only done good things."

Cassia put an arm around Zoe. Her glowing words made Cassia want to be the hero the child saw in her. Starting tonight, she would be, she vowed.

Not the heartless survivor she had once been, who would sell out anyone to save her own hide. The years before she had met Lio had been bitter ones, when she had lived through her father's wrath by the skin of her teeth and had not had the luxury of being scrupulous about it.

Until the night she had realized some things were more important than her survival. She had become willing to give up her life for Lio. For love. That had given the precious gift of life back to her.

Her future had not slipped through her fingers during all those dangerous human years. How could she imagine that the miraculous transformation she was about to attempt would end her life?

Cassia, who had once believed in nothing and hoped for even less, once again found herself aware of the new but healthy seedling inside her: hope. She would continue to nurture it under the light of the Queens' ward over Orthros. It would grow stronger than all her bad memories.

"What else do I need to do, Zoe?"

"That's all. If you've done all those things, you're ready." Zoe frowned, peering at Cassia. "Do you want to go over the questions again?"

"I don't think so."

Zoe took her hand. "Why don't you feel ready yet?"

Cassia hesitated. This was her last opportunity to lay old grievances to rest. To make amends.

Lio rubbed her back again. "You made your peace with everyone in the Tenebran embassy before they left Orthros."

"Yes."

"You're not still worrying about any of them, are you?"

"You mean am I worrying about what I never went back to Tenebra to finish?"

They rarely spoke of Cassia's onetime ambition of making herself queen. She didn't want her old life to interrupt the new one they were building together here. But now past worries haunted Lio's eyes.

She took both his hands. "When I think of what I don't have to do, I feel only relief. You saved me from that...life sentence."

"You don't regret letting someone else have what could have been yours?"

Even now, Lord Flavian of Segetia might be enacting the peaceful takeover she had created for him and claiming the crown she might have worn.

Even now, he might be deposing the king responsible for Solia's death and Cassia's suffering.

Cassia didn't know. She had made a point to avoid any and all news about Tenebran politics since the embassy had sailed away from Orthros without her.

"Lio," she said, "I want nothing I could have had in Tenebra. Everything I want for the rest of eternity is right here within arm's reach."

He pulled her close again. She rested her head on his shoulder.

Whether the king remained on the throne was no longer within her power. No longer her responsibility.

It was time for it not to matter to her anymore.

It was all right for it not to matter to her anymore.

Her breath caught, and a fraught mix of emotions gripped her chest.

Solia would understand. She would want Cassia to be safe and happy. Being a good sister to Zoe was a better way to honor her than vengeance.

Cassia didn't have to control their father anymore. She didn't have to fear him, either.

"That's it," she whispered, drawing back.

"What is?" Lio's brow furrowed.

"That's who I need to talk to."

"Who?" Zoe asked.

"Zoe, I need you to ask someone to meet with me before my Gifting."

WELCOME GIFT

CASSIA WENT ALONE. LIO would have gone with her. He and Zoe had both offered, but she even left Knight with them. She must do this on her own.

She made her way through the corridors of House Komnena, avoiding the main gathering in the Ritual hall. More sounds of celebration echoed through the quiet passages, along with the burble of fountains. But Cassia only encountered the statues, the portraits of the Goddess in her many guises that Lio's father had sculpted. Apollon's works of art greeted her with enigmatic smiles from alcoves, corners, and galleries, dappled with colors in the light of the stained glass windows Lio had crafted.

At last Cassia found herself at the back entrance of Apollon's workshop. She took a deep breath and stared at the door.

It was unlocked, she knew. At any hour, on any night, Apollon's children could simply walk in to seek his help. Or just his company. Zoe ran in and out of here all the time, as Lio had at her age. They had never known any differently.

Cassia had.

It all rose in her mind like smoke, choking. The silent corridors of the palace and the menacing faces of the guards at the door. The man on the throne, his once-golden hair, his piercing, sky-blue eyes. Her longing to run as far from him as she could. The inescapable demand that she approach him.

The king. Her father. The man who could sentence her to death anytime he chose, as he had her sister.

Cassia pushed the vision away with all her might. She had left the king behind in Tenebra months ago. She had escaped him. She was safe and free in Orthros, where he could not reach her. She would never have to see him again.

And she would *not* let him keep taking things from her.

She reached out a shaking hand and opened Apollon's door.

She strode in like she lived here. Because she did. This was her home now. The only person who made her unwelcome in this room was her.

From the moment she had set eyes on Lio's father, her fear of him had crippled her. Ever since, she had wrestled with the mixture of terror and guilt that came over her in his presence.

She had no cause to feel this way. Apollon was one of the elder first-bloods who had founded her beloved Orthros. For centuries, he had fought as one of the Blood Errant, the notorious Hesperine warriors who protected mortals from the cruelties of Tenebra.

He was Lio's father. The Hesperine who had rescued Komnena and her unborn child. The father who had raised his son to be a protector and who adored his little daughter. He was more than the architect of this house and the rest of the city's monuments. He had built so much of what Cassia loved about her new family.

Cassia walked between mystery statues covered in white fabric, past uncut blocks of marble and granite. She navigated around the "cave" Apollon had made for Zoe out of a table, chairs, and sheets. Inside the play shelter lay Apollon's familiar, a golden lion befitting his legend. The mighty creature napped peacefully amid a pile of Zoe's storybooks.

It was an injustice to him that Cassia couldn't be near him without thinking of the king, the cruel hand who had wrought all the worst moments of her life. Every time she looked at Apollon, the powerful, blond father figure evoked all her worst fears, rather than the reassurance and love he inspired in his children.

At last she reached the center of the Lion of Orthros's den.

Apollon sat waiting for her on a stool at his worktable. Her gaze fixed on his sandaled feet and the end of his floor-length, curly blond braid, visible under the table. Then his broad, honed hands, relaxed and folded atop a tidy pile of his sketches. Then his barrel chest and his massive shoulders. Instead of his usual work robe, tonight he wore formal robes of golden silk befitting the Gift Night of a new addition to his ancient and prestigious bloodline.

Cassia made herself look at his face.

Her heart pounded, and she broke out in a sweat.

There was no judgment in his expression. "Imagine my delight when Zoe said you wished to have a word with me, before any of the friends and family awaiting you."

"Thank you for meeting me here."

"How can I help?"

Cassia couldn't meet his eyes. Her gaze dropped and went astray amid his beard. Much was said of it, for he had been growing it out for centuries. He kept it braided along his face and down his back with his hair.

At the corner of his mouth, trailing across his cheek, ran the jet-black Grace braid of Komnena's hair, which she had bestowed upon him at their avowal. As if he kept her close enough to kiss, even when she wasn't in the room. As if he cherished her so dearly that she was woven into him, as her braid was into his beard.

Lio's father cherished women as surely as Cassia's father destroyed them.

Apollon didn't even look like the king. A life of war and cruelty had weathered and hardened Lucis's brutish features. His beard failed to hide the burn scar that had marred his face since she could remember. His eyes were as cold as that empty place inside him where his heart should be. His once-blond hair wisped around his face, thinning and white after his years of holding the throne at any cost.

Apollon radiated power without the trappings of a crown and sword. His kind gaze and ready smile said he wielded his strength wisely and well. His immortal visage was unmarred by scars. He looked larger than life, Goddess-touched. Because he was.

"I realized how fortunate I am," she began. "I'm about to become the most recent recipient of Hespera's Gift, and the first Hesperine ever Gifted is right here. I'm sure many newgifts come to you for advice, but..."

"None of them are my Grace-daughter." He got to his feet and pulled an extra stool up to the side of the table for her before returning to his seat.

He didn't make her sit across from him, with the table between them. She took the invitation.

She cleared her throat again. A silence fell between them. An uncomfortable one, but only for her, she knew. "I thought talking with you might help me prepare for tonight."

"What would you like to know?"

How to stop fearing you. "Well, I wouldn't want to cross the veil by prying into your past…"

"You have every reason to ask. My past is about to become our shared past, the story of our people and this family."

"I never thought of it that way. Not that I am insensitive to the great legacy your bloodline bestows upon me tonight."

"Tonight you become, in your own right, one of my heirs. But what you bring to our bloodline is as great and precious as what we bestow upon you."

She risked a glance at his face again. She froze in astonishment, her scalp prickling with discomfort.

There was a sheen in his eyes.

"A new member of the family," he said. "We could not ask the Goddess for a truer or braver heart to make one of our own. When I am the recipient of a blessing so immeasurable, I find that crafting is the only way of marking the night that feels sufficient. But sometimes even creativity is not enough. Tonight will not fit in granite."

Cassia's mind went blank. She scarcely knew what to say.

Elder Firstblood Apollon had tears of joy in his eyes. Because of her.

"We are so proud of you, Cassia. We will do everything in our power to make this night wonderful for you. What can I tell you about the Gifting that will set your mind at ease?"

She realized she was knotting her hands and tried to relax her fingers. "Will you tell me about your Gift Night? Your story of how you became the first Hesperine to receive the Gift from the Ritual Firstbloods?"

He gave a nod. He was quiet for a moment, stroking his beard absently. Then he began, his tone reminding her of when he told bedtime stories to Zoe, but his words acknowledging the gravity of the subject.

"Sixteen hundred years ago, I collapsed on the front steps of a temple of Hespera, certain I would not survive the night.

"I was riddled with the burns of fire spells after a battle with war mages of Anthros. My enemies had fallen at last to my stone magic, but more would come in their place.

"The worshipers of Anthros would stop at nothing to secure their authority and make all other mages bow to their god of war and order. Although some of us refused to submit, we knew we lived on borrowed time.

"The world I had loved for the forty-two years of my human life was burning around me. The new Order of Anthros would rule whatever they built upon the ashes, and I did not regret I would not live to see such an era. All that mattered was that I complete one task before I died. I needed to get a message to my brother."

"You were trying to reach Uncle Argyros?" Cassia asked.

"I never would have made it to Hagia Anatela, the Great Temple of Hespera in the East, where he was one of the leading mind mages. But I managed to survive long enough to reach a closer Great Temple, Hagia Boreia in the north. I knew the mages of Hespera there would send word to him of what had befallen our parents."

A sense of dread unfurled in Cassia. She hesitated to ask her next question. "What happened to your family?"

"Our father was a mage who worshiped Demergos, god of stone and soil, our mother a mage of Chera, Demergos's wife, goddess of rain and spring. They had served as village mages for a lifetime, tending to the needs of one generation after the next. They were the two most loving people I have ever known, full of generosity for each other, for Argyros and me, and for the village. The neighbors cared for them in return so they could spend their old age together in their home, surrounded by friends.

"Then the cult of Anthros began the Ordering. As you know, they declared that all mages must practice magic in sanctioned temples and remain celibate. I was an itinerant mage of Demergos, traveling to take my magic wherever it was needed. I will forever regret that I was not with my parents when the Order came for them.

"The mages of Anthros tore them from their home and forced them into separate temples. The Order justified it with recitations of new doctrine and official scrolls, approved with the seal of mages of Demergos who had once been brothers to my father and me."

Heat and the smell of burning roses flashed in Cassia's memory, and her eyes stung. She had seen the destruction war mages were capable of. But they did not need fire spells to destroy lives. Sometimes they committed cruelty with the stroke of a quill and the silent closing of a temple gate.

"But you found them," she said with certainty. The Lion of Orthros would tear through the walls of the temple to save his family.

"I was too late." His voice was rough with emotion. "By the time I found the temples to which they had been banished, they had already joined the gods. At their age, they could not withstand the ordeal. The loss of everything they knew and loved—the loss of each other."

Cassia's throat ached, but she made herself speak, her gaze fixed on his folded hands. "Your grief runs in my veins."

"Thank you, Cassia."

She shared a moment of silence with him for those two people from a distant time, whom his memories brought near. They would live on in him, Lio, Zoe, and soon, Cassia.

"We could have saved them," he said. "The cult of Demergos was a powerful brotherhood of mages committed to building, not destroying."

Despite the emotion in his voice, his hands remained relaxed. They were the muscled hands of a craftsman and a warrior. She only ever saw him lift them to create. She knew he wielded them in defense of those who needed his protection.

"If all of us had stood together against the mages of Anthros, we could have prevented the Ordering and all the horrors of the Last War that resulted from it. We had the strength to temper the war mages—and they knew it. So they began a campaign of terror and temptation, of intimidation and strategy to break our power and bring all the men of our cult into their own.

"Some mages of Demergos reacted with fear and capitulated to the Anthrians. Others of my brethren saw the power they could have in the new Order and welcomed the enemy with open arms. Then there were those of us who held fast to our courage.

"We were too few. Scattered and broken, we fought on." He sighed deeply. "Our cause was just, but I will not pretend that my deeds in those grim days were merciful.

"I destroyed everyone who had played a role in my parents' betrayal, from the mages of Demergos who had once been our friends, to the Anthrian temple scribe who had drawn up the paperwork. Declared an apostate, with warbands of fire mages on my trail, I sought refuge with Argyros's cult. The mages of Hespera welcomed all outcasts and refugees, despite the retribution they would face.

"I was so near death when I arrived at Hagia Boreia that they called in the most powerful healer, the Prismos of the temple—Anastasios."

"Was he a Hesperine yet?" Cassia asked.

"Yes. This was after he and the other leaders of the four Great Temples of Hespera had performed the Ritual that turned them into the first Hesperines. But not long after. They still did not fully understand the miraculous transformation they had experienced when they had combined their blood magic. They had revealed their new natures only to a trusted few."

"Did he tell you what he was?"

"Not at first. I only knew his healing magic was more powerful than I thought possible. He tended to me hour after hour, night after night, leaving me in the care of others only during daylight hours.

"Anastasios could not have been more different from me. He was a healer, I a warrior. He was a temple mage, I a wanderer. But we had one important thing in common. We would spend the last drop of our power for the people who needed us. Despite our differences, respect and friendship grew between us.

"But at last it became clear that even his healing magic, great as it was, could not restore me. Even then, he did not give up. He asked for my permission to try a dangerous magical experiment on me.

"I had nothing to lose, but he did not want to lose me. I knew he could not let me go unless he tried everything. So I agreed.

"He placed me in a secluded room and sent all the other mages away."

"That was when you found out he was a Hesperine," Cassia guessed.

Apollon nodded. "He explained everything the Ritual Firstbloods knew at that time about their power. He wished to give me his own blood in the hopes that its magical properties would heal me, but he couldn't predict the consequences."

Cassia waited, listening, her mind far away from the workshop and the father before her, imagining a secret chamber in a temple where a wounded warrior languished.

Apollon spoke calmly, matter-of-factly. "Anastasios pierced his wrist with his fangs and held his vein to my mouth. As soon as I swallowed, magic surged through me as I began to experience what we now know is the beginning of the Gifting."

"Partaking," Cassia murmured, "one of eight phases of transformation, when you first drink Hesperine blood and share in the Goddess's power."

"Yes," Apollon answered with a chuckle. "Anastasios named the phases based on his observations of me that night."

Cassia couldn't imagine facing the Gifting blind. She was grateful for the plentiful advice the Hesperines had given her in preparation for tonight. She had listened, memorized, meditated over their wisdom. "Everyone has explained the process to me so many times. But you had no idea what was happening to you. It must have been…a shock."

"Your experience will not be so harrowing, for you know what to expect, and you have Lio to guide you. I admit, in my case, I believed I was dying. I thought my life was flashing before my eyes as I departed for the realm of Hypnos. But the god of death never came for me. Hespera had other plans."

"The Divining," Cassia said, "the second phase, when you have visions of your past."

Apollon nodded. "As I witnessed my past deeds, I realized I was not only reliving my memories. I was revisiting each of my choices with new insight, new empathy for those I had affected. Grief, anger, and revenge had brought me to Anastasios's doorstep, and those were the foes I had to defeat during the third phase of my transformation."

The Reckoning. Dread pulled Cassia out of Apollon's tale and back to the realization that she must face the Goddess's verdict upon her heart. Tonight.

"Cassia." Apollon's mighty voice, softened to a tone of comfort, sounded just like the Hesperine magic she had trusted all her life. "You don't need to worry about that."

The simple statement was impossibly reassuring. He made the most dangerous moment of the Gifting sound like something only other people must fear, as if it had nothing to do with her at all.

But there was a reason the fourth phase was called the End. It would either end her mortal existence so her Hesperine life could begin—or it would be the end of her.

"Cassia," Apollon said again. "You are not the kind of person who suffers that fate."

"How can I be sure?"

"Phaedros was once my friend. He sought to pass on the power the Ritual firstbloods had given us. I remember when he discovered that the Gifting can be fatal to mortals whose hearts are full of evil. I witnessed his tragic and misguided campaign to force all mortals to become Hesperines. You are nothing like the criminals of the Last War who faced his retribution."

Cassia had done many things that might be called criminal. Not so long ago, she had even planned to assassinate the king.

On the edge of her vision, she saw Apollon lean closer, his elbows on the table. Not looming. Bringing himself to her eye level. "I survived the End."

"You're a hero."

"So are you."

Cassia drew in a breath that was shaky with unshed tears. "What is it like? When you survive the hard part, and you know everything will be all right?"

"Well, on that subject, my Gifting with Anastasios offers little comparison to what you will experience with Lio tonight. But I trust Komnena has given you some insight into what the Fangs phase is like when your Grace is your Gifter."

Cassia's cheeks flamed. She had become more comfortable talking about romance with fellow females. She was completely unprepared for the notion of discussing it with a father figure. In Tenebra, even a kind father's intervention on the matter usually amounted to an arranged marriage.

In Orthros, did fathers give advice to their daughters about love? She supposed they did. She had no trouble imagining Zoe confiding in Apollon about such things when she grew older. This was a world where Cassia was living unwed under Apollon's roof with his son, and he was nothing but happy for them.

Apollon released a deep sigh. "You know I waited fifteen hundred years for my Grace. I understand what it's like to drift without an anchor. Every time I think of your impact on Lio's life, I say a prayer of thanks to the Goddess. And I rest easy knowing you are in the best of hands, because my son is the finest Grace any young newgift could ask for. Admittedly, I may be slightly biased in that opinion."

"Well, that makes two of us."

"Lio will take such good care of you tonight. He has been most diligent in seeking advice from those of us with experience, though I think he didn't need much guidance."

Cassia laughed a little, despite her nerves. "Of course Lio had done his research, even though he is already an expert on taking good care of me."

"Alas, when my Gifting visions broke, I had no Grace to dote on me. But I did have a trusted friend to mop my brow and make notes to himself about my suffering."

Another laugh escaped Cassia, relieving a bit of the grim tension of the subject.

"The pain of my wounds was gone," Apollon continued, "replaced by the pain of a thirst I had never known. I had a new set of fangs with which to quell it. Anastasios offered me his wrist again, and I became aware of the changes in my body."

"The Renewal, when you need to continue drinking blood while your body is transforming."

"That's right. Strength suffused my limbs. My senses grew so keen that I could hear every heartbeat in the temple. My magic surged with power I couldn't have imagined. I'm afraid there were quite a few repairs to be done on the temple after that. Gifting a lithomagus is rather damaging to the masonry, as it turns out."

Cassia covered her mouth with her hand. "Oh. Is that why Giftings happen in seclusion now?"

"If you're already a mage, or your affinity awakens during the Gifting, the results can be eventful. I'm glad to hear Mak and Lyros warded Lio's residence for you two. You can discover your magic in safety."

Even Apollon was convinced Cassia was a mage. Her fears receded still more, giving her hopes more room. "I understand why they call the seventh phase Completion. I think it must feel remarkable to be your whole self for the first time."

"I cannot describe it. At that point, you are fully transformed, but still delirious from the Gifting. Drunk on your Gifter's blood and your own power. Komnena's seventh phase was the best fun."

Cassia tried not to blush again, but to no avail. She asked him about a less private topic instead. "When you regained lucidity in the eighth phase, the Awakening, you must have been astonished about what had happened."

"To be sure. When it was over and I came to, Anastasios and I realized his blood had done far more than heal me. His experiment had accomplished what the first Hesperines had believed impossible, after many attempts to replicate the Ritual. He had found a way to grant others their power and nature. He had bestowed Hespera's Gift upon me."

The silence that fell between them this time was less difficult, Cassia found. Countless questions ran through her mind, but she asked not about magic or the Gift or history, but about the more personal aspects of Apollon's story. "Did you manage to contact Uncle Argyros?"

"He arrived at the temple to find me much changed. You can imagine my scholarly brother's reaction to Anastasios's discovery. I think the real reason he asked his Prismos, Eidon, for the Gift was so he could write a research treatise from firsthand experience."

They both laughed. Cassia realized she was laughing with Apollon.

"If the decision had been mine," he said, "I am not certain I would have deemed myself worthy of immortality. But it was the Goddess's choice, and here I am. She is the greatest sculptor there is. She cut away all that did not suit her, revealing the best of me. She saw fit to give me great power, and I have tried to use it well ever since."

He had endured so much, trying to do the right thing. All in the name of protecting those he loved. He had fought hard for what was right, but for revenge, too. He had suffered and caused pain. He had been far from perfect. He had lost nearly everything that mattered to him.

Then Hespera had given it all back to him and more.

She understood his story. It was every Hesperine's story. It was her story.

"Thank you," she said. "For everything you've told me tonight. I needed to hear it."

"I hope you will remember that the painful past is how we all arrived at this wondrous present."

She swallowed around a lump in her throat, nodding.

Apollon's presence felt so big, so close. "I wish I could have made the past that brought you here easier for you. I promise your future will be bright. I understand why it is difficult for you to trust others' protection, and I respect that you are capable of protecting yourself. But I hope you will be patient with those of us who want to keep you safe because we love you. I will never let anything happen to you, Cassia."

Her breath hitched. "I think you understand...the name 'Father' is forever tainted for me."

"What a lesson I would teach to the one who ruined it for you," Apollon growled. "Let me into his palace for but a moment, and Tenebra would never forget the justice I would bring down upon Lucis's head. I have thought of it many times, Cassia. It goes against my every conviction to leave his many wrongs against you unanswered. I resolved to rescue you from that man as soon as Lio told us about you, and it was only my dear son's insistence on diplomacy that stopped me."

"You almost came to get me?"

"Of course."

She had never realized. That's what Lio had meant when he'd told her their people had wanted to remove her from Tenebra to keep her and Lio safe. The Lion of Orthros had nearly descended upon Solorum, the capital of Tenebra, to pluck her from the king's grasp.

Apollon sighed again. "I must constantly remind myself that any action against Lucis would cause a war between Hesperines and humans. I would hate to undo all the hard work you and Lio have devoted to forging peace between our peoples. Otherwise I would ride out tomorrow and knock the king from his throne with my hammer. It would only take a little tap."

Apollon spoke the truth. He could do that. He would do it, for her.

"Can you forgive me for not doing more?" he asked her.

She was so surprised that her gaze darted to his face again. "There is nothing to forgive. You have done so much for me. Every time you've given Lio advice or played with Zoe. You've shown me something I never knew. I don't want to miss it. I won't let Lucis ruin it." She looked into Apollon's dark blue eyes, the eyes he had given Lio. "Perhaps...could I...call you Papa, like Zoe does?"

He gave her the same smile he gave Lio and Zoe. "That would make me very happy."

Cassia reached out. He let her. Holding her breath, her heart hammering, she slid her small hand into his big palm.

When she did not pull away, Apollon wrapped his hand around hers and held it gently.

He sat there like that with her until her heartbeat slowed.

"Do you remember what I said to you your first night at House Komnena?" he asked.

"You told me it was all right to take my time letting go of my fears."

He nodded, an encouragement for her to continue.

"You also mentioned you had a welcome gift for me, which would be ready for me when I was ready for it. I'm sorry it's taken me so long. I hope you don't feel I dishonored your gift."

"Of course not. I'm immortal, and so shall you be after tonight. We have all the time in the world for me to give you presents."

They laughed together again.

"I think this would be an appropriate time," he suggested, "if you're willing. I should warn you, it is a gift that may stir some powerful emotions in you. But in the name of honoring your past—and moving forward—it could be good for you to see it tonight."

She took a deep breath. "Very well."

"Let us tell Zoe. She has been looking forward to this."

Cassia relaxed. If Zoe was excited about it, it must not be anything too difficult to face.

Apollon got to his feet. "Would you like to wait in Komnena's study? I'll go get the rest of the family."

"That's fine."

He gave her hand a pat before releasing her. Then he disappeared before her eyes. She had grown used to Hesperines stepping in and out of sight all around her as they traveled from one point to the next with effortless magic.

She left through the front door of his workshop and crept into the family library. Hearing no one, she darted past the sparsely occupied shelves of the collection Komnena and Lio were trying to build. She made it across the room without meeting any of her guests and peered into Komnena's study.

The only occupant was Komnena's familiar, Anna. As Cassia entered, the eagle ruffled her feathers and began to preen, eying her as if evaluating her fitness to join the family.

"I have already secured the seldom-bestowed approval of Uncle Argyros's owl. Surely you cannot be pickier than he, proud bird."

Anna sneezed.

"When I get a familiar, you must first approve of it."

At the sound of Lio's voice, Cassia turned. He stood in the light of the stained glass door he had crafted for his mother's study.

She smiled at him. "My heretical sorcerer. Why don't you have a familiar yet?"

"I have yet to acquire one on my adventures."

She padded across the thick Imperial carpets to him. "Too late, then. We are done with adventures."

He pulled her into his arms. "I'll have to find a nice, boring familiar here at home."

"What sort of cozy creature do you have in mind?"

"I've always thought it would be nice to have a cat to purr on my lap while I'm reading."

"Oh dear. I will approve, but convincing Knight will be another matter entirely."

He looked into her eyes, and his teasing tone faded. "How are you?"

"Better than I hoped. Things will be different between Papa and me from now on."

At the word "Papa," Lio gave her a surprised smile. "I can tell."

At that moment, Zoe stepped into the library with Knight and her goats, and her parents appeared behind her. Komnena's dark gold formal robes, combined with her height and elegant features, made her look as regal as a princess. But she had begun her life as a starving, illiterate peasant. She had fought her way to this life, just like Cassia.

Komnena pulled her long hair over her shoulder and showed Cassia a new braid she had added. Like the ones she wore for Lio and Zoe, it was woven together with Apollon's thick golden Grace braid.

"Is that new braid for me?" Cassia asked.

"And all my promises to you, Grace-daughter. I'm here for you, now and forever, anytime you need me."

Cassia embraced her. Getting to know Komnena had been wonderful. Cassia was triply fortunate, despite her losses. She'd had a mother who had loved her, even though she had never known her. She'd had a sister who had mothered her. Now she had Komnena.

Komnena pulled back, taking Cassia's hands. "You will do well tonight."

"Is that your professional opinion as a mind healer?"

"Yes, and my confidence as your Grace-mother and encouragement as your friend. But what's even more important is your confidence in yourself." Komnena looked at Cassia with insightful brown eyes. "I think Apollon's gift will help with that. Come."

Something settled around Cassia, relieving her breathtaking, quivery anticipation. It was the contentment she had come to feel with the family, and this time, no troubled feelings toward Apollon dimmed it.

She turned to Zoe. "What is this welcome gift Papa has been keeping under his hat all this time?"

Zoe giggled. "It won't fit under his hat! But that's all I'm going to give away."

With Zoe and Apollon in the lead, the five of them and, of course, Knight and the goats exited Komnena's study through the stained glass door. They crossed the outdoor terrace and passed the cozy barn and paddock where Zoe's familiars lived.

She and Apollon struck out along the snow-covered path that led into the untamed stretches of the grounds. Lio illuminated their way with spell light as they meandered under massive evergreen trees. Cassia could not guess where they were headed or what sort of gift might be hidden in the woods.

Then Apollon took the fork in the path that would lead to the cliffs and the memorial statues of his fellow Blood Errant. Were they going to see Methu, his late Ritual son? Or Nike, his niece who was still missing in action somewhere in Tenebra? Nike had saved Cassia's life and given Solia her last rites. It would be fitting to pay tribute to her role in Cassia's past tonight. But she suspected that Apollon had something else in store for her.

A hush fell over all of them as they emerged from the trees. On the horizon, the moons were two mysterious glows just appearing over the waves, like a white spell light and a red blood enchantment.

Lio pointed up at the shifting, translucent colors above the cliffs. "Look! A crimson aurora, the rarest of all. That's a blessed sign."

Cassia watched how the lights of the Goddess's sky touched his pale skin with color. "A sign I take to heart, considering the first time I ever saw an aurora, it was crimson."

"That was your first night here in Selas."

She had watched the aurorae dance over Orthros's northern capital while he had held her in his arms. She had listened to the bells chime across the city and known she never wanted to leave.

"A *very* fitting sign for tonight," she agreed.

Apollon halted them at a ledge sheltered from the wind by the higher cliff beyond it. "Ready for me to lift the veil spell I've been keeping over your gift?"

Cassia put one arm around Lio and her other hand in Knight's ruff. "Yes."

Before their eyes appeared Apollon's latest addition to the memorial statues. He had given Solia a place in the company of Hesperine heroes.

Cassia beheld a portrait of her sister carved from golden stone. Solia shone in the spell light of Orthros, an image out of Cassia's best memories. Solia was kneeling, her beautiful gown pooling around her, looking with delight upon the flowerbed before her. A profusion of rimelace grew there, its dainty white petals and soft green leaves spilling over the sides.

Zoe broke the silence. "I know it's supposed to be delphinium, goldenrods, and white daisies. That's what you put in the first garden you planted for Soli. I tried so hard to get them to grow out here with everything you've taught me about taking care of plants, but it's too cold."

"You planted this?" Cassia asked.

Zoe nodded, gnawing at her lip with her new front teeth and baby fangs. Cassia pulled Zoe to her and held her tight. "Rimelace is even better."

Cassia held her little sister and looked at the statue of her elder sister, seeing rimelace and remembering delphinium, goldenrod, and daises.

She met Apollon's gaze. "She's perfect."

"She will always be a part of our family," he replied.

Cassia studied the likeness again. Of course, Apollon had given Solia one red eye and one white eye, in imitation of the moons, the Goddess's Eyes. "Everyone always likened her beauty to a goddess. I find this portrayal of her most fitting of all."

"When you told Zoe the story of the first garden you planted, and Lio conjured illusions to match the tale, I had a perfect reference to work from. The surprise was almost ruined once, though, when you wandered into my workshop and caught a glimpse of my sketches."

"Oh," Cassia breathed. "I remember that. I did see some half-finished drawings of a kneeling girl."

She had misinterpreted them through the eyes of her fear. They had made her think of the king forcing her to her knees. But all along, they had been evidence of Apollon lifting her and Solia up.

She reached out a hand to him. "Thank you so much, Papa."

He took her invitation and came to her side. He put his other arm around Komnena. Lio gave Cassia a squeeze, reassuring her he was there. They all stood close before Soli's memorial for a long, peaceful moment of silence.

At last Komnena spoke, her beautiful, quiet voice as sure as the tide below. "Cassia, it's time to begin."

With one last look into her sister's eyes, Cassia nodded. Her future was waiting for her.

EVERYTHING NEVER IMAGINED

L IO CARRIED AN IMMEASURABLE amount of magic inside himself at
every moment. But there wasn't room enough within him for the joy
he felt tonight.

As soon as he and Cassia entered the Ritual hall, their friends and
family began to shower her in congratulations. She didn't shrink under
the attention or armor herself in a false, courtly smile. She blushed and
beamed, and her aura soared higher, her worries receding.

He savored his Grace's emotions in the private Blood Union he shared
with her alone. He wanted to soak up and remember everything she felt
tonight. The invisible, intangible aura emanating from her was like a light
shining upon his magical senses. She was blooming in his veins now, the
thorns of her hesitation easing their grip, letting go.

She had overcome her emblematic fear of his father. If she could do
that, she could overcome any fear she faced during her Gifting. She had
decided she was ready.

Dear Goddess. My prayers are answered.

Tonight, Cassia would become a Hesperine. They would have everything they had ever wanted.

The realization overflowed him, and her gaze found his as her
body eased instinctively closer to him. He was probably flooding their
bond with so much emotion that she could feel it, even without the
Blood Union.

There wasn't room enough inside him alone. But the two of them
together could experience everything without limits.

He couldn't seem to stop smiling. He dared anyone to make him try.

He had earned these foolish, besotted smiles, and he would enjoy every minute of them.

"No one seems bothered that I'm late," she murmured with evident relief.

He chuckled. "Immortal perception of time."

He escorted her through the crowd. Knight navigated at her side with ease, raising his hackles at no one. He had left his past behind as surely as Cassia had. No one could accuse him of being a Hesperine-hunting dog anymore, and indeed, none of the guests shied away from him.

The large chamber was packed with powerful magical auras, the air packed with fragrance all the way up to the high, vaulted ceiling. There were flowers *everywhere*. Garlands wrapped every pillar and draped every arch, and vases occupied every spare surface. His mother had availed herself of all the gardeners and floral artists in Orthros, it seemed, to fill the house with Cassia's favorites.

The powerful smells made Lio giddy. Then again, that probably had more to do with the beautiful woman at his side.

He leaned down so she could hear him better. "We could have kept the affair small, you know."

"Blood Komnena has responsibilities. We had to invite not just relatives and friends, but also all the Ritual tributaries Apollon has Gifted."

"You don't seem very dutiful at the moment, my rose. I think you actually wanted a big party."

She gave him a remorseless grin. "Being surrounded by our people is nothing like being at court."

"I know even our people can be overwhelming at times."

"It is taking me time to adjust to not being alone, to having so many people in my life. I'm still learning how to respond to everyone's kindness. But tonight is one of those nights when it isn't hard."

As they strolled further into the room, deeper into the gathering of well-wishers, Lio felt no answering rise of anxiety in her aura. In fact, the crowd seemed to have the opposite effect, as if their love overflowed into her and filled her with strength. "I'm so glad. After your strained court appearances in Tenebra, I was afraid this wouldn't be the ideal experience for you."

She put her other hand on his arm, so closely intertwined with hers. "Lio, the night has barely begun, and it is already marvelous. But there is one thing I must ask of you."

He leaned closer. "Of course. Anything you need."

"Don't try too hard. We don't want perfect, remember?"

"I love you, Cassia."

"I love you, too."

Right there in the middle of everything and everyone, she halted him to press a sweet kiss to his lips. The guests' applause roared in his keen Hesperine ears.

Cassia's place of honor awaited her at the center of the hall, a chair draped in silk and roses inside the Ritual circle. As soon as Lio escorted her onto the beautiful mosaic, the magical echoes of past blood rites swept through him, along with good family memories. Cassia paused, gazing down at the blood-red Hespera's Rose at her feet and at the white stars that overlaid its five petals in the pattern of the constellation Anastasios, the sign of Lio's bloodline.

"You feel it, don't you?" Lio asked.

She nodded. "I feel like...I belong here."

"Well, of course you do." With Mak in the lead, their circle of friends was waiting to ambush them by Cassia's chair. He grabbed her up in a bear hug. "Cup and thorns. Happy Gift Night, Cassia."

Her aura filled with reassurance and good humor, as it always did around Lio's cousin. "I'm glad you're here," she mumbled, crushed against Mak's broad chest.

"Easy there," said Lyros. "She still has to breathe for a few more hours."

As soon as Mak released her, his Grace swooped in. Lyros looked into her eyes, his gaze perceptive, his voice steadying. "How are you, Cassia?"

"Better, now," Cassia answered.

Lyros put an arm around Cassia's shoulders. "You have your Trial circle at your back tonight. Nothing can go wrong."

Cassia looked at all their friends. "Thank you all for supporting me through my Gifting, even though I wasn't here for the Trial of Initiation when you formed our circle. I'm proud to officially become your Trial sister and a member of the Eighth Circle."

"Someone as notorious as you belongs in our circle." Xandra blew on the tips of her fingers and dusted them on her robe. "The eighth generation of the founders' children already has a reputation for stirring things up."

Nodora took Cassia's hands, the earnest sweetness of her presence lighting up the Blood Union around them. "Tonight will be unforgettable. I've chosen all the music myself and made sure every dance is one of your favorites. Whenever you hear these songs in the future, you can relive all the memories you make tonight."

Kia tossed her mantle over her shoulders. "I won't even lecture you on the Gifting. Tonight is for celebrating!"

"I'm so glad you're finally going to be immortal." Xandra's eyes lit with a spark of mischief. "Lio won't be so intolerable for the rest of eternity now."

Lio joined in their laughter and happily endured a couple of elbows in his ribs.

While their Trial sisters were talking with Cassia, he cast a quick veil around himself, Mak, and Lyros. "Did you have time to finish setting everything up?"

Mak clapped him on the shoulder. "It's all waiting for you."

Lyros grinned. "The hard work was already done, thanks to my talented Grace."

"I can't thank the two of you enough."

Lyros chuckled. "This definitely falls under the 'what are Trial brothers for' category, and I'm glad we could help."

"I wouldn't entrust such a...personal...request to anyone else, that's for certain."

Mak wiggled his eyebrows. "Have fun."

"Oh, we will. We definitely will."

Kia inserted herself into their huddle, and Lio adjusted his veil spell to include her.

"Now, about the ceremony," Kia said. "We have everything planned out, and it will all be ready by the time Cassia comes out of seclusion. As soon as she's adjusted to her new power and can rejoin everyone, we'll induct her properly into our Trial circle."

They finished their plotting as Aunt Lyta was offering her congratulations to Cassia. "My Gift Night was on the eve of battle. I only had hours to gain command of my new power before facing an onslaught of war mages."

There was a gleam in Uncle Argyros's eye more intense than his powerful mind magic. "It was my honor to awaken such a ferocious defender of the Goddess. Needless to say, the Order of Anthros still rues the night."

"Mortal armies still march to songs about the horrors of my Gifting," Aunt Lyta mused.

"Here in Orthros," Uncle Argyros said, "our minstrels sing a love ballad about it."

"As romantic as the ballad is, it does not do you justice, my love." Aunt Lyta twined her arm in Uncle Argyros's, sharing a conspiratorial look with Cassia. "Despite the rush, Argyros managed to make it an unforgettable experience for me. Mind mages excel under duress."

Uncle Argyros's famously intimidating gaze was now focused solely on his Grace with a different kind of intensity. "And you have made every night since unforgettable for me."

"There are very specific benefits to a mind mage Gifting you," Aunt Lyta continued, "which we will leave you two to discover for yourselves."

As Aunt Lyta and Uncle Argyros stepped aside to let others near, Lio squeezed in close to Cassia again. Her cheeks rosy, she murmured to him, "I appreciate all this frank advice I'm receiving tonight, but I think I already have an inkling of your specific benefits."

"I've been saving a few for us to discover tonight."

Her eyes rounded. "You have? Really?"

"It's your Gift Night. I intend to make it special."

There was no more time for whispered words of anticipation. The rest of the family took their opportunity to spend a moment with Cassia before the other guests. Kadi and Javed handed little Thenie back and forth so they could each hug Cassia. Even Bosko looked genuinely happy. The ten-year-old suckling might struggle with his adjustment to Hesperine life, but Cassia was now a hero in his eyes and no longer a target of his angry outbursts.

Cassia scanned the crowd. Her gaze fell on Alkaios and Nephalea standing nearby, and she urged them to join the family inside the Ritual circle.

They glowed with happiness and health, wearing their formal silks as naturally as if they had lived in Orthros all their lives and not spent their first decades of immortal existence Abroad as Hesperines errant on the battlefields of Tenebra. It was good to see them recovered from their arduous homecoming and thriving in their new lives here.

"I want to thank you both again," Cassia told them. "It's important for me to say that tonight. If you two hadn't protected me all those years ago, I wouldn't be alive today. I wouldn't have known to trust Hesperines. My Gifting would never have been possible without you."

Lio embraced them both in turn, sending them all his gratitude through the Blood Union. "I can never thank you enough for protecting Cassia and opening her heart to our people."

Alkaios clasped his wrist. "Not many of our deeds Abroad resulted in such happy endings. Tonight's celebration is…a balm. To both our hearts."

Nephalea touched Cassia's arm. "I have no doubt your sister would be very happy for you tonight. Remember that she is with you, in all the light around us."

Cassia pressed her hand. "Apollon has made a statue of her on the cliffs, down the path from Nike's. Perhaps we could all go there together one night?"

"Of course," Alkaios answered.

Nephalea nodded. "We will take a moment to remember her together."

A sigh escaped Cassia. "I wish I could give Nike my gratitude tonight."

"I know," said Nephalea. "But what if there's a child like you in Tenebra this very night who needs her protection?"

"You're right," Cassia answered. "I respect her reasons for not coming home when you did. Perhaps fifteen years from now, that little girl will grow up and come to Orthros, and I will be at her Gift Night celebration, all thanks to Nike."

At length, Lio eased his Grace from the arms of their closest friends and family and seated her. Standing next to her chair, he spotted his father over by the gift table and lifted a hand, giving him a nod.

"Good moon, everyone." Apollon didn't speak loudly, but his voice carried throughout the Ritual hall, and everyone hushed to listen. "It is with the greatest joy that we welcome you all to House Komnena tonight.

This past century has seen the long-awaited arrival of my Grace, the true beginning of our bloodline, and the birth of our bloodborn firstgift. This past year has seen the beloved addition of our Secondgift, Zoe, to our family. And now, the Goddess blesses us with another daughter. How glad we are that you can all join us in welcoming Cassia into our bloodline."

A cheer went up throughout the hall.

Apollon went on with a jovial laugh, "And thank you especially for conspiring with my son and me these many weeks without alerting Cassia to our plan."

Cassia looked from Apollon to Lio. Lio put on an innocent expression.

"Cassia," his father said, "we hope you will enjoy this Gift Night present from all of us."

He lifted a hand to gesture above the table. The velvet drapery there pulled back, revealing the diagram underneath. Cassia gasped and jumped to her feet, darting forward to get a better look. Lio went with her, holding her hand.

Her face alight, she studied the architectural drawing on the wall. "Greenhouses!"

"Your very own," Lio said, "one for Orthros Boreou, to enjoy while we are here in our northern residence, and a matching one in Orthros Notou for when we migrate south. Father planned the architecture and will build the foundations. I'll handle the glassmaking, of course. Mak has already promised his skill for the metalwork. Where on the grounds we build will be your choice, but we've selected a few suitable sites for you to consider."

"I would say it's what I've always wanted, but...I never imagined I could have my own greenhouse, much less two."

Lio drank down the emotions pouring out of her. Since the night they had met, he had felt so much of her anger, grief, and pain. He had made it his quest to fill her life with love and happiness instead. Tonight he tasted her joy. "You deserve everything you never imagined."

She threw her arms around him. "Oh, Lio. Thank you so much."

Then, with only a moment's hesitation, she turned and embraced his father as well. A look of reverence came over Father's face as he held her.

At last she turned and beckoned to Mak. "Come over here!" He laughed and joined them, accepting another hug from her.

Lio gestured to the scroll rack by the greenhouse plans. The documents were beautiful gifts in and of themselves, the finest paper with elegant wax seals. "The greenhouses are a gift from all of us. Everyone here tonight has brought a written promise of a plant they'd like to contribute. They'll all be brought in when the greenhouses are ready for them."

"So many." Her hands were folded in front of her, as if she couldn't decide which scroll to read first.

"I may have told them what was on that list you've been making of everything you want to grow."

Her lips rounded in the most endearing expression of astonishment. "That list was full of…ideas. I wasn't even sure it would be possible to get my hands on half of those varieties."

He rested a hand on the scroll rack. "They're all here."

Cassia turned to the watching guests, her emotions filling the Blood Union. "You all know I am not accustomed to plenty. For many years, my life was devoid of generosity. That makes these gifts mean all the more to me. They are of extraordinary value, yes, but it is the consideration and meaning in every one of them that makes them treasures. I haven't the words to properly thank all of you. But in the amount of time I will have among you, I will find the words."

Cassia's heartfelt, unrehearsed speech was met with kind auras and another round of applause.

Lio wrapped an arm around her again. "Let's have a seat so everyone will have a chance to greet you and tell you which plant they brought."

He guided her back to her chair and took the one beside her. His mother brought them plates heaped with food and poured them goblets of wine, the first of many, for the toasts were yet to come later in the night.

One by one, in pairs or by family, all those connected to Blood Komnena came into the Ritual circle and took a seat with Cassia. Elders dispensed advice, their fellow youngbloods jested to put her at ease, and sucklings sat on her lap, when they weren't playing on the floor with Knight.

Lio was in tune with her emotions moment by moment, as if he held his fingers on her pulse. He watched for any sign that she was overwhelmed or anxious. But she was genuinely enjoying herself.

As Firstgift Komnenos, he had found himself at the center of many important occasions, from Gift Nights to sacred festivals. But tonight his duty was not to his bloodline or their tributaries. Right now, he had one responsibility, and one alone. The well-being of his Grace. His mind and magic, body and heart were entirely devoted to her.

She had met with about a third of the guests when Lio sensed the Queens and the Second Princess at the door. Auras all over the room lit, as they always did upon the arrival of the Annassa and their eldest daughter. The guests vacated the chairs nearest Cassia to make way.

Queen Alea and Queen Soteira approached, arm-in-arm, with Princess Konstantina at their side. Cassia and Lio stood and bowed, their hands over their hearts.

"Annassa," Cassia greeted them with the customary honorific. "Second Princess. You honor my Gift Night celebration with your presences."

"Annassa." Lio echoed, then addressed the princess. "Aunt Kona."

A smile graced the princess's dignified expression at the affectionate name, which she allowed him to call her in honor of their families' closeness.

Annassa Alea looked upon Cassia with evident delight. The onetime Prisma of Hagia Boreia and only surviving Ritual firstblood still wore her simple white temple vestments as proudly as any royal robe. "An addition to Anastasios's bloodline is a rare and precious occasion. I wouldn't miss it."

"You have brought great joy to so many tonight, Cassia." Annassa Soteira rested a smooth, dark hand at her Grace's pale waist, clearly enjoying Annassa Alea's happiness.

"Do you have time to join us for a moment?" Cassia invited.

Annassa Soteira treated them to the kind music of her beautiful, deep laugh. "Of course, child. Everyone here has unlimited time."

Once the Queens and Aunt Kona had taken their seats, Lio and Cassia sat down again.

"Annassa Alea," Cassia said, "I realized that Anastasios's affinity has yet to manifest in our bloodline. It seems strange that no one in our family is a healer. I plan to have another affinity reading for healing after my Gifting."

Annassa Soteira considered her with the gaze of a theramancer and healer. "You should indeed repeat all your affinity readings. But I do not think healing will be your path."

Annassa Alea shook her head, a smile at the corners of her mouth, as if she knew a secret. "No, I don't see my old friend's affinity for healing appearing in you. Whatever power you possess, it is something unexpected."

Far from being disappointed at their pronouncement, Cassia turned eagerly to Aunt Kona. "Second Princess, would you have me read for garden magic again after my Gifting?"

"Of course I will repeat your affinity reading with the Circle of Rosarians." Aunt Kona relaxed back in her chair, the dark coils of her hair like an aura around her figure. As always, she was the epitome of royal beauty and Orthros's elegance, her moonstone pendant pale against her night-dark skin, her robes of ceremonial Imperial stripweave. "I would insist on that first if I didn't know Argyros will read you again before I have the chance. He is determined to snap you up for his next diplomacy student."

"I will certainly have my second reading with you," said Cassia.

Aunt Kona made a gracious gesture toward the gift table. "Your new greenhouse will aid you greatly in your studies. When it is complete, I will give you my Gift Night present: a cutting of the Sanctuary Rose."

Cassia gasped. "You would spare a branch of the mother rose? For me?"

Aunt Kona gave a regal nod. "I know you will give it proper care."

"Of course I will. To be entrusted with a piece of the last surviving rose from a Great Temple of Hespera...the one you revived and have tended for a millennium and a half..."

"It will become a thriving new vine in your greenhouse. Lio will be able to provide the necessary light spells, having studied with my mother Alea and me."

"It will be my honor, Aunt Kona," Lio replied.

"It's too much," Cassia breathed.

"When we ask Hespera for a little something, she always answers with magnificence. I try to show the same generosity to her people."

"You have my gratitude, Second Princess."

"I am to be your mentor in rose gardening. We will get dirt under our fingernails together. You must call me Master Kona, as all my students do."

"I would be honored," Cassia blurted. "Thank you."

Lio had no doubt his Grace was an excellent fit for Aunt Kona's tutelage. The princess might not be officially mentoring her in politics, but she was still the Royal Master Magistrate, Orthros's foremost legal authority and political influence. She was sure to include more in their lessons than rose gardening. An excellent opportunity, given Cassia's hopes of joining Lio in the diplomatic service.

Lio hesitated to change the subject, but the celebration was well underway, and he was growing concerned about who was missing.

"Aunt Kona," he ventured, "you wouldn't happen to know when Ioustin will arrive, would you?"

"He is coming." She sounded confident about her brother's plans.

Lio let out a breath. "Thank you."

"He is hard at work on something in Tenebra, and that is all I shall say. He holds out hope of achieving his goal by tonight, but if he cannot, he will come home for Cassia's Gift Night in any case."

Cassia frowned. "I still think we should have asked someone else to be my Ritual father. Of course I want it to be Ioustin, but as the First Prince, he has so many responsibilities. Lives depend on him Abroad."

"It has to be him," Lio protested.

"It is a very important tradition," Queen Alea agreed. "Our eldest son is always Ritual father to Apollon's children, in honor of our shared origins at Hagia Boreia."

Queen Soteira raised a brow at Lio. "As our Ritual sister, Kassandra, is mother to them. You have not asked us when she will arrive."

"I know she will arrive at the moment she deems best," Lio replied. "I would not presume to question our oracle's timing."

"Such a respectful boy," Kassandra said. "Tell that to the foolish young things who doubt my prophecies."

Kassandra had appeared at the edge of the Ritual circle. Lio was surprised to see her in Imperial purple, the deep, vivid hue bringing out the warm undertones in her mahogany complexion. She seldom flaunted her mortal origins as an Imperial princess, although she had played a key role in securing the Empire's alliance with Orthros. In the centuries since, she had embraced her role as the Queens' Master Economist, who oversaw all of Orthros's trade relationships.

"Ritual mother." Lio stood to kiss her cheek.

Before Cassia could get up, Kassandra patted her knee to stay her. "Sit and enjoy yourself a moment longer."

Cassia gave her a curious look, but did not question her remark. Apprehension came over Lio.

The celebration was supposed to last all night. Cassia was supposed to sit there and enjoy herself for hours. Why did Kassandra speak as if she had only a moment longer to savor this?

Kassandra pulled her floor-length locked hair out from behind her and took a seat beside the Queens. Perhaps Orthros's oracle simply wanted to sit down with her loved ones and not have them hang upon her every word.

Lio should know better than to read too much into his Ritual mother's remarks. He shouldn't let old fears ambush him tonight. Despite everything they had been through, Cassia was here now, safe at his side. Nothing would get in the way of her Gifting.

"I'm looking forward to calling you Ritual mother," Cassia said to Kassandra.

"As honored as I am by the invitation, my dear, I'm afraid I can't accept. Don't misunderstand. I would love to count you among my Ritual children with Lio and Zoe."

Lio stared at Kassandra in consternation. He had thought all this settled weeks ago. How could something as monumentally important as the choice of Cassia's Ritual mother change at the last minute on her Gift Night?

"I don't understand," Cassia said carefully.

"I am not to be your Ritual mother. That role is already someone else's. Don't worry. She'll arrive just in time. She always does." Kassandra closed her eyes, holding up a finger. "Wait. I love moments like this. They come along so seldom, but everyone's reactions are priceless. Right…now."

Two auras flared in the Blood Union. Gasps erupted near the front doors.

One of the auras was Ioustin's. The other…

She was…a bastion. Powerful. Adamant. Ancient. She felt familiar, but Lio didn't know her. How could he not? He should know any Hesperine elder of her stature.

A hush fell over the room, spreading and growing heavier until absolute silence reigned.

The crowd parted. Ioustin strode toward them in a formal robe thrown over his Tenebran riding boots. When Lio saw who was at his side, he recognized her, although he had only seen her carved in stone.

Nike. She was alive. And she had returned to Orthros.

HOMECOMING

F OR THE FIRST TIME since she was seven years old, Cassia looked
upon the Hesperine who had saved and changed her life.

Somehow Nike seemed just as tall now. She wore the very same
black robe as she had that night, but her hood was gone. Her vibrant red
hair was visible in a tousled braid that swayed behind her as she walked
with Hesperine grace and a warrior's determination. There was a furrow
on her pale brow, a hint of vulnerability around her full lips.

In a crowd full of people who had loved her for centuries and missed
her for decades, her gaze locked on Cassia's.

So much sadness in her dark gray eyes. Cassia recognized that, too, as
if she looked into a mirror at their shared past.

A cry broke the silence. Lyta stepped in front of Nike. The Guardian
of Orthros reached out, touching both hands to her daughter's cheeks.
"My girl."

"I'm home, Mother." Nike's voice, quiet and husky, offered comfort.

A sob tore out of Lyta. She pulled Nike to her, holding on. Nike
wrapped her arms around her mother.

"Hello, Papa." Nike smiled at her father over the top of her
mother's head.

Argyros didn't speak. Cassia thought he probably couldn't. He and
Nike looked at each other, and whatever wordless understanding the two
mind mages shared needed no words, perhaps. In silence, he wrapped his
arms around both his Grace and their first daughter. He pressed his eyes
shut over the tears that trailed down his face.

Master Kona went to her brother's side. "Well done."

Ioustin let out a sigh and put an arm around his sister.

Queen Alea's face shone. "Oh, welcome home, Nike."

Nike and her parents drew nearer the Ritual circle. Nike clasped a fist to her heart and bowed deeply to the Queens. "Annassa."

Queen Alea touched her head with affection and benediction.

As Nike straightened, Queen Soteira held her gray gaze with her own deep brown eyes, which saw everyone's hearts. "You're safe."

The rest of Nike's family crowded around her and her parents.

"Don't you dare apologize," said Kadi. "You're safe. You're here. Goddess, it's so good to see you."

Nike's mouth quirked at that. She grabbed her sister in a fierce hug. When Kadi finally let her go, Nike clasped Javed's wrist and pulled him in for an embrace as well.

"Aunt Nike?" Bosko was breathless with excitement before his idol. He clutched Thenie on his hip.

Nike blinked down at the sucklings. Her gaze flicked to Bosko's speires, the symbolic hair ties awarded to each new student of the Hesperine battle arts. Bosko never took them off, determined as he was to become the next great warrior of his bloodline. The few Stewards of Hippolyta's Stand comprised the peaceful Hesperines' entire standing army, and Cassia knew how much it meant to her loved ones that Bosko would carry on their tradition.

"Clearly I am your aunt," said Nike, "for I can tell you are a warrior and my sister's son."

Bosko stood taller. "This is your niece, Thenie."

"Hullo, Thenie."

Thenie, with her unique mind, seldom responded when spoken to and never met anyone's gaze, except Argyros's. But now she looked up, wide-eyed, at her aunt and cooed.

"Congratulations," Nike murmured to Kadi and Javed. "They're beautiful."

Mak stood waiting for his turn at their family reunion, and Cassia's heart was fit to burst for him. His sister was standing right there, the sister he had thought he'd lost before he ever knew her. And she didn't even know who he was to her.

Lyros took his hand and tugged him forward.

Mak cleared his throat. "I'm Mak. Your brother."

It was a testament to the strength of Nike's emotions in that moment that they showed in her eyes, despite how heavily veiled the ancient warrior must keep herself. Cassia saw astonishment in Nike's gaze.

"And this is my Grace, Lyros. Stewards, full rank, at your service, First Master Steward." He saluted her, then offered her his hand.

She ignored that and gave him one of the bear hugs he was always so generous with himself. "Thank you for keeping our home safe in my absence."

Mak let out a huff of relief, and a huge grin lit his face.

Nike embraced Lyros as she had the rest of the family. "Already Graced at your age, and to such a fine warrior. Goddess bless."

When Nike let go of Lyros, Apollon was waiting for her.

"Was it a good season errant?" he asked.

"Rather longer than usual. But my best."

Apollon laughed and held out his arms. She went into them without hesitation, and Cassia heard her laugh for the first time.

Holding his niece under one arm, Apollon threw the other around Ioustin's shoulders. The three surviving members of the Blood Errant were together again at last.

"Let's hear a welcome for my niece!" Apollon called out.

The cheer that rose up was worthy of her legend.

Apollon's joyous response had broken the spell. The crowd came back to life. Now greetings and the sounds of celebration surrounded Nike as well as Cassia. Nike paused to embrace Komnena, then ignored everyone else and faced Cassia.

Cassia became aware of Alkaios and Nephalea at her side. And there she stood, surrounded by her three Hesperine rescuers.

"Iskhyra." Nephalea greeted Nike by the assumed name she had used Abroad. "You decided to join us."

Nike's mouth twitched. "You two look comfortable in your silks."

Alkaios laughed. "Join us in your mother's fighting ring, and we'll show you how comfortable we are."

"I never refuse a challenge, especially from my own trainees."

Cassia watched the exchange. Did that mean Nike would stay long enough for a sparring match?

"We're not trainees anymore," Nephalea warned with a smile. "We're Stewards."

"Tied up in speires now, are you? I knew I was a bad influence." The comfort with which she spoke to them revealed her affection for them more effectively than any kind words. "How do you like it?"

"Right well," Alkaios said.

Nike put a hand on his shoulder and her other on Nephalea's. "It's good to see you in one piece."

Nephalea gave Nike an indicative look. "So. You changed your mind."

Nike's gaze settled on Cassia again. "I couldn't miss our Cassia's Gift Night, could I?"

Cassia's breath caught. It was for her sake that Pherenike, Firstgift Argyra, the Victory Star, had ended her ninety years errant.

Cassia stepped forward. She was vaguely aware of everyone watching them, of Zoe telling Knight to stay and wrapping her arms around his neck, of Lio's reassuring hand at the small of her back.

She closed the distance between her and Nike. She had thought so many times of all the things she wanted to say to her savior if she ever had the chance. Now all of those words and years caught in her throat. The ones that made it out first surprised her. "I tried to fight as you would."

Cassia recognized Nike's answering silence. She had many more words and years to struggle with. "You won."

Tears trailed down Nike's cheeks. Cassia reached out and touched them, as she had when she was seven.

And as Nike had then, she pulled Cassia into her strong arms and held her close. Her warding magic whispered across Cassia's senses, dark and mighty, the first Hesperine magic Cassia had ever felt, which had taught her to recognize the Goddess's power.

"I'm so sorry about Methu," Cassia said. "Your grief runs in my veins. I understand it now."

Nike's arms tightened a fraction, then she released Cassia. "Thanks to you, one Hesperine remains to us who is bloodborn like Methu."

Cassia reached for Lio's hand and drew him near.

He gave his head a shake, looking at Nike with wonder on his face. "It's an honor to meet you at last."

Nike tilted her head, looking up at him. "Uncle Apollon's Firstgift... and mentored by my father. Ioustin has told me a great deal on the way here. I understand I am no longer one of the two most powerful Hesperine thelemancers, but one of three."

Lio actually blushed. "I can only imagine how much I could learn from you."

"From what I hear, the two of you don't need much training at this point. I'm told a mage of dreams breached Orthros's defenses." The ferocity in Nike's voice made Cassia wish she had been there to unleash her power on the evil mind mage who called himself the Collector. "You defeated him with thelemancy and an artifact imbued with Sanctuary magic. You must tell me of the battle. But not now. That's not what tonight is for."

"True." Kassandra lounged in her chair, observing the exchange. "Where did you put it, by the way?"

Nike's jaw clenched.

"You couldn't bring it with you." There was a reassuring undertone to Kassandra's words.

"I feel like I'm missing a limb," Nike gritted.

Cassia glanced between them, then exchanged a curious look with Lio. It wasn't unusual for Kassandra to seem omniscient. But it did seem strange for Nike, after ninety years of not seeing Kassandra, to carry on a conversation with her as if they were continuing a discussion.

Were they perhaps talking about Nike's famous shield, the Chalice of Stars? Did that count as a weapon, making it subject to the ban on all arms in Orthros? If so, she would be required to leave it at the border fortress of Waystar before coming to Selas.

"You are in one piece," Kassandra said. "It will be fine with your shield."

Well, apparently "it" was something else.

Nike hesitated. "It's not at Waystar with the Chalice."

"Even better," Kassandra replied. "Next time you can put it in my silk box."

Nike's brows rose. "Your box is full."

"I've let the Akron's Torch out to get some exercise lately. You should have seen Lio brandish it before the Firstblood Circle."

Nike eyed Lio. "You wielded the artifact Methu stole from the war mages? You properly appreciate your legacy as a bloodborn, I see."

"I hope so," he said.

Kassandra leisurely got up and came over to drop a kiss on Nike's cheek. "You've laid it down for tonight. Try to feel like you have."

"If you are satisfied, then I will try."

"Satisfied? Tonight is a triumph, and don't you doubt it. I will leave you and Cassia to your chat, now."

Aunt Lyta cast a searching gaze between her daughter and the oracle. She put an arm around Nike again, pulling her close. On Nike's other side, Uncle Argyros did the same, holding her as if to reassure himself she was really here, and not an illusion.

"Cassia," said Nike, "I came here tonight for you, to shed light on your past before you face it during your Gifting."

Amid the happy celebration, a pall came over Cassia. "I have left my past behind."

"You cannot, until you fully understand it. What I have to say may change what you believe about the night we met."

Cassia didn't want anything to change. Except the fact that she was mortal.

Somewhere deep within her, there rose the voice of doubt. Apollon had beaten it back, and everyone's well-wishes had drowned it out. But she hadn't quite banished it.

What if she still wasn't ready?

Nike might prove to be her rescuer once again.

The warrior's gaze swept the crowd again, as if surveying a battlefield. "Where can we talk?"

Cassia gestured around them at the family. "We can go to Lio's library."

"I think you and I ought to discuss this privately."

Aunt Lyta's arm tightened around Nike.

Nike held fast to her parents for a long moment, resting her face on her father's shoulder. "Cassia saved your lives. Let me honor my bond of gratitude with her tonight."

"There will be a fresh pot of coffee in my library after the celebration." Her father let the statement hang, the implications unspoken, neither asking nor demanding.

"Set a cup out for me," Nike said.

Uncle Argyros placed a kiss upon Nike's brow.

Aunt Lyta let her go with obvious hesitation, but nodded. "You saved Cassia on the most dangerous night of her life. Who else could make the Gifting safer for her tonight?"

Cassia squeezed Lio's hand. "I'll take Nike to our library if you take care of the guests."

He shook his head. "I'm staying with you."

"Yes," Nike agreed, "Lio should join us."

"Lyros and I excel at fending off anyone, including guests," Mak broke in. "You three go. We'll smooth things over here."

"Mak," Cassia protested. He had barely gotten to look at his sister. It was he who should get to have a private talk with her.

He shook his head. "The Stand is on duty tonight, and our mission is to see you safely through your Gifting. Go. Let Nike help you with your past."

Cassia gave him another hug. "We'll visit Nike's statue with her later. I'll make sure of it. She should see what you've done for her there."

"I'd like that."

With Mak and Lyros standing fast against the crowd, two of the three most powerful mind mages in Orthros stepped Cassia away from her Gift Night celebration.

FRAGILE CHOICES

LIO COULDN'T HELP BUT stare at his famous cousin. It was surreal to
see her standing here in the library of his and Cassia's residence. In
person, as in the stories, Nike seemed larger than life.

Her gaze darted over the bookshelves that lined the walls from floor
to ceiling. The coffee table and silk cushions in the center of the room.
The piles of scrolls on his desk, Knight's chew toy. She took in her surroundings in less than the blink of an eye. There was a readiness in her
tense limbs, as if Orthros's luxuries were a threat, and she didn't trust
the mundane.

Lio had seen the same signs in many of the returning Hesperines errant
who were his mother's patients, and they had been in the field far less than
ninety years. This legend needed a mind healer.

And yet he couldn't read her aura. He had never sensed a veil like the
one she kept over her emotions. She was as unreadable as Uncle Argyros,
and Lio never would have known she hid her emotions with thelemancy, if
her veil weren't crafted of warding magic, too. That ward was like a curtain
wall. She had no qualms announcing she was well-defended.

How fractured was she under those graceful protections?

"'The Gift is both a petal and a thorn,'" Nike read from one of his
stained glass windows. "One of mine and my father's favorites."

"Mine, too," Lio said. "He spoke of you often while I was working on
that panel."

"Glass and diplomacy and the mind. Ioustin said you have the hand
for fragile work."

"In the end, I had to take Mak and Lyros's invitation into the training ring, where I can hit things that don't break. Except my nose. That's been broken plenty of times."

He managed to surprise a laugh out of Nike with that. The longer Lio knew Mak, the more he came to value the role humor could sometimes play in diplomacy.

"Would you like some coffee?" Cassia gestured to the glass coffee service on the table, following his jest with a simple social ritual.

Between the two of them, they might manage to put the returning Hesperine errant at ease.

Nike took a step closer to the coffee table. "I would always like some coffee."

"My sentiments exactly." Cassia took a seat on her and Lio's favorite couch.

"I'll make it." Lio joined her and reached into a storage basket under the table to select a jar of coffee. "Uncle Argyros said you used to like Starfrost Brew."

Nike lowered herself onto the chair across the table from them. "I wouldn't mind a cup of Polar Night Roast tonight. Strong."

"I need one, too," Cassia agreed.

Lio pulled out the jar of the darkest, strongest coffee in Orthros. "Polar Night Roast it is."

Nike glanced down at herself and let out a huff. She plucked at the sleeve of her robe, a beautiful antique formal, its black embroidery fraying. "I want to apologize for appearing tonight like some...harbinger of death. What must you think of me, coming to your Gift Night in the robe I wore the night you lost your sister?"

Lio started. He hadn't realized it was the same one.

"It's all right," Cassia said. "She's been present in all our minds tonight. This is a happy occasion, but a heavy one, too."

"I didn't have time to..." Nike waved a hand at the robe in resignation. "...make myself more presentable."

"That's the last thing you need to apologize for," Cassia assured her. "You could have arrived in dusty fighting robes, and no one would have given it a thought."

Nike paused, then stood. "Very well."

She pulled off the formal silk and tossed it over the back of a nearby chair, revealing what she wore underneath. A knee-length black fighting robe, like Stand regalia without the emblems. There were dark stains across the front, still wet. The scent told Lio it was blood.

"Oh, I see," said Cassia.

Nike gave them a rueful smile and sat down again.

"Even better than dust," Cassia added with relish.

Nike barked a laugh.

"But I suppose it's best the sucklings didn't see it." Cassia raised her eyebrows. "Whose is it?"

"And what do you need it for, if I may ask?" Lio couldn't imagine why she required the blood of her enemy, but clearly Nike had her reasons for keeping the stains on her robes. Otherwise she could have worked a cleaning spell on them already.

"I'm afraid that's a tale for another time," Nike replied. "As you can see, Ioustin didn't catch up with me until tonight. We wasted no time returning. I had to get here before your Gifting, Cassia."

"How did he find you?" Cassia asked. "We all know you eluded him for nearly a century. It's astonishing that he was able to make contact with you just in time for my Gift Night."

"Oh, that was no coincidence. Apparently Alkaios and Nephalea decided that your Gifting was the right occasion to give Ioustin new information about where I was likely to be. Meddling Newgifts." Affection was evident in Nike's tone.

"Oh." Cassia looked chagrined. "I hope you don't feel as if they betrayed your cause because of me."

"Of course not. I should thank all three of you. I understand you have been a great comfort to my family."

"No more than they have been to us."

"If I'd known…" Nike gave her head a shake. "Imagine my surprise upon seeing my Trial brother for the first time in nearly a century. He cornered me, not to halt my quest or beg me to think of my family. He didn't even ask me to come home. He just wanted to tell me that a little girl I had rescued from an archer's arrow fifteen years ago was about to become a Hesperine tonight. And what a dangerous path you took to get here."

"I tried to honor what you did for me, Nike."

"You have been a shield between the Hesperines and our mortal enemies." Nike's voice grew husky with emotion. "You saved my family's lives. None of them would have survived the Equinox Summit, had you not warned Lio about the assassination attempt. You have honored our bond of gratitude many times over."

Lio smiled at his Grace. "Ioustin has told you of Cassia's deeds?"

"All of them," Nike said. "Goddess bless, you are a woman after my own heart."

Cassia's aura swelled under the praise. "Lio and I did everything together."

"Yes, I have heard Glasstongue's legend as well. I would expect no less from Uncle Apollon's son." Nike turned to Lio. "I am not surprised. But I am thankful."

Lio put a hand to his heart. "So am I. At last, I can give you my gratitude for saving Cassia's life."

The Blood Union grew potent with unspoken emotion, uncomfortably so. Lio deemed it a good time to set large mugs of coffee in front of all three of them. Nike took refuge from their gazes, glancing into her drink.

Once they had all taken a swallow of the brew, Cassia filled the silence with more kind words. "I can scarcely believe you came back to Orthros after all this time because of me. It means more to us than we can say."

"Tonight also holds meaning for me beyond my expectations." Nike set down her coffee, and the soft thump of her mug on the table seemed to toll through the library. "I have remained Abroad for a very specific purpose. Or so I thought. I don't know, now."

The Victory Star doubted her purpose? To that monumental admission, Lio could find no reply. Cassia didn't ask Nike to elaborate, either.

But Nike did. "You are familiar with Kassandra's prophecy that 'the bloodborn will return to Orthros.'"

"Yes." Lio hesitated.

"Our people believe it refers to you," said Nike. "When you were born among us after Methu's death, there was once again a bloodborn in Orthros."

"I would not presume. Kassandra has said the prophecy refers to

Methu. She holds out hope he was only captured by the war mages, not killed, and that he will somehow return to us."

"No one in Orthros believes her."

"You do," Lio said in realization.

"The fateful words you have heard all your life are only half the prophecy," Nike told him. "The other half was for me."

Cassia and Lio listened.

"'The bloodborn will return to Orthros,'" Nike pronounced, "'and you shall deliver his rescue.'"

"You've been looking for him." Lio leaned forward.

Nike's hands tightened around her mug. "For almost a century, I have been prying evidence from places I will not describe in your pleasant library."

Lio took a breath so he could speak. "What have you found?"

"So much. But not my Trial brother."

Once again she looked at the window with its double-edged quote about the Gift. She leaned an elbow on the arm of her chair, her fingers pressed to her pursed lips. This was what a century of grief and crushing disappointment looked like under bloodstains and a veil of warding and thelemancy.

"I'm so sorry, Nike." Cassia's simple words carried the earnestness of a prayer.

"I might have been wrong," said the Victory Star. "For here is the bloodborn, brought home to Orthros. I delivered a girl from danger, and she grew into this woman before me, who saved the bloodborn and all Hesperines. She proved to be the partner whose blood your life depends on."

His Grace. Lio looked at Cassia and the fresh tears trembling in her hazel eyes in the soft light of his stained glass windows. "My rescue."

Nike's distant gaze returned, and she observed the two of them. "We are bound together by choices more fragile than glass. Somehow they fused together into something good. Whether my quest is over or not, tonight, my place is here with you, Cassia. I am a piece of your choice to become a Hesperine. I hold a piece of your past. Like the night we met, tonight I have a responsibility to do everything in my power to protect you. In this case, from the dangers of your own memories."

"I thought I was ready," Cassia said, "but now I understand that I couldn't have been. Not without you."

Lio felt a sense of reassurance he hadn't known he needed. One of Orthros's greatest heroes was fighting for his Grace tonight. His father had led the charge against Cassia's fears, and their family and friends had rallied to her defense. Who better than Nike to help Cassia lay any lingering doubts to rest?

Solia's death had been the most heartbreaking event in Cassia's life. Even after all the healing she had done since, Lio knew it would be painful for her to experience that loss yet again during her Gifting. If Nike's revelations tonight helped soften the blow, he would be grateful.

Nike spread her hands. "I have come to offer you the opportunity to relive your past. Ioustin tells me you have already done something akin to what I'm proposing, thanks to Lio's thelemancy. But I can make it possible for you to experience that night as no one else can, because I was there."

Cassia swallowed. "You can use your mind magic to put me in that place and time."

Lio squeezed her hand. "It will do you good to revisit these memories consciously, before your Gifting. It gives you the opportunity to resolve your feelings now and reduce the possible struggles awaiting you during your transformation."

Her hand tightened in his. "I must do it."

"Do you remember what I said to you that night?" Nike asked. "That even though you were a child, you deserved answers, and that I would tell you truths that might be difficult."

"You said that if they were too hard to hear, I only had to ask you to stop, and I should not be ashamed of my fear."

"The same holds true tonight. If at any point you wish to return to the present, call out to me, and I will cease the spell."

"I'm not a child anymore. You're going to show me truths you couldn't reveal then, aren't you?"

"How much do you want to know?"

Emotion quivered in Cassia's aura. Lio drew her closer.

"Lio explained to me later that when a Hesperine gives a human the Mercy, the transformation of their mortal remains into light causes a powerful effect. A release of spirit that conveys their final thoughts and feelings."

"That's right. Each time I give someone the Mercy, I become a steward of their memories."

"Were Solia's final moments...difficult?"

"Many people suffered that night. Especially you." Nike paused. "You know I had no idea who your father was. Consumed by my search for Methu, I paid little attention to politics and diplomacy. Alkaios and Nephalea left human society in an earlier reign and knew nothing of the current king. Our work took us most often to the fringes, where evil seeks to do its work unseen."

"Hesperines' motivations are pure," said Cassia. "I have always known you saved me out of the goodness of your heart, and not because of the political implications."

Nike's jaw clenched. "I had less than pure thoughts about what I would have liked to do to your father. I could tell he was a monster. The circumstances made that clear. You don't know how many nights I've thought back to my decision to return you to him."

"You kept the Equinox Oath," said Cassia. "Hesperines aren't allowed to take children who aren't orphans. If you had broken the treaty, the Tenebrans could have taken revenge on all Hesperines errant."

"I kept the letter of the Oath," Nike replied, "not the spirit of it. I couldn't escape the feeling that I should have found a way to save you from him. I could have sent you to Orthros and let your father believe his enemies were to blame for your disappearance."

"You don't know how many times I've imagined that. What my life would have been like if you'd brought me home then, and I had grown up in safety in Orthros."

"Should I have taken you away from him?" Nike asked.

Cassia's aura ached for all those years.

But then she shook her head. "Do I wish I could have been spared the suffering he caused me? Of course. But you couldn't do it, Nike. We needn't ask Kassandra how that version of the future would have looked. I wouldn't have been in Tenebra to stop the assassination at the Equinox Summit or any of the disastrous consequences that would have followed."

Lio had pondered these what-ifs many times, wishing his Grace's heroism had not come at such a cost to her. She had paid so dearly to rescue him. "I would have traded places with you if I could have."

Cassia gripped his hand. "Don't think about such things. We're here now, and we're both safe. Thanks to Nike's decisions."

Nike gave a nod. "I understand that now."

"I hope it gives you peace about that night," Cassia said. "As Apollon reminded me, the painful past is how we all arrived at this wondrous present."

"Uncle Apollon should know." Nike's expression softened. "I would not ask you to relive that painful past without cause. You need to see for yourself. You will understand what I witnessed, in a way even I do not. There are answers there that only you can glean."

"What kind of answers?" Cassia asked, apprehension hazing her aura.

"When Ioustin told me you and Solia were the king's daughters, that shed an entirely different light on what happened. But I do not wish to influence your interpretation of events, not until you confirm what I suspect."

"Do you think this will give me peace?" Cassia asked.

"If I'm right, it could give you something much more than that—hope."

COURAGE THEN AND NOW

"ARE YOU READY?" Nike asked.

No. Of course Cassia wasn't ready. Nothing could ever prepare her to witness her sister's suffering.

Over the years, Cassia's worst imaginings had threatened to fill in all that she didn't know, but she had found refuge in the shadowy corners of her childhood memories. Comforting Hesperine darkness obscured the most painful details because Nike, Nephalea, and Alkaios had kept the worst of it from her.

Now Nike would reveal all of that. But she promised it would ease Cassia's pain, not add to it.

Cassia would never want to know. But she was willing.

"I am not ready for this," she said, "but I must be ready for my Gifting. I'll do it."

"Take heart, Cassia," said Nike. "I have seen your courage then and now. You are equal to this challenge."

Hearing the Victory Star say that about her, Cassia couldn't help but believe it of herself.

Lio held her against his side, his arm unwavering around her. "May I assist?"

"Yes," Nike answered. "I thought Cassia would want you with her on this journey."

She leaned into him. "I do."

"I'll not leave your mind," he promised. "I will be right there with you every step of the way, my rose."

"Since you're a mind mage," Nike added, "you can lend your power to my working while you're at it. Cassia is highly acclimated to your magic, I assume. It will make the experience more comfortable for her."

"Certainly." He kissed Cassia's brow.

Nike rested a hand on each arm of her chair. "Let us begin."

She didn't say any incantations or inscribe any arcane symbols in blood. Cassia had learned long ago that the most potent Hesperine workings were acts of pure Will. Even with her dull mortal senses, she sensed the magic in the room waxing full. The library around Cassia began to haze, as if she were looking at her surroundings through rough Tenebran glass.

"Goddess bless," Lio murmured. "It's a privilege to cast a spell with you, Nike."

"I'm impressed," Nike replied. "You and I never have the opportunity to collaborate with thelemancers on our level, except Father."

Lio's familiar magic enveloped Cassia's mind. Along with him came Nike's presence. Until now, no thelemancer but Lio had ever been a visitor in Cassia's thoughts. But Nike didn't feel like an intruder. Hers was the first Hesperine magic Cassia had ever encountered. It wrapped around her now like a strong, protective embrace and snatched her up.

THE FIELD

THE FIELD.

Where Solia had met her fate. Where Cassia still waged her inner battles.

The fortress of Castra Roborra and the snowy grounds surrounding it looked smaller than the monolithic place she recalled. Viewed through the eyes of Nike, who had seen centuries' worth of battlefields, the place shrank in contrast to the mighty Hesperine.

Her keen ears detected the sounds of men and horses at rest in the camp some distance behind her. She could track the footsteps of each scout that haunted the surrounding woods. She could count the racing heartbeats of the guards on the walls above her.

When one man's shaking hands loosed an arrow at her, she halted it midair with a touch of levitation. She concentrated on his aura. Yes, that was the one who had tried to kill the child. She turned the arrow around and drove it into his heart. There came a grunt, and then his heart was silent.

Nephalea eyed her.

"I know," Nike said, "I taught you that Hesperines don't kill needlessly. That wasn't needless."

"Of course it wasn't," Nephalea replied. "The next time he aims at a child, you may not be there to move her out of the way."

Alkaios looked up at the slit the archer had fired through. "I only wish I'd done it myself."

"Iskhyra," Nephalea said, "if it is Cassia's father you really wish to aim for, you might as well send him the way of the archer, too."

Alkaios turned to Nike. "There's still time to go back for her. We could get her out of camp as easily as we put her back."

Nike rubbed her arms, thinking of how Cassia had fought her, then reached for comfort. "The Oath forbids us to take her. She's not an orphan. We must not make her one."

Nephalea shook her head. "What sort of father would leave his older daughter to the scavengers, driving his younger daughter to risk her life to search for her sister's remains?"

"What other heartless deeds has that man committed?" Alkaios wondered.

Nike could pluck the man's crimes from his thoughts easily. But such an evaluation of a person's soul was for the Goddess to perform.

"We must adhere to Hespera's tenets and the treaty," Nike reminded them—and herself. "We do not steal children. We must never behave like the monsters humans believe us to be."

Her father had striven for peace for too long, and her mother had instilled too much honor in her for Nike to compromise now.

Goddess, I pray that we are making the right choice.

Nike must set an example for her Newgifts. "It isn't always easy to know when to wield our power and when to refrain. What is clear is that we must keep our promise to Cassia and give her sister the sacred rites."

Alkaios grimaced. "You're right."

Nephalea rubbed his back with a comforting hand.

In reverent silence, they began their duty. The catapults had scattered the fallen, but the Hesperines' senses led them to each body on the field or at the perimeter of the surrounding woods.

Alkaios retrieved the only mortal who had still been alive upon their arrival. The young Hesperine's aura was still haunted after fulfilling the man's last request for a merciful death. At least Cassia had not been here for that.

Gently they laid the broken warriors in respectful positions on either side of the smaller form covered in Alkaios's cloak. In death, as in life, the soldiers should flank the woman they had sworn to protect.

Cassia's emotions flashed painfully, overlaying and echoing Nike's.

"I'm sorry you have to see this." The words emerged from Nike of the past, but Cassia could tell it was Nike of the present who spoke. "But this is important. Observe carefully."

Nike walked along the entire line of the fallen, gazing at each man's face. Cassia recognized them from her childhood. Solia's bodyguards.

All her bodyguards. Not a single man was unaccounted for.

When the rebel free lords had waylaid Solia, their numbers had been far superior. In the skirmish that followed, some of her guard must have perished, or so Cassia had always assumed. Only the survivors would have been captured with Solia, taken to the fortress, and executed with her.

How could her entire guard be here?

"Keep that in mind," Nike instructed.

At last she halted before the cloaked figure. Despite her efforts at courage, Cassia quailed. That was Solia. That was her sister. The bundle under the fabric looked so small. So alone.

In fact, she was the lone woman on the field.

Where was Lady Iris? Solia's handmaiden, her dearest friend, her most trusted confidant. She would have followed her princess anywhere, and had done so, going into that fortress at her side, never to return.

So why wasn't her body here?

"I knew you would understand more than I did," said Nike. "Now brace yourself." Her words faded into the voice of memory. "Oh, Cassia. I'm so sorry."

Alkaios and Nephalea joined her over Solia.

"Alkaios," Nike bade him, "if you would uncover her for us. Let the Goddess's Eyes see her, for Hespera looks upon suffering only with compassion."

With a heavy sigh, he knelt and pulled back the cloak.

Cassia's heart lurched, sending pinpricks through her limbs that made her remember her body. She felt Lio's arm steady her.

That's enough. His anger shook the foundations of Castra Roborra.

"It is Cassia's choice to leave this place," Nike reminded him gently.

She wanted to flee. Her panic was driving her back into her awareness of the library. But the truth was here in the memory. The key to her future was in the past.

"Lio," she choked out. "Help me stay."

"As you Will."

His power steadied the vision. His presence was everywhere, filling the night. He was here with her, for her. She was no longer alone in that night, and she never would be again.

She wouldn't have been able to hold all the pain without him there to feel it with her.

It was so much worse than Cassia had imagined. Where Solia's beloved face had been, there was a butchered mask. Blood from countless knife wounds crusted her golden hair and spidered across her golden gown. It was less horrifying to follow the trails of blood than to look at what remained of her face.

There was a pristine circle over her chest, where her pendant had surely rested, before Alkaios had retrieved it and placed it in Cassia's small hands. He must have cleaned the blood from it first.

Nephalea knelt and placed Solia's head on her lap, smoothing her hair back from her destroyed face.

Nike sank her fangs into her wrist. Holding her open vein over Solia, she let her blood splash onto the stains on her gown. "We shed our blood for her, as she shed hers for those she loved."

Nephalea opened her wrist and combed it through Solia's hair. Alkaios placed his bleeding hand where Solia's pendant had been.

Their libation complete, Nike began to speak. The ancient Ritual words in the Divine Tongue flowed through Cassia's mind, eddies of familiar verses she had heard in the hallowed halls of Orthros, mysterious but comforting words she didn't quite comprehend.

The sky above felt near. The darkness seemed to become magic. The Hesperines' fresh blood started to glow, forming a halo of bright white around Solia's head, garbing her in light, shining out from her heart. Then she became the aura. Brilliant and powerful, she flashed, lighting up the night.

Magic quaked through Nike's veins and brought images, sounds, sensations to life under her skin.

Through Nike's memories, Cassia was drawn deeper, down into the memories of Solia's final moments.

THE SHAPER OF THE WORLD

THE GUARDS ESCORTED HER in silence, keeping their part of the bargain. A few flakes of snow threatened from the flat white sky, but she would soon reach the shelter of the trees. Just a little farther, and she would make it past the strategically cleared area around the fortress, out of the archers' range. She would be on her way back to camp. To Cassia.

She had to get to Cassia. To protect her and the secret. She must not allow anything to stop her.

She drew nearer and nearer to the safety of the woods. She could almost feel the fortress receding behind her. With each step, her tension became a little less unbearable.

When she heard hoofbeats behind her, the tension reared up again. She kept her gaze fixed ahead and walked onward as briskly as she could.

The thuds of the horse's hooves swept around her. One of her captor's knights drew rein in her path. "That's far enough."

She stood with perfect posture and spoke in her most feminine, dignified court tones. "I beg your pardon?"

The guards sank back a step, staying out of the negotiation.

The knight's face was as pale and hard as that threatening sky. "My lord wishes for you to return to the fortress."

"We have an agreement. He promised me safe passage back to camp."

"Now you are to come with me."

"What is the meaning of this? There is a frightened child waiting for my reassurance. All I have asked of your lord is that I be allowed to return to Cassia. I am of no consequence in his siege."

The knight looked past her to the guards.

She took that as a warning that negotiation was futile. She ran.

Three long strides and a heave of breath, and she was under the trees. She focused on not tripping, on getting as far as she could. If only she could come within range of a friendly forward scout, an arrow might find the knight before he could snatch her.

The ground shook with the approach of his horse. But she was smaller and could maneuver better than the beast. She darted between two close-growing trees and heard the horse angle away in another direction.

Ahead of her, a man she recognized leapt down from a tree. She gasped in relief. She threw herself toward the scout.

He landed limply on the ground before her. She couldn't stop in time and stumbled over his twisted body. She went down, catching herself on his bloodstained chest.

Arms clamped around her from behind, cutting off her breath. The enemy scout yanked her to her feet and held her fast. She heard the knight ride toward them.

The world slanted as she was hauled up onto the horse. The knight set her before him on his saddle, his hold like a vice, and kicked his horse into motion.

Retracing her slow, anxious escape took only a few breathlessly fast moments. She barely had time to plan what she would say to her captor before his men brought her back into the grip of the fortress through a postern. Soon the narrow back halls squeezed her into the chamber where she had been a prisoner before.

When she saw that it was empty, her heart came back to life in her chest.

The others had escaped.

The room's only occupant was the lord of the fortress. His men joined them inside and slammed the door.

"They're gone," her captor growled.

"They were here when I left, my lord."

"You are her most trusted confidant. You think for a moment I believe you had nothing to do with this?"

"How could I, my lord? She made her wishes clear. I was to go straight to Cassia and stay out of the conflict. Once I have answered your questions, I am sure you will once more uphold our agreement and let me see to the child's care."

"That depends on your answers to my questions."

"I am of no use to you in this standoff, my lord. You have nothing to gain by ransoming me, and everything to gain by leaving me be. My family is on good terms with you. Just send me back to the camp, where I may see to my domestic concerns."

He took one threatening step closer. "How did they escape? Where did they go?"

"I don't know, my lord. All I am certain of is that a frightened little girl awaits me in camp. Despite what you think of her, you must at least acknowledge she is worthy of your pity. Think of the steps you've taken to keep your son safe tonight. Cassia is even younger than he is. She needs me."

"Don't you dare invoke my son!" The flash of desperation on his face revealed the shaky foundations on which this fortress now stood.

"Benedict is a dear boy," she said softly. "You've seen how fond of him we are. You know I will look after him as well. I will be in a position to do so."

"There is only one offer you can make that will buy your way out of these walls," he rasped. "Tell me where I can find them."

"As I said, my lord, I do not know."

"I could get it out of you, given time. But there is no time. I owe my enemy a dead hostage by dawn." He spread his hands to indicate the empty room. "Lo, there is no hostage to be had."

Her breath whipped dryly into her throat. "You intended to murder her? I did not think you would stoop so low."

"I do not relish the ugly outcome of my best intentions."

"Even after your betrayal, I thought better of you."

"I have no choice. I must make a show of strength. I swore to execute her by nightfall, and I will keep my word. Now it is your turn to make your decision. You can tell me where she is, and quickly." His gaze started at the top of her blond head and traveled all the way down her figure. Not in a leer, but with cold calculation. "Or you may die in her place. It will not be difficult to substitute your corpse for hers."

Her own heart began to pound with the certainty of what she must do.

No tears came, as if her body knew she could not afford such an expense in this crisis. The sourness in her belly disappeared, and strength spread through her limbs.

"You've given me a very easy decision to make," she answered. "I swore long ago that I would give my life for her. I have lived each day with the knowledge that this might very well be how I meet my end. I will die in her place. I have always been ready."

Shock crossed his face. "You cannot really believe in her mad plan."

"Not the answer you expected? Did you think the threat of death would frighten me into spilling her secrets?" A laugh escaped her, madly triumphant. "Some of us have kept our honor."

"You do not deserve this fate." He took a step toward her.

She held her ground. "Then do not send me to it."

"I have no choice."

"You have had many, many choices. I'm not sure how much longer you'll have to live with them, but live with them you must. I have no regrets. Her friendship has been the greatest treasure of my life. Her trust the greatest reward for my service. I will not survive to live in the world of her making, but I will die knowing it was my counsel that shaped it. I am proud of my legacy. Can you say the same?"

He would not meet her gaze now. "I will return with the guards in a moment. I expect you to change into her clothing. I do not wish to have my men dress your corpse."

"Do not think you will subject me to such indignity. I go to this fate with my head high. I am proud of all I have accomplished in this life and the impact my death will have. I count myself fortunate to meet such an honorable end."

He turned his back on her and marched out, his men following him. The door sealed her in the windowless room.

Her hands did not shake as she divested herself of her clothing. She laid out her dress, her tunica, her undergarments on the bed. On the table beside it, her family signet ring and the ear baubles her sweetheart had given her. Vague footprints of the life she had lived.

She had written who she was in a longer-lasting medium than gowns and jewels. Tenebra would bear her mark forever.

She stood there in nothing but the wooden ivy pendant.

And the other side of the truth struck her.

She had not finished her work. Many choices still lay ahead of her dearest friend, and she would not be there to help her navigate. The cause still needed her.

Cassia needed her.

The vision of Cassia alone and frightened almost brought her to her knees.

The ivy pendant. That was the only thing still in her power to protect. Its secret must never fall into enemy hands. It must not be lost. Cassia would need it someday.

She could only hope her body was indeed the safest place for this ancient, irreplaceable treasure. If she carried it to her crypt, perhaps there was still hope that one day, a trusted hand might retrieve it from within her tomb.

She opened her friend's travel trunk and retrieved what she would need. She put on the fine undergarments, the whisper-soft tunica. She donned the golden gown she had put on her friend so many times. This part was easy. It was not the first time they had traded places so she could serve as a decoy.

She looked down at herself, garbed like a goddess.

We would have failed long ago without you, her friend had so often said. *Never doubt you are as necessary to our cause as I. I look forward to the day when I can elevate you to the position that befits you, so all of Tenebra will bow to your wisdom, and laud you as the adviser of queens.*

She held those words in her heart as the door swung open and Lord Bellator entered to deliver her fate.

THE TRUTH

CASSIA ROSE FROM THE vision with a hollow gasp, as if filling her chest with her own last breath.

Lio had gathered her onto his lap. He stroked the side of her face with his smooth fingers. His touch oriented her.

She sprang to her feet, and he let her go. She stared at Nike. The elder Hesperine did not speak, as if waiting for Cassia's verdict.

"That wasn't my sister."

Nike rubbed a hand over her face. "So I suspected, after Ioustin explained things. But only you could be sure."

"Cassia." Lio spoke. "This means…"

The truth was roaring up out of her, but she held it in. It was too much to imagine. Too much to hope for. She began to pace, reasoning it out. She had to make sure, before she dared speak it aloud and let it feel real.

"The memory we all just saw…the final moments of the woman you gave the Mercy to, Nike…the woman who experienced that was not my sister."

"Do you know who she was?" Nike asked.

"Yes! That had to be Lady Iris. She was taken captive along with my sister because she was her handmaiden, who never left her side. But I remember now…her family *was* at one time in the same faction as Bellator, the lord of Castra Roborra, who captured Solia."

Lio joined in, her patient ally now, as in every crucial moment. "Would Lady Iris have been in a position to secure her release from the fortress?"

Cassia nodded, her neck popping with the motion. "Given her rank and status, she could certainly have made an argument that she should be treated as a non-combatant and allowed to return to the king." Cassia halted, her gaze seeking Lio's.

There was encouragement in his dark blue eyes. "She and Solia did everything they could to protect you. Lady Iris was trying to get to you—with the pendant. She must have known its history and power."

"What is the pendant's significance?" Nike asked. "Alkaios, Nephalea and I always wondered."

"It is connected to the Changing Queen in some way," Lio explained, "imbued with Lustra magic."

Nike whistled. "The old nature magic is all but lost. Few artifacts of it have survived. That pendant could be sixteen hundred years old."

Lio nodded. "It was secretly passed down from one Tenebran queen to another and finally, from a princess to her sister." Lio looked to Cassia again. "Solia wanted you to have access to the artifact's power, but most of all, someone to look after you."

Cassia's throat ached. "My sister gave up her best ally for me. Iris left Solia—her dearest friend, her future queen—so I wouldn't be alone."

"She was so focused on you," Nike said. "You can understand why I didn't doubt I had just witnessed your sister's memories."

Cassia resumed her pacing, treading back and forth between Nike and Lio. "Iris was a few years older than Solia, but they were the same size, had the same figure. I used to watch them in the mirror with their golden hair and fair faces. They were so beautiful."

"So they looked truly alike," Lio concluded.

"Iris knew all Solia's secrets. I don't doubt she was her chief adviser in their plans to overthrow the king. The shaper of the Tenebra that Solia wanted to build. She died a hero. She died."

Lady Iris had faced the prospect of her own death and shed no tears. Cassia knew how that felt. She had found that strength more than once. Now the loss of that brave and powerful woman welled out of Cassia. The tears Iris had never shed poured down her cheeks.

Lio stood and caught her in his arms, stilling her with his gentle embrace. She rested her face against his chest, unable to stop her sobs.

She felt Nike's strong hand between her shoulder blades. Nike and Lio were always the ones who reminded her tears were no cause for shame.

When she caught her breath and lifted her head, Lio was holding out one of his white silk handkerchiefs, embroidered with a black Rose of Hespera. Resting one grateful hand on his chest, she took the handkerchief in the other and wiped her face.

As soon as she could trust her voice, she spoke her faceted thoughts, the many small, sharp truths that were taking shape into the whole truth. "Iris refused to betray Solia to the very last. She did deserve a better fate. Lord Bellator was a monster. The way he and his men desecrated her...to make the king believe... I'm glad you gave her the Mercy, Nike. The rites you gave her were worthy of her."

"I have always considered it an honor to be the steward of her final thoughts. I feel it all the more, now that I know who she really was."

Cassia met Nike's gaze. "That was Iris's body on the field. It wasn't my sister."

Nike gave a nod. Lio gazed down at Cassia, his eyes intense and shining.

She looked between the two Hesperines who already saw the truth and were merely waiting for her to acknowledge it.

Cassia spoke it. "Solia escaped."

EVERYTHING ONCE BELIEVED

L io felt Cassia's aura rise like a shout of triumph over every
moment of every year she had mourned.

"I have to know. Where did she go? What happened to her after
that?" As quickly as her joy struck, it quelled. "She was never seen or heard
from after that night. It can't be good news. But I have to know."

It *was* good news. Nike had just reported a miracle. Solia had escaped.
Anything seemed possible.

Lio wanted to tell Cassia that now, of all times, was the time to get her
hopes up. It was his instinct to shower her with hope.

He gritted his teeth. He mustn't. He couldn't promise her this meant
everything would be all right. That was not in his power. He must allow
her to feel this in her own way and wrestle with her hopes however she
could bear.

What was in his power was tearing apart the world until he found the
answers she needed.

"It should be possible to step to her," Lio said.

Cassia's eyes widened. "Surely not. It couldn't be so easy."

He took her hands. "With some help from mind magic, a Hesperine
could use your memories of her to achieve sufficient focus on her aura,
wherever she might be in Tenebra."

"And if her aura is not..."

He gave her all the information, as he knew she wanted. Cassia drew no
comfort from ignorance. "If auric focus is no longer possible, we could use
your blood tie with her as a physical focus, but success with that method
is less certain."

"Depending on how long it has been since living blood flowed through her?"

"We will try everything," Lio promised.

Nike held up a hand. "Hold your horses, youngblood. I won't sit here and let you step into unknown conditions in hostile territory."

Lio had no intention of letting his cousin volunteer herself for another quest Abroad, either. "No, I will not leave Cassia's side tonight. What I can do is establish whether focus is possible. Then we can ask Ioustin to send whomever he sees fit."

Nike nodded her approval. "You know Solia best through Cassia's memories, so if anyone can achieve focus on her, you can. I'll stand by in case you wish to draw on my power, although I doubt you'll need it."

"Thank you." Lio closed his eyes, opening his mind's eye.

His awareness of the library faded, except for the nearby nova that was Nike's aura and the powerful touch of his Grace's small hands in his. Cassia held him a little tighter, drawing in a breath, which she didn't let out. He gave her hands a reassuring squeeze.

Solia already had an aura in his mind, one crafted through many conversations with his Grace. He concentrated on Solia's bright spirit and loving heart, her fierce determination and graceful nobility. It was easy to connect with the traits she and Cassia had in common.

But his meditation was only that. It did not take on life as an auric focus that would guide him to Solia.

He kept trying the futile spell a moment longer because he didn't want to open his eyes and tell Cassia he couldn't find her sister.

Nike's power stirred and joined to his. Molten thelemancy poured into his spell, promising to form a link stronger than steel. The surge of power would have rocked Lio on his feet, if Nike had not delivered it with such control and precision.

But even her great power did not forge a link they could follow to Solia.

Lio gritted his teeth, his fangs unsheathed, and tried the blood spell. Cassia's blood ran in his own veins, the most powerful focus of all.

He felt an opening, a path through the Goddess's good world with an unnatural monster lurking at the end of it. He could step to the king from here. Lio shuddered.

"Are you all right?" Cassia asked.

No, he was not all right. He could find the sunbound king, but not Solia.

Nike was patient, waiting for him to acknowledge the truth and end the spell first. He sent her his gratitude through their connection, then let go.

He gave his frustrated power something useful to do, wrapping Cassia in reassurance. "Our first attempt was not a success, but take heart, my Grace. This is only the beginning of our search, not the end."

"Of course. It would take more than one spell to solve this mystery after so many years." Her back was straight, her face composed, but Lio felt how her heart sank.

He caught it in his magic, holding her in his arms. "There are a number of obstacles that can prevent a Hesperine from stepping to a person."

"That's true," Nike confirmed. "Concealing spells, for one. Either Hesperine veils or a mortal mage's deflections. Certain wards can stop us, too."

"If Solia is in hiding somewhere," Lio reasoned, "trying to stay safe, it would make sense for her to rely on such spells. We should ask Ioustin to send Kalos. If anyone can find her, he can."

Nike gave them a bemused smile. "Is Kalos the one who has been following me like a hunting hound?"

Lio nodded. "He is the best scout in the Prince's Charge." The Hesperines errant who served under Ioustin maintained a permanent, if secret presence in Tenebra at his fortress, Castra Justa. Kalos was seldom home in Orthros, but always willing to come to their aid when needed.

"His skills are impressive for a young Hesperine," Nike said. "He came close to finding me a number of times. He should have no trouble locating a mortal."

"I'll go find Ioustin right now," Lio said.

At Cassia's nod of assent, he stepped back into the crowded Ritual hall. There was one person he needed to speak with before anyone else.

She came to him first. His mother pulled him aside in an alcove and swept a veil around them. "How is Cassia?"

"Mother, you will scarcely believe the tidings Nike has brought. I will let Cassia tell you in her own words, but…"

"Moon hours are waning. Soon the celebration must end and you must begin her transformation—if you are to do it tonight."

"I know."

"Cassia has a difficult decision to make, doesn't she?" his mother asked.

"I wish it weren't so," he answered, "but I can't guarantee how we will proceed. I refuse to let anyone in this room, no matter how well-meaning, make her feel she has already made that choice."

His mother touched a hand to his face. "I am so proud of you, Lio. From the moment this night began, you have thought only of what's best for her. You are a fine Hesperine and a wonderful Grace. But remember that you're allowed to feel disappointed."

"Thank you, Mother. I think I should cross that bridge when—if—I come to it."

On his way to Ioustin, Lio located his Trial brothers. They were busy deflecting every question about Cassia's absence with good humor that brooked no argument. "Thank you for holding down the fort here. But now Cassia would be very grateful for your company."

Mak's aura clouded with protectiveness. "What did she find out from Nike?"

"She'll tell you."

Lyros asked urgently, "Lio, she *is* still going to—?"

"She'll tell us. Let's get Ioustin."

As they approached, Ioustin turned from his conversation with Lio's father, his brow furrowed. "What can I do?"

"Can I help?" Father asked.

If there was anyone Cassia needed in this moment, it was their Trial brothers, the Blood Errant, and Mother. He spotted Alkaios and Nephalea nearby and realized something else. They might be who Nike needed tonight. He beckoned in invitation. Without a word, they nodded and join him. Lio stepped all of them to the library and sensed his mother join them on the way.

Mak beat the rest of the family to Cassia's side.

"Mak," Cassia said, wonder on her face. "Your sister is home—and mine escaped. Solia got out of the fortress before—before the catapults."

His head whipped around as he looked to Nike for confirmation.

When she nodded, he let out a whoop and swung Cassia off her feet in a hug.

At the joyous questions from everyone, Cassia palpably pushed her hopes back down again.

Lio put a hand on Cassia's arm. "Before you and Nike explain the details to everyone, we need Kalos. Ioustin, is there any possible way he could put his current tasks on hold and help us discover what really happened to Solia that night?"

"I will bring him immediately." Ioustin stepped out of sight.

Cassia sank down onto their couch. "Kalos is usually scouting far afield. There's no telling how long it might take for him to get here."

Lio remained standing, keeping a reassuring hand on her shoulder.

But it was a mere moment later that Ioustin reappeared, Kalos at his side. The quiet Hesperine's dark hair was tied back, his green eyes as guarded as ever, but he didn't sport his usual woodland gear. He dusted what appeared to be toast crumbs off a comfortable-looking beige linen robe. Lio had a sneaking suspicion they had caught the indefatigable scout relaxing for once.

Lio suppressed a wince. "Welcome to our residence, Kalos. Please sit down and make yourself comfortable. There's coffee for everyone."

Without meeting anyone's eyes, Kalos took a seat catty-corner from Cassia, as if there might be knives on the silk cushion. He gazed at the floor at Cassia's feet. "Knight isn't with you?"

"He's with Zoe," Cassia answered. "When they're together, he can withstand my absence."

"That's remarkable. Uh. Nevermind. You didn't bring me here to talk about dogs."

"It's always nice to talk about dogs." Cassia smiled. "It's good to see you again."

Kalos was silent for an uncomfortably long moment. Then he cleared his throat. "You as well."

Everyone quickly took a seat and the coffee Lio passed around, which no one touched. He sat down next to Cassia and once again held her close. She adopted a factual tone as she explained what they had learned. But every Hesperine in the room could hear her heart hammering away.

"I'll start tonight," Kalos said when she was finished.

"Our bond of gratitude grows deeper still," Cassia told him. "It means so much to me that you're attempting this."

The scout shrugged. "I succeeded in tracking Nike, Nephalea, and Alkaios from Castra Roborra over fourteen years after the fact. I can certainly pick up Solia's trail now."

Cassia hesitated. "It was Nike's magic you were able to trace. Solia wouldn't leave that kind of evidence behind."

"Mortals leave plenty of their own marks. And it sounds as if I'll have more than one trail to follow. I gather she wasn't traveling alone."

"That's right. Iris felt confident 'the others' had escaped."

"Do you have any idea who could have been with her?" Kalos asked.

"Not any of her guards. They were all accounted for on the field with Iris." Cassia's brow furrowed. "I have it on good authority that Lord Evandrus and his son, two of the men implicated in Solia's kidnapping, were actually on her side. It's possible they tried to protect her from Bellator. If they helped her escape, they most likely sent some kind of escort with her."

"Where are they now?" Kalos asked.

"To my knowledge, they perished in the siege," said Cassia, "but I suppose that could also be a false assumption."

"If they or someone loyal to them escaped with Solia, where would they go? What do you think your sister would do once they got away?"

"She would seek aid from her and Iris's allies. Unfortunately, I don't know who. I never learned the names of her other co-conspirators."

Cassia's shoulders tensed. Lio slid a hand across her rigid back. He could feel her mustering all her inner defenses against her own emotions. He hated that she needed to.

"If Solia had made it to safety and rallied her supporters," Cassia said, "I would have known."

Hearing her talk around the possibilities, Lio knew she was not ready to let herself hope or to look her fears in the face. But he hoped for her, even as he feared more grief might be in store for her.

Had Solia escaped the fortress, only to meet her end another way? Or could she still be alive? If she was, where had she been all these years?

The bloodborn had returned to Orthros, and the Victory Star had delivered his rescue. Hespera's Will, glimpsed by her Oracle, wrought miracles against all odds. Couldn't the Goddess have a reunion in store for Solia and Cassia?

"We must question everything about that night," Lio said.

"Yes." Cassia's hands clenched. "Except this. Bellator was a murderer, and so is the king."

Lio wrapped a hand around her fist. "The stain of their evil remains. But it may not have wrought as much damage as we once believed."

Kalos leaned forward and lifted his gaze to Cassia's. "I'll find her."

Cassia's breath made a little hitching sound in her throat. "Thank you."

"You've waited fifteen years already," said Ioustin. "We won't have you wait a moment longer for answers. Kalos and I will return to the field right away."

Kalos gave a little bow before he departed.

Ioustin hesitated a moment longer, eying his Trial sister. "I'll be back."

"I'll still be here," she said.

Lio had seldom seen such a smile on Ioustin's face. "Good. I'm not done with you yet."

"Is that a challenge?" Nike returned.

"Of course."

"Hurry back."

He lifted a hand in farewell.

"And Ioustin," Nike added, "give my regards to your fortress masters. Especially Baru."

Ioustin stood still. "You're acquainted with my fortress masters?" His brows descended. "Well enough to call my librarian 'Baru?'"

"She's very well acquainted with Baru," Nephalea said innocently.

Nike gave her a steely glare. "He and Jaya helped me keep Nephalea and Alkaios out of trouble when they were foolish Newgifts."

Alkaios rubbed his chin. "You still owe Jaya a sack of coffee beans."

Lio suspected there was a long story there. He sensed his Ritual father's consternation that Nike had associated with any of the Charge under his very nose, without him knowing.

Ioustin shook his head. "I'm not done with you," he said again, then stepped away.

"'Acquainted' with Fortress Master Baruti, nemesis of necromancers." Mak whistled a few notes of a tune. A very popular coffeehouse ballad about a Hesperine errant who claimed and broke hearts everywhere she adventured. Since it had been written during Nike's absence, she was unlikely to recognize it. But all of Orthros knew it was based on her.

They could only imagine how many adventures—and secrets—Nike had accumulated over her long time Abroad.

Cassia's aura did not share in Mak's humor. She was still trying valiantly to guard her emotions. Her inner defenses had always been strong for an untrained mortal, and she had gained finesse spending time around Hesperines, especially mind mages.

But the effect in her family's company was rather like holding a scarf in front of her face and expecting none of her loved ones to notice she was there. "Lio, could I talk to you for a moment?"

"Of course." Yes, they needed to talk.

She drew him away from the family to the relative privacy of the window where she kept her potted plants and sequestered him behind a fern. "Veiled, please? Oh. You already did. Thank you."

Her gaze fell. The struggle raged in her. Would it be easier for her if he brought it up first, or if he let her approach it in her own way?

"Lio, I don't know how to ask you this."

He cupped her face in his hand, stroking a thumb over the plethora of freckles on her cheek. He drew her petite form a little closer, until she had to tilt her head back to look at him and she ended up resting her head against his hand.

"I love you so much," she whispered. "I want you so much. I've been dreaming of and longing for tonight so much it hurts."

"You know I feel the same."

"Everyone has gone to so much effort for me tonight. The Queens and Master Kona are here! Your mother worked so hard, and all our tributaries are waiting on us, and I haven't even spent enough time with them to properly recognize their generosity to me. I—"

He caressed her face. "They're here for you. Not the other way around."

She trapped her lip between her blunt mortal teeth. How he longed to feel her bite. To see her canines lengthen, sharpen, unleashed by her power.

"It's all right, Cassia. I know what you're trying to say, and it's all right."

Frustration and guilt riddled her aura. "How can I even be considering this?"

"How can you not? One of the most defining events of your life has just shifted around you. Everything you once believed about the Siege of Sovereigns has been turned on its head. How could you possibly continue with our plans for tonight as if nothing has happened?"

"You always understand. But Lio, how can I do this to *you?*"

"Cassia, your Gifting is too important for you to undertake it with any doubts. For us to attempt it when you're uncertain about your past would be difficult, even dangerous. At worst, your unanswered questions would make your visions more difficult to endure. At best, they would hang over your head during your seclusion. And what if Kalos brought news while we were apart from everyone?"

"I don't think I can wait to know what he has to say."

Lio shook his head. "Of course not."

"Are you sure, Lio?" she asked in a small voice.

"This isn't…this night has not turned out as I imagined. When I Gift you, I want there to be nothing on your mind but your future. Us." He brushed a wayward tendril of her ash brown hair back from her face. "When I take you to our bed, I don't want you to be worrying about Solia. When you first taste my blood, I don't want you to be wondering what happened in Tenebra. And when your fangs pierce me for the first time? Goddess. I will not allow *anything* to detract from that moment."

Her pulse was racing, her lips parted, her scent flush with her response to his words. "When I finally taste you, I promise, *you* are all I'll be able to think about."

"I won't have it any other way. Which is why I agree with what you're trying to say."

"If you keep on like this, I may be able to get into the spirit of the night after all."

"But you shouldn't have to try, my rose."

"Do you really think we should do it?" She swallowed and finally said it. "Delay my Gifting?"

"It is your decision, and yours alone. I will not allow anyone to talk you into or out of it. I will support your choice, even if it means we have to wait."

"You are a wonder, Lio. How is it I have the good fortune of being your Grace?"

He smiled at her. "I got one whiff of you, and I was taken."

That actually fetched a laugh out of her. "You and your Hesperine sense of smell."

He rubbed his nose in her hair on the top of her head.

He could feel her drawing comfort from him, as if her aura drank from his. Her Gifting must wait. But they had this, their powerful Union.

At length she turned toward their loved ones. "We have to tell them."

Her steps dragged as they rejoined everyone in the lower center of the room. The others left off their conversations as Lio and Cassia approached.

She took a deep breath. Her aura flared as if every word were like walking on broken glass. "This is one of the most difficult things I've ever had to do, but I think it would be wise to delay my Gifting."

"Are you sure?" Mak asked her.

Lyros elbowed him.

Mak was undaunted. "She deserves for someone to ask her that. You don't have to wait, Cassia. Not for Solia. Not for anyone."

"But it's perfectly all right for you to wait if you need to," Lyros insisted.

"That, too," said Mak.

"I'm sure." She didn't sound like determined Cassia. She sounded miserable.

Mother sent a wave of bolstering magic through the room. "I think you're being very responsible, Cassia. I know how hard this is for you. There isn't a mind healer in Orthros who wouldn't respect your decision."

"How will I tell everyone?" she asked.

"Shall I tell them?" Nike's eyes glittered, the tips of her fangs visible.

Mak grinned. He kept glancing at the blood on his sister's robe.

Cassia shook her head. "You've done more than enough for me already, Nike. You sacrificed so much to come here tonight, and we haven't had a chance to welcome you home properly. What can we do for you? Do you need anything?"

Nike sighed. Reluctantly she stood and picked up her silk formal to cover her bloodstained fighting robes again. "I think it's time for me to face the rest of the family."

"If Mother and Father get to be too much," Mak offered, "just stick Thenie in their arms. Works every time. Being grandparents has mellowed them."

Nike quirked a brow at her brother. "The Guardian of Orthros and Silvertongue have '*mellowed?*'"

"Only when they're holding Thenie. When we had mages to visit at Winter Solstice? Not so much."

Nike's lips twitched. "I hereby appoint you my strategic adviser in the coming confrontation."

"Oh, if it's strategy you need, that's really more Lyros's area." Mak's gaze warmed with affection for his Grace. "He's the level-headed one who gets along with Mother and Father much better than I do."

"Most of the time," Lyros said.

"Then I'm glad to have you at our sides, Lyros. We have hope of not being overwhelmed by superior forces."

Father put on an all-too-good-natured smile. "I will make Cassia's announcement to the guests. No one argues with me."

Cassia relaxed a little. "Thank you, Papa."

"Don't worry about it a moment longer," he said.

"Shall I let your parents know you're back at House Argyros?" Mother asked Nike, offering her an unspoken excuse to avoid the crowd.

"Yes, thank you," Nike answered, a hint of relief in her posture.

"We'll see you there later," said Nephalea.

Alkaios nodded. "Your parents have offered us a residence in the main house."

Nike shook her head, half smiling. "You two are always underfoot."

"Count on it," Nephalea promised.

Nike looked to Mak and Lyros. "Well. Shall we…go home?"

Lio gripped Mak's shoulder, encouraging him through the Union. With his sister and his Grace, he stepped away.

"We're going to see if Kadi and Javed need any help with the sucklings.," Nephalea said before she and Alkaios took their leave.

Mother put a hand on Cassia's arm. "I'll explain things to Zoe."

"Thank you," Cassia replied. "It's best if you decide what to tell her."

"She'll be happy she doesn't have to be separated from you right away. One benefit of waiting is that she'll have more time to adjust before your seclusion. Don't worry."

"I'll try."

"I'll have her bring Knight back to you after we've talked."

Cassia shook her head. "Ask her to keep him for me tonight."

With an understanding smile, Mother accompanied Father back to the Main House.

The silence that descended over Lio and Cassia reminded him of the quiet after a spell exploded.

THE BRIDGE

CASSIA DREW BREATH TO speak, but Lio held up a hand. "You know you can always be completely honest with me. Tonight you can tell me anything, even the messy things. Because nothing about all of this is clean and tidy. But there is one thing I will not let you say—that you're sorry. You have nothing to apologize for."

She pulled him to her, her arms circling his waist, and rested her face on his chest. They held each other like that for a moment, and he realized they were both leaning into each other with weariness.

A cool, sweeping thing suffused their Union. Cassia was *relieved*.

Lio discovered it was time to cross the bridge of disappointment, but the bridge had already burned and fallen into the chasm below in an ugly heap.

She was relieved.

Of course she was. She had been about to face a life-altering, life-threatening transformation, and now she didn't have to do it right away.

But his disappointment burned through his every vein.

He had thought this would be the last night he would ever spend worrying about his vulnerable mortal Grace. He had thought his first breath tomorrow would be a sigh of relief that she was powerful, immortal. Safe, forever.

He had thought he would spend this night with her fangs buried in his throat.

Bleeding thorns, they had come *so close*.

He sincerely wanted to break something.

Her hands roamed over him, as if she could hold in the unruly power trembling to escape him. But her touch only made control more difficult. It took an act of Will for him to keep his magic from rattling the windows.

Her hands slid down between his shoulder blades. "For the rest of the night, I want to give you my undivided attention. No dog on the bed."

A laugh squeezed out of his throat. "I would appreciate that."

Her fingers traced little circles low on his back. Oh. She wasn't trying to help him with his self-control.

She reached her other hand up, sliding her warm, calloused fingers along the nape of his neck. "You've been amazing tonight. What do you need, Lio?"

"Well... I have a surprise for you upstairs that we can still enjoy, despite everything."

"No, you've done enough for me. I asked what you need."

It became a little easier to keep his mind magic from blasting his windows right out of their frames. "Believe me. I'll enjoy the surprise."

"If you're sure."

He slipped behind her and covered her eyes with one hand. He slid his other arm around her waist and pulled her to him, tucking her buttocks against him.

"All right," she said, "I can see you are enjoying this."

He stepped them up to their bedchamber on the topmost level of the tower. The fragrance of roses enveloped them, sweeter than any of the flowers that had decked the main house tonight. *Their* roses. The Sanctuary ward that dwelt in their room pulsed with both their heartbeats, ensuring shelter and privacy.

Lio positioned Cassia in front of the surprise and slid his hand from her eyes. The sight stirred her aura, even after all the revelations of this night. This still had the power to move her.

The new wrought iron bed dominated the center of the circular chamber. It had turned out exactly as he'd wished. The young, potted rose vines, which had quickly been outgrowing their stakes, were now positioned at each of the five bedposts and trained to the poles that swept upward over the round mattress. No fabric covered the rails above. In time, the roses would climb up and grow together, overtaking the iron frame until their five-petaled, blood-red blooms formed a canopy.

At the center of the curved headboard, fitted into a precisely designed setting, rested their glyph stone. The irreplaceable relic Cassia had pried from the ruins of their shrine of Hespera, moments before its destruction, now had a place of honor in its rightful home. The rose seeds, the glyph stone and the Sanctuary ward it carried were all that survived of that sacred place. They would endure here forever.

Cassia ran her hands over Lio's arms, then reached one hand up to tangle in his hair. "Now our shrine is complete. I'll make an exception for perfection after all. This is perfect, and I want it with all my heart."

He grabbed her up and tossed her onto the bed. Rose petals scattered around her as she landed. The room filled with her bright, hiccuping laughter that he loved so much, and all the cares of the night lifted away for a moment.

Lio prowled toward her, halting at the footboard. He gazed down at her, his lovely Grace. She looked so small in their big bed. Her freckled olive complexion seemed to glow against the crimson silk bedspread. The stained glass windows on one side of the chamber splashed her with light, while the empty window frames on the other side cast her in darkness, turning her hazel eyes to one gleam and one shadow. Her beautiful party braids were unraveling around her. Her black silk robe, embroidered with the very roses that framed their bed, twisted around her splayed knees.

"Did you think I would Gift you in a nest of blankets on the floor?" he asked.

"I wouldn't have minded. But I admit..."

The corners of his mouth turned up, and he realized how far his fangs had already unsheathed. "This is better."

"It's magnificent. The largest bed I've ever seen."

"Big enough for a bloodborn to lie down in any direction without his feet dangling. I wanted us to have all our options."

She leaned up on her elbows, her gaze drifting over him. "You mentioned some options you'd saved for tonight." But then the heat in her eyes dimmed. "That is, if you didn't mean things you were saving for after I'm...if we can still try them while I'm..."

Her guilt threatened, an unwanted weed in the garden they were desperately trying to protect from the storm of the night.

He circled the bed. His shadow moved over her as he passed in front of the windows. Joining her upon their bed for the first time, he lay on his side and pressed his forehead to hers. "Our love…our need…is eternal, whether your heart is mortal or Hesperine. A power greater even than the Gift has made it so."

She clutched his face, holding him to her, her aura swelling with the righteous fury that had altered Tenebra and Orthros's history. "I'm so disappointed. Does that make it any easier for you? To know we're disappointed together?"

There it was, under the relief. The agonizing burn of being cheated out of what they had wanted to share tonight. There wasn't as much room for her disappointment because she was so full of the thelemantic memories of a fallen hero and a lifetime of questions about her sister. But she *was* disappointed.

"Yes, that makes it better." He lowered his mouth to hers.

He kissed her with all his frustration and disappointment and love. His fangs sliced her lip, flavoring their kiss with her blood. She bit down on his lower lip in answer. A groan vibrated in the back of his throat.

He rolled atop her, pressing her into the bed. She bit his lip again, then his tongue, and he plunged it into her mouth to devour her. She ran her tongue over his fangs and tangled it with his, feeding him little droplets of her blood.

Her knees tightened on either side of him, cradling him in the silk constriction of their robes and her thighs. Her hands clutched at his shoulders, opening and closing, as if grasping at something she couldn't have. She tore her mouth away for a breath, then kissed a hot, wet trail across his jaw, trailing her blood through his beard and down his throat.

She opened her mouth on his vein, lipped and tongued him. Suddenly she stopped and turned her head. "I'm sorry. I don't mean to taunt you."

"It's instinct, isn't it?"

"Yes. It's become natural."

"You know how much I desire your bite."

"Even tonight?"

"Especially tonight."

She struck and bit down on his vein. Even her dull canines were enough to make his skin tighten and his rhabdos harden.

She scraped her teeth up, then down his throat, as if compelled. "I wish I could do it right now," she confessed against his vein. "I wish I could finally know what it's like."

"I can give you an idea."

"Like you did the night you told me I'm your Grace? When you used your mind magic as you sated your Craving to let me experience it with you?"

"We've already inundated you with thelemancy tonight."

"And you've spent a great deal."

He had magic to spare. He always had more of it, ready to flood out of him. At the moment, though, he would find it difficult to form a coherent spell out of the raw power raging through him. "I was thinking of a more physical demonstration."

"Oh?" Her breath whispered over his sensitive flesh as the mark of her bite healed. A shame he wouldn't have a bruise to admire later.

He rose to his knees in front of her. "Your blood is...like filling my mouth with you, but you pleasuring me. To answer your earlier question, yes, we can do this as a mortal."

He took hold of her ankles. One of his hands circled the delicate joint where she wore the thin braid of his hair, the physical symbol of their arcane Grace bond. He dragged her lower on the bed. The motion hitched her robes up around her hips, revealing...

"Oh, Cassia. I didn't realize you'd expanded your Orthros wardrobe quite so much."

"When in Orthros, dress as the Hesperines do. Have I chosen the appropriate attire for this event, Ambassador? Am I sending the right message?" She let her knees loll playfully from side to side, teasing him with the view of her new undergarment.

Green silk embroidered with a single, lush little rosebud trembling on the verge of opening. A scanty length of fabric, wrapped round and round. Something that would take time to unwind, to make the enjoyment last.

"You couldn't have chosen better, my lady. I understand your intentions perfectly."

He began to slide her robe off, and she rolled to a sitting position, lifting her arms. Tossing her clothes aside, he discovered she hadn't constrained her small breasts in any undergarments at all.

"Excellent choice again," he said.

"I'm glad you agree."

She was a feast of bare, perking nipples and feminine desire wrapped in a scrap of green silk. His mouth watered, his fangs lengthening still more.

She began drawing his formal robes off of him, first the stiff, heavily embroidered outer one. She piled it on her own, and their clothes slid off the bed in a tangled swirl. Then she peeled off his close-fitting underrobe.

Her gaze fell below his waist, and her swollen lips parted. "I always knew you aren't the basic white underlinens fellow you pretend to be. A red silk Hesperine seducer has been hidden under there all along, trying to get out."

His laugh was cut short when she cupped his arousal in both her hands through the red silk. His erection strained against the simple, classic subligaria wrapped around his waist, which covered his rhabdos and little else.

The roses shivered, and he realized his magic was getting away from him. He took hold of her wrists. Her pulse raced under his fingertips as he drew her hands away from him. He gave his power an outlet, levitating them both and throwing back the bedclothes with his Will, then lowering them to the black silk sheets.

Seeing the blanket layered beneath the new crimson bedspread, Cassia smiled. She reached out and ran a hand over the Tenebran army blanket of rough wool they had made love on for their first time. "Our bed wouldn't be complete without this."

"It stays, always."

"This can't be my Gift Night…but it's still the anniversary of the night we met. We can celebrate that."

For a moment they just knelt there before each other, tasting and touching. Her hands roamed his skin as he skimmed his palms over her thighs, her hips, the sides of her breasts. The only sounds in the room besides their heartbeats were her soughing breaths and the damp meeting and parting of their lips and tongues.

He broke the kiss to slide around behind her. He eased her down and back until she had her head on his lap. She rested her head on his thigh, turning her face up to him with eager trust.

He bent and dusted a kiss over each of her eyelids. Then the upturned tip of her nose. Then her smile, when he returned his lips to hers. As he stroked the tops of their tongues together, the air filled with the musky perfume of her desire.

He slid backward, easing her head onto the bed. He braced his hands on the sheets, supporting himself above her, and kissed his way down her chin. Her neck. The spray of freckles under her collarbone.

"I begin to see where you're headed." Her voice was low and velvety, her bedroom voice that only he ever heard.

"Do you like my direction?"

"Keep going."

Light played on one of her pebbled areolae. He fastened his mouth on her other, shadowed breast. She rolled her hips up off the bed. He splayed one hand below her navel, feeling the quivering tension in her. He laved her nipple with his tongue, then sucked at her breast, letting his fangs press but not pierce the tender skin. Her lower belly flexed up under his hand.

He teased a finger under the top of her green undergarment, but returned his hand to the bed. He sampled her other breast, teasing her nipple between his teeth, rolling and nipping it. Her hands found his chest. She hooked a finger in her braid around his neck and tugged him down closer.

He licked the undersides of her breasts, then kissed his way down her torso. He couldn't count her ribs anymore. She was still thin, but no longer dangerously so. He relished the way her figure had softened, now that she had eaten properly for weeks. When she could have her fill of his blood, what size and shape would she settle into?

The feeling of her mouth on his chest soothed his bittersweet longing. His senses focused on the sharp pleasure-pain of her teeth on his nipple. With languid, thorough kisses and sudden, surprising nibbles, she awakened sensation in each part of him that came within her reach.

"Can we manage this?" she asked with a breathless laugh. "You're very tall, and I'm very short."

"We will more than manage." He dipped his tongue into her navel. "Stretch for me."

He watched her heels slide over the sheets and her legs extend. She arched and lengthened her torso, lifting her silk-clad krana in invitation.

"Mmm. So beautiful." Very slowly, he kissed his way along the final stretch, following the trail of hair that guided him from her navel to the top of that strip of green silk.

She spread her thighs. Her arousal had already dampened the fabric, darkening it along the lips of her krana. The plump red rosebud invited him. The fragrance of her made his fangs ache. His blood burned at the thought of how long it would take to unwrap her.

She tangled her fingers in his hair. "It's like I'm hungry, although you will feast on me."

He took the edge of the pretty fabric in his teeth and gave it a tug.

"Do it," she urged. The words, like two heartbeats, pounded through him.

He did what he had never done in their bed and ripped her clothing from her body with his fangs.

He heard the fabric tear and the crescendo of her heart.

"Arch for me," she bade him.

He curved his back, his knees pressing deeper into the bed. Her nails combed over his shoulders and down along each side of his spine. Then silk was slipping away across his hips, and his rhabdos sprang into her waiting hands.

He laid claim to her kalux, making a banquet of her most sensitive point.

With a soft impact on the bed, she threw her head back. She guided his rhabdos to her lips.

With a deep groan, he sank into the soft, wet welcome of her mouth. His fingers dug into the sheets and his back tightened with his effort at self-control. She kept one hand on his moskos, caressing him and guiding him about how much of him she could take. She began to suck, setting a rhythm that scattered his thoughts.

He feasted on her krana in long, hungry strokes, but never let his fangs so much as prick her. Her hips rolled in time with each draw of her lips and tongue on his rhabdos. The taste of her and the searing pleasure of her mouth on him flooded together into one tide.

With his face buried in her curls, he felt the tremors of her climax against his lips. She bowed off the bed, and her ecstasy slammed through their Union. He suckled her kalux relentlessly. Her mouth closed over his rhabdos, holding him hard. Sensation and magic flared within his body and mind, searing the edges of his control.

She let out one more whimper in the back of her throat as her climax trembled to an end. He raised his head, gasping, his head filling with her scent. Her mouth clutched at him again and again, as if she were starving for the sensory power she drove through him. He shook with the effort not to push too deep into her kiss.

He sank onto his elbows, grasping her thighs in both hands. She parted wide for him again, and he pressed her legs back against the bed. He kissed her inner thigh, letting his fangs touch her skin to show her what he wanted. Her free hand tangled in his hair and pressed him to her there.

He opened his mouth, unleashing the full length of his fangs, and sank them into the large vein on the inside of her thigh. It gave forth a river of her blood flavored with her thrill at his bite where she had never felt it before. Her thighs pressed up against his hands as he held her down.

He drank her with abandon. It took all his control to hold back from the brink of release while his fangs speared her. He flexed his jaw, biting and releasing with every motion of her lips and tongue on his rhabdos.

She braced both her hands against his hipbones. Then she increased the pressure of her mouth, clamping around him. He roared against her vein as he lost control.

She cradled him in her hands, guiding every jerk of his hips. Her blood streamed into his mouth as he spilled himself into hers.

When he was complete, she parted her mouth from him, her breaths ragged. He sank back on his knees, moaning into her thigh.

Her hips still swiveled in little circles under his hold with every swallow of her blood that he claimed. Anchoring her on his fangs, he moved one hand over her krana. He covered her curls and palmed her kalux, applying gentle pressure.

Her next climax enriched her blood and stirred his arousal. Her panting breaths became soft cries as her krana rubbed slickly against his hand for long moments.

When he had savored the last aftertaste of her climax, he slipped his fangs carefully out of her. He kissed the wound thoroughly, licking until it was completely sealed, leaving swirls of blood behind on her skin. He rested his face against the inside of her thigh, sighing.

"That's what the feast is like," he said at last.

"More," she breathed. "I want you to have more."

She pushed against his hips, urging him to turn over. "Your magic is still shaking out of you. More."

"Yes," he confessed. He fell back, stretching out over their tangled bedclothes.

She turned to face him and straddled him. Her blood had reawakened him. The sight of her naked and ready to ride him had him aching hard again. The determined set of her chin filled him with affection. She knew what he needed, and she was going to give it to him.

She braced her hands on his chest and mounted him in three fast, strong pushes of her hips. He hissed as her flesh gloved him. When he was buried deep, her knees splayed a little wider, her toes curled, and her eyelids dipped. But still that determined set of her chin.

She began to rotate her hips. He watched her move and felt her moving him inside her. She tightened her krana around him, turning each swivel into a pull that had him groaning with her every move.

He let his head fall back, let fistfuls of silk fill his hands, let his feet rest on the headboard. His body and his magic and his mind relaxed into her rhythm.

She leaned forward, tilting her buttocks back a bit, altering the pressure and rubbing her kalux against him. She rode him harder, now rocking her hips forward and back, forward and back. She filled their Union with her own pleasure, serving it up to him.

He clamped his hands over her hips. Bracing his feet against the headboard, he thrust. And thrust. And thrust. Their rapid breaths harsh together, she rode out his need.

When he levitated them and flipped her onto her back, she wrapped her legs around him the way she knew he wanted. He pounded into her.

All the magic he had held, all the magic he had meant to pour into her veins tonight, blasted out of him.

Cassia screamed and climaxed under him, her heels digging into his lower back and her hands clawing at his shoulders.

Her aura opened up and sucked him down. All the unruly power inside him crashed into her. He let out a roar of relief. His body answered, surging into her in long pulses. His release robbed him of deep control, and another wave of raw magic swept out of him.

That and the first blast rebounded within the safety of their Sanctuary ward. His own power descended back over him, now a gentle darkness. Cassia's aura seemed to spread open and welcome its weight down upon her. She cried out, short, sweet calls of satisfaction, as her climax rolled into another and her krana tremored around him.

He sank down over her, every nook and cranny of him limp with relaxation. His face landed in the crook of her neck and shoulder. He heaved a sigh. No power racing through his veins and pushing against his skin. His magic was silent.

All he sensed in him was Cassia. She emanated, deep as night and shining bright. No yearning or frustration now. She was replete.

Her laughter bubbled through their quiet bedchamber. "Would it be terrible of me to say that was *magical?*"

He laughed. They were both giddy from passion, clearly. "But it *was.*"

She didn't move, her legs hanging limply around his waist. "Just when I think I know all about being a mind mage's lover, you take me by surprise again."

"And just when I think I know all about being a human's lover, you surprise me."

At the mention of her humanity, a little pang went through her aura. He pressed a tender kiss where her neck and shoulder joined, trying to soothe away her pain.

But the regret was still there. His, hers. They wrapped their arms around each other, hiding from it all in one another's embrace.

THIEVES

S HE WOKE FROM HER mortal sleep sometime in the depth of veil
hours, stirring against him. He wasn't sure what time it was. He had
stopped counting the tolls of the city bells, lost in thought with no
sunrise to plunge him into the Dawn Slumber.

She lifted her tousled head from his chest, and her hand caressed his
breast. "I'm sorry it's impossible for you to sleep at this time of year."

"Why would I want to sleep when I have a beautiful, naked woman
draped over me?"

A smile flitted across her face, but there was concern in her drowsy
gaze. She traced his lips with one finger. "Tell me all the messy things."

He propped his arm behind his head. "I don't want my mess to make
your mess worse."

"That's not how our Oath works. We promised to always speak openly
and honestly with each other. We did not include any exceptions for
messiness."

"But I can't bear adding even the smallest bit to your pain, Cassia."

"Silence is no way to protect each other. Tell me."

He fondled her small hand, kissing her fingers. "I'm afraid this news
about your sister will cause you more grief."

"It won't. You know I excel at managing my expectations."

Her words went straight to his heart. Of course it would hurt her if
she learned Solia had escaped, only to lose her all over again. It would
crush her.

"I don't want you to have to manage your expectations," he said. "I
want to lay all your greatest expectations at your feet."

She rose up, caressing his face in a way that made him feel like the most valuable treasure in the world. "My Grace. You are my greatest expectation."

He kissed the words of love from her lips. His worries were thieves, stealing into his thoughts and snatching at the joy they had found in their bed tonight. He tried to snatch it back. "There's something I want to show you."

"If it's anything like what you showed me earlier, let's please forget everything else and try it."

That brought a smile to his face. "Not something in bed."

"Oh. Come to think of it, I was so busy enjoying our new bed with you that I didn't ask you where this masterpiece came from. Is conjuring a dream bed one of your magical skills of which I was unaware, my nocturnal sorcerer?"

"In truth, I had to commission it from a smith like anyone else. But he kindly made it exactly to my specifications."

"Of course he did. Mak is such a romantic under the warrior."

"I hope you don't find it awkward that he made our bed and Lyros helped him install it."

"It would be awkward if anyone else had done it."

"While you were talking with Father, the three of us sneaked up here to fix the bedchamber for tonight. I'm sure you have a suspicion about what else I added to our room for the occasion."

"Kassandra says one should never try to foresee gifts. It ruins the fun."

He pointed and, with a touch of magic, pulled away that cloth hiding the fourth window frame.

She looked beyond him and the bed to the new panel, his intended stained glass tribute to her Gifting. "You chose cassia flowers for this one."

"What better way to honor who you have been and who you will become?"

Her gaze roamed over the panes of glass that portrayed a majestic cassia tree rife with bright blossoms, like yellow freckles upon its verdant foliage. "The craftsmanship is exquisite. You're so talented, Lio, and every time you craft something new, you manage to amaze me yet again. Each of your creations is more beautiful than the last."

"What do you sense in it?" he asked.

She slid off of him and knelt at the headboard, where she would have a better view. But her eyes drifted shut, and she turned her arms over in the vibrant light of the window as if she could feel the colors on her skin. "It's more than what we see. You infused it with your light magic, as always. There's something else, though. It's strong and vast like that tree, and it's reaching out, growing, making itself new like the leaves. But like the flowers, it's pretty and fun."

"I worked your blood into the glass."

"You mean…I'm sensing…"

"You. This is the closest I can come to portraying your aura."

"I feel like *that?*"

He knelt behind her and wrapped his arms around her waist, holding her and her ragged emotions. "This is your mortal self, captured as best I can with my craft."

"But wouldn't you rather have waited and used my Hesperine blood?"

"As much as I long to discover how you will be as a Hesperine, I want to remember every detail of your human nature. I wanted us to always have this reminder of that you."

She turned in his arms, her mouth a breath away from his own. The lights of Orthros, shining through the cassia flowers, kissed her skin with gold. "You have always seen so much more in me than anyone else has."

He ran a finger down her cheek. "I would be blind not to. You are so bright."

"Thank you for reminding me to look for that in myself."

"Do you need to be reminded, my rose?"

"Sometimes. Tonight, yes, when I don't want to be human."

"I will keep reminding you." He pulled her back under the covers with him, wrapping her up with him in Orthros silk and Tenebran wool. He gathered all of her close in his arms, binding her to him. His hand fisted in her hair.

"Oh, Lio." She cradled his head against her chest. "Tell me the rest."

He pressed his face to her breast. "I'm such a mess, Cassia."

She stroked his hair. "Don't be frightened for me. Nothing will happen to me before my Gifting. We're in Orthros now, where everyone is safe."

She spoke his every silent fear, reminding him that although she had no Blood Union yet, she always understood him. Always knew what he needed to hear.

"I know it's foolish," he said. "If you fell ill, our healers would cure you. Gardening lessons do not cause fatal accidents."

"You're not worried about those things."

"There are no enemies here. No king can order your execution. No war mages can burn you for heresy. No assassin can poison you."

"The Collector cannot take me from Orthros. It's not foolish at all to still be frightened. All our close calls were so recent. But I'm safe. Nothing and no one will take me from you, and the Craving will not take you from us."

"This isn't about—"

"You almost died without my blood. Don't you dare say it isn't about that. I'm still afraid from your close call, and so is everyone who loves you."

So was he. Cursed survival instincts, reminding him of his scrape with Hypnos. The god of death seemed near, as long as Cassia was mortal.

Cassia stroked his hair. "I don't want you to live with this fear. How can I make it stop?"

"Let me protect you."

She nestled down in his arms, tucking her head under his chin, letting him enfold her completely. "I'm right here, where you can keep me safe."

She spoke the truth. He didn't know what it would take to convince him that she was not in danger.

He only knew that he would pay any price to ensure that nothing and no one threatened his Grace ever again.

POETRY

CASSIA, WHO HAD SPIED on the king every hour of the day and leapt into action every moment of the Solstice Summit, wanted to stay in bed for once.

If she had gone through with her Gifting last night, she and Lio would be in seclusion now. She had no desire to face the world. But she had made a promise to Mak, and she did not break promises to her new family.

That was how she found herself downstairs in the library, sitting on Lio's lap at his desk, trying to think of what to say in a note to the Victory Star.

She gripped one of Lio's quills. "It was easier to invite mages to a Hesperine dinner party. How does one ask a living legend to do something? I know she's my Grace-cousin, and our powerful bond of gratitude draws us close. But she's also…her."

Lio rested his chin on her shoulder. "I don't think it matters what you say. It matters that the note is from you."

"I hope you're right. Thank you for helping me with this."

"Of course. I want us to do this for Mak, too." He adjusted her fingers on the writing instrument, loosening her death grip.

"Nike was in Tenebra saving my life while he grew up without his sister. But of course, he was nothing but supportive when Nike spent her first hours back home focused on me."

"No one in our family would have it any other way. But I am glad we have this opportunity to support Mak in return."

"Nike needs to see the spell he kept alive for her all these years. She needs to understand how much he cares about her. I'll do everything I can to make sure he doesn't miss his chance at a bond with his elder sister."

"No one understands the importance of that better than you do." Lio set a piece of fine notepaper in front of her.

She eyed the stack he'd pulled it from, wondering how many sheets she would ruin in her attempts to choose her words and spell them properly in penmanship that was actually legible to other people.

She pressed the quill into Lio's hand. "You'd better write it."

"Are you sure you don't want to? It's your idea."

"Nike could leave Orthros again in the time it takes me to scrawl out three sentences."

"You can dictate, then, and we'll put both our seals on it."

After much debate with herself and patience from Lio, they had a note in his elegant handwriting, which she could dispatch to House Argyros without mortification.

Dear Nike,

There is a sight not to be missed while you are here with us. Your brother has dedicated a marvelous work to you, which we would dearly like to show you. Could you find the time to join Mak, Lyros, Lio, and me for a walk up to the cliffs over House Komnena? We will gladly meet you there at any hour you find convenient.

With gratitude,
Cassia

She sighed. "I hope Mak is finding it easier to talk to her."

"Knowing Mak, she's finding it easy to talk to him."

"Indeed. Let's write a note to him next."

Mak,

We've sent a note to Nike in the hopes of persuading her to visit her statue with us tonight. I'm sure a little of your good humor would go a long way in convincing her to accept.

If she agrees, we'll meet you, Lyros, and Nike on the path to the cliffs at the hour of her choosing. I can't wait for her to see your ward.

Love,
Cassia

Cassia held out the glass seal Lio had crafted for her, which bore a glyph in the shape of a spade, her private symbol for communicating with their Trial circle. He pricked his thumb on his fang, then pressed it to the seal. She stamped her spade on the note to Mak in their combined blood. Lio did the same with his seal, a moonflower.

"I'll leave these in the entry hall and light a summons for the courier." Lio sounded no more in the mood than Cassia to see people tonight.

By the time she had fed Knight and Lio had made coffee, a single reply arrived, sealed with Mak and Lyros's glyphs of matching speires.

Ho you turtle doves,

I'm sure you two don't want to leave the love nest generously provided by yours truly. But I won't say no to visiting the statue with Nike while we have the chance.

She said yes. We'll meet you there at sixth moon. Thank you for doing this.

- Mak

By sixth moon, Cassia managed to collect her thoughts and make herself presentable. She joined Lio in the entry hall with Knight in tow. Lio hadn't been waiting for her long. He had gotten ready only a little less slowly than she had, even with his Hesperine speed.

He was frowning, his gaze distant. She hated that. Ever since last night, he hadn't stopped worrying.

"What's wrong?" She feared she would be asking him that often for the foreseeable future.

He sighed, his attention returning to her.

"Are you sure you don't mind doing this tonight?" she asked.

He shook his head. "I think it's a wonderful idea."

"Then what's troubling you? Besides...everything." She threw up a hand.

He caught it in his. "We have no idea when Nike will leave again. Migration is only a month from now, and I have to wonder if she will go south with us. She might not even stay long enough to see us off...she could be gone tomorrow. I'm concerned about how everyone will take it if she disappears again. Especially Uncle Argyros. They were always very close."

At least Cassia hadn't put the furrow on Lio's brow this time. "I know you don't want him to be hurt."

"Especially so soon after he and I mended our own rift. That made me realize just how much more he feels things than he lets on."

Nike answered to a call her loved ones couldn't hear. Cassia, of all people, respected the clarion that guided her rescuer. But that call had brought Nike to her last night, and if she could do anything to influence the Hesperine errant to stay, she would.

"Only she can give herself permission to stay," Cassia said, "but we can show her all she has to stay for. Like the brother she never knew. Perhaps it would be better if Nike and Mak visited the statue on their own, but I want to go with them to see if I can help."

"If we stayed home, I suspect they would still have an audience. Everyone wants to spend as much time as possible with Nike."

Lio fussed with her cloak, checking to make sure she was properly wrapped up, as he always did before she poked her nose outside. Even if the only enemy was an imaginary case of frostbite, she let him indulge his protectiveness. She knew he needed to right now, and she had promised to let him.

If she weren't still human, she wouldn't need the cloak. "I swear, as soon as I'm a Hesperine, I shall dance naked in the snow."

"My lady, may I have that dance?"

"I'm saving it for you." She stared at the empty wall next to his Gifting chart, where hers should hang. "Hypatia will have to re-read the sky for my star chart on another night. Do you suppose Orthros's greatest astronomer will be cross with me about the wasted effort?"

"I'm certain she'll enjoy the excuse for another elaborate vigil atop her Observatory." Lio sounded as deflated as Cassia felt. "Ready?"

Even after multiple cups of coffee, she covered a yawn with her hand, but nodded.

They exited their residence and descended the front steps of the tower. The flagstone terrace was hidden beneath a fresh layer of snow, which cloaked the surrounding garden in white. Lio levitated them to the shelter of the arbor.

They had just entered the tunnel of vines when Zoe came running toward them from the other end, Knight and the goats racing after her. At least someone was happy they weren't in seclusion tonight.

Cassia dropped to her knees for Knight's tail-wagging, face-licking greeting. She rubbed his ears and returned his kisses. "Oh, my dearest, it's so good to be missed. I missed you, too. Yes, I did, with all my heart, my good Knight. Did you have wonderful fun with our *kaetlii* while I was busy?"

Zoe glued herself to Cassia's side. "He played fetch with me and Moonbeam and Aurora and then Papa let me Slumber in the barn!"

"That was a very special night indeed." Lio ruffled Zoe's hair. She didn't notice him wince, but Cassia did.

Despite Zoe's frequent pleas to bed down with her goats, her parents always insisted she sleep in her room. She must have been unusually anxious for them to relent and let her sleep in the barn, the place she felt safest.

Zoe hugged Cassia with all her might. "Will you come help me water my window garden later? And practice my reading?"

"I'd love to, Zoe flower," Cassia answered.

Lio said, "We'll finish reading *Marina's Magical Mind* together."

Zoe clung to his hand. "You'll be here when I get back from Bosko's?"

"Of course." Lio knelt and straightened her mantle, then retied a ribbon on one of her slippers. "You have your spyglass with you, so you can find us when you're done playing?"

She nodded and pulled the spyglass out of a pocket of her play robe. It was so like Lio to concentrate his immense magical power in this little artifact to ease Zoe's fear of separation from her family.

"Do you want to take Knight with you?" Cassia asked.

Zoe thought for a moment, then shook her head. "He missed you too much. And my goats will be jealous if I don't give them all my attention tonight."

"Very diplomatic." Lio's mouth twitched.

Cassia swallowed a chuckle, so very grateful for the joy that was Zoe. "Have fun with Bosko. I'm sure he'll have many exciting things to tell you about his Aunt Nike."

Zoe hugged each of them one more time, then stepped away with the goats.

"I'm not going to tell her," Cassia announced.

Lio helped her to her feet. "It's difficult to decide what would be best for her."

"We can't tell her," Cassia insisted. "She idolizes Solia. If she finds out what we learned last night, she'll get her hopes up. A disappointment would set her back, when she has just now made so much progress coping with the loss of her human family."

"That's what worries me as well. And yet, I know there are times when telling children the truth, even when it's hard, is better for them."

"Not this time. She already had to face the realities of loss too early in life. How can we tell her the truth, when we don't even know what the truth is?"

Lio sighed, then nodded. "We'll wait till we have news."

"It's my fault for telling her so many stories about my sister. I thought it would help her for us to speak of loss together, but…"

Lio rubbed her arms. "It has helped her. We'll wait."

Knight nudged his nose under her hand with a whine, and she ran her hand over his head to his ruff. "Let's go."

Lio wrapped his arm around her waist and stepped them and Knight from the garden. They arrived at the trailhead to find Nike, Mak, and Lyros awaiting them. They would not have this walk to themselves, as Lio had predicted. But Cassia was glad to see that their Trial circle had come to support Mak, and that Apollon, Alkaios, and Nephalea had joined the party to put Nike at ease.

"Thank you all so much for coming." Cassia found a smile for everyone.

Apollon returned it, his own encouraging. "I should thank you. How kind of you youngbloods to spend an aftermoon walk looking at my work, when you could be off dancing at the coffeehouses instead."

Nike raised a brow at Apollon. "So, a statue of me. Really, Uncle?"

"Think how many mallets and chisels you've smithed for me over the years. How could I not make you a statue?"

"You could have sculpted me a nice horse or something to look dashing outside my residence. A statue of myself makes me feel old as a monument."

"Nonsense. You're in good company with my young Grace. Komnena isn't even a hundred years old, and I've already made a statue of her."

"Cradle robber," she teased, as if it were an old joke.

"I must maintain my infamy somehow." Apollon gave a cheerful, fanged grin.

Yes, it was good that Apollon had come.

There was the crunch of a footstep. A heavy boot. Cassia turned to see that the third member of the Blood Errant had also decided to attend.

"Glad you could join us, Ioustin," Apollon welcomed him.

Cassia tensed with apprehension. Lio checked her cloak again. She had grown used to the little signs of his attentiveness to her feelings, but she never took them for granted.

"No news yet," Ioustin told her before she asked. "I'm sorry."

She shook her head and spoke with a confidence she didn't feel. "Kalos needs time to work. I'm glad you could get away from the Charge and come home again so soon."

Ioustin looked at Apollon. "The union stone in my sword lit up, but not with a distress signal. It was rather nice."

Cassia and Lio exchanged a glance. They had seen the enchanted stone in the hilt of Thorn, Ioustin's renowned two-hander, which the Blood Errant could use to communicate. Not that they would divulge to anyone that he had brought it into Orthros before, despite the Queens' laws to the contrary.

"You didn't have to come for this," Nike said.

"Neither did you," Ioustin replied.

"Cassia and Mak are persuasive."

Mak winked at Cassia, and she gave him a victory salute like the Stewards did after a battle.

Knight was leaning forward in Ioustin's direction with his whole body alert, his tail poised to wag. Cassia patted him twice behind his shoulder, silently giving him permission to stop heeling. He sprang from her side to show his adoration for the two royals present.

He raced over to Xandra first, who laughed and petted him with her usual blitheness. The perfectly beautiful princess with her snow-pale skin, rosy lips, and dark coronet braid never shied away from liege-hound drool.

Cassia thought Knight might stop there and melt with happiness, but it seemed he hadn't given up on winning the notice of the First Prince himself. Knight trotted over and lowered himself to his belly at Ioustin's feet, wagging his tail, and looked up with his most pathetic, longing eyes.

Ioustin looked away first. "Have mercy, dog."

Nike pointed at Cassia's hound. "That's Knight?"

Ioustin sighed. "So he is."

Nike's brows rose. "He certainly looks like a liegehound. He *smells* like a liegehound. But that overgrown puppy begging for the Blood-Red Prince's attention cannot possibly be one of the Hesperine-hunting menaces we've fought countless times over the centuries."

"I'm teaching him to overcome his prejudices," Cassia said.

"He's much bigger than the last time your saw him, isn't he?" Nephalea asked.

Alkaios chuckled. "Quite different from when we tucked Cassia into her bedroll next to her new puppy."

"Indeed," Nike mused. "Back then, I was sorry to realize he would grow up to hunt us one day. I'm glad that wasn't his future after all."

"So am I," Cassia agreed. "His destiny changed the night he met the Queens of Orthros. He fell completely in love with them and, by extension, every royal in Orthros."

"Don't say it," Ioustin warned his Trial sister.

Nike's half-grin showed one of her fangs. "You've had all sorts of admirers over the centuries, but a liegehound? That's a new one."

"Oh, Rudhira." Xandra used the affectionate name Methu had given Ioustin, which most young Hesperines now called him. "Look at that face. At least say something to him."

Ioustin sighed. "Good dog."

Knight wagged his tail harder and drooled on his paws.

Cassia swallowed a laugh and decided she'd best intervene before Knight drooled on Ioustin's boots. *"Dockk dockk."*

Knight returned to her side and the affectionate pats of their Trial circle.

"Nicely done." Lio scratched Knight's tail.

She trusted Lio to veil their quiet words. "I thought everyone might benefit from a laugh. I don't think a solemn occasion is what anyone needs tonight."

"I really must stop referring to you as Lady Circumspect and start calling you Lady Diplomat."

That brought a smile to her face. "I like the sound of that very much."

Cassia was glad to hear the conversations flowing a little more easily now. She hooked her arm in Mak's, and they led the way up the cliffs.

She sensed the patchwork of veil spells running through the gathering, as was customary among Hesperines. She thought the Blood Errant were probably talking amongst themselves as much as the Eighth Circle was.

"I'm amazed Lio let you out of his lair tonight," Mak said.

"I'm not really here," she replied. "This is his illusion of me, while he's keeping the real me captive in his tower."

"I would never," Lio protested with a laugh.

"His very willing captive."

"In that case, I definitely would." He flashed his fangs at her.

"Lio, don't you think it's much more surprising that Lyros and Mak set foot outside the gymnasium tonight?"

"Indeed. I thought the warriors would spend every waking moment watching Nike fight. How many times has someone invited her to spar since you all went home last night?"

Lyros shook his head. "We lost count. But she's not committing to any matches."

"She's good at it, too." Mak sounded admiring and exasperated at the same time. "I've never heard someone avoid a challenge without actually backing down from it. This is what happens when mind mages are warriors."

"See here," said Lio, "I've never avoided a challenge, even when I knew you were going to break my nose."

"Maybe you should learn some of Nike's avoidance tactics, scroll-worm," Mak teased.

Cassia was glad they had left the residence after all.

They all strode out onto the narrow promontory of rock known as Victory Point and approached the back of the statue.

Nike circled her portrait with her hands behind her back. She had the same tell as Uncle Argyros and Lio. Cassia widened her eyes at Mak, who nodded, his eyes glinting with amusement.

The Victory Star faced her own statue. The black granite portrait of her stood fast, unmoved. Her Stand regalia and loose-flowing hair were caught forever in motion, billowing out behind her, her face frozen in fierce joy.

Nike reached out one pale hand and pressed it palm-to-palm with that of her stone self. Tonight's wind tugged her rufous hair and simple black fighting robes out behind her toward the sea.

Like an impossible mirror image conjured by Hesperine magic, Cassia's past and present stood across from each other.

Nike's expression was closed, her eyes shuttered. But for a moment, Cassia thought she caught a glimpse through the window there to Nike's soul. She looked into her statue's eyes as if she sought the answer to a question. Just as Cassia had done one night here not so long ago.

What did Nike see, confronted with her own past and present?

I don't know now.

How well Cassia understood those simple words that could fracture the ground beneath one's feet.

"This is how I discovered who you were," Cassia said. "When Mak first showed me the statue, I recognized you, and we realized you were the Hesperine who had saved me. His ward feels just like your magic did that night."

Abruptly Nike lowered her hand and dusted off her palms, standing back in the shelter of Mak's magic. His ward hovered in the air before her statue, a shield of shadow that echoed the shape of her famous armament. "It's a fine ward you've conjured here, Mak."

"Thank you." He bowed. "For your portrait to really resemble you, it needed a ward at hand."

"You must have put a great deal of time and magic into maintaining this casting. I'm honored that you spent your power on this. I sense our blood tie in your spell."

"A family resemblance to the Victory Star?" Mak puffed out his chest.

Kia tossed up her hands. "His pride was already inflated enough."

"Hardly," Lyros scoffed. "All his boasts are entirely justified."

Alkaios pondered the statue, a hand on his chin. "I still say it needs more bloodstains."

Nephalea tilted her head. "And perhaps some mages cowering at her feet."

Apollon laughed. "That can be arranged."

"We've been very glad of your statue, Nike," said Nodora. "It enabled us to know you before we got the chance to meet you."

"That way, we could imagine you when Rudhira told us about your adventures," Xandra said.

"Did he fill your ears with tales?" Nike raised a brow.

"Only the truth," Ioustin answered. "It is grand enough."

Apollon winked. "I did all the embellishment for him."

Nike went to stand beside Apollon. "It's a flattering statue, Uncle. Thank you."

"I want you to like it."

"Of course I like it."

He put an arm around her shoulders and said nothing more.

Cassia could tell Nike was unable to like the statue, although that had nothing to do with Apollon's work, and everything to do with Nike's. It must be difficult to like that magnificent stone woman, so sure of herself, when in reality, she was no longer certain of her quest.

"The Blood Union feels like a star about to explode," Lio murmured. "I think they're trying to decide if we're going to Methu's statue next, but neither of them wants to be the first to say it aloud."

At last it was Nike who announced, "I want to see Methu."

"You don't have to on my account," Apollon said.

"I want to."

Cassia suspected that tone of Nike's had settled many dilemmas and arguments over the centuries.

Nike turned soft gray eyes on Ioustin. "You don't have to come."

"I only let you tell me that once, when you went errant alone without me. Never again."

They all headed farther up the cliffs. When they came to the memorial, they found someone already waiting for them.

Cassia had never seen Kassandra at her son's statue.

Nike hesitated for a moment.

"Come," Kassandra invited. "See the beautiful portrait Apollon has made of our Methu."

Nike, Apollon, and Ioustin joined her before the statue of Prometheus,

Orthros's first bloodborn and martyred hero. Cassia, Lio, and their Trial circle hung back with Alkaios and Nephalea, giving the elders space.

Nike studied the smaller statues that surrounded Methu's, the childhood portraits of the Eighth Circle. All the sucklings who had been brought to Orthros during the surviving Blood Errant's quest for vengeance against the mages who had captured Methu. The blessings Hespera had brought out of that curse, so the legend said.

Her gaze lingered on Methu's hands, which were carved as if to hold swords, but held the children's hands instead.

At last Nike lifted her face to her Trial brother's. Her fangs gleamed.

Did Nike show her fangs instead of tears? Cassia had done that many times. Sometimes only anger was powerful enough to keep you standing in the face of a loss so wrong.

Ioustin took Nike's hand, and their fingers intertwined, tightened.

"My prophecies aren't like Kia's math problems," Kassandra said, "which have only one right answer. They aren't like Mak and Lyros's disciplined battle arts. Or like Lio's negotiations, in which the outcome is uncertain. They are not even like Nodora's music, which can be written down and played exactly, or improvised and elaborated on."

"Your prophecies are like poetry," Mak guessed. "They have form, but are open to interpretation. They have many possible meanings, but a beginning and an end. Is that why Methu was a poet?"

Their Trial circle all looked at Mak as if he had just made a prophecy himself. Although he and Lyros enjoyed reading military history, Cassia didn't think he had ever talked about poetry before.

Kassandra gave a nod of approval. "Everyone has to decide for themselves what the words mean, and if some people arrive at different conclusions, they aren't wrong."

Ioustin's face seemed etched in stone, as if he were a statue himself.

Nike looked away from Methu. "Add a statue of Cassia here. I'll use my thelemancy to show you what she looked like when she was seven."

Apollon looked at Cassia with fondness in his eyes. "An excellent decision. Her portrait belongs here, too."

Lio traced a finger over her temple, tucking her hair behind her ear. "Next to mine."

Cassia hadn't quite realized that until now. She, too, was a child brought to Orthros by Nike's quest on her Trial brother's behalf.

Nike turned to Cassia. "Shall we visit your sister, too? For years, I thought I knew her, believing Iris to be her. Now I'd like to know them both."

"I want you to see her." Cassia just wasn't sure if she could bear to see Solia right now.

But if Nike could bear to look upon her Trial brother, Cassia could visit her sister's statue long enough to fulfill Nike's request. Cassia was doing this for Nike and Mak.

She led the way back to the trail, and with Lio holding her close, her steps didn't drag. He glanced over his shoulder at Ioustin and Kassandra, who stayed behind at Methu's memorial. The rest of them took the path back in the direction of the House, to the statue of Cassia's sister.

"So this is Solia," Nike said.

"I'm so glad all of you are here," Cassia told her rescuers.

Alkaios smiled, and Nephalea squeezed her hand.

Cassia struggled for words. The last time she had stood here, when Apollon had presented the statue, she had felt such peace. "Papa?"

"Yes, Cassia."

"I'd like to commission a statue. You can do mine later, if you don't have time to make two new ones."

"You don't have to commission statues, my dear. You can just ask for them, and I will make the time."

"Thank you." She swallowed. "Iris deserves a statue. A monument to her heroism and the power of female friendship. I think she would want to be right here next to Solia forever."

"Consider it done."

A moment of silence fell over their gathering. Not a vigil for her sister's memory. Robbed of the certainty of mourning, Cassia felt uprooted. Not knowing was a petal and a thorn.

Here they all stood, not grieving, but waiting for news. All these strong, dear people in suspense for Cassia's sake, wondering about Solia.

The silence seemed full. It was packed with everything they hadn't asked her, all they had not said, all she refused to acknowledge.

They knew exactly how to support her.

The wind sighed among them. Then Ioustin's voice sliced through like an icy gust. "Cassia."

She turned. He had joined them at Solia's statue. When she saw who was at his side, a chill swept over her.

Kalos was back.

She should have been glad to see him. But dread uncurled in the pit of her stomach.

She should welcome him, or thank him again, or ask him if he could tell her what had really befallen her sister. She just looked at him while Lio held her.

She could read nothing on Kalos's face. He was always that silent and solemn and still. But he didn't hesitate to meet her gaze tonight.

"Kalos has given me his report," Ioustin said. "Are you ready to hear it?"

No, she wasn't. She nodded.

At that moment, she appreciated more than ever that Kalos was not someone who made small talk. "I found her trail."

Cassia took a breath, but couldn't quite let it out.

"She definitely escaped," Kalos announced.

Cassia found her voice. "How far did she get?"

"Past the siege perimeter."

"Past Bellator's scouts? And the king's surrounding army?"

"That's right. She got clean away."

Cassia's mind told her this was good news, but she only felt angry and frustrated. Things had seemed easier a moment ago, before Kalos had returned. Everyone around her was waiting for a reaction, she could tell. She didn't know what to say.

"I haven't followed the trail to the end yet," Kalos explained. "I didn't want to keep you waiting for news, so I came back to give you a report after confirming a few things."

"Thank you, Kalos." There. That was the most important thing to say. "It was so kind of you to come all the way back so I wouldn't be in suspense."

"There's more. It's very interesting." There was a hint of animation on his face. Although he always seemed uncomfortable around other people, he must truly enjoy his lone hunts. "About her escort. She left in the company of one other person. A male mortal. They hid some distance from the fortress in a mill—in disuse in that season, I presume. After a few days, they headed south."

Cassia's mouth hung open. "You were able to find out all of that since last night, fifteen years after the fact?"

"Yes." His eyes glittered as if someone had a surprise for him. "That's the most interesting part. I was able to discover so many details because someone used magic."

"Magic!" Lio rubbed his beard. "What affinity?"

"Not sure about the affinity, but magic is how they escaped. A mortal mage performed a difficult traversal spell to get them out of the fortress, to a safe location beyond the siege."

"So the man with her was a mage," Cassia said.

"Do you know of any mages who were in the fortress?" Lio asked her.

She shook her head. "To my knowledge, the only magic involved were the catapults the king used to besiege the fortress."

Nike frowned. "The king used magical catapults at the Siege of Sovereigns?"

Mak nodded. "Illegal ones he got from the Aithourian Circle."

At the mention of the circle of elite war mages who had captured Methu, Nike's gaze hardened. "I wish I'd known they were involved that night."

"They built siege engines based on ancient designs," Lyros explained, "from before the Mage Orders mandated that men could not be both warriors and mages. King Lucis's allies in the Aithourian Circle violated their own religious laws to build spell-enhanced catapults, which enabled him to demolish Castra Roborra in a matter of days."

Nike's frown deepened. "There were even wider-reaching political implications to that night than I thought."

Cassia no longer had to concern herself with the politics, only the personal. "The Mage Orders were on the king's side. The man who helped my sister escape must have been an apostate who practices magic without their sanction."

Kalos rocked on his feet. "They might have rested in the mill so the mage could recover from the traversal. Possibly also to evade troop movements. The early end of the siege would have confused matters. I'll resume my search at the mill. With your permission, I'll stay on their trail longer this time and not return until I know their destination."

"Yes, of course. You must be free to do your work without having to interrupt yourself to bring us news. Please, stay as long as you need to."

"I'll let you know when I'm sure." He bowed to Ioustin. "My Prince." Without pleasantries, he disappeared.

Cassia looked at the statue and met Solia's happy gaze.

That gust of something, like a painful breath or a bird shooting into flight, tried to take off in Cassia's chest. She shoved it back down before she could entirely feel it, much less put a name to it. Each time it happened, she got a little better at trapping and silencing it.

She had to re-learn how to master it, as she had always done so well. Had she really forgotten how so easily?

She dare not let it rise. For that was less painful than if it took wing, only to be shot from the sky.

THE STRONGEST ALLOY

M AK WAITED FOR NIKE in the last place she would expect
to find him. The last place in the world she would expect
to find anyone, really.

Any minute now, she would reach her limit on how much of the family's company she could take for one night. He was certain this was where she would escape to.

Try as he might, he couldn't stop staring at what she had left here. It had to be what he thought it was. It *felt* like what he thought it was.

She's there? Lyros asked through their Union.

It had been years since they had first exchanged blood and fully awakened their Grace bond. But each time Lyros's voice rolled through his mind, Mak relished it more.

Well? He sensed Lyros's calm, raised eyebrow and deep concern.

Not yet, Mak answered.

Then why are you as excited as a trainee at the Hippolytan Games and as reverent as a pilgrim on the Vigil of Mercy?

Maybe because the pride of Orthros's warriors is touching my mind, and the Goddess has ordained that I be his personal blood supply for the rest of eternity.

Cup and thorns, Lyros's laughter felt good. *I'll touch more of you later and you may worship as long as you like, but don't think you can distract me so easily.*

Mak sighed. *She's not here now, but she's been here. And she brought something with her.*

Something dangerous?

The truth is, I'm not sure what it is.

He could almost hear Lyros's huff. I can see your suspicions, my Grace. No wonder you're practically levitating. Wait. Are you actually levitating?

Mak glanced down at his sandals. *No. Knowing the First Master Steward is about to find me where she may not want me to be has a sobering effect.*

You don't have to do this. Give Nike a chance to get to know you better before you tell her what you've done.

This is how I want her to get to know me.

By risking her anger for her respect? Lyros smiled. *I love you.*

It's a good thing you do, because I may need lots of your blood to put me back together if she leaves me in pieces.

She won't, but I'm happy to give you lots of blood in any case.

Are you back at our residence now?

Reading in bed. Naked.

You certainly know how to distract a fellow from his troubles. Mak rubbed a hand over his mouth. He couldn't greet his sister with this fangy grin.

Hurry home. Lyros's presence receded from his mind. Giving him room, but always there, within reach.

And always worried of late. Mak grimaced. Grace ought to be a petal and a thorn on Hespera's Rose. You couldn't keep from dragging the love of your eternity along through all your risks, too.

Mak stood and waited for his confrontation with the Victory Star.

He couldn't see her arrive in the antechamber, but as soon as she stepped in, her aura filled the whole place like a hand fitting to a well-worn shield grip. Of course, she would already know he was there.

Not that he could sense a sunbound thing through those veils of hers. Warding *and* mind magic, and sixteen hundred years of it. He shook his head. Mother and Father were a deadly combination, and their firstgift had gotten a double dose.

Her sandals padded in his direction. The inner door swung open. Perfectly silent. No squealing hinges on his watch.

She emerged from the shadowed doorway and strode to the large worktable that stood between them. Her hand went to what she had left there, her knuckles white.

Mak held up his hands. "On my honor, I did not disturb it."

The door eased shut behind her with a thud that did not reverberate here underground. She gazed at him with her unreadable gray eyes and stood at relaxed attention. And he had thought Father was opaque.

Mak stormed the hill. "It wouldn't take you long to realize I've been here, and I wouldn't keep it from you. I've tried to take care of the place in your absence. I hope I haven't crossed the veil."

She strolled around the circular chamber. She peeked in a toolbox and perused a shelf of scrolls. Took a quick inventory of the bins and racks of raw materials. Then rounded the worktable. Mak turned as she passed him.

She went to stand before her crucible. The heat rising from the forge made her waver before his eyes. The round, deep well of geomagical power cupped her anvil where, he was sure, she had made some of the most powerful Hesperine artifacts in history. He drew nearer, standing to one side by the pool of polar runoff that served to cool her creations.

"The temperature is regulated," she said. "You've kept the spells tuned."

"I'm no geomagus, but I know how to work a forge."

She looked at him. "You're a smith?"

"When the family told me that was your craft, I could see the benefits of it." He didn't let on about his silly childhood hopes that she'd come around to mentor him. "When I first started learning, Mother and Father gave me permission to use your forge—the one they know about, in your residence."

"I see."

"It's a fine setup, and I've done some of my best work there. But the more I used it, the more obvious certain things became. As I learned our craft, I grew into the forge. The more I pushed my skills, the more I pushed what the forge was capable of. I learned everything it can do. And what it can't. There were things I know you've made that you couldn't have made there."

"That forge is excellent for making anything from furniture to tack, in any metal from bronze to steel."

"But steel isn't your specialty."

"Admittedly, I prefer the more traditional iron."

"That's not your specialty, either, though, is it?" He slid his hand into the pocket of his robes and drew out the little item he'd brought with him. The size of his thumbnail, it weighed on his palm heavier than an iron bed knob. The gleaming material looked like a blend of silver and steel with a dash of pearls.

Nike's gaze fell to the four-pointed star. Her voice was low. "Where did you find that?"

Mak sighed. "In your library. Tied to a bookmark in a volume of Methu's poetry." He placed it in her hand.

She closed her fist around it.

"You see," Mak tried to explain, "Mother and Father kept your residence spotless for a long time. After a while, though, they stopped going in. I offered to run some cleaning spells through from time to time. Not the warded areas, understand. I wouldn't meddle in your private rooms. Father was mostly worried about your library moldering. I spent a lot of time dusting your books over the last few decades."

"*This* is a warded area."

Mak rubbed the back of his head. "So it is. You were very thorough. That star was the only evidence anywhere in your residence that this place exists. But when I found it, I knew you couldn't have made an alloy like that in the forge I was using. It's heavier than any known material. It resists damage, rust...everything." What he'd done next was harder for him to justify. But he told her. "So I tried using it as a focus and stepping to... wherever it had come from."

Her eyes flashed. "You could have gotten yourself killed."

Her concern for him almost made him smile. "I was careful. And it's a good thing, too, because the wards on this place put me through my paces."

"Decades-old, untended wards of mine are usually enough to leave war mages in pieces."

"But not someone who shares your blood and your affinity and has a link to this forge in his pocket. I still can't get in unless I bring the star with me."

Her hand uncurled a measure around the key to her Sanctuary, which he had just returned to her.

"I won't come here again," he promised. "Unless, of course, you invite me. I don't expect it. I've told no one of this place, although I couldn't keep it from my Grace."

"Mak...thank you for being such a good steward, in all senses of the word. I was worried the forge had suffered from my absence. It was a risk I had to take, but if the spells had faded, it might never have been possible to restore it exactly the way it was."

Now he did smile, with relief. "You're most welcome."

"But this forge is dangerous. For many reasons. I would not be a good sister or a good Master Steward if I encouraged you to return here."

That sounded a lot like what Lyros had tried to tell him. Not that it had worked. "If that's your decision, I respect it. I'd like you to have this, as a gift to make amends for my intrusion and to show my gratitude for the time I've spent here."

From his other pocket, he pulled out the trinket he had made for her, a bauble of blackthorn leaves and berries. When he dropped it on her palm, her hand dipped, and so did her jaw.

"Adamas," he said. "The strongest metal in the world, so heavy only Hesperines can handle it. Its inventor is still the only smith who knows the secret of how to make it."

"Except for my little brother."

Mak grinned. "Took me years, even with the detailed notes you keep down here. When I finally managed my first, tiny triumph, it only seemed right I make something for you."

She shut her eyes, and he sensed her massive magic concentrate on his small creation. "Goddess. It's perfect."

He couldn't help the rush of triumph he felt at her words.

Her eyes snapped open. "How many of my notes have you read?"

"All of them, I'm afraid." He lifted a hand, and the journal he had left on the worktable behind them levitated into his grasp. "Fair is fair, so here are mine."

She stowed both their charms of adamas together in her pocket and took his journal from him, her brows drawn. She opened it and scanned a page. Flipped to the next. And the next.

Her gaze leapt to his. "Mak, do you know where we are? The location of this forge?"

"Under a remote stretch of the Umbral Mountains. Inside the border of Orthros and the Queens' ward."

Nike closed his journal with her measured, graceful motions that reminded him of a wary warhorse. She held his notes for a long moment, as if she was taking time to make a decision. "I seem to have arrived to the battle too late."

"Would you have tried to stop me?"

"*Yes!* I would have tried to protect you, not...lead you astray."

"Don't worry, Lyros did everything possible to talk me out of what I've been doing down here. Obviously if my Grace couldn't change my mind, then neither could you."

"You have other considerations than I did. More to lose."

"All of Orthros has more to lose right now. If we're to protect our people from new threats, we need new ways of countering them. During the Equinox Summit, Lyros and I were solely responsible for the safety of the border while the rest of our family traveled to Tenebra and almost got embroiled in a war with the mages. Then the Stand had to keep Orthros safe with those mages inside the ward, right here in Selas. Rudhira told you about the mage of dreams who got in here during the Solstice Summit. Lio almost died, and Cassia was almost kidnapped, while the entire Stand was tied up at the ward!"

"Yes. I know another Old Master was here."

"*Another* one? Wait...that's not your first one?"

"Didn't you know about the others?" she asked mildly. "According to the scrolls, there are six."

The way she had said *another*, it sounded as if she spoke from personal experience, not the arcane riddles in ancient texts that told legends of the hex of powerful necromancers. Most people believed they weren't real. The fact that one of them had actually manifested was only known to Hesperines and still a secret from mortals.

As a warrior of the Stand, it was Mak's duty to apprise the First Master Steward of all he knew of the danger. If, in the course of conversation, she happened to reveal something she knew, well, that didn't mean he had pried.

"This Old Master calls himself the Collector," Mak reported. "As one of the god of death's mind mages, he uses his necromancy and thelemancy to collect *people*. He takes control of them through possession or rips their magic out of them using a ritual called essential displacement. He and the King of Tenebra seem to be working together."

"Ioustin didn't have time to explain the details. Sometime I'd like to sit down with you, Lyros, Lio, and Cassia so you can tell me what we currently understand about this enemy."

Did that mean she planned to stay long enough to become involved in the defense of Orthros?

Or was there some other reason she knew so much about the Old Masters and wanted any additional information they could give her?

Mak was certain there were only so many of her adventures Nike was willing to discuss as yet, and he had best indulge his rabid curiosity carefully.

He pointed to what she had left on the worktable. "Is that what I think it is, if I may ask?"

Her lips flattened in a stubborn line.

"It feels like it belongs here," he said. "You've returned it to where you made it, haven't you?"

She slapped her hand with his journal and stalked away. But she didn't head for the door. She walked back around to the other side of the table, setting his notes down. He almost did levitate in his haste to join her there and stand across from her over her mysterious prize.

It was a long, narrow bundle wrapped in dull black fabric and thick, dark wards. It sat there between them on the scarred, polished wood of the worktable. The magic shielding it didn't quite conceal the power emanating from within, the way it seemed to hum with the same warmth as the forge behind him.

Nike reached forward and unwrapped the artifact.

There before them was one of Methu's two famous swords, the Fangs, separated from its match.

Mak gasped, then let out the breath in wonder. He had known it. But seeing it with his own eyes was something else. He flattened both his hands on the table and studied it.

The hilt was of gold, with an ornate filigreed sphere at the top and the base forming a grip in between. Prometheus's own hand had rested there, wielding this weapon through countless legendary battles. The adamas blade widened along its curve, and along its broadest edge were engravings and cutouts Mak recognized as Imperial symbols.

"Where did you find it?" he asked. "Dare I ask how you got it?"

"Hm," she answered. "That is a tale for another time."

Another time was not never. "Does the other survive?"

"Yes."

"That's amazing, Nike. Do you know where it is?"

"No. But I will."

Her voice was as deadly as the blade's edge, and he knew she would rend the world to find her fallen Trial brother's other sword.

Mak eyed the milky crimson stone shaped like half of an egg that was embedded in the hilt. "This piece of his union stone survives. Perhaps it can help you locate its other half."

"That is my hope."

"You must have been on the hunt for a long time. Cassia saw this bundle on your back in her childhood memories. Even the few of us who know that detail have been left to wonder what you were carrying with you that night. But when I felt it, I just knew."

"It hasn't left my side since I reclaimed it."

"I dare say you would have carried it into House Komnena last night if you could have. But if you had to leave it somewhere, well, there's nowhere safer than right here."

"Thank you for showing his sword the proper respect."

"Of course."

She traced a loving hand over the flat of the blade. "I asked his permission before I forged it for him. The sword arts are a sacred tradition among his mortal ancestors. But he said as a Hesperine, he wanted me to craft his blade. We followed the rituals closely and made these in the image of his father's sword. He commissioned two, adapting some of the dual wielding techniques of his grandfather's people into his personal fighting style."

"All his heritages, brought together in his weapons. Beautiful."

"Crafting these was one of the greatest honors of my life."

"Did he know about this forge where you made the Fangs? Do Rudhira and Uncle Apollon know this is where you made Thorn and the Hammer of the Sun, as well as your own Chalice of Stars?"

"They all spent time here so I could make the weapons according to their requests."

"Thorns. I'm glad neither Rudhira nor Uncle Apollon ever caught me down here."

"They are as complicit as you and I in breaking the Queens' ban on weapons in Orthros."

"I know they wouldn't turn me in. But they might have tried to lock me out."

"Actually, they couldn't have gotten through the wards without me."

Mak made sure his sandals were still on the ground. He had gotten in, where the Blood-Red Prince and the Lion of Orthros couldn't even tread.

"After you and I met last night," she said slowly, "I wanted to castigate Ioustin for not telling me I had a brother. Walking into House Komnena for Cassia's Gift Night, I knew more about Apollon's son than about my own parents' son. Not that I blame Ioustin for what I was not here to learn. That is my burden to bear."

"You just thought he should have…prepared you?"

"No. I thought it unjust to you that he didn't fill my ears with your praises."

That would have been nice. "You two didn't have a lot of time on your way here."

"That's not why." She smoothed a hand over his journal. "I think he wanted to let you introduce yourself. Discovering you firsthand has proved to be much better than anything he might have said."

Now Mak couldn't stop grinning. He wouldn't be going home in pieces, after all.

He held out his hand anew. "Well met, Sister."

"Well met." She clasped his wrist. "I *love* brothers, Mak. I grew up with two Trial brothers, but I've never had a blood brother before." Her grip tightened. "You could have grown up with me."

"We could have…" He shook his head, at a loss for words to describe the years. "But you will always have my gratitude for saving Cassia's life. I'm her favorite relative, you know."

Nike chuckled at that. "You aren't angry that I didn't at least visit?"

"Look at it this way. You know what would have happened to Lio without Cassia. Thanks to you, I didn't lose my Trial brother."

"I'm glad. So glad you didn't have to face that."

"I'm sorry you had to. Your grief runs in my veins."

"I wish Methu could have known you." She opened his journal again to flip through his notes. "I have a confession."

"You're holding all my dangerous secrets in your hands, and I've read quite a few of yours. It can't be much worse."

A spark of mischief lit her eyes, and Mak felt like he'd just seen a shooting star. A celestial sign of who she had once been and still was and could be again. "I've known you for mere hours, but I feel closer to you right now than anyone else in our family."

Mak wanted to make a jest. Light remarks ran through his mind, all promising to unwind the tightness in his throat. But he couldn't.

"I know hours can't make up for years," she said.

"I know they can."

She pulled the star of adamas from her pocket and put the key to her forge back in his hand. "Let's find out."

25

nights until

BOREIAN SPRING EQUINOX

16 Khariton, 1596 IS

INTENTIONS

WHEN LIO ARRIVED AT his uncle's terrace, the door leading inside to the library stood open in invitation. Snowflakes swirled busily over House Argyros, turned away by wards protecting the terrace and the surrounding orchard. The paths between the fruit trees were quiet. The sucklings must be playing somewhere else this moon.

Lio crossed the terrace and entered his uncle's library. The smells of paper and ink enfolded him.

His uncle's desk caught his eye, and he paused to stare at the state of it. Uncle Argyros was usually the most organized person in Orthros, but tonight his desk was a chaos of scrolls. Lio sensed the veiled blood seals on them and dutifully walked away from the confidential documents. If Uncle Argyros was letting his work pile up while he spent time with Nike, he had certainly earned it.

Lio strolled between the stately iron bookshelves and racks of scrolls to the center of the library. His uncle waited with coffee set out on the large, round table.

"Good moon, Lio."

"Good moon." Lio took a seat next to his uncle. "It's quiet tonight."

"I thought you and I could do with a quiet talk over coffee."

Uncle Argyros could be spending time with Nike, but he had made time for Lio instead. "Thank you. I was very glad when I received your note."

Lio found himself relaxing, and only then realized just how tense he had been in the three nights since Cassia's interrupted Gift Night. It was good to join his uncle for their familiar tradition of talking over coffee, as they had done since he had been a student.

Lio sensed his uncle relaxing, too, as he concentrated on his pour. Uncle Argyros filled two delicate, filigreed cups from the copper pot. Lio knew his uncle enjoyed every detail of his coffee making craft, but now he could sense it. The small rituals brought calm to the complicated depths of his uncle's aura.

Since their reconciliation at Winter Solstice, Uncle Argyros had made a habit of letting down more layers of his veils around Lio. It had been a welcome surprise, and Lio cherished the new trust between them. He was still growing accustomed to the intricate, sometimes volatile currents in his powerful mentor. And yet every one of them was so true to who he knew his uncle to be.

Lio paused to show his appreciation for the Midnight Roast his uncle had prepared. He inhaled the rich aroma of the coffee before taking a sip, then rolled the coffee to different areas of his tongue to fully experience its bold flavor. "Mmm. Dark, but not burnt, with a nice, acidic kick. I remember us drinking quite a lot of this in a certain fortress in Tenebra."

Uncle Argyros raised his cup to Lio. "On the momentous journey when you met Cassia."

"I can look back on that now with such relief." It was what had happened in the intervening year that Lio didn't care to think about too closely. "As can you. You need no longer wonder where in Tenebra Nike might be."

Uncle Argyros gave his head a shake. "I can scarcely express my gratitude."

"In this instance, I dare say Silvertongue is entitled to be at a loss for words."

His uncle chuckled at that.

Lio took another sip of coffee. "How is Nike adjusting?"

"She isn't. Nike is not a person who adjusts. She forges everything around her into shape."

"Well, it's family tradition to put the world back together on the Goddess's terms, isn't it?"

"And sometimes to be the ones who break it into little pieces."

Lio winced. "That's excellent when dealing with Anthros's unjust order, but it sounds painful when surrounded by family."

"Indeed. Nike hasn't quite lowered her fists since leaving the battlefield."

"She'll be ready to see a mind healer eventually. Aunt Kona and my mother are working on that, after all."

His uncle nodded. "There are few opponents who can best Nike in a contest, but her battle to avoid the mind healers is one I predict she will lose."

"How is Aunt Lyta taking all of this?"

Uncle Argyros sighed. "Nike and Lyta haven't spoken."

"Hespera's Mercy."

"I don't mean to say they aren't speaking; they exchange words as one might expect while the whole family is together. In fact, they are quite busy using the rest of us as shields."

"I'm so sorry, Uncle."

"Nike is safe. Everything else can be mended. With time."

Lio hesitated. "Has she said how long she's staying?"

"No. But she also has not left."

"How are you?" Lio finally asked.

"We took a walk in my orchard at first moon. Nike and I. Together, this very night. I couldn't ask the Goddess for anything more."

"I'm sure she's confiding in you," Lio said.

"She knows she can, when she's ready, and I know she will."

"With your support, she and Aunt Lyta will come together again."

"Thank you for everything you and Cassia have done for Nike. You and Mak and Lyros are quite a solace to her."

"Cassia is determined to honor their bond of gratitude and help Mak grow closer to his sister."

Uncle Argyros's aura gentled with concern. "How is Cassia?"

"She's with Aunt Kona tonight for a gardening lesson."

"It's good for her to stay busy while she waits for further news, and I believe Kona's wisdom is precisely what Cassia needs at present."

"Just as I need yours," said Lio.

His uncle's aura softened. "I thought you might wish to discuss Kalos's last report. What do you make of it?"

"It's difficult to draw conclusions until we learn more. But I've thought through the possibilities."

"As have we all," his uncle agreed.

Except Cassia. She didn't even want to think about them, much less speak of them. "We now know that Solia made it past the siege perimeter. It is clear she escaped death that night."

"But you fear what might have happened to her afterward."

"We can't rule out the possibility that when she went to her other allies, they turned on her as Bellator did." Lio grimaced. "Or that the king hunted her down."

"While I cannot disagree with your logic, my long-lost daughter took a walk in my orchard with me this moon. This is a time of wonders that defy reason."

"I could believe that Solia survives still. But if that's true, where has she been all these years? The one thing we know with absolute certainty is that she would do anything for Cassia. Something prevented Solia from coming back for her, and whatever it was, it wasn't good."

"Given the political situation," his uncle suggested, "perhaps she was forced into hiding to avoid the king's retribution."

"Or worse. She could be a prisoner somewhere."

"Do you think there is any dungeon in Tenebra that would pose a challenge for Hesperines?"

"No." Lio relaxed slightly. "You're right. Wherever she might be, the Charge would certainly rescue her and deliver her safely to Orthros. I have to let myself believe it's possible. If we could bring Solia home, then Cassia's happiness would be complete, and so would mine."

"Try not to let the other what-ifs play on your mind. Worry is a tremendous waste of energy."

"I'll try to put that effort into praying for good news instead."

"Our family understands what you and Cassia are experiencing right now."

"You had to endure this uncertainty for nearly a century, hoping for good news about Nike."

Uncle Argyros smiled. "But see how that turned out. I hope Cassia is drawing comfort from that."

Lio shook his head. "She's fighting so hard not to get her hopes up. But I'm not sure it's possible for her to protect herself from this. If Kalos brings news that deals her a new wound, it will reopen all her old ones from her sister's loss."

"And of course, what bothers you the most is that you cannot protect her from it, either."

All Lio could do, if that night came, was be there to pick up the pieces of her and hold them for her while she put herself back together.

Lio slumped in his seat. "I would join Kalos in the search, if I thought it would help. If I could be there and here to hold Cassia at the same time."

"You are exactly where you need to be."

"Cassia and I are together. Everything else can be mended. Can't it?"

"With time." The way his uncle looked at him made Lio realize they were no longer talking about Cassia. "How are your sessions with the mind healers progressing?"

He truly did not want to bring his mess with him to the table. It made him feel much better to help everyone else with theirs instead.

"Lio." His uncle laughed kindly. "Don't look as if I've suddenly served up your soul on the coffee tray. You have your battle scars, just like everyone else in this family. We know and love you."

He sighed. "Thank you for reminding me."

"Goddess knows I've needed mind healing often enough over the centuries."

Why had Lio never thought about this before? Of course his uncle would need mind healing, after everything he had experienced in sixteen centuries of life. After simply living as a mind mage.

Lio should have known, but he had been too busy idolizing Uncle Argyros. Now his mentor's simple statement tore down many more veils, but only built up Lio's admiration for him.

"I'm glad to hear you sought out healing, Uncle. And thank you for discussing it with me."

"I usually see Annassa Soteira. She's been patching up us ancients since the Last War. In recent decades, your mother has also lent me her ear. Her mind healing methods are a breath of fresh air."

"When Cassia was preparing for her Gifting, we went to many of her mind healing sessions together. Just as we fought the Collector together. It has helped."

"What about the things you cannot say in front of Cassia?"

There hadn't been any, until recently. "I have a session with Master Baruti upon his next visit home. That was Ioustin's recommendation. Cassia has been encouraging me to take him up on it."

"Ah, excellent. I'm glad you'll have the opportunity to get to know Baru. Scholarly discussions with him are a true pleasure. And I think Ioustin is correct that the Charge's mind healer is exactly who you need."

"I have felt like a Hesperine errant often in the last year. But Cassia and I are both home for good now."

"And how are you adjusting, Lio?" his uncle asked, his dark eyes full of concern.

"I suppose I don't adjust, either. I make stained glass windows out of the shards of glass."

"And is your latest work taking shape?"

"I can't make the pieces fit." Lio wrapped both his hands around the little coffee cup, holding it tightly. "Until Cassia is a Hesperine, I don't think anything will seem right."

"Your feelings are natural."

"So Cassia has told me."

"And yet you avoid talking with her about it, because you don't wish to make her feel guilty for postponing her Gifting."

"Precisely. But she gets it out of me anyway."

"Of course she does. As long as both of you are trying to arrange the pieces together, take heart."

Lio's own guilt stung him. "There are still things I haven't said to her. And that is not right."

"Be patient with yourself. I know how difficult it is to be an open book. Grace is good for mind mages, Lio. Think how closed we would become if that bond did not force us to change our ways."

Lio had always thought of himself as the open one, helping Cassia learn to stop closing herself off. He had never been unable to keep their Oath before. Until now.

"I can't bring myself to tell her about the dreams I'm having," Lio confessed. "As soon as the sun started rising for a few hours each day, I began having day terrors in my brief Slumber."

"Day terrors are a common affliction after a thelemantic duel."

His uncle topped off his coffee, giving him an excuse to drink another sip and gather his thoughts.

Lio rubbed his brow. "As much power as we have over the minds of others, using that power does not leave our own minds untouched."

"It can take time to cleanse echoes of a powerful enemy's magic from the recesses of your mind. Baru can help you with this. His expertise will be especially beneficial, considering that the Collector blends necromancy with his thelemancy."

"It's bad enough that I must confront the Collector again in my dreams, without subjecting Cassia to him as well."

His uncle gave him a rueful smile. "Like Nike, you hide your wounds to project an image of strength, because you want to make those around you feel safe. You learned that from me, I'm afraid."

"It worked, Uncle. To everyone who loves you, you are part of why Orthros feels like the Goddess's Sanctuary. I'm sorry for what that may have cost you over the centuries."

"Don't be. I embrace my role, like one of Hespera's gargoyle familiars who defend the gates of her sacred realm." Amusement glinted in Uncle Argyros's gaze. "How else would I keep up with the Guardian of Orthros?"

That gave Lio a much-needed laugh.

"But I remember how I felt when Lyta was still human," Uncle Argyros went on. "I couldn't bear to let her out of my sight. I hated the Dawn Slumber for rendering me helpless to protect her. Even then, she was a force to be reckoned with, and yet it seemed as if anything might happen to her in a world full of so many dangers."

"You'd think that here behind the Queens' ward, I would not fear anything. But it's not just any danger. It's the Collector."

"The enemy who trespassed in the Goddess's Sanctuary."

Lio swallowed. "We banished him. I know that."

"You defeated him, Lio. I am still in awe of your duel with him, although we have discussed it at length. I am so proud of how you handled yourself in the greatest thelemantic battle of your life. I will keep reminding you of that, if it helps."

"It does. So much. But he's still out there."

"He is out there, and Cassia is here, thanks to you."

"He's an Old Master, and he targeted her. He still feels like a threat." Lio took a deep breath. "But as long as Cassia never sets foot in Tenebra again, it won't matter."

"You and Cassia need never return there again. I want to impress upon you both that this is within your power. It is your decision, and only yours. Even if someone gives you a reason to go back."

In the refuge of his uncle's library, Lio felt that an invasion once more lurked beyond the Sanctuary, drawing nearer. "You're speaking of the possible political implications, if Solia is alive."

"It's perfectly all right if you haven't considered those yet."

"Helping Cassia sort through the personal implications has been my sole focus."

"I wouldn't have it any other way. However, I am honor bound to tell you that Basir and Kumeta are coming to my library shortly with a report from Tenebra."

The Queens' Master Envoys, the spymasters of Orthros. They only left their fieldwork when they discovered information of grave importance. If they were about to make a personal appearance, it meant they needed to discuss current affairs in Tenebra with Uncle Argyros in his capacity as the Queens' Master Ambassador.

"Have the envoys learned something about Solia?" The question jumped out of Lio.

Uncle Argyros was already shaking his head. "No, no. If they had any news about Cassia's sister, they would have already told her."

"Of course. Searching for Solia is Kalos's task. But I assume the envoys are following the situation closely."

"They continue to advise me of their findings so that the diplomatic service can prepare for possible outcomes."

Lio's awareness returned to the wisps of spells on his uncle's desk. Those veiled blood seals in the far corner of the library seemed to breathe down his neck.

That was why the dispatches were piling up. The envoys were preparing Orthros's diplomats for whatever might happen, and the Queens' Master Ambassador was handling it all without the only other diplomat who specialized in Tenebran affairs.

Lio straightened and made himself ask the question. "Do you need me to end my leave of absence, Uncle?"

"I want you to savor every moment with the people you love and ignore everything else as if it doesn't exist."

"But what do you need?"

"I also need to do precisely what I just suggested to you."

"I hate that pile of documents on your desk."

"I confess, I wouldn't mind letting Moonbeam and Aurora have a go at them."

Lio had to laugh, but it was half groan. "What is to be done about the dispatches, then?"

"Let me worry about that for now. Unfortunately, I can't help you avoid the decision you must make tonight. Before the Solstice Summit, I excluded you from conferences with the envoys, thinking that was to your benefit. I promised you I wouldn't do so again. It is your choice whether you wish to stay for Basir and Kumeta's report."

Lio set his coffee cup aside. "When will they be here?"

"In a quarter of an hour, I'm afraid. I didn't intend to cut our coffee short, but they must come when they can and leave again soon after."

"Of course. Lives depend on them. Time is always of the essence for the envoys."

Lio had a quarter of an hour to decide if he was ready to face politics again.

He and Cassia had been wrapped up in rose gardening and glassmaking, affinity readings and language practice, playing with Zoe and nights out with their friends. All their projects and routine pleasures seemed painfully precious suddenly.

"We thought we were finally done with politics. At least, until we were ready to serve as diplomats together, either at home or in the Empire."

"That is still possible."

"I should make this decision with Cassia."

"If you believe she is ready to consider it, we will by all means invite her. I'm sorry to put you in this position, Lio, but you are the best judge of whether she would want to join us tonight. She has yet to give me her decision about her official involvement in diplomacy."

She was his Grace. They were partners. They didn't keep things from one another, and they didn't make decisions without each other.

But right now, Cassia was barely ready to talk about her sister. She was even less ready to talk about politics.

If Lio must stand between her and the political forces that threatened to encroach on her hard-won peace, he would.

"She has seldom had the luxury of tending to her own feelings above practical and political considerations. I want to do what I can to give her that time. Let's not say anything to her yet."

"Very well. Do you wish to stay, in that case?"

The powerful auras of the Queens' Master Envoys loomed on the terrace. Lio was out of time to make his decision.

His uncle pinched the bridge of his nose. "They're early."

The elder Hesperines swept into the library with a gust of cold air. Lio fortified the veil spells over his emotions and stood with his uncle to greet Basir and Kumeta.

No illusion disguised them, whatever their most recent mission in Tenebra had been. Their true identities were revealed in their night-black complexions and their hair, which they each wore in seven braids to commemorate their centuries together. The two Graces, who led Orthros's eyes and ears the world over, approached with their hands intertwined, dressed in brown cotton travel robes.

Uncle Argyros clasped Basir's wrist and embraced Kumeta. "It's always good to see you, my friends. Do you have time to sit down for coffee?"

Kumeta gave him a wry smile. "We might as well deliver our news sitting down, sipping coffee in between pronouncements of doom."

Lio was glad to hear Kumeta jesting. At least, he hoped that was a jest.

As the master envoys joined him and his uncle around the table, Basir took the time to ask, "How is Cassia faring?"

He seldom paused for such pleasantries, as dedicated as he was to their service. He and Kumeta carried the burden of all Orthros's secrets, on constant vigil for information from the human world that could endanger the Hesperine people. And yet he was making an effort to show consideration for Cassia.

"Thank you for your concern," Lio said sincerely. "The wait for news is very difficult for her, but she knows the search for her sister is in the best of hands."

"And how are you, Lio?" asked Kumeta.

"As well as can be expected."

Basir's voice was neutral. "Argyros tells us you have extended your leave of absence from the diplomatic service and that once you return, you are likely to apply for permanent reassignment to Imperial affairs."

"Pending agreement from my prospective partner. Cassia is very happy that Uncle Argyros has offered to mentor her. She's only waiting for her affinity readings so she can take her magic into consideration before making a commitment to the diplomatic service."

Basir exchanged a look with Argyros. "Have your plans for your future careers changed in light of what you have learned about Cassia's sister? We need to know before we make you privy to this meeting."

Kumeta touched a hand to Basir's arm. "We understand that it hasn't been long since Nike brought the news, so you've had little time to make decisions. But we can only divulge our information if you and Cassia intend to become involved in Tenebran affairs again."

Basir crossed his arms. "Orthros cannot wait to prepare for the possible results of Solia's escape."

Lio felt ambushed. It seemed much too soon to be discussing any of this. "We still haven't determined whether Solia is alive."

Kumeta nodded. "It's possible Kalos's discoveries will change nothing, but in case they do, we must be ready."

"If Solia did survive," said Basir, "there could be another contender for the throne of Tenebra."

No. Please, Goddess, no.

The very idea sent dread through his veins. If Solia wanted the throne, Tenebra was not done with him and Cassia.

No. That part of their lives was over. It had to be.

"Cassia has handed Flavian the kingship, and that's the end of it. If

Solia still wanted to be queen, she would have come back to take the crown by now."

"We don't know that," Basir said.

"We don't know anything yet," Lio protested.

But such an assertion was useless before the envoys. Of course the Queens' spymasters had already considered the political implications of Solia's survival. That was their cause. They considered every human activity in Tenebra and its every possible impact on Orthros, teasing out every secret that could help them protect the Hesperine people from the consequences.

Basir's gaze was heavy on him. "We need to discuss crucial developments with the Queens' Ambassador for Tenebran Affairs. We need to know who that is."

Silence reigned around the table.

For centuries, his uncle had been the Queens' Master Ambassador, who oversaw the entire diplomatic service. The Queens' Ambassador for Imperial Affairs served directly under him as Orthros's representative in the Empress's court. Numerous other Hesperine diplomats nurtured the many ties between the Empire and Orthros.

There was only one Ambassador for Tenebran Affairs. That title had been appended to Uncle Argyros's since he had negotiated at the first Equinox Summit sixteen centuries before. Orthros needed but one diplomat to handle the few negotiations the Tenebrans consented to hold with the Hesperines they hated.

Of all his uncle's students, Lio alone had chosen to focus his career on Tenebra in the hopes that the situation might improve. He had thought his uncle might create a new position in the service for him, perhaps Deputy Ambassador for Tenebran Affairs.

"I have always sought to support my uncle's efforts in Tenebra," said Lio, "never to wear his title."

"During the Solstice Summit," Basir replied, "you stepped into the role of Ambassador for Tenebran Affairs."

"The Queens never officially appointed me in any capacity. They merely gave me permission to carry out my proposal for the Solstice Summit."

"You are the diplomatic service's leading expert on current relations with Tenebra. The appointment is a formality."

"My uncle stepping down as our foremost negotiator with Tenebra is not a formality!"

Were they speaking of his uncle's retirement?

Uncle Argyros shook his head. "Basir, my friend, I know it is your responsibility to be prepared for all eventualities, but do not put me out to pasture yet, in any version of the future."

Basir huffed. "I would hardly call your work overseeing the entire diplomatic service 'out to pasture,' even if you did delegate your duties in Tenebra to Lio, as you discussed with the Queens."

Lio stared at his uncle. "You and the Queens have been discussing this?"

"This was not the occasion when I planned to share this news with you," his uncle said with a heavy sigh.

Kumeta was giving her Grace a look. Whatever she said to him through their Union, Basir's veil spells suddenly became thicker, although they failed to disguise the embarrassment that crept into his expression. "My apologies, Argyros. I assumed you had already told Lio."

"We'll give you two a moment." Kumeta took Basir's hand and stood. He offered a slight bow and let her lead him out of sight behind the bookshelves.

Lio threw veils around the table so quickly that his spells tangled with his uncle's. With a furrowed brow, Uncle Argyros refilled his and Lio's coffee cups. He set one in front of Lio and raised the other in his hand with an air of ceremony.

"Let us pause to mark this for the occasion that it is. Congratulations, Nephew. In recognition of your extraordinary service to the Hesperine people, the Queens of Orthros and I have agreed that you are my rightful successor as Ambassador for Tenebran Affairs."

With no sense of triumph, Lio touched his cup to his uncle's and took a bracing swallow of the brew.

"Lio, I am not telling you this because I expect anything from you. I want you to know you've earned the recognition. You have every reason to feel proud of your accomplishments as a diplomat. I hope you gain some joy from that, whether you actually want the position."

"I never had any idea that you were considering appointing me Ambassador for Tenebran Affairs."

"It's been on my mind since your first boyhood treatise on Tenebra."

"I'm not even a master yet."

"Yes, well, I had intended to bring this up rather later in your career. But when you proposed the Solstice Summit, the topic naturally arose between the Queens and myself."

"You discussed this with them based only on my proposal? Before we even knew the Solstice Summit would succeed, long before we secured the treaty?"

"Of course. The Solstice Oath will go down in history as one of our most pivotal treaties and one of your greatest accomplishments. But the fact that you organized the Summit at all was evidence enough. You should take the lead in all of our future diplomacy with Tenebra."

"I thought you would make a new position for me and let me be your right hand."

"I planned to establish a new position for Cassia, so you could both be the Ambassadors for Tenebran Affairs as partners and equals. Of course, all that changed when you told me you would prefer to be reassigned."

"I'm so sorry, Uncle. You trained me for this my whole life."

"Hmm, yes, and all you have done with your education is craft a treaty with the mortals who once wanted to murder us, change history, and make way for a new king of Tenebra. Oh, and you found Cassia while you were at it. Not much to show for your career, eh?"

Lio let out a breath. "Honestly, Uncle, if Cassia was all I had to show for my years of dedication to Tenebra, I would be satisfied."

"Remember, we've established that you could not possibly disappoint me, and that your safety and happiness are more important to me than your success as a diplomat. But you still have your future career to think about. Whatever your goals become, Cassia will always support you, as you do her."

Lio wanted his future in a cozy home service office, showing Imperial dignitaries around Orthros by moon hours and making love to Cassia by veil hours.

They had fought so hard for that simple future. He wanted it with every drop of blood in his veins, and he felt how Cassia longed for it with all her heart. Less than a week ago, it had been within their grasp.

Now the envoys talked as if Lio and Cassia's future might hold a return to Tenebra, where an Old Master lay in wait for her.

He was one of the most ancient and powerful necromancers in history. He could possess anyone, anytime, anywhere. His reach was limitless, and his power knew no bounds.

The Master of Dreams wanted Cassia for his own ends, and King Lucis had promised her to him as payment in their devious bargain. If she ever set foot in Tenebra again, he would come to collect.

All the what-ifs and questions that had plagued Lio the past few nights melted away. It became crystal clear to him that there was only one possible outcome, because he would make sure it came to pass.

No matter what they learned about Solia, Cassia would never return to Tenebra.

Lio would allow nothing and no one to drag his Grace back there. Not pressure from Hesperine elders. Not a cry for help from the mortals. Not even news about her sister. He would keep fighting for the future they had chosen, as he always had.

Starting here, now.

He must stay for this conference, not as an ambassador for Orthros, but as Cassia's protector.

Ignoring events in Tenebra would not make her safer. That would only leave her undefended. Just as the envoys must analyze every event in Tenebra for possible threats to Orthros, Lio must do the same to prevent any danger to Cassia. Only then would he have the knowledge he needed to stop Tenebra from sinking its hooks into his Grace.

He could announce to Basir and Kumeta right now that he had no intention of ever becoming Ambassador for Tenebran Affairs. But if he did, they would never discuss any of their confidential reports with him.

Lio would never don that mantle, but the envoys didn't need to know that yet.

"My goals are clear to me," Lio said. "I will stay for this and all the envoys' conferences with you."

Uncle Argyros clasped his shoulder. "The truth is, I'm glad to hear that. I think you will be better off knowing."

"Forewarned is forearmed." Lio looked into Silvertongue's perceptive gaze. He needn't announce his decision to Basir and Kumeta tonight, but Uncle Argyros probably already knew.

His mentor nodded. "Very good."

As soon as they lowered their veils, Basir and Kumeta approached the table again.

Lio offered the Master Envoys a bow. "I cannot make any final commitments regarding our future service until I consult further with Cassia. However, I am prepared to represent us both in these matters for the time being. If Orthros calls upon Cassia and me to accept the Queens' appointment as Ambassadors for Tenebran Affairs, I wish to ensure that we are fully prepared."

"Thank you for your service to our people," Basir told him.

"A wise and admirable decision," said Kumeta.

Uncle Argyros gestured to the coffee table. "Have a seat again, everyone, and we will discuss what has happened in Tenebra since their embassy left Orthros."

OUTCOMES

"**Y**OU ARE DISTRACTED TONIGHT."

Master Kona's comment was mild, but Cassia felt chastened. She carefully put down her spade on the potting bench and folded her hands.

One did not handle a cutting of the Sanctuary Rose while distracted.

Master Kona considered Cassia over the pot they were preparing for one precious limb of Orthros's oldest rose vine.

"I'm sorry," Cassia said. "You know how honored I am that you're giving me a daughter vine of the Sanctuary Rose. Even more so that we're starting it together. I'm glad we can begin tonight, so that it can grow strong here in your greenhouse while mine is built."

"I thought some time in the greenhouse might be a comfort to you. Perhaps a less demanding project would be more suitable for tonight."

Surprised, Cassia relaxed a little.

Master Kona laughed. "Did you think every one of our gardening lessons would be like your first visit here?"

"I accepted that possibility along with your offer to mentor me."

"I see. You imagined all our meetings would involve you declaring yourself the unconditional opponent of my plans for Orthros's future?"

"Certainly not, Prin—Master Kona."

Her eyes sparkled. Cassia realized that Orthros's legal mastermind and most brilliant politician was teasing her.

Or testing her?

Knowing Master Kona, she could easily do both at once, while analyzing their interaction on a level Cassia didn't even know was possible.

"Relax, Cassia." Master Kona handed her a pair of shears. "Here, let us deadhead the bushes."

They began making the rounds with their clippers, removing spent blooms from the lower rosebushes around the greenhouse.

Master Kona started on a slender bush with scarlet blossoms. "Tell me, are you looking forward to your first Migration?"

"Yes. I can't believe it's less than a month away." Cassia tended to a bush of ivory roses.

"It must be exciting for you."

"There are so many wonders here in Orthros Boreou. And yet this is only half of our homeland. To think, there is another entire land of ours in the south. I look forward to seeing Orthros Notou for the first time."

"I remember how I felt upon my first Migration from Orthros Notou to here. Of course, I was a suckling and slept through much of the actual transition. But when I awoke on the other side of the world, I was amazed to discover just how big the world was."

"It is hard to imagine," Cassia confessed, glad she didn't sound like an ignorant peasant. "Lio showed me a globe. I can't believe we'll be on another continent, on the opposite pole of the world. I'd never left Tenebra until recently."

"Fortunately our magic will make the journey easy."

"Is it true that the seasons are reversed in Orthros Notou?"

"Yes. Here in the north, winter is ending and spring will soon begin. Then summer will come, along with the midnight sun, which would banish us all into Slumber for days on end. But we will be long gone by then. We will leave here after Spring Equinox and that very night, arrive in Orthros Notou just after the southern Autumn Equinox."

"So winter will be on its way again, and we can look forward to another Winter Solstice?"

"Yes, and the return of polar night."

Cassia looked around the greenhouse, her gaze lifting to the vast rose that climbed the central iron trellis, as if ascending a staircase to the heavens. Its white blooms covered much of the ceiling, like many-petaled stars. "How can your plants survive for half a year while you're gone? Does the Sanctuary Rose suffer in your absence?"

"Preparing the garden for Migration is one of the most important skills a Hesperine rosarian must learn. We take certain steps to maximize the benefit our flowers receive from the Queens' magic. The ward provides protection for our plants, animals, and structures. Of course, that is no excuse not to provide proper care. A healthy plant can better endure our absence."

Cassia applied herself to deadheading the next bush. "The gardens in Orthros Notou must be in need of maintenance by now. When we arrive, will my lessons also include the steps to take after Migration?"

"Most certainly. You'll enjoy learning about the fauna native to that part of the world. About our human neighbors, as well, once you and Lio become diplomats involved in Imperial affairs. If I can be of assistance, please don't hesitate to ask me about the land of my mortal heritage."

"Thank you, Master Kona." Listening to her talk about those plans as if they were a certainty, Cassia felt a weight lift off her chest. An evening in the garden really was comforting.

"Such a sensible human civilization." Master Kona lopped off a cluster of shriveled yellow roses. "None of Tenebra's selfish kings and bumbling lords. No offense."

"None taken. I couldn't be happier to leave behind the kingdom where I was born." Cassia inspected a rose cane, counting the clusters of leaves to find the best place to cut. "I want to understand everything about how the Empire's female leadership works."

"The Empress's power is eminent. However, that power ultimately rests in the hands of the Queen Mothers. There is one from each land within the Empire, and she possesses the sacred artifacts that symbolize power to her particular people. No Empress can rise to power without the Queen Mothers' blessings."

How marvelous that such a land existed, where women wielded power as both queens and mages. Cassia couldn't have imagined such a place scarcely a year ago. But now, the little kingdom of Tenebra that had once been her entire world seemed to shrink and lose importance all the time.

"For generations," Master Kona continued, "the Queen Mothers, in their wisdom, have conveyed leadership upon one dynasty of successful Empresses after another. In return, the Empresses have striven to heed the Queen Mothers' counsel about the needs of their peoples."

"So instead of the Council of Free Lords choosing a king, the Queen Mothers choose an Empress."

"The Empire has an entirely different understanding of leadership. While the free lords bicker out of self-interest and the king tries to be the master of all, the Queen Mothers care for the futures of their families and their people. The Empress is called their eldest daughter, and their lands are her sister states."

Cassia could not imagine anything better than having your elder sister rule and care for you.

Master Kona snipped another yellow bloom. "Over the millennia, several dynasties of Empresses have received the Queen Mothers' blessing. Various sister states have held the Imperial throne at different times in history. The throne does not belong to one particular people of the Empire, but to all of them. No matter what state the present Empress comes from, all her citizens are symbolically part of her clan."

"No wonder the Empire and Orthros do so well. They let females decide things."

The author of Orthros's legal code smiled, her fangs white against her cool black skin. "You will not regret making the Empire your focus. You and Lio should travel there as soon as you can. You will find some consolations to remaining mortal. The Sun Market on Marijani is wondrous, and you will get to enjoy it."

"Have you been there?"

"I always wanted to go as a child."

"Perhaps Lio and I can go to Marijani, even though we had to delay our tour of goat country with Zoe."

Another disappointment of postponing her Gifting. They couldn't provide for Zoe on a long journey, since it took two Hesperine Graces to keep up with a suckling's thirst. Cassia's human blood wasn't enough.

Zoe had been so glad Cassia wasn't going into seclusion that she hadn't even complained, but guilt still rankled Cassia.

"Don't worry about delaying your Gifting," Master Kona reassured her. "You are so young. You have plenty of time. You will be free of your mortality soon enough, so you might as well enjoy the diversions it has to offer."

"Lio worries about me."

"And you worry about him." Master Kona's expression softened.

"We are both bundles of worry for each other at present."

"My Grace is centuries old, a fearless thinker, renowned scholar, and powerful Hesperine. I still fret over him every time someone writes a harsh critique of his latest treatise. With the one you love, objectivity is an exercise in futility."

Cassia chuckled in surprise. But she could see the usually logical Master Kona bristling in biased defense of her Grace, to be sure.

"Lio has nothing to fear," Master Kona said. "You are healthy and strong. He should be glad you can enjoy mortality as much as you do."

Wise advice, coming from Master Kona, whose childhood as a mortal had been a misery due to an incurable illness. "I'll try to help him keep that in mind. Thank you for reminding me."

"Of course, being a Hesperine will be much better."

"I confess, I have pinned so much of my...confidence, I suppose, on the expectation of my transformation. Now I feel..."

"Vulnerable."

Cassia nodded.

"That's natural. You have endured many close calls as a mortal, some very recently. The mind takes time to heal from those ordeals. You're talking with Komnena?"

"Yes."

"Good. Keep reminding yourself that you emerged from all those trials victorious. You have accomplished great things as a human."

Cassia could scarcely believe she had just received such high praise from the Second Princess. "You have my gratitude."

"There is more than one kind of strength. Your greatest power will come from your ability to influence outcomes—not to let outcomes influence you. You need only choose where to apply your power, then cultivate the rewards."

Cassia came to a decision. She pruned an entire cluster of spent blooms, shortening a branch of Master Kona's rosebush. She looked to her mentor for confirmation.

Master Kona stood back to admire the bush's new shape. "You understand already."

"I'm glad you approve."

"You have shown yourself adept at winning my approval."

Earning Master Kona's support for her first proposal before Orthros's government had been one of the most difficult challenges Cassia had ever faced. The result promised to be one of the greatest rewards of her life.

But she knew she had only convinced Master Kona to delay the Departure, not rule out the possibility. The princess might still decide it was necessary to cut off Orthros from Tenebra forever. "I appreciate that your support requires repeated effort."

"But my friendship does not. That is something you can rely on."

Cassia stilled her shears. "Thank you, Master Kona."

Master Kona continued to the next bush. "Do not be troubled if Kalos doesn't return before we migrate. He can step to Orthros Notou to bring us tidings."

Cassia almost nicked a healthy new bloom. She had to do better. "Does the Charge always remain in the field when everyone at home migrates?"

"I'm afraid so. Ioustin is planning to visit more often this season, however."

"I'm so glad."

"So am I." Her love for her brother was evident in her voice. She and Ioustin seemed to be enjoying a thaw in their complicated relationship. "It's doing him good to spend more time at home."

Did she still aspire to keep him home permanently and bring the entire Charge out of the field? She would announce her decision when they all returned to Orthros Boreou next year. Cassia had stopped dreading that, until now.

What if Kalos's search took longer than that? What if time ran out, and Master Kona once more proposed the Departure? The truth about Solia's fate would be out of reach forever.

Master Kona pursed her lips. "It's important not to plan the shape of the bush before it has grown. You can't prune branches that aren't there yet."

Cassia rubbed her eyes, getting a bit of soil and rose fragrance on her face. Her gardening metaphors failed her. "Sometimes I think not knowing is going to waste me away. I want to enjoy going south. But we're going farther away from Kalos and whatever answers are still there for him to find."

"I understand. We lived with that every night Nike was away. But now she is here, where I can do something to help her." Master Kona paused in her pruning. "I cannot tell you how good it is to have my friend back."

"I remember you saying that she's like an elder sister to you."

"Yes, Cassia. And she returned because of you."

"That was all her decision. But I'm glad to be the reason."

Master Kona glanced at the Sanctuary Rose. "I am almost always right. I say that without arrogance. It is a fact that magical insight and centuries of wisdom promote sound judgment. But not all theories become laws. Not so long ago, I stood here with you and deemed it unlikely that Nike would ever return. And yet she is now among us, safe."

"Are you...trying to encourage my hopes, Master Kona?"

She met Cassia's gaze. "It has nothing to do with hope. Make the most educated guesses you can, test them and form theories, but always remember—they are not laws."

SPRING EQUINOX

7th Night of the Month of Annassa
1,597th Year In Sanctuary (IS)
New Year's Night

NEW YEAR

Last Spring Equinox, Cassia had listened to the Tenebran festival dances from her window, a prisoner in her rooms in the king's palace. Tonight she would dance in Orthros' festival, free in Lio's arms.

He had brought her to a vantage point on the docks where she could behold the breathtaking sight of Harbor. Knight's tail wagged in anticipation, as if he too could feel the excitement from here. The sprawling celebration occupied the decks of every ship. The Hesperines' pale, sleek vessels sat heavy in the water, loaded for tomorrow night's Migration, their crimson sails furled as yet.

Tonight, moon hours were bright with northern twilight, the arctic blue horizon aglow. Far above, in the inky center of the sky, the stars hovered, still watching over them all even though polar night was gone for the season.

Selas's pantries were empty, the city's provisions spread out atop crates and barrels in a banquet such as Cassia had never seen. Hesperines stepped with their human companions from ship to ship, everyone free to sample the delicacies offered on each deck.

Other decks were reserved entirely for dancing. Jubilant music echoed across the water. As the dancers leapt and circled, their braids and festival silks glittered in the colorful spell lights of the stained glass lanterns.

Cassia turned to Lio. "Where do we start?"

He looked dashing in his crimson festival attire. A gentle wind blew off the sea and stirred his hair. The lights shone in his reflective eyes, making them glow with an intensity that stole her breath.

Perhaps they should have started alone in the bedchamber.

"That's where we're going to finish," he said.

"Oh. Was I projecting that thought?"

"I love the mental images that came with it, too." He lifted her chin and placed the most tempting, chaste kiss on her lips. "Is your Craving too much?"

"I can wait."

"Are you sure?" he asked, suddenly quite serious.

She twined her hand in his. "Yes, my love."

His long lashes dipped, and she glimpsed a hint of doubt in his eyes. "This is your first Spring Equinox celebration in Orthros. I want you to get to enjoy it."

"I'm determined to."

He brought her knuckles to his lips. "The new year is best welcomed surrounded by family and friends."

Spring Equinox was the beginning of the new year in the human and Hesperine calendars, but she had never had much cause to celebrate it in Tenebra. She had only to look out across Harbor to see that she had as many reasons to celebrate in Orthros as there were lights in the bay.

She squeezed Lio's hand. "Let's go enjoy the festival."

He stepped them to the deck of the *Lion's Wings*, Blood Komnena's ship. Knight's nostrils went wide, and he immediately turned his begging eyes on her.

"Oh," Cassia groaned, "every ship is liegehound paradise. He shall look at me like this all night, and I shall make him a very fat dog."

Lio put a hand over her eyes, shielding her from Knight's pitiful stare. "No, you won't. You'll be too busy letting me feed you."

Of course Lio wanted to feed her first. "Any mortal's ship would sink under this much food."

He laughed. "My mother takes pride in the Spring Equinox banquet every year. Let it never be said that the Queens' Chamberlain didn't have the best spread."

Lio led Cassia from crate to crate, watching expectantly while she filled her plate with all manner of foods. "You don't have to save room on that plate. You can get a new one on each ship."

"My Grace, if I eat half of what's already on this plate, I will be too full to move, much less dance." She held her food out to him. "You'll help me finish it, won't you?"

He looked somewhat abashed. "If you're sure it's too much."

She pulled a grape off the bunch on her plate and popped it into his mouth.

He nibbled her finger. "Just save some room for when we go to Uncle Argyros's ship. He'll be disappointed if we don't taste his coffees."

"I *always* have room for coffee."

They paused at the prow to say good moon to the family and give their compliments to Komnena. Apollon sat beside her with Zoe fast asleep on his lap. Lio took his place beside his mother as firstgift and spent some time greeting visitors to the ship. Cassia found herself sitting with Apollon and Zoe.

She caressed Zoe's head, looking forward to when the deepening twilight would release her from the Slumber. Knight stretched out at their feet, gazing up soulfully at his sleeping playmate.

Apollon smiled. "Every member of the family is ready to migrate so we can enjoy the lengthening nights and more time with Zoe."

"I can't believe she sleeps for three-fourths of the Equinox." Cassia shook her head.

"But she makes up for it in energy while she's awake." Apollon laughed.

Cassia couldn't help laughing, too. Now that she really saw her Gracefather when she was in his presence, she realized how often he smiled and laughed and gave those around him reason to do the same.

At last she held up her empty plate to Lio and shot him a teasing glance.

He bent to inspect it. "You fed some of it to Knight."

"He'll never tell. Let's go get some coffee."

Lio stepped them across the short stretch of water that separated Blood Komnena's ship from Blood Argyros's, the *Wisdom's Steed*. Mak and Lyros lounged at the rail, passing a cup of coffee and kisses back and forth. They welcomed Lio and Cassia on board and took them to the prow to say hello to Uncle Argyros. Nike occupied her place at his side.

He took Cassia's hand in both of his. "When I said that reviving my coffee plant was the greatest gift you could give me, I was mistaken. It has been a long time since I had my firstgift at my side on a night like this."

Nike had been home for nearly a month, and no one had stopped thanking Cassia. It was still new, this realization that she could give the kind and powerful people around her so much happiness, as they had done for her. She could truly be part of her new family.

She squeezed Uncle Argyros's hands and smiled at Nike. "It's good to see you."

Cassia couldn't stop herself from saying it, although Nike was probably tired of hearing that each night they discovered that she was still in Orthros.

Nike gave Cassia a wrist-clasp. "I'm only here for the coffee. The beans I had stashed in errant Sanctuaries have gone stale as rocks over the decades."

Everyone laughed at that, even Uncle Argyros, and Lio looked so relieved to see his mentor happy.

Mak nudged Cassia and pointed out Bosko and Thenie's sleeping forms behind Nike. The sucklings were wrapped up in blankets and draped cozily across a bed formed of two crates.

"Yes," Nike admitted, "I might also be assisting with the sucklings while my happily exhausted sister and Grace-brother enjoy the festival."

Uncle Argyros's expression softened. "I believe I can handle two unconscious children if you wish to go dancing yourself."

She sipped on the goblet in her hand. "I can't dance and drink Starfrost Brew at the same time, so I think I'll stay here."

Cassia did not have the heart to ruin the mood by asking if Nike was planning to migrate with them tomorrow night.

Mak and Lyros led Lio and Cassia on a round of coffee tasting. When they were halfway across the deck, Cassia sensed the veils go up and knew they were going to talk about Nike after all. They gathered around the Twilight Roast barrel.

Mak poured them all cups of coffee as if nothing were amiss, but his expressive face gave away his concern. "Nike's love for dancing is famous. I can't believe she won't budge tonight."

Lyros wound his arm in Mak's. "She must still need time before she feels like dancing."

"She hasn't left our ship tonight, except once, to visit Kassandra's."

Cassia raised her eyebrows. "I have to wonder what she's consulting the oracle about, especially after their exchange the night she returned."

"Do you think it could be about…" Lio trailed off and shook his head.

Cassia knew what he was thinking, and she was also afraid she would cross the veil if they asked.

"…her quest to find Methu?" Mak finished for them.

A month of worry lifted from Cassia. "She told you. Thank the Goddess. Not that I'm surprised she confided in you."

Lio let out a relieved sigh. "We hated the thought that we must keep secrets from you two."

Mak looked unusually solemn. "I know what you mean."

"Thorns," said Lyros, "we've been worrying about the same thing for weeks. I'm glad we cleared the air."

"Do you think anyone else knows the purpose of Nike's quest?" Cassia wondered.

"Surely Ioustin and Father do," said Lio.

"No," Mak said, "but Kassandra does."

Cassia glanced toward the oracle's flagship, the *Far-Seer.* "Does this mean Nike hasn't given up on the prophecy?"

"I don't know," Mak replied. "I don't think she does, either."

Lyros's brow furrowed in thought. "What I still want to know is what she's writing all the time."

"She's making notes of some kind?" Lio asked with interest.

"She fills a scroll every night," Mak explained. "And keeps them veiled, so even her favorite little brother can't get a glimpse if he happens to look over her shoulder—accidentally, of course."

"Do you believe it's related to her quest?" Cassia asked.

"Possible," Mak answered. "That's why we didn't tell you before."

"Hmm." Lio raised his cup to his lips. "Nike is as eminent a scholar as she is a warrior. Perhaps she's analyzing some research she did in the field. Magical innovations she's developed, perhaps?"

"Or new fighting moves," said Mak.

"Secrets about our enemies?" Lyros suggested.

Cassia had a different suspicion. "Perhaps she's trying to appear busy so she'll have an excuse as to why she won't set foot in the gymnasium."

Mak's disappointment was written all over his face. "The Victory Star back in Orthros for weeks, and we still haven't seen her fight a single time. Not that I'm complaining about how much time she spends with the four of us."

Lyros topped off Mak's cooling coffee. "Just idling in the library or taking walks with the Victory Star seems miraculous. But I admit, when I envisioned us spending time with her, I always pictured us in the gymnasium."

Remembering the cup of Twilight Roast in her hand, Cassia sipped the rich but smooth brew. "I haven't seen Nike and Aunt Lyta together a single time, except when everyone else is near."

Mak's expression became grave. "Let's just hope none of us are around when the Guardian of Orthros and the First Master Steward decide to have it out with each other."

She patted Mak's arm. "It must be difficult for Aunt Lyta that Nike let her worry all those years."

Mak nodded. "But Nike stands by her decisions about the importance of her quest."

Kadi joined them at the barrel, and they left off their furtive conversation. Knight wagged his tail and looked at his training partner expectantly.

Kadi obliged him with a good scratch at the base of his tail. "If you're whispering about sisters, I want in on it."

Cassia poured Kadi a cup of Twilight Roast. "We were just talking with Mak about how Nike is doing."

Kadi exchanged a glance with Mak. "It was painful at first. Some aspects of it will be painful for a long time, and that's all right. The important thing is, we aren't angry at her."

Mak nodded. "When you spend years of your life without your sister, you get used to missing her. Then suddenly, there she is, safe and well."

"You've been agonizing over what might have happened to her," Kadi went on. "You've mourned her. You've watched others suffer their own pain at her loss. It would be easy to blame her for putting everyone through that."

"Anger is a natural reaction," Cassia agreed.

"Exactly." Mak nodded. "Nothing to be ashamed of."

"But that's not how you feel," Cassia said earnestly. "It would be unjustified. You're too glad to see Nike to be angry at her."

Mak held her gaze. "Or to wonder why she deprived us of her all those years."

"Sisters have excellent reasons for doing these things," Kadi said. "They make sacrifices. Even though it's hard, we understand the necessity—and that they do it for us."

Mak slung an arm around Cassia's shoulders. "As we've often said, if Nike had come home sooner, she wouldn't have been there to save you. It's easy to imagine all the reasons why sisters would stay gone, and know that it's worth it."

The warriors had effectively cornered Cassia. She had to credit them for some degree of subtlety, although their strategy had quickly become obvious. She hadn't expected this. She hadn't come prepared to talk about Solia.

"I'm so glad you're at peace about Nike's absence." She tried to sound as innocent and sincere as she could. Then she drained her cup. "What ship are we going to next?"

Goddess, now who was being obvious? Lady Circumspect was losing her touch.

Lio took her hand. "Let's find our Trial sisters."

Cassia was relieved when no one protested.

Kadi gave her shoulder a squeeze. "Javed and I will see you in the dance."

"How about we head to Xandra's?" Lyros suggested. "Cassia should see the royal fleet."

Cassia stood on tip-toe and peered across the water toward the ships at the center of Harbor. Their black sails clearly marked them as the royal ships. It was easy to spot the Annassa's flagship, the *Eternal Grace*, by the emblem on their sail: two braids intertwined to form a figure eight.

"Can you guess which one is Xandra's?" Lio asked.

There was exactly one ship in all of Harbor that had torches instead of lanterns. Cassia laughed at the sight of a Hesperine vessel bristling with flames thanks to Xandra's singular affinity for fire. "That's quite a lot of torches."

"It's actually Ioustin's ship, the *Restless Rose*, but it's been on permanent loan to Xandra for decades." Lio cleared his throat. "I sense his aura on deck, too."

She shouldn't need a forewarning that they were about to see their Ritual father, but it did help. "He would already have come to tell us if there was any news."

"Yes."

But the illogical urge to ask him was almost too powerful for Cassia to resist.

They stepped onto Xandra's ship, and Cassia blinked in the ring of bright firelight. Ioustin and Xandra were strolling the deck among their visitors. On her arm was Harkhuf, her human share, her companion for blood and romance. The handsome, richly dressed Imperial aristocrat looked like he belonged among the Hesperine royals.

Xandra rushed over to the four of them who had just arrived. "Isn't this wonderful?"

"Knight couldn't agree more." Cassia laughed at her hound, who was once again delighted to be in the presence of two royals. "*Hama*, Knight. Don't shed your entire coat across the princess's festival robes."

"I have a rival for your affections." Harkhuf frowned with mock ire. "A very determined rival."

Ioustin watched Xandra pet Knight. He looked away, rubbing his chin, then at Knight again. With a sigh, he extended a hand toward the dog.

Everyone stared at him.

"It's New Year's," he said. "Let bygones be bygones. If he intended to take off my fingers, he would have already."

"*Ckuundat,*" Cassia called Knight to attention.

She held her breath as her hound politely sniffed the prince's hand. When Knight made no further move, Ioustin dared rub his ears.

Knight's tail wagged so hard that his whole rump swayed. His drool dripped onto the deck, but thankfully not Ioustin's boots. Then he flopped his entire body down at the First Prince's feet, rolling onto his back in pure bliss.

"Good dog," Ioustin said with the frown of someone trying desperately not to smile.

Cassia put a hand over her mouth to keep her laughter in as she watched the Blood-Red Prince succumb to temptation. Ioustin crouched and rubbed Knight's belly fur.

"See," Xandra said, "aren't you glad you're actually sailing on the *Restless Rose* with me this year instead of just letting me borrow it? Isn't the Equinox more fun when you spend it with a lot of impertinent youngbloods instead of the elders?"

Now he did smile. "Indeed."

Lio gave his Ritual father a wrist clasp. "It's wonderful that you're here."

Ioustin looked between Lio and Cassia. "This year, I can migrate with some peace of mind, since all the Hesperines errant who were missing in action are now accounted for."

"We can all rejoice together about that." Lio put an arm around Cassia. "Last year, the Queens canceled the festival due to the dangers in Tenebra. Instead of marking the new year at midnight, they summoned everyone to safety behind the ward."

Ioustin got to his feet. "We expected this to be the deadliest year for the Charge in centuries. And yet we didn't lose a single one of our people—thanks to our diplomats. Keep that in mind."

Cassia was glad Lio said all the right things in response to Ioustin's praise while she struggled for words. The words running through her mind were the ones she was trying so hard not to say aloud.

If all of our Hesperines errant can make it back safely, after all these years, then perhaps it's really possible that...

Cassia was glad for the distraction when Harkhuf spoke to her. "The pleasures of being a Hesperine's companion are sweet on a night like this, are they not?"

"Very," she agreed. "I know you're glad your studies in Orthros won't be over for another year."

He turned a warm gaze on Xandra. "Perhaps I'll extend my stay even longer."

Xandra's eyes lit. "I'm looking forward to visiting your family with you after we go south. I can't wait to see your bees."

He laughed. "So easy to please, My Princess. Just show you some bees, and you're happier than if I gave you silk shoes."

"Only you think bees are easy compared to shoes." Xandra chuckled, her cheeks pink.

While she and Lio were engaged in conversation with Ioustin, Harkhuf turned to Cassia again and winked. "Have you been to the ship where they're serving spirits?"

"No," she scolded with a laugh. "I've never been as drunk as when you and your friends took me out, and I never want to be that drunk again."

"It's a rite of passage for humans about to leave the mortal world. We had to treat you to the pleasure of getting drunk one last time. Admit it. It was fun."

"The part I can remember was great fun."

"Look on the bright side. You have a little longer to enjoy alcohol before your Gifting, eh? Let us take you out again soon. No hard liquor this time, just some nice, relaxing wine."

She had to appreciate his efforts to cheer her. The Imperial students who were guests in Orthros, men and women alike, had all been good friends to her. "You are excellent company, the finest human company I have ever encountered."

"Much preferable to those close-minded Tenebrans. Humans like us need the company of other mortals our own age who are also friends of Hesperines. There's no reason to be bored during the long daylight hours when our nocturnal companions must Slumber."

"You'll have to show me your favorite drinking house in Orthros Notou."

"Excellent. Some more of our friends will be arriving from the Empire to begin their studies in Orthros this season. I'll introduce you. Ah, speaking of my fellow scholars…"

Kia joined their gathering, her favorite turquoise-and-white silk mantle draped around her shoulders. The slender Hesperine had pinned up her blond curls for the festival and looked quite elegant, except for the insolent slump of her shoulders. "Yes, please, let's speak about scholars. What's the most scandalous academic controversy you heard this week? I need something good."

The goblet in her hand let off such fumes that Cassia wondered if the alchemists had a ship where they served something even stronger than hard liquor. Cassia didn't seem to be the only one seeking distraction from her troubles tonight.

"Is everything all right?" Lio asked, joining their conversation.

"Nothing is more wrong than usual," Kia said darkly. "Don't bother going to my family's ship. It's just like it is every year. I think my mother counts the mince pies to make sure it's the exact same number as she served at first Floating Banquet."

Mak shrugged. "Some people like tradition."

Kia's scowl deepened. "Some people are so determined to preserve tradition, they turn off their brilliant minds. It's horrifying to imagine all the innovations that will never occur to them. Tradition is the assassin of future ideas."

Mak waved a hand. "Eh, tradition isn't so dangerous. A few good punches would probably teach it a lesson."

Kia laughed and bumped Mak's shoulder with hers. "Let's go to Nodora's and dance."

"I'll hold down the fort here for us," Ioustin said to Xandra.

She looked up at him, hesitating. "I can dance anytime."

"I'll be here. Dance with your Trial circle and that swain of yours."

Harkhuf put his hand on his heart. "I will offer you a whole hive of bees for a dance."

She laughed, then kissed her brother on the cheek before letting Harkhuf lead her away.

"We'll meet you there." Lio turned to Cassia. "Perhaps Knight would like to watch over Zoe while we dance."

"Good idea."

Once they had delivered Knight to his *kaetlii*, they rejoined their friends. Stepping to Nodora's ship, they landed at the heart of the magnificent music filling Harbor.

Their Trial sister was dancing in place, her eyes closed and her flute trilling, her long, straight black hair flying about her. Several other young musicians were at her side, devotees of Nodora's musical innovations or rising artists whose styles interested her. She seemed lost in her song, but must have sensed them arrive, for she opened her eyes and tossed her head in greeting, her gaze alight.

Cassia's foot started tapping. The music around Nodora was always in the newest styles, weaving together sounds from Tenebra, the Empire, and the faraway Archipelagos where she had been born. Sounds Cassia had never imagined before she had come to Orthros. The rhythm raced, the drums stirring her blood. The lutes pounded, and the flutes lifted her spirits to the heavens.

Lio took her hand and pulled her against him. "Let's dance for the rest of the night."

His arms felt so good, so sure around her. "That's all I want."

"Come, I'll show you the Equinox Step Dance."

Rows of celebrants were already dancing across the breadth of the ship. Lio took a position beside her, holding her hand at shoulder level. Laughing and smiling, Mak and Lyros formed up beside them, then Xandra and Harkhuf, then Kia and her share.

Lio looked over at Cassia. "Ready?"

"I think so?"

Together, everyone leapt forward, forming a new row in the dance, and Cassia followed their lead.

The steps were simple, easy for anyone to learn. The energy of the crowd was powerful, sweeping her up, making her part of something larger than herself. She watched Lio's graceful feet, learning the lively, leaping steps, and they swept across the deck together with their friends.

The railing drew nearer. And nearer. She watched for how they would turn and move back the way they had come.

They didn't turn. As they danced toward the edge of the ship and the water below, her feet touched nothing but Hesperine magic for an instant. She set foot on the deck of the next ship, still hand in hand with Lio.

She laughed in delight. "Oh! It really is a *step* dance!"

"Look." Lio tossed his head to the side.

She gazed in that direction, out across the decks of the next ship and the next. Suddenly she saw it, the grand pattern of the dance.

"It goes around the entire harbor! We aren't in a line at all—it's one, great circle."

He smiled at her and swept her to the next deck.

The dance had no beginning, and it never ended. Hesperines and humans joined the ring and left it, but the dance went on unceasing. And though it might end at dawn, Cassia knew it was a tradition that would continue as long as Orthros.

She lost herself in the music and the invigorating steps and Lio's touch. He began to elaborate, adding little flourishes to the basic pattern. A spin here, a twirl there, an excuse to lift her in his arms and set her down again. Her body responded to his effortlessly, as if she possessed a deep instinct for his next move. She stopped thinking and just danced with him.

She was breathless and euphoric by the time they drew to a halt. She felt like she was still moving, although he had stilled them. She realized their friends and everyone else around them had paused, too.

"It's almost midnight," he said. "The lightworks will begin any moment."

They crowded with their friends at the stern of the ship and looked toward the center of Harbor, where the royal fleet lay at anchor. Lio stood close behind Cassia and wrapped his arms around her.

A hush fell over the bay. The bells of House Kitharos began to toll.

"One," all of Selas counted together, their voices carrying across Harbor. Cassia knew her numbers in the Divine Tongue now and could join in.

"Two," they all counted.

It became a chant to the tolling of the bells.

"Three. Four. Five. Six. Seven. Eight."

Just a few tolls away from the end of the old year.

"Twelve!" she said with Lio and their friends and family and all their people.

The bells erupted into the joyous, booming peals of deepest midnight.

"Happy New Year, my rose," Lio said in her ear, his voice low, resonating through her blood.

She reached up and caressed his cheek. "Happy New Year, my love."

A single spell light, like a shooting star, rose from the Queens' ship. Then another. And another. Then a whole orb of brilliant white light sailed into the sky and burst apart into a thousand sparkles of every color.

Cassia lifted her face, watching the beauty of Hesperine magic fill the night. Light snowed down over them all.

It was over. The year when she and Lio had been apart and fought to be together again. The mages and the king and all of it was over.

A new year had begun. She was starting it in Lio's arms. She would spend it in Lio's arms. What had once seemed impossible was now her nightly reality.

Anything was possible.

Cassia had tried so hard to train her hope. But the trust she had mistaken for a tender seedling was an uncontrollable vine that had burst out of the soil of Tenebra and taken root in Orthros.

She couldn't control it any longer, no matter how much it might hurt to let it grow. She *wanted* to believe.

Thorns climbed out of her, shredding her, and bloomed.

A sob tore at her throat, and the words unfurled. "Solia might be alive."

"Yes, Cassia," Lio said. "She might."

"She might be looking at these same stars right now." Cassia turned to wrap her arms around him, laughing and crying. "I may not have lost my sister."

THE SAFEST PLACE IN THE WORLD

THE JOY BURSTING OUT of Cassia's aura felt more brilliant to Lio than all the lightworks in the night sky. He held her in his arms, his wild rose, his brightest light.

"I might actually get to see her again," Cassia said through her tears.

"Wherever she might be, we can find her, and the Charge can bring her home to us."

"I can scarcely imagine it. Solia, alive, safe. Here with our family."

"Imagine it. You deserve joy tonight," he murmured to her fiercely.

At last, she let herself have it.

She kissed him. He tasted all her hopes and happiness on her lips and let himself have them, too.

She pulled back, looking into his eyes. "You deserve joy tonight, too. You began last year alone with your Craving. Never again."

Never again. Her vow to him that nothing would part them.

The mate to his own promise that he would always protect her.

It pained him not to tell her about the circles he attended with the envoys while she was gardening with Master Kona or playing with Zoe. But her words tonight reminded him that he was defending what she wanted.

She joined her fingers behind his neck. "Show me where you were on this night last year. Exactly where you stood when you cast the illusion of yourself that I beheld in Tenebra."

With a step, he carried her away from the celebration and took her to his glassmaking workshop in the cellar of their tower. There was an eerie hush over the room without the hum of his furnace, which he had cooled for the season. Cassia's breath puffed pale in the darkness.

He had already doused the spell lights, but reawakened one dim one for her mortal eyes. It sparkled on the panes of finished glass in their storage racks.

"That night, my magic shattered every piece of glass in this room." He circled his worktable, trailing a hand over the surface. When he stood where he had sent his illusory message to her, he swept out his hands.

Her arms came around him tightly. She buried her face in his chest and breathed. "I tried to hold your illusion."

"Don't think about it anymore."

"I don't. Except to remind myself we can hold each other every night. Every moment."

She held him like she was sure she would never have to let him go. He held her like she was the illusion who might disappear.

"I'm here," she whispered.

He closed the distance between their lips, closed out the world. He staked his claim on her mouth.

She kissed him like she was parched, and he was water. Like she was Craving, and he was blood.

Without parting their lips, he turned them. He didn't levitate her. He picked her up by the waist, feeling the reassuring reality of her body between his hands, and set her backside on the worktable.

She pulled her mouth from his. "We can't do this here, my love. Your magic will break all of your beautiful glass again."

"I don't care about my glass. But there is something I want to discuss with you."

She trailed her hands through his hair, eliciting delicious sensation along his scalp. "Oh. I didn't think talking was what you had in mind."

One thing was more powerful than his need for her tonight. His need to keep her safe. He could not rest until he wrote his promise to protect Cassia on her very mind.

But now wasn't the time. She had only just accepted, at last, the possibility that her sister had escaped death. He should let her enjoy that.

Cassia buried her hands in his hair. She parted her legs, holding him between her knees. "Lio. Tell me what you're thinking. Let's not begin the new year with words unspoken."

How sweetly she invited him to give her the truth. He couldn't resist when she asked him like this. "I'm still afraid for you."

Another rhythmic stroke of her hands through his hair. "Because I'm still human?"

"Yes."

"I can tell. I know you're having day terrors."

"What? I sleep peacefully beside you every day."

She pressed a hand to his chest. "Your heart pounds in your Slumber, and I feel the way you hold me when you wake. Do you want to talk about the dreams?"

"I have told Master Baru."

"Would it help to tell me, too?"

"I don't know if it would help you."

"It's the Collector, isn't it? The battle? I would have nightmares about it too, if you didn't use your mind magic to help me sleep. Let me help you, too." She nuzzled his nose with hers and planted a kiss at the corner of his mouth.

Goddess, she made it so easy. He touched her hips, holding her vulnerable human frame in his powerful hands.

"Would you do something for me, Cassia?"

She pressed her lips to his throat. "You know I would. Anything to banish your fears."

"It wouldn't be easy for you. It's not something I would ever ask of you lightly." But it might be the only thing that could give him peace.

She pulled back, a frown between her brows. "I'm listening."

"I've always noticed that your mental self-defenses are highly effective for someone with no formal training. I would say, for someone who is not a thelemancer, but...we don't know that for certain."

"You think that could indicate I have mind magic? I'm still not sure that would be my affinity."

"It could be. Or it could simply mean that your inner self-discipline and your responses to the threats you've faced in life have made your mental protections strong."

"I see. I have walls around my mind, just as I once had around my feelings."

His smile softened. "How I enjoyed persuading you to let me through your emotional defenses. Now allow me to help you strengthen your mental ones."

"Can you teach me how to shield my thoughts?"

He sighed. "There's only so much a non-mage can do against a mind mage. Even if you strengthen your mind in every way possible…" Old fears rose in him, and he fought to keep his voice even.

"The Collector is gone, Lio." Her voice fell.

"But when I think of what he could have done to your mind during his attack at Rose House…"

"Don't think about it. It's over now." Her frown deepened. "Besides, a more useful question is, why didn't he?"

"What?"

"He didn't spare anyone else. He invaded the minds of the entire embassy to use them against us. One would think he'd take over my mind and force me to stop casting the Sanctuary ward that was protecting us from him."

"I admit, I've been too relieved he didn't to wonder why." And trying to keep his thoughts out of his nightmares.

"Sanctuary wards can't shield a person's mind, can they? Not unless they're modified, the way Annassa Soteira put her theramancy in Annassa Alea's ward over Orthros."

"And the way I added my thelemancy to your Sanctuary ward during the battle at Rose House."

"Even before that, the Collector didn't attack my mind."

"Perhaps he was so overconfident in his other powers, he thought to use more direct attacks first," Lio said, although he felt a deep hesitation.

"Why would a mind mage throw lightning at Sanctuary magic when he could simply command the Will of the person casting the ward? It makes no sense." She was tense under Lio's hands. "I would have been defenseless against him."

"Maybe you wouldn't," Lio said slowly. "You said yourself he talked as if he knows what your affinity is. Perhaps it's something that prevented him from harming you."

"I just need to know what it is." Frustration gripped her aura. "I wish it would hurry up and show itself and not make me wait to become a Hesperine to discover it."

"You will achieve your true power. But in the meantime, I want to discuss an additional option with you."

"If it will ease your fears."

"Just as a warder can shield your body, with my magic, I can create mental defenses for you. This would be even more powerful than the temporary mind ward I maintained for you while we were under attack. I want you to have a permanent one that is sustained at all times."

"Lio, that's wondrous. I want you to do it."

He held up a hand. "You need to understand the implications before you agree to it."

"What is there to understand? It's your magic, protecting me. Just as you always do." She put her hand on his chest.

He covered her hand in his. "There are...consequences."

"All right," she said reasonably, unperturbed.

Lio took a deep breath, choosing his words with care. He wanted to reassure her. But he also owed her honesty. "To make an active casting last indefinitely without the mage's attention, it requires special steps. It's an enchantment, not a casting, actually."

"Can you make a mind ward pendant?" she asked. "Perhaps a glass infused with your thelemancy? Something for me to wear and keep with me always."

"I'm afraid it's more complicated than that. The sort of magic I used to enchant Zoe's spyglass, for example, wouldn't be sufficient to protect you from a powerful attack. I'm not sure there are any materials compatible with thelemancy that would hold up under an onslaught from the Collector."

"So...*I* am the material."

"That's right, Cassia. I would enchant *you*. I would anchor my spell in your mind."

"So it will draw power from...my aura? My life force?"

"No. Wards that siphon life force are dream wards."

"Ah, I remember us talking about those before the battle with Skleros at Rose House."

"Yes. Dream wards are what Gift Collectors like him use." Lio's lip curled at the thought of the assassins who hunted Hesperines for the Order of Hypnos. Now Orthros had learned that Gift Collectors like the infamous Skleros truly served the Master of Dreams. It still made Lio's blood boil that Skleros had escaped after trying to harm Cassia. "I would never subject you to any magic of their perverse variety. I would cast a Hesperine mind ward that draws strength from your blood."

"Of course. Blood magic."

"Even so...it is no small thing to take such a spell inside yourself, Cassia. It is an enormous amount of trust to place in someone. To protect every part of your mind, I would have to touch every part of your mind. Even your innermost Will."

"Oh. That's not something you've done before, is it?"

"As deeply as our minds intertwine when we feast together, no. You know the sanctity of your Will is where I would never trespass."

"That's where you go to deprive someone of their Will. Does this mean you'd have to actually...take over my mind? That I wouldn't have my own volition during the spell?"

"Never. I will never allow that to happen to you. Not by my hand or anyone else's. But for a brief time during the casting, I would place myself in a position where I *could* master your Will. You would remain in full control, but to feel my magic there would be...disorienting. You would be more vulnerable to me in those moments than you've ever been to anyone."

"With or without such a spell, you have the power to take over my Will as easily as looking at me. And yet, the safest place for me in the world is right here." She wrapped her arms around him.

He held her close. "Always."

"You earned my trust long ago, complete and unconditional."

She had such faith in his power to protect her. He must never fail her. "The process of casting the spell would be intense. It wouldn't be particularly comfortable for you."

She frowned. "I've never known your magic to be painful."

"Oh, no, it wouldn't hurt. In fact, considering the nature of our bond, it would be extremely arousing. The entire experience could be rather overpowering."

"Overpowering, intense arousal? Let us proceed."

He framed her face in his hands, stroking her. "You must be absolutely sure. Because it isn't reversible, Cassia."

Her brows rose. Still he sensed no fear in her, but she did pause to consider. "I suppose I should take that seriously."

"Yes, you should. The ward would be sealed to your mind for as long as I live."

Her heartbeat sped in the quiet darkness. "Then it would endure forever, just like you."

"Yes. Nothing could remove it, except my death."

Her hands tightened on his shoulders. "Don't even say those words. You are my immortal."

"I will always be with you, Cassia. I will always be within you. As close as I can get." He pressed a kiss to her brow.

She rested her forehead on his, holding his hands to her cheeks. "Promise me. Right here, inside me."

"This magic would change you. Your mind wouldn't ever be the same. Such a powerful spell, woven so deeply into you, would leave a mark. Forever."

"Your mark?"

"My mark."

She took his hand and placed his fingers on her pulse, on the vein where his fangs pierced her each night. "Why wouldn't I want that?"

He kissed her there upon her delicate skin. "Think about it for a little while."

"I don't need time. There is no doubt in my mind. And I can tell there is none in yours, or you would not have asked."

"None," he confirmed. "I will do whatever I must to keep you safe."

"Then do this."

"Take some time to consider your decision. That is also something that will reassure me."

"Whatever you need, my mind mage."

She offered him her mouth again, and this time, he gave into his need for her.

97

Nights Until

NOTIAN WINTER SOLSTICE

8 Annassa, 1597 IS

FULGURITE

ENEATH LAYERS OF VEILS and wards, Rose House was a skeleton. On the docks just outside the spells, all of Orthros laughed and talked and boarded the ships for Migration. The magic over the destroyed guest house hid painful reminders from sight and discouraged young Hesperines from braving the dangerous ruins.

They were not enough to discourage Lio. He stood on the last intact, bloodstained bit of floor and let the silence around him fill his senses.

With the roof gone, he could see the stars overhead. Through the empty frame where his rose window had been, the Harbor Light blazed in the hands of the Goddess's statue, a spell that had shone for centuries to guide Hespera's worshipers home.

He still dreamed of the vision the Collector had showed him, where the Harbor Light had died and the Goddess had lain shattered.

Hespera's Sanctuary was more fragile than he had ever imagined.

He looked around at the devastation that remained from his and Cassia's duel with the Collector. What had been a beautiful edifice of his and his father's design was now a heap of rubble in the crevasse surrounding the surviving floor.

The whole ruin was covered in scattered fragments of red glass. All that remained of his finest creation. A parting insult from the Master of Dreams.

Lio must finally admit he had lost something else that night.

He rubbed a hand in the empty place on his chest where he usually felt the weight of his medallion of office. No one had commented on him not wearing it during his leave of absence, not even Uncle Argyros. Thankfully. He would have had to tell them he had no idea where it was.

The medallion he had worked his entire life to earn. Crafted by Hesperine artisans, bespelled with his and his mentor's blood, first bestowed upon him by the Queens.

He had turned the residence inside out and scoured the main house. He had even managed to hunt at House Argyros with his uncle none the wiser. He had searched everywhere he could think of in the entire city. It had taken him that long to realize the last time he remembered wearing it: when he and Cassia had been negotiating with the Dexion of the Aithourian Circle here in this room, just before the battle with the necromancers.

The fact that his own memories of that night were so disjointed unnerved Lio. The fact that his mind shied away from it all threw him off balance. His mind was his strength. And yet how fallible it seemed, when he couldn't even recall the moment he had lost the symbol of his life's work as a diplomat.

The truth was, he would rather let the medallion lie wherever it was under this rubble than set foot here again.

But he would need it to continue his ruse as the future Ambassador for Tenebran Affairs. If he didn't want to leave Orthros Boreou without it, he must find it tonight. And if he wanted to find it, he must search here.

He grimaced, bracing himself, and cast his senses out. Nausea rose in his throat at the echoes of necromancy that remained here.

The floor on which he stood was still stained with his Grace's blood, here in the spot where she had nearly died protecting everyone. He bared his fangs at the memory.

He pulled his senses back. He would never find the medallion this way, even if it did resonate with his own blood. He conjured a hovering spell light over his shoulder, rolled up his sleeves, and went to work.

He retraced his steps from that night as best he could in the ruined room. He stirred the debris with brushes of telekinesis, lifting chunks of broken marble out of the way with his hands. He levitated over shards of crimson glass because he couldn't bear to crush them under his feet. No gleam of silver caught his eye in the spell light.

Minutes turned into an hour. The family would be boarding the ship soon. He was running out of time.

He sank to his feet, crouching on a fallen pillar over a hole full of rubble. The site crackled with residual energy. Black burn marks marred the stones where the Collector had wielded Eudias's lightning magic against them. This had been where Eudias stood during their mind-duel to free him from the necromancer's possession.

That experience would always make Lio feel connected to the apprentice war mage, and the young man's courage and honor would always have Lio's admiration. Lio wondered how Eudias was faring now that his mind and his destiny were once more his own.

If Lio was suffering nightmares just from that battle, how much worse must it be for Eudias, after enduring possession by the Master of Dreams for months?

The Collector had broken so much beyond repair. It was impossible for Lio to find the medallion under all of this magical refuse. His power flowed with his frustration.

He felt an answering echo. His medium, glass, responding to his power. The destroyed bits of his window gave a soft, sad auric chime.

But there was another resonance, too. It felt like glass, but strange to him. It wasn't any glass he had made.

He leapt from the pillar in search of the strange material, carefully levitating down into the crater. When the hunk of rubble beneath his feet held, he let his weight rest on it. The burns formed a pattern, a swirl of striations that met right here. They marked the path Eudias's magic had taken as he had pulled it back into himself. Lio knelt, running his fingers through the soot.

When his skin brushed it, an uncomfortable, thrilling current traveled up his arm. At the touch of his magic, it came free, and he was able to pull it from the rubble.

It was a chunk of rough black glass the size of his hand. None of the smooth colored glass he crafted. How had this gotten here?

Of course. Lighting and sand made fulgurite.

Lightning magic had forged this from the remains of Rose House. This was a piece of a glass tube that had been shaped when Eudias's power had shot through the dust and debris with incredible heat and speed. The room was probably full of fulgurite, tracing the paths of every lightning bolt Eudias had reclaimed with Lio's help.

Lio recalled the wooden artifact Eudias carried, a carving of a lightning bolt, which had been the young mage's talisman during the duel. Lio tucked the fulgurite into his pocket.

With a sigh, he abandoned the search for his medallion. He must tell his mentor he needed a new one made. A task he would put off for as long as possible.

Right now, he must join Cassia and the family for Migration without letting on he had been here. He would smile so much that it would hide any tension in his expression. He would hold her so tightly, she would mistake the tension in his body.

When had he developed strategies for hiding his unease from his Grace?

He stepped away, leaving a little piece of their Oath in the dust at Rose House.

MIGRATION NIGHT

HE DECK OF THE *Lion's Wings* leapt under Cassia's feet, as if the ship were eager to fly from her mooring. Cassia petted Knight and dawdled Zoe's hand in hers. She felt she should help with the loading, but Apollon and Komnena had given her the much more pleasant task of watching Zoe while the Hesperines used magic for the heavy lifting.

Watching with Zoe from the deck, Cassia marveled at the sheer logistics of Migration. Harbor was an organized chaos of activity. Every bloodline hurried to finish their last-minute preparations for departure from the northern hemisphere. Hesperines stepped to and fro, trunks levitated, and the sucklings old enough to be awake at this time of night were as wild as ricocheting spells.

Cassia was sure she had forgotten something. She would spend half the year frustrated over that one little item she had left at the opposite pole. She felt the urge to go through her trunks one more time, but seeing them disappear into the hold, she knew it was too late.

She adjusted her gardening satchel against her body. The most important things were right here, including Solia's pendant.

Zoe kept up the stream of excited conversation she had started the instant she had awoken a few minutes before. "Every family is responsible for their own things and their own ship. Some families are so big, they get more than one ship, but we just have one."

"Your first Migration last year clearly made you an expert."

Zoe blushed. "It takes too much magic to step all our trunks and animals and humans to southern Orthros. So we put everything and everyone on board and then step all the ships."

"That must take a lot of magic. Why don't we sail there?"

"It's too far to sail. Unless you're a privateer!"

"A privateer? Zoe flower, do you mean there are pirates on these seas?"

"You didn't know about the privateers?" Zoe's eyes widened. "They're good pirates who sail all over the world and steal things from the bad mages and take treasure back to the Empress!"

At that moment, Lio finally arrived. He stepped into sight on the docks and said something to his father, but Apollon waved Lio away. Ignoring the gangplank that was purely for Cassia's benefit, Lio levitated onto the deck.

He joined her and Zoe at the stern, his sleeves rolled up over his elegant scholar's hands and lightly muscled forearms.

Zoe tugged on his hand. "What took you so long?"

Lio picked her up, propping her on his hip. "When did you wake up?"

"Awhile ago!"

"All of ten minutes," Cassia said seriously.

"That's ages." Lio shook his head. "I'm sorry I wasn't here when your Slumber ended. I was checking to make sure we didn't forget anything."

"You must have made a very thorough search of the house," Cassia said. "I thought we might have to come search for you."

He kissed her cheek. "Someone new to Migration has been fretting about leaving things behind. Rest assured, I found no forgotten botanical texts or rubber chews."

"You didn't have to spend all that time checking just for me." She slid an arm around him, smiling.

It still amazed her that she had the love of someone who would lay waste to an entire army with his magic for her sake. But somehow, his willingness to search through the house for any lost scrolls on gardening or Knight's favorite toys was all the more powerful and surprising.

He gave her a squeeze. "I thought you might like it better if I checked, so you won't have to worry about asking someone else to come back for things."

"You can always ask Papa to get something for you," Zoe said. "Last year he stepped back to find my doll."

Cassia didn't doubt Apollon would scour the ends of the world to make sure his children wanted for nothing. But Cassia would be embarrassed to ask the Lion of Orthros to return to the empty city for a trifle of hers.

Lio said, "The Blood Errant have all been known to stay Abroad in the northern hemisphere when our people are not in residence here. Compared to going errant, retrieving something for you would be easy."

She arched a brow at him with sudden curiosity. "Did you ever ask him to come back for anything when you were a boy?"

"I have to keep some secrets, lest I ruin my image as a mysterious and dignified heretical sorcerer."

"I'll get it out of you yet."

"You won't. But I'll enjoy you trying."

"Well," she announced. "If I forgot anything, I shall do without. I want you to spend the rest of the night enjoying my first Migration with me."

Cassia had been looking forward to this night for months. This ship would carry her farther than she'd ever been from Tenebra. She could leave the king and all her foul memories of him on the other side of the world. She and Lio would sail toward the Empire and their future career as ambassadors to Orthros's allies.

But now she might also be sailing away from her sister.

Zoe took her hand. "Isn't this exciting?"

Cassia focused on Zoe. It was hard not to get caught up in her enthusiasm. For her sake, Cassia could let herself enjoy the festivities.

Lio set the fidgeting suckling down, and Zoe pulled him and Cassia to the front of the ship. Apollon and Komnena closed the hatch at last, and the crew released the ship from its mooring.

All across Harbor, crimson sails unfurled. The whole fleet was on the move, like a flock of beautiful, seagoing gargoyles with pale breasts and brilliant red wings. Their white hulls cut easily through the deep arctic waters. The stained glass lanterns that lit each ship's way reflected off the ocean, colorful stars in the twilight sea, their celestial counterparts twinkling in the purple sky.

Cassia's throat tightened. "I'll never forget sailing into Harbor for the first time. It was one of the best moments of my life. I'll never forget this either."

Lio brought her hand to his lips.

Blood Argyros's ship pulled alongside theirs. An equine gargoyle with the wings of an owl graced the prow of the *Wisdom's Steed*, a fitting relative for the figurehead of the *Lion's Wings*, a creature whose body resembled a lion, with the head and wings like an eagle.

Mak and Lyros waved from where they stood at the rail and pointed at the person next to them.

"Nike is coming with us," Lio exclaimed.

Cassia let out a laugh and waved back. Nike lifted a hand in greeting.

Bosko, who had become his famous aunt's shadow, called out something Cassia couldn't hear, but Zoe clearly did. The suckling bounced on her feet, shifting her weight first in Cassia's direction, then Bosko's.

"Has Bosko invited you to go over to their ship?" Cassia asked.

"He and some of the other sucklings want to play Empress's Privateers."

"That sounds fun," said Lio. "Why don't you go play with Bosko and your friends?"

Zoe went quiet. Never a good sign when her newfound openness gave way to her previous silence. "We should check on Moonbeam and Aurora again."

"We checked on them as soon as you woke up, Zoe flower," Cassia reminded her, "and Papa checked on them while you were asleep. They're all snug in their bed of hay belowdecks. They like it much better down there and won't mind if you go play."

Zoe didn't reply.

"Are your friends kind to you, Zoe?" Under Lio's gentle tone was the promise of doom to anyone who mistreated his little sister.

"Everyone's nice." Zoe hesitated. "But they're really Bosko's friends. The Eriphites are my friends."

Cassia stroked Zoe's hair. She knew the child still felt responsible for all the sucklings with whom she had come to Orthros. The twenty-four of them were all that remained of their people, after all, and she and Bosko had raised the younger Eriphites after their elders had died.

"It's wonderful that you are still friends with the other Eriphites," Lio said, "but they're much younger than you. It's all right to play with children your own age. Perhaps Bosko's friends will become yours, too."

"They're all couriers already," Zoe said shyly. "Maybe someday if I get to join the Queens' Couriers, I can play with them then."

Lio could tell Zoe was set on her goal to become one of the sucklings who delivered letters and packages throughout the city. She might still doubt herself, but now that she had overcome her fear of open spaces, he knew she could succeed. "*When* you join the couriers, you'll already have friends among them, if you start playing with them now."

Cassia eyed the deck of the *Wisdom's Steed*, where all of Blood Argyros was migrating together with Alkaios and Nephalea. "Zoe, we have more room on our deck. Wouldn't this be a better place to play privateers?" Perhaps Zoe would feel more comfortable on home territory.

"Yes," Lio encouraged, "you could invite the sucklings over here and show them what a nice ship we have."

"You're right...we do have the best ship for playing privateers..." Zoe hesitated a moment longer, but then called out to Bosko.

"I get to be Diviner Mmoloki!" Bosko called back.

"Then I'm Captain Ziara!" Zoe said in a rush.

Sucklings were soon stepping onto the ship from various vessels around the harbor. Zoe swept Knight into their game, and he bounded across the deck alongside her. The crew continued their work with concentration and good humor as a gaggle of sucklings and a liegehound rampaged about.

Cassia watched the children and Knight play. "Lio, could there really be pirates who sail all the way from the Empire to the Magelands of Cordium?"

"Oh, yes. But they are no mere seagoing brigands. They are the Empress's privateers."

"I'm not sure I understand the difference between a pirate and a privateer."

"Privateers sail with the sanction of the Empress, a document from her called a letter of marque. She authorizes them to rob her enemies for the benefit of her lands. They don't steal for personal gain or attack ships that belong to Imperial citizens. They get their spoils from the unsuspecting mages of Cordium—who don't even know they exist."

"What about the Empress's strict policy of isolation, keeping her lands and people separated from Tenebra and Cordium?"

Lio explained, "Tenebrans and Cordians are not allowed in the Empire, but the Empress does allow the privateers to make forays into the Magelands."

"Oh, I see. Is information one of the commodities those in their profession acquire for her?"

"To be sure. But she also sees no reason why her people should do without goods from the Cordian and Tenebran side of the world, and trade with Hesperines is not the only way she obtains them. I once saw an Aithourian master's entire collection of golden spoons for sale in a privateer market."

Cassia laughed. "Now I see why Zoe calls them good pirates."

The front of Orthros's fleet was almost out of the bay. In the lead sailed the *Far-Seer*. Kassandra stood at the helm with the captain, guiding their people toward the land of her mortal origin.

Lio pointed back the way they had come. "The royal fleet always sets sail last."

The numerous vessels bearing the extensive royal bloodlines lingered at the docks. Then their black sails caught the wind, and they too set sail.

The sheer amount of magic in the auras surrounding Cassia made her pulse race. The whole city of Selas was packed into this sprawling, magnificent fleet.

The city cupping the crescent bay was deserted. All the beautiful buildings were silent. The streets were empty. Cassia thought of the herds of deer left to their spring foraging, of the gardens readied for the midnight sun of summer and left in the shelter of the ward. Of her and Lio's own little Sanctuary ward in their bedchamber, which must remain here.

Lio's hair whipped around his face in the wind. "You once feared the night when you would sail away from these shores, thinking you would be on a ship bound for Tenebra. But here we are, leaving together, and only heading toward another part of home."

As their ship slipped out of the encircling arms of Harbor, she took him in her arms and kissed him.

It was a new year, and a new world lay ahead of them. In that moment, her hopes were stronger than her fears.

A flare of magic came from the back of the fleet. The Queens stood hand in hand on the deck of the last ship. On the leading ship, Kassandra lifted her face to the moon, and another swell of magic came from her direction. More power rose all around them, from every Hesperine on every ship, as Hespera's children joined their magic together in Blood Union.

Lio wrapped his arms around Cassia. "Hold on tight."

The air around them seemed to turn inside out. Where sky and sea met, a blanket of stars appeared, but one that didn't match the sky under which they sailed. The unfamiliar constellations swallowed them up, and Cassia's stomach dropped.

The current changed, tossing the boat. The wind came from a different direction, smelling of ice. Vertigo made Cassia's head spin.

Lio steadied her and checked the security of her cloak and scarf. "Changing hemispheres in a matter of seconds is disorienting."

Her vision cleared, and for the first time, she beheld the southern pole of the world.

They sailed between massive ice sculptures. A frosty white whale leapt from the sea, frozen forever mid-jump. A leopard stalked impossibly over the surface of the ocean, its claws dipping into the water. A bear towered over them, its front legs outstretched, but it seemed more protective than threatening.

Cassia expected Lio to begin his historical commentary on everything they were seeing, but he stood quietly behind her, holding her against his chest.

Zoe darted back over to them with Knight at her side. "Aren't the big animals beautiful?"

"They're marvelous!" Cassia petted her hound, rewarding him with affection as she always did after playtime.

"Lio, tell Cassia about the treaties."

"You go ahead, Zoe flower."

"But you know all about diplomacy," Zoe protested.

"I like how you tell the story," said Lio.

"If you're sure." Zoe pointed up at a sculpture of dolphins artfully strung together on a flourish of ice representing a water current. "Every ice statue is from a treaty with one of the places in the Empire. They all have different types of leaders, but mostly Queen Mothers. Every Queen Mother has a sacred animal that's special in her family."

"That's fascinating." Cassia kept her gloved but chilly fingers tucked into Knight's ruff. "Will you help me learn the names of the different places?"

"We can share the book Aunt Kona gave me. It says that as long as the statues don't melt, the treaties aren't broken. Because the Queens' magic changes the land and the weather. We have to keep all the magic inside the ward so it doesn't melt the ice animals or bother the real animals."

"Oh, I see." Cassia nodded. "When plants that like the cold get too warm, they die. So we can't come in and make it warmer, or it could hurt the plants and animals, which people in the Empire surely depend on."

Lio put in at last, "The Queens' ward seals the increased warmth associated with Hesperine activity inside Orthros, leaving the surrounding ocean and landmasses unchanged. Also, the light magic in the ward has highly reflective properties that repel solar heat, which has a cooling effect."

Cassia was impressed, if not surprised. "The Annassa think of everything."

Zoe pointed at an ice sculpture of an eagle. "Lio says making the treaties with the Empire took even longer than with Tenebra. There were lots and lots of meetings. But Ritual mother Kassandra and Annassa Soteira get along a lot better with the Queen Mothers than with the stupid free lords."

"No doubt," said Cassia. "My respect for the Queen Mothers grows all the time."

The fleet emerged from between the sculptures, only to plunge into a blanket of mist that hovered over the water. Cassia could scarcely see past the prow, and the voices from the other ships were muffled. But their tones were happy. The air seemed to swirl around Cassia in welcome.

"It feels like the blizzard in Martyr's Pass," she murmured in the hush. "As if there are wonders hidden within it."

"There are," Lio promised. "That night in the pass, I stepped you into Orthros. But this time, you will feel us cross the border."

His arms were strong and warm around her as the Sanctuary magic enfolded them and welcomed them in. Cassia's heart leapt, and tears sprang to her eyes at the power of the Queens' spell. She knew it in her blood, which she had shed to awaken Sanctuary magic before. It was dark and bright, old and new, safe and dangerous and everlasting. Lio let out a sigh and relaxed against her.

She pulled her scarf away from her face to smile at him and Zoe. "We're home."

That brought a smile to his face as well. But she wondered at his silence of a moment before.

Zoe and Knight ran off to play veil and step in the mist with the other sucklings. Cassia took the opportunity to kiss Lio again. "A cassia roll for your thoughts."

That roused a laugh from him. He nibbled the tip of her nose. "I'll take a cassia roll tonight when I show you our southern bedchamber."

The mist thinned, and their moment of privacy slipped away with it. The other ships came into view again, and then the land toward which they sailed.

Cliffs of dark ice rose ahead of them, cloaked in pale frost. Deep passages opened in them, channels that appeared to lead far into the ice. The mist obscured their twists and turns and cloaked the tops of the bluffs above.

Hesperine magic swept over them again. Orthros's weather mages must be at work, for the mist swirled and rose. Nature's veil lifted, and Cassia beheld the city built on the heights.

"Welcome to Haima, my Grace," Lio said.

She gasped at the wondrous beauty above them. Orthros's southern capital was a city of delicate spires, mighty pillars, and elegant domes that gleamed with exquisite colors. From brilliant turquoise to sapphire blue, vibrant red to emerald green, all were adorned with a mantle of glittering white snow.

"Did your father design this, too?" Cassia asked.

"Oh, no. Haima is the masterpiece of the architects who accompanied Kassandra to Orthros from the Empire. The founder of the Haiman style is Firstblood Yasamin, from the same sister-state as Javed."

"How fortunate for Orthros that she brought her gifts here."

Zoe popped into sight next to them to continue her excited narration, while Knight raced to catch up to the stepping suckling. "The channels are called the Veins, and you can sail through them to anywhere you want. Then you can step back up to the city on top. But Moonbeam and Aurora love climbing the stairs instead!"

The ships of the elder firstbloods and the Queens drew together and sailed for the central Vein. Here at the gateway to Orthros Notou stood a magnificent red marble statue of Kassandra dressed in Imperial finery. She faced statues of the Queens. Kassandra and Soteira's hands were outstretched, almost touching, in a gesture that bespoke the moment the Empire and Orthros had joined their destinies.

Zoe leaned out over the railing, pointing up at the statues. "This is Sisters' Port, because Kassandra is the Queens' Ritual sister, and the Empire and Orthros are like sisters too."

The *Far-Seer* and the *Eternal Grace* pulled alongside each other and sailed between the statues. Kassandra stood at the rail, reaching out both hands to Annassa Soteira, who reached back in echo of their monuments. Then the Queens lifted their joined hands, and all the lights in the city above them flared to life at once.

Across every deck, their people cheered. Cassia joined in, her spirits lifting with their voices.

The *Lion's Wings* docked next to the *Wisdom's Steed*. Lio went to help his parents, only to be back at Cassia's side in a moment. "Mother and Father will oversee the unloading. Why don't I show you the city?"

Apollon and Komnena were levitating Zoe's purple travel trunks out of the hold in anticipation of suckling Slumber. Zoe, Bosko, and the other children seemed bent on making the most of their fun before they must sleep.

Cassia had no intention of sleeping tonight. "I'd love a tour of the city…and our residence. And you."

He gave her a sweet grin, turned sultry by his fangs. "Let's say good veil to everyone and be on our way. As quickly as possible."

They interrupted the children's game to embrace a pouting Zoe.

"Could Knight stay with you and the goats?" Cassia asked. "I think it would help him get used to our new home."

"Really? I can keep Knight tonight? Are you sure?" Zoe leaned closer and whispered. "You won't be scared in a new place without him?"

"Lio will help me not feel scared," Cassia whispered back. "But who will help Knight feel at home?"

"Moonbeam and Aurora and I are already used to Orthros Notou. We can make Knight feel better. And he'll have plenty of room to run around in the goat paddock."

"That's the perfect place for him until Lio and I prepare our residence for a dog. Thank you so much, Zoe flower."

The suckling hugged Cassia tightly before rejoining the children's last-minute game with Knight.

Cassia took Lio's hand. "Let's go."

"Are you sure about Knight?" he asked. "I have a dog run for him at our residence."

"No dog on the bed tonight," she said.

He gave her a fast kiss. Pausing only to snatch up his travel pack, he levitated them off the ship. She gasped and laughed as he spun them midair.

They met their Trial circle on one of the stone piers that ran along the base of the cliffs. Xandra beckoned to them. "Let's be the first into the city. There's nothing like seeing it before anyone else disturbs it."

And they were off, Cassia following the graceful Hesperines as they set an inhuman pace up the stone stairs that ascended from the docks. Whenever it seemed Cassia might fall behind, Lio scooped her up and carried her part of the way. She didn't ask them to slow down. Laughing and jesting with each other, they escaped all their duties and ran off together as surely as the sucklings had.

They passed guest houses and coffee shops built along the inside of the cliffs. When they attained the top at last, the noise of the docks below faded. The city before them was silent, nascent, just waiting to burst into life.

The capital ascended in tiers built along the rise of the cliffs. At Haima's summit was the statue she had been looking for. This rendition of Hespera sat on an intricately carved stool, a goddess on a sacred throne. She had the features of an Imperial woman and wore a wrap dress of ceremonial stripweave. Her hair was a myriad of braids, like all her promises to her people. She watched over the domes and towers of the city as if greatly pleased with the Sanctuary her children had laid at her feet.

"We get to live here," Cassia breathed.

Streets buried in snow invited them onward. They walked between stately round pillars carved with intricate geometric designs and under low, wide archways with graceful points. Lio levitated her over the drifts while their friends took turns pointing everything out to her.

"That gateway leads to Steward's Rise. We'll take you riding there."

"The musicians parade on this roadway during festivals."

"You have to cross ten bridges to get to the library. Only those with true dedication are rewarded with knowledge."

They took her across Haima's central bridge, a massive span of stone and brick with two levels of arcaded galleries that offered shelter from the snow. They paused with her at scenic viewpoints, where she looked down from impossible heights at flat roofs and hidden courtyards. Tucked away under wards, dormant plants waited, and fountains ran unfrozen in the polar night.

As the Eighth Circle roamed, the voices from below drew nearer and nearer. Soon the streets began to fill, and they were no longer alone. They halted on a wide road in one of the highest tiers of the city.

Mak nodded toward elegant walls visible through the evergreens lining the way. "House Argyros is just right here, and House Komnena is over there. In Haima, we're next door."

Lyros gestured down the street. "And the rest of our circle isn't far. The homes of the elder firstbloods occupy this entire district."

"How lovely," Cassia said. "We're all neighbors here."

Xandra pointed over their heads to the structures visible on the level above, which ringed the goddess's feet. "I'm up there with the other royal houses, but it's not far, either. And Hespera is our nicest neighbor of all."

Cassia gave each of their friends a hug, and they said their momentary farewells before taking off in different directions. She wound closer to Lio as they walked under the evergreens toward House Komnena.

Cassia studied their thick trunks, spreading limbs, and branches heavy with cones. "These must be as old as the city. What kind of trees are they?"

"Take a deep breath," he replied.

She inhaled the icy air and their woodsy scent. "Oh! Cedar trees."

"This variety is from the high, cold mountains of the Empire."

"Do we have some on our grounds?"

"See for yourself."

He led her through one of the broad pointed archways into a large courtyard framed by galleries. Hand in hand, they strolled between orderly clusters of cedars and past a central pool toward what must be the main wing. It was topped with a golden dome like a great, elegant bulb waiting to sprout.

The entrance was deeply recessed under a grand arch, its honeycomb of vaults richly decorated with gold and blue tiles. Cassia gaped at the complexity and opulence of it. But when she spotted the stars of Anastasios's constellation engraved amid the intricate patterns on the double doors, she knew they were home.

Lio pointed to one of the galleries on their right. "Our wing is this way. No tower. I'm afraid we're attached to the main house here."

"That's what veil spells are for," she teased.

He winked at her. They passed through the gallery into an adjacent courtyard nearly as large as the central one. Cassia's jaw dropped again at the entrance to another sprawling wing topped with its own blue dome.

"This is ours," Lio said.

"This entire…palace?"

"I think we're expected to be prolific."

They burst out laughing. She had a sudden image of them together here for hundreds of years making sucklings, and her worries seemed farther away than ever.

He pointed to a flat section of the roof at the base of the dome. "The rooftops and balconies are wonderful for watching the auroras at night."

"Rooftop gardens! That's what I shall have here."

"Consider them your gardens-to-be."

They approached the front doors, and the two panels swung open ahead of them. Her breath clouded into the shadows within.

He paused on the threshold. "Let me awaken the spells with my blood—which carries yours. Ever since I first gave our combined blood to the magic here, this residence has been truly ours."

He bared his fangs and brought his hand to his mouth. Then he knelt in the doorway and pressed his bleeding palm to the floor.

The promise of heat rose from the floor, a sign the geomancers' enchantments were warming. Flashes of light raced over the outlines of objects within, and the fragrance of moonflower and sandalwood cleaning spells overpowered the air. At last, the spell lights awoke.

One globe after another lit up to reveal thick, round pillars and vaulted ceilings, all covered in tiles of cerulean and aquamarine. Warm glows illuminated inviting alcoves filled with floor cushions, coffee tables, and writing desks. Cedar screens divided the room, the lights shining through their lacey, cutout designs.

Of course, the spacious chamber was full of books and scrolls. She spotted empty slots in the shelves and scroll racks, surely waiting for the volumes they had brought back with them from the north.

"Lio, you have been keeping secrets from me. You have twice as many titles in your library as I thought. You've just hidden half of them here."

"Well, not really. I keep two copies of the best ones so I don't have to cart them back and forth. But there are plenty here you've never seen before."

From the nearest rack, she pulled out a pretty scroll with a blue tassel. She unrolled it to stare at the beautiful, flowing script inside. It beckoned her, promising answers to mysteries, if only she could decipher it.

"Most of these are in Imperial languages." Lio sounded apologetic.

"Perfect. You can help me study for our new diplomatic assignments."

"Let me show you the rest of the residence."

Ah. Sir Diplomat had forgone the chance to wax poetic about the treaties the statues represented, and Sir Scholar could not even be tempted by the promise of cuddling up with scrolls.

Lio did not wish to think about diplomacy at present, and especially not about his lost medallion. That was what weighed on his mind.

How like him not to say anything. He kept their Oath with great devotion when it concerned her well being, but not always for the sake of his own. She had almost asked him about it so many times. But she hesitated to rush him if he wasn't ready yet. She understood what it was like to need time.

If only she had been able to find the medallion herself. She was quite proud that she had managed to spend so much time searching without her mind mage finding out. But even Knight's nose hadn't been able to track Lio's talisman anywhere in Selas.

Should now be the moment when she finally said something? What did Lio need?

The happiest he had been all night was when they escaped their responsibilities and focused on each other.

Rolling up the scroll, she made a show of searching the room, peering into the alcoves and up at the tops of bookcases.

He watched her with a bemused expression. "What can you be searching for, my rose?"

"Why, the bed, of course."

He laughed and shook his head. "You won't find one in this room."

"You don't mean to tell me you sleep apart from your scrolls in Orthros Notou?"

"When you arrived in Orthros Boreou, I was using the window seat in the library as a bed because I'd had no opportunity to prepare the tower for you. But I spent half a year in this residence wishing you were here. We have a proper, furnished bedchamber."

She teased the tip of the scroll rod down Lio's chest. "We will spend some time in this room, won't we?"

His gaze followed the progress of her hand. "I hope so. But not time sleeping."

"We'll have to spend at least as much time at your desk here as we do in our other residence. Only…I happen to notice there is more than one desk in this room."

He plucked the scroll from her hand and brought her wrist to his lips. "We'll have to take a tour of the desks. After we have thoroughly explored the bed."

His grin had reappeared, and the light was back in his eyes. Distracting him was the right choice. For now.

"Do show me this proper bedchamber," she invited.

He drew her deeper into their wing, through a cocoon of empty rooms and inner courtyards. Stained glass windows transformed the moonlight into warm colors, and it reflected off the cool shades of brilliant glass mosaics. Their steps were quiet on the thick rugs, their words echoing impudently loud in the tiled halls. At every turn, Cassia tried to make Lio laugh and listened to the rich sound filling their vacant residence with promise.

She pulled him against a pillar and kissed him slowly, because she could, and because she knew every kiss made him forget his worries a little more. But soon she would give him something better than a distraction. This very night, she was determined to give him a solution. The mind ward would banish his worst worries for good.

Their hands and mouths roamed until they were both panting. His lids heavy, his eyes bright, he pulled away. "Feasting on you right here is tempting, but perhaps we will save our tour of the pillars for later as well. There are two more stops on the tour."

"Another stop before the bedchamber?"

"Of course. The bath." He gave her a wicked grin.

"Yes, please."

He showed her out into the next courtyard. It was roofed with crystal clear glass, offering a stunning view of the night sky and shelter from the cold. Balmy warmth filled the air, rising from a bathing pool. Water splashed up from a fountainhead in the center. She took a step closer and examined it.

"It's not a reflection of the marble," he said. "The water really is red."

"Is that magic?"

"No, it's entirely natural. The city is built on mineral hot springs. The geomagi and water mages tapped it and coaxed it up through the ice. All the natural fountains and baths run red."

She gasped in delight. "It's like a sign from Hespera that this place was meant for her people."

"So we have always believed."

"You know, plants will grow so well in this warmth and humidity. What do you think of some ferns around the bath…?" Just then, she spotted a collection of empty pots in the corner of the courtyard, and she kissed him again.

"Mmm. Clearly, the way to a woman's heart is through gardening tools."

"You've discovered the secret to keeping a mortal trapped in your lair forever, my Hesperine. An eternal supply of empty pots, and I shall never want to leave."

"There are more pots in the bedchamber." He scooped her up in his arms and carried her past the bath, into the luxurious room beyond. "I tried to imagine exactly what you would want. If you don't like any of it, we can change it, of course."

Everywhere she looked, vibrant pots waited for new houseplants. Screens with curling floral motifs framed a deep, raised alcove where a thick mattress waited. Tiny spell lights dotted the top of the recess, filling it with a soft, magical glow. Their roses would grow perfectly here in the light of Lio's spells, climbing all over the screens.

She shook her head. "How could I not adore it?"

"Well, I know it feels strange without our Sanctuary ward."

"And I do miss your stained glass windows," she admitted.

"I thought you might." He lifted his gaze to the ceiling, and the spell lights rose to illuminate it.

Four of the eight vaults were filled in with mosaics, each with a different floral design. Countless tiny, colorful tiles were pieced together into cassia flowers, Sanctuary roses, betony, and Hespera's Roses to match the windows in their northern residence.

"Oh, Lio, they must have taken you so much time and patience."

He turned in a circle, making the garden above her spin until she grew dizzy. "I needed to make them. Every little fragment I placed was for you."

She put her arms around his neck and brought her face to his. "You have a gift for putting broken things together into something whole and beautiful. Stained glass and mosaics. Alliances. My heart."

He lowered his gaze. "You were always a work of art, all on your own."

"But I wasn't whole."

"Neither was I."

"I know this is where you spent most of our half-year apart, and I will spend the next half-year erasing every single one of those memories." She brushed her fingers across his brow. "Are they starting to fade yet?"

"Oh, yes. But perhaps you can hurry them along."

She heard a rustle, then their Tenebran army blanket levitated out of his pack and spread itself onto the bare mattress.

He tossed her into the bed alcove, and she pulled him in with her.

MIND WARD

Lio covered Cassia's body with his and rested his face against her neck, just holding her there for a long moment, breathing her scent.

"I'm here," she reminded him, running her hands over his hair, down his back.

He breathed a sigh. She nuzzled her way under his collar. Her sudden bite on his throat sent pleasure-pain shooting through him, a sharp reminder of the reality of her nearness.

"Cassia." He put his mouth to hers.

She opened for him, soft and welcoming. He delved in with his tongue, needing to taste the reality of her, too.

When she put a staying hand on his shoulder, he parted their lips and propped himself on his elbows. "Is everything all right? Is there anything you need?"

She smiled, shaking her head. "Always so thoughtful of me. Tonight, it's time for us to do what you need."

His body responded to her invitation, his arousal stirring amid the layers of silk between them.

She touched her thumb to one of his extended fangs. "We have no Sanctuary ward in our Notian bedchamber. This is the place for a different kind of Sanctuary. Here, now, you should cast your mind ward upon me."

He rolled off of her, caution cooling his desire. "You haven't had enough time to think about your decision."

She propped an arm behind her head, her hazel eyes bright under his spell lights. "It's all I've wanted to think about since last night."

"You planned this. That's why you sent Knight off with Zoe."

"I was uncertain how he would respond to blood magic as powerful as you describe this spell to be. I didn't think we could manage him and the mind ward."

Lio rubbed his brow. "No, we couldn't. But, Cassia—"

"I am in conflict about so much right now, but of one thing, I am certain. I want us to do this."

"With so much else unresolved, perhaps now isn't the time to make a decision about something so permanent. I should have waited to ask you." And yet, even now, another part of him asked why in the Goddess's name he was trying to talk Cassia out of what he felt so driven to do.

"No," she said vehemently, shaking her head. "You shouldn't have waited. No more withholding your needs. Now is exactly the right time."

"I'm grateful for your care, my Grace. But this must be for both of us, not only me."

"It is for me, too." She rolled closer, pressing their bodies together once more. "I cannot have your blood in my veins, not yet. But I can have your magic in my mind."

"It won't be like the fleeting connection I create between us when we feast together. As I told you, it will leave a permanent mark."

"Like your bite? Like your body? Like Grace? You have left your mark deep within me already, my love. Your magic is in my blood from every time you have feasted on me. I am already bound to you by our Craving, and I will never, ever be the same. I wouldn't wish to be. I will gladly carry the mark of your protection on my mind. It will reassure me in a way I cannot describe to know that your magic is inside me, and no one can tear it away."

He placed a gentle kiss on her throat. A shiver passed through their Union and over his skin. "I want to make my mark on you. I need to give you a piece of myself. I need to know I am with you, even when you're in the next room. Even when I'm asleep. Even when you're human."

"I want that, too."

"I have never created such a spell in reality, only practice models. But my training has made me fully prepared to perform such a casting if ever necessary."

"I have no doubt about your ability."

"So much of what I can do has always been theoretical. The Goddess gave me all this power, but it was not to be used, except in hypothetical threatening circumstances. I was to save it for situations I would never encounter in the safety of Orthros or, so I thought, on any diplomatic mission."

"But the hypothetical has become all too real of late, hasn't it?"

"I am not a book to be left on a shelf unopened. I have this power from Hespera for a purpose. I will use it." He caressed her cheek. "This is exactly the kind of application my power is made for. *I* was made for this, Cassia. I will protect you, inside and out."

Her certainty strengthened their Union. "Cast the spell, my Grace."

"Goddess bless. Your permission, each time you give it anew, is one of the sweetest gifts of my existence, Cassia. I would do anything to earn that over and over again."

"Gifts don't have to be earned," she reminded him. "I've chosen you."

He eased her onto her back again. Tenderly, he kissed her until she relaxed in his arms, creating a moment of reassurance for both of them that offset the magnitude of what they were about to do.

She looked up at him, her lips rosy. "If I can't keep my hands off of you while you're casting the ward, will that disrupt your concentration?"

That brought a smile to his face. "Oh, no. Feel free to act on your arousal. In fact, joining our bodies during the casting will strengthen the magic."

"Ohh. That makes sense."

"The use of physical intimacy to enhance magic is an entire area of practice. It has been explored since ancient times and plays a role in sacred magical rituals involving pleasure worship."

"We may have left the glyph stone in Orthros Boreou, but let us begin to rebuild our shrine here as well."

He took a deep breath. They were really going to do this. "Is there anything you need before we begin?"

"Do you need time to prepare? To…gather any supplies or such?"

He shook his head. "I have been preparing for this my entire life. Eighty-nine years of Hesperine blood and training." He tapped his temple. "All my supplies are right here."

"You've been thinking about this, before we talked about it last night."

"A great deal, yes."

"Then we're both ready."

He pushed her hair back from her face. "Don't be afraid."

"I won't be."

"After the spell, I mean," he said softly.

"I won't be. And neither will you." She let out a deep sigh. "Thank you for doing this, Lio."

"To say it is my pleasure would be an understatement."

"Is there anything I'm supposed to do?" she asked.

He slid a hand into her hair. "Just relax."

Her pulse pattered. "I'm too full of anticipation."

"Then just place your trust in me."

"I already have."

"Your work is done. Now mine begins." He began to take her clothes off. "You won't need these."

"What a nice task you have. You're already enjoying your work right well, I can see."

"I realize your work is not done after all. I won't need clothing, either."

She started to divest him of his robes. "I'm enjoying your spell very much already, as well."

When they were skin to skin, he lay with her for a moment, letting the intimacy of it build between them. Her aura bloomed within the private moment, opening for him as she never did anywhere else, with anyone else. Her heart fluttered against his chest, and she ran her hand up his arm with the ease of familiarity.

"First, I will drink from you," he explained. "I will blend our blood for the spell. Then you will feel me in your mind, just like always. Most of the actual casting will take place then."

"So it is all an act of Will?"

"Essentially, yes."

"According to what I'm learning about magic, isn't that the most challenging way to cast?"

"Yes. Thelemancy is nearly all Will. It neither requires nor allows for as many casting aids as other affinities. I will apply my magic directly to your mind. I will be in complete control of the spell at all times, with no other components but our blood. That is the most powerful and careful way to cast."

She nodded. He sensed not a trace of apprehension in her aura. Only trust—and no small amount of excitement.

Her faith in him was complete. Like the night he had first bitten her, like the night they had first made love in spite of all her fears. He did not know anymore just how much of his faith in himself he had built on the foundation of hers.

He lowered his head and kissed her between her breasts.

Her heart leapt, and amusement danced in her aura. "Is that how the spell begins?"

"Yes. It's a very important preliminary preparation. The part where I appreciate your beauty and make sure you're enjoying yourself." He turned his head, kissing first one of her nipples, then the other with a lingering tongue.

"Oh, yes," she said, her voice breathy, "I can see this is a very significant part of magical theory."

He dove under the covers and between her legs. "Is it all right with you if we make this step last a little longer?"

"We ought to be thorough about every part of the spell."

Her laughter turned to a gasp of pleasure as he fastened his mouth onto her krana. He ravished her kalux with his mouth for several moments, relentlessly pleasuring her with the pressure and strokes he knew she liked. This purely physical spell worked its magic quickly. She climaxed with a shuddering cry, her hips bowing against his mouth.

She heaved a sigh. "Will that make the ward stronger?"

"No." He planted a kiss on the inside of her thigh. "That was just for you."

"Let it never be said that you cast a spell on a woman without making her feel thoroughly appreciated first."

He moved back up her body. She claimed a kiss from his damp mouth.

"Mmm." He licked his lips. "Let it never be said that you let a heretic cast his blood magic on you without making him feel appreciated."

He nuzzled her temple, then kissed his way down to her throat. Her fingers roamed down the small of his back. The spirals of sensation her touch wrought heightened his pulse to meet hers, and the throb of their heartbeats filled the space around them.

"First, drink," she said.

"Yes, Cassia."

When he slid his fangs into her flesh, she sighed and pulled him closer. Her blood was spicy with her recent pleasure and sweet with her trust. He took a long drink to fortify himself. His magic and his body rose in answer, but he focused on his goal. He could not allow the smooth skin of her thigh against his rhabdos to distract him.

Then her hand found his shaft and gave him a smooth caress.

He took her wrist in his hand and disengaged from her vein. "Best let me get the spell properly started first."

"I thought you said it wouldn't distract you," she said, her voice a husky tease in his ear.

"I have excellent concentration and self-discipline, but I'm not a god."

She chuckled and settled her hand on his shoulder. "I'll try to behave myself."

"For now. There will be plenty of opportunity to misbehave later."

He gave her neck another gentle bite, drinking until words failed her and his magic hummed. He tasted that she was on the verge of another climax, but had to stop himself.

She made a sound of protest as he withdrew his fangs. Her gaze fastened on his mouth, her eyes dilated. "Lio."

He felt her blood dripping from his fangs and down his chin. He brought his wrist to his mouth and bit. His own blood welled on his tongue, mingling with hers. She shivered against him, her whole body going tense, her aura sharp with longing as she watched, riveted to the sight of their blood blending.

He lowered his head again and kissed her between her brows, streaking her skin with their blood. He pulled back to observe the stain.

"Ready?" he asked.

Her hands closed around his arms. "Yes."

He let her heartbeat summon his power. With the rhythm of her pulse, he pulsed his magic into her. Time seemed to stop as every throb of her heart brought them closer together, and his power built within her.

Her chest rose and fell, as if she breathed him in. "So slow and gentle this time."

"I must go very deep, Cassia. I must be more gentle than ever."

Just then she moaned, her head falling back on the pillows. "Come deeper, my love."

At that exquisite invitation, he fought the urge to plunge inside her. He kept at his delicate pace, sinking slowly, slowly, his magic growing as he held his body in check.

Images flashed through his mind. The book she had been trying to read the other night, all fine, frustrating black print. Zoe's smiling face. A week's worth of a seedling's progress, sweeping through her thoughts in an instant, from its first peep out of the soil to it attaining the height of her hand. He shut his eyes for a moment, savoring the sights that made up Cassia's life.

Every other image was of him. He smiled. "Am I always in your thoughts, my rose?"

"Mmhm," she confirmed.

Then came smells. Fresh soil and damp greenery. Coffee and cassia spice. Sandalwood and moonflower and pleasure.

"Mmm," he agreed.

He heard the laughter of their friends. The howl of winter wind through the top of their tower.

Then his own laughter. His words, which she hung on. His groan at the taste of her blood.

"Cassia," he said, and heard the echo in her thoughts.

Now sensations. The way his hands felt on her skin. The way his fangs felt in her throat. The way her body felt when he...

Her next moan of pleasure reached his ears. "Lio. I need your body inside me, too."

"Soon, darling. Soon." His magic was flowing hard, demanding attention from the tightness in his body.

He blanketed her with more thelemancy. They sank together into older memories. Tenebra was a shadow lurking in her thoughts, a desolation that stank of death, where the voice of her father echoed.

She gave a sharp gasp and turned her head away on the pillow.

"Shh. No need to linger there." He stroked her hair and overshadowed the memories with his magic.

She breathed a sigh, and her eyelids fluttered shut. He carried her down deeper. They groaned together as they fell into the realm of her instincts and desires.

Her eyes flew open again, her lips rounding. Her arms twined around him as her leg sought his waist. He slid his hand between them to keep her from sliding her krana right onto his rhabdos. When his hand met her wet folds, she gave a guttural sigh and rubbed against his palm eagerly.

She bared her teeth. The sight made his own gums ache.

"Soon," he promised.

The powerful fantasy of her slaking herself from his vein unfolded in her mind.

"Oh, Goddess. Cassia." He curled his free hand into a fist around a handful of the sheets.

She arched her body off the bed, and he let his fingers sink inside her as her krana clutched around them.

He wanted to live all night in the images and sensations in her mind, to lose himself in the dream of what it would be like when she was a Hesperine. But he could not linger here. He had work to do.

He held his magic in check and drew out her pleasure a moment longer. She rode out her climax on his hand and was rocking her hips to beg for another.

"Soon," he rasped.

She mewled, letting her arms fall back on the bed, delirious with his magic.

"Cassia," he murmured, "now I must go deepest of all. Look and me and tell me you still want me to."

She blinked, her gaze sharpening. He waited for her to think through the intoxicating layers of his magic in her mind. When she spoke at last, her voice was clear. "Yes, Lio. I want you to continue."

"Do you want my body now?"

She hooked her other leg around him. *"Now."*

He braced himself above her on his arms, drew his hips back, then plunged inside her. They each gave a shout.

Pleasure stoked his magic, and he rallied his Will to bolster his control. "I must touch your Will now."

"I trust you," she affirmed once more.

He channeled all the power of their joining and held it ready, seeking her innermost reaches.

There it was, the most precious of all treasures—the freedom of her spirit, her power of choice. Fragile as glass, strong enough to break the world.

Lio held her unbroken Will in his hands.

She looked up at him, her soul bared to him in her gaze. Her body relaxed under his in reflexive surrender, her legs sliding apart, her hips shifting. The motion sank him deeper and altered their angle to give him leverage.

He gazed down at her. She was so vulnerable with her legs spread and his body buried deep in hers. Her mind was laid open for him, his magic filling nearly every corner. There was no part of her he could not touch. There was no power over her he could not wield.

Awe came over him. The Goddess had made him so powerful. But Cassia's trust had made him strong.

I will always protect you. He spoke the words through their Grace Union. *I will always do right by you. I will always love you.*

I know. Her inner voice rang out into the depths of his magic.

You are still in command, Cassia. No matter how powerful my magic feels inside you, remember that. Your Will is your own, and I will obey.

Don't stop. Don't ever let go.

I'll never let go.

He began his spell there, in her innermost being. The blood on her forehead glowed red, then brightened to white. Her eyes rolled back, and she let out a long, sensual moan.

She levitated off the bed, magic bearing her up onto his shaft. He leaned his weight on his fists and braced his hips, anchoring her. Their pleasure, flooding together through the Union, immersed him.

He pushed back against the current with his Will. The friction, the give and take, sharpened all his senses to an overwhelming keenness. His mind was perfectly clear, his power aroar, his body so alive.

He spun his magic round and round, as if shaping molten glass. He would enclose the Sanctuary of her mind within a barrier so powerful that it would repel the hand that had laid waste to Rose House with the flick of a finger.

He felt her mind harden, shining and crystalline.

You are so strong, he marveled. *You will make my spell upon you strong as well.*

With every new layer of magic, her body undulated beneath his in slow, rhythmic strokes. Her wet channel stroked around his shaft, hardening him, sharpening the pleasure.

He spun their ethereal materials together, his magic and her blood, sealing them with the strength of their combined Wills. He felt the moment when his spell tapped the power in her veins and took on life.

An ecstatic scream broke out of her. Her thoughts scattered in a thousand directions, countless prisms shining their fractured colors into his spell. Her body twisted and bucked with the force of her climax.

Cassia. My rose. It's all right. Shh. I'm here. He cradled her under his body and held his incomplete spell steady as she came apart.

Her teeth fastened onto his shoulder, and her nails scored his back. Her krana pulsed around his rhabdos, demanding everything of him.

He couldn't give it to her until the right moment. He clamped down on his body's need with an iron Will and focused on his spell. He prepared to pour more magic into the ward and strengthen it.

Where his spell and her blood met, an impossible current opened up and began to draw on his magic. Without any intervention from him, her mind laid claim to his power and channeled it into the protections he had begun to build.

He gasped, yanking back on his magic. He had to regain control before he hurt her.

She groaned in protest. Her head tossed on the pillow, and whispered words passed her lips. He couldn't understand the unfamiliar syllables. But he sensed her unmistakable meaning, felt the need in her blood. The yearning... The Craving?

He almost laughed in relief. It was not some magical anomaly. His Grace was making a feast of his magic.

He let her have it, easing the current of his power to a manageable flow. Her mind sipped at him, and his spell grew stronger.

The most challenging thelemantic casting of his career was astonishingly easy. They navigated her mind together in perfect Union, him guiding the spell, her pulling his power into it.

He was aware of their bodies moving together, their tangled limbs, the searing pleasure radiating from where they joined, but he lost track of what was her and what was him. There was still a physical world where their breaths mingled, her sweat slicked his skin, and his fingers dug into her hips.

But what he saw in his mind's eye was the abstract order of her mind, the complicated perfection of her thoughts. He crafted the spell with every attention to the finest details, spinning tiny flourishes of thelemantic protection around her memories, layering heavy, brilliant bands of mind magic over her senses. He plunged his molten power into her, conforming his spell to her form, until her Will set it in a shape perfectly matched to her inner self.

At last they left no facet of her undefended. His construct was everywhere, powerful and flexible, resting lightly in her thoughts with the strength to repel any trespasser. He had only to seal the spell with one wave of power to complete the work.

He needed no words to tell her he must drink from her again. She needed no words to tell him she wanted his fangs in her throat. He sank his canines into her and sucked long draughts of blood from her vein to feed the final surge of magic. It was safe now to lose control.

He let go. His magic crashed through the veins of the spell. The ward held her fast, and he knew nothing could ever hurt her. Not even him.

His climax shattered every nerve and muscle in his body into fragments of pleasure. He ground into her, his body, mind, and magic pounding with release.

Her fortified mind enclosed the cascade of his magic. She drank him and contained him. He replenished himself long and hard on her blood and their climax.

At long last they lay still together. He flexed his jaw, peeled his tongue off of her, and remembered how to separate his fangs from her flesh. He lifted his head.

Before his eyes, the bruising at her throat began to heal. With a pang of concern, he licked his bite until there was no trace of it except the lingering smears of blood on her skin.

He had to recall how to separate their bodies. He pushed against the bed and eased back so he could slide out of her.

She clutched at him frantically.

He stilled. "Not ready to be parted from me, my Grace?"

She let out an inarticulate moan and held him to her.

He needed to care for her in the aftermath of the spell, but he could see he would need to untangle himself from her gradually. He rolled over, keeping their bodies joined, and let her rest on top of him.

She went limp on him, resting her face on his chest, and breathed easy. He sensed the inebriated confusion in her mind. He stroked her hair and waited for her to surface. As they lay there together, he slowly gathered up the tendrils of his power that still threaded through her. Carefully, so she wouldn't feel a shock to have their deep Union severed.

She was so quiet. He monitored her mind to make sure she didn't lose consciousness. At last he sensed her thoughts clearing and her mind returning to awareness.

"Ohh," she muttered. "Ohhh."

"It's all right, my rose. Just take it slow. Give it time." He infused his voice with calm. He wouldn't use his mind magic to calm her, not right now. She needed time and space in her own head. She needed him to give her strength in other ways while she recovered from the spell.

She tried to lift herself on him, but sank back down again.

"Dizzy?" he asked.

"Yes?"

"Are you ready for me to pull out now?" He stroked her hair.

"Suppose we must. Can't spend eternity like this. Alas."

He laughed softly. If she had her sense of humor in this moment, she would be all right. "Well, we can certainly spend a lot of eternity like this. But right now I want to take care of you."

As gently as he could, he separated their bodies and laid her on the bed beside him once more.

"Just lie still and rest," he said.

He went to the washstand and filled it from the tap of clear water. Feeling that the geomagic had sufficiently warmed it, he reached for a cloth and realized the linens weren't unpacked yet. Cursing his thoughtlessness, he summoned a handkerchief out of a pocket of his fallen robes.

He returned to Cassia with the warm, wet cloth. He washed her face, then her neck, then continued down her body with gentle strokes. "All right?"

She gave a slight nod.

When he cleaned her between her legs, he was relieved to find she was not as sensitive as he had feared. There were also no signs of bruises on her hips matching his fingers. Their joining had given her a powerful infusion of his Gift's healing properties. Even so, what they had done had not been easy for her body.

He put the cloth away and wrapped their wool blanket closer to ward off her shivers. "How do you feel now? Honestly."

"That was…"

"Overwhelming?"

"Worth it."

He smiled. "I'm very glad you think so. Because it was one of the most exquisite experiences of my existence, and I would hate to think you didn't enjoy it just as much."

"Seems I enjoyed it a few more times than you did." Her eyes twinkled.

"That's as it should be. I was well compensated, I assure you."

She swallowed. "I'm not sure how I'm going to feel when I try to sit up, though."

"You need to drink some water when you can."

"I'll try."

He helped her sit up. She let out another moan and held her head.

He propped himself behind her, letting her rest against his chest. "Is this what it feels like after a long night of drinking too much?"

"I hate to impugn your excellent care, but this is worse, I'm afraid."

He sighed. "We have just used your mind and body to the extreme. You can expect to feel dizzy, tired, and ill. You will need copious amounts of rest and food."

"I don't want to eat anything at the moment, thank you."

"Some broth later. Your mind mage's orders."

She paused. "I still have the volition to turn my nose up at broth. Clearly my Will is one piece."

His love for her seemed to overflow all the pathways through which his magic had just raged. "As promised."

She reached up and touched his face. "I lose count of your promises, my love. But the ones made with you so deep within me…I am changed."

He held her hand to him. "So am I."

"I would do it again. I will never regret this."

"Then neither will I."

96

Nights Until

NOTIAN WINTER SOLSTICE

9 Annassa, 1597 IS

CHERA'S TEARS

CASSIA WATCHED LIO FALL asleep. She heard his breathing cease and felt his chest go still. Pressing her cheek to his breast, she listened to his heartbeat. Steady, calm. No day terrors. Yet.

This had become her ritual since daylight had returned to Orthros. But this time, she didn't miss him the instant she lost him to the Slumber. She felt him with her, within her. His presence was in her mind, as if he were working thelemancy on her even now.

A relief she hadn't known she needed sank deep into her.

The casting of the mind ward had left her feeling like Knight's training lure after a wrestling match, but it was worth it.

The spell lights joined Lio in sleep as dawn reached into their alcove. Pale winter sun gleamed into the room through the screens that separated their bedchamber from the bathing courtyard.

Even if she had been able to put her foot to the floor, she had no desire to go out into the day. She couldn't imagine getting out of arm's reach of Lio. The spell had left her with a powerful compulsion to be as close to him as possible.

She nestled against his body under the blankets he had unpacked. His skin was warm from the Feast. She lay there with him and waited for sleep.

But no rest gave her reprieve. She was exhausted, but shivery with alertness. It seemed it would take some time for the stimulating effects of Lio's magic to wear off.

She looked up at the ledge over the bed, which served as a shelf, where he had set out a few necessities for her. Books in case she felt equal to reading, flasks of water, and a supply of broth on the geomagical warming plate.

Dutifully, she raised up on an elbow to drink a few sips of water, then collapsed onto the bed with the effort. Without sitting up again, she reached up and got the dictionary Komnena had given her.

Lately she seemed to have hit a wall in her progress learning to read. On a good day, it frustrated her and gave her a headache, so trying it while her mind felt like jelly was most likely a bad idea.

But if she didn't give her mind something to do, it would only wander to what-ifs about her sister.

Besides, if she hoped to learn to read those tempting scrolls in Imperial languages, she must improve her Divine first. Spoken Divine had come naturally to her. She hardly ever spoke Vulgus anymore and was doing her best to forget the language of her birth entirely. But reading was still like pulling teeth.

She had no illusions that she was suited to be a scholar, but she had higher hopes than this for her education. She must do better.

She flipped to the back of the small, thick book, searching for the section of useful common phrases. She would review them again, matching up the words she spoke so often with their written forms.

The dictionary fell open to the parallel calendars of Orthros and Tenebra. The spine was worn there, evidence that Komnena and Cassia had used the section often during their adjustment to Hesperine life. But Cassia had not needed to refer to it in some time.

She was about to turn the page when her eyes fixed on today's date.

She had forgotten. It had not even occurred to her what day this was by Tenebran reckoning.

Far away on the other side of the world, this was the third day of the month of Chera's Tears. The day Cassia had been born, twenty-three years before. The day her mother, Thalia, had died.

Strange twists of fate had ended her mother's life as soon as hers had begun. Lucis had deigned to appear in his concubine's room shortly after the birth. An apostate mage hired to assassinate him had made it through all the palace's defenses. Their duel had taken place at her mother's bedside. Before Lucis's sword had gutted the assassin, the fire spell meant for the king had killed Thalia.

Had Cassia been in the room when it happened? She didn't even know.

For many years of her life, she had stopped thinking about her mother. Without Solia to tell her who Thalia had been, the woman who had given birth to Cassia had become nothing but a weapon for the court gossips to use against her.

She still didn't know very much about her, but she was certain of one thing. Whoever Thalia had been, it was a disservice to her that Tenebra only remembered her as the king's concubine.

Worse still was Cassia's failure to remember her at all.

Tears slid down her face.

"I'm sorry," she whispered into the sacred silence of Hespera's hours of rest.

A DISPLAY OF POWER

"A RE YOU SURE YOU'RE all right on the couch?" Lio asked for
the third time.

"I like it here in the coffee room," Cassia answered. "It's
an entire room for having coffee. Why would I want to be anywhere else?"

"I really think you should be in bed."

"Zoe will be here any minute," Cassia replied, "and she'll worry more
if I'm in bed."

Lio sighed and did not mount further protest. Cassia knew invoking
Zoe settled the matter. What was more, she was exactly right.

"You are a mighty negotiator, my rose," Lio said darkly.

She gave him one of her arch smiles. Then she stuck her tongue
out at him.

He smiled back, but he knew she was trying to be cheerful so he
wouldn't worry. He bent to fluff her cushions and tuck their blanket closer
around her legs. "I'm so sorry that this is the price you must pay for what
we did last night."

"Lio, stop. You talk as if I had to sacrifice an eye. I'm just a little under
the weather, that's all."

He knelt beside the low couch. "Promise me you'll tell me if you feel
worse, so I can take you to the healers?"

"I will most certainly tell you."

"I am giving your mind a complete rest today, and I won't be prying
to see if you're withholding anything from me. Don't tell me you're fine
if you are not."

She put a hand on his arm. "I won't. I'm just achy, and the dizziness isn't gone, and that makes my stomach feel strange. In short, I am worn out." She arched a brow at him. "What a terrible fate, to exhaust myself in a Hesperine's bed."

He kissed her cheek. She would be all right. That didn't mean he felt all right about it. "I'm sorry."

"My love, you should not apologize for anything you did to me last night. It was marvelous. And now we must stop talking about it, because Zoe will be here and we mustn't discuss such things around the sucklings."

Mollified, Lio took a seat on a floor cushion beside the couch. He checked on the coffee brewing on the low, round table. He already had Cassia's broth and Zoe's milk on the warming plate, along with some of their favorite breakfast rolls stuffed with cheese and savory vegetables. Many of their trunks were in the main courtyard, more crates in the hold of the *Lion's Wings*, but he had retrieved the essentials.

"Ready for me to lift the veil and invite the goats to coffee?"

That got a chuckle out of her, and he was glad he had made an effort to find his good humor for her sake. "Yes."

No sooner had he raised the privacy spells than Zoe and the goats galloped into the room. "Lio—?" Whatever she had been about to ask, she halted mid-question, seeing Cassia on the couch. "Cassia, are you all right?"

Lio tried not to look guilty.

Knight had already crossed the room in a flash and was sniffing Cassia all over, whining. She petted him and let him check her over. "I'm fine. Just a little under the weather, but it will pass."

"Has Javed been to see you? Is Lio taking you to the Healing Sanctuary?"

"I don't need a healer, Zoe flower. Just rest." Cassia held out her arms. "Come here."

Zoe was soon snuggled under the blanket with Cassia. Knight lay down faithfully beside the couch, and the goats tucked themselves halfway under his fur. They all made an endearing sight.

"What are you sick with?" Zoe asked.

"Lio said Migration can sometimes make humans sick. The change of atmosphere is a bit sudden for us."

"You have to get enough sleep," Zoe said earnestly. "Humans can choose when to sleep but if you don't decide to sleep enough, you'll get sicker."

"You are a very good girl. Much better than me."

"Well, I can't help falling asleep. If I could stay awake, I guess maybe I might stay up too late sometimes."

Cassia and Lio exchanged amused glances over Zoe's head. Zoe was notorious for resisting the Slumber, asking for more bedtime stories until her eyes closed and sleep claimed her.

"No wonder you didn't get enough sleep," said Zoe, "with Lio casting that spell last night. What was it, Lio? Did Cassia help you? No, wait, Bosko is coming over. He won't want to miss hearing about it. You have to wait and tell both of us so it's fair."

Lio put on his calmest big brother expression and handed Zoe her milk. "What spell?"

"The big spell!" Zoe squealed. "Heaps of magic came through your veils, but we couldn't tell what kind of spell it was. You didn't tell us you were going to cast a big spell last night."

Lio was saved, or perhaps the danger increased, when Bosko charged into the room.

"Did I miss it?" the suckling demanded.

Zoe shook her head. "Lio was just about to tell us."

No, he most decidedly was not. He really was saved when he saw who had brought Bosko. "Uncle! Good moon. Would you like some coffee?"

Uncle Argyros gave him a knowing smile. "I hope I am not intruding on your morning ritual."

"Not at all," Lio said gratefully. "Please, join us."

Uncle Argryos took a seat on one of the couches. Lio poured his uncle some coffee while the sucklings stared at him expectantly.

"I was practicing an advanced mind magic spell," Lio said. "Cassia was helping me. Uncle Argyros taught me how to do it, but I had to put it into practice to get really good at it."

Bosko's face fell. "You mean you were studying?"

"Yes," Uncle Argyros chimed in. "Advanced studies. Only for after initiation."

"I can't wait until our studies are that exciting." Zoe sighed, undimmed.

That made Bosko's expression light up again. "It sounds like learning gets a lot more interesting when you grow up."

Lio's father appeared in the door, like a nocturnal sun blazing into the residence. "Zoe! Bosko! Are you ready to help me unpack the workshop?"

Zoe hesitated. "Maybe we should help another time. Cassia is sick and she might feel left out."

"But Papa promised to make a new cave for you two," Cassia said. "You don't want to sit on the couch all night with me, when you could be building a cave. I'll be happy knowing you and Bosko are having fun."

"I'll keep Cassia company," Aunt Lyta announced, strolling in, "while Apollon helps the sucklings with their cave and Argyros and Lio discuss his studies."

Lio thanked the Goddess that all his family members were expert strategists. He exchanged a grateful look with his father, who appeared amused, although Lio could sense the concern in his aura. The sucklings dashed off with Father and the goats without asking any more questions.

Aunt Lyta sat down beside Uncle Argyros and gave his knee a pat.

"Another successful maneuver, my Grace." He kissed her cheek before he rose to his feet. "A walk on the balcony, Lio?"

Aunt Lyta made a shooing gesture. "The females would like a chat."

"Far be it from me to intrude." Lio tucked Cassia's blanket one more time. "I am being banished from our coffee room, my rose."

"Go and enjoy a mind mage chat with Uncle Argyros. I think a female chat with Aunt Lyta will do me all the good in the world."

Lio didn't want to let her out of his sight, but he knew she was right. He stepped with his uncle up onto the roof.

"Well." Uncle Argyros leaned on the railing, taking in the view of the goddess's statue above.

Lio joined him there, the ice on the rooftop slick beneath his shoes. He would have to clear that off before Cassia could enjoy it up here.

"I have no intention of stirring the veil," his uncle said. "If you have no desire to discuss your casting of last night, it is really no one's affair but yours and Cassia's. Lyta and I simply wished to make ourselves available, should you find us helpful. Or reassure ourselves that you are well, if you do not."

"Thank you, Uncle."

His mentor gave a nod.

Lio started walking, and Uncle Argyros joined him. They followed the curve of the dome around to the other side of the roof.

Lio raised his brows. "So, you could all feel the spell?"

"It was rather like a muffled seismic event."

"Even with all the extra veils I cast."

"All of Haima knows that Firstgift Komnenos was putting his power into practice last night."

Lio gazed down at the rest of the city spread below them. "Let them."

"Indeed. It has been a long time since your youthful experiments caused notorious explosions. Your performance last night was most certainly not a practice session. Attributing it to your studies is an entertaining excuse to divert the sucklings' interest, but every elder Hesperine who took an interest in your casting last veil knows it was the work of an expert. There is no shame in a display of power. In fact, I think we elders need to be reminded more often that you are not a student anymore."

"They cannot know what spell I performed last night."

"No. I have my theory, but again, you need not confirm or deny it unless you so choose."

There were few people in the world, even powerful Hesperines, who could understand the choice Lio and Cassia had made last night. Uncle Argyros and Aunt Lyta might be the only ones.

"Cassia allowed me to cast a mind ward for her."

"A great privilege."

"Yes. We made the decision together. She is very confident in her choice."

"And you?"

"I hate subjecting her to even a moment of discomfort." Lio braced his hands on the railing. "But I am also so deeply relieved."

"I pray Cassia will never need the ward. But I, for one, will Slumber more peacefully knowing you have done this."

"I am very glad to hear that."

"You do not need anyone's approval but Cassia's. However, Lyta and I would like you to know that she granted me the same privilege."

"Have either of you ever regretted that decision?"

"Not in all the centuries since. It was a choice we made in a moment of fear, but not motivated by fear."

"No," Lio said. "By love. And trust."

"Yes," his uncle replied with conviction. "Of course, Lyta also placed her ward on me in return. I have no doubt the night will come when Cassia, whatever her affinity proves to be, will leave her indelible, magical mark on you."

"That night can't come soon enough."

"In the meantime, I believe you will both be pleased with the results of your decision."

"Uncle..." Lio tried to decide how to broach the subject, without discussing anything too private. "The casting surprised me in a number of ways that were not consistent with my academic expectations. I found that Grace influenced the process in ways I did not predict."

"Oh, yes. Grace always does."

He tried to think of how to describe the way Cassia had fed on his magic. The ease with which they had constructed the ward in Union. "She had as much influence over the spell as I did. And it was so much easier than I ever imagined."

"Yes, that is consistent with Lyta's and my experience."

Lio relaxed somewhat. He wanted to ask if Aunt Lyta's Craving had been as severe as a human as Cassia's, but perhaps that was not his place to ask. He would leave it to Cassia to raise the topic with Aunt Lyta if she wished.

At least Lio no longer had to worry about losing control of his magic while he sated her. The ward would contain his power as they feasted. His next magical display for the city wouldn't take place in the bedchamber.

"I plan to cast more master-level spells," Lio said. "I need to be comfortable with their real applications, not just theory."

"Excellent. I like everyone talking about how impressive my nephew is."

Lio laughed. "Thank you for your vote of confidence."

"You always have my vote, Lio."

The arrival of two auras in the courtyard below interrupted their conversation. A head of crimson hair had appeared, and beside it, a shorter figure with dark hair.

Ioustin and Kalos had returned once again.

What would the news be this time? Would it lift or sink Cassia's spirits?

Lio's resolve hardened. He would protect her from anything that could hurt her. Even her sister.

THE STRENGTH IN EVERY SPELL

CASSIA WRAPPED HER COLD fingers tightly around her warm mug of coffee. Her stomach wanted none of it. But she could still hold the cup and smell the coffee, even if she was deprived of drinking it.

She felt wretched, she couldn't have her moon hours coffee, and now all of this.

"Well, let everyone gossip," Cassia said. "This is Orthros, not a virgin mage's vestibule in Tenebra. It shouldn't surprise anyone that Lio and I were up to something last night, and we needn't apologize."

Aunt Lyta had a good laugh. "Hear, hear. But if it reassures you, all anyone knows is that Lio was showing off his power last night. No one but Argyros and I have a real idea what the nature of his spell was."

"Oh." Cassia hated that she was blushing.

"I didn't come to pry," Aunt Lyta reassured her. "I just wanted to ask if you're doing all right. I was weak as a kitten after Argyros cast his mind ward on me, and weakness makes me miserable. And angry." She smiled fondly. "Of course, I did use quite a bit of magic myself, putting my own ward on him."

"You can do that?"

"Yes." Her smile widened, although she didn't elaborate on the nature of the spell she had exchanged for her Grace's mind ward.

Cassia looked away. "I hate this. I don't have the power to protect Lio in return. I'm not even a mage, as you were when you were human. Weakness does make me miserable and angry."

"I know. Although I had magic as a human, I still felt...young. Untested compared to Argyros. His Hesperine nature seemed so much more powerful than my human one. I was only eighteen, you know. He was two decades older in years and much more advanced in magical study, not to mention cultural sophistication. He was a temple scholar, I a horse trader from a country village."

"I didn't realize how different your lives were before you met."

"The Last War had a way of equalizing Hespera worshipers. We were all reduced to refugees."

"But soon you were both Hesperines. You chose that power so you could defeat your enemies."

Cassia had to wonder if Lyta's Craving had been so troublesome as a human. But perhaps she hadn't been human long enough after meeting Argyros for it to become so severe. Komnena had told Cassia that she had pined for Apollon terribly before her Gifting.

Aunt Lyta touched her hand. "Don't underestimate your importance to this family. To Lio. You have great power over him, Cassia. No less than he has over you. You're the reason he is alive. You are the strength in his every spell."

That reassurance, at last, quieted Cassia's doubts. She nodded. "Thank you for reminding me."

Aunt Lyta took a swig of her coffee. "There's another thing that will remind you how strong you are."

"What might that be?" Cassia needed all the encouragement she could get.

"Battle training," Aunt Lyta said. "When you've recovered from the mind ward, why don't you join us in the arena? Take it from me. Strengthening your body will make you more confident about everything."

For Aunt Lyta and the other warriors, perhaps. Cassia doubted she was suited to the battle arts, but Aunt Lyta was kind to offer. "Thank you for the invitation. Once I'm feeling better, I'll try to do that."

"The speires I gave you are ready when you are."

"I'm sorry I haven't yet used the Stand's gifts."

"You were busy defeating enemy necromancers. You're forgiven."

Cassia laughed a little. But she had to wonder, was Nike forgiven? When would she and her mother make peace?

She was trying to think of how to ask, when her attention from the conversation wavered. She felt a familiar warmth in her mind, drawing nearer.

Whenever Lio was in the room, she usually had the feeling that he was near, even if she couldn't see or hear him. But this was something more. She could sense his presence approaching, as if something within her own mind brightened the nearer he came. It was more powerful and more precise than any vague awareness she'd ever had of magic at work around her.

"Already enjoying your new mind ward?" Aunt Lyta asked.

Cassia focused on her physical surroundings, a blush coming to her cheeks again. "With this, I might be able to endure the remaining time I must spend as a human. I can sense that Lio will walk through that door in three…two…one…"

"He's not alone," Aunt Lyta warned her, the instant before the others entered the coffee room.

Uncle Argyros had returned with Lio, but so had Ioustin and Kalos.

And there Cassia was, barely able to lift her head, feeling utterly unequal to hearing whatever Kalos had to say.

Lio was already at her side, pulling his cushion closer to the couch so he could hold her hand. Uncle Argyros returned to his seat beside Lyta, their presences a powerful support.

Ioustin sat down on the unoccupied couch across from Cassia. "Kalos has not finished his search, but he has some information for you."

Kalos stood at the edge of their gathering, looking uncomfortable. Did he ever feel at home in their homeland? Perhaps Castra Justa was home to him, and the Charge his people. But here he was in Orthros, standing apart as if he were an interloper. There was room around Cassia's dread for empathy.

She chose which one should grow. "Welcome home. Please, come join us."

Kalos glanced around at the silk couches and tasseled cushions and plush carpets. "I…I shouldn't stay."

"We haven't seen you in weeks. You've come so far."

"Our door is always open to you, Kalos." Lio poured two more cups of coffee.

Knight was clearly ready to break the ice. His nostrils were flared, his ears perked. Cassia reached down under the cover of her blanket and gave him a surreptitious double-tap behind his shoulder.

He jumped up to greet Kalos, his tail wagging. The scout dropped to a crouch and rubbed Knight's ears with both hands. As Knight licked his face, Kalos muttered to him in the ancient liegehound training language, which none of the other Hesperines understood. Only Cassia could tell he was praising Knight with as much silly affection as Zoe showed her goats.

Knight's display clearly put Kalos more at ease, and it helped Cassia as well. A little kindness was an antidote for anything, even what she might be about to hear.

Kalos took a floor cushion, crossing his legs. "I came to ask the prince's permission before I continue my search."

Ioustin looked at Cassia. "I thought you would want to know what he has found so far."

Kalos scratched Knight's chest. "With all respect, My Prince, part of a trail can often be misleading about where it will end up."

"Indeed, but Cassia has often made it clear she does not find ignorance to be bliss."

Cassia's stomach turned over. She truly didn't wish to be sick in front of the First Prince, even if he was to be her Ritual father. She swallowed hard. "I'd rather know what information you have, even if it is incomplete. Thank you for not withholding anything."

"If you're certain." Kalos sighed. He hesitated so long, she wasn't sure if he would go on. "She and the man went south, as I said before. They kept going. All the way to the border. Their trail leads into Cordium."

"*Cordium?*" Cassia choked out. "Why would she go to the Magelands?"

Amid her own horror, she felt something else. Like a storm ready to rise around her, one that made her safe, wrapped in the eye of such raging power.

Lio. Where his magic intertwined with her mind, she was aware of the furor in his thoughts, his determination to protect her. She gripped his hand.

Kalos studied the rug at his feet. "I'm sorry, Cassia. When I tracked her departure from the siege site, I...I missed something."

Once again, empathy welled out of her. She had never suspected, in the cruel years of her life, that empathy could make difficult things easier for her, as well as for others. But it did. So very much. "You've been following the fifteen-year-old trail of a mortal. It would be easy to miss something. I'm just thankful for your skill, because any other scout would have found nothing at all."

He cleared his throat. "It was the siege engines that threw me off. Fire magic residue everywhere. That's why I didn't realize that the mage who performed the traversal had an affinity for fire."

This was the problem with hope. It burned easily.

"A war mage took her?" Cassia hated how her voice wavered. "To Cordium?"

Kalos's shoulders slumped. "So it appears."

Lyta let out a furious curse against their enemies. Her anger comforted Cassia somehow. Anger was always easier than despair.

"We shouldn't make too many assumptions until we have all the evidence." Lio's voice was so calm. Her comfort.

But the evidence was clear. The man with Solia had been a fire mage. His destination had been Cordium. Those details recast her victorious escape into a fate worse than Cassia had imagined. A war mage, one of the king's allies, had taken her prisoner and made her disappear.

The Aithourian Circle wanted Lucis on the throne for their own ends, and they had no scruples about what they must do to keep him there. They had given him the catapults that violated their own laws. What would they do to a traitor princess, a woman who dared defy Anthros's Order?

Cassia's head spun, and her ears roared, threatening that she might faint. "Did he hurt her? Can you tell from their trail?"

"I know she was alive when they reached the border of Tenebra and Cordium."

Cassia mustn't lose consciousness, not until she finished asking the important questions. "What happened to her after that?"

"I don't know yet," Kalos answered kindly. "I could not cross into Cordium until I secured the prince's mandate. As you know, no Hesperine errant is allowed to enter the Magelands unless authorized by the First Prince."

"Of course." Her vision was starting to fade.

A cool, bracing current flowed through her. The spinning stopped, her belly calmed, and her mind cleared. Ioustin hadn't moved, but she recognized Hesperine healing magic. Javed's was strong, but Ioustin's was deep as all the snow in Orthros and as gentle as a single flurry.

"Cordium is not a death sentence for everyone," Ioustin said.

Those words would not have meant much from anyone else, but hearing them from Methu's Trial brother was powerful. She knew what it cost him to encourage her hope. "Thank you."

"Kalos." The prince was grave. "Would you consider traveling with allies for the rest of your search?"

"I work best alone, My Prince. Company will only slow me down—and make me easier to detect."

"Would you not accept assistance from the envoys?"

"Their way of searching is different from mine. But I'll share my findings with them when I return."

"Very well. You have my permission to enter Cordium. You are currently the only Hesperine who is sanctioned to go errant there."

"I appreciate what a sign of your trust that is, My Prince."

"Do not put it to the test. If you must choose between your safety and completing your search, retreat."

"Yes, My Prince." Kalos glanced in Cassia's direction. "I'll do my best."

"You don't have to go." The words pained her, but Cassia would never forgive herself if she failed to say them. "I won't ask anyone to risk their lives for my answers. The war mages are even more dangerous to Hesperines than to my sister. Orthros has already lost enough of our people to the Aithourians."

"You never asked," Kalos said.

Cassia wanted to throw her arms around him and hold him and tell him to be safe. But she doubted he would appreciate that demonstration as much as he liked Knight's greetings.

Kalos's trail would be much less lonely with a liegehound at his side. Why must Cassia be the only Hesperine who had a faithful companion like Knight? Then and there, she decided she would find a hound for Kalos. That was a gesture that would mean something to him.

"May the Goddess's Eyes light your path," Lio told Kalos.

Argyros completed the blessing. "And her darkness keep you in Sanctuary."

"I'll go now." Kalos didn't stop to brush the liegehound fur from his clothes before he stepped away.

"Cassia." Lio put his finger under her chin, tilting her face toward his.

She searched his gaze, wanting to find what she needed there.

"It's not over," he promised.

There was her solace. Even when she was ready to surrender, Lio would not.

"Lio is right," said Uncle Argyros. "Nike's safe return is proof that miracles are possible."

Aunt Lyta nodded. "Everything you've told us about Solia makes it clear she's always been a fighter. Don't give up on her."

"Thank you," was all Cassia could say. She appreciated their words, even if she couldn't bring herself to believe them.

"I'm sorry." Ioustin had seldom appeared so downcast. "There is little I can do to soften such a blow. But I can perform more healing on you to help you feel stronger."

"Would you please consider it?" Lio asked her softly.

All Cassia wanted was for everyone to leave and let Lio hold her. But she couldn't refuse Ioustin's aid when Lio pled with her so tenderly.

"Well done on the mind ward, Lio," Ioustin put in. "I can tell how careful you were. Not that I'm surprised. That's why Cassia is doing so well."

Apparently Cassia was not too ill to blush again.

"I'm a mind healer," Ioustin said kindly. "Naturally, I can tell there's a mind ward on you."

"She's doing well?" Lio asked.

"Remarkably well," Ioustin confirmed.

Lio let out a breath.

"I'm afraid I can't entirely banish the mental effects," Ioustin went on. "That would require healing in all the reaches of your mind where Lio worked his magic—where I would never trespass. The best I can do is assuage the physical effects, which should speed your recovery."

Ioustin was right. She could bear all of this better if her body was not so beleaguered. "I would appreciate that."

This time, the flurry became a gust, one that filled her sails. Uncle Argyros and Aunt Lyta stayed with them for the duration of Ioustin's healing session. After half an hour, her illness had lifted, leaving her only with a deep weariness of spirit. At last, their concerned elders left them to themselves.

Lio rearranged the cushions, joining her on the couch so she could lean back against him instead. Knight rested his head on her belly, within easy reach for petting.

Cassia lay there in silence for a long while, fighting the tears, unable to put words to the roil of feelings within her. She, who had once been able to armor herself against the very worst, was laid bare by this disappointment.

"Why did it have to be today?" were the words that finally came out of her.

"I know." Lio stroked her hair. "It was much harder to hear all of that when you're still ill from the mind ward."

"No! That's not what I meant. The mind ward is…" Her only armor left. "I'm glad I had that today."

"Cassia…" She heard the frown in his voice. "Is there something I don't know about today?"

She stroked his arm where it was draped over her, her vision blurring with tears. "The day my mother died."

He startled against her. "Your birthday?"

"No. I don't have a birthday yet. But I will once we choose a new night for my Gifting."

He kissed the top of her hair, his arm steady around her. "I'm so sorry, my Grace. Your grief runs in my veins."

A vigil they had shared in Solia's memory had been the occasion when Cassia had begun to remember her mother. She had talked about Thalia with Lio as she had never done with anyone. Then, as now, he had been her comfort.

"I had started to hope I wasn't the only woman who has survived Lucis. But it seems I am, after all."

"Don't give up, my rose."

"I won't," she swore.

Cassia was still standing. And with Lio's mind ward, she was less vulnerable. Less mortal. More Hesperine.

Her hope for Solia had been dashed. But she hadn't given up on herself.

94

Nights Until

NOTIAN WINTER SOLSTICE

12 Annassa, 1597 IS

A BRANCH OF THORNS

MAK RARELY BOTHERED TO keep a veil spell on his emotions. He usually spoke his mind and made his feelings known. In his experience, secrecy just overcomplicated things that could be easily solved by getting to the point.

He paused in the doorway of his father's Notian library, letting his unconcealed aura announce his presence. From within the layers of veils that wrapped the quiet room, his father's aura brightened. "Come in, Son."

Mak could remember many occasions in the past when his father had not sounded so cheerful upon his arrival in the library. He had dreaded getting summoned to Father's sanctum for one of his stern-but-loving talks. Since then, Mak had come to appreciate that those had always been more loving than stern, but it didn't feel that way to you when you were a naughty suckling and your father was Silvertongue. Mak was glad he was no longer the naughty suckling of the family, although he was none too pleased that Bosko had taken on the role.

Now Mak eagerly crossed the room with a step to the back alcove where his father sat at his desk. "Nike took my suggestion about going for a ride. Did you manage to convince Mother to go to the stables so they 'accidentally' end up there at the same time?"

Father set down his quill, slumping back in his chair. "Your mother was just there. As soon as she and Nike encountered each other, they both decided they had urgent duties elsewhere."

"Thorns. I thought that if anything could ease tensions between them, some time around the horses would. You've said how many happy memories they have there."

"It was worth a try." His father heaved a sigh.

Mak's gaze fell to the mess all over the desk. Father was buried in dispatches from diplomats and envoys. There were two empty cups abandoned in the chaos. He was very busy indeed if he wasn't stopping to rinse out his precious coffee cups. The whole room smelled like stale Polar Night Roast and paper stained with Tenebran rain.

Mak glanced around at the state of his father's usually immaculate library. Light shone through the half-moon stained glass windows near the ceiling, gleaming on black, red, and silver inlays, which adorned the gray stone walls and the shelves carved into them. The Goddess Eyes peered into scroll racks there, revealing many to be empty.

Half the reference texts in the library had found a new home on the desk and the side tables in the alcove. Mak had to wonder how even so great a scholar as his father could read that many scrolls at the same time without confusing himself.

It seemed the whole world was having a fit, and it fell to Father, as usual, to be the voice of reason. Mak wished his loved ones could have a moment's peace so they could enjoy having Nike home and try to cheer up Cassia.

Mak scowled at his father's correspondence. "Is this Imperial or Tenebran?"

His father appeared pleased, although there was a hint of surprise in his aura. Mak didn't blame him. It was only recently that he'd made a point to ask Father about his work.

"I may have no interest in diplomacy," Mak said, "but I do have an interest in whether you're all right."

"Thank you, Son."

The warmth that filled the Blood Union told Mak his father had lowered some more veils. Thorns, that was a good feeling.

"Well," his father said, "there is more than the usual business to attend to with our Imperial allies upon our return to the south. The Empress's policy of isolation from Tenebra is still very much a subject of discussion between the Empire and Orthros."

"I'm sure it is, since Orthros's mortal guests from both the Empire and Tenebra had contact during the Solstice Summit. I know it was a point of contention."

"And yet, that discussion is almost relaxing compared to the dispatches from the envoys."

Mak gestured at a pile of dispatches bearing veiled blood seals. "This the latest onslaught since we found out the war mages took Solia to Cordium?"

"As you can imagine, the envoys are reevaluating everything. The mere suggestion that Hesperines might infiltrate Cordium to rescue the rightful Queen of Tenebra from the Mage Orders allied with the current king is…" His father shook his head.

"Like putting all the most volatile materials in the forge and watching the explosion. And you get the lovely job of regulating the temperature."

"Are those ingredients safe at any temperature?"

"No."

His father gave him a salute and a wry smile.

Every time another dispatch landed on that pile on Father's desk, Mak only became more determined to be the one who helped him heal the rift between Mother and Nike. At least they could have peace in their home while the world went up in flames.

"All right," Mak said. "Next plan. What else can we try to get Mother and Nike to talk to each other?"

"Patience."

Mak sighed. "Not the strong suit of us warriors."

"I beg to differ. You were very patient about helping Lio and me reconcile this past Winter Solstice."

Mak smiled at the praise. "For a couple of mind mages, you two were a lot less stubborn about it than Mother and Nike."

His father chuckled. "The tenacity of diplomats is great, but no one is as stubborn as the Guardian of Orthros and her First Master Steward. Except perhaps the other Stewards."

Mak huffed a laugh. "I try."

His father's dark eyes gleamed with amusement. "I begin to think you inherited a taste for conspiracy from me, though. Thank you for helping me try to bring your mother and sister together."

"I'm glad to help."

Mak had tried to make peace years ago with the fact that his father would never completely understand him. He had done his best to accept that it was all right if he did not win his father's approval in all things.

But he still wanted it, and right now, he had it. They were on the same side in family matters for a change.

It would stay that way as long as Father didn't find out what Mak had been up to at Nike's forge. Guilt crept in on him, and this was one of the rare occasions when he pulled a veil around his emotions.

It wasn't hard to disguise all of that under his very real frustration. "Mother is so happy that Nike's home. And I can tell Nike missed her something fierce. They love each other. What will it take for them to admit that and realize their anger is just getting in their way?"

Father stroked his chin. "Nothing short of a conversation with their fists, I think."

"Oh, Goddess." That settled it. The world had definitely exploded. "Really, Father? *You* think a fistfight is the best solution?"

Father laughed, his fangs flashing in the spell light. "Not a mere brawl. They are both too disciplined to resort to simple violence to vent their tempers. We need to bring them to what has always been their negotiation table, where they can speak with each other in their mother tongue. They need a debate on their home ground, with the battle arts as their mediator."

"You're talking about a proper sparring match in the arena." Mak shook his head. "I'd love to see that. But Nike hasn't practiced with us once since she's been home, even though Kadi has begged her to. Not even Alkaios and Nephalea can talk her into it."

"Have you asked her?"

"I didn't want to…push her too much, I suppose." No matter how tempted he had been to ask her to show him some moves when they were at the forge without an audience.

"Trust your wisdom about people, Mak. You have a great deal of it."

"It means a great deal that you think so, Father." Yes, Mak could grow used to that approval. He tried not to think of the forge.

"If you find the right time to ask Nike about sparring, I think she'll respond differently to an invitation from you."

Mak paused to consider. "If I can convince Nike to come to the arena, do you think you can persuade Mother to stay for it?"

"Certainly. Lyta would never stand down from any challenge in her own arena."

"Good plan. I'll do everything I can to cajole Nike into giving us a demonstration of her skills." Mak's grin returned. "Goddess knows I'm looking forward to it."

"To think, you've never seen Nike in battle. She is an artist, as surely as your mother is. Their match will exceed your expectations, and I know how high they are."

The horns that marked the hours in Haima now sounded beyond the library, their stirring tones echoing over the city from House Kitharos.

"Time for my patrol," Mak said.

"Is it? You and Lyros were on duty last night. I thought Alkaios and Nephalea were due to check the ward."

"There's a new residence they wanted to view, and tonight was when the architect could meet with them. Lyros and I offered to cover their patrol."

"That was kind of you two. I admit, I'd rather our newest tributaries establish a permanent residence here in House Argyros, but it's good for them to explore and decide what their future should hold."

"I hope they decide to stay, too."

"Their presence would be most welcome to Lyta and me, especially since you and Lyros have your southern residence at House Timarete. Of course, you must have a residence in both the houses of your elder bloodlines. We do not begrudge Lyros's family your company…much."

"Bosko is enough to fill ten residences." But it was nice to be missed.

His father laughed. "True."

"After Lyros and I are off duty for the night, I'll find Nike and try again."

"Thank you, Mak." His father stood and rounded the desk, pulling him in for an embrace.

Mak hugged him back. "We'll get them talking yet."

"Between the two of us, I believe we will."

Mak left through the back doors that led out to the rooftop terrace, letting them shut behind him. He paused to enjoy the sight of his Grace waiting for him. Lyros lounged against the railing, his lean, muscular arms crossed over his chest, his long, tan legs stretched out before him in the warm glow of the lanterns.

Mak strolled closer. "You seem relieved to have escaped your sister's art symposium."

Lyros sighed. "I don't know how my siblings shackle me into these things."

"It must have been at least a little bit interesting. All that talk of sculpting buttocks."

"They spent too much time on breasts."

"Oh, well that's boring."

"You, on the other hand, didn't seem in a hurry to escape your father's library. You had another good conversation."

"Yes, actually."

"I'm glad, my Grace. It's good to see the two of you in agreement about things that matter. Besides me."

"True, Father and I have always seen eye-to-eye about that. You're the best thing that's ever happened to me."

Lyros smiled at him slowly. The left side of his mouth always lifted a little higher than his right, showing off more of that fang. "Suddenly you look like a newly avowed youngblood who just got back from his Gracemoon."

"Can you blame me? You know what the sight of you in regalia does to me." Mak rested both hands on the railing on either side of Lyros. The Stand's short, black fighting robes had always seemed made for his Grace's athletic body. Lyros might come from a family of artists, but he had been destined for the art of battle.

Lyros didn't uncross his arms, his green eyes teasing. "You see me in regalia every night."

"And every night is our Gracemoon, as far as I'm concerned. I plan to be newly avowed to you for the rest of eternity."

"Say that to me again later when we aren't headed out on patrol." Lyros gave Mak's chin a gentle bite.

A shiver traveled over Mak's skin, and he leaned closer. "How about the minute we're done with our patrol?"

"At a certain deserted cove, perhaps?"

Grinning, Mak stood back and gave Lyros a salute. That was one of the benefits of being Stewards. They found all sorts of remote places along

Orthros's edges where no one else set foot. Border patrol could be very romantic when you served with your Grace.

Hand in hand, Mak and Lyros stepped away from House Argyros to begin their routine. They landed at the first checkpoint, the bluff over Sisters' Port that stretched farthest out to sea. Ice crunched under their sandals as they walked out on the narrow outcropping. Far below, the docks glittered with spell lights, and ships slipped in and out of the Veins.

Like an affectionate greeting from the Queens, the nearest node of the ward called to Mak's magic from where it was anchored out to sea. The Annassa had built up points of concentrated magic at intervals along their defenses, nodes that both strengthened their spell and offered the Stand powerful gateways for connecting with the ward.

One could levitate or sail out to the ward's perimeter if need be, but the nodes were so powerful, the Stewards could make use of them from the nearest shoreline. Besides, with solid ground under their feet, they could devote all their concentration to the ward.

Lyros slid his fang over his palm and offered his hand to Mak. The libation to join with the ward was sacred, but they hadn't technically started the spell yet. And Grace was sacred, too. With a mischievous grin, Mak snatched Lyros's hand to his mouth and licked the blood slowly from his Grace's skin.

Lyros tugged at his grip half-heartedly, laughing. "That blood was dedicated to the ward, you heretic."

"Not anymore."

"You had a snack before we left our residence."

"Now I've had another one."

Lyros laughed again and made a lunge. Mak knew this move, but he let Lyros make it and was rewarded with a bite on his earlobe.

"Ouch," he said happily. "No biting in the arena."

"We're not in the arena." Lyros stepped back, licking a drop of Mak's blood off his lips.

Mak cleared his throat. "All right. Libation. Patrol."

"Cove."

"Patrol first, you handsome distraction."

"I seem to recall you're the one who started the distractions."

Mak dutifully bit his palm and held it out. Lyros repeated the gesture and clasped his hand. Their blood mingled, and Lyros's magic came to attention in their Union. Mak raised his own warding magic and joined it with his Grace's matching affinity. Comfort surrounded him, and their combined power flowed through him, making him feel as tall as the cliff they stood upon.

Together they stretched their senses out toward the Queens' masterpiece, and its currents drew them in. Although they only shared Annassa Alea's affinity for warding, not the combination of warding and light magic that defined her rare status as a Sanctuary mage, the sacrificial nature of Sanctuary magic invited them to participate in her spell.

Mak supposed most Hesperines thought of the ward as a monolithic thing, but it wasn't. It was complex, with variations in pattern and texture, eternal and changeable. Like a shield forged of adamas, but also like one of the waves crashing into the Veins, or the frost in the ground that never melted.

They connected with the node. Power surged through Mak's veins, but he and Lyros stood steady, trained to withstand the massive magic. A thrill traveled through him, filling his lungs and pebbling his skin. If he had felt tall as a cliff an instant before, now he felt as vast as Orthros.

He could encircle the whole land with his arms. He held all their people within his magic. He saw and knew every precious stretch of frozen ground, every powerful Hesperine heartbeat.

Each night that he served as a Steward only strengthened his conviction. He would go far beyond the call of duty to protect his home. Lyros's hand tightened in his, a silent promise that they would always stand together.

Mak's eyes slid shut, and he opened his auric gaze. Queen Alea's light magic gave him sight, and Queen Soteira's affinity for the mind turned the ward into one great vein of the Blood Union.

As if he flew over the water, his mind's eye swept along the perimeter of the ward. He sensed every nearby sea creature with a heartbeat, their auras flowing and leaping through the Blood Union. Although he and Lyros cast their magic in opposite directions, Lyros felt close, bound up in the ward with him.

Mak scanned the waters below and the horizon afar for anything eventful, such as a lost boat or a whale that swam too far into the warmer waters inside the ward. He performed the required check for cracks or melting on the ice sculptures, although he had never found one.

There were no heart hunters with vicious mongrels to worry about. No mages bent on setting Hesperines on fire. Border patrol in the south was so relaxing.

"All clear," Mak announced.

"All clear," Lyros confirmed.

They surfaced from the ward, both panting a little from the sheer force of the magic.

"It's going to be a quiet night," said Mak. "You want to take the western nodes while I do the east?"

"Then meet at the cove?"

"Mm hmm."

Goddess, how did Lyros manage to make a salute look suggestive? He stepped away at record speed.

Mak stepped eastward to the next checkpoint, a stony stretch of beach at the foot of the bluffs. It was narrow, but at low tide you could ride all around the base of the Veins here. Perhaps he would suggest that to Lyros for after their next patrol.

Mak paused to savor the quiet. Nothing but the rush of the waves and the power of the ward nearby. He supposed he could see why some warriors found border patrol boring. But Mak enjoyed it out here. When he was on patrol, he was always comfortable in his own skin. He knew his place in the world. His purpose.

The flash of another aura nearby disrupted his thoughts.

What is it? Lyros asked.

There was no mistaking the Victory Star. *Nike is out here.*

Nike is joining us for border patrol? Now it was Lyros who sounded as excited as a green trainee.

Mak had never forged a connection with a node so quickly. But the magic that flowed into him linked him only to his Grace. His sister had not joined with the Queens' spell. *I'm not sure she's here for Stand duty.*

He sensed Lyros's agreement. *She's also not using the ward to check and see who else is out here.*

She must not be expecting to meet anyone.

Mak, are you about to try to sneak up on the Victory Star?

No. I'm going to find out what she's here for.

By sneaking up on her.

Mak hesitated a moment, then veiled himself. Sneaking up on your elder sister and nosing in her business were expected behaviors from younger brothers, he reasoned.

Also, he was a Steward on border patrol, and it was expected that he would have a friendly word and check on the welfare of any Hesperine approaching the border on his watch.

Not that anyone ever chose a spot like this to cross. The gates to the Empire hadn't even opened for the season, and once they did, all traffic would come and go from the docks.

Maybe she's just out here for a ride, Lyros mused.

Maybe. But he doubted it.

On the dry, icy air, Mak caught an incongruous scent.

What do you smell? Lyros asked.

Myrrh? Mak sniffed again. *I think? It's not quite like the stuff Orthros gets from the Empire. There's something off about it.*

Do you want me to come with you, my Grace?

I think this is another occasion when I should try to talk to Nike alone, especially since I'm going to ask her questions she doesn't want to answer.

You can probably get away with it, Lyros said, *since you're her favorite brother.*

I'm her only brother. Blood brother, anyway.

Exactly.

Mak levitated around the cliffside toward Nike's aura. He held his veils steady, and like a little spell hiding under a bigger one, let the ward obscure his approach.

Even so, he was rather shocked that he did, in fact, manage to sneak up on her. She had let down her guard tonight. Was that a good sign?

No, it was a bad sign that the only place she lowered her defenses was a deserted beach where she expected to be the only soul for miles.

He landed soundlessly a couple of paces away from her and frowned at what he saw.

"I cannot believe you made it this far, you mangy thing." She cradled a bird in her arms.

It was a vulture. Mak wrinkled his nose at the sight. There was no death in Orthros. There were no scavengers, either.

There was something even more unnatural about this one than its mere presence in the land of immortality. It was docile in Nike's hold, as if there were nowhere it would rather be. When it shifted in Nike's arms, as if making itself comfortable there, the fragrance of myrrh puffed into the air.

As Mak watched, she removed a metal cylinder from its leg. Tightly rolled papers levitated out of the document case and hovered at her shoulder while she refilled the tube with the very scrolls Mak had seen her writing all week.

She paused to run a hand through the bird's feathers. Something about it bothered Mak. It was too still. Too quiet.

Silent, in fact. Because it didn't have a heartbeat.

No heartbeat. No blood flowing through its veins. It was bloodless, an undead creature with no life of its own, reanimated by a necromancer's power. There was a reason "bloodless vulture" was the foulest insult a Hesperine could think of.

"Nike?" Mak asked. "Why in the Goddess's name are you holding a *literal* bloodless vulture?"

She stared at him, frozen, like a suckling caught raiding the gumsweets.

"Cup and thorns," she said calmly. "You should know better than to startle a Steward. I might have flattened you."

"Your hands are full."

"I could flatten you with my hands in blood shackles behind my back."

"What is that thing doing here?"

"What are you doing out here, Mak? It's Alkaios and Nephalea's night to patrol."

"Lyros and I swapped with them." He rubbed the back of his head.

So she hadn't expected to run into anyone out here—except Alkaios and Nephalea. They must already know the secret of the undead creature. A secret Nike was hiding from her own family.

"I have a standing invitation to your secret forge," said Mak. "You might as well tell me about the bloodless vulture."

"No, Mak. Knowing about my forge does not mean I'll tell you everything." She sighed and released the bird. It flopped down to the pebbly beach at her feet and ruffled its feathers, then began to preen a bit. "But since you are a Steward and you have sighted a bloodless vulture in Orthros on your patrol, I am required to give you an explanation."

"And I'm required to report it."

"Will you?"

"Of course I will. I might just…wait a few years, or decades."

"This is why you don't get to know everything, Mak. Because it will only add to the list of what you aren't reporting to Mother. I won't be responsible for tarnishing your service record any more than I already have."

"Let me worry about that. On behalf of the Stand, I have to ask you to please explain your undead avian, Firstgift."

She pressed her lips together, narrowing her eyes at him. "Stubborn youngblood."

He grinned at her.

"It's a messenger," she said.

"From where? Hypnos's realm?"

"From Cordium."

Mak stared at the bird, which cocked its head and gave him a friendly glance with its beady little eye. "That flew all the way from Cordium? *Through the ward?*"

"I levitated out and brought it inside the ward." She gave it a smirk, clearly impressed. "But yes, this bag of bones did hold up from Corona to here."

"You brought a necromancer's pet from the capital of the Magelands into the ward. Cup and thorns, if you weren't you, Nike, I really would have to report this."

But Mak knew, the way he knew the ward would stand forever, that Nike would never do anything to endanger Orthros. If she thought it was safe to bring that thing inside the ward, then it was.

The vulture spread its wings, hopped a couple of times, then unceremoniously took flight.

"No rest for the weary," Nike said. "Goddess light your path, old thing."

"That's what you've been writing? Letters? To…a spy? A contact?"

She pursed her lips, watching the strange bird fly away. "An ally," she admitted.

Mak was silent for a moment, stunned. What kind of ally used a bloodless creature for a messenger? With allies like those, Nike hardly needed enemies. He had known she would search for Methu at any cost, but he hadn't imagined this.

"Does this mean you haven't given up on your quest?" he asked.

"I am evaluating. I hope my ally can provide me with information to aid me in making a decision."

No wonder she had been so engrossed in those letters. "I'm glad you had someone helping you Abroad."

Her eyes returned to him, opaque again.

"Oh, thorns, Nike, you can ease up on the veils a bit, you know. I already know your worst secret, and it's hard to have a conversation with you when your aura is as hard as adamas."

At that, she laughed, and he added a point to his score. He was even better than Kadi at getting a laugh out of Nike.

Her combination of wards and veils eased off, lightening the pressure on his magical senses.

And there she was, the real her. She was as patient as a steed about to burst from the starting gate of a race, as powerful as a blow on the nose from the Chalice of Stars, as hot-tempered as her forge. But under all of that, she was as deep and soulful as the snows of Orthros. She could be so still, like that snow. But when a snowstorm arrived, he'd best watch out.

Mak grinned. "Well met, sister."

She tossed her hand up in the salute to the victor. "You don't know my worst secret, though."

"Oh? Care to share?"

Her gaze drifted after the bird again. Mak could just make out its black wings on the horizon, at the edge of his sharp Hesperine eyesight. Her eyes narrowed, and he felt a hint of that storm in her aura, as if she really was about to tell him a dark secret.

But she seemed to change her mind. "Orthros's meatless mincemeat pies aren't my favorite food."

252 ❧ *Vela Roth*

He put a hand to his mouth in mock horror. "Are you even a Hesperine?"

"I've been Abroad too long, clearly."

"Next you'll tell me Father's coffee isn't the best beverage in the world."

"Never! I'd fight a duel in defense of our bloodline's fine coffees."

Mak heaved a dramatic sigh of relief. "You haven't entirely become an errant barbarian, then." He scratched his head. "What is your favorite food, though?" He could already imagine him and Cassia coming up with some kind of picnic to make Nike feel welcome.

"Vegetable soup."

Well, that would be easy. "How can you possibly like vegetable soup better than mince pie?"

"Not just any soup. It's the secret recipe of a mage who only serves it out of his own kitchen."

"My sister, frequenting some mage's soup kitchen? Where is this apostate holed up?"

"Oh, he's no apostate. Quite cozy with the higher ups in the Orders. He has a nice place in the manor district in Corona."

Oh. Soup was her worst secret after all.

Nike hadn't merely been corresponding with a mage in Cordium. She had been there herself.

Mak had surmised as much. Where but Cordium would she search for Methu? Where else would she have found his sword?

But now she had admitted it aloud.

Mak let out a low whistle. Her eyes dared him, but there was a hint of bitterness there.

He nodded. "That's why you couldn't let Rudhira find you."

"I had a choice between letting him wonder if I was dead or letting him drag me out of Cordium and arrest me for regularly entering the Magelands without his sanction."

"He wouldn't have arrested you, surely."

"He's the Prince Regent of Orthros Abroad. He can't bend his own Charge Law for his Trial Sister. Least of all for me. And I'm the First Master Steward of the Stand. I can't be seen bending laws."

"Wouldn't he have given you his sanction?"

"I asked him. He told me, 'When Corona freezes over.'" She sighed. "How can I blame him? He was having visions of me meeting Methu's fate."

"That was the subject of your last conversation with him before you went errant alone, wasn't it?"

"So it was."

"You're back now, and he hasn't arrested you yet."

"Fortunately, when he finally caught up to me, it was one of the occasions when I happened to be in Tenebra. He officially doesn't know where else I've been. Unofficially, I'm sure he has drawn conclusions, but I've been careful not to inflict any proof on him."

Mak hesitated. "You were trying to protect Mother, too."

"I don't want to put her in that position, Mak. I won't make her choose between me and the law."

"I don't think she would see it that way."

"She is too angry to see anything right now. I know what all of you must think of me. I spent nearly a century collecting Newgifts and forging alliances from Tenebra to Cordium, while you held vigils and wept at my statue."

"That's not why I'm angry, Nike."

"But I can feel your anger, Mak. You almost never bother with veils."

"Oh, I'm furious. You had to rely on..." He waved a hand after the bird. "...someone with a bloodless vulture to help you with your quest. You had to Gift Alkaios on your own, and your Newgifts had to help you save Cassia. While your family sat at home and cried." He took a step forward. "Your *family* should have helped you. Everyone is so angry that you were gone that they don't seem to realize they could have gone with you! Or at least given you their blessing. If they'd supported you in the first place, you wouldn't have needed to hide your quest from us. If they had never stood against you, they could have prevented all of this pain."

She let out a breath, a sheen in her eyes. "They were trying to protect me."

"Well, that's stupid. Everyone should know they can't keep the Victory Star from doing what she believes is right. They should know the only way to keep you safe is to fight at your side."

Her voice sounded thick. "I can think of some battles when I would have been very grateful to have you at my side."

That declaration from her was better than winning the branch of thorns at a competition, the highest achievement in the battle arts.

"Mak...Mother and Father had an important task to do here. Raising you. I wouldn't change a thing that might change who you have become."

"They could have at least cheered you on with a spare hand while using the other to keep me out of trouble."

"Hm. Something tells me they needed both hands for that."

"Only the time I stuffed Father's formal robes to use as a practice dummy."

Nike burst out laughing. Oh, points for him indeed. "Goddess, I'd like to have seen that."

"I'd give you a demonstration, but I think it might set a bad example for Bosko."

"Listen to you, so responsible now."

"Only when Bosko is watching." He winked. "Send letters via undead messenger bird on my watch anytime, sister. Maybe have him bring us back some magical soup next time, though?"

"I think dragging it across the ocean and expecting it to still be edible would be a disservice to excellent soup."

"You'll have to honor our bond of gratitude another way than soup, then."

Her expression softened. "I certainly will. What would you have me do, little brother?"

Well, if there was ever a right time, this was it. "Spar with me."

93

Nights Until

NOTIAN WINTER SOLSTICE

12 Annassa, 1597 IS

ALL ASSEMBLED

Lio looked so very tall when he stood over the couch like this. He dropped a small, folded paper on the coffee table at Cassia's elbow. "A courier just brought another note for you."

Cassia turned a page in her gardening book and studied a botanical diagram of a lilac. "I wish our Trial circle would stop inviting me to things. It makes me feel guilty when I have to say no. I thought they knew I need to rest."

"It's not from our Trial circle."

Cassia glanced up at Lio. "Ioustin promised he would make my excuses to Master Kona about my gardening lessons."

He picked up the note and slid it into her book. "It's not from Master Kona, either."

Knight stuck his head on her lap to sniff the paper. It didn't have any mark on the outside at all. She unfolded the note.

The Stand will be training in the arena at third moon. Will I see you there?
- Nike

Cassia gasped. "Mak finally convinced her!"

"I have no doubt it was Mak."

"I can't say no to this invitation."

"Indeed, if you tried, our Trial brothers would come and carry you to the arena."

"I thought you wanted me to stay in bed."

"My protective instincts will have to be satisfied that you've been resting for a few nights, and that Ioustin healed all the physical effects of the mind ward."

Cassia sighed. She had to admit, her body felt fine. Even so, she still wanted to spend every night curled up here on the couch in her most comfortable robe and wool socks. That might not be entirely the fault of the ward's residual effects on her mind, however.

She fingered the note from Orthros's prodigal. "Third moon. That's in half an hour. I'd better get dressed."

Lio stepped away and back in a blink to offer Cassia her athletic tunic.

"Oh." She shook her head. "I'm just going to watch."

"You know they'll be disappointed if you don't wear it. It was a gift from Kadi in her capacity as the Stand's outfitter."

Cassia sighed. "Those Argyroi."

"Expertly cornered," Lio agreed.

"At least it will be an excuse to see you in your athletic tunic."

"Happy to oblige, my rose. We can change here and step to the arena, which is heated. That way, you won't risk catching a chill going through the city."

"Still feeling protective, I see."

He propped a hand on the back of the couch and crouched beside her, bringing his face near hers. His voice was low and smooth as silk, echoing through the mind ward within her. "Very protective."

She closed the distance between their lips and gave into her own instincts for a moment. She still wanted to spend every night curled up here on the couch with Lio.

"Very well," she said with a sigh. "If you, as my protector, can reconcile yourself to it, we will go and reassure our friends and family that I haven't become a hermit."

Once they had gotten ready, Lio stepped them into a small room filled with warm, moist air. There were steam benches and taps like the private bath chambers at Hippolyta's Gymnasium back in Orthros Boreou. But she could tell from the red tint around the drain that here, one could enjoy the mineral hot springs of Orthros Notou.

Cassia recalled when she and Lio had stolen a quick and unforgettable tryst in a room like this during the Summit Games.

"Care to stake our claim on this bath before we leave tonight?" Lio asked.

"This time I won't have a Tenebran gown to keep tidy or human spectators waiting for my return."

"Definitely not a Tenebran gown." His gaze swept over her.

Her athletic tunic fit her perfectly, crafted for her by Kadi in the color of cassia spice. The only trouble was, it was less clothing than Cassia had ever worn in Tenebra, where women lived under layers of skirts and covered their hair. The simple cotton garment stopped at her knees. The sleeves didn't even go past her elbows. Her sandals showed her bare toes.

She looked better than she had when she'd first come to Orthros, but she still didn't think Hesperine athletic attire suited a short, scrawny human with no figure. There was a reason she hadn't worn this in public yet.

Lio's tunic, on the other hand, offered an eyeful of Hesperine to admire. His long legs were strong and limber from his nightly runs. The jewel-blue fabric matched his eyes.

"You should wear that more often," Lio said. "You'll get more freckles. I promise to find and kiss every new one that appears."

"Well, in that case, I won't hide in my cloak."

He knelt at her feet and rested his hand on his braid. Veiling magic circled her ankle, and the braid became invisible. But she could always feel it there. She would have felt far more naked without his Grace braid than in any new clothing.

Rising, he touched her braid at his throat, as if saying the same, before his veil concealed it from sight.

The night when they could exchange braids publicly and wear the symbols of their Grace bond openly was even farther away now. Postponing their avowal was one of the worst consequences of her remaining mortal.

Knight's whine interrupted their thoughts. He had his nose pressed to the door, his fur plastered to his body in the humidity.

"Poor darling," Cassia said with a laugh. "Steam rooms were not made for liegehounds."

They went out the door, and Cassia found herself in dry, open air. The baths were a row of small buildings behind them. Before them lay the arena.

Rows of seats were hewn into the dark bedrock of Haima, descending to the fighting ring, which was open to Hespera's night sky. There was plenty of spell light, and the air a comfortable temperature. The snow flurries beyond the arena never blew their way. The whole area must be warded.

"Another feat of Hesperine engineering," Cassia said. "An open-air arena at the south pole that won't give humans frostbite."

"Is it warm enough for you out here? I can ask them to adjust the geomagic."

She took his hand, shaking her head. "I'm fine."

The only reason she longed for a warm blanket at the moment was so she could cover up all her exposed skin. But that wouldn't fend off the concerned Hesperine friends and family, to whom her emotions were just as bare.

Mak, down in the arena, spotted them and stepped to their sides with Lyros. She glimpsed the concern in their eyes, but Mak didn't ask her any questions. He just gave her one of his bear hugs.

"Cup and thorns, we're glad to see you out of bed," Lyros said.

"Who stays in bed when the whole Stand is together in Hippolyta's Arena for the first time in nearly a hundred years?" Cassia didn't have to struggle to smile. She knew how much this meant to them. "We have you to thank for this, don't we, Mak?"

He beamed. "You may all line up and give me your gratitude. After the match. Right now I need to concentrate on losing to my sister as skillfully as possible."

"Who says you'll lose?" Lyros spoke up.

"Everyone except you, my Grace."

"And us." Lio gave Mak a wrist clasp. "We'll be cheering you on, Trial brother."

"I'll do my best for the Eighth Circle," Mak promised.

He and Lyros levitated back down to the ring to rejoin the others waiting for them in black fighting robes. And there, in Hippolyta's Arena, stood all seven surviving members of the Stand. Hippolyta with both her daughters, her son and Grace-son, and her daughter's Newgifts, Alkaios and Nephalea. Orthros's entire standing army.

"That's a sight for the history books," Lio murmured. "But especially for our family memories. You helped make it possible, my rose."

Cassia watched Nike and Mak. He appeared to be keeping up a steady stream of jests. She kept replying with a sly grin.

Cassia mustn't succumb to her grief for her mother and sister. Not when she could do so much for her Hesperine family.

She and Lio went to find their seats among more of their loved ones. The section reserved for Blood Argyros was the only one occupied, but it was packed. The audience there to witness the Stand's reunion was actually larger than the number of Stewards, even if one didn't count the goats leaping and climbing the tiered seats.

Before Cassia and Lio reached everyone, Zoe ran up to meet them. "Cassia! You're out of bed!"

"All better, Zoe flower. See there, it only took me a few nights to recover from the journey."

"Reading on the couch with you all that time was fun, but now we can start our southern garden!"

Bosko had strolled up and now scratched the base of Knight's tail. "We didn't get to watch Knight practice with Mother during the Summit Games. Do you think he'll join the Stand in the ring tonight?"

"Let's see what the Stewards decide should be tonight's order of events," Cassia said.

Zoe and Bosko dragged Cassia and Lio to their seats. They squeezed onto the bench between the sucklings, with their Trial sisters in the row behind them.

Xandra threw her arms around Cassia and squeezed. The air around the princess was warm with her magic. "The First Circle is having a reunion! And the Eighth Circle is here to see it!"

The founders of the Trial circle tradition were indeed here. Ioustin was in attendance for Nike's return to the ring. He sat in the front row in a crimson fighting robe. Was Methu here in spirit, observing with a smile from his place among the stars?

Beside Ioustin sat Apollon in a gold battle robe. Komnena wound her arm around his, talking with her Grace and his fellow Blood Errant with obvious contentment.

Uncle Argyros occupied the seat on Ioustin's other side, their rift over Nike's absence well mended. Javed was also on the front row. Thenie crawled back and forth between his and Argryos's laps.

"I never saw Ioustin in the gymnasium," Cassia remarked.

"I know, isn't it amazing?" Xandra bubbled. "Our mothers don't come to the gymnasium or the arena, of course, so I'm usually the only royal who sets foot here. But now that Nike is back, so is my brother."

"The Queens don't ever attend Stand events?" Cassia asked.

Kia, ever ready with answers, shook her head. "It's part of the symbolic relationship between the Stand and the Queens. 'The Stand shoulders the burden of violence for the Hesperine people.' The Queens ensure peace."

"Rudhira does enough fighting for all of us," Xandra said.

Nodora studied him as if she perhaps recalled how sweet she'd been on him when she was younger. "At this moment, he almost seems relaxed."

The First Prince leaned back in his seat, his legs stretched out before him. No Tenebran riding boots tonight. He was barefoot, like the other fighters.

No Stand regalia tonight, either. The Stewards were wearing their simple black training robes. Nike looked like she belonged—no, like she commanded. And yet she traced her sandal over the sand as if standing on uncertain ground.

Nike lifted a hand to Cassia in greeting, and Cassia waved back.

Alkaios and Nephalea stood at Nike's shoulder. Mak stood at her other, tossing good-natured taunts back and forth with her.

Kadi stood to one side, running through a quick stretch. Lyros did the same on Mak's other side.

Right across from Nike, separated from her by a stretch of the ring, stood Aunt Lyta.

Cassia murmured to Lio, "the layout of the battlefield is pretty clear, isn't it?"

"I'm afraid so," he answered.

"Alkaios and Nephalea are trying to keep Nike from escaping. Mak has her back. Lyros has his back. Kadi's the mediator."

"And Aunt Lyta and Nike are on opposite sides of the field."

"Well," came Uncle Argyros's voice from the front row. "We are all assembled. Now we can begin."

A PROPER CONVERSATION

WHILE THE WARRIORS IN the ring began a few warm-up exercises, their family and friends in the stands passed spells around, along with words and emotions, according to the patterns they were all accustomed to.

Lio quickly found himself ambushed by a veil of Nodora and Kia's. Xandra was talking with Cassia for all to hear, something about soap wax.

Nodora leaned down over one of Lio's shoulders. "What will help Cassia more? If we bring it up or not?"

He sent his Trial sisters his gratitude through the Union. "I think we should let her decide when to bring it up."

Nodora nodded, but her brow furrowed. "I just want her to know we're here for her."

"She does. She knows she can confide in you when she's ready."

"Does she need distractions?" asked Kia at Lio's other shoulder. "Or would she feel imposed upon if we took her out after this?"

"It took Mak and Nike to get her to leave the house tonight."

Kia sighed. "Enough said. We'd best give her time."

Nodora shook her head. "But we can't let her become too withdrawn. We need to keep coaxing her out. Gently."

"Thank you."

"And you, Lio?" Nodora asked. "Do you need distractions?"

"My focus is on Cassia right now."

His Trial sisters exchanged glances. He raised his eyebrows at them.

"You're allowed to leave the residence, Lio," said Kia. "You're not a liegehound."

"Kia—" he started.

"Come to Harkhuf's symposium," she broke in. "The topic is the history of the Imperial High Court. He'll be talking about all the most exciting political intrigues there."

"I wouldn't want to commit when Cassia may need me near."

"Cassia might enjoy an evening of gardening or playing with Zoe," Nodora said.

"All the other diplomats will be at the symposium," said Kia, "and it would be excellent preparation for your reassignment to Imperial affairs."

"All the more reason I shouldn't go without Cassia."

"Then bring her."

"Look." Lio nodded to the ring. "Nike is about to spar with Mak."

The Steward's voices carried up from the floor of the arena, easy for Hesperine hearing to detect. Nike beckoned to Mak. "Come, Brother. Show me what you can do."

Mak took his position across from her. "Sister, you honor me with your first challenge since your return."

The other Stewards fell back in a loose circle around them.

Lio cheered for Mak. "You'll do us proud!"

Kia's whistle nearly split his ear. "Show the First Circle what the Eighth Circle is made of!"

Mak waved to them, and Cassia clapped for him. Zoe sat on Cassia's lap, her face bright with excitement, letting Knight jump up onto her seat.

"He does have an advantage of size over Nike," Nodora said, "even if few can match her experience."

Kia nodded, a finger to her chin. "And he has experience using that against a shorter and lither opponent after all his matches with Lyros."

Lio had no doubt that whoever was the victor, Mak would thoroughly enjoy the fight.

Nike and Mak bowed to one another. A moment of complete stillness followed.

Mak made the first move. A powerful but graceful attack. Nike dodged easily and waited. He stayed on the offensive; she eluded him, posing a real challenge, giving him the opportunity to demonstrate what he was truly capable of.

"Lio, do you know which attacks they're using?" Bosko asked.

"I recognize them from watching Mak and Lyros practice. Those are the highly advanced moves only Stewards learn."

Bosko's aura leapt with eagerness, his wide eyes riveted to the fight. When either Mak or Nike landed a blow, he cheered.

Mak delivered a jest with every attack, and his sister laughed as they battled. Their banter and their moves came fluidly. She transitioned from agility to the hard wrestling Mak often preferred. The match became a high-impact battle of strength.

Lio could tell when Mak stopped showing off and started pushing, testing his sister. She adhered strictly to the advanced moves Mak had studied, her skill enthralling, but her counterattacks unsurprising.

Mak kept testing. Teasing. He wanted *her* to show *him* what she was capable of. Trust Mak to be so impudent.

Finally she wrestled him down in a headlock. The potentially fatal position signaled her victory and the end of the match. But Mak was beaming.

She thoroughly ruffled his hair before she released him and helped him up.

Mak clasped her wrist. "Cup and thorns, that was marvelous. Thank you for giving me a real challenge."

"I'm impressed. You managed to surprise me."

Mak showed one of his good-natured grins, his aura giving away how much her praise meant to him.

Nike clapped Mak on the shoulder and turned to Lyros. "Grace-Brother, care to acquaint me with your skills?"

"It will be my honor."

Lio smiled, watching Nike get to know Lyros. Their match was a deep conversation in the language of warriors.

Nike battled her way through the entire Stand, emerging the victor each time. Next a friendly three-way match with Alkaios and Nephalea, which demonstrated how well they had fought together Abroad. Then with Kadi, a joyous reunion of confidences and differences and private jests told across the entire arena in beautiful, mighty battle art.

At last, only one warrior remained unchallenged. The Guardian of Orthros herself.

Lio leaned forward in his seat and gripped his uncle's shoulder. He swept a veil around them, just another one weaving in and out of everyone else's. He hoped his uncle would take the invitation to confide in him.

"How are they?" Lio asked.

"I knew we had to get them into the fighting ring together, although it would take some time and effort."

"You and Mak conspired to arrange this?"

"He had the more difficult task, and see how he succeeded. Now my Grace and our adamant girl can have a proper conversation."

Relieved, Lio gave his uncle's shoulder a squeeze.

Nike and Kadi had strolled back to the center of the ring, an arm around each other's shoulders. Kadi drew her sister to a halt in front of their mother.

Xandra blew out a breath. "The Guardian of Orthros and her First Master Steward are about to spar."

Kia leaned forward. "For the first time in almost a century. Most of us here haven't seen this in our lifetimes."

Lio's father let out a low laugh. "A sight sorely missed. You're in for quite an experience."

"They're so well matched," Nodora said, "after sixteen hundred years of sharing the battle arts. How will one of them possibly best the other?"

"Won't Aunt Lyta win?" Zoe guessed. "She's Nike's teacher. She knows all the secret moves."

"Aunt Nike might still win." Bosko tightened his own speires in preparation. "A teacher always wants her student to become even better than she is."

"You'll see," was Ioustin's prediction.

Kadi stepped back, leaving her mother and sister facing one another.

"Did you learn new skills in the field?" Aunt Lyta asked.

"Did you develop new tactics to teach these trainees?" asked Nike.

"Let us find out, shall we?"

They bowed to one another.

When they disappeared from sight, Lio jumped. They made their first moves so fast, they eluded even Hesperine eyes. Grains of sand fanned up from the floor, casting the two wrestling warriors in relief for an instant.

Then they rolled, Nike's body leaving an imprint in the sand, and blurred with speed again.

Lio couldn't begin to name all the fighting moves Aunt Lyta and Nike put on parade before them. By the looks on Mak and Lyros's faces, they had only heard about them in legends. Ioustin and Lio's father sat on the edge of their seats, their heads turning, as if they could guess where the battle would appear next. Uncle Argyros watched with his quiet intensity, and no hint of surprise.

The arena was silent except for sounds of battle. The rush of sand. The impact of flesh on flesh when one landed a blow. A grunt of effort when the other escaped from a powerful grasp. They sped in and out of sight, dancing around each other, striking, fleeing, embracing.

Aunt Lyta trapped Nike against her in a complex grip. Her eyes flashed, and her lips moved, saying something in her daughter's ear. Nike bared her fangs and freed herself with a pirouette and a fist.

"Can you read their lips?" Lio whispered to Cassia.

"No, they're moving too fast. Can you hear them?"

He shook his head. "Veiled."

Nike seemed to go on the offensive, her moves deliberate, confident. The other Stewards stepped back, giving room to the tight but ever-widening spiral of battle. The whirl froze with Aunt Lyta pinned to the ground. Nike stared down at her, her eyes wide.

Then Aunt Lyta made a move, and Nike flipped. She was on her back for a mere instant before the two warriors were fighting it out on their feet again. Footprints trailed behind the invisible combatants, and more sand splashed up, flowing along the path of their contest.

Nike planted her feet, bringing her forearms up to block Aunt Lyta's rapid strikes. Her eyes dancing, Aunt Lyta launched one feint after the other. Nike parried, her laughter echoing through the ring.

She ducked under her mother's guard, landed a blow and skipped away. Aunt Lyta spun and chased after her into the unseen realm of their fight.

Quivering points of light appeared in the air. The spell lights sparkled off the droplets of moisture. First a few, then many, then four trails of them that guided Lio's gaze along the same path as the footprints in the sand. Tears.

Nike and Aunt Lyta stilled. They lay on their backs, shoulder-to-shoulder. A tendril of Aunt Lyta's hair was plastered to her tear-streaked cheek. Nike scrubbed a dusty hand over her eyes, and wet sand streaked her face.

They lay there for a moment. A few more words passed between them, then another laugh. Then they helped each other up.

The battle was over.

Uncle Argyros sighed, a smile in his aura.

"That was *fast.*" Bosko sounded awed.

Lio's father laughed again. "They usually stop their match when they've demonstrated what they set out to."

"But who won?" Zoe's asked.

"They both did," Ioustin answered.

WITH MORTAL STRENGTH

CASSIA WATCHED KADI AND Nike standing together, talking with their mother. *Nike. My example to live by. My best friend.* That was how Kadi had described her, one night when she and Cassia had confided in one another about their lost sisters.

"Are you glad you came?" Lio asked.

She rested her head on his shoulder. "Very."

Suddenly Zoe giggled.

Cassia hugged her. "What?"

"Your tummy is growling."

"Oh. So it is."

"So is mine."

"Why don't you ask Papa for a snack?"

Zoe climbed down a row, and Apollon scooped her onto his lap. She whispered in his ear, and he offered her his wrist. Bosko was already in the front row, trying to have a casual conversation with his father about the fighting match. Javed was patiently waiting for the suckling to admit he was hungry too.

Nodora chuckled. Cassia slapped a hand to her belly. Traitorous thing.

Xandra reached for something at her feet and produced a picnic basket. "I brought everyone's favorites. Cold starflake pudding...hot lentil soup...some Notian red wine...mince pies, of course..."

Cassia felt less impatient with her mortal needs when all her friends were so good-natured about them. Even though the Hesperines drew no nourishment from the food, sitting and sharing it with them was festive. It was a good thing Nike and Mak had pried her out of the house.

He must have sensed her feelings, for he winked at her before the Stewards began a group drill.

By the time the training exercise ended, the sucklings had full bellies, and the rest of them had decimated Xandra's picnic basket.

"Do you think they'll run some laps next?" Cassia asked Lio. "You've missed so many of your morning runs lately. You could join in."

"Perhaps."

"Your legs are longer than Nike's," Kia teased. "Maybe you'll be the first of our circle to beat her at something."

"A squishy scholar like me? I dare not try."

Xandra gazed at Ioustin and Apollon with a sigh. "I hope the Blood Errant spar tonight."

"Cassia!" came Nike's voice from below.

All conversations hushed, and Cassia cast a startled glance down at Nike. "Yes?"

"I understand you haven't yet joined a training session with the Stand."

"It's true," Cassia called. "I'm afraid I haven't done justice to the fine attire the Stand has given me."

"Would you like your first lesson from me?"

Tension filled Cassia. "I'm honored! But I'm not even a proper trainee."

"Everyone is welcome to pursue athletic excellence here. Come, join us."

At the encouragement from her family and friends and the sucklings' excited urging, Cassia found the nerve to stand up and descend into the ring with everyone watching her exposed freckles.

Mak and Lyros parted to invite her into the group of warriors, each giving her a welcoming hand on her shoulder. She found herself at the center of the circle, facing Nike.

"Should I call Knight down?"

"Hmm," said Nike. "Kadi told me about her match with him during the Summit Games. You actually convinced him to partner with a Hesperine for an exercise session."

"I know there's a particularly painful history between the Stand and liegehounds." Cassia didn't mention Master Steward Atalanta by name. She wasn't sure how much of a reminder Nike wanted of her bloodborn friend and comrade whom heart hunters and their liegehounds had brought down. "Kadi and I wanted to prove that history can change."

"Not this time," Kadi answered. "This session is for you."

"He doesn't look interested tonight," Nike added.

Zoe had now taken Cassia's seat, and Knight lay with his head on her lap. If he kept this up, he would become as lazy as Apollon's familiar and forget how to fight. Cassia didn't begrudge him that one bit.

"Have you ever been caught in a dangerous situation without him at your side?" Nike asked.

Cassia swallowed. "Rarely."

"But those situations made you feel vulnerable. Helpless, even. Would you like to know how to protect yourself? No liegehound required. No magic required. Just a woman and her fists."

Cassia remembered watching a war mage who wanted to burn her for heresy light a bonfire before her eyes. Knight hadn't been at her side that night. She recalled falling alone into a chasm during a heart hunter attack, torn from him again.

Knight, trapped within a necromancer's magic. Her, facing the Collector on her own.

Lio holding her tight, hiding his tears against her breast, afraid he might lose her.

She glanced down at herself. For most of her life, she had been stashed uselessly in her chambers behind Knight and the king's commands, except when she could get out into the garden. "I'm not much of a warrior."

"Every woman is a warrior," Aunt Lyta said.

Cassia looked over her shoulder at the Guardian of Orthros, and their gazes met, reminding her that the great Hippolyta was not a hair's breadth taller than Cassia herself. But she had been studying war for sixteen centuries. She had invented the Hesperine battle arts.

"I'm afraid I'm getting too late a start to become truly skilled," Cassia said. "All the warriors I've known trained for years. Many started when they were children."

Nephalea spoke up. "I didn't. Nike turned me from a lady into a warrior."

"I didn't either," said Aunt Lyta. "When I started learning how to fight, I was only a few years younger than you are now."

"Really?" Cassia asked. "I never knew that."

Aunt Lyta nodded. "The Hesperite village I grew up in was strictly pacifist. My whole human life, battle was foreign to me. During the Last War, I realized there are times when we must fight in Hespera's name."

Cassia knew those times well. "I do have some strength from gardening."

"Being a liegehound's handler is also a demanding physical pursuit," Kadi pointed out.

"And I climbed through a murder hole once," Cassia added.

Nike half-grinned. "First, practice. Then you must tell me the story of that adventure over coffee."

Cassia looked around her at the four disciplined female warriors of the Stand. "How much can I achieve with mortal strength?"

"A great deal," Nike answered. "A very little practice goes a long way. It may take years to become a professional, but in a short time, a mortal woman can learn skills to rely on in a life-or-death situation."

"Can I learn to knock a crossbow out of a man's hands? Land a blow on a mage if he's concentrating on a spell? Evade a Gift Collector long enough for help to arrive?"

"I want to hear *all* those stories. We'll devise a strategy for each one and practice them until they become your instincts."

If Thalia had known these skills, would she have survived the assassination attempt on the king that had claimed her life instead? If Solia had been a fighter, could she have escaped the fortress as she and Iris had planned, instead of getting dragged to Cordium?

"Yes." Cassia surprised herself with the decisive answer. "I would *love* to know how to protect myself."

Nike smiled. "You have just met the only requirement to begin. You have demonstrated that you have the Will."

Cassia reached into her pocket and pulled out Aunt Lyta's welcome gift to her, a pair of speires of her own. She tied her hair back. "I'm ready."

Nike motioned her forward. "New trainees normally start with preparatory exercises to condition their bodies. Once in fighting shape, they begin studying the actual moves that comprise the Hesperine battle arts. Learning proper technique, and in the proper order, is paramount."

"But?"

"But this is your first time in the ring, and I want us to do something fun."

Laughter rippled through the Stewards, Cassia sharing in it.

"How about I show you how to throw a punch?" Nike proposed.

The Stewards and their audience called out enthusiastically.

"Yes, please." Cassia stepped closer to Nike.

The Hesperine took her hands. "I don't have to tell you to make a fist, I see."

Cassia hadn't realized that she had balled up her hands.

Nike pried her fingers apart and pulled her thumbs out from under them. "Thumbs on the outside. Always. Otherwise you'll break them."

"Oh. Good to know."

Nike wrapped Cassia's hands into fists again, looser this time, but firm, with her thumb tucked on the outside of her fingers. "Imagine you're holding something precious in your hands that you don't want to break—but you want to protect it from anyone trying to take it away from you. That's the kind of fist you want to make."

Cassia imagined a shard of the glyph stone in each of her hands. Suddenly her fists felt right, and so did the entire exercise.

"You've got it," Nike approved. "Now, feet shoulder-width apart."

Cassia followed her instructions.

"Are you right- or left-handed?" Nike asked.

Cassia had to pause to think. She was still so bad at writing with *any* hand. "Right-handed, I suppose."

"In that case, you'll want your right foot back, left foot forward." Nike released her shoulders. "Turn until you're facing Nephalea. Stop. Perfect. See how your left toe and right heel are aligned with the center of your opponent's—my—body? You don't want to face your opponent directly and leave yourself vulnerable to attack, but you don't want to turn away, either."

"That makes sense."

"Now tuck your right fist against your cheekbone, ready to protect you. Elbow in, shielding your ribs." Nike walked around her, adjusting her elbow here and shoulder there. "Left fist up in front of you. Now bend your knees a little." Nike shook her head. "So tense. Relax. In a moment I'll teach you which muscles to tighten to protect yourself from blows. Only certain portions of your body need to be tensed, and only at the right moments."

Cassia tried, but she wasn't sure how to separate the parts of her body that should relax from the tense ones. She was one knot of tension from head to toe.

"It will work out as we go," Nike reassured her. "Training teaches you discipline—but also how to relax."

In Nike's patient, direct instructions, Cassia could hear how the Hesperine had taken solace in the battle arts over the years. It was clear she was an amazing teacher.

Facing Cassia, Nike held up her hand, palm out. For a moment, she looked just like her statue, hand braced to shield Orthros from the world.

"I want you to land your knuckles right against my hand," Nike instructed. "Extend your fist straight outward, and at the last moment, before you hit me, give your hand a twist so your thumb is facing downward."

Slowly, Cassia attempted the motion Nike had described, until her knuckles met Nike's palm. The Hesperine's hand was cool and firm and reassuring.

"Very good. Most beginners wave their elbows too much, but you punch straight as an arrow. Now withdraw your hand."

Encouraged by the praise, Cassia pulled her hand back to the position guarding her face.

"Very well done. You were wise to return your hand to where it was before instead of pulling it back too far and leaving your face vulnerable. Now do it again, faster."

Cassia tossed a quicker punch, only slowing her hand right before she touched Nike.

Nike gave her a look. "I don't have to ask if you have more fight in you than that. I *know* you're a fighter."

"I thought this was just practice."

"You can't hurt me, so don't hold back."

Javed waved from the stands. "Ready and waiting, in case any split knuckles should need healing."

"We'll make sure Cassia doesn't hurt herself, either!" Kadi scolded.

"You're starting out the same way I did," Nephalea said to Cassia. "Many of us have developed a deep instinct that physically lashing out at someone is inappropriate. Especially females raised in Tenebra—and especially those of us who were taught how to be 'ladies.' You need to break through that inhibition."

Nike raised her palm again. "Imagine my hand is the nose of your least favorite person."

Everyone burst out laughing.

"I'm afraid I have a long list of least favorite people," Cassia confessed. "Hespera will have to help me work on compassion."

"Sometimes compassion demands that you throw a punch," Nike replied. "Who will you pick from your list to be today's punching bag?"

"Dexion Chrysanthos," Cassia announced.

Mak and Lyros booed.

Lio joined in from the stands. "*Your* turn to break his nose, Cassia!"

The cares in Nike's storm-gray eyes had lightened. She was actually enjoying this.

"All right, Florian," Cassia muttered. "This is long overdue."

She envisioned the war mage's pretty face, his supercilious smile, the burn of hatred in his eyes. She swung.

Her pulse leapt. Her fist connected with her target with a satisfying impact.

"Now *that's* a punch!" Mak said.

His voice brought her back to where she was.

Nike nodded. "I knew you had it in you."

"I think I might actually have a lot more in me where that came from."

"A lifetime in Tenebra will do that to you," Nephalea agreed.

"Let's work some of that out." Nike clapped her hands together, then began instructing Cassia on cross punches so she could use both her fists.

Once she thought she had the gist, Nike held out both palms.

Cassia envisioned the Dexion again. Her surroundings faded.

She felt the force traveling up through her from the ground. The bedrock of Orthros. She spun on her foot as Nike had instructed. Power moved up her leg, through her core, and down her arm. Her power. Her fist met flesh.

One blow. Two. One. Two. One two.

The short, measured breathing steadied her. Tightening the muscles of her abdomen braced her. The sweat breaking out on her skin was a release.

One two. One two. One two.

She *could* learn to protect herself.

One two one two one two.

She could learn to protect the people she loved.

Even if she was still mortal. Whether or not she had magic.

She wouldn't be helpless ever again. She had promised herself that when she came to Orthros. What Nike could teach would help Cassia keep that vow.

She would never again be that girl alone in the king's camp, waiting for someone who loved her to return, helpless to stop the catapults.

"*There* is the fight in you." Nike's voice sounded close. Cassia could scarcely hear the others, as if she and Nike were wrapped in a blur of magic and sweat and her pounding heart. "Let it out."

Cassia didn't want to stop. It was so satisfying, such a relief to pound out the years and the unspoken terrors.

A loud whistle and a roar of applause broke through her haze. She slowed, taking a deeper breath. Her vision and her thoughts began to clear as she eased to a halt.

Her arms felt like lead. Sweat trickled down her back. Her hair was plastered to her head, but had not escaped her speires.

Everyone was cheering for her.

"You are a natural," Lyros pronounced.

Mak grinned. "What did we say when we met you? Ferocious."

79

Nights Until

NOTIAN WINTER SOLSTICE

26 Annassa, 1597 IS

ROSES ANEW

LIO SMILED AT THE sight of his Grace kneeling by their bed alcove amid a clutter of gardening supplies. She looked adorable with a bit of potting soil on the tip of her nose. He hoped she wouldn't realize it was there and ask him to work a cleaning spell.

"The pot is ready," she announced. "You can take the rose out of the wrapping now."

Sitting beside her, Lio carefully held the precious cutting of their roses. It was still swaddled in the damp, bespelled cloth that had protected it during the journey from Orthros Boreou. As she had instructed him, he removed the long, green cane from the wrapping.

"Now we cut a bit off the end." Using the sharp edge of her trusty gardening spade, Cassia trimmed the rose. "There."

She placed her small hand on his big one. He let her guide him. Together they placed the cutting in the pot and started their roses anew.

With their hands still on the rose cane, they shared a kiss over the new vine.

"Now it just needs three things," she said. "Keep holding it for me."

"All right."

While he kept the rose steady, she filled in the rest of the rich, moist potting soil around the cane. Then she watered it from the can she had ready.

Before she told him, Lio knew what the third thing was. He offered her his wrist. She nodded.

He brought his wrist to his fangs, then made a libation of their combined blood over the pot.

As soon as his wrist healed, Cassia took both his hands in hers, her aura suddenly determined.

She had sent Knight off with Zoe again. He should have realized she had something in mind.

"What is it?" he asked.

"Lio, there is something I need to ask you. Well, I've asked you before. But I need to ask you again, and kneeling here before our rose is the most sacred place I can think of to do it."

He was so very tempted to kiss her smudged nose. "Yes?" he asked gravely.

"Lio, my love, will you Gift me?"

His breath caught. "Cassia, are you saying you want to try again?"

She nodded. "I know so much is still unresolved. I don't care. I think we were wrong to postpone my Gifting after all. I...got caught up in my hopes. In the end, nothing has really changed, and yet I remain mortal."

Now it was Lio who did battle with his hopes. He wanted to sweep her into his arms and tell her yes and forget everything else. But he said what she needed to hear. "Don't do this because you've given up hope."

"I haven't. But I don't want to stop living and wait upon my hopes. Think how long Nike has been searching for evidence of Methu in Cordium. How long might it take Kalos to discover what happened to Solia? Even if there is hope, I will still be waiting here for the Charge to rescue her, and what good will my humanity do anyone?"

He squeezed her hands. "Can you face your visions during the Gifting with so many questions unanswered?"

"Better to face them on the night of my transformation than endure them for who knows how long as a mortal."

"Are you sure, Cassia?" *Please, let her be sure.*

"Your mind ward has made me realize how wonderful it is to have a magical connection with you. Training with the Stand for the past fortnight has made me realize how much I want to be powerful. I can't bear to wait any longer."

Yes. She would let him Gift her after all. She would be a Hesperine. The future they wanted would begin.

Lio slid a hand into her hair and held her to him. Their thighs pressed together. He opened his mouth on her vein, kissing her there, slow and hard. The fragrances of her blood and her hunger curled around him.

"Gift me," she asked for the third time.

"Yes," he said against her throat. "I'll spend the rest of the night inside you, and come moonrise, we'll choose a new date for your Gift Night."

She wrapped her arms around his neck and began to feast on his mouth, climbing onto his lap. He grasped her hips, pulling her against him until his arousal met her core through the layers of their work robes. The combined pulses of their racing hearts filled his hearing.

Another percussion reached his ears, out of time with their rhythm. He gasped as he pulled his mouth away.

"Bleeding thorns," he swore. "Not tonight!"

"What? What's wrong?"

"There's someone knocking at the sunbound front door."

"Now?" she demanded. "Who is it?"

He pressed a thumb and finger into his eyes, turning his head away, and tried to focus. "It's Ioustin."

Cassia climbed off Lio's lap, her aura suddenly cold. "What do you sense in his aura?"

"Nothing. He's veiled his emotions."

Her jaw clenched. They looked at each other for a long moment.

Lio wanted to take Cassia to bed, feast on her slowly, take a bath with her even slower, then wake up next moon to their long future together. But Solia's fate was knocking at their door.

THE ANSWER

"K ALOS HAS YOUR ANSWERS," Ioustin said as soon as they
opened the door.

Cassia's heart began to pound. This was it. The moment
of truth, the whole truth of what had befallen her sister in Cordium.

"He is on his way to House Annassa to give his report," Ioustin told
them. "I came to get you."

She held fast to Lio's hand. She had endured so much and not only
survived to see another day, but to make a new life for herself. Now she
must do this. She could do this.

She drew herself up and raised her chin. "I am ready."

Lio rubbed her nose, then wrapped an arm around her and
stepped them.

Her surroundings were a blur through her emotions, but she registered
that they were on a broad, flat rooftop. White roses everywhere. Black
marble and red fountains. Ioustin had arrived beside them and crossed
the roof to approach his mothers.

Nike was waiting for them, with Mak and Lyros at her side. "We
thought you might need reinforcements."

Gratitude swelled out of Cassia, and she must have made quite a wave
in the Union, judging by Mak's smile.

Cassia tried to take in the tableau before her. The Queens together
on a low couch; Master Kona and Kassandra seated at their right; Uncle
Argyros and the Queens' Master Envoys on their left. And before them
stood Kalos, the rugged field scout, wearing incongruous formal silks
for his presentation to the Annassa. An exalted company, wrapped in

starlight, Sanctuary magic and the fragrance of roses, in which to find her life altered forever.

She went forward with Lio at her side, unable to care that they were still wearing their work robes. Ioustin and Nike stood aside to let them approach. Cassia and Lio gave the heart bow to the Queens.

Cassia and Kalos faced each other. Lio held her hand.

Annassa Alea commenced the circle. "Go ahead, Kalos. Tell us what you have learned."

Kalos cleared his throat. A silence ensued.

"Please start at the beginning and explain in order," Annassa Soteira invited, "so we can follow your excellent work."

At her gentle suggestion, he seemed to find his voice. "As you Will, Annassa. As soon as I crossed into Cordium, the tracking became much easier, because the residue of fire magic was more obvious and more frequent. The trail led deeper into the Magelands. I feared they were headed for Corona itself, but they went around the capital and headed down to the large port city of Obruza."

"Why would the mage take Solia there?" Cassia asked.

"I'm not sure. The trail got harder to follow there. It outright disappeared most of the time, under years' worth of human comings and goings. I might have lost her altogether, except a big magical explosion made matters clear."

Cassia's stomach clenched. What had the Orders done to her?

"In a tavern on the docks," Kalos went on, "there was an incident involving very powerful fire magic. She fled the scene, still tracking a bit of the spell's leavings."

"Does that mean the fire magic injured her?" Cassia forced out.

Lio put his arm around her. "Not necessarily. She could have picked up magical residue simply by being in the vicinity of such a powerful spell."

Kalos gave a nod. "As I followed her trail from the tavern, I ran headfirst into someone quite unexpected, who witnessed what happened to Solia all those years ago."

Cassia sucked in a breath. "You met someone who saw her alive?"

He gave a bow in Basir and Kumeta's direction. "Namatsi sends her regards."

Kumeta appeared impressed. "Well. She's one of our best contacts in Cordium. You must have made an impression on her if she revealed herself to you."

Lio frowned. "I thought Kalos was the only Hesperine errant in Cordium at present."

"Namatsi is mortal," Basir explained. "She is an Imperial citizen."

Cassia's thoughts raced, trying to put the pieces together. "One of the pirates the Empress allows in Cordium?"

Basir nodded. "Namatsi is a privateer and a trustworthy source."

"What did she tell you?" Kumeta asked Kalos.

"It's really quite extraordinary. A minstrel couldn't invent a more unlikely tale. But I have it firsthand." Kalos glanced at Cassia. "She says a Captain Ziara found Solia in a bad situation and saw fit to rescue her."

Rescue. Cassia's mind and heart hung on the word.

The eight-hundred-year-old envoys were visibly astonished. An incredulous laugh escaped solemn Basir. A smile flashed on Kumeta's face. Kassandra appeared to be enjoying herself immensely.

"Captain Ziara?" Lio asked quietly, as if he were afraid to scare off the answer.

"Ziara." Cassia knew where she had heard the name before. "Zoe's favorite pirate?"

Kumeta's smile widened. "One of the most accomplished of the Empress's Privateers."

"Imperial pirates aided my sister?" The words sounded preposterous coming out of Cassia's mouth.

"They did more than aid her." A real smile lit Kalos's face. "They took her with them."

Impossible. Cassia couldn't take it in, even as Lio hugged her close and she felt his elated laugh in his chest.

Kalos's smile widened. "They brought her on board and set sail for the Empire."

Cassia found her voice. "This…changes everything." She had to say it aloud for it to even begin to seem real. "My sister escaped to the Empire."

Lio rubbed her back. "With every mile the privateers put between her and Cordium, she became safer."

Next she found herself enveloped in one of Mak's well-timed hugs. "See there? Elder sisters have a way of thumbing their noses at the mages."

"She's your sister, after all," Lyros exclaimed. "She wouldn't let the Mage Orders stop her any more than you did."

"Solia sounds like a woman after my own heart," Nike declared.

"Remember what I told you, Cassia?" Ioustin had seldom appeared so unburdened. "Cordium is not a death sentence for everyone."

Annassa Alea smiled at her, holding Annassa Soteira's hand in both of hers. "The Empire is where I evaded the war mages sixteen hundred years ago. If a fugitive Sanctuary mage can find safety there, so can a lost princess."

"Especially a princess who has Ziara's help." The corners of Kassandra's mouth curved. "This wouldn't be the first time she lent a hand to a lone female in trouble on the docks of Cordium, but she doesn't usually adopt them."

Kumeta shook her head. "How extraordinary that in this case, that girl was the heir to the throne of Tenebra."

Kassandra tapped her lips with a finger. "I suspect Ziara knew precisely how extraordinary."

"Are privateers allowed to bring Tenebrans back with them?" Cassia asked. "Or would my sister face penalties for entering the Empire?"

Kumeta answered, "The privateers are only permitted to smuggle goods and information."

Kassandra chuckled. "If anyone could smuggle a Tenebran into the Empire, Ziara could. The more the mages want something, the more pleasure she takes in stealing it from them. And she is a consummate thief. She also commands great respect among certain influential Imperials."

"If someone found out Solia was there illegally, what would happen to her?" Cassia asked. "Harkhuf told me that if a Cordian ship is ever sighted in Imperial waters again, it will be given one warning, and if it doesn't turn back, it will be sunk."

"Your sister didn't arrive on a Cordian ship," Kassandra said. "She arrived on the *Wanted*, Ziara's notorious vessel. She's known in every Imperial harbor. No port is closed to her."

"What about after they docked?" asked Cassia.

"Take heart, Cassia." Annassa Soteira gave her Grace an almost mischievous smile. "There are Imperials who will offer refuge to those in need, no matter where they come from."

Queen Alea raised Queen Soteira's hand to her lips. "Like a certain healer who kept me safe."

Master Kona looked from her mothers to Nike, and finally to Cassia. "Sometimes in the face of all our best theories, the Goddess makes her own laws that exceed our hopes."

"Her wonders never cease," Uncle Argyros agreed.

"Rest assured, Cassia," said Master Kona, "mortal justice in the Empire is kinder than the tyranny of Tenebra. The Empress would not subject Solia to the same treatment as an expedition of hostile mages. If your sister were discovered, the worst consequence she would face is deportation."

A humorless laugh escaped Cassia. "So it's entirely possible she made it all the way to the Empire just to be packed off back to Cordium."

"I found her there once," Kalos said. "I can do it again."

Cassia would not rest until she got him a liegehound.

Basir shook his head. "With Ziara's aid, I deem it likely that Solia has succeeded in remaining hidden in the Empire."

"Regardless of Solia's legal status," said Kumeta, "all of this is good news."

"Good news!" Basir exclaimed. "We so seldom have any news that isn't tragic. Surprises are almost always a crisis. Let us find a worthier word for this revelation than *good*."

Kumeta laughed. "Any suggestions, my Grace?"

"Miraculous comes to mind," Basir replied. "At best—"

Uncle Argyros's lips twitched. "Are *you* about to volunteer a best-case scenario, my friend?"

Basir huffed a laugh. "I do have a few shreds of optimism in reserve for an occasion such as this. I don't consider it outside the realm of possibility that the Empress might hand off an unwanted Tenebran to Orthros. A perfect opportunity for Hesperine intervention." He gave Lio and Cassia a pointed look.

Cassia had arrived in Orthros with her own shreds of optimism, all of which the Hesperines had given her. Now it seemed the Goddess was determined to spin them into silk. "Thank you, Basir. We'll keep that in mind, should we discover that the Empress has a Tenebran problem. She might appreciate her Hesperine allies offering an amicable solution."

"I have one more piece of information that will help you," Kalos added. "According to Namatsi, Captain Ziara was last in Cordium about a year and a half ago."

"She makes that voyage faster than anyone," said Kassandra. "She and her crew are extraordinarily skilled, and their ship is heavily bespelled not only for speed, but to withstand everything from storms to krakens to magefire."

Kumeta nodded. "I would estimate she's due back in the Empire some-time this month, barring unforeseen delays."

Just then, a Hesperine stepped into sight near the railing of the rooftop garden. Cassia recognized him as one of the Chargers she had met during the Solstice Summit.

"My Prince," he said, "you instructed me to interrupt if necessary."

Ioustin beckoned the Charger to join the circle, his expression grim. "Of course. What has happened?"

"The Hesperites have received a plea for help. Another family of mortal Hespera worshipers has fled their life of secrecy in Tenebra. They took their chances trying to reach the Hesperite settlement. Only one of them made it. The rest are lost in the wilds."

Ioustin grimaced. Cassia knew how protective he was of the Hes-perites, who kept mortal traditions of Hespera worship alive in Tenebra despite the constant threat of persecution. Their settlement in the wilds of the eastern Tenebrae was a place they could escape the Orders' notice, but life there was harsh.

Before he could say anything, Kalos spoke up. "Already on my way, My Prince."

Ioustin clasped his wrist. "I promised you leave."

"This will feel like leave compared to chasing a lost princess or a mem-ber of the Blood Errant." He offered a bow to Nike. "Begging your pardon, Master Pherenike."

She shook her head. "I know the name of every Hesperine errant who is no longer missing in action thanks to you. You need never beg pardon from anyone."

That made him shift on his feet and look away. "Leave the lost Hesperites to me."

Ioustin clapped him on the shoulder. "Very well. After this circle, I'll be back at Castra Justa to oversee the rescue parties."

Kalos turned to Cassia and gave her a Hesperine wrist clasp. "My work here is done. Now it's time for you to finish the search for Solia."

Cassia had once run to the battlefield too late to save Solia. She had spent these weeks sitting at home, helpless against unknown dangers to her sister.

Now, at last, she could act. "We'll go to the Empire, and we will find her."

Lio's hand was strong and sure in hers. "Yes, we will."

TENEBRAN AFFAIRS

BASIR WASTED NO TIME letting the hammer fall. "Annassa, other matters awaiting your counsel cannot be delayed. We need to make plans concerning the situation in Tenebra."

Lio gritted his teeth. There he stood before a most eminent gathering of Hesperines on the roof of the Notian House Annassa, with Hespera herself looking on from the nearby summit of Haima. And he asked the least responsible, most undiplomatic question of his career. "Can it wait?"

The elders considered him.

"Cassia only just learned that her sister really is alive. Can't everything else wait for one moment?"

Basir answered him. "Orthros only just learned there is a real possibility a contender for the throne of Tenebra is alive. Can our preparations for the consequences wait?"

Cassia let out a breath, her hand tightening around Lio's. He sensed the strong words she wanted to say run through her mind before she chose more diplomatic ones. "I know it is the envoys' duty to consider such matters, but it is my duty to find my sister and ensure she is safe and well before a throne from her distant past even enters the conversation."

Every defensive throb of her aura gratified Lio. "Cassia and I have already agreed that our first conversation with Solia will concern her coming to Orthros with us to take her rightful place in our bloodline."

"She belongs here, with us," Cassia said.

Mak crossed his arms. "Of course she does."

"Clearly," Lyros agreed, "Orthros's goal should be to offer Sanctuary to Solia."

It was a relief, after all these secret circles, for his Grace and his Trial brothers to stand with him.

"A moment, Basir," Uncle Argyros requested of his friend. His silent support for Lio hummed in their Union. "If our attendees from the Eighth Circle would prefer to discuss these matters at a later time, it is perfectly all right for you four to retire for the night."

Cassia and Lio looked at each other. He understood her unspoken request, and he knew the elders would understand when he swept a veil around the four of them.

Cassia was strung tight as a bowstring with tension and much too quiet. Lio recognized the fraught currents of her aura that arose when she was feeling too many things at once, and was still sorting through it all.

"Are you ready to talk about this?" Lio asked.

"I don't know," she admitted.

Lio's uncle had given him the opportunity to make that decision for himself weeks ago. Cassia must now do the same with an even more demanding audience. "Let's take a moment and think it over."

Mak grimaced. "Far be it from me to drag us into a political discussion, but it's clear the envoys think this concerns the safety of Orthros."

Lyros nodded. "We came to support you, Cassia, and we're prepared to stay and represent the Stand with Nike."

"And to support Father." Mak glanced at Lio. "He's been buried in veiled dispatches about all this. You've probably seen the pile on his desk when you come for coffee. But you two are on leave. You don't have to deal with any of this yet."

Cassia rubbed her face. "That's what the dispatches are about? All this effort to plan for the imagined possibility of Solia taking the throne, before we were even certain she's not in her grave?"

Mak winced. "Father is not pleased."

"But of course the envoys are making calculations, and Uncle Argyros must be aware of them. You mustn't feel guilty about it, Lio. No matter how much he would have benefited from your help, you needed your leave. We both did."

It was sweetly painful that her first thought was for his sake, when he was about to admit something that might hurt her.

He knew now was the moment when he must confess that he had kept secrets from her to preserve her respite, even as she confirmed she had needed it.

"Mak, Lyros, we need a moment."

"Oh, thorns," Mak said. "That's why there were two coffee cups on his desk."

Lyros shook his head. "Veil us in if you need us."

They joined Nike a couple of paces away, sliding out of Lio's veil. He and Cassia and the truth stood in the little bubble of silence.

"We never have coffee at his desk," Cassia said quietly. "Only at the table. Together. What were you doing at his desk?"

"Uncle Argyros felt strongly about keeping his promise not to exclude me from his meetings with the envoys anymore. He gave me the option of hearing Basir and Kumeta's reports from Tenebra."

Her eyes and aura flashed. "We should have done that together."

"You weren't ready. You needed time. I was trying to give it to you."

"You should have told me."

"How could you expect me to drag you into it, when it was clear you wanted to avoid it?"

Her anger lashed higher. "Is that what everyone has been saying about me?"

"We were trying to help. *I* was trying to help. Facing the news from Tenebra for both of us was all I could do to protect you from—all of this."

"We've talked about this so many times before. We don't keep secrets to protect each other."

"Think of the times when there was something you weren't ready to tell me. You needed to wait until the right time to keep our Oath."

"That was entirely different." Her anger dissolved into a deep sense of failure.

She was angry at herself, he realized.

"I should have been with you," she said. "I let you shoulder *our* burdens. Alone. For what? So I could whine on a couch in our residence while you all tiptoed around my *feelings*."

He laid his hands on her shoulders, which had carried the weight of a kingdom. "Don't be so hard on yourself."

"I was off potting flowers when *you needed me.*"

"Sometimes I *need* to protect you. Won't you let me?"

"Only if you let me protect you. This ends tonight, Lio. If Tenebra is trying to drag you away from me and shove a crown at my sister, then by the Goddess, no one will keep me out of the discussion. I don't have fangs or magic, but one thing I do have is a head for politics, and I will use it."

Her anger flashed at him like a storm in the night, and he let it drench him. She was always so beautiful when her temper ran high.

This was her cleansing anger, the kind that drove her to act. He loved it, even when he was the reason for it.

"I'm glad," he confessed. "Goddess knows I missed doing this together."

"Then stop trying to do it alone."

He pulled her to him and held the storm. "By our Oath, we'll face the politics, then get out of here and find Solia. As partners."

Her anger melted away, leaving behind pure determination. Her arms came around him. "What can you tell me about the situation?"

"I'd best let you hear it firsthand from the envoys and Uncle Argyros so you can draw your own conclusions. There's a question you should be prepared for, though."

"What?" Her gaze dared anyone to question her.

He took a deep breath. "Uncle Argyros and the Queens were planning to promote me to Ambassador for Tenebran Affairs. They had a matching title ready for you, if you wanted it. I had no idea until Basir let it slip in my uncle's library."

Her eyes were wide. "Your uncle was going to pass his position onto you?"

"To us."

"That would have been a dream come true for you."

"If that were still my dream. We already made that choice. We're done with Tenebra. But Basir and Kumeta seem to think it isn't done with us." He hesitated. "I haven't officially declined the position, because remaining under consideration was the only way I could gain admittance to the envoys' conferences. But I want to make it clear to you, my Grace, that I will accept that title when Corona freezes over."

She hooked her finger in her braid, where only the symbol of their bond hung now, no medallion. "Good. Because I would have had to thaw Corona myself to rid you of it."

He tightened his veils and his arms around her and kissed her. "Basir and Kumeta will try to talk you into donning it yourself."

"I will set fire to Corona if I must. I want to become a diplomat, but the only negotiation table I'm interested in sitting at is the Queens' and the Queen Mothers'."

He drew back, keeping her in his embrace. "Cassia, you've decided for certain that you wish to enter the diplomatic service?"

"I have. Tonight has made my decision clear. We don't need to wait for my affinity readings. Whatever my magic is, it won't change this. Diplomacy has always been the best way to protect each other and the people we love, and I want us to keep doing it together."

Lio had eagerly awaited her decisions for months. He had looked forward to the moment when she would formally accept his uncle's invitation and officially become his partner. He had envisioned that medallion around her neck.

Now alarm gripped him instead of the happiness he had expected to feel. He could only think of his own medallion buried under the ruins of Rose House. He realized he wasn't entirely sorry he had left it there.

Cassia drew her fingers across his brow. "Don't worry, my love. My becoming a diplomat will not make it easier for anyone to stick the Tenebran mantle on me. But it will ensure that I am at every one of you and Uncle Argyros's conferences with the envoys from now on."

"You'll announce your decision tonight?"

"I think this is an appropriate time. At the very least, it will reassure Uncle Argyros he'll have another pair of eyes on those bothersome dispatches."

That brought a chuckle out of Lio, easing the tension in his chest. "I'm glad there will be three coffee cups at the desk from now on."

Hand in hand, he and Cassia faced the circle. Lio let their Trial brothers back into his veil first. Mak and Lyros drew near again.

"Are you two all right?" Mak asked.

"We have resolved the matter of the unexplained coffee cups." Cassia gave Lio a look, her lips pressed together. He wanted to kiss them again.

Lyros's relief was palpable. "Have you decided whether you two are going to stay?"

"Not even a gargoyle could drag me off this rooftop," Cassia threatened.

Mak laughed and gave her a salute. "Oh ho, the king's worst enemy has returned from leave. Tenebra had best watch out."

Lio lowered his veils, and the voices of the debating elders rose around them.

Kumeta was speaking. "The envoys are responsible for keeping Orthros informed and advising our leaders regarding our people's response to events. I cannot in good conscience fail to point out our good fortune in stealing one of Tenebra's former ambassadors for our own. Cassia, should she choose to do so, is a perfect candidate to continue influencing the relationship between Orthros and her previous homeland."

Aunt Kona's aura glinted with her enjoyment of a good debate. "Tenebra is such a limited sphere of influence for so promising a Newgift. Why shouldn't she seek broader avenues for her talents? The Empire offers much better opportunities for her future."

Nike seemed as formidable in a verbal contest as she was in a sparring match. "Cassia's return to Tenebra isn't only a diplomatic question. An Old Master is so determined to take her, he tried to kidnap her from the heart of Orthros. It is out of the question for us to send her outside the ward and make her an easy target. I did not save her life fifteen years ago for us to hand her over to an Old Master now."

"Of course Cassia's safety is paramount," Kumeta replied.

"Whatever the Old Master intends," Basir said, "Cassia is clearly necessary to the outcome. The best way to foil his plans is to keep her out of his hands."

Nike's eyes flashed. "It's also the best way to keep her alive."

"No one is suggesting we put Cassia in harm's way," Basir returned, "we're simply acknowledging that she and Lio are already deeply involved in the situation, and it would benefit Orthros for them to continue to be."

Ioustin stood at his Trial's sister's shoulder. They were an intimidating pair. "As Prince Regent of Orthros Abroad, Cassia's return to Tenebra cannot occur without my approval, as it will be the Charge's responsibility to ensure her safety."

"Cassia will be safe in the Empire," Aunt Kona pointed out.

Nike nodded. "The Old Masters are not active in that part of the world. Cassia and Lio can travel freely anywhere in the Empress's domain without fear of the Collector."

Kassandra leaned back in her chair and popped another mince pie in her mouth.

Had Aunt Kona, Ioustin and Nike all just taken the same side in the argument? They had. And they all wanted Cassia to stay safe in Orthros and the Empire. She and Lio had powerful allies tonight.

Cassia extended her hand, palm up, in the age-old circle petition that signaled her desire to speak.

"Cassia," Annassa Soteira invited, "have you and Lio come to a decision?"

"Yes. Lio and I will remain for this circle, in light of our future plans." Cassia went to Uncle Argyros's side. In her work robes still fragrant of potting soil, she stood with dignity befitting an ambassador and touched his arm with the gentleness of a Hesperine. "Uncle, it would be my honor to serve Orthros as a diplomat. With gratitude, I accept your offer of mentorship."

Uncle Argyros's intense eyes rested on Cassia, as if his thelemantic gaze saw an eternity of potential in her. He rested his hand on hers. "You keep giving me the most marvelous gifts."

The fraught debate dissolved into applause, and the Blood Union filled with genuine appreciation for the moment.

Lyros clapped Lio on the shoulder. "You'll love being in the same service with your one and only."

Mak chuckled. "With Nike and Cassia around him all the time, Father might mellow in truth."

Cassia turned to the Queens and offered them the heart bow. "Annassa, I hope the night will soon come when I stand here before you and receive my medallion of office as a Hesperine diplomat."

Annassa Alea smiled. "You have already served our people with courage and generosity. We know you will accomplish great things on this new path."

Kumeta nodded in satisfaction. "Congratulations, Cassia. A worthy service, and a position well deserved. The envoys will enjoy working with you for many years to come."

"Excellent," said Basir. "The time for action will approach quickly. We need you in the positions of Ambassadors for Tenebran Affairs."

Queen Alea answered him. "My Grace and I will make no appointments tonight."

"However, Cassia and Lio will remain privy to these matters," Queen Soteira said, "while their future commissions are under consideration."

"Thank you, Annassa," Cassia told them, gratitude in her aura. Lio echoed her thanks.

He joined her beside Uncle Argyros, and their mentor clasped his wrist, pulling him close. "We all have much to look forward to."

What Lio looked forward to was Cassia standing here as a Hesperine, diplomat or not.

A WHITE SANCTUARY ROSE

ASSIA WAS ABOUT TO break her months of silence on Tenebra. She would know if her struggles there had made a difference.

"Have a seat, Cassia." Kassandra patted the couch cushion next to her.

Cassia took the oracle's invitation to sit on the plush silk in the circle of elders who ringed the Queens. Lio posted himself beside her, as if to stand sentinel against whatever they were about to hear. She tugged his hand. With a sigh, he sank down next to her.

Even restless Nike settled on one of the couches, looking suddenly like a dignified diplomat rather than a prodigal Hesperine errant. Mak and Lyros joined her.

The questions Cassia truly wanted to ask ran through her mind. Was Perita having an easy pregnancy? How was Callen enjoying his freedom now that his leg was healed? Had Ben finally told Genie that he loved her? Were the spring gardens at the Temple of Kyria in bloom?

But this circle concerned politics. What she could ask about were the changes she had tried to make in Tenebra, which might improve the lives of the people there who still mattered to her.

"Did Flavian commence the plot I designed for him? Has he begun securing the allies I cultivated in order to gain enough support for a peaceful transfer of power? How is the mood of the Council of Free Lords—do they appear to favor revoking their mandate from Lucis and approving Flavian as king instead?"

Kumeta began to answer her. "A very short time after the Tenebran embassy returned from Orthros, someone entered the royal crypt. Princess

Solia's tomb was disturbed, her sarcophagus opened—and revealed to be empty."

"They heeded me," Cassia said.

"The king has yet to identify the culprits," Basir informed her. "He has decried their act as a desecration, but he cannot reverse the damage. Now all of Tenebra knows he refused to ransom the princess and failed to retrieve her body. Everyone believes her tomb is empty because Hesperines gave her the Mercy."

"Iris would approve," said Nike. "Her sacrifice has turned into her queen's legend."

"Yes," Cassia agreed. "I believe she would be proud."

"So should you," Uncle Argyros told her. "The lords and knights of the embassy have spread the truth you gave them, and not only about the Siege of Sovereigns. The free lords no longer doubt that Lucis conspired with the war mages to assassinate them all at the Equinox Summit. The exposure of Lucis's lies has made a real crack in his armor."

Lio met her gaze. "It worked."

She let out a breath. "I knew it would, but seeing it work is different."

"Better."

"Much better."

"Congratulations, Cassia," said Lio, her partner through it all. "You have begun Lucis's downfall."

She always tried to avoid thinking of the king. But in this moment, she pictured him. He sat alone in his solar, surrounded by swords and banners that meant nothing, watching everything he had fought for fall apart around him. And she let herself enjoy it.

If only the new king would rise to the occasion. "Is Flavian doing his part?"

"He has been quietly maneuvering among the free lords," Basir answered. "To his credit, he is using his charm and popularity to their full advantage, but he has been subtle. Now that the tide of opinion has sufficiently turned against the king, the suggestion has been made to call a Full Council. It is impossible for Lucis to pinpoint exactly where this proposal originated, and the free lords have not given any indication that revoking their mandate could be their reason for assembling."

"But in the current climate, Lucis is sweating," Cassia said with relish. "He knows this is no innocent council. He knows they are coming for him."

"Without a doubt," Lio said, "and yet nothing they are doing is treasonous. Under Tenebran law, the Council of Free Lords may convene without the king's summons, if they have a quorum."

"Have enough free lords committed for the Full Council to take place? Does Flavian have enough supporters?"

"As we speak," replied Uncle Argyros, "he is camped at Patria, where the Free Charter was first laid down and all Full Councils are traditionally held. The free lords are on their way, more gathering there by the day."

Her eyes widened. "Matters are so far along already?"

Basir steepled his fingers. "The Full Council will commence on Summer Solstice."

"The next Winter Solstice here?" That was no time at all.

"Yes, Cassia," said Kumeta. "The free lords will vote on the king's mandate in less than eighty days."

Lio brushed his fingers across Cassia's temple. "Your plan didn't simply work. It's afire."

She took a deep breath. "We can only hope violence doesn't break out as a result. How has Lucis responded to the lords assembling?"

Uncle Argyros smiled. "He has sent Hadria's forces to make camp between Patria and Solorum. Lord Hadrian moved in when Flavian arrived and has been there ever since. Simply been there."

"His mere presence is a strategy," Lyros put in. "The other free lords will not dare armed rebellion when they'd have to go through him, and the king will feel no need to attack the Council while his loyalist is breathing down their necks."

Cassia breathed a sigh of relief. "He has devoted his life to ending the feuds, even when it means supporting a king he does not respect. He will not allow a revolt on his watch."

"Impressive," Lyros said. "I can see why Lord Hadrian is considered Tenebra's greatest military commander. He can decide a war without drawing his sword."

"Where is Lord Titus in all of this?" Cassia asked.

"Sweetening the king's ears," Kumeta answered, "characterizing the

Full Council as an altruistic effort by the free lords to come together against the threats Tenebra has recently faced. Or so he said, before he departed court and made himself scarce back in Segetia."

"Clever fox," Cassia murmured. "He always knows how to slip out of the trap. Where is Sabina?"

Kumeta exchanged a glance with Basir. "Lord Hadrian's heir? At home in his domain, presumably."

Cassia shook her head. "I don't think she's there."

Basir gave her a curious look. "Where, then?"

"I'm not sure," Cassia mulled. "Like her father, she may be waiting for Flavian to prove himself before she chooses her side."

"Good luck to him," Lio muttered, without much feeling.

Cassia knew he could muster few well-wishes for the man who had once aspired to marry her. Flavian might be secretly in love with Sabina, but Lio still regarded him as that man who had tried to steal his Grace.

Cassia rubbed his arm. "I'm sure he has already dissolved his betrothal to me. It was merely a political arrangement, one that served Lucis's interests."

"Flavian hasn't dissolved it," Lio bit out.

Cassia blinked at him. "What?"

"He's using it." Lio's fangs showed as he spoke. "Using *you* to curry favor. You are a moving tale for his supporters to rally around. Humble, devout Lady Cassia, who sacrificed herself for the good of mankind to bring holy teachings to the heretics. Flavian's Cassia, the Goddess Kyria to his Anthros, torn from his loving bosom."

"That is the tale that's circulating," Kumeta confirmed, "however, it's unclear exactly who has played the most active role in cultivating it."

"Benedict," Cassia said. The knight was sincere in his faith, and in his grief over her decision to stay in Orthros. Her friend would have a chivalrous desire to keep her memory alive.

"Benedict is honorable," said Mak. "He would say such things about Cassia without self-interest."

Lio scowled. "But Flavian is reaping the rewards."

"You know Flavian," Cassia said. "He hasn't kept his breeches on long enough to feel my absence from his bosom. In fact, his bosom isn't usually his guide."

Lio choked on a laugh, while Mak and Lyros snickered. The elders' eyes gleamed with amusement at Cassia's frank analysis.

Now she came to the most difficult question of all, and she must try to raise it without making Lio's nightmares worse. He had already heard this, she reminded herself. He had faced it all. Without her. Now she could try to make it easier for both of them. She could try to shrink their vast enemy down to something they could discuss reasonably in the light of the Queens' circle.

Cassia raised her chin. "And that theatrical parasite who calls himself the Collector? Does he think to play with his pieces and defend the king on his little game board?"

Lio laughed. She looked at him in relief and saw the love and appreciation in his gaze.

Ioustin appeared eager to crush the parasite beneath his boot heel. "We can't find him."

Tension crept through Cassia at the thought of the Collector lurking, but she kept talking to shine a light on the monster. "I wish I could say I'm surprised, but that is his way."

"Ha," Mak said, "sounds to me like he's scared of a few Hesperines."

Ioustin crossed his arms. "We do hope the Charge will be an effective deterrent."

"And he certainly won't try to sneak into Orthros Boreou again, not even in our absence." Mak bowed in the Queens direction from his seat. "The modifications the Annassa made to the ward will ensure that."

Queen Soteira nodded. "When we established the ward, I placed theramantic protections against necromancers in our spell to ensure the Mages of Hypnos would not threaten Orthros. Now I have adapted those defenses to the Collector's unnatural tactics. If he ever tries to deceive me again, he will be most surprised."

Master Kona tapped a stack of scrolls on table by her couch. "Our theramancers and thelemancers have been researching the Old Masters. We've held a number of circles to collect and analyze our available texts and oral history, to make the most of the scant knowledge we have."

Cassia couldn't help looking to Lio, her worry and no small amount of her anger returning. Had he been attending those circles, too?

Lio sighed. "I've already told Uncle Argyros, Ioustin, and Master Baru everything I know about the Collector. They took that information to the circles in my stead."

At least someone had been protecting Lio, while he wouldn't let her.

Ioustin said, "I've passed all of our research on to the Charge. Every band of Hesperines errant is now required to travel with at least one theramancer trained in Imperial techniques for combating necromancy. If the Master of Dreams tries anything, we are ready. But he has not."

"How are relations between the Charge and Flavian?" Cassia asked.

"Mage Eudias and Sir Benedict are our intermediaries. They have assured us that Flavian is in favor of the treaty." Ioustin's expression softened. "Sir Benedict has asked us to tell you that Perita is out of harm's way, serving as one of Lady Hadrian's handmaidens until her lying in, while Callen is currently in Lord Hadrian's camp after earning a promotion. Genie is safe at Segetia, where she occupies herself with thirteen puppies. The Mages of Kyria are reaping a bountiful harvest of rimelace."

The words went straight to her heart, a message from her friend, as if he had read her mind. "Tell him I am well and happy in my new life."

"We have."

"Thank you." She looked at Lio, knowing this news about his friend would also be welcome to him. "Eudias isn't an apprentice anymore?"

Lio smiled. "The Tenebran mages of Anthros have awarded him his mage robes in honor of his deeds."

"Can they promote a Cordian war mage?"

"They can promote a Mage of Anthros. We're not certain of Eudias's status among the war mages."

"Please tell me they haven't sent Dexion Pretty Shoes back to Cordium yet, and that he is learning some life lessons as a hostage in the 'squalor' of Tenebra."

Lio's grin widened to display his fangs. "Chrysanthos is Flavian's 'guest.'"

"Brilliant," Cassia said. "I knew Flavian had that in him. Instead of riling the Orders about their Dexion's captivity, he's making it look like he has tacit support from the war mages. Showing that he has Hesperine support as well will be a stunning precedent."

But Ioustin was frowning. "Unfortunately, all Hesperine support must remain unofficial for now."

"What?" Cassia protested. "The lords who signed the treaty asked for Hesperine support."

"And they have it," Ioustin assured her, "quietly. However, welcoming Hesperines with open arms is still too controversial among some of the lords whose support Flavian needs."

"How can they be so entrenched?" Cassia demanded. "They know Hesperines saved their lives at the Equinox Summit. Their fathers, brothers, and sons came to Orthros and saw for themselves what Hesperines are like."

Lio shook his head. "You and I understand how difficult it is to drag the free lords out of their age-old prejudices. We know how long it takes."

"I know. I'm not surprised. But I am angry."

He took her hand. "They're willing to consider that we are not the enemy."

"They just don't want us in their kingdom." She gritted her teeth.

Uncle Argyros sighed. "A Hesperine embassy to Tenebra will leave. A human embassy to Orthros will return. It is another matter to officially open the kingdom to Hesperines for the first time since the lapse of our truce centuries ago. Many Tenebrans still consider that too close for comfort. They will continue to find Lucis's promise of war with Hesperines appealing."

"But they want to be rid of Lucis himself," said Lio.

Cassia grimaced. "Which means any number of Hesperine-hating free lords will look for an alternative to Lucis and Flavian, if pushed too far."

"Naturally," Uncle Argyros said, "the Full Council creates a feeding frenzy among predatory lords. Many will regard the weakening of Lucis as an opportunity for anyone to seize the throne."

Cassia's frustration boiled. "And they will see the disruption of his status quo as their chance to bring back the days of weak kings, when free lords had the freedom to cause havoc."

"Such contenders won't have the support Flavian does," Lio assured her.

"No," she said, "but the threat they pose is instability. He will need to win support from at least some of them to secure the kingship."

Argryros concluded, "He cannot do so if he is seen openly courting a Hesperine alliance."

Cassia looked to Ioustin. "But Flavian has assured us he will uphold the Solstice Oath once he is king?"

The prince gave a rueful half smile. "He has assured us he is in favor of the new treaty."

Agreeing with something and promising to do something about it were two entirely different things. Flavian was infuriating in his desire to please everyone. That could turn him from a good king into a bad one, and it still made Cassia sweat about her choice. "If he curries favor without exhibiting strong leadership, the lords will use him instead of respecting him. And if he proves unwilling to risk the lords' ire for what he knows is right, everyone will suffer. If I have misjudged him, I hope all of you can forgive me."

"Cassia," Lio protested, "you have worked wonders in Tenebra. You of all people are not responsible for Flavian's flaws."

She shook her head. "If Flavian fails to make the treaty with Orthros a cornerstone of his new reign, it will ruin everything we've worked for."

"No, it won't." Lio squeezed her hand. "He cannot ruin our lives here."

"You have given the Tenebrans an opportunity," said Master Kona. "We can care for them, but we cannot force their hands. Their Will must determine their future. If they squander this chance, you are not to blame."

"Thank you, Master Kona. I begin to understand why you have not withdrawn your proposal for the Departure."

"As agreed, I will not decide whether to reintroduce the measure until we return to Orthros Boreou and evaluate the situation in Tenebra at that time."

The closure of the border was not outside the realm of possibility. What was out of the question was for Solia to go back to Tenebra.

Basir spoke again. "Having the sister of a Hesperine on the throne would be preferable to Flavian, of course."

"Imagine," Kumeta said. "It would be unprecedented. A blood tie between one of Orthros's first bloodlines and the dynasty holding the Tenebran throne? Such a thing was unimaginable—until you and your sister, Cassia."

"It is already spring in the northern hemisphere," Basir cautioned. "If you do not wish for Flavian to wear your sister's crown, you have less than a season to search the vast Empire for the rightful queen."

Cassia drew herself up. "I understand why the envoys and the diplomatic service must consider such eventualities. But I object to any presumptions about my sister's desires before we have a chance to ask her. I want her to have the same choice I did. She should get to choose freedom and safety in Orthros. She doesn't owe a thing to the kingdom that reduced her to a fugitive, and I won't rest until I put a white Sanctuary rose in her hand myself."

Lio brought that hand to his lips, and the kiss he pressed on her knuckles felt like a silent declaration. "There came a time when the Hesperine people had to place Cassia's personal importance to us ahead of our diplomatic interests. We must do the same for Solia without hesitation."

Nike gave Mak a nod, and he addressed the circle. "The Stand's official position is that Solia's plight represents an unfulfilled request for Hesperine aid. Fifteen years ago, Cassia begged the help of Hesperines errant in recovering her sister. That is a sacred request, regardless of the fact that Orthros would be safer with Solia on the throne of Tenebra. The Stewards must always be willing to face danger to bring a human to safety."

"That is also the official position of the diplomatic service at this time," Uncle Argyros announced. "Our first course of action will be any negotiations necessary to bring Solia to Orthros from the Empire."

"But our initial search for her does not necessitate an official approach," Lio said. "It would surely be preferable for Cassia and me not to travel as representatives of Orthros for the time being."

Uncle Argyros frowned. "Diplomatic status would benefit you if trouble arose."

"True," Lio replied, "but our actions would reflect on the Hesperine people. If Orthros's diplomats were seen to be aiding a fugitive, it could create tensions in our alliance with the Empire."

Uncle Argyros looked thoughtful. "Diplomatic passes would open more doors for you."

"Searching for Solia through official channels might only bring her status to Imperial attention."

"And make it clear she had Orthros's protection."

"The Imperial authorities would not throw open the doors and let us search where we please. They would expect us to let them find her on our behalf. We would be in a fancy palace somewhere, rubbing elbows with officials while we waited for them to tell us where Solia is. If they did find her, they would have all the leverage in the situation."

Cassia hesitated. "I'm concerned the authorities could drive her further underground. She might not realize we were behind the search, trying to protect her."

It was unlike Lio not to pursue a diplomatic solution first, but Cassia saw his point. The thought of turning over the search to anyone else, even their allies, was unbearable to her. Her sister needed her, and this was the first time she could lift a finger to help.

Lio went on, "If we present ourselves as a Hesperine youngblood and a Newgift of Orthros sightseeing in the Empire, the authorities need not concern themselves with us. Such things happen all the time."

"Not when the Newgift is of Tenebran origin," Uncle Argyros pointed out.

"No one can question Cassia's origins," Lio insisted. "She will not be a Tenebran trespassing in the Empire. The Queens have already granted her Sanctuary."

"But if we find Solia in trouble," Cassia said, "we'll have no influence over her situation without diplomatic credentials."

Lio put a hand on her back. "If we discover that to be the case, we can return home to coordinate our approach with the elders, then reenter the Empire as diplomats."

Cassia gnawed on her lip. How could she stand by and let the Imperial magistrates take matters into their hands?

She only hoped she could avoid a disagreement with her Grace-uncle and new mentor over this. "Uncle Argyros, you know I have always favored a circumspect approach, and that Lio and I have accomplished much that way. As eager as I am to don my medallion, in this situation, perhaps it is best if I wait a little longer."

The elder diplomat did not try to to dissuade her. "I'll have your diplomatic passes ready, should you change your mind," was his only reply.

Lio turned to the Queens. "Annassa, this is a personal matter. With your permission, Cassia and I will not travel as official representatives of Orthros."

"My Queens," Cassia requested, "on this journey, may I go to the Empire merely as your Newgift?"

Annassa Soteira twined her hand in Queen Alea's. "Our people have the right to travel freely in the lands of my mortal origin. If that is your wish, go with our protection, and let none of our Imperial allies challenge you."

Uncle Argyros bowed. "I'll make sure this matter escapes my thoughts whenever I correspond with our ambassador at the Empress's court."

Annassa Soteira nodded. "Should we confirm, however, that a Tenebran is dwelling in the Empress's lands in violation of her laws, you must seek our counsel about how best to handle such a delicate situation. Go in search of answers, but return to us before you act."

"We understand, Annassa," Cassia replied.

"Now you have a journey to prepare for," said Kassandra. "Ziara doesn't stay in port for long. You'll want to be waiting for her arrival so you can catch her before she sets sail again. Your ship leaves tonight. I have it waiting for you."

With the words of the Goddess's oracle speeding them along, there was no time to waste.

THE PURPLE SAIL

AFTER THE CIRCLE'S SWIFT conclusion, Lio stepped Cassia
back to the quiet of their residence.

She looked at their newly planted rose. "This is wrong, Lio.
I can't disappoint you again."

He wrapped his arms around her, pulling her back against his chest,
and studied the rose. "You have done nothing."

"I keep raising your hopes, only to dash them."

"We have many reasons to be hopeful right now. But we can't stop for
your Gifting and risk missing Captain Ziara while she's in port."

"Lio, I…" He could sense the apology she didn't speak.

As if she should apologize for wanting to race toward her sister. Or
for the fact that she and Solia were unwillingly intertwined with the king
and all the politics that came with him.

"Just think how much better your Gift Night will be with Solia here."

"Oh." She gasped softly. "That does feel worth waiting for."

"Her memory brought us together. It's only right that she be here for
your Gifting and our avowal."

"It sounds like a dream."

"One we will make come true."

"I know the risks she still faces, wherever she may be. But even Basir
believes she has avoided deportation and remained safe in the Empire. It
finally feels safe to hope."

Lio placed a kiss on her neck. "I was so afraid you would have your
heart broken again. But years of despair have begun to lift from you
tonight. I can feel it happening. The Goddess has answered my prayers."

"At least one of the fears you've carried for me has been lifted." She reached back and touched his cheek, her fingers chilly on his skin.

He caught them between his hand and face, warming them. "You will be safe in the Empire. That reassures me as well."

"It will be remarkable to travel in a land welcoming to Hesperines, on the far side of the world from the Collector. But we'd best hurry. Missing an oracle's ship sounds like a very bad idea."

"Don't worry. I'm an experienced traveler, and you're fairly well prepared, since you already have most of what you would have needed for our trip to goat country. I'll have us ready in time. We can make it to a nice inn in one of the Imperial port cities before sunrise."

With a hasty cleaning spell, they changed into travel robes. The calf-length robes Hesperines favored on journeys were much more practical than formal silks. They paired them with Imperial trousers, the loose, blousing legwear gathered at the ankle that Orthros had adopted from their allies.

As Lio and Cassia packed, they found a rhythm, tossing each other what they needed, repacking what they'd brought from the north at record speed.

Cassia offered him his astrolabe more carefully, holding out the elaborate brass instrument. "Would this help?"

"We wouldn't want to leave without it." He checked the compartment inside for all the necessary parts. "I'll need it to calculate how many hours of darkness we'll have each night. Not to mention it's useful for navigation."

"I wish I knew how to use one, but I'd never make it through one of Hypatia's lectures on her invention."

He tucked the astrolabe into a secure pocket of his pack. "Kia and I can teach you instead. I knew we survived her mother's lectures for a good reason."

Cassia sighed. "I should probably start with basic geometry."

"While we travel, you'll have the chance to learn many things, the way you learn best—by practical experience." Lio levitated a scarf her way. "Here, you'll need head and face protection to prevent sunburn."

"Do Hesperines get sunburn?"

"No, the sun has no effect on our skin at all. It stays the same from the night of our Gifting."

"Oh. So I get to keep however many freckles I have upon my transformation."

He grinned. "May I suggest you sunbathe while we're traveling?"

"I'm happy to do so for both of us."

"Sorry I can't join you. The more daylight Hesperines are exposed to during the Dawn Slumber, the harder it is to wake up."

She grimaced. "I hope Imperial inns have thick curtains."

"They have accommodations that cater to Hesperine guests."

They had almost finished packing when a goat bleated beyond the side door. Lio sensed Zoe and her familiars there in the private courtyard that gave friends and family direct access to the coffee room. She paused just outside, probably to herd a wayward kid.

Cassia buckled her pack with a dismal click. "What are we going to tell Zoe? It will devastate her for us to leave."

"Perhaps it's time for us to explain everything to her about Solia."

"Yes, now that we have more hopeful news, I think it is."

Lio carried their packs out to the coffee room as he lifted his veils. Zoe burst into the room with her spyglass in hand. In her haste, she didn't even notice that her goats were misbehaving by jumping onto the coffee table.

The suckling threw her arms around Cassia. "I can't believe it! The good pirates took Soli to the Empire!"

Lio's father entered the room and plucked the goats off the table. Right behind him, Mother worked a cleaning spell and placed a tray of finger foods where the kids had stood. "Argyros told your father and me about the circle, and we thought it best to explain matters to Zoe."

Lio sighed in relief. "Thank you, Mother."

Cassia held Zoe, rocking them both on their feet. "It's the most wonderful news, isn't it?"

"We can find her with my spyglass!" Zoe held up her prized artifact.

Cassia's eyes widened, and she looked at Lio. "What a wonderful idea. Let's ask Lio if the spyglass can be used for that."

They had been so occupied with politics and chasing privateers, something so simple hadn't occurred to Lio. When he had enchanted the spyglass, he had never considered that Zoe might use it for such an ambitious purpose. He was unsure what the effect might be if she tried. He couldn't bear to think of how she would feel if it didn't work.

"Of course it can," said Zoe. "Lio enchanted it so it will show me the way to whatever I'm looking for. And right now, I want to find Solia more than anything. My spyglass can reach all the way to the Empire, right?"

Lio put a hand on Zoe's shoulder. "Well, I tested to make sure it would reach all the way across Selas or Haima, so you could find anyone you were looking for at home. It might be possible for it to reach farther than that."

"Let's try right now!"

Zoe took Lio's and Cassia's hands. She stepped to the roof, and Lio brought himself, Cassia, and Knight along with her. He sensed his parents and the goats arrive behind them, the whole family gathered to comfort Zoe if she was about to be disappointed.

His little sister faced north, toward the Empire, and put the spyglass to her eye. Her face scrunched in concentration.

Cassia's heart beat a little too fast, and his parents' auras tensed with concern. Moonbeam bleated.

Zoe lowered the spyglass, still staring north. Her chin trembled. "I don't see anything."

Lio knelt beside her and rested a hand behind her neck. "Try one more time, Zoe flower, and show me what you see."

She nodded and put the spyglass to her eye. With the gentlest touch of mind magic upon their Blood Union, he observed the vision through the glass that only Zoe could see with her eyes.

He let out a breath of relief. He recognized the strange image, which resembled a night sky turned inside-out and full of haphazard stars. "What does that remind you of, Zoe?"

She frowned. "It looks like whenever I try to find you and Cassia, but you're already under a veil for the night."

Lio had made very sure his innocent sister could not use the spyglass to peer at any adults behind veil spells. "Yes, exactly. I think what we're seeing is concealing magic of some kind. Wherever Solia is, she's hidden."

Zoe gasped. "You think Hesperines could be veiling Solia?"

"Or an Imperial mage could be protecting her with some kind of spell."

"Maybe a sneaky privateer!" Zoe exclaimed.

Lio exchanged a glance with Cassia. It made sense for a Tenebran in the Empire to be under such magic—especially if she was safely hidden.

"Thank you so much for looking, Zoe," said Cassia. "That's very reassuring."

Zoe turned away from the view. "I guess you'll have to go on a long trip to search for her after all."

"I'm sorry we have to leave so suddenly." Lio felt the words were terribly insufficient.

Until Zoe looked at him as if he had just suggested that mince pies grew on trees. "You have to hurry! You have to find Solia. Then I'll have two big sisters to visit goat country with."

Lio smiled and touched her hair. "Thank you for understanding, Zoe. You're so brave."

"I'm not afraid of open spaces anymore." Zoe took a deep breath. "But that's not why I can't go with you."

Lio and Cassia exchanged a look. He had been dreading trying to explain to Zoe why they couldn't take her with them.

Her face was so solemn. "Courier training starts next week. It wouldn't be honorable to miss out on a chance to serve the Queens."

Lio beamed at her. "I'm so proud of you, Zoe. Of course you must stay and start courier lessons."

"And I have to practice first, because even though they'll teach us, I want to be extra good at stepping before I start learning. At the end of training, they have the official tryouts to pick who gets to be a courier!"

Cassia knelt beside her, too. "We'll be back before courier tryouts. When you apply, we'll be here to cheer you on."

"I know."

Lio pressed a kiss to the child's forehead. *Goddess, let us never disappoint Zoe's unconditional faith in us.*

"I'll water your flowers for you while you're gone," Zoe promised Cassia.

"Thank you so much," Cassia replied. "I won't worry about them, knowing they're in your care."

"I would take care of Knight, too, but he can't stay with me." Zoe hugged the dog's neck. "You'll need him to help you find Solia. I read about it in *Dimitri's Daring Dog*. He let his dog sniff something that belonged to the missing girl, and then they were able to find her."

"You're exactly right," Cassia said. "Knight's tracking skills will help us very much."

Father rubbed his beard. "A search and rescue mission in the Empire. That's an easy task for the Blood Errant."

Mother put her hand on his arm in a staying gesture Lio had often seen over the years. "You know we cannot go with them, my Grace."

His father's presence in the Blood Union rumbled. "I keep misplacing daughters Abroad, and everyone expects me to sit at home and twiddle my thumbs."

"I too hate that our hands are tied, but we will be of greater help to Cassia and Lio sitting in the Firstblood Circle." His mother's aura flashed.

Lio rose to his feet. "What's happening in the Circle?"

Whatever it might be, the look in his mother's eye said that Blood Komnena would be a formidable obstacle. "Do you have time to talk to Xandra before you leave? She can explain."

"Mak and Lyros are coming back with our Trial sisters any time now." After the conference with the elders, they had quietly agreed it was time for an Eighth Circle conference.

Father wrapped an arm around Zoe and touched a hand to Cassia's head. "We may not be going with you, but we will be waiting to welcome Solia into our bloodline."

Cassia didn't flinch. Her aura softened as she drew comfort from his gesture. "She never had a Papa, either."

"Now she does."

Lio's mother embraced him and Cassia. "Three daughters in one year. The Goddess's cup runs over. Travel safely, my dear ones. May the Goddess's Eyes light your path."

"And her darkness keep you in Sanctuary," his father echoed, clasping Lio's wrist and pulling him close.

Zoe clung to Lio for a long moment. "Can I check on you and Cassia with my spyglass while you're gone?"

"Of course." Lio began to suspect that the range of the artifact was not a concern, if Zoe's experiment just now was any indication. The capabilities of his magic could still surprise him.

"You have to write to me every night," Zoe told Cassia.

"I promise, Zoe flower. It will help us both practice our reading and writing."

Komnena herded a precocious Aurora away from the railing. "After Zoe's first courier lesson, we should all celebrate together. Your father and I could bring the sucklings over, and we can all choose a place to meet in the Empire."

"That would be wonderful." Cassia didn't appear anymore eager than Zoe for them to let one another go.

Their parents waited patiently for Zoe to get enough affection from Lio and Cassia, and Lio trusted that the oracle would know to schedule her ship around the suckling's insecurities.

"Zoe," Mother suggested at last, "why don't we go to Kadi and Javed's so you can tell Bosko the good news about Solia?"

Zoe gasped. "Oh, I can't wait to tell him. Now he has to let me be Captain Ziara every time we play privateers! Because she saved my Grace-sister."

Apollon lifted Zoe on his hip. With a look of determination, she waved at Lio and Cassia as their parents stepped away with her.

Lio handed his handkerchief to Cassia before her hands were halfway to her face. She clutched the handkerchief and dried her tears. "Ugh. I'm in worse shape than Zoe."

"That's perfectly all right." His own throat was uncomfortably tight. He wrapped his arms around her and waited for the lump in this throat to ease.

They had just stepped back down to the coffee room when their Trial brothers came in through the side door.

"We sensed tears," Lyros said with concern.

"Aw." Mak enfolded Cassia in one of his hugs.

"This is the first time I've had to leave Zoe," Cassia fretted.

Mak patted her back. "You'll return with Solia. It will be worth it."

Cassia nodded and dried her face with a mighty sniff that Lio found so very endearing. When she handed his handkerchief back to him, he worked a cleaning spell on it, then filled it with fruits and nuts from the food tray and handed it back to her.

She gave a laugh muffled by her stuffy nose. "Of course."

He patted her midsection. "You can't start a journey to the Empire on an empty stomach."

Shaking her head at him with affection in her eyes, she sat down at the coffee table to eat.

As they all took a seat around her, Lio was surprised at the dilemma in Mak's aura, which was becoming more and more evident on his face. It was unlike his cousin to feel so conflicted. Mak usually felt sure of his course of action right away and pursued it with all his strength and heart.

"Mak," Lio said, "we all know you need to stay here."

"Cassia brought my sister back. I have to help find hers."

Cassia put a hand on Mak's arm. "Nike returned to Orthros for my sake, but we all know you are the reason she has stayed."

"That may be, but—"

"It is true," Lyros said. "She'll only attend a sparring session if you're in the arena. What's to stop her from going errant again the moment you aren't here to give her a reason not to?"

Mak blew out a sigh. "Then we should tell Lio and Cassia why Nike isn't first in line to help them search the Empire for Solia."

There was some worry in Lyros's aura, but also amusement on his face. "Going to be that little brother again, are you?"

"They deserve to know. Besides, I can get away with it."

Lyros's shoulders shook with quiet laughter. "I don't disagree."

"Is this about Nike's quest?" Lio asked.

"Yes," Mak answered. "But only I—and by extension, Lyros—know anything about it."

"Nike's secrets are safe with us," Cassia assured him.

Mak nodded. "All those scrolls she's been writing? They're correspondence with a contact of hers Abroad. She says he has information that could inform her decision on whether to concede defeat in her quest to find Methu."

"Well." Lio sat back. "The fact that she trusted you with this, but also has not gone to speak with the contact herself, proves why you need to stay."

"You see why she can't leave for the Empire," Mak said. "Secret letters from behind enemy lines aren't something the couriers can deliver. She must be here to receive the messages when they arrive."

"How is she communicating with her contact?" Cassia asked. "Never mind. We won't cross the veil."

"Thank you," Mak replied.

"Mak, stop feeling guilty," said Lio. "You're holding your family together and possibly aiding Nike on her quest for Methu. That is just as important as Cassia and me putting her family back together by finding her lost sister."

"Lio is right," she said without hesitation. "Nike has already done her part to help us find Solia."

Mak looked at her, all his regret on his honest face. "I haven't."

"You do your part all the time," she replied. "You and Lyros already canceled your own romantic getaway to the Empire to be here for your family."

"And don't apologize for it again," Lyros said. "You don't hear me complaining about getting to spar with the Victory Star, do you?"

Mak chuckled at that. "Well, we can travel anytime, but we can't always train with the First Master Steward, can we?"

"Besides," Cassia said, "Zoe will cope much better with you and Lyros here."

"It will ease our minds," Lio agreed.

"Bosko needs you too," Cassia went on, "especially right now, when the family that still feels new to him is changing."

Lio waved at the coffee pot in front of him. "And Uncle Argyros needs one of us to peer over the pile of dispatches and check on him."

"Steward Telemakhos," said Lyros, "clearly you must answer the call of duty and remain on the home front."

"Well, when you all put it that way, I suppose you're right." Mak sighed. He hesitated a long moment. When did Mak ever hesitate? "And you're not wrong, Lio, about me helping her with something... I can't tell you what it is yet, not till I'm certain it will work. But it could help keep all of us safe, no matter what is to come."

Lio rested a hand on his cousin's shoulder. "Mak, that sounds truly important. How can you doubt that we would understand?"

"I knew you would. I just wish I could be in two places at once."

"The Stand always knows where our place is," Lyros said, "and diplomats know they have to go."

Cassia sighed. "We diplomats will try to restrain our voracious curiosity about Mak's secret endeavor."

Lio held up a hand. "I make no promises. My scholarly inquisitiveness may result in pestering Mak with questions."

Lyros groaned. "When he doesn't answer them, I'll be your next victim."

"Of course," Lio said.

At that moment, their Trial sisters swept in and joined them. The whole Eighth Circle was gathered, and by the determination in Xandra's aura, the coffee table was to be their council table.

Nodora reached across and took Cassia's hands. "Mak and Lyros told us all about Solia's escape on the privateer ship. We are so happy for you."

Kia's eyes were alight. "A defiance for the history books. Imagine her laughing all the way to the Empire while the mages wrung their hands!"

Xandra squared her shoulders. "I wish we could all go with you to find her, but the Eighth Circle will soon be called upon to defend our political position. Since I'm our vote in the Firstblood Circle, it ought to be me."

"What storm is brewing in the Circle now?" Cassia asked.

"My mother," Kia answered.

Lio winced. "Hypatia has been apprised of Kalos's latest discovery?"

"Along with the rest of the elder firstbloods," Xandra confirmed.

Lio rubbed his brow. "Of course. The traditionalists' blood must be boiling at the mere thought of Hesperines involving ourselves in a dynastic dispute in Tenebra."

Cassia's stubborn chin was set. "The only future the firstbloods should prepare for is giving Solia a seat in Blood Komnena's section of the Circle. Not a throne in Tenebra."

"I couldn't agree more," said Xandra, "but unfortunately the elder firstbloods take the same position as the envoys and the diplomatic service. They deem it necessary to prepare for all possible outcomes."

Cassia threw up her hands. "Is it too much to ask that they all wait to bare their fangs until we ask my sister what she wants?"

"Yes," Kia confirmed, "that is far too much to ask of my mother. You know how she is. At the first hint of progress, she must batten down the hatches against the winds of change."

Nodora patted her hand. "She's still recovering from when Lio demolished the status quo by inviting the first Tenebran embassy here."

Xandra grinned. "And when Cassia convinced Kona to table the Departure."

"Yes." Kia smirked. "That did come as quite a shock to my mother, when her greatest political ally gave an ear to a rebellious Newgift."

"Traitorous, heretical, and rebellious?" Cassia arched a brow. "Do stop, Kia, or my pride shall become insufferable to you all."

Lio planted a kiss on her cheek. "Become as insufferable as you like, my rose. You earned it."

"Hear, hear," said Kia. "It is the Eighth Circle's sacred duty to be as insufferable to the elders as possible."

There was a gleam in Xandra's eye. "We'll certainly have a chance to do so during this vote."

"Hypatia is calling a vote?" Cassia asked. "Oh, no."

"Oh, yes." Kia scowled. "My mother is putting forth a proposal to enforce her vision for Orthros, which is anathema to all our circle's hopes for the future."

"We haven't even set eyes on my sister," Cassia protested. "What is there to vote about?"

Xandra answered, "We don't know the details of her proposal, but we do know it's coming."

Lio clicked his tongue at Kia. "Surely you have not been engaged in scholastic espionage against your mother."

Kia crossed her arms. "I cannot take credit for this discovery. Unfortunately."

"Kona warned us," Xandra said.

Lio's brows shot up. "Aunt Kona told you in advance that her dearest friend and partisan is preparing to propose a vote that we will disagree with?"

"Not in so many words," Xandra replied, "but essentially, yes. Tonight was the first time Kona has ever given me a list of the podium requests. Including Hypatia's. It's perfectly acceptable to make another royal firstblood privy to the roster of who will speak at the next Circle, but she never shows it to me, her youngest sister, especially not this many weeks in advance."

Lio smiled. "When you promised to make the Circle spin, you meant it. Even Aunt Kona has taken notice."

"I think she's pleased that I've looked up from my silkworms to take an interest in politics. 'Coming out of your cocoon,' she said." Xandra rolled her eyes, but her aura betrayed that she was pleased.

"Does Hypatia's podium request provide any hints about the nature of her proposal?" Cassia's aura glittered with calculation.

Lio was reminded just how much his Grace was suited to politics. Seeing her rise in the Firstblood Circle was a pleasure compared to watching Tenebran politics drag her down.

Xandra shook her head. "We have no details, but considering her political position, we suspect she aims to place some kind of limit on Hesperine involvement in Tenebran affairs."

"She cannot propose the Departure, can she?" Cassia asked.

"No," Xandra said firmly, "only a member of the royal family can invoke that."

"A vote like this could still tie the Charge's hands," said Lyros. "If the firstbloods vote that Hesperines cannot increase our role in Tenebra any further, then the Charge will never be able to expand their mission. It would limit their ability to respond to new threats to our Hesperines errant, the Hesperites, or other mortals in need."

"Would Hypatia's vote erode the Solstice Oath?" Cassia demanded.

"The treaty is sworn," Lio said. "The Firstblood Circle cannot revoke it by a simple vote. But a motion like this could preclude any revisions of the terms that might strengthen Orthros's alliance with Flavian, once he is king."

Xandra bit her lip. "Of course, it would also mean we could never assist Solia in taking the throne, should she want it. Not that our circle is in favor of that in the first place. But it must be the real reason for Hypatia's proposal."

Cassia shook her head. "So the firstblood circle is threatening everything we've worked for due to something we don't even support?"

"Alas, yes," said Lio. "Welcome to the complexities of immortal politics."

Nodora put a hand on Xandra's shoulder. "Our cause needs a voice. Songs have great power to sway minds. I can't let Epodos control the narrative of this political situation. I want the Eighth Circle's commentary sung in the coffeehouses—preferably louder than my brother's."

Kia placed her hand on Xandra's other shoulder. "You also need an instigator. Someone who isn't afraid to set a fire under the elder's tails, while you're warming their hearts. Everyone expects me to cause trouble. I can rally all the younger malcontents who feel unheard by the elders. Not all of them have votes, but their partisanship will still make a statement."

"They're right," Lyros said. "If too many of us are absent from Orthros in this climate, we'll leave our position undefended."

"We all worked so hard to change things during the Solstice Summit," said Cassia. "We mustn't surrender the ground we gained."

Lio sighed. "Politics won't stop while Cassia and I are looking for Solia."

Cassia nodded. "We need our views represented in the debates and votes, and we must make sure our partisans know they can rely on us, lest we lose them."

Xandra gave Lio and Cassia miserable look. "I think we'd best hold down the fort here."

"We need you to," said Cassia. "I'm sorry Lio and I won't be able to help you, especially since I'm officially a diplomat now."

"Leave it to us," Xandra assured them.

"And let us handle the search," Lio replied.

Cassia handed his empty handkerchief back to him. "All we'll be doing at first is waiting for Ziara to arrive, then asking her for information on Solia's whereabouts. We are equal to a negotiation with privateers, aren't we, my love?"

He took the handkerchief and kissed her hand. "To be sure."

"It may benefit you two to travel on your own," Lyros pointed out. "There are advantages to a smaller party, situations where you'll draw less notice and be able to respond faster to what you learn."

Mak leveled a stern gaze at Lio and Cassia. "But if you need any kind of help from us at all, you must promise you'll call in reinforcements."

"Of course." Lio clasped his cousin's wrist.

Mak gripped his wrist firmly. "We have your backs."

"We know." Cassia smiled.

Lio added, "My parents want to bring Zoe and Bosko over for an evening after her first courier lesson. Perhaps all of you can get away for a little while then and meet us wherever we happen to be in the Empire."

Lyros glanced at Mak. "I don't think Nike will disappear, if we're only gone for a few hours."

Mak stroked his chin. "I wonder if I'm powerful enough to cast blood shackles on her to make her stay put."

Lyros shuddered. "Let's just ask Nephalea and Alkaios to keep an eye on her while we're gone."

"Until then," Xandra said, "hopefully these gifts will help you on your journey." She reached into a pocket of her robes and held out her hand to Cassia and Lio.

On her palm rested a moonstone the size of an eye. Lio recognized the spark of magic resting rather uneasily inside it.

"A fire charm!" Cassia accepted it, turning it over carefully in her hands. "Thank you so much, Xandra. These are rare enough, but this one even more so. It's the only one I've ever seen that isn't made of sunstone."

"I make all mine from moonstone," Xandra explained. "Lyros used his knowledge as a jeweler to help me adapt the spell."

Lyros gestured to the tiny artifact. "Xandra is the only known fire mage who can make charms out of moonstone, bringing her affinity and blood magic together."

Xandra blushed. "You never know when you'll need a fire on a journey."

"I brought you a dictionary of major Imperial languages." Kia slid a small, fat book across the table to Cassia.

"Oh, this is perfect. I'll treasure it."

Nodora smiled with some amusement as she offered Cassia a small wooden flute. "Here's mine. Don't worry, you don't have to learn to play it. It's a dog flute."

Cassia's eyes lit with delight. "For Knight."

"Only dogs can hear the sounds it makes. You can experiment with different notes and see how he reacts. Some will calm him if he's anxious in a new environment, while others will call him if he loses his bearings."

Cassia looked at Knight and put the flute to her lips. Lio heard her breath move through the wooden instrument, but Nodora was correct. Even his Hesperine ears didn't hear any music.

Knight, on the other hand, leapt to his feet and wagged his tail, then let out a happy bark.

They all laughed.

"You all have our gratitude," Lio told their Trial sisters.

When another aura filled the still-open door, silence fell.

Xandra straightened. "Kona."

Her eldest sister raised a brow, a glint of amusement in her eyes. "Am I interrupting an Eighth Circle plot? Excellent."

Excellent that she was interrupting, or that they were plotting? Lio wasn't entirely sure.

"Master Kona," said Cassia, "Xandra has told us of the upcoming vote. I was under the impression nothing would be decided until our return north."

"I will decide nothing for the time being," Aunt Kona replied, "but the rest of the circle has the freedom and the authority to make their own decisions."

"Freedom?" Kia protested. "There's no freedom in my mother's faction. She wants to make Orthros as traditional as her mince pie recipe and her hair."

Aunt Kona raised her brows at Kia. "Her mince pies are second to none. Don't tell me you'd really like to change that recipe."

Kia offered Aunt Kona a bow from her seat. "Nevertheless, I hold to my argument."

"I would expect nothing less from you, Kia."

"Master Kona," Cassia asked, "may I ask what your position is on Elder Firstblood Hypatia's vote?"

"I am keeping my promise to withhold judgment until our return to Orthros Boreou. In the meantime, I will hear all arguments and weigh them fairly. I am especially interested to hear the points my youngest sister will make."

"You mean you're abstaining from the vote?" Xandra asked.

"Indeed. I pledged myself to a course of action. On my honor, I will not make an exception, even for a dear friend. Hypatia should know that, and if she chooses to make this motion at this time, she must accept that she will not have my vote."

Xandra's eyes widened. "That means the yays will be one royal vote short, and the nays will have mine."

"Why yes, it does. I suppose the newest voting member of the royal bloodlines will have to take on a greater role."

Xandra sat up straighter. "I'll do my best."

Aunt Kona smiled. "I look forward to it."

"I wonder if I can persuade Rudhira to stay for the vote."

"I have already secured his agreement that he will."

"But he'll vote against Hypatia as well."

"You know I like to see him at home, involved in royal matters. The potential impacts of Hypatia's measure on the Charge's mission in Tenebra happened to come up in conversation."

Now Xandra's eyes gleamed with no small amount of admiration for her sister.

"Everyone has a right to be heard in the Firstblood Circle," Aunt Kona said.

Xandra's mouth twitched. "Is it appropriate for you to be party to this discussion of rebellion?"

"I am but an impartial observer. One who comes bearing papers and the tidings that Lio and Cassia's ship is waiting."

Lio heard Cassia take a deep breath. It was time to go.

He felt a pang at the knowledge that they would not have their Trial circle with them to help bring Solia home.

But he couldn't deny he felt an instinctual satisfaction that he would have Cassia all to himself on this journey.

Aunt Kona waited patiently while they took leave of their circle and thanked them again for their gifts.

Mak gave each of them another embrace. "One more for the road. May our Union remind you that your circle is always with you."

Cassia held onto him a moment longer. "Don't worry. One night—perhaps not very long from now—both our families will be here in Orthros together, in one piece."

After their friends reluctantly stepped away, Aunt Kona offered Lio and Cassia each a scroll case. "Your papers. Documents for private persons, just as you asked."

Lio accepted his. "I've never had papers approved that quickly."

"You would be amazed how quickly they work with me looking over their shoulders."

Cassia studied her scroll. "Newgift Cassia. Citizen of Orthros." A smile came to her face, and her aura swelled with emotion.

"The proper permits to bring an animal into the Empire are also there, for Knight. The letter from Orthros's animal healers exempts him from inspection and quarantine."

Cassia lifted her head and met her mentor's gaze. "Thank you, Master Kona."

She gave Cassia a nod and smile. "Are you two ready for your first mission in the Empire?"

Cassia tucked her papers in her gardening satchel and secured it across her chest. "I only need provisions for Knight."

"We can purchase those when we arrive," Lio said. "I have our funds in order."

"Excellent." Aunt Kona beckoned. "Follow me."

Cassia yanked on her cloak. Lio put his arm around her, focusing on her, Knight, and their small collection of belongings. When the princess stepped, Lio went in her wake.

She brought them to a small, private dock. One of Kassandra's boats was waiting for them with no one but the oracle herself on board.

"There's my cargo." Kassandra put her hands on her hips. "Why, Kona, have you brought me contraband to smuggle out of Orthros?"

"Innocent contraband, Ritual mother, unfairly taxed by well-meaning elders."

"Well, in that case, I won't report you to the magistrates."

Aunt Kona's aura sparked with mirth. "You wouldn't get far with the Royal Master Magistrate. She will attest that my activities are justifiable."

Kassandra nodded. "Thick as thieves with the Queens' Master Economist. No telling what those two get up to."

Aunt Kona turned to Lio and Cassia once more. "Off you go."

Cassia smiled at her. "Thank you again for all of your help."

"Recall that it is in my interest to settle the matter of the missing heir to the Tenebran throne, so I may steer Orthros's future accordingly. Not to mention, I intend to endear you to the Empire. I have plans for you, and I will not have you poached by those who wish to embroil you once more in Tenebran affairs."

"Well," Cassia replied carefully, "at least abstaining and watching our Trial circle lead a discussion will be one of the easier tasks you've had to perform in the pursuit of your political aims for Orthros."

"Oh no, the Eighth Circle has a special place on my list of extreme and unpredictable factors in current events."

Lio swallowed a laugh. Cassia had succeeded in teasing her mentor, and Master Kona had teased her back.

"In that case," Cassia said with even more confidence, "I appreciate the lengths you're going to for my political future."

"You have our gratitude, Aunt Kona." Lio offered her his hand. Instead of giving him a wrist clasp, she took his hand in both of hers and patted it.

"How can we thank you?" Cassia asked.

"Bring me a souvenir, if you like." The princess lifted a hand, then stepped away.

Lio hastened to levitate their two trunks into the boat. "You're sailing us over yourself, Ritual mother?"

She grabbed the trunks as they came over and guided them to the deck. "I wouldn't miss this for all the mince pies in Orthros. Come aboard."

Lio helped Cassia onto the small vessel, one of Kassandra's personal craft that she enjoyed sailing on her own. Knight leapt from the dock and landed beside them, clearly eager for whatever this new activity with his lady might be.

Kassandra let out the single purple sail. "This will get us through the main port and the spirit gates."

"Spirit gates?" Cassia gripped Lio's hand.

"They're nothing like a displacement gate," he hurried to reassure her.

Kassandra shook her head. "That hole the necromancers ripped in the world at Rose House hadn't anything to do with Imperial magic. Spirit gates are the work of sacred ancestral power. After every Migration, our allies open them to connect Orthros to key locations throughout the Empire, so trade can resume, and Imperial guests can go home or arrive in Orthros."

"Don't you need to be there for the gate ceremony?" Lio asked Kassandra.

"That's what I have tributaries for," she replied. "Learning to delegate is key to living forever without losing your mind. It's more fun to take a little voyage with you two."

"What ceremony is it?" Cassia asked.

Visions filled Lio's head of all the Imperial ambassadors he'd ever met trapping him in lengthy diplomatic discussions. "When the Empress's representatives open the spirit gates for the season, they come to officially welcome us back to this hemisphere. The port will be swarming with dignitaries here to meet the Queens. Won't someone stop us?"

"I've foreseen their faces when they watch us slip through, and I can't resist seeing it come true." Kassandra laughed. "Relax and try to enjoy yourselves, you flighty youngbloods. No one stops a purple sail."

Kassandra guided her craft through the maze of the Veins. The noise of the city drifted down to them from above, but no one seemed to notice their passage. The boat slipped out of a narrow opening and sailed into the main port.

Hesperine elders waited on the docks for the Imperials who would soon arrive. More officials occupied the decks of Orthros's ships, which were drifting out to their positions for the ceremony, the banners of their bloodlines and circles whipping in the breeze. The Queens overlooked the port from a balcony in the cliffside that was draped in black and white velvet.

Kassandra's boat sneaked up on the ships, then slid right past them, a little rebel cutting through the pomp and circumstance. Lio laughed aloud, the wind blowing through his hair. The ships' lanterns sent colors cascading across Cassia's face, lighting her gaze as she looked ahead.

Kassandra sailed her craft between the great statues of her and the Queens and into open waters.

THROUGH THE SPIRIT GATE

ONE MOMENT, CASSIA WAS looking out at the meeting point of Orthros's dark, icy waters and Hespera's night sky. Then that horizon transformed. The eternal sky and constant sea changed.

As if a celestial hand had given it a tug, the world itself seemed to ease open before them. She could see where the cold, blue world of Orthros Notou faded into a calm indigo sea under a sky where clouds drifted across the moons.

Whispers reached Cassia's ears, gentle as that sea, soft as those clouds. But the sounds did not come from the sea or the wind. She frowned, rubbing her ears.

Then another portal opened up, and another, until at least a dozen rose in a semicircle before the entrance to Sisters' Port. And through each one, a different group of Imperial ships sailed out into Orthros's waters.

Vessels of every shape and size, flags of every color. Cassia had never seen such a magnificent display from humans before. As the fleet engulfed Kassandra's craft, a dozen different languages reached Cassia's ears. But none of them were like the whispers she had just heard.

Kassandra sailed against the sea traffic without slowing down. On the larger decks above, the elegantly clad Imperial ambassadors, traders, and nobles looked properly scandalized. But they all bowed as the purple sail passed by.

Kassandra's craft broke free of the Imperial fleet and sailed straight toward the central spirit gate.

Suddenly Cassia couldn't see anything around her but black sky and white stars. She felt Lio's nearness, but couldn't hear his voice.

A whisper touched her cheek, and a caress murmured in her ears, tender as she imagined a mother to be. She had never heard the voice before, but it felt familiar, speaking words she didn't understand.

The boat slowed, and she could see again. They were gliding through the smooth, moonlit waters under the cottony clouds.

Cassia peeled out of her cloak, which suddenly felt oppressive in the balmy air.

Lio draped the garment over his arm. "All right?"

She wasn't sure. "Well, it didn't make me ill like a mage's traversal."

"Spirit gates use fundamentally different magic. They allow passage through the spirit phase, rather than forcing a way against the laws of the natural phase."

A shiver went down Cassia's spine. "The spirit phase? You mean...the afterlife?"

"It is the plane of existence where our spirits originate and return. One of the great mysteries." He took her hand, his flesh and blood touch reassuringly solid. "The natural phase is the world we can see and touch."

"Did you...hear something?"

"No," Lio said gravely. "Immortality binds Hesperine spirit and flesh together, preventing us from being torn from the natural phase, but also from fully communing with the spirit phase. We hear nothing when we go through spirit gates. But mortals do."

"What was it?"

He smoothed her windblown hair. "Echoes. From the spirit realm."

"You mean..."

"Your ancestors."

Cassia startled. "I don't want to hear anything the king's rotting ancestors have to say."

Kassandra laughed. "Imperial wisdom teaches us that we have a much stronger connection to our mothers' ancestors."

"I don't know anything about my mother's family."

"They know you," Kassandra replied.

Cassia wasn't sure if she wanted to forget the eerie message or hang on to every incomprehensible word.

Who had her mother's ancestors been? The king had taken Thalia from a Temple of Hedon in Cordium, where she had been a handmaiden of the god of pleasure and chance. The playthings of the powerful men of the Magelands. Had Thalia been born to a prostitute, with no possibility of a different future? Or had she once been free? Perhaps something had befallen her that had doomed her to a life of service to Hedon.

Where had Cassia's forebears been then? What kind of family would fail to rescue Thalia from that fate?

Cassia could only guess. In Tenebra, communication with the spirits only happened in tales so old, they were twisted, gnarled versions of whatever seed of wisdom had once given rise to them. Even the necromancers of the Order of Hypnos, the experts on death's secrets, agreed the shroud between life and the afterlife was impenetrable.

But clearly, the Imperial side of the world had her own rules.

Kassandra watched the horizon, sailing her small craft with relaxed, practiced motions. "My mother and father had very different ancestors. She was one of the earliest Empresses of the Owia Dynasty, the lineage that still holds the throne. He was from Vardara, which you know as the Silklands. When she had a child with him, it sealed her alliance with his homeland, joining Vardara to her Empire, ending centuries of war."

So much had rested upon Kassandra from the moment she was born. That was the life of any royal offspring. "So it was a political union?"

"Love is a more effective basis for politics than most people assume."

Kassandra had always seemed comfortable talking about her past, but it must be difficult. Cassia listened, unwilling to ask a question that might cause pain. Lio didn't say anything, either.

"I was born into my mother's dynasty," Kassandra went on, "but in Vardara, heredity is traced through the father."

Cassia started to have an inkling of the dynastic dispute that had landed Kassandra in Orthros and her sister on the Imperial throne.

"Many in my father's homeland were not satisfied with Vardara's new status as a sister state of the Empire. They saw in me an opportunity to exert their influence. They hoped to sway the Queen Mothers to transfer their mandate to me, so that I might start a new dynasty in the name of the Silklands." Kassandra smiled, her fangs showing. "You see how well their plan worked."

Cassia knew what it felt like to be someone's puppet. She had also chosen the Hesperine path instead. But was that the decision that had cost Kassandra her sister?

"My father had a grove of trees from Vardara planted at the Imperial palace as a gift for my mother. My sister and I loved to sneak away from our duties and watch the gardeners work. We even planted one tree together. I'm quite sure it's still there, for the current Empress is my sister's direct descendant and would preserve anything her ancestor erected. It's a cassia tree, you know."

"Oh! I'd like to see that, but I don't suppose just anyone may tour the Empress's cassia grove."

"You will see many wonders while you're here."

Cassia caught sight of what appeared to be land in the distance. Her first glimpse of the Empire.

Kassandra adjusted the sail, and Hesperine magic sparked in the air. The purple cloth suddenly appeared crimson, like all the other ships from Orthros. "There we are. My status makes an excellent ticket through the spirit gates, but would become something of a bother once we make port. You should see the pile of annoying invitations I receive all the time. If we arrive under a purple sail, there will be no end of state dinners. Drawing so much attention is not the way for you two to start your getaway."

Definitely not. They couldn't search for Solia with the wealthy and powerful looking over their shoulders. With her legal status in doubt, the less scrutiny, the better.

Lio peered ahead. "Ritual mother, may I ask where we're headed?"

"We're a few minutes out from Captain Ziara's first port of call."

Lio stood up straighter. "You know where Captain Ziara will arrive?"

"Hesperines and privateers are the only ones engaged in the transport of goods from Cordium and Tenebra to the Empire. Ziara and I have great professional respect for each other."

Lio and Cassia exchanged a grin. Perhaps innocent youngbloods weren't the only contraband his Ritual mother was familiar with.

Kassandra went on, "Her ship has quite the reputation among the privateers and Orthros's sailors. You'll know the *Wanted* by her flag: a gull with an acacia branch in its claws."

Cassia's spirits lifted. "I thought we'd have to hunt all over the coast, but now we know where to start and what to look for."

Kassandra pointed at the large island that drew nearer and nearer. "There is Marijani."

"Marijani," Lio echoed. "That makes sense."

"Where are we on your globe?" Cassia asked him.

"You remember the line that runs around the middle of it, dividing the northern and southern hemispheres?"

"The equator."

"Right. Marijani is sitting on it."

She let out a wondering laugh. A mere week ago, they had crossed the world. Now they had crossed half of it again!

Lio smiled, appearing to enjoy her reaction. Seeing that his smile had returned made her feel even better.

"The Kwatzi City States," he explained, "forty or so of them, occupy a series of islands off the eastern coast of the Empire. Marijani is the largest, wealthiest, and most powerful."

Marijani came into proper view at last. The city sprawled across a sizeable island, its shores dotted with groves of trees and bustling piers. The buildings of smooth white stone almost seemed to glow softly in the moonlight. As their boat neared the docks, rich smells of verdant plants and spices joined the smell of the ocean.

"What kind of trees are those?" Cassia asked.

"Mangrove trees," Lio answered. "They produce strong wood that's excellent for making ships and the rafters of the homes you see here."

"The city is beautiful."

He put an arm around her and gestured to a row of buildings on the waterfront. "The architecture here is quite famous. It's built of coral quarried from the ocean."

Cassia closed her gaping mouth and tried not to ask any questions about how mortals could have a quarry in the ocean. She didn't want to seem like an ignorant Tenebran.

But she felt like one. None of the places that passed for cities in Tenebra held a candle to Marijani, and she'd never seen so many ships in one place. She could hardly believe humans had built all of this.

"Look there. Those are dhows." Kassandra pointed at a line of slender, pointed ships with triangular sails.

"Their construction rather reminds me of Hesperine ships," Cassia ventured.

"Our fleet's design draws inspiration from them. The ones you see here are from Vardara."

Cassia was looking at something that had come all the way from the Silklands. She herself had come all the way from Orthros. Just breathing the air of Marijani made her feel connected to the whole vast world.

"And the other kind of ship?" Cassia asked. "The ones with the square sails and the wider hulls?"

"The mtepe," Kassandra answered, "the pride of the City-States' master shipwrights. They're made of mangrove planks sewn together with coconut fiber and caulked with sap. Makes them flexible and durable— and fast. Excellent for trade. Kumeta owned a very successful trading fleet of mtepe in her human life."

"She never mentioned she was a trader before," said Cassia, "but she did tell me that Tradewinds, the language of the City-States, is the tongue of commerce all over the Empire."

Kassandra rested a hand on her hip, a rope in the other. "I'm still grumpy that she became an envoy instead of entering the economic service with me. But it's no wonder she has an instinct for intrigue, coming from Marijani. This island commands the sea trade between the Empire and Vardara, and it's also the most strategic port for the privateers' voyages to and from Cordium. And the merchant council knows it."

"Merchants advise the ruler here?" Cassia asked in surprise.

"No, the merchants rule," Kassandra said. "The Kwatzi City-States don't have kings or queens. Each one is governed by a group of the most successful merchants in that city."

"So...people buy their way to power?"

"Essentially, yes."

"But birth doesn't matter?"

"Also true."

Cassia's thoughts were still busy with the benefits and dangers of such a system when the boat slowed. They were approaching a long pier that was strangely deserted compared to the others. She guessed it was reserved for incoming Hesperine ships.

With their journey almost complete, Cassia couldn't resist asking another question while the oracle was being so forthcoming. "So where did Basir come from?"

"A different side of life on Marijani." Kassandra nodded ahead at the man on the pier, who wore an official-looking white robe and a stiff white hat that looked like someone had folded up a piece of paper on top of his head. "Basir was an Imperial administrator stuck in his office all day, even more boring and stuffy than the fellow you see waiting for us there."

Cassia and Lio exchanged a glance and laughed.

He squeezed her waist. "No wonder he wanted a life of travel and adventure with a beautiful partner."

While Kassandra moored their boat, the official glanced around as if expecting something more. Nevertheless, he bowed, managing to do so without toppling his hat. "Welcome to the Empire, friends from Orthros. It is my privilege to welcome the first Hesperine vessel to arrive this season. To what do we owe the pleasure of your visit?"

Kassandra answered him, "My girl and her intended are here for a little getaway. Her last chance to soak up some sunshine before her Gift Night, you know. I didn't want them to get caught behind the trading fleet and have to wait forever to get through."

"Ah, a personal visit." He looked disappointed. "Wise to be first in line at the entry office. Rest assured, however, we have increased our staff again this year, and wait times have been reduced by thirty percent. Allow me to direct you to the proper administrative structure."

"I'm not staying. Just my girl and her intended."

"I hope we can welcome you for a visit another time."

"I look forward to it."

Lio offered Cassia his hand to help her from the boat. Before she took it, she paused to embrace Kassandra. "Thank you so much for everything."

"My pleasure, truly. By the way, I'm keeping the banner safe for you."

Cassia knew the one Kassandra meant. A banner from the Mage King's time, emblazoned with the ancient coat of arms from Tenebra's early history. Cassia thought back to when the oracle had first placed the banner in her hands during the Solstice Summit. She had thought it a portent that she would spend her future trapped in Tenebra as their unwilling queen.

"I don't want that banner to be a trap for my sister," Cassia said, "but you have often reminded me that choices determine the future."

"It's only a choice if the white rose is not all you offer her."

Cassia pulled back. "I hate the thought of even suggesting it to her. I'll do anything to give her the freedom of choice that I've had."

"Then why don't you do your best to find her before Summer Solstice? Not for Tenebra's sake. For hers."

Cassia looked into the oracle's eyes. "You knew. When you told me, 'My sister and I loved one another as you and Solia will.'"

"I'm sorry it wasn't time for you to know yet." Kassandra smiled, but the expression seemed sad on her beautiful, ancient face.

"Did you ever get to see your sister again...after?" After she had exiled Kassandra to Orthros to secure her throne.

"No. I was not allowed to return during her lifetime or that of her heir. The terms of my exile. I wouldn't have had time in any case, for I was so busy building Orthros's economy from the ground up."

She had told Cassia that Solia was in her future, knowing that her own sister was in her past. "I'm so sorry."

Kassandra embraced her, then let her go. "May the Goddess's Eyes light your path to your sister."

Cassia made a vow against her fears then and there. No matter what happened, she and Solia would not face the same fate as Kassandra and the Empress.

Lio embraced his Ritual mother as well. Then he and Cassia shouldered their packs and disembarked with Knight. Lio levitated their trunks onto the pier and turned them over to two dock hands.

While he was paying them in what looked like quartz, Kassandra gave them a parting wave and sailed back out of sight.

The official provided Lio and Cassia with instructions, then turned back to his post as if hopeful of more important visitors. She held onto Lio's hand and heeled Knight close as they hastened along the pier. The official didn't give them a backward glance.

They were here. She was setting foot on Imperial soil for the first time. Was she retracing Solia's steps even now?

Looking out across the forest of masts in the port, she wondered if there was any possibility that Captain Ziara was already here. She couldn't make out any flags resembling Kassandra's description, at least from here. "There are so many ships. How will we ever find her?"

"Don't worry. We will search every dock on Marijani if we must."

"There are more docks?"

"Around the whole perimeter of the island. But I have an idea of where we should start. Not here."

He didn't elaborate, and she knew this was not the place to discuss their clandestine search. This also wasn't the time.

She glanced at the sky. "Will it take long to get through the entry office and find lodgings?"

"I hope not."

"How long do we have until sunrise? Do you need to check your astrolabe?"

He shook his head. "Here in the equatorial zone, there are eight Hesperine hours of night and eight hours of day all year round."

That was twelve human hours. She would have to do without him for half their time here. It was just like the Equinox in Orthros, but that had only lasted for one day. After the wealth of time polar night had given them, she couldn't help feeling disappointed.

"Don't fret, my rose. There's so much to do here. You'll enjoy your days, I promise."

She doubted that. "I'll make our nights together worth the wait."

"Mm. You always do."

They followed the official's directions to a line of wooden buildings built right on the harbor, some on stilts. It was a good thing Lio could read the signs. He ushered Cassia into a spacious room, where many administrators waited behind a long counter. Before the door shut behind them, Cassia glimpsed a wall of Hesperine ships approaching the harbor.

"Let's hurry," Lio suggested.

They approached the nearest administrator. Cassia listened carefully to his rapid conversation with Lio, but it was impossible to follow. Thanks to her Imperial friends in Orthros, she did recognize the tongue as Dynastic, the language of the Empress's court and administration. But they had started teaching her Tradewinds first, the easier of the two to learn.

When Lio indicated for her to, she presented her and Knight's papers.

The administrator peered over the counter at her hound and said in Divine, "A most unusual animal companion for a citizen of Orthros."

"He is very well behaved." Cassia tried not to sound nervous. Time to make a good impression. She held Knight's gaze. *"Ckuundat."*

He drew himself to attention, his whole focus on her.

The administrator gave her a courteous smile, but there was something about his gaze that made her uneasy. "And what is the purpose of your visit to the Empire?"

Cassia took Lio's hand. Only he would be able to tell her palms were sweating. She looked into his eyes and hoped her smile appeared excited, not nervous. "Lio is taking me traveling, just the two of us. It's so romantic."

The administrator studied her face and her hair. "Your first time on Marijani?"

"Yes. Your city is beautiful."

"Wait right here, please." He departed through a door behind him, taking their papers with him.

Cassia looked at Lio. "Is that normal?"

He frowned. "It does seem to be taking longer than usual. But then, I've always traveled with a diplomatic pass."

He gave her hand a reassuring squeeze. They both cast glances at the main doors every time they opened. The room began to fill with Hesperines, many of whom Cassia recognized as Kassandra's tributaries. A few of their acquaintances waved at them, and she felt more at ease among people from home.

At long last, the administrator reappeared. He handed their papers back to them. "Enjoy your stay."

With relief, they thanked him and left.

"Now we pick up our trunks, and then we find lodgings." Lio's step seemed lighter as they returned to the pier to reclaim their packs.

Until they found the pallet where the dock hands had left their possessions. It was empty.

Lio frowned and picked up the slip of paper where their trunks had been. "They took our things through inspection?"

"Is that unusual?" Cassia asked.

"The Empire inspects every sack of gumsweets that goes in or out in the hands of her own citizens. But Hesperine luggage is never inspected. It's a courtesy to Annassa Soteira, a gesture of trust in her people. Our reputation in the Empire is such that it's assumed we would never bring in anything dangerous or take something out that doesn't belong to us."

"It must be because I'm human. Do you suppose there's any chance they mistook me for a former Imperial citizen?"

She looked down at her hands. Her olive skin was lighter in tone than the Imperials she had met. But her complexion didn't stand out here the way Lio's fair skin did. His fangs and his preternatural beauty made it obvious he was from Orthros, though. If only she had fangs, no one would care what she looked like.

Lio took both her hands and kissed them. "You might be mistaken for someone from the far northwest by people who don't travel much. If they didn't pay attention in geography class at university."

She sighed. "Are experimental soaps on the Empress's list of contraband?"

Affection lit his gaze. "No."

"Good. Then there's nothing in my trunk that will raise the inspectors' eyebrows."

"I beg to differ. I caught a glimpse of some of the underlinens you packed."

Heat rose to her cheeks. "Oh, thorns."

"Very clever, Lady Circumspect. Those will give the inspector reason to believe we really are here on a romantic getaway."

"Those are for your benefit, not the inspector's! Only you were supposed to see them!"

He grinned, his fangs much in evidence. "Only I will see them on you."

"Your eyebrows are not what I intend for them to raise."

His low laugh made her blush even more. "You don't need fancy underthings to do that, my rose, but I'll enjoy them nonetheless."

Cassia reached up and touched his face. "We can't have my Gifting and seclusion, but I can give you a journey through the Empire, just the two of us."

"I will accept that as a consolation more eagerly than I care to admit."

"Admit it. You're glad we came alone."

He turned his face into her hand. "I am. I want you all to myself."

"You are going to enjoy yourself on this trip." She pulled him closer. "This *is* a romantic getaway, Lio, even if that's not the reason we set out on this journey."

He lowered his head nearer to hers. "I love it when you say things like that with your kingdom-destroying look on your face."

"My...kingdom-destroying look?"

"It's the look of determination you get when you're planning to dethrone a monarch or start a rebellion against the religious authorities."

"I don't mean to look that way on a romantic getaway."

"What could be more romantic? Imagine how I feel when you wear that look and swear to me I'm going to enjoy myself."

"Let's find an inn so I'll have time to keep my promise before you fall asleep."

They forged their way through the increasingly crowded docks. It took longer to get to baggage inspection than it had to get from the pier to the first office. They waited in line in the open air before an enormous warehouse. When it was their turn to approach the inspector's stand, Lio presented their claim slip to her.

The sleeves of her brown official robe were rolled up past her elbows, revealing intricate tattoos that fit her hands and arms like gloves. "Your bag, please, Newgift Cassia."

Cassia froze, her hands closing around the strap of her gardening satchel. It was pure instinct from the many times when the contents of this bedraggled canvas bag had saved her life.

She didn't carry the glyph stone in it anymore, she reminded herself. And she was perfectly safe in the Empire. Sensing her distress, Knight pressed closer to her legs.

Lio quickly deployed his diplomacy, covering her lapse. "My intended is carrying family heirlooms. She is very anxious about them becoming lost on our travels."

The administrator gave Cassia a kind smile. "I handle everything from precious gems to children's favorite dolls. Your heirlooms will be in good hands."

"Thank you." Cassia made herself take the bag off her shoulder and slide it across the stand to the inspector. "Ah, they are magical artifacts. I hope that's all right."

The inspector paused. "Mind healers' medicine bags and talismans are exempt from inspection."

"No, none of them are theramantic in nature."

"Nonetheless, rest assured I will handle them with care."

Cassia watched the inspector spread the talismans of her life across the counter. Her battered spade, which had begun as a favorite gardening tool and become an artifact imbued with blood magic. A collection of Lio's handkerchiefs that he had given her at memorable moments. The green hair ribbon he had gotten for her at the Crafters' Festival during the Solstice Summit. A paper wrapper with a design of cassia flowers that had once covered the first bar of soap he'd ever given her.

She blushed at her romantic mementos like the lovestruck fool she was. He grinned.

His smile faded as the inspector dug the rest out of the bag. Blood-stained linen garments. A vial of flametongue oil. The wooden pendant that Alkaios had taken from Iris's body.

The inspector must see many strange things, for she didn't raise an eyebrow at any of it. She handled the pendant carefully, turning it over in her hands, and magic rose gently in the air. "Your family is blessed with powerful gifts from your ancestors."

In truth, these had belonged to Solia's ancestors, to whom Cassia had no blood connection. But her sister's love had made them hers. "I feel very fortunate."

The inspector put everything back in Cassia's satchel the way she had found it, working with amazing speed but no less care. "May your fore-mothers guide you on your journeys."

Cassia slung her bag gratefully over her shoulder while the inspector had their trunks brought from the warehouse. Lio paid another pair of dockhands, arranging with them to have the packs delivered somewhere.

Cassia stood and observed the well-practiced rhythms of the docks. The Imperial administration ushered Hesperines and returning guests in, and Marijanians enriched their coffers by assuaging the inconveniences of travel, from baggage transport to getting lost to being hungry.

By the time they left the harbor, Cassia had bought a map of the city, and Lio had bought her three snacks.

"I'm not going to fit in my old gardening dress if I keep eating like this."

"Kassandra will let it out for you."

When they broke free of the busy streets surrounding the docks, Lio breathed a sigh. He had brought her to a quiet lane that meandered between the smooth, pale coral stone buildings. The houses here were lovely in their simplicity, their walls like veil spells sheltering everything within, broken only by small, high windows.

"We made it," he said, "and with time to spare before dawn. Do you feel like a walk? If not, I can hire transportation so you can enjoy the city, or we can step directly to the inn."

"Oh, let's not hire anyone. A quiet walk sounds lovely."

He took her hand again, and they set off through the side streets of Marijani. His nearness, their unhurried pace, and the warm night all conspired to ease the tensions of their arrival from her body.

"You know your way around here," she observed.

"Ritual mother has brought me here often since I was a boy. I loved tagging along on her trading negotiations. I think you'll like the inn where we're staying. I hope you don't mind that I already chose one."

"Of course not. We left in such a hurry, when would you have had time to ask me about it? I'm glad you know where we're going. Your experience traveling here will make things much easier."

"I've never actually stayed at this establishment, but I know it well." He gave her a rather self-effacing smile. "I always had ambitions of bringing my Grace here on a romantic getaway sometime in the future. Now I can."

At this reminder that she had proved to be the Grace of his lifelong imaginings, Cassia felt as if she could levitate.

The simple houses gave way to small manors with fountains burbling behind their walls. Then the small manors became large estates where brightly colored flowers spilled over the rails of verandas and music drifted down from the roofs.

"Are these where the merchant governors live?" Cassia asked.

"No, their palaces are at the center of the city. These are accommodations for visitors."

Lio led her along a stone avenue beneath beautiful wooden walkways and balconies that crossed over their heads. He brought her to a luxurious carved wooden door twice as tall as she was. It was covered in beautiful, intricate floral designs, a rich, dark contrast to the white walls.

The door swung open on silent hinges. A young man in a flowing white tunic ushered them inside and greeted them in Divine. "Welcome to the Coral Star, honored guests."

The white hallways and mangrove timbers overhead enclosed them in privacy and luxury. Cassia soon felt more like a family guest than a customer thanks to the hospitality of the young man, who proved to be the owner's son. It became clear that Lio had sent word ahead and made all the arrangements.

They were soon left to themselves in a suite. Their rooms were appointed with elaborately carved wooden furniture, and greenery grew in fine ceramic pots. Shelf alcoves in the walls displayed treasures of the sea trade. A small stair even led to a private rooftop.

Cassia went out onto the balcony, running her hands over the smooth curves of the railing. She looked down at the courtyard below, where a stately fountain splashed. "This is all very fancy for a human like me."

Lio joined her and leaned on the railing at her side, one around her. "You're becoming accustomed to the luxuries of Orthros. I have to maintain some standards."

"Ah, Lio, this place is clearly very expensive. We never talk about money, because Orthros thrives on gifts, but…"

"It's true Orthros has no official currency and maintains a gift economy. But we do make use of currency in our dealings with the Empire." He turned to her and pulled a large coin purse out of a pocket of his travel robes. "I meant to give you this before we left, but didn't have time."

She weighed the purse in her hands. It was heavier than the one she had once spent to save Callen's life, and that had been all the wealth she had ever expected to possess in her life. "I never imagined diplomacy paid so well."

"Oh, this isn't mine. It's the bloodline's. Father, and now Mother as well, accumulate gifts over the centuries as a result of their various relationships with people from the Empire. Every coin belongs to every member of the Komnenoi, and our tributaries can of course avail themselves of these resources as well."

"Sixteen hundred years of gifts is…probably quite a lot."

A gleam came to Lio's gaze. "Tell me, who is the wealthiest lord in Tenebra?"

Cassia rolled her eyes. "Flavian, of course. Because his father is clever in his dealings, their farmland is good, and…"

"And money follows Flavian's charm and pretty face?"

"I'm afraid so."

"It is perhaps un-Hesperine of me, but I feel entitled to a moment of gloating. House Komnena could buy Segetia without bruising our bloodline's treasury."

She ran a finger down his chest. "I didn't run away with you for your money."

He propped his elbow on the rail, leaning close. "But the money is nice."

"It rather is. But I'll be a responsible steward of our bloodline's resources, I promise."

"Don't. You've had to be responsible all your life. If you see something you like while we're here, buy it. Enjoy yourself. Let me…indulge us."

She rose up to kiss his mouth. "My promise starts now. You're going to enjoy this."

"Mmm. I already am." He rested his hand on her neck.

"Are you? I know it's not my seclusion, and we're in suspense about Solia, but we can—we will—make our time here special in its own way."

"I fully intend to distract you from your suspense."

"I intend to distract you from your disappointment."

He pulled her against him and began to do very distracting things, and no more words were necessary.

A NEW THREAT

THE WARMTH OF THE forge bathed Mak's skin. His blows on the anvil traveled up his arm with satisfying force. Through the wards on his ears, the rhythmic clang of his hammer reached his hearing. He found the noise satisfying, too, banging out his messy thoughts until they didn't dare bend out of shape.

Usually I'm the one overthinking things, Lyros commented. *If you need to pound something, you could save that energy for me.*

I'll bring my needs home to you when I'm fit company, my Grace.

You could at least vent your frustrations at your forge in our residence, so I can watch.

Steel wouldn't hold up. I need some adamas to beat.

Mak, we made the right decision.

Dilemmas are for diplomats. How did we end up caught between our Trial circle and our family?

The same way Nike did.

On Mak's next strike, his hammer cracked in two. He cursed and tossed it aside. *I decided to stay home for the family instead of going after my Trial brother. What does that say about me?*

"Mak? What are you doing here?" Nike had finally arrived.

He shoved the abused length of adamas into the frigid water and turned to face her. "I'm here for my smithing lesson."

Concern emanated from her. "You didn't go with Lio and Cassia?"

"Lyros and I are staying here."

She rested a hand on the worktable, her brow furrowing. "Is this about the vote? I didn't realize you had an interest in politics."

"It will help our Trial sisters to have two partisans from the Stand."

Her frown deepened. "This isn't about the vote."

"Zoe and Bosko need stability."

"This isn't about the sucklings, either." She pushed away from the table and walked over to the trough. Yanking his project out of the water, she studied the pockmarked paddle of the rarest metal in the world.

"I told you I was here for a smithing lesson," he said.

She raised an eyebrow at him over the piece. "You need a few more."

"Ha. I don't deny it."

"Mak, you should be with Lio and Cassia, looking for Solia."

"And miss my chance to learn your secret smithing techniques from you firsthand? Not likely."

"You've read my journals."

"You said yourself there's far more in your head than in your notes."

"You already know how to craft adamas."

"You also said I can't keep it stable when I try to craft something larger than my hand."

She thrust his failed experiment back into the water. "Solia's life is more important than a hunk of metal."

"Says the person who was gone for nearly a century to find one sword."

"That's a different matter, Mak. Your Trial brother is alive and well and currently headed to the Empire without you."

"A sword is more than a sword. It represents a life."

Her gaze went to Methu's blade where she had hung it on the wall above the forge.

"How many lives did that sword save?" Mak asked.

She shook her head. "I couldn't count them."

Mak took a step closer. "No matter how the Firstblood Circle votes, Hesperines already have a new role in Tenebra. No matter who sits on the throne in Solorum when all is said and done, the world has already changed. That means new threats. That means changing tactics."

"I know why you believe in doing this, Mak, but it must wait."

"No," he said gently, "it can't. Unless you can promise me that the next time a messenger bird arrives from Cordium, you're sure you won't follow it right back where it came from."

"You know I can't promise you that."

"Lio and Cassia will be fine in the Empire, and it doesn't take two extra warriors to ask Captain Ziara questions. Even when they find out where Solia is, they'll need diplomatic passes, not fists." Mak dragged his failed project out of the trough. "This is my only chance to learn what you have to teach me."

"I agreed to teach you to craft adamas, not weapons."

"It leads to the same thing."

She snatched the length of metal faster than his Hesperine eyes could see. Taking it in both hands, she brought it down across her knee. The adamas snapped under the force of her strength. Mak couldn't help staring.

She held up the broken pieces. "It will lead nowhere if you become reckless. First, you learn to craft adamas properly. But before that, you learn patience. Go home. Don't come back until tomorrow. Yes, I'll still be here."

Mak smiled. "Understood, First Master Steward."

That wasn't an agreement about the weapons, but it wasn't a refusal, either. And she had promised to be here tomorrow. Trusting her word was not something he had to learn.

Mak saluted her and stepped home to Lyros. He found his Grace stretched out on the thick rug, which covered the floor where their new reading chairs were supposed to sit. Once Mak actually crafted them.

Moonlight shone down from the skylight, illuminating the page in front of Lyros's nose. He was staring at it, but not reading it. Mak knew that look, and he knew he was the reason his Grace was preoccupied.

Lyros set his book down and rolled onto his elbow. The light blanket draped over him slid lower on his waist. "You're back sooner than I hoped."

Mak sank down onto the rug next to Lyros. "I was dismissed. Smithing lesson tomorrow, though."

"She's going to teach you."

"Patience first. Then adamas, she says."

"And then?" Lyros's worry rose in their Grace Union.

Nike's hidden forge and the distant Empire, the family's needs and their Trial circle's goals, all of it receded from Mak's awareness. His attention fixed on the furrow between Lyros's brows. That frown on his face made the whole world seem to fall into place.

If Mak went too far, with his hope of crafting weapons or anything else, his Grace would pull him back. When he wasn't sure where he ought to stand, the answer was always at Lyros's side.

Lyros reached out and ran a hand through Mak's hair, tugging on his Grace braid. "Do you feel better?"

Mak slid his fingers over the back of Lyros's hand, tracing the tendons there. Then along Lyros's forearm and up to his bicep, feeling the strength in his muscles. "Yes."

Lyros's lashes slid closed over his green eyes. "Hitting things works."

"That didn't help." Mak let his hand continue, now following the chiseled lines of Lyros's chest, more perfect than any of the sculptures the artists of his bloodline ever produced.

A frown appeared on Lyros's handsome mouth. "What did, then?"

"I realized why my choices are so different from Nike's."

Lyros's eyes came open, and he looked at Mak with his thoughtful gaze. "Why, Mak?"

Mak rubbed his thumb on that furrow on Lyros's brow. "I have you, my Grace."

Lyros smiled, his fangs descending to gleam in the moonlight. Just that smile could still make Mak's breath catch in his chest. "You don't regret you have a Grace chaining you to hearth and home at such a young age?"

"You're no Mortal Vice. You're a Pilgrim's Anchor."

Lyros's expression softened. "If the night does come when it is time to go errant, I won't hold you back."

"I know. Because that will be the night we both agree it's time to go errant together."

Lyros tossed the blanket over both of them. "I'm glad you came home early."

"So am I."

78

Nights Until

NOTIAN WINTER SOLSTICE

27 Annassa, 1597 IS

THE SUN MARKET

THE FIRST TIME CASSIA had held Lio in his Slumber, in the depths of Solorum Fortress, she had known she must let him go. It had seemed an enchanted and aching moment. Now he fell asleep in her arms every sunrise. But each time, such an act of trust from her Hesperine felt magical.

In their airy rooms on Marijani, she ran a finger down his peaceful face. She rested her head on his chest and listened to his heart beating, as was her wont.

So much power, sleeping in her arms. But he looked young and vulnerable in his Slumber.

She sat up, looking from Lio to the heavy drapes over the window. She had never once seen him in full sun.

After a moment's hesitation, temptation overcame her, and she crawled out of their large bed. The sheer curtains ruffled with her passage. She padded to the window and opened the carved wooden casements.

The warm, brilliant light of Marijani's morning sun flooded the room and struck Lio's pale skin. Cassia stared, scarcely breathing. How many mortals ever beheld a Hesperine in daylight?

His skin looked almost translucent, the sun warming the cool rosy undertones of his fair complexion. His black hair had brown highlights she had never seen before. Her gaze followed every elegant angle and contour of his long, lithe body, from the lips she loved to kiss, to his feet that moved with hers when they danced, and everything in between.

But the price of this stolen moment would be the Dawn Slumber keeping him from her for a moment longer. He had warned her that the more sunlight touched him while he slept, the longer it would take him to waken. She shut the casements quickly and returned to his side to cover him with the blanket.

Longing to slide under it with him, she cast one more anxious look at the curtains. Her answers were waiting out there in the city. Solia might be waiting, in need of her aid after all these years.

But what could Cassia hope to accomplish on her own today? Lio knew the best places on Marijani to make inquiries, and her language skills were insufficient, in any case. Even though she had been trying to study Tradewinds in preparation for their trip to goat country with Zoe, she had made little headway.

That wasn't the only reason she hesitated. A part of her, not so very deep down anymore, admitted that she simply needed to be near him. The certainty that they would not lose each other still felt new.

But there was more to it than that. She had the Craving for his mere presence, and ever since he had cast the mind ward, that had become a compulsion.

She had relied on herself for so long, survived so many hardships on her own, perhaps this dependency on another person should alarm her. It would have, at one time. But she had felt him feast on her, knowing his life depended on her. With every layer of the spell he had cast on her mind, she had felt how desperate he was to keep her close to him.

She needed him no more than he needed her. His soul was as bare to her as hers was to him. There had never been any danger in promises so pure.

Like a moth to starfire, she darted under the covers to press her body to his.

He should be glad you can enjoy mortality as much as you do. Master Kona's words came back to her.

She could enjoy her mortality, such as it was, right here with Lio.

You are so young. You have plenty of time.

They had not yet been together as long as they had been apart. Every moment with him still seemed precious.

You will be free of your mortality soon enough, so you might as well enjoy the diversions it has to offer.

Well, she supposed she might as well enjoy their suite, since Lio had gone to so much effort to treat her.

She got out of bed again. Knight, sleeping off the finest meal of his life, woke and lifted his head. He watched her open her trunk to find a robe.

Boldness overtook her. She was no longer a modest Tenebran lady. She was Newgift Cassia, and she was in the cosmopolitan City-State of Marijani with her Hesperine lover.

Without getting dressed, she walked up the narrow, private stairway to the rooftop. Engraved wooden panels and tall potted plants shielded her from every prying eye. Even at this early hour, the air was warm. The moisture in the air was a balmy humidity, nothing like the chilly, creeping dampness of Tenebra. When she stepped out from under the shady leaves, the sun struck her full force.

The sun had never felt this way to her before. This was something even more than warm afternoon rays on a bright day in the garden. The power of the Empire's sunlight seemed to radiate into her bones.

She didn't want to love it, but she did.

She put a hand over her eyes, looking as closely as she dared at the brilliant orb. Anthros did not rule the skies here. To think, Cassia had made it to a part of the world where even the sun was beyond his command. Her father's god suddenly seemed small.

She stretched out on her back on one of the lounge benches and lay naked in the sun.

After a while, she rolled over on her belly and sunned her backside. Knight now lay on the ground beside her bench. He sprawled on his back, one leg askew, panted happily.

She laughed at the image. "Good boy. You deserve to relax, too. No threats to watch out for here."

Lio wouldn't mind if she left their bed for this, once he saw what sunbathing did to her freckles.

She lay there, careful not to fall asleep, until she started to bake. Then she retreated inside for a drink of cool water. But she found herself still thirsty for more of the sunlight.

She rounded up her clothes and her map of Marijani.

The Sun Market was clearly marked. It took up a large section of the city, centrally located between the estates and the docks. It shouldn't be hard to make her way there.

"*Dockk, dockk.* Time for an adventure."

Knight wagged his tail and raced to the door.

Cassia pressed a kiss to Lio's forehead. "I'll be back before you wake."

Before she set foot out of their suite, she wrapped a silk scarf around her head and neck, covering her hair. If she spent enough time in the sun and kept her hair out of sight, she might not raise quite so many eyebrows.

Cassia left the inn and joined the flow of pedestrians outside. She realized that all the traffic was heading in the direction she wished to go. She let it carry her along and soon found herself in an even larger crowd, which squeezed into the grand plaza that was the epicenter of the Sun Market.

A thrill of energy traveled through her. She had never been in such a crowd before, not even in Tenebra's busiest cities. And there ended all the comparisons to Tenebra her mind could make, for what she saw around her could never have existed there.

There were people around her of every shape, size, and skin tone. Black, light brown, and every color in between. She saw hair in locks and braids and knots. She saw clothes of silk and cotton and raffia in colors so varied and vibrant that they made her feel the same way the sunlight did. Some people wore long robes that covered them from head to toe, except for their eyes, while others wore nothing but a simple waist-wrap and sandals.

The variety of people and the number of languages flowing around her would have reminded her of being home in Orthros. Except that it was all so human.

And everywhere she looked, there were women. Women buying, women selling, women asking, women ordering.

No one stopped Cassia to ask where her husband or father or brother was. No one called her a whore for being in public unaccompanied. In fact, no one looked at her twice.

An involuntary smile came to her face, and she felt she had taken a deep swig of strong spirits.

This was what freedom felt like.

She plunged deeper into the crowd and began to explore. The plaza was a maze of market stalls and pavilions, rolling carts full of wares, and open corners where street performers danced. She recognized some of the dances from Orthros, while others were new to her.

She drifted from one bubble of music to another and heard a dozen different styles within just a few minutes. Thanks to the time she spent around Nodora, Cassia recognized the instruments. There were Imperial-style lutes and tambourines, grass rattles, drums, and thumb pianos. Many were accompanied by women singing poetry in Tradewinds.

And the scents. She didn't recognize half of them, but they all smelled delicious. Her stomach rumbled, reminding her she hadn't had breakfast. She followed her nose to the nearest food stall.

She felt betrayed when she discovered they were selling grilled goat skewers. Comforting herself with thoughts of Moonbeam and Aurora safe in Orthros at that very moment, she moved on quickly. She had first chosen to give up meat on Lio's behalf; no Hesperine wanted to taste death on his lover's lips. But life in Orthros had rendered her own heart too tender to allow her to eat animals any longer, even if she didn't yet have an empathic connection to them through the Blood Union.

To think, the once-heartless Lady Cassia couldn't even bring herself to touch a bite of meat. She had come a long way. She would enjoy the Sun Market as long as she was human, but she wouldn't leave her Hesperine principles back at the inn with her Hesperine.

She joined the line at a food stall that appeared to be selling some kind of vegetable fritter. She watched carefully to see what size of quartz each of the customers ahead of her offered the proprietress. When it was her turn, Cassia offered a smile and a small piece of quartz from her purse, and received a smile and a basket of fritters in return.

Drifting out of the way of hungry customers and passersby, she bit into one of the deep-fried morsels. Flavor exploded on her tongue, and she stood in the sun, savoring what tasted like a thousand spices. A moment later, she felt the burn in her throat. She curled her toes, waiting out the heat, and wondered how Tenebran society had survived as long as it had on such bland food.

After that, she armed herself with a flask of water, prepared for a thorough tour of the food stalls. Coconut-cassia rice proved a delicious surprise, but she discovered her favorite was a fried pastry made with coconut milk and cardamom, dusted with sugar. When she was unable to endure Knight's begging eyes any longer, she relented and bought him a meaty bone from some kind of game animal she was fairly certain she had never seen alive.

They were both stuffed by the time she found herself in an open area where crafters and artists were at work. She passed women making ceramics at their potting wheels, men carving elaborate wooden sculptures, and children advertising their parents' wares.

She passed them by and consulted her map. "There's an area for animal trading, Knight. We'll have to visit the kennels. Everyone will love you. Perhaps you'll even take a shine to a puppy."

His wagging tail stilled.

"I jest, my darling. Of course I would never expect you to share my attentions. Ah, here's what I was looking for! Past the animal pens are the herbalists."

She forged her way there, and as she had hoped, the herbalists didn't only sell medicine and dried plants. There were many live plants on display as well. She lost track of time as she studied one Imperial variety after another. Whenever she found a merchant who spoke Divine, she asked questions. When she couldn't, she pointed, and the sellers taught her new words.

Anything would grow under the Queens' magic. The trouble was, everything already did. Master Kona had added countless Imperial treasures to her garden over the centuries. How could Cassia hope to find something suitable as a gift for her?

She wandered on without direction and soon found herself in the textile section of the market. Even with her miserable weaving skills, she could appreciate the value and variety of the fabrics.

Clothing had always been a tool to her. She had never much cared for finery; she wore the right thing to accomplish the right goal, whether making herself unexceptionable to the king or impressive to the free lords.

Now she was used to living in Orthros silk, which she valued for what it represented, more precious than wealth or power. Happiness. Comfort. Feeling beautiful, whether she looked beautiful to others or not.

But she supposed there was also no shame in finding herself a little more affected than usual by the sight of pretty clothes.

Indulge yourself.

She ducked into a clothier's pavilion, where cool shade and the scent of incense enveloped her. A woman who appeared to be from the Silklands glanced at Cassia's robes and offered assistance in Divine. The Vardaran stood Cassia before a mirror and helped her decide what to buy. Cassia had just enough of a sense of the value of Imperial currency to feel a bit dizzy at what she spent, but left happy to have patronized such a skilled and friendly seamstress.

She shopped for cotton next, then shoes and gloves, then got lost amid stands draped in scarves. She hesitated outside a tent decked in suggestive silks, from which women emerged with discreetly wrapped packages. Was there really an entire seller devoted only to underlinens?

Telling Knight to heel at the door, she marched in, and when she left, she was smiling at the thought of Lio's expression when he saw her in what she'd purchased.

She paused to watch at a stall where women were tending to other women's hair. They were artists, expertly creating the braid designs and beaded styles Cassia saw all around her. Surely the value Hesperines placed on braids was based on Orthros's Imperial heritage.

Cassia rubbed one ankle against the other to feel Lio's braid. Her eyes drifted shut, and she reached within. His mind ward made him feel so close, she could almost imagine him standing next to her here in the sun. Later, she would let him deep into her thoughts so he could walk these streets in her memories.

Next she stumbled upon the beauty vendors. She didn't even mind all the scent oils, for there was so much soap. She was so busy trying to decide which ones to buy, so dizzy from the fragrances, that it took her some time to notice the woman behind her.

Cassia had seen her before. Yes, the woman had definitely been in line behind her at the rice and pastry carts. Now she shopped several paces behind Cassia.

On instinct, Cassia urged Knight closer to her, while trying to maintain the appearance that she was casually browsing the soaps.

She surreptitiously studied the woman. Average height, a build that was neither thin nor curvy, a face that was neither plain nor beautiful. She had the deep brown skin tone of many Imperials and a neutral expression. Like countless others here, she wore a long tunic, Imperial trousers, and sandals in earth tones.

She could have been a regular who was no longer surprised by her city's wonders. Or a merchant from elsewhere, preoccupied with her business.

She could have been anyone. In fact, she was so ordinary that Cassia felt foolish for noticing her.

Cassia shook her head and returned to her soaps. This wasn't Tenebra, where she had to watch her back, and the king had always sent someone to follow her.

The woman was keeping pace behind her because they were both doing the same thing—moving from one soap booth to another. The only danger she posed was to the rice and pastries they had both polished off.

But two booths down, Cassia couldn't stop herself from taking another glance at the woman. She was haggling with a man over a bottle of scent oil.

Cassia moved on. But when she looked again, the bottle of scent was still at the man's stall, and the woman was the same distance away from Cassia as she had been all along.

Cassia would simply take a few detours. Only to verify that the woman was not following her. It was foolish to do so. She would humor her fears, but only for a moment. She would look behind her, and the woman would be gone, and it would prove to her that all those worries from her old life were unnecessary.

It was instinct to fall into her pattern of evasion. To keep up the appearance that she was doing nothing out of the ordinary. To complicate her route to test the woman's skill. To take her measure. Then to start trying to lose her.

The woman was very skilled. Far better than any of the runners the king usually sent after Cassia. More than once, Cassia thought it was her own imagination chasing her through the Sun Market. She would have believed it was all in her mind, except that she was very skilled, too.

Who was this woman?

Cassia's mind kept circling back to the delay over her papers. Had the port authorities decided to keep an eye on her? If so, she'd best not give them any reason to believe she was acting suspiciously.

Cassia buried her hand in Knight's ruff. His hair was standing on end. He leaned against her legs. She trusted his instincts and turned down a different aisle of the market in the direction he urged her.

If Knight was alarmed, there was cause for alarm.

The hairs on Cassia's arms stood up. Curse all the different magics at work in the market. She didn't need them tickling her senses when she must train all her awareness on the woman.

There really was a great deal of magic here. So much that she wouldn't know if some of it was being used on her.

Her heart beat faster, and she clutched her gardening satchel closer. There were no secret passageways to duck into. The ivy pendant's magic was impotent here.

The Sun Market was an excellent place to get lost in. But if a mage was following you, what use were nooks, crannies, and drapery?

Breaking out in a sweat, Cassia kept walking through the market, running her options through her mind.

She didn't know enough. The woman held the advantage. She could hardly do Cassia visible harm in broad daylight in the Sun Market. But if there was magic at work, visible harm might not be what Cassia had to worry about.

Just before her fear turned into panic, she noticed that the woman was gone.

Cassia took a breath and looked around again. No sign at all of the woman who had been following her.

Or whom she thought had been following her.

She took a couple more turns, just to be sure. No one around her now but busy, shifting crowds full of parents and children, scholars and warriors.

When she saw a tiny girl playing with a glittering magical talisman, she realized that the soap and perfume were just on the other side of a flimsy wood-and-fabric divider from the mages' stalls. Scrolls, staves, artifacts, and spell casting services had been one aisle over all this time, while she and the other woman had been browsing the soap. No wonder Cassia and Knight's hair had stood on end.

Cassia heaved a sigh and had a good laugh at herself.

She was perfectly safe in the Empire.

"Is everything all right?"

The question made Cassia jump and spin to face the speaker. A young man leaned against the nearest market stall, a skewer from one of the food vendors halfway to his mouth. He gave a pleasant laugh and held up his hands in reassurance.

In Tenebra, she had trained herself out of startling like a rabbit. She really was losing her touch. She drew a deep breath and found a smile for the friendly stranger.

Knight let out a growl, his hackles still up from their false alarm. Poor darling, accustomed to a more dangerous life than they led now.

"*Het.*" Cassia held his ruff. "Be polite, dearest. We're all friends here." She gave the man an apologetic glance. "Knight is a very faithful protector."

"Good dog." The young man pulled off the last juicy bite of meat on his skewer and tossed it to Knight.

Knight leapt on it as if it were a prize kill, then licked the stone path after it was gone. He turned to the young man, wagging his tail.

Cassia relaxed, laughing. "Clearly, you have his gratitude."

"I hope that will make up for startling you two just now." The man spoke Divine with an accent that reminded her of some of her Imperial friends in Orthros.

He dressed like the fashionable university students as well, wearing a tunic with vibrant geometric patterns, Imperial trousers, and sandals with metal discs decorating the straps. He had added a pair of tight-fitting gloves to the look, which left a strip of his warm amber skin visible at his wrists.

But he was too muscular to be someone who spent all his time studying. His hair was cropped pragmatically close to his head, his face clean-shaven.

"I'm sorry," Cassia said. "I'm usually more…composed."

"Not from around here?" One side of his mouth lifted in a charming smile.

"You'd think I'd be used to city life, coming from Orthros."

"Marijani can be a bit overwhelming if you've never been here before."

"Selas and Haima are quieter."

"Indeed. Hesperines are so…somber." His glance skipped over her in a rather flattering way. "What is a beauty like you doing draped in their robes?"

Cassia laughed in response to give herself time to think.

He glanced at Knight and tilted his head. "You like dogs, and you have gentle hands. You're studying animal healing with the Hesperines?"

"Ah, no." Gentle hands? Really? Did he try that one on all the girls?

"Hmm." His gaze swept appreciatively to her feet. "I've got it. You're a dancer learning new styles in Orthros."

"Definitely not."

"Let me think…" He took a step closer.

Thorns, she had never been in this situation before. She knew how to handle a Tenebran lord flirting for his own advantage, or even Flavian's outrageous romantic gestures. She was unaccustomed to a human flirting with her without an ulterior motive.

The time she had spent with her Imperial friends in Orthros offered little guidance. They never tried to flirt because they knew she was staying with Lio, and they only had eyes for their Hesperine shares.

Since this was not court—thank the Goddess—she decided she would simply be straightforward. "I'm a gardener. Newgift Cassia. Pleased to meet you."

"Newgift?" He let out a dramatically woeful sigh. "Another lovely woman, lost forever to the dull life in Orthros."

"On the contrary, my Hesperine is great fun, and he's much less somber than I. But hopefully I'll improve my sense of humor over the centuries with him."

"Ah." He gave her a regretful smile. "So it isn't opportunity or immortality that has lured you?"

"Oh, those are nice, too. But love is the reason I'm staying."

"Well, there's no arguing with that. I shall gracefully concede defeat."

She returned his smile. "I'm sure you'll have no trouble finding someone more fun to get to know in the Sun Market." He really wouldn't, with his good looks.

"But it wouldn't be very honorable if I failed to assist a guest of the Empire in trouble. You seemed so worried a moment ago. What was the matter?"

I thought an innocent woman shopping for soap was following me because I'm so accustomed to my father sending spies after me. I have a tendency to do things that make him want to execute me. Oh, excellent conversation starter. "I...I'm worried about my little sister."

He frowned and glanced hastily around. "Did you lose her in the market?"

"Oh, no. She's at home in Orthros. Actually she's my Hesperine's little sister. I fear she is anxious, with both of us gone."

His smile returned, soft with kindness this time. "You two must be very close."

"We've never been apart since the night we met. We both know what loss feels like." Cassia closed her mouth. What was it about this genial man that made her want to tell him her thoughts?

Then again, perhaps it was a good sign that she was less secretive these days. Her friendships in Orthros had helped her realize how many people in the world could be trusted.

He pursed his lips. "Would it make you feel better to write her a letter?"

"I promised to write her every day. We're traveling light, so I planned to purchase writing supplies once we arrived."

"Perhaps I could help you find some? My friends and I frequent the Sun Market when our classes aren't in session. I can show you where everything is."

"Oh, I'm sure you'd rather enjoy your time off than escort a stranger about."

"Fear not, I promise I will make no attempt to poach you from your Hesperine." He smiled with both sides of his mouth this time. "I swear on all the scrolls in the Capital University library."

"Capital! I knew it. My soon-to-be Ritual parents both graduated from there. They say it's where all the innovative research happens."

"We're also the friendliest, unlike those snobs at Imperial University. Let me show you around. We might even run into some of my classmates who are here on holiday like me, and then you'll have even more friends on Marijani."

Well, this would be just like spending time with Harkhuf and his friends. She supposed it couldn't hurt. "That's very kind of you."

"Think nothing of it. I'm Dakk, by the way. There. Now we are not strangers." He straightened and took a step nearer.

Cassia gave Dakk a Hesperine-style wrist clasp.

"Look at you, mostly Hesperine already." Dakk shook his head again, but his frown was teasing.

"I hope so."

They set off along the busy aisle, and she let him take the lead. They appeared to be going deeper into the magic section of the market. It made sense there would be paper aplenty here.

"So, what's your Hesperine's name?" Dakk asked.

Cassia blushed. "Lio."

"Lucky fellow. Is he as besotted with you as you are with him?"

Her blush intensified. "Yes."

"He'd better be." Dakk winked. "So, do you two have the kind of bond you can't talk about?"

"Yes. I'm Lio's intended." How lovely to be here, where Hesperines needn't keep Grace a secret from their Imperial allies, unlike their Tenebran and Cordian enemies.

Dakk made a face. "That's very…permanent."

She laughed at his expression. She supposed a young man sowing his wild oats might find the prospect of Grace rather intimidating. "Wonderfully permanent."

He shook his head. "How do you like it in Orthros, really?"

"I'm happier than I have ever been anywhere. It felt like home the moment I set foot there."

"Is it as cold as they say?"

"Colder! But beautiful. Have you never been to Orthros?"

He shook his head. "My field doesn't offer many study abroad options."

"What is your area of study?"

"Mind healing. But not like the ambitious High Court hopefuls who need a stint in Orthros on their qualifications. I'm on a more traditional program. Mostly hands-on study with diviners in villages across the Empire."

No wonder she felt like she could tell him anything. Mind healers had that effect on others. "I have the utmost respect for mind healing in all its forms. Lio's mother and our Ritual father are both mind healers."

"I can't resist asking. Have you met the mind-healer Queen? All of us here read about her."

"Oh, yes. Everyone meets Annassa Soteira, and Annassa Alea too." Cassia paused to think. "It's hard to do them justice in words. The first time Annassa Soteira spoke to me, I felt like she knew me better than anyone ever had, and she helped me to know myself."

"Interesting."

"She's kind and beautiful and…the Queens make you feel as if all is right in the world."

"You really do love Orthros."

"I…came there by a difficult path," Cassia tried to explain. "I had very little faith in anything when I arrived. And yet the Queens inspire my faith."

"They've built something very impressive in Orthros, no doubt about it. But I can't help wondering what Soteira might have built if she had stayed here."

Cassia looked at him in surprise. "She couldn't stay here. She and Alea cannot be apart."

"She threw away so much for love. Mind healing scholars write volumes about how she left and took her power out of the Empire, instead of staying here to contribute to our future."

Ah, so he wanted a debate, did he? "Who would help the refugees who arrive in Orthros, if she didn't?"

"Other Hesperines, I suppose."

"There would be no other Hesperines without her. She saved our entire kind."

"They could have all stayed in the Empire, too."

Except the Tenebrans. Dakk hadn't brought up her origins yet, so she certainly didn't plan to draw attention to them.

"Sorry," he said. "I don't mean to question your choice to leave. Especially if you weren't happy where you came from." He peered at her face. "Are you from the northwest? I hear there are villages so remote up there, births don't even get recorded, and few people have Imperial citizenship. It can't be an easy life."

Inwardly, she thanked Dakk for every geography class he had napped through. "It's true, I wasn't born into Imperial citizenship. But I'm a citizen of Orthros now."

"I'm glad you found a place you feel at home. What was it like for you before?"

"My mother died when I was a babe, and my father…" *Tried to kill me several times, when he wasn't shouting at me.* "…was not kind. My sister was the only true family I had until…we were separated when I was a child. That's why Lio and I are here, actually. Through friends in Orthros, we received word of my sister. We're hoping to find her so we can seek her blessing before my Gifting."

"You still have family in the Empire? That's wonderful."

"It is. But the Empire is a very large place, and finding her will be a challenge."

Goddess, now she was telling the man her life story. Perhaps her time with Harkhuf and his friends had made her too relaxed, too open.

But where was the harm in mentioning her sister to Dakk? He thought they were bumpkins from northwestern Empire, not two of the infamous Tenebrans.

She waved a hand. "Enough of my sad tale. Tell me more about your studies."

He regaled her with tales of university life while they spent a while among the mages' and scholars' stalls. She found plenty of scrolls Lio and Komnena would like, as well as storybooks for Zoe. There were fascinating artifacts of all kinds, although she saw nothing she would feel confident bringing home to Master Kona.

Dakk helped her haggle with the paper seller, and they walked away with a box of fine notes, new quills, and vials of ink.

"This way." He beckoned to her. "I know a place where you can sit down and write."

He led her to an open area of the market, where elders idled at tables, playing some kind of game with wooden pieces. They borrowed an unoccupied table, setting the game board aside so Cassia could spread out her paper.

She hesitated with her quill over the page. Heat crept up the back of her neck, and it had nothing to do with the warm day. Her new friend, an accomplished university student, was about to witness the horror of her limited literacy.

"This might take a while…"

He laughed. "I've seen the letters the girls at university write to their sisters at home. I know how it is—always so much to tell each other. Why don't I go find us something to drink in the meantime?"

"That would be lovely, thank you."

With only Knight as an audience, Cassia found herself able to relax and concentrate on the words and phrases she and Zoe had practiced.

Dear Zoe flower,

 Lio is asleep, so I'm writing you our first letter.

 Knight and I are at the Sun Market. He likes being outside—and the food of course! I hope you like the storybook I bought for you.

 We have not met any privateers yet, but we made a new friend named Dakk. He goes to school where Rudhira and Nike went.

 Are you and Bosko having fun playing privateers?

    Love,

    Cassia

Cassia tucked her note into the storybook, where no one would see how short it was.

Just then, Dakk returned with two open coconuts full of milk. "Ready to go find the Office of the Imperial Mail Administration?"

"That sounds very…official."

They sipped the rich, refreshing coconut milk as he led her back through the Sun Market. The Imperial Mail office turned out to be a permanent construction of mangrove timber amid the stalls and pavilions of the ever-changing market. Behind the building was a small spirit gate, where people in short, tan robes rushed in and out, laden with heavy packs.

"Oh," Cassia said hopefully, "that looks fast."

Dakk nodded. "Timely correspondence with Orthros is important, especially this time of year. The deliveries only pause during Orthros's hours of daylight. The Mail Administration keeps fancy charts of that sort of thing."

"Haima only gets a few hours of sun right now. It must already be twilight back home, although the sucklings won't be awake yet."

"Well then, let's make sure your package is waiting for her when she wakes."

Suddenly Cassia felt much closer to home and less worried about Zoe.

But when Dakk guided her into the crowded, humid office, her heart sank. Several administrators in longer tan robes were hastily accepting payment for packages, but there were long lines at every single one.

Dakk caught one young administrator's eye, and the other man's face brightened in welcome. Then he waved Dakk and Cassia ahead of the line.

Cassia glanced nervously at the disgruntled patrons. "Is that allowed?"

"If anyone asks, it's official university business." Dakk winked at her. "He graduated last year, thanks to my help studying for exams."

The young administrator greeted them warmly in Tradewinds, clasping Dakk's hand. This man also wore gloves, and Cassia thought it must be yet another university trend.

The administrator switched to Divine. "Who's your pretty friend from Orthros?"

Cassia blushed again and resigned herself to their unserious compliments. Dakk's friend packed the storybook with great care, and she was fairly certain he gave her a hefty discount. At last, he and Dakk had to stop reminiscing and teasing her because the rest of the patrons in line became so impatient.

As she and Dakk went out into the fresh air again, a yawn overtook her, and she glanced at the sun. She was usually sleeping during this time of day, like Lio. She had now been up past their bedtime for hours.

Dakk raised an eyebrow at her, and she blushed in anticipation of a rowdy comment about her Hesperine keeping her awake at night. But all he said was, "Spirit gate fatigue?"

"Changing climates so suddenly is rather tiring. I'd best get back to the inn for a nap. But thank you so much for taking time to help me today. I'll sleep much better not worrying about Zoe."

"How long will you be on Marijani?"

"I'm not sure. It depends on our search for my sister. How about you? When does your holiday end?"

"I have plenty of time on my hands. Thank you for helping me spend some of it so pleasantly." He gave her a gallant bow. "Will you return to the Sun Market tomorrow?"

She hesitated, but she would have to come back the next day, she reasoned. "I'll need to mail another letter."

"Then allow me to help you ahead of the line once again! Meet me at the mail office in the morning?"

"If you're certain you really want to spend more of your holiday keeping a foreigner from getting lost."

"I would never abandon anyone's little sister in her time of need. If you had to wait in line, it would leave Zoe in such terrible suspense."

Cassia smiled. "Thank you, Dakk. I wasn't sure what kind of reception I would have while traveling here, not being a citizen. But you have made me feel so welcome."

"Don't worry about that, Cassia. Everyone in the Empire loves to show hospitality. Shall I walk you back to your inn?"

Her wariness resurfaced, and she found she didn't want to lead him to where she and Lio were staying. That was as foolish as suspecting that woman of following her. But she could only fight so many battles against her misguided survival instincts in one day.

"I'm sure you'd rather go find your other university friends," she said lightly.

"They can get drunk this early in the day without any help from me. You, on the other hand, could benefit from some assistance with your parcels, perhaps?"

"I've got them. We gardeners have muscles, you know. Not like those gentle-handed animal healers."

He laughed. "If you insist."

He took his leave with a wave. Cassia returned to the inn, her arms full of her purchases, and shook her head over the student who had pulled her into his lark in the market. What a different world than Tenebra.

PIECES OF TIME

L IO WATCHED CASSIA FOR several minutes before she realized he
had woken.

She was perched at the dressing table before the mirror, her hair
flowing unbound around her. Barefoot. But she was wearing a silk dress
luxurious enough for a party at the merchant governor's palace. The whole
room smelled like the open jar of cassia butter she had been eating out
of with a spoon.

When she noticed his eyes were open, a blush spread across her cheeks.
He had caught her in the act of putting on vivid red lip color. Only her
upper lip was red, her lower one damp and pink. He smiled at her slowly.

Her flush deepened. "Yellow is my worst color."

"If that dress is your worst color, your beauty in your best color would
stun me so much I would fall unconscious back into Slumber."

"Oh, dear. I missed you all day and don't want to knock you unconscious." Her fingers still stained from the lip color pot, she stood up and
spun for him. The yellow dress swirled around her. "So this dress is just
safe enough to keep you awake?"

"Wide awake." He propped his head on his fist, letting his gaze make
another trip from her head to her naked toes. "Wear your new dress to
bed, and I'll show you how beautiful you are in that color."

She swayed toward him.

"Bring the cassia butter," he suggested.

She snatched the jar off the table before joining him in bed.

He welcomed the bundle of yellow silk into his arms. "I promise I
won't get bloodstains on your new dress."

"I can't promise any such thing about cassia butter stains."

He kissed her red lip, tasting fruit and crushed rose petals. "I'm glad you've been enjoying yourself. Tell me about your day."

"Don't you want your breakfast first?"

Sometimes other needs were more urgent than blood. Like making up for the hours he could never spend with her. Getting back little pieces of that time, which she could give him in words. "I can wait while we talk."

She bit her pink lip. He sensed her hesitation and a weight in her aura. Duty. For a moment, he thought she would bring up where they should start searching for Ziara.

But she didn't. She slid her leg over him and started talking about the food she had eaten today.

Satisfaction rushed through him. She needed to make up for those hours, too. She would even set aside their quest for the sake of these moments, when they tried to weave her dawn into his dusk.

"I like Marijani," she said. "Women can go anywhere they please here."

"Where did you go?"

Her gaze drifted away from his. "Master Kona made some suggestions about sights to see."

"You included the famous Sun Market on your itinerary, didn't you?"

"She told me I should."

"Did it live up to what you've heard?"

"I wish you could have been there. I got you some new titles for the library from the scroll sellers."

"Scrolls too? But you already brought me so many nice things."

The scent of cassia butter and Cassia made his fangs lengthen. He twirled one finger in the sash dangling from her dress and rubbed his other thumb at the corner of her mouth, where their kiss had smudged the brilliant color. Her lips curved into a smile under his touch.

He listened to her describe all the wonders she'd seen at the Sun Market and the package she had sent to Zoe. The more questions he asked her, the more at ease she became.

She shouldn't have to hide how much she'd enjoyed herself just because he had missed it. Feeling it in her aura now, he wasn't missing it, not really.

"It's good for you to have independence, Cassia. You'll be stuck with me for centuries. Enjoy your time alone while you can."

She gave him a playful swat. "I worked very hard for the privilege of being stuck with you."

"I'll try not to wear out my welcome."

She ran a hand down his chest, her palm lingering above his navel. The warmth of her touch shivered down over his skin. "But you're so very welcome, and I enjoy it so much when you wear me out."

He slid his hand along her calf. "Are you lonely during the day?"

She sighed. "I always miss you when you Slumber."

His hand tightened on his braid at her ankle. "I'm sorry."

She shook her head. "It's normal. I wouldn't have it any other way. And I'm fine on my own. You know I am."

"I want you to enjoy your days."

She rested her head on his chest. "This is a different kind of solitude than I had before. Not the isolated, lonely kind. The independent kind."

"You do like it."

She smiled. "I suppose I do."

"Well, I will enjoy imagining you enjoy it."

Her gaze fell again as she traced a circle in his chest hair with her finger. "I did make a new friend at the market. I hope that's all right with you."

He sat up and pulled her onto his lap. "Cassia, you don't have to ask my permission to meet people and make friends. It doesn't have to be all right with me."

"But I don't want you to feel you're missing something."

"Thank you, my rose. I appreciate your consideration. But you know I would go to any length to ensure your freedom. That includes all areas of your life. Even spending time with humans."

Her discomfort felt like a briar patch in her aura.

Lio's eyebrows rose. "Yes, even male humans."

She let out a frustrated sound. "He's a student from Capital University on holiday here. He reminds me of Harkhuf. I made it very clear to him in the first few minutes that I am taken, and he was strictly friendly after that."

"But he tried to flirt with you when you met."

Her blush returned, prettier than ever. "I'm sure he does that to all the girls."

"He would be a fool not to flirt with you. You're magnificent. I'm sorry I wasn't there to see you set him straight." He tickled her behind her knee until she squirmed and laughed instead of looking distressed. Dropping his voice low in his throat, he caressed her with his magic. "Cassia. I am your Grace. I do not feel threatened by university students in the marketplace."

"You were jealous of Flavian. You threatened violence."

Lio's smile deserted him, and he pulled her tighter against him. "That was different. He tried to marry you. You went into the woods alone with him, and I didn't know if you wanted to go or what kind of unwelcome advances he might have made."

"I seem to recall you had some worries they might not have been unwanted."

"We had made no promises yet. That was then." He slid his hand up her thigh. "This is now. You have given me your trust. I will always honor that gift by giving you my absolute trust, as well."

She trailed her hand down his neck to her braid and rested her forehead against his. "How I love you, my Grace."

"My Grace. How I love you in return."

"You needn't miss anything," she said earnestly. "I'll give you a tour of the Sun Market in my mind any time you like."

"And I'll give you a real tour of the Moon Market. You haven't experienced Marijani until you see what they sell at night."

She teased her toe over his leg. "That sounds like our kind of place. Shall we go tonight?"

"Yes." He wanted to sweep her into the moonlight, even as he savored the taste of sun on her skin. But there was another reason they should go. "It's the best place to ask around about Ziara."

"Oh. The Moon Market does sound like a place where privateers would do business."

"It's their bazaar. Their territory."

"We'll mix pleasure and purpose then." She straddled his lap, running her hands through his hair. "Pleasure first. It's difficult to be purposeful on an empty stomach."

His fangs descended. He should take her invitation and forget everything else. But he didn't. "No, my rose. First, we find out when Ziara is due back and settle that question. Then you can enjoy the Moon Market, and I'll enjoy it straight from your vein."

Her hands tightened in his hair. The arousing tug and the want in her aura almost made him change his mind.

But he let her go. She slid off his lap and went to fix her lip color. Her finger teased over her mouth, taunting him with the doubt and promise of this night.

THE MOON MARKET

CASSIA FOUND IT CHALLENGING to dress for the Moon Market when her instincts demanded that she and Lio shed their clothes and return to bed. No matter how the imperative to find Ziara hung over her, the Craving had a way of winning all debates.

But Lio was right. They could linger over their pleasure after they had tried to locate the *Wanted*.

She was straightening the collar of his dashing red festival tunic when one of the inn's runners appeared at the door with a delivery. Lio took the small scroll, then sent the boy off with a coin and a tin of gumsweets.

Cassia's heart lifted at the sight of the purple ribbon tied around the missive. "A letter from Zoe already!"

She and Lio unrolled it together and read it by the warm spell light of the inn's lamps.

Dear Cassia and Lio,

    We played privateers and then I feel asleep. Then I woke up and got your letter. Thank you for my new storybook! It's about goats that save the day! It's my favorite book now! Papa and me are reading it in the new cave and he helped me write this letter!

    Write me back all about the privateers!

                Love,

                Zoe and Papa

Lio smiled at her. "Choosing storybooks is clearly another of the Brave Gardener's talents."

"I'm so relieved she seems more excited than despondent. Perhaps it will be good for her that we're traveling. It could help her learn that when loved ones go away, it can be safe and even enjoyable."

"And that we'll return." Lio tucked the cherished note from Zoe into their new writing supplies on the desk.

"Well, let us go meet some of these privateers. Their devotees in Orthros are eager for news." Cassia consulted her map of Marijani, only to frown at it. "The Moon Market isn't on here."

Lio folded the map closed and slid it into her satchel. "Everyone who is welcome there knows where it is."

She raised her brows. "And everyone who doesn't know where it is, isn't welcome?"

"Precisely. There are only two ways to get in. The first is to arrive by ship, as most privateers do. It's quite hazardous, I understand. Easy to wreck on the reefs, if you don't know where you're going. Every privateer must learn the route from another. They're careful to show the way only to those they trust."

"Has anyone ever betrayed that trust?"

"Yes. If someone causes trouble, they and the privateer who invited them in are both forbidden to return. Ever."

"I see. Any privateer who doesn't want to lose access to the market had best be sure they only invite the right people. Profit is a powerful motivator. But what about the second way in?"

"Hesperines can step in, but only those the privateers consider friends."

"How does a Hesperine win the friendship of the privateers?" Cassia asked.

"By winning the approval of their favorite Hesperine trading partner."

"Kassandra," Cassia concluded.

"My Ritual mother is a more effective deterrent than any coral reef. Only Hesperines she vouches for set foot in the Moon Market. Fortunately for me, she's been taking me there since I was a suckling, so I know the ropes."

"Upstanding Firstgift Komnenos, experienced in the ways of a pirate den? Really?"

"I'm quite wicked when I want to be, I assure you."

"You ruined your wicked image the night we became friends."

"On the contrary, I'm a notorious heretic wanted in two countries across the sea."

Cassia gave him a mischievous smile. With his stubble, his knee-length tunic and loose black Imperial trousers, he looked beguiling. "A dashing fellow with fangs is about to take me into a secret privateer hideout full of rum and treasure, and I won't know the way out. This sounds like an undoubtedly dangerous and possibly very romantic adventure."

"Undoubtedly romantic. Only maybe a little bit dangerous. Allow me to show you the real lifeblood of Marijani—the city's dark side." He turned over her hand and kissed the inside of her wrist.

Even as her want for him heated, his resolve to make her wait for their tryst sweetened her anticipation. How would she concentrate on their quest with her Craving like this?

He smiled, his own hunger sharp in his gaze. He pulled her nearer. "Stay close to me tonight, all right?"

"I thought you said the Moon Market was only maybe a little bit dangerous."

"Which is why you should stay close to someone more dangerous, like me." He tucked her under his arm, and the familiar sensation of stepping swept them up.

The next thing she knew, they were standing in a moonlit sort of courtyard. The ground was covered in planks, and wooden walls curved upward from where they stood. Vines grew over the timbers. Even with her mortal senses, she could tell the whole place had a distinct and complex magical aura.

Before them, a sword with a curved blade rested on a stand made of bones. The edge was stained with blood.

Knight leapt forward to sniff the morbid arrangement. His whole body went on the alert, as if ready to bound off on a hunt. Cassia was suddenly reminded he was a predator.

Lio nodded at the blade. "I added my blood to the stepping focus the first time Ritual mother brought me in."

Cassia eyed the finger bones wrapped around the hilt of the sword as they passed. "The privateers are very serious about gatekeeping."

"Blood is always the most powerful way to seal an agreement. I could do without the bones, though."

They walked through a jagged doorway that led out of the courtyard, and Cassia realized it hadn't been a courtyard at all. It was the belly of a ship, long since installed on land. She looked all around her.

The entire Moon Market was built of the pieces of beached, wrecked, or retired ships. It was a maze of hulls and gangplanks. Sails had been turned into awnings, people talked and laughed on plazas that had been the decks, and lovers idled in crew hammocks. Balconies that had been crows' nests held musicians playing a beat that made Cassia's heart leap and her feet want to dance.

The aromas of brine and rum and spices floated through the market. The ocean soughed, never out of sight or earshot. The moons and the water conspired to cast a glow over the city within a city, while torches and lanterns were bright spots of orange in the indigo night.

She breathed in the ocean air. "We could get lost here."

"We should do that as soon as possible. Let's take care of our business quickly so we can."

"Where should we start?"

"The Plundered Heart is the tavern the famous privateers prefer. Someone there should be able to tell us when Captain Ziara's ship is expected to dock."

Lio held Cassia against him as they wound through the Moon Market. Knight stayed alert, taking in the scents, alive with energy, as if a hunting game awaited him around any corner.

Could Captain Ziara or her crew be somewhere in this bustle? Even now, Cassia might be walking past people who knew about Solia—who had *known* Solia.

Lio led her between two boats that formed an archway, into a nest of tiered ships. The courtyard before them held a bubbling fountain, tables, and a counter made out of barrels where a woman with short, locked hair was serving drinks.

Lio greeted her in Divine. "Moon's blessings upon you."

"And you, stepper," she answered in the same tongue, considering him. "You're not one of my regulars."

"Alas, on my previous visits to the Moon Market, I didn't have the opportunity to visit your establishment."

She raised an eyebrow at him. "You're too polite to be one of my regulars."

Lio smiled, an expression that often looked boyish on him. But tonight, it looked roguish. He leaned an elbow on the bar. "I can be less polite, if you like."

Cassia had the urge to drag her Hesperine back to the inn and ask him to be very impolite with her indeed.

The bartender chuckled, grinning at Lio. "What can I get for you?"

"A mint rum," he replied. "Should I refrain from saying 'please?'"

"You'd better not thank me, either." The bartender winked.

When the bartender mixed the drink, Cassia was glad he'd ordered them one to share. That tankard was big enough to drown in.

The bartender threw Knight a smile and a scrap of meat and didn't bat an eye when he devoured the messy treat on the floor of her tavern. "Anything else?"

"We and Captain Ziara have a mutual friend," Lio said, "who tells us the *Wanted* is due to return soon. Any idea when we might find her here?"

The bartender laughed. "When Ziara's back, you won't need me to tell you. You'll know."

That was all? They had come halfway across the world and entered a pirate den for that frustrating non-answer.

"How will we know?" Cassia asked, struggling to keep the frustration out of her voice.

"You'll see," the bartender replied.

"Is there anything else you can tell us about Captain Ziara?" Cassia pressed.

The bartender stopped smiling. "If she hasn't told you herself, she doesn't want you to know."

Cassia bit her tongue, lest she pry their only source of information until she locked her secrets up even tighter.

Lio's charming smile and generous overpayment smoothed Cassia's blunder. He found them a table near the fountain and pushed her chair up for her. "Why don't you have a little rum? It will relax you."

On second thought, perhaps she could finish this entire drink. "You're right. Waiting for news will definitely be easier at the bottom of this glass."

Knight stretched out on her feet under the table. Lio, instead of sitting down beside her, pulled his chair behind her and began to rub at the knots of tension in her shoulders.

She let out a little groan and let her head fall forward. "Have I told you that you're magical?"

"Not tonight." He chuckled. "I'm happy I live up to Hesperines' magical reputation."

"Not just Hesperine magical. Lio magical."

His hands gentled, pressing tenderly but firmly into the spaces between her spine and shoulder blades. "I wish there weren't so many things I can't fix with magic."

"You fix me."

"Do I?" He leaned close, his breath touching her neck.

"Every time. You have to let me fix you later."

He planted a kiss on her neck. "Just how are you planning to fix me?"

"Any way you like."

"Mmm."

The rum was nice, but forgetting everything in Lio's arms would be even better.

She was a third of the way through the drink when the pleasant, soft, warm-all over feeling took over her. Two thirds of the way through, she giggled. "I suppose my humanity isn't useless after all."

Lio reached around and stole her drink, finishing it for her.

"I wasn't done."

"Save room for the next tavern."

"We're going to another one?"

"I thought we'd take a food tour. There are many places with excellent meatless fare that cater to Hesperines. And you won't want to miss the banana beer."

"Banana beer sounds like good cheer in a bottle."

They began a nocturnal counterpart to her tour through the Sun Market's food stalls. Cassia let Lio thoroughly indulge his need to feed her, and she allowed herself more indulgence in alcohol than usual. As the night wore on, she was stuffed and more tipsy than she could remember.

"Getting drunk is nice."

"You're adorable when you're drunk."

She rested a hand on Knight's shoulder to steady herself. "I hate to disagree with you, Sir Diplomat, but I think in this case, your argument is invalid due to your bias."

Lio's chest shook with laughter. "You can still talk like a diplomat yourself, even after that many drinks."

"Oooh. If I'd realized I could still be competent like this, I would have gotten drunk so much more often in Tenebra." She swayed.

Lio put a strong arm around her waist. "I'm glad you feel safe enough to enjoy yourself. As long as you don't make yourself sick."

"Not sick. I feel *marvelous!*" She took a step away, holding out her arms and turning in a lopsided circle that ended in Lio's arms.

She followed the drinks with a very large coffee. Then they ran into a crowd of dancers. Laughing, she slurred a sit-stay command at Knight and pulled Lio into the dance. He led, using his levitation when needed to keep her from losing her way in the steps. They danced and danced and laughed and whispered to each other and laughed some more.

"I'm fairly certain my jokes are only funny to me because I'm drunk. And you're only laughing because you're sweet."

"I'm laughing because I feel a little drunk myself."

She caressed his neck. "You haven't even drunk a drop of me tonight."

"I'm drunk on irresponsibility."

"Oh, yes. Better than rum."

There was still more to see. They retrieved Knight and continued on, wandering past market stalls and twisting alleys and shadowed doorways. Cassia suspected the most important negotiations went on out of sight, but the wares on display were intriguing, too.

Silk from its namesake Silklands, fine porcelain from the Archipelagos, scrolls of poetry and spells and swords of every variety, as sharp and beautiful as the night itself. The jewelers were enough to dazzle even Cassia, and she didn't much care for jewels. She paused to ogle a golden nose ring studded with diamonds that glowed with a halo of magic.

"It would be unwise to make a decision about piercings when you're this drunk." Lio looked at her nose protectively.

She laughed so hard she snorted. "My Gifting would heal it later. It would only be temporary."

"Not your nose," he pleaded.

"Shouldn't I enjoy piercings while I can?"

"I'll shower you with clip earrings to make amends."

She patted his chest. "Not to worry. I like my nose the way it is."

He kissed the tip of it. "That's a relief. Because I adore it."

"In truth, it's all the magic I noticed, not the nose ring."

Lio raised his eyebrows. "Is that so? I believe your magical senses may be getting stronger."

That made her feel more alert. "Really? Could that be a side effect of my mystery magic?"

"Yes. Improved ability to sense spells could only come from an awakening affinity."

Cassia felt like dancing again. "I've been paying attention when everyone else casts spells, in case it sparks something."

"Is that why you were so interested the other night when Lyros was enchanting a ring?"

"Yes. I couldn't feel what he described, though. Even so, it was interesting to learn about how artifacts are made. He said he sets the enchantment in the gem."

"Yes, the inherent magic of the stone sustains the spell."

"So…" She chuckled. "My mind is a rock for your mind ward?"

"The most precious diamond," he assured her.

"Can I be an emerald instead?"

"Ah," he said with interest, "Do you prefer emeralds to diamonds? I'll remember that."

She felt herself blush. "There are many things I prefer to gems, though. You know how much I loved the bar of soap, the first gift you ever gave me."

"I know riches have never been your greatest temptation, my love. I saw what you were looking at the night the Tenebran embassy was ogling cases full of jewelry."

"You." She pulled him closer. "And now I no longer have to covet what I may not have. For you are mine."

"But it does not make you petty to enjoy receiving luxuries from me. You're allowed to want emeralds."

Her brow furrowed. "I suppose I think of gems as things men pay to buy a bride or mark a woman as a concubine."

"If jewels will always mean that to you, I will always get you something else. But if we could change your feelings about them, I would be happy to do that, too. I don't want you to miss out on anything because Tenebra tainted it for you."

"Oh no." She put her hands to her face. "You've already commissioned something from Lyros, haven't you? And now you think I won't like it."

"We may have discussed it. Would you object very much to a piece of jewelry crafted by a heretical artist, infused with blood magic, and given to you by your shameless fanged lover to signify our profane bond?"

"Well, when you put it that way, it's rather the opposite of marriage and concubinage, isn't it?" She grinned wickedly.

He kissed her there in front of the passersby, and the Moon Market crowd didn't bat an eye.

"I'll take you to see the flowers next," he said.

She beamed at him and bounced on her toes. "Which way?"

"All we need do is follow my nose. I smell their fragrances from here."

Soon, Cassia could smell them as well. She didn't know how the air held so much scent, and she felt twice as drunk. Sellers in costumes as colorful as their blooms charmed passersby into buying cut flowers, while other merchants with fragrant hands and dirt under their nails hawked seedlings in pots. Flowers in every color surrounded Cassia and Lio, a wonderland of exotic treasures and familiar faces.

Lio passed a coin to a little girl selling moonflowers from a basket. He tucked the big, silky white bloom behind Cassia's ear, and its delicate, fresh fragrance reached her nose.

"They're all night bloomers!" she said in delight. "Every single plant for sale here. Anything we buy will give us flowers all through polar night. Oh, but how will I choose which ones to get? And where will we put them while we're traveling?"

"If you can't decide, get them all, and we'll have them shipped back to Orthros."

"You shouldn't trust me in a flower market while I have no inhibitions."

"If I cannot walk for all the potted plants in our residence, I shall levitate, my rose. If flowers increase your happiness, let us fill the entire house with them."

"Do you know what makes me happier than flowers?" she asked.

"Do they sell it here?"

She looped her arms around his neck. "No, he's not for sale."

Her inhibitions slipped away even more as a fanged grin spread across his stubbled face, his hair blowing in a gentle sea breeze. "And he is already yours."

Cassia lost track of time while they flirted and explored every stall in the flower section of the market. She discovered blood moon lilies that only flowered at certain phases of the red moon. Night-blooming jasmine made her long to craft a new soap so she could bathe in its scent. Everywhere, there were more moonflowers, as pure as her beloved diplomat. He didn't protest when she bought a bloom to match hers and attached it to the front of his robe.

She concluded it would take her tonight to discover what was there, the next night to decide which to buy, and another night after that to make all the arrangements for having her choices sent home.

"We've seen my favorite things," she said at last. "Is there anything you'd like to look at?"

He looked down her body, and heat rushed through her everywhere his gaze touched her. "She's not on the market either."

"Definitely not. A Hesperine stole her." Was he going to steal her away from the Moon Market right now and step her back to their bed?

Her teasing immortal merely took her hand, despite the heat in his eyes. "Shall we see what the glassmakers have on display?"

They found their way through the artisans. The glaziers occupied an open-air stage in front of a clay furnace, its openings gleaming orange in the blue night. Bare to the waist, the muscular men sweated in the coastal warmth and the heat of their fires. As the audience watched, they crafted the vases that were for sale nearby.

Lio struck up a conversation with one of them in Tradewinds, too fast for Cassia's fuzzy mind to follow. Before she knew it, the glassblower motioned for Lio to join them.

Lio stripped off his tunic and handed it to Cassia. She held the garment to her, breathing his scent. She watched him leap onto the stage wearing only in his trousers.

He accepted a spare blowing iron from the glass makers and dipped it into the furnace. He pulled the long metal rod back out with the end coated in gleaming hot glass. With the glass aimed downward, he began to swing the iron, letting it arc in front of him like a pendulum.

He took advantage of his height and the stage, letting the end of the rod sweep below the platform. The force of the motion coaxed the molten glass down into his desired shape.

His lips touched the iron, and his breath filled the glass, giving it shape, life. Muscles in his arm and torso flexed as he spun the rod not with magic, but pure physical strength. Mesmerized, Cassia watched his whole body work to coax one delicate piece of glass to life.

When the vase was complete, he used a sharp blade to make a cut around the top, then with precision, snapped the glass from the iron. The other glassblowers spoke to him in complimentary tones, and he gave them each a wrist clasp. After setting the vase to cool on a nearby stand, he leapt down to rejoin Cassia.

"For you, my Grace," he murmured under the noise of the crowd. "To hold bouquets from your garden."

She held his hands to her heart and held his gaze until she saw the gleam of satisfaction in his eyes.

"We can come back and retrieve it when it has cooled," he said. "In the meantime, how about we lose our way?"

She nodded. He took his robe from her and tossing it back on, leaving the garment open over his bare chest. As they headed away from the onlookers, he slung an arm around her waist.

He urged them toward the alluring privacy of a nearby empty alleyway. Cassia pulled him into the shadows there, taking hold of his open collar and bringing his mouth down to hers. He braced his hands on the wall on either side of her, kissing her just as hungrily.

His veil spell descended upon her, smooth and heavy, and she moaned. She ran her hands down his chest, then his arms, feeling the strength she had seen at work upon the glass. Then his hands were upon her, caressing and working and teasing her out as carefully and powerfully as he had shaped the vase. She kissed his breath from his mouth and felt his mind magic sigh into her.

She took him into her, into all her hollow, empty places where only he could reach. The sunlight wasn't enough to warm her there. But Lio filled her and made her overflow.

77~74

Nights Until

NOTIAN WINTER SOLSTICE

DEAR ZOE

27 Annassa, 1597 IS

Dear Zoe,

 I was so happy to get your letter when I woke from Slumber!

 Cassia and I visited the famous Moon Market tonight, where privateers sell their treasure. We saw many good pirates, although Captain Ziara is not here yet.

 Here are some beads for you and Bosko, just like the privateers wear in their hair. We also bought some privateer headwraps for the goats. We hope you have fun with these when you play.

With love,
Lio and Cassia

28 Annassa, 1597 IS

Dear turtle doves,

 Zoe and Bosko won't take off their privateer beads. Now all the sucklings in Orthros want some. Just imagine the raised eyebrows at the Moon Market when they get so many orders from Hesperine parents come Winter Solstice.

 The goats are not as excited about their headwraps, but Zoe hasn't admitted defeat in her attempts to dress them up.

 Lyros and I found some information in one of his military strategy books that we think may help you. We're sending you a transcription with this letter. It's a collection of search strategies the Imperial army uses to find soldiers who are missing in action.

We think you could adapt it to almost any location in the Empire. Maybe it will help you follow up on whatever leads you get from Ziara. Hopefully by then we can join you to help.

Now we're off to keep the sucklings out of trouble while they play privateers (again).

Yours,
Mak and Lyros

29 Annassa, 1597 IS

Dear Mak and Lyros,

Thank you so much for the search strategies. Tonight we spent time at a table in the Moon Market, where we pored over the information while Lio made me eat too much.

(Cassia insists that I write that in, but for the record, I protest. I didn't have to make her eat that much dessert.)

This will undoubtedly help—if Ziara ever arrives to give us any leads.

How is the mood of the Firstblood Circle as Hypatia's vote approaches? And how is the mood at House Argyros?

Cheers,
Lio and Cassia

30 Annassa, 1597 IS

Dear Lio and Cassia,

With Xandra's eminent sister abstaining from the vote, the Firstblood Circle is in a mood we've never seen. Without the Second Princess as a deterrent or a shield, her opponents and allies must make their true positions clear and stand on their own.

Xandra's residence has become the rallying point for our partisans from the Solstice Summit. Kia is turning it into a hotbed of rebellion, of course.

Mak and I have secured a number of fellow youngbloods as partisans, who feel reassured that the Stand is confident in our ability to protect Orthros in a new era of Tenebran politics.

Everyone on both sides of the debate is sick of hearing Epodos's cloying songs all over Haima. The elders will never admit it, but we believe even Hypatia's supporters find Nodora's music sweeter to their ears.

Plenty of time with the whole Stand together in the arena continues to help the mood at House Argyros. We spar with Nike every night. It now takes her a few more minutes to beat us than before.

We'll keep you informed.

Yours,
Lyros and Mak

31 Annassa, 1597 IS

Dear Lio and Cassia,

Courier lessons are only five nights away!

Everyone is helping me practice stepping. Tonight I stepped from Uncle Argyros's roof all the way to the big dome at our House.

Mama says I'm not allowed on top of the dome. But I stepped so far! With my goats!

Love,

Zoe

P.S. Papa had to help me down. Then Mama helped me with my spelling.

73

Nights Until

NOTIAN WINTER SOLSTICE

32 Annassa, 1597 IS

A GIFT FOR A PRINCESS

"Y̶OU SPEAK TRADEWINDS WITH the accent of a lost goat,"
Dakk told her at the smiths' stalls later that week.

Cassia replied with one of the few phrases she could say
with confidence, which she and Zoe had learned together. "I like goats."

Dakk pointed at the planting axe in her hands. "You just called that,
well, the word for a woman you're on intimate terms with. Should your
Hesperine be jealous?"

Cassia carefully returned the axe to the smith's display. "Ah. No. I'm
not wed to my craft."

"Clearly, you aren't in love with your language studies, either," he teased.

"I spent weeks trying with my Tradewinds primer in preparation for
traveling here, but I don't learn languages from books very well. I'll pick
it up much faster in the market like this."

He raised an eyebrow. "Are you saying you never spoke Tradewinds
before you went to Orthros?"

Had it been a mistake to admit that? Did even people in the northwest
speak Tradewinds for commerce? "I was, ah, very sheltered."

Tension ached between Cassia's shoulders. Thorns, what would she
do if he found out she didn't know whatever language was spoken in the
northwest?

He looked at her intently. "In that case, your Tradewinds is very good
for someone who just started learning. Rather unbelievable, in fact."

Inwardly, she sighed in relief. "That's encouraging to hear. Would it be
too much to ask for you to help me practice?"

"Well, I did make excellent marks in that class. Never once mistook a gardening tool for a woman's embrace." He scratched his beard. "That could be a very painful mistake."

"Please, help me avoid such uncomfortable errors."

"Practicing with you sounds fun." His eyes twinkling, he reached into his pocket and pulled out a little wad of cheese. He held it up, saying a new word. Then he offered it to Knight and told her another word she hadn't heard.

She laughed, watching Knight gobble the cheese out of Dakk's hand. Her hound relaxed into a food daze. To Dakk's credit, he didn't bat an eye at the mess on his glove.

"You have made a friend for life," she said, "and I shall never forget the words for 'cheese' and 'dog.'"

They made a game of it all through the market. Dakk told her a few words for items at one stall, and when they came to another stall with similar wares, asked her to recall their names. When she stopped to mail her and Lio's latest letters to Zoe, Dakk taught her how to talk about writing and correspondence. Cassia's practical Tradewinds vocabulary grew at record speed.

"What's next on your shopping list?" he asked. "Can I teach you the word for puppy?"

Cassia covered Knight's ears. "Perish the thought. What I really must find is a gift for my mentor."

"A teacher of yours back in Orthros?"

Cassia nodded. "She can't come to the Sun Market, of course."

"Right. The operative word being 'sun.'"

"I'm not sure what would be special enough for her."

"I find myself in the same dilemma every time I need a gift for my mentor. She's also my grandmother, so that makes it doubly important to show my consideration for her."

"That does sound like a challenge."

"You have no idea. But the last time I gave her a gift, she actually cracked a smile. I must be doing something right."

"Are her standards equally high regarding your studies?"

"Oh, yes. She's a mind healer of great eminence, and I'm lucky to have such a teacher. But she doesn't make it easy."

"Pressure to follow in her footsteps?"

He winced. "Only countless generations' worth."

"So what do Imperial matriarchs with immense magical power like as gifts?"

"My grandmother prefers fine liquor."

Cassia laughed again. "I'm afraid if I got my mentor a nice bottle of something like that, she would already have more of it in her cellar. She keeps one of the most elegant houses in Orthros. No, I want it to be something you can only get here...something that makes her feel as if she's been here. I want to take a little piece of the Sun Market home to her."

She was shaking her head at an enchanted geode when she felt a drop of water on her forehead. She lifted her face to the sky. Where had those clouds come from?

"Best find some shelter," Dakk advised. "Fast."

She followed him as he ran for cover under a nearby tree. They made it beneath the mangrove's spreading branches just as the sky open and dumped a steady downpour on the Sun Market.

Cassia frowned up at the dripping leaves. "I wasn't expecting that. It mustn't rain very often on Marijani."

Dakk laughed. "The rainy season is about to start. It will rain for months."

"No sun over the Sun Market? I can't imagine."

"The sun will return."

As if eager to prove his words, the heavy shower ceased within a few minutes. The warm, golden rays of the sun spread over its namesake market. Cassia stood back from Knight as he shook himself off.

Dakk nodded to a nearby statue. "I need to thank Jua for the return of the sun."

The figure, carved from gleaming, dark wood like the doors of the city, depicted a woman with a heavy basket on her head. Dakk crossed to her and added a quartz to her basket, murmuring something in Tradewinds.

Cassia joined him by the statue. "What would be more respectful to her—giving her an offering, or refraining because I'm not from here?"

"My ancestors aren't from this area, either, but Jua has never expressed displeasure at my offerings. She gets all kinds here. She's the goddess of the Sun Market, after all."

"The Sun Market has its own goddess?"

He adjusted his gloves. "Well, I think at first she was the goddess of the swamp the market was built on. Now she's the patron of all the commerce that goes on here. In seasons when trade is good and people give enough offerings, she'll sometimes delay the rainy season."

Cassia placed a quartz into the basket, and Dakk repeated the prayer.

Her gaze drifted up to the tree that sheltered them and Jua's statue. She could only imagine how long the venerable mangrove had been here, soaking up the sun over Marijani, building all that light and warmth into its bark.

That was a treasure you couldn't buy.

Her gaze fell to the litter around the base of the tree. Seed pods.

"Dakk, is there any custom or law against taking some seed pods from the ground beneath this tree?"

He raised his brows and glanced down, as if noticing the litter for the first time. "No one will care if you make the street sweepers' work easier for them. But why would you want those old things?"

Cassia leaned down and collected a gift fit for a princess from the ground. She stowed the seeds carefully in her satchel. "This is something my mentor will appreciate."

"She must be a great deal more forgiving than my grandmother."

Cassia chuckled. "I wouldn't say that. I'm sorry to have dragged you all over the Sun Market looking for a gift, though."

"It was my pleasure. But you hardly needed my help after all."

"No, you've been a great help." She smiled. "It's nice to have a friend in the city."

"So it is." He grinned back.

"Do you suppose…" Cassia chose her words carefully. "The northwest is so far removed from everything. I didn't grow up with the lessons taught to children who are born Imperial citizens. Even our local gods are different."

"Well, you'll soon be a Hesperine, so it won't matter."

"But I don't wish to remain ignorant. I hope to become better educated not just about my new people in Orthros, but about the Empire as well. Could you teach me more than just language?"

"What would you like to know?"

"Everything."

He laughed as they began to walk again, strolling along a sunlit aisle of the market. "That would take a while."

She lifted her face to the warmth shining down from the sky. "Who is the deity of the sun here?"

"That's Zalele, of course. She is the deity of the sun everywhere, she who hung the sky. The nurturer, creator of all that is."

The sun seemed to shine right into Cassia's chest. Imperials believed the sun belonged to a goddess, even as far away as Tenebra. Just hearing about Zalele made Anthros sound like a weak little pretender, laying claim to something that had never been his.

"You should see Zalele's temple in the capital," said Dakk. "Magnificent."

"Perhaps I'll have the opportunity to pay my respects there."

"Just don't expect her to involve herself in day-to-day matters, as do goddesses like Jua. Zalele is too powerful and important for that. She leaves the affairs of mortals to the lesser deities and the ancestors."

Cassia gnawed her lip, remembering the eerie voices coming through the spirit gate. "How exactly do the ancestors involve themselves here?"

He gave her a curious look. "I suppose every lineage would give you a different answer to that question. All our traditions vary so widely in different parts of the Empire, depending on what our particular ancestors expect."

"I'm sure there are many traditions here that we never heard about in the northwest."

"Well, most citizens give offerings to their ancestors and include them in family activities. For example, it's often a custom to pour the first sip of coffee on the ground for them, before filling the cups of living family members."

Cassia liked the thought of the Eighth Circle being able to share some of their coffee with Methu. "That's a lovely practice."

"Everyone has their own rituals, prayers, and spells for communicating with the ancestors, but all of us seek their guidance often. We ask them for protection, for wisdom. Of course, their messages to us are not always easy to understand or interpret."

The thought of seeking advice from the whispers, on the other hand, gave Cassia a chill. "Do you…talk with your ancestors often?"

His expression was quite serious. "Every day."

Cassia couldn't imagine that. "Is it difficult?"

"Why would it be?"

How astonishing that such things were normal to him.

"Have you never heard your ancestors?" he asked.

Only in the spirit gates. "I admit, I am not on good terms with my forefathers."

"And your foremothers?"

"They are unknown to me."

"Yours is a great loss, Cassia. I am sorry." He sounded as if someone had died, or the world was broken beyond repair.

She suppressed a shrug. There was only one thing she appreciated about Tenebra. There, all the king's forebears were in a crypt, reassuringly dead and silent.

"It's all right," she said. "I am Hespera's now."

FIRST TASTE

THE LIGHTS OF MARIJANI glittered at Cassia from beyond the balcony, tantalizing her with the island's beauty and its secrets.

Tonight, once again, the jewel of the City-States had revealed not a hint about Captain Ziara. Although Cassia and Lio had haunted the Moon Market all week, it had been all beauty and no secrets. They had finally given up for the night and returned to their rooms at the inn with a few hours to spare before dawn.

She wrapped her veil hours robe closer around herself, sliding her cheek against the smooth green silk that reminded her of home. She sensed him come up behind her, his presence warming her within. Sometimes she couldn't tell the mind ward was there, it was so deeply fused to her, resonating with his every move.

He wrapped his arms around her waist and kissed her behind her ear. She ran her hands along his forearms over the brilliant blue of his veil hours robe.

"Don't lose heart," he said. "There are many factors that could make the length of Captain Ziara's voyage unpredictable. It's difficult to know exactly when she'll arrive. But when that night comes, we'll be here, ready and waiting."

"When Kassandra hurried us over here, I suppose I didn't expect more waiting."

He nuzzled the top of her head. "The oracle's timing is often mysterious. But always for a good reason."

"You're right. We know that from experience." She turned in his arms. "Thank you for your faithfulness on this wild quest, as in everything, Lio."

Surprise flashed across his face. "Cassia, why do I sense guilt in you when you say that? There's no reason for you to apologize about searching for your sister."

"Even though it interrupted my Gifting and our family trip and the rest of our eternity? It seems the mess the king made of mine and Solia's lives is always affecting yours—or endangering it."

"Which, as usual, is his fault, not yours."

"Your Grace comes with so much messy past attached. I'm all sharp edges sometimes."

That made him laugh. There was so much love in the sound. "Of course. Roses have thorns."

"Your patience never ceases to amaze me."

"Cassia, I want to find Solia too."

Her gaze fell. "You're so selfless."

"I'm not. Not at all." He took her face in his hand and lifted it. "Remember what I said on your almost-Gift-Night."

She thought back over all the momentous events and intimate moments of that night. "Which thing? 'Your bite gives me pleasure'? Or 'so beautiful'? Or perhaps you mean the way you shouted at the end? I remember that especially. I so enjoyed listening to you."

His fangs descended, and his magic stirred. If she had a kingdom-destroying look, this expression was his heretic sorcerer look. "I said I want there to be nothing on your mind but our future. I don't want you to be worrying about Solia. I will allow nothing to detract from this. From us. I'm selfish, Cassia. I want you to have peace about your sister, so you'll be free to live our life together."

"So do I," she said.

Drumbeats drifted up to them from the courtyard below their balcony. The yearning strains of an Imperial lute joined the call of a flute and the jingle of tambourines.

He took her hand and kissed her palm, and the sensation flowed through her entire body. "Dance with me. Lay it all down for the night. Let's go up to the roof and dance under the stars."

Cassia gave into the call of the music and the invitation in his gaze. She let him lead her up to the rooftop.

He was a vision in the moonlight, with his fangs unsheathed and his veil hours robe hanging halfway open. She forgot how the heat and light had felt at the Sun Market earlier that day. She thought she could feel Hespera's moons on her skin, or perhaps that was just her shiver of wonder and desire at the sight of Lio.

He caught her close and swayed with her, leading her through various steps plucked from their favorite dances. The musicians shared their song, even as the privacy of the moment enfolded her and Lio.

Every step with him was a temptation, luring her farther from her cares. When he twirled her, she spun away from him with a laugh, and a little more of her doubt flew away on the warm night breeze. He tugged her back into his arms, driving away her fears. With his strong arms around her and his ardent gaze upon her, it was easy to let go.

There was a part of her that did not abide by doubt or duty. That part of her knew only that being in his arms was right, and everything else was wrong. That part of her lived by only one law, the law of her need for him, and when that was satisfied, all must be well in the world.

With every motion of their dance, every brush of his body against hers, that part of her woke a little more. She became a little more breathless. A little more heat coursed deep within her.

He whirled her away from him again, and every fiber of her body protested. But when he pulled her close once more, the satisfaction of his arms around her was all the more intense.

He performed a step from a Hesperine dance, and she followed his lead, moving her left foot backward as he moved his right forward. Their thighs brushed, and need coiled between her legs.

He strung together one dance step after another that tantalized her with his nearness. His reflective eyes glowed at her, catching the spell light of the lanterns like all of it belonged to him. He held her gaze with an intensity that drugged her, as if he worked mind magic on her with just a look.

She couldn't look away. She could see in his eyes that he could not bear for her to. If she looked away, he would be jealous of the entire world beyond the circle of their arms.

"I can't do anything but dance with you," she breathed. "If you ask, I'll dance and dance and never stop. You have that power over me, Lio."

His mouth was so close, he seemed to catch her words on his lips. "No more power than you have over me."

He dipped her, his mouth hovering over her throat. Her head spun with the motion and her need. She lifted her knee, caressing his body with her inner thigh.

He swooped her upright. Holding her tightly, he turned in a circle as their feet left the ground. They spiraled midair, bound together. Their hearts thundered against one another.

The taste of his lips made her moan in the back of her throat. Her tongue dove between his lips. He opened to her so she could taste the sweet wine there and the hot spices and all the things she could not name that only he could give her.

She tightened her leg around him, arching to bring her body flush against his. His arousal met her core through their silk robes. His hand tightened on the small of her back, pressing her closer against him.

She nipped his lower lip, the music a distant, sweet urging in her ears. She bit again, and then it was his low growl that urged her on.

She searched for the ground with her feet, and he set them down. He let her pull him toward the nearest piece of furniture. She thought it was a bench. Too short. But the bed was too far away. Why didn't he step her or lift her in his arms? It would be faster.

"I want you to need me so much you'll take me where you want me," he answered.

She drew him back inside, sparing only enough thought from their kisses to make sure she didn't trip down the stairs. But he held her steady. He wouldn't let her fall, except further in love with him.

There, at last, the bed. She drew her Hesperine into the shelter of the gauzy curtains. She felt his magic sweep over her skin, and the curtain ties all loosed at once, letting the sheer silk fall around them and cut them off from the world.

They landed on their knees with one of her legs still tangled around him.

"How many veils have you cast over this room?" she panted.

"Plenty."

"Good. I don't think I can be quiet."

His fangs lengthened, white and visible in the semidarkness within the bed curtains.

She was hungry for every part of his body. She couldn't keep her mouth off of him. The feel of his shoulder between her teeth made her moan. When she nipped her way across his chest, it was his turn to utter his pleasure into the shadows. With quick, greedy kisses, she traveled down his belly.

Fumbling to unfasten the rest of his robe, she scraped her teeth down the hair below his navel.

"Goddess, yes, Cassia. Feast on me."

With her hands on the mattress on either side of his knees, she leaned down and snatched his rhabdos between her lips. His gasp was harsh in her ears. She filled her mouth with him, sucking, relishing the heat and flavor of him.

Already so hard and long, his erection leapt at her ravishment. Impatient for more, she took one last, long taste of him, then rose up with a gasp.

She pushed him back against the pillows and climbed onto his lap. His hands fisted in the silky folds of her robe, and she felt his knuckles pressing into her hips.

His gaze caught hers again, riveting. She licked her lips and looked into his eyes as she joined their bodies.

She gave a ragged groan of satisfaction. The pleasure parted and stretched her, and she bared her teeth.

Lio wrapped his hand behind her head. "You are a Hesperine in human form, my Grace. Never forget it."

He pulled her mouth to his. His tongue laved each of her dull canines, reminding her of what they would have. Of who she would be.

No, of who she was.

She grasped his shoulders and rocked her hips, filling herself with him again and again like the lustful heretic she was. Every thrust of him deep within her body fed her Craving. They bit at each other's lips and tongues, and when his fangs drew her blood, his body surged beneath her, driving him up harder inside her, driving his mind magic down into her thoughts.

His mouth parted from hers, only to go for her throat, she knew. Her mouth felt so dry without his kiss.

She wanted him to show her what it was like again. To open their minds wider so she could feel and taste it when her flesh gave under his fangs and her blood filled his mouth.

Cassia. Oh, Cassia. I heard that.

Lio! She reveled in the rich tones of his voice in her mind. She hadn't heard him like this in weeks, not since the last time their Grace Union had awoken in defiance of her humanity. *It's happening again, at last.*

It was faster this time.

Her heart leapt. *Has the mind ward made it easier?*

I hope so.

I hope it doesn't stop.

His magic expanded in her mind in a rush, seizing on the brilliant connection between them.

Her head fell back. She tightened her krana around him, gripping him inside her, her loins trembling with the exquisite pleasure-pain just before release.

Keep talking, he purred, *just so I can hear you.*

She felt the caress of his voice from her head all the way down to her toes, and everywhere in between.

Lio. It's too much, and not enough. I need you. I'll die if I go one more night without tasting you.

Taste this.

His fangs penetrated her. She tasted pleasure, and her heart raced. She licked her lips, moving on him to the rhythm of the liquid pulse between them.

She rested her face in the crook of his neck, panting. The beat of magic and blood echoed in his throat. Everything she wanted, just beneath that layer of skin. So close, and yet out of reach.

She fastened her blunt mortal teeth onto his throat and sucked his skin.

His fangs clenched. *That will make a glorious bruise.*

For all of a minute.

I'll thoroughly enjoy it for that single minute.

Only with Lio could she laugh while experiencing pleasure so intense it made her want to...

Bite something?

She bit down harder, and he shuddered under her. Their enjoyment of each other cycled through her blood and his mind and back into her heart. She closed her teeth harder on his vein, holding on as the intense layers of pleasure spun her into release.

You were right, he said. *Definitely not quiet.*

Her scream gave way to another laugh.

His fangs left her flesh. Her jaw aching, she pried her teeth from his neck. She lifted her head, her lids heavy, to give him access to the other side of her neck.

His gaze fixed on her mouth. His face froze in horror. "Don't. Swallow. *Don't swallow.*"

That was when she saw the one impossible thread of crimson on his pale neck.

She had broken his skin.

She felt dampness on her lower lip and knew it was his blood.

So close. So close. So...

On instinct, her tongue darted out.

He hauled her off of him with immortal speed. The next thing she knew, she was sitting on the side of the bed, and he was putting a basin and a flask of water in her hands.

"Spit it out. All of it. Then rinse your mouth. *Don't swallow.*"

Tears sprang to her eyes. She followed his instructions.

Her first, priceless taste of his blood. Gone.

The windows rattled with his frustrated power. He was out of reach on the other side of the bed now. She looked over her shoulder at him. He had his fist and the edge of the sheet wrapped around his erection, his other hand covering his face. With a silent shudder, he took care of his own release. His pleasure and his blood, wasted.

With their Grace Union once again severed, he felt so far away.

"Your blood was in my mouth..." The tears poured faster down her cheeks.

"That was too close a call. I never thought—I didn't realize—"

"I didn't even get to taste it."

"Cassia. We couldn't have. Not here, not now. I can't Gift you at an inn on Marijani where sunrise might find us, when we're...."

"I hate this." Miserable, she set the basin and flask away from her on the bedside table and curled her arms around herself.

His weight left the mattress.

"No," she forced herself to say. "Don't come over here."

A moment of Hesperine stillness. "Why not, Cassia?"

Her gums throbbed, her heart ached, and the Craving inside her told her the truth. "If you come within arm's reach right now, I'll have my teeth on you again in a heartbeat."

"I won't let that happen again. Not until it's time." Then he was there in front of her, kneeling before her in the soft light, taking her hands. "I'm so sorry, Cassia."

Her whole body tensed with her fear of what she might do, even as she clutched his hands. "You have nothing to apologize for."

"Neither do you. What you did just now was natural."

She drew a sharp breath. "I want to do it again."

"May I give you some help with my thelemancy?"

"You must."

"Is that all right with you?" he insisted.

She stared at the column of his throat. *"Please."*

His mind slipped into hers again. For an instant, the intimacy of it made her lean closer, lowering her mouth toward his neck. Then drowsiness, like a comforting blanket, fell soft and heavy over her.

She swayed where she sat. He held her up. Her thoughts drifted. What had she been worried about a moment ago?

"You're so handsome naked in the sunlight," she blurted. "But maybe more handsome in the moonlight. I can't decide."

His smile was handsome, too, but a little sad.

"It felt so good to bite you while I rode you." She stared at the smear of drying blood on his neck. "Did you enjoy it?"

He brushed his fingers over his throat, as if trying to touch a spell. "Yes."

"Why did we delay my Gifting again?"

He eased her back onto the bed. "You need your humanity a little longer."

She let him tuck the covers around her. "But I don't want it. I don't even like it."

He placed a tender kiss on her forehead. "I love everything about you."

"I love you, too."

"Sleep, Cassia."

"Ohh. It feels…so good…" She yawned. "…when you say that with your magic."

The music seemed to recede, and all she could hear were the lulling tones of his power in her mind. Her eyes drifted shut. The last thing she remembered was the touch of his finger on her canine.

72

Nights Until

NOTIAN WINTER SOLSTICE

33 Annassa, 1597 IS

THE WANTED

CASSIA WOKE FEELING DEEPLY rested, with the vague sense that something lovely had occurred.

When she remembered what had actually happened, the pleasant effects of Lio's sleep spell wore off.

Holding the blankets under her chin, she sat up and cast a miserable glance around her at the bed. Empty, except for Knight. She wrapped her arms around his furry neck, and he licked her ear with concern.

She spotted Lio in a chair on the other side of the room. Too far away.

The casements were open, and the lights outside cast shadows over his face that made him look tired. "Good moon, my Grace."

She rubbed her eyes with one hand. "How long have I been asleep?"

"The rest of last night and all day, I'm afraid."

"Did you spend the entire Dawn Slumber in that chair?"

"No, I slept with my arms around you. Once I was completely awake again, I lifted the sleep spell from you. I thought I'd sit over here while you wake up, in case that makes it easier for you."

It did. And yet it was also terrible.

"How do you feel?" he asked.

"Cheated."

He sighed. "Me too."

They gazed at each other across the room.

"What are we going to do?" she asked.

"I think a night out in the Moon Market is exactly what we need."

"Don't you need breakfast?"

"I'll be all right for now."

He would have to feast on her again soon. She would have to control herself. How?

"If I move, will you feel the urge to chase me down and pounce?" His tone was teasing, but the way he looked at her told her he took the matter seriously.

"I think my ravenous instincts have calmed for the moment, thanks to your spell. I can't say the same for Knight's, though. I should feed him."

"And have something to eat yourself."

Her stomach felt hollow with hunger, as if mocking her Craving.

Cassia went through the motions of eating the food the inn staff brought, feeding Knight, and getting herself ready to go. Lio went into the other room to change.

When he returned, her whole body tensed.

Anger and determination flashed in his gaze, but his voice was as gentle as ever. "This won't do, my Grace. You've never jumped at the sight of Hesperines before. We can't have you start now."

"I don't know what I might do if you come closer."

He crossed the distance between them. She took a step back. But then he took a Hesperine step and was suddenly right in front of her with his hands on her arms.

"Relax, Cassia. Controlling your bloodthirst is something that must be learned. There's a reason self-discipline is central to the training all new Hesperines receive. I know neither of us thought you would need to learn this quite so soon, but it's nothing to be ashamed of. I know how it feels. Let me help."

His calm and confidence were so reassuring, his lack of judgment a balm to her as ever. She let out a sigh. "Thank you, my Grace."

"For now, going somewhere crowded is a good tactic. Deeply held inhibitions around others tend to assist with self-control. By the time the calm from the sleep spell wears off, we'll be surrounded by people, where you'll feel less of an urge to tear all my clothes off."

She choked on a laugh. "I hope so."

When he slipped his arm around her waist, she was not overtaken by any sudden compulsion to give his throat another bruise. Yet.

He stepped them and Knight to the bone focus at the entrance to the

Moon Market. As soon as they landed, he went as still as only a Hesperine could, his head cocked. Listening.

"What is it, Lio? What do you hear?"

"Cheers from the pier. They're calling out to a new ship that's arrived. I think—" He met her gaze. "They're welcoming Ziara."

She raced forward. "Let's go."

He grabbed her hand, and they hurried from the courtyard with Knight at their heels. Before she could ask, "Which way?" they were swept up in the crowd. It seemed the whole Moon Market was on the move.

The musicians came, still playing their instruments. The glassblowers came, carrying lanterns of their making. The eaters and drinkers came, and everywhere Cassia could hear them toasting Captain Ziara and the *Wanted*.

"Another safe voyage under the shadowlanders' noses!"

"Wonder how many mages she robbed blind this time?"

"Do you hear those sails snapping? That's the sound of money lining everyone's pockets."

"A good year for Ziara is a good year for all!"

Cassia kept Knight heeled close to her as the crowd carried her and Lio along. Masts came into view ahead, but the people around her blocked her view of the docks.

She felt the subtle lift of a levitation spell from Lio, and suddenly she could see over everyone's heads.

There, docked at the end of the crowded pier, was the *Wanted*, the vessel carrying all Cassia's hopes. The sewn plank boat was battered, proud, and beautiful. Just the sight of her sent a thrill through Cassia.

That ship had been to Cordium and back, and not through any convenient spirit gate. She had explored uncharted horizons and sailed waters few mortals or Hesperines had ever seen.

She had once carried Solia.

How had Solia felt when she first laid eyes on the *Wanted* and knew she would carry her away from danger?

Had she arrived at this very pier? Had she listened to these cheers and heard this music and breathed this air? Had she first set foot on Imperial soil right here in the Moon Market?

Seeing that brave and capable ship, Cassia felt hope that her sister had found welcome here.

A woman stood on board, hands on her hips, her crew arrayed beside and behind her. She wore a curved sword at her waist, and every inch of her was honed with strength, her deep brown skin weathered and marked by her many adventures. Her long, locked hair whipped behind her in a sudden ocean wind. This must be the famous and infamous Captain Ziara.

She lifted her arms. "My friends, my colleagues…my enemies!"

A roar of laughter went up.

"Are you glad to see the *Wanted?*" she called.

The crowd cheered, the noise sweeping over Cassia.

"Did you miss her?"

An even louder cheer.

"Do you want a piece of what she's carrying?"

Cassia's ears rang with the shouts.

"Well," Captain Ziara snapped, "you can't touch anything on her till I've felt Imperial ground under my feet and had a proper drink."

To more laughter from her admirers, she bowed. Then there came an eddy of wind, and she floated to the pier with her braids blowing around her. The rest of her crew leapt down after her as if they too had wings on their feet.

One woman came up beside Ziara, and the captain slipped an arm around her waist. They walked down the pier together to whistles and more cheers. The rest of the sailors followed, and Cassia studied each member of the all-female crew. They appeared to be from all parts of the Empire, garbed in eclectic and vibrant clothing, hairstyles, and tattoos.

Cassia's feet touched the ground again as Lio gently set her down.

"The captain is a wind mage?" she asked.

"A very powerful one," he confirmed. "Let's step to the Plundered Heart and get ahead of the crowd."

Her nod was lost in the transition as he stepped them. They landed in another press of people. Everyone else was also waiting for Ziara to arrive at her favorite establishment. The man next to them jostled them, and Knight snapped at him.

Cassia held her hound back, rubbing a soothing hand over his head. "There's no way you can step us closer to her when she comes in."

"Not without us landing on someone," Lio muttered.

"We'll have to be diplomatic."

"No." He shook his head. "No diplomacy allowed."

"Oh, of course, that's too responsible. We'll have to be polite," she amended.

"I'm not sure politeness is accepted as currency in the Moon Market."

Cassia watched helplessly as Ziara and her companion, barely visible in the middle of the crowd, came through the courtyard and disappeared up the stairs.

Lio's eyes drifted upward. "I think there is a happy medium between polite and bold."

She followed his gaze. "And I think a privateer would agree that fortune favors the bold."

CONTRABAND AND SECRETS

L IO STEPPED THEM OUT of the Plundered Heart, aiming for a space where there were fewer auras. They landed on an unoccupied balcony across the street. He and Cassia fit in the former crow's nest with room to spare—room that Knight took up entirely.

Another couple, coming up the rope ladder that led to the balcony, gave Knight annoyed looks and climbed back down the way they had come. Lio called a gracious apology after them, although he felt no remorse about using his Hesperine abilities to beat them to this excellent vantage point.

He gave Knight an appreciative pat. "Who knew a liegehound and a Hesperine could work so well together?"

"I did." Cassia leaned out over the railing for a better look.

From here, they could see Ziara and her entourage ascending the tiers of the ships that comprised the Plundered Heart. The privateers sat down around a table large enough for the whole crew.

"It looks as if they've reserved the entire top level," Cassia said.

"You're right." Lio pointed. "The tavern staff is turning away most of the crowd at the ladder so the sailors can relax over their meal."

Cassia gave him her secret smile. "We don't need a ladder."

"My lady, my levitation services are all yours."

She turned to Knight. "*Baat.* Stay here and guard our retreat, dearest."

Lio offered her his arm.

She took it. "Your skills are excellent not only for storming damsels' balconies, but also for approaching famous privateers."

"As I recall, the damsel was much more welcoming than privateers are likely to be."

"You snatched said damsel from the under the mages' noses. That should impress the privateers."

He levitated them both across the short distance, over the crowd, and drew near the top deck of the tavern. The privateers' gazes all turned toward them, assessing.

Lio paused, hovering just beyond the railing. Holding Cassia steady with one arm, he bowed midair. "Captain Ziara, may we have a word?"

She raised an eyebrow. "I have a ship full of treasures, and you sneak up here for a word? You Hesperines have strange taste sometimes."

Lio smiled. "Alas, my taste is not as refined as that of my Ritual mother, Kassandra."

Captain Ziara would never doubt he told the truth about his connection with Kassandra. Here in the Empire, Hesperines were known for honesty. More than that, no one lied about the oracle, who saw all deceit.

The captain gave him a considering look. "You're one of Kassandra's boys? No wonder. The oracle plays by her own rules. I see she's taught you a thing or two."

"I endeavor to heed her lessons."

"What's your name, then?"

"Lio. This is my intended, Cassia. I am here on her behalf."

Captain Ziara sighed. "That's the hardest adjustment every time we dock. Not the floor suddenly being still. Not the food being fresh for a change. The *males* everywhere."

"I will make every effort not to be vexing, I assure you," Lio promised. "My younger sister, Zoe, holds you in the highest esteem. When the children play privateers, she insists on pretending to be you and reenacting your legendary deeds. I will not be able to show my face at home if I cross you."

Ziara tilted her head back and laughed. "Sounds like your little Zoe is quite the handful. A girl after my own heart. She'll cause all sorts of marvelous trouble when she grows up, I dare say."

"I certainly hope so. In the meantime, she will demand bedtime stories of our meeting for years to come."

Ziara leaned her head on her companion's shoulder. "What do you say, love? Shall we tolerate one male among our company for the sake of his sister's bedtime stories?"

She crossed her arms. "I suppose, as long as it's just one. Since Kassandra taught him his manners."

Captain Ziara waved for them to join her. He set himself and Cassia down on the deck.

Standing before the captain and her banquet table of privateers, Lio had the distinct feeling he was at a queen's court with a petition. He was thankful his Ritual mother's name had gained them an audience.

The renowned privateer lived up to her legend. Her famous wind magic swirled in her aura, never still. The many-colored beads in her hair swayed and clinked, as if in a breeze only she could feel. There was gray at her temples and a world of wisdom in her eyes. Her full lips lifted in a crooked smile.

Cassia offered her own bow to the queen of the privateers. "It is an honor, Captain Ziara. Everything I have heard about you leaves me amazed."

Ziara looked back across the way they had come and pointed. "Is that your dog?"

"Yes, Captain," Cassia answered. "You said I am only allowed one male, though."

Ziara's lover chuckled. "We won't hold it against a dog."

"I'll bear that in mind," Lio said with a smile. "Allow me to retrieve Knight for Cassia."

When he returned with the hound, Ziara was looking Cassia up and down. "Well, well. Kassandra has sent us some prohibited goods."

"Not at all, Captain." Cassia gave one of her arch smiles. "I am a documented citizen of Orthros."

"All papers and no bite."

Cassia scratched under Knight's maw. "I bite. Soon enough I'll have fangs, too."

The privateers laughed at that.

Ziara gestured to two of the unoccupied chairs across from her. "You may look like a shadowlander, but you talk like a Hesperine. Have a seat."

Lio and Cassia joined the privateers at their table, and she murmured to Knight, who sat politely at her side. Lio did not miss the quick but inquisitive glance she gave him.

"Shadowlander," he explained, "is a term Imperials often use to refer to people from Tenebra or Cordium."

"Those lands are shadowed by evil," said Ziara's companion, "but you are not the kind to bring it here with you."

Ziara stroked the other woman's hand. "This is Huru, my first mate, partner...and greatest weakness. Try to keep that secret between us."

First Mate Huru laughed. She was a very short woman with a joyful, round face and a stocky frame. "Everyone knows I'm your weakness, Ziara. It's a good thing I can protect you."

She appeared to pull a knife from Ziara's ear, then hurled it without looking. It sailed past Lio's head, its passage ruffling his hair. Schooling his expression, he turned to see where it had landed. The portrait of a man hung on a nearby mast, the drawing pockmarked with many knife punctures. Huru's dagger was currently lodged right in his nose.

"Who is this fellow," Cassia asked, "who has been so unfortunate as to earn your ire, ladies?"

Ziara smirked. "Gomba, *former* privateer."

"Late privateer?" Cassia guessed.

"Oh, no. I cannot kill him yet. We still have unfinished business." Ziara savored a swallow of her wine.

Lio could smell that it was Moon Market Night Rose, the most expensive wine on Marijani. One of the most expensive anywhere in the Empire. Ziara had excellent taste. She could certainly afford to, reigning over her queendom of contraband and secrets.

She swirled her glass. "Speaking of unfinished business, I believe we have some to attend to."

THE CAPTAIN'S PRICE

WERE THE MYSTERIOUS CAPTAIN'S words a hint about Solia? Cassia couldn't be sure.

She took a deep breath. "Kassandra is not our only mutual acquaintance. I have it on good authority that my sister was once aboard your ship."

She watched the privateer for a reaction, but even with her skill at reading people, she could glean little from the captain's face and body language.

"Whose authority?" Ziara asked.

"Namatsi's," Cassia answered.

"Our sister privateer," the captain mused. "What did she tell you?"

"She says you met my sister fifteen years ago."

"I see." Ziara sipped her wine. "Many women have been on board my ship over the years."

Very few had come on board in Cordium, Cassia would wager. But the illegality of what Ziara had done for Solia was not the place to start a negotiation.

"What is your sister's name?" Ziara asked.

"I know her by the name of Solia, although it's possible she has also used different names."

"There are many forms of sisterhood. What is the nature of your bond with her?"

"We are sisters by birth. Well, half sisters. We have the same father, but different mothers."

"What does she look like?"

With Captain Ziara's razor-keen gaze on her, Cassia had no doubt that the privateer remembered every person who'd ever set foot on the *Wanted*. She wasn't asking questions to aid her own memory.

She was testing Cassia somehow. Cassia would just have to keep passing until she understood what the test truly was.

"The last time I saw her," Cassia continued, "her hair was long and blond. She is blue eyed and fair skinned, half a head taller than me and curvier. She would have been seventeen when you met her."

"Tell me about your father."

She didn't want to think about him, much less talk about him. Where to begin describing such a monster?

A hard smile came to her face. "If I had a picture of him, we could hang it there with Gomba, and I'd be obliged to you if you'd teach me to throw a knife with such good aim."

That won her another round of laughs from the privateers.

"She was running from him," Cassia explained, "and probably from the mages. I haven't seen her since she escaped. Now that I've made it to safety too, thanks to Lio, I want to find her."

"Hmm," Ziara said. "I will answer your questions—for a fair price, of course."

Cassia's heart swooped. A privateer might be offering her a dangerous bargain, but she had just promised information that could help them find Solia. "I'm sure we can come to an agreement."

Ziara shook her head. "I name the price, and you and your Hesperine pay it—or don't."

Lio's steady hand didn't move from Cassia's back. His signal that he trusted her to negotiate, and he would back her.

"Tell us what you would have from us," Cassia said, "and we will consider it."

"I'd like a small advance tonight, as a gesture of good faith. I'll ask for the full price tomorrow."

The survivor in Cassia was wary of betrayal. But she reminded herself Ziara was a privateer in service to the Empress. She stole from the mages, their common enemy. She did business with Kassandra. These women were thieves, but there was great honor among them.

"That is fair," Cassia replied, "but we reserve the right to decline after hearing your full price tomorrow."

"Fair," Ziara agreed. "In that case, we'll all walk away with only what we exchange tonight."

"That suggests you'll give us something tonight, in exchange for the advance."

Ziara smiled. "That depends on whether I'm satisfied with the payment."

Cassia studied the rows of jeweled rings on Ziara's fingers and the goblet they held. The captain's idea of a fair price was sure to be high. But if Blood Komnena could buy Segetia, she was certain they could afford a pirate's secrets.

Paying the advance seemed a safe bet. Cassia glanced at Lio, projecting her thoughts.

"Family is priceless," he agreed.

She squeezed his hand, meeting Ziara's gaze. "Name your price for the advance."

"A vial of flametongue oil," Ziara replied.

Cassia's brows shot up. "Captain, such a thing is a rare commodity where I come from, to be sure. But as extraordinary as it is, could you not find something like it on any corner of the Moon Market? I would pay a fairer price for information on my sister's whereabouts."

Ziara scowled. "Those cockbrained mages in Cordium do a surprisingly good job hoarding the stuff for themselves. But I suspect you can provide me with one vial."

Ziara knew about the hidden vial of flametongue Solia had left behind for Cassia. One of her sister's most valuable and closely-guarded secrets. That was how much Ziara knew.

Cassia's hand tightened on the strap of her gardening satchel. There was no reason to hesitate. She would never again have to walk through fire to spy on the king. She didn't need the flametongue oil to protect her anymore.

But she did hesitate, for the same reason she had brought the vial with her in the first place. It was still Solia's precious store of flametongue, a piece of the legacy her sister had left her.

But it wasn't all she had left of Solia anymore.

It was time to let it go, and it was fitting that it should pay her way toward seeing her sister again.

Cassia pulled out the tiny tasseled bottle labeled with an embroidered lily. "I know it looks like perfume, but the smell will assure you it's genuine flametongue."

She put it in Captain Ziara's hand.

The privateer held it up to catch the light, turning it in admiration. Then she held it under her nose, flaring her nostrils, and let out a hiss at the smell. "Lovely."

"Does that mean you have something to offer us tonight?" Cassia asked.

"Indeed. A confirmation. You are correct that Solia sailed with us, and we have information about her that will be useful to you. Come back tomorrow night, right after sundown, so we'll have plenty of time. We can settle the rest of the cost, and then I'll tell you everything you want to know."

A DISCOURSE ON TRUST

THE DOOR OF THEIR suite shut behind Cassia, and she leaned back against it. The carvings pressed into her palms, while the reality of the night sank into her mind. "We found Ziara, and she will tell us what she knows of Solia."

Lio went further inside to drop their belongings on a chair. "Yes."

"This is really happening."

He sat on the edge of the seat and took off his silk shoes. "Congratulations, my rose. You handled that well."

"So did you." She tried to keep her eyes on his face. She was no longer a modest Tenebran maiden. Why did the mere sight of a Hesperine's ankle make her blood hum? "But what more will she ask us to pay? If flametongue oil is what she considers an advance, what could the full price be?"

"I have to wonder why she wants to keep us guessing. We'll just have to find out tomorrow." He unfastened his collar.

Oh thorns, she must *not* let her gaze slide down his throat. "Do you trust Ziara? Is that even the right question to ask about a woman like her?"

Lio appeared to consider his answer while he continued to undo those little fasteners, revealing the dusting of hair at the top of his chest. "She is honorable. But she doesn't play by anyone's rules but her own."

"Well, we are heretics." Cassia's fingers curled into the grooves of the wood behind her. "That could just as easily describe us."

"My rules are very strict." Lio strolled toward her, his black travel robe now hanging open to reveal the smooth contours of his chest and his slim waist.

She pressed herself back against the door.

He rested his hands on the door on either side of her, his sleeves sliding back to reveal his forearms. "One of my rules is taking care of my Grace. You need me to feast on you."

Her tongue was dry, her skin hot, her body prickling with tension at his nearness. "How do you live with it, Lio? I did this to you for months. How did you even think with the Craving an undercurrent to your every waking moment?"

"The same way you managed to conduct yourself before the privateers tonight."

"We've been alone for minutes, and I'm already about to fall apart."

"Just like I did as soon as I was in your arms again." He brushed his lips over hers with delicate control.

That barest contact lit her body like starfire. It had been a long time since a simple kiss from him had felt this dangerous, since she had feared the consequences of letting desire overtake her.

She let her head fall back to put the barest distance between their mouths. He hovered over her, giving her that space.

She shook her head. "We need to make sure I don't bite you too hard again."

"I'll make sure." His hand drifted down her neck.

She shivered. "Do you mean you can use your mind magery to keep me from drawing blood?"

"No. That would require inhibiting your Will to an extent I would not consider."

"I suppose you can't cast sleep spells on me all the time, either. It calmed my Craving for a while, but now..." She swallowed, squeezing her legs together. "We need a strategy."

She saw the telltale signs of amusement around his eyes and mouth, but he gave her a serious reply. "What did you have in mind?"

Her voice rose, belying her attempt to sound reasonable. "If we cover my mouth, I won't be able to bite you."

He looked at her quite seriously now. "Is that something you find exciting?"

"What?"

"Bondage games in bed."

Her eyes widened. "That's something people find exciting?"

"There's a whole section of the *Discourses on Love* devoted to it—the 'Discourse on Trust.'"

"Ah, no, that's not something I would suggest for enjoyment. It reminds me of…nevermind. But it seems like the only solution."

Lio straightened, pulling her away from the door. "What does it remind you of?"

She bumped into his chest, her hands tightening on the front of his partly open robe. "Nothing. It's a solid plan."

He took her hands, and she couldn't bring herself to resist as he drew her toward the bed. He sat down on the edge of the mattress, easing her between his knees, and her plan felt less and less sure in her mind.

"It's not nothing," he said.

Why did she even try to avoid confessing everything to him?

"To be honest, it reminds me of that vision I had when Skleros poisoned me. I dreamed I was strapped to a bed. But we have to do someth—"

Lio pulled her onto his lap. "Cassia. You think I would even consider doing something that reminds you of *that*? While we're together in bed? Never."

She kept her head turned away from him, even as she drank in the feeling of his arms around her. "We have to find a way for me to continue giving you what you need without another close call. I have to get what I need from you, Lio. I can't go one night without our pleasure feeding my body and your magic feeding my mind."

"Shh." He stroked her hair. "I know what you feel right now. You feel as if you're being so logical, when really the Craving is driving you."

"We have to find a way."

"Cassia." He caressed her face. "We don't need a gag for that."

"You know what it's like to fear losing control."

"Yes, I do. And you are always the person who is safe for me to lose control with. You've shown me that many times. Now you must relax and feel that it's safe to lose control with me. I will make sure of it."

"I can't make you responsible for my actions."

"You aren't, my rose. But now that we know to be more vigilant, I'll do my part to help you avoid another mishap."

"I can't trust myself," she whispered.

"Then trust me."

Trust in him was one of the beams that held up her world. That she could always do. She nodded.

"Come here." He drew her onto the bed with him, and she didn't have the power to protest or overthink any more.

When she was sitting on the blankets on her knees, he slid behind her. His thighs framed hers. He gave her legs a reassuring caress. "Is *this* something you might find exciting?"

"Ohh." Her fears began to dispel in a rush of desire. He was right. Craving was addling her wits. "All the gossip I've heard about this does make it sound very exciting."

"I admit, I've been wanting to try it."

"Why didn't you say so earlier?"

He paused, his hands drifting up and down her thighs in smooth strokes. "We will be lovers for a very long time. We can afford to explore slowly."

"Lio…" She looked over her shoulder at him. "Did it actually cross your mind that I might grow bored with you?"

"Well, I thought it couldn't hurt to save something new for later."

She shook her head. "Do you think your parents are bored with each other after nearly a century together?"

"Considering how they sneak off together all the time? No."

"Do you think the Queens are bored with each other after sixteen hundred years?"

He laughed. "It is respectfully agreed throughout Orthros that the Queens have more fun with each other than any of the youngbloods with their shares."

"Lio, my worrier. A thousand years from now, all you will need to do is look at me, and I will go wild for you like the first time you bit me."

He bowed his head, bringing his mouth to the bare skin of her shoulder, just above the collar of her travel robe. He ran a finger along the inside of her thigh through her robe. Sitting here with her knees splayed and her backside tucked between his legs, she felt bared to him, even though she still wore her clothes.

He pulled up her robes, and she lifted her arms so he could undress her. His hands ran over her body, guiding her. She let him position her. He wanted her on her hands and knees.

A feeling of self-consciousness swept down her spine, but it was fleeting. A primal thrill traveled through her, chasing away any hesitation and pooling between her legs in an aching desire.

"You have freckles back here, too." He caressed her buttocks with both hands.

"All that sunbathing."

They laughed together, and she just wanted him more. He was going about this so slowly, it was going to kill her.

"I love you," she said.

"I love you."

He massaged the base of her neck, sending two kinds of pleasure through her every nerve. He continued to her shoulders and back. The pressure of his hands eased the last traces of her anxiety away while building a far sweeter tension inside her.

Then his hands slipped under her, and he took her breasts in his palms, fondling them where they hung. Still playing with one of her nipples, he slid his other hand between her thighs from behind. His fingers delved into her krana. It was pure instinct to bow her back and lift her hips up for him.

"Do you like that, Cassia?"

"It feels natural."

"You're beautiful." He pressed his thumb into the roof of her intimate channel.

She moaned and rolled her hips again. He worked her perfectly with his fingers and thumb, pleasuring her kalux and the depths of her krana. His mind magic descended upon her. A new rush of wetness between her legs made his hand glide faster.

Trust me.

At his words in her mind, she gave a ragged sigh. *You know I do.*

His hands left her on the verge of climax. Fabric rustled. His robe fell onto the bed at the corner of her vision. Another rustle, a dip of the mattress. His trousers landed on her other side.

His hands came to rest on the bed on either side of her. At last his body came down over her. With his chest molding to her back, she felt sheltered under him. The head of his rhabdos pressed into her. Her whole body relaxed beneath his, and she offered herself up for his taking.

Divine, came his voice in her thoughts.

He stroked into her slowly, entering her in a way she had never felt before, awakening places he had never touched quite like this. She felt her body stretching for him, changing so his hard thickness could penetrate her deeper and he could become a part of her anew.

For long moments, he just made love to her. Her hips rocked with the gentle rhythm he set. Her thighs trembled, and she fisted her hands in the blankets. His mind magic enfolded her. She breathed deeply, as if she could drink his magic from the air, and her senses opened wider without her even trying. He filled her with a fresh rush of magic and another deep thrust.

His weight felt so good on her, his powerful hips pushing against hers. She sank down onto her forearms, resting her forehead on the blankets, and let him take control.

She felt his kiss on her shoulder blade. He began to pump into her more firmly. His pace made her heart race faster and her krana tighten around him. She breathed through the pleasure, spots dancing on her vision.

As her climax started, she rose up on her hands again with a cry. His fangs sank into her neck, capturing her pleasure in his mouth. She succumbed, keening his name.

He kept pounding into her, giving her as much as she could hold, even as he drank his fill of her. She shuddered up under his rigid body, and he drove deepest of all. Then he was no longer in control, either.

He spoke his surrender, a rough whisper in her ear. "Cassia."

She watched little droplets of her blood fall onto the white bed linens. He released her vein. "Better?"

She panted for breath. *"Yes."*

He rolled them onto their sides, their bodies still joined. She hadn't thought their intimacy could deepen. But spooned with him inside her, she felt even closer to him.

He fanned sweet kisses over her neck and shoulder. His hand dawdled on her breast first, then returned to her kalux. The barest brush of his fingers on her wet, sensitized flesh sent a raw wave of pleasure through her.

"Lio—!"

"You need more."

Her hips jerked back against him. "Oh, Goddess. I need more."

His teeth scraped her shoulder, breaking the skin, and he laved away tiny tastes of her blood as his finger circled her kalux. He was teasing them both.

She reached back and caressed his hair. "Will I ever get enough of you?"

"I hope not."

She felt him hardening inside her again. She couldn't lie still. With a moan, she moved on his length, reveling in how he filled her, savoring the caress of his body behind hers as they rubbed against each other.

Working her kalux relentlessly, he pumped forward into her. Caught between his fingers and his rhabdos, she clutched his hand, her nails digging into him. She threw her head back, crying out for release.

His fangs sank into her exposed throat, and his magic surged through her. Their Union carried them over the edge, and their bodies writhed together.

And then she could breathe. She felt safe again. She was ready to start a new night and take on the world.

His lips curved in a smile against her shoulder. "I'll always give you what you need, my love."

"I see I had nothing to worry about." Tangled up with him, she lay there savoring the relief and the pure comfort of him.

71

Nights Until

NOTIAN WINTER SOLSTICE

34 Annassa, 1597 IS

A DIFFERENT WORLD

WHEN LIO AND CASSIA joined the privateers on the top deck of the Plundered Heart the next night, Captain Ziara was wearing a fluttery gown of the most delicate silk. She and First Mate Huru smelled of the same luxury bath salts. The entire crew was playing a knife throwing game at Gomba's expense, and only Huru had scored more points than Ziara so far.

The captain gazed down the gleaming blade of her dagger, taking aim. "Ah, Cassia has arrived with her charming hound and tolerable male companion. Let us get down to business."

"Tolerable is high praise from you, Captain," Lio said.

Laughing, she threw. Her knife hit Gomba in the eye.

The privateers applauded her, and Lio found himself and Cassia joining in.

"Beautiful hit." Huru smirked. "I still win."

Ziara narrowed her eyes, smiling. "For now."

"No time for another round. We have customers."

Cassia offered a slight bow. "By all means, Captain Ziara, please tell us what you'd like us to pay you tonight."

She beckoned to them. "Come. I'll show you."

Lio began to suspect the payment was not something he could find in his coin purse, after all.

Followed by her first mate and a handful of the crew, Captain Ziara led them down from the top of the tavern via a twisting wooden staircase. Lio kept Cassia close and braced himself to be mobbed by the privateers' admirers again. But Ziara cut down side streets, ducking through doors even he hadn't noticed, and led them through the clutches of moldering ships turned into gardens. They made it to the shore without anyone the wiser that the great Ziara had passed among them.

This was a quieter stretch of beach beyond the Moon Market. The shallower waters appeared inconvenient for docking ships.

Ziara slipped off her sandals and strolled barefoot across the damp sand, holding Huru's hand. "I've been chatting with my Hesperine friends about you, Newgift Cassia."

"I hear you have many friends among Kassandra's tributaries, Captain."

"They're quite well informed about you. You're an infamous traitor to the King of Tenebra and a heretic in the eyes of the Mage Orders. I'm impressed."

"I am glad to hear it."

"It sounds as if your fellow here has made himself rather useful through it all, as well."

Lio exchanged an amused glance with Cassia. "I endeavor to be helpful."

The captain stopped them at a sandy spit. "The sea looks calm from here, doesn't it?"

"Relaxing, in fact," Lio agreed.

"You would never know there are deadly coral reefs beneath the surface." Ziara aligned her arm with a star on the horizon. "That's where I lost my old ship. The mother of the *Wanted*, if you will. Not through any failure on my crew's part. Through treachery."

"I pray no lives were lost," said Cassia.

"No. Trust and treasure were the casualties."

Lio didn't envy the enemy responsible for that. Could he be the one with Ziara's knife in his picture?

"I'll never see my old ship again. My air magic lets me dive deeper than many, but not deep enough." Ziara turned to Lio. "How lucky you are, that you don't need to breathe underwater. You can swim into places mortals can't reach."

"Ah." Lio offered a slight bow. "I might be of service to you, then, Captain?"

"Are you willing to pay for information about Cassia's sister with a favor?" the captain asked.

He would do anything, he wanted to say. But that was a dangerous boast to make to a privateer. "I will help her find her answers, no matter the challenges we face along the way."

"Then dive into my ship's final resting place and retrieve something for me."

There must be many skilled divers among Ziara's acquaintance. He had to wonder why he was her choice for the task. Cassia's face was neutral, but the concern in her aura suggested she had questions, too.

"What would you like me to find?" Lio asked.

"You'll know it when you see it."

That sounded too easy. "I am surprised none of your Hesperine friends have performed the service for you already, Captain. Has Orthros's generosity failed you?"

"You look generous enough."

"Lio and I would like to discuss it first, if we may," Cassia suggested.

Ziara gestured with a flourish. "Of course."

Cassia pulled him aside, and he cast a light veil to muffle their words.

There was a furrow between Cassia's brows. "What favor would Kassandra's tributaries decline to perform for Ziara? What is she asking you to do?"

"Those are excellent questions. If it were something to which I wouldn't object, I suspect she wouldn't be so mysterious about it."

"Do privateers engage in activities that go against Hesperine principles?"

"Besides pillaging and sinking Cordian ships? Ziara has probably sent more mages to Hypnos than the Blood Errant ever did."

"Ah. Common enemy, different methods."

"But we defer to the Empress's laws, which say that whatever Ziara brought back from Cordium is hers by right, minus the Empress's cut. I can't imagine why Hesperines would fail to help the captain recover something of hers from her own shipwreck. Unless..."

Cassia raised her brows. "What?"

"...perhaps it didn't belong to the mages. Competition between privateers can be fierce."

"You think Ziara stole something from a rival? Gomba?"

"If so, Kassandra would stay clear of the situation. She wouldn't risk losing her trade contracts with Ziara by awarding them to a rival, but she would ensure Orthros's fleet didn't get involved in their feud." Lio shook his head. "I wish Kassandra had given us more advice about negotiating with Ziara."

"We'll have to make the best decision we can based on what we know."

"And it's clear Ziara won't reveal anything else to us."

Cassia rested her hands on Lio's arms. "If you have any concerns that this could affect relations between the Empire and Orthros, we should think twice before agreeing."

"Cassia, this is the price of finding your sister."

"We must find her without causing a diplomatic incident. The Queens want us to consult with them before we do anything that might anger the Empress."

"Ziara was clear. She names her price. We pay it, or we don't get her information."

Cassia touched his cheek. "Your conscience is not for sale. If that's what she expects us to pay, she'll be surprised what a hard bargain you and I can drive."

Lio hesitated, thinking of the difference between a privateer's moral compass and a Hesperine's, of his Ritual mother's careful weaving of contracts and alliances. But also of the moral compass that had led him to break every rule of diplomacy for his Grace's sake, and the resulting shift in the fabric of Orthros's history.

"I think this is a small price to pay to guarantee Solia's safety. But if I find anything down there that I cannot condone, I will return without it."

"All right." Cassia hugged him, then stepped back. "Be careful."

"No need. Ziara is right. The ocean is no threat to me."

Hand in hand, they returned to the privateers.

"I'll dive for you," Lio announced.

"We'll take good care of Cassia while you're gone," Ziara said.

He held the privateer's gaze. "I entrust her safety to you."

It wasn't a statement of trust. It was his promise he would hold her to her word. A Hesperine's promise.

She smiled, reminding him she was dangerous. But not to Cassia.

"Stand down, youngblood. Kassandra's girls are always welcome—and safe—among us."

He inclined his head. Cassia gave him an encouraging nod. Reluctantly, he approached the edge of the water.

No use dragging layers of robes down there with him. He stripped to his trousers, leaving the rest of his clothes and his shoes in Cassia's keeping. He gave her a quick kiss before wading out into the surf.

The water surrounding Marijani was warm. The sort of water he could play in with Cassia before they spent a lazy evening lounging on the beach. It was hard to imagine that this placid sea held destruction.

He stroked over the surface. Growing up with Nodora had made their entire Trial circle good swimmers. They had to be, to keep up with a water mage. Using the star the captain had pointed out as a guide, he made for the location of the shipwreck, covering the distance quickly.

Ziara was right. There was no hint of the dangers below.

He dove. Moonlight followed him down, sparkling on the surface behind him when he glanced back, shining ahead of him into the depths.

A school of fish danced around him. He swam with them down to the reef. Formations of brilliant coral formed what seemed like a whole city, a wild counterpart to the city of people above the surface.

He followed the spine of the reef, looking for any sign of a ship. There was none. He would have to go deeper.

The reef dropped off suddenly, and he gazed into the impenetrable darkness ahead of him. It looked like a long way down.

He conjured a spell light just bright enough to guide him without blinding any of the marine life. Or attracting too much attention. This was a different world with its own kings and queens. Lio would be safe, but he still wouldn't want something with sharp teeth to distract him from his task.

The moonlight faded farther and farther behind him as he dove. He found he felt very small, encased in the tiny bubble of his spell light, with the vast ocean all around him.

The blow came out of nowhere. One minute, he was making good progress down the trench. The next, the impact hit his entire body. He went surging through the water as if he'd rebounded off a stone wall. Then his back hit something rough and sharp, and new pain awoke there.

He blinked. He was in total darkness, except for the sparkles that danced on his vision from the blow. His light spell had gone out when the impact interrupted his concentration.

He didn't conjure the spell again, and he mustered a veil around himself as best he could.

The rules weren't the same beneath the sea, not even the rules of magic. This was another paradigm than the one of blood and stone and snow in which his power had been born. Nodora had taught him this as well. The natural magical forces of the ocean were as vast and deep as the water itself, and it took years of expertise to wield magic properly under these conditions.

He couldn't entirely trust his veil, but he kept it around himself all the same and cast his senses out. Where was the creature that had run into him? It had to be something large.

He felt the fluttering presences of the fish and even the barest hint of some dolphins at the furthest reach of the Blood Union. Much of the rest of the marine life was beyond his ability to sense. The Union only connected him to living things with blood. Who knew what mysterious substances flowed in the bodies of the creatures down here?

It seemed whatever had struck him didn't bleed. At least that meant it wasn't a shark. Because he certainly was bleeding.

Or had been. Lio rubbed his back. He thought he had run into some coral. The broken skin had already healed, but his blood drifted in the water around him, a temptation to hungry sea monsters.

He ran through the bestiary in his mind. This trench wasn't deep enough for a kraken, at least.

He would have to rely on other senses than the Blood Union to protect himself from whatever it was.

Which way was down? He cast a spell light flying away from him in various directions until he could make out the edges of the trench below him. Then he swam downward, away from the source of his lights, in case they had given away his position.

He focused on the currents of water around him, hoping a shift in temperature or water flow might give him a warning before the creature struck again.

But nothing prepared him for the water to close around him like chains.

On instinct, he thrashed against the invisible manacles binding his limbs. The water tightened around him. The band of pressure around his chest sent a jolt of alarm through him. He didn't need his lungs. But if something damaged his heart, all was lost.

Lio forced himself to be still and think. He tried to calm his racing pulse.

This was not the work of any beast. He was dealing with a water mage. Someone with an affinity for water could easily use the ocean to conceal themselves. His unseen enemy was in their element here.

This couldn't be a random attack. The mage didn't want Lio to find that shipwreck. So much that they were willing to trample over the Empire's alliance with Orthros and attack a Hesperine.

How generous it would have been of Ziara to warn him he might meet some resistance down here. Was one of her competitors after her sunken prize? Was someone from the Moon Market willing to risk her ire to recover treasures from her lost vessel?

Or was someone trying to recover what was rightfully theirs, something she had stolen? Would they see Lio as the one who had trampled on the treaty first?

The answer was in that shipwreck. Cassia's answers were waiting for them on the beach. The only way forward was down.

Cassia's sister was at stake. Lio couldn't let the privateers' games stop them from finding Solia. He had faced the worst enemies Tenebra had to throw at him. He wasn't about to let this water mage come between Blood Komnena and one of their own.

The water mage was a fool. They had trapped Lio's body, but not his mind.

Thelemancy might be twice as challenging under the sea as it was on land, but Lio had used it enough on larks with Nodora that he could manage something. Tonight their Trial circle's youthful games would come to his aid in a dangerous situation.

Lio let his vast power seep out of him, adding his own current of magic to the depths, and trawled the ocean around him for a hint of a human mind.

The school of fish swimming nearby him scattered. Disturbed sea creatures rose from their sandy beds, while others dove for their dens.

The water mage was a slippery presence, darting out of reach as soon as Lio caught up to them. The watery manacles tightened, and Lio winced.

He brought up more magic from within himself. It felt like trying to force a fountain to run against the current of a raging river.

Another solid wall of water slammed into him, striking his back this time. He couldn't throw up his arms to protect his head. And if he blacked out, he couldn't use his mind magic at all.

Spending the last of his air on a shout of effort, he pushed his power out of himself, one determined wave set against all the waves in the sea. The rough blast of thelemancy crashed out of him with a force that should stun anyone nearby.

He struck the reef headfirst, and everything went dark.

A PRIVATEER QUEEN'S RANSOM

LIO'S EYES OPENED. HE raised a hand to his face.

He was able to move his hand. He was free.

His mind magic must have hit the water mage. Right before they had rammed Lio face-first into the coral, hard enough to kill a mortal.

It was a good thing Ziara hadn't hired a mortal diver. Lio suddenly lost any sympathy he might have had for her rival, whoever they were.

He tested his limbs and felt his skull. The Gift had healed whatever damage had been done.

Anxiety swept up from inside him, a tide that even the ocean could not control. Not his own emotions, but Cassia's. If he'd been unconscious long enough for a wound like that to heal, he had been down here long enough to worry her.

And for any human water mage to be in serious danger, if they hadn't recovered from Lio's mental attack. Their affinity would keep them alive longer than average down here, but even a water mage could drown.

He conjured a powerful searchlight to illumine a wide radius around him. He saw that he was halfway down the trench. And there below him, he could just make out the uppermost tip of a proud, ruined mast.

Not far above him, two humans dragged a third, limp person between them. An unseen force propelled them quickly toward the surface. *Three* water mages. They had clearly decided to cut their losses.

He sent a warning wave of thelemancy their way and felt another current of their magic as they propelled themselves away from him even faster.

It was a shame that levitation couldn't propel him underwater. But he had the advantages of his immortal body. He swam with Hesperine strength and speed down to the wreck.

She had been a beautiful, powerful ship. Now she was a broken heart at the bottom of the ocean. But still the echoes of magic lingered around her remains—wind and water, alchemy and healing. The benedictions of the women who had sailed her, with her always.

Cassia's fear crept down his spine and whispered like a voice from the depths.

Even as her worry made him grit his teeth, he didn't rush his search. He knew he shouldn't risk missing something.

What did Ziara intend for him to find? He began looking through the debris for anything that stood out.

With his nose of no use, he let his other senses dive in and out of the nooks and crannies of the hull, seeking everywhere a treasure might have come to rest. He dared disturb the ship's tomb, running magic over the sand to uncover anything hidden in silt.

There was a privateer queen's ransom in lost cargo. He found temple artifacts from Cordium whose loss the Akron himself, the supreme leader of the Order of Anthros, must still regret. Broken vessels had once held precious oils or wine. The glaziers of the Moon Market would kill for the scrap glass alone. And oh, the jewels.

Captain Ziara must lay awake at night thinking of all she'd lost down here. But she had sent him after something specific, not piles of treasure. She hadn't even suggested he bring a sack.

Which of the extraordinary fables before his eyes would yield not just riches, but answers?

She had been right. When it caught his eye, he knew.

It was a metal document case, still emanating powerful wards against water and theft. He would bet all the rest of the precious cargo that this held the captain's log and other papers even more valuable than gold.

He retrieved it from the ruins, but for good measure, also took a small cloth purse filled with jewelry.

He swam for shore and the beacon of Cassia's emotions.

NO TURNING BACK

CASSIA'S EYES BURNED FROM watching the undisturbed surface of the sea. Kneeling on the sand, she kept her arms wrapped around Knight. She tried to focus on his steadiness and the texture of his fur.

Not her wild imaginings of what might have happened to Lio.

They were supposed to be safe in the Empire. But the longer he was underwater, the higher her fears rose. Had unexpected danger found him?

When he rose from the water, she breathed and started running to him.

He levitated out of the shallows, scattering surf and sand. Water ran down his shoulders and chest, catching the moonlight and slicking his trousers against his hips and legs.

She threw her arms around him. "What happened?"

He held her, although his hands were full. "I'm all right, my rose."

The seawater soaked through her clothes as she ran her hands over Lio to reassure herself he was whole. She reached up, stopping herself before she touched the dark stain on his pale brow. "Is this your blood?"

He sent a cleaning spell over them both, banishing the blood and seawater and the sweat of Cassia's fears. "The Gift has already healed me."

"It *is* yours! Who hurt you?" Cassia hated this. Goddess, why must she be a mortal without magic, unable to face an enemy at Lio's side?

"The headache my mind magic gave them will last considerably longer than my injuries did. I think they were after this, the ship's documents." Keeping one arm around her, he handed her a metal case. In his other hand, he held a cloth bag that looked heavy.

"Documents," she said. "I can imagine many reasons why those would be priceless."

"Unfortunately, we can't check to see what they are. The box is warded, and deconstructing the spell is not within my magical abilities." He looked toward the waiting privateers. "We must either send it back to the depths or hand it over without asking questions. And considering what I had to go through to get it, I'd rather pay Ziara's price."

"Are you sure?"

"If I were mortal, I would have died down there." Her arms tightened around him. He ran a soothing hand down her back. "Whoever Ziara's rival is, I'm inclined to trust the privateer who sends mages to the bottom, not the one who attacks people on Imperial shores."

"They attacked you. She saved my sister. We know whose side we're on." She took a deep breath. "We just don't know if Orthros is supposed to take a side."

"Well, Blood Komnena is taking a side now. Let us give this to Ziara."

They walked back toward the waiting privateers. Knight circled them, kicking up sand and drips of water. Happy fellow, oblivious to the stakes, he knew only that his people were hugging and would pet him next.

They rejoined Ziara and her crew by the campfire they had built on the beach while Lio was underwater.

Captain Ziara looked him over. "Run into some company down there?"

"Anyone you know, Captain?" Lio asked.

"Gomba's coinlickers. Nothing a Hesperine couldn't handle, I trust?"

He gave her a slight bow and gestured to the document case Cassia now held. "I believe this is what you meant for me to find."

Ziara held out her hands, and Cassia turned over the prize. "Lio has fulfilled our end of the bargain."

"Thank you," Ziara purred. She ran her hands over the metal box. She and Huru opened it together, and the captain gave a satisfied sigh.

Cassia couldn't endure the suspense any longer. "What's in there?"

Ziara held up a scroll in pristine condition. "This is a letter of marque, the document from the Empress granting her permission to operate as a privateer. No captain may sail for the shadowlands without one."

"Might this one belong to Gomba, former privateer?" Lio inquired.

Ziara smiled. "I relieved him of it some time ago, and he's been try-ing to get it back ever since. Now that it's safely in my hands again, he never will."

"It's not as if he can ask the Empress for a new one," Huru jeered. "No privateer would dare admit before her that he was foolish enough to lose the letter of marque she bestowed upon him."

The crew shared a derisive laugh. Cassia bit back her protests, afraid if she let out just one, all her angry questions would follow. Ziara *had* tricked Lio into involving Orthros in a theft from an Imperial citizen and a privateer feud.

Lio was tense at her side. "Is the letter what the water mages were looking for?"

"Yes," the captain answered, "Gomba has hired himself some thugs."

Oh, even better. Gomba could deny that he had attacked a Hesperine. The thugs were responsible for that.

Ziara thumbed through the other papers in the case. "Those water mages he dredged up can dive deeper than an air mage such as myself."

"Ah," Lio said. "A Hesperine can dive even deeper than they can."

Captain Ziara saluted him with Gomba's letter of marque. "You're a very useful advantage to have in a diving contest."

The privateers laughed again, but Cassia couldn't. What would she and Lio tell Kassandra?

"Well done," the captain told Lio. "I've been hoping to get this back for over twenty years."

"In that case," Lio said calmly, "perhaps we should keep this favor between us."

"Some secrets are better left at the bottom," Ziara agreed.

No matter what they said or didn't say, Kassandra would know. That felt even worse.

But she had sent them to Ziara. Had she known what Ziara would ask Lio to do? Had she expected Lio and Cassia to respond differently—or known and approved of what they would do tonight?

Cassia couldn't puzzle out the oracle's thinking. She only knew there was no turning back now. "I have questions about my sister."

"Of course," said Ziara. "Huru and my Hesperine contacts assure me it will be safe for Solia if I answer you. What they told us about you makes it clear you are the true enemy of the king and the mages, just like your sister."

"And I'm a mind healer," Huru revealed. "I can tell that you really are looking for your sister for personal reasons. Not with an ulterior motive."

"You were protecting her." Now Cassia understood the testing questions, the delay while the privateers verified her and Lio's assertions.

"We have been protecting her ever since we met her," Huru replied. "We know how many factions in the shadowlands would seek to exploit her. It would have been dangerous to assume they're not using you, and foolish to imagine you wouldn't use her for your own purposes, even though you are her sister."

"You believed me about that, at least?"

Captain Ziara gestured at Cassia and Knight. "Oh, yes. I recognized you the first time we saw you. There's no mistaking your freckles and the dog."

A surprised laugh worked its way out of Cassia. They had recognized her. That must mean Solia had told them about her.

Ziara gestured to the fire. "Sit with us, and we will tell you the whole story of Solia's time among us."

Cassia and Lio joined the privateers around the fire. Knight lay down against her leg, and she slid her hand in his ruff, leaning against Lio.

She was about to learn the truth, or at least, a new and important part of it.

The light of the flames played over Captain Ziara's face as she settled cross-legged on the other side of the fire. First Mate Huru stretched out with her head on Ziara's lap.

The captain ran a hand over her companion's close-cropped hair. "It was Huru who first noticed your sister. Mind healers! Always unable to turn away from a hurting soul."

Huru scoffed. "This from a privateer who can never resist a chance to do mischief, especially under the mages' noses!"

Ziara's wicked grin flashed. "We were having even more fun than usual working the Cordian coast that year. A vessel carrying a shipment from the Order of Anthros's mint went missing without a trace."

"Are there coins stamped with the Akron's face in the Empress's treasury now?" asked Cassia.

"Oh, the Empress's palace is full of gifts I've brought her. That's a privateer's business: stealing anything that will weaken the mages and strengthen the Empire, all without alerting the Orders to the fact that they have an Imperial pirate problem. And every member of my crew is the best at her business. We bring Her Imperial Majesty all sorts of unusual treasures that we know she'll find useful."

Cassia knew that none of that was a boast. "How did my sister have the good fortune to be rescued by the Empress's foremost privateers?"

"We picked up some information that a full war circle of Aithourian fire mages had arrived in one of the port cities, straight from Corona. That meant loot ripe for the picking."

Cassia had to admire that. Only women like Ziara and her crew would see seven elite war mages and think "easy money."

"We went ashore in Obruza," the captain continued, "in disguise, of course, thanks to the illusionists among our crew."

Huru snickered. "The war mages truly believed we were librarians sent by the Akron to return their artifacts to a temple for safekeeping. Us, librarians!"

A roar of the privateers' laughter went up around the campfire.

Ziara smiled fondly. "We conned them out of four spell scrolls, three enchanted artifacts, and the most hideous pair of jeweled slippers I've ever seen in my life. In the process, they offered up quite a bit of information about what they were doing—chasing a fugitive girl."

Chasing her. That meant she had gotten away from her captor at some point. Cassia added escaping from war mages to her sister's list of accomplishments. "But they caught up to her at the tavern, didn't they?"

"That was quite an incident." Ziara clicked her tongue. "Drew attention from all sorts. We could have gone quietly back to our ship with our spoils, but a certain tenderhearted first mate thought we should investigate."

Huru raised a brow. "I seem to recall it was you who decided we should run toward a fiery explosion."

"I promised you our life together would never be boring."

"And that you would trust my instincts."

Ziara smiled. "So it was, Cassia, that we put ourselves conveniently in the path of your sister as she fled the scene, and we helped her disappear."

"Thank you," Cassia said. "I haven't told you that properly yet."

Lio nodded. "You have our gratitude for saving her life."

"Our pleasure," said Huru. "I hate to think about what would have happened to her if we hadn't gotten to her first. There was nowhere safe for her in Tenebra or Cordium."

Ziara shook her head. "They were looking for her in every city, town, and pigsty. War mages everywhere, arrest warrants with glowing seals, the whole bit."

"Even so," Huru went on, "she would have gone right back ashore if she could have. She was determined to stay and make the best of it, she was so devoted to you."

Ziara shrugged. "What could we do about a runaway princess with a suicidal desire to get back to her little sister? It was no easy task to persuade her to come with us, I can tell you. But once we made it clear we could help her, she realized she didn't have much of a choice. It was either come with us to the Empire, or go back ashore into the welcoming arms of the Order of Anthros."

"She didn't thank us," Huru said, "not at first. But the longer she was aboard, the more she came to trust us, and the more she revealed about her past. Eventually she told us everything. And she came to realize the wisdom of letting us take her away from it all."

"She proved to be an excellent sailor," Ziara mused. "She learned fast, and she never complained. I think it was the easiest thing she'd ever had to do in her life."

Huru nodded. "She needed that time. The freedom, the hard work… it gave her a kind of peace she had never had in her life. By the time we arrived home, she had come to terms with some things."

Ziara sighed. "I would have kept her on permanently, if circumstances had been different."

Huru laughed, fondling her knife. "Even if she was completely useless in a fight."

"True," Ziara said. "We had to keep her away from the sharp things."

"Oh dear," said Cassia. "There must be a lot of sharp things on your ship."

"She wasn't even safe around the wrestling matches and rounds of fisticuffs," Huru added. "If she came within arm's reach of a scuffle, dangerous misfortune was sure to occur. She was like a walking accident waiting to happen."

Cassia knotted her hands. "I hope she didn't hurt herself or any of you."

"We managed to keep her out of trouble," Ziara reassured her.

"Most of the time." Huru waved a hand toward the sea. "All that violence in the shadowlands. The least thing that reminded her of it set her off."

Cassia had a vivid mental image of her sister aboard the *Wanted*, nursing her inner wounds. A blade would flash in the sunlight. She would jump out of her skin and knock something valuable overboard. Then her mind would catch up, and she would remember that the sword meant nothing more than a friendly challenge between her rescuers.

Lio wrapped his arm closer around Cassia. "Solia went through so much in Tenebra, as did you."

Ziara leaned forward. "It's important that you know, Cassia. She didn't want to leave you. She would have done anything to get back. But there was no way she could without putting herself and you in mortal danger."

Cassia let out a shaking breath. The mages had cheated her and Solia out of all this time. But the privateers had given her back so much with this one reassurance. "Thank you. I needed to know that more than I was willing to admit. I crossed the world to hear it, and you're the only ones who could have told me."

Huru had a kind smile hidden under the dangerous ones. "She talked about you all the time. Even before she revealed all her secrets to us, she talked about you with such pride. We respect a woman who places sisterly loyalty above all."

Cassia blinked back tears, and as always, Lio was there to hold her. "I've tried to carry out everything my sister would have wanted me to do."

"Clearly you did," Ziara said. "You found the flametongue and the other resources she left for you."

"Is that why you asked for the vial? To find out if I was aware of her plot against the king?"

"Not only that, although it did let us know you were either a devotee of her cause—or you had discovered it and betrayed it to the king."

"*Never*. I've fought tooth and nail to make sure that man watches his precious power crumble around him."

The privateers answered her declaration with rowdy calls of approval.

"Thanks to Cassia," Lio told them, "a new monarch will soon sit on the throne."

"Solia is our rightful queen," Cassia said, "but she can be free of all that now. She can come home to Orthros with us."

A corner of Ziara's mouth turned up in a crooked smile. "Now isn't that interesting."

"Where did she go when you docked?" Lio asked. "Why didn't she stay with your crew?"

Huru sat up and dusted some sand off of herself. "She would have loved to hop the next privateer ship right back to Cordium, I can tell you. But she knew that wasn't a solution. There was no point in going back to the same mess she left. She needed a better plan."

Ziara stretched. "We entrusted her to a friend of ours. Ukocha has done us many favors over the years, no fewer than we've done for her. We knew she was just the person who could help Solia."

"She is another privateer?" Lio inquired.

Ziara shook her head, laughing. "That landlubber wouldn't know an oar from a sail. She's the first blade of the Ashes, her band of mercenaries. As deadly and secretive a woman as you'll ever meet outside of a privateer crew."

First privateers. Why not mercenaries next? At least they sounded like the kind of people who were both skilled and discreet enough to keep Solia safe.

She would need fighters like the Ashes to protect her. By the sound of it, she had arrived here with a crippling fear of violence. Even before that, her strengths lay in her cunning and politicking, her way with people and persuasion. She had been a princess, with bodyguards to handle physical threats while she fought her battles of strategy with whispered words.

"What was Solia's new plan?" Cassia asked. "How could the Ashes help her with it?"

"You'll have to ask Ukocha," Ziara answered.

Cassia tried to keep the desperate excitement out of her voice. "Is Solia still with her?"

"Another question for our friend," was Ziara's reply.

"Where can we find Ukocha?" Lio asked.

"The Ashes are in high demand across all parts of the Empire," Ziara explained. "She could be anywhere at the moment. I'd like to be more precise, but we haven't been on shore long enough to hear any word of her."

"We can tell you where to ask around, though," said Huru. "Many mercenaries find work escorting trade caravans between the Kwatzi City-States and our sources of gold, ivory, and copper far to the southwest. The Sandira Kingdom controls that route. Their capital, the Sandira Court, draws traders and mercenaries from all around. I can guarantee you that any number of people there will be able to give you news of the Ashes."

Cassia looked at Lio. Her ever-faithful Grace, who had just leapt into a shipwreck without hesitation and fought off rogue mages with scarcely a complaint, all so she could find her sister.

He only seemed more determined than when the night had begun. "Then the Sandira Court is where we go next."

THE MOON GATE

LIO KNEW THE REPUTATION of the Sandira Kingdom. This part of their journey would require them to tread carefully.

Cassia shifted to her knees, as if she were ready to spring up and go that instant. "How far is the Sandira Court from here?"

Lio smiled. "About three times as far as Solorum is from Waystar."

Undaunted, Cassia asked, "Can we step there?"

"We can, but we may not," Lio answered. "When Hesperines are in the Empire, it is understood that we won't use stepping to bypass the authorities. It would be an offense for me to step us over kingdom borders instead of us properly presenting ourselves and our papers at the spirit gates."

He may have quietly helped one privateer steal another's letter of marque, but that didn't mean he was about to throw all respect to the winds.

"Of course," Cassia said. "Is there a spirit gate from here to there, then?"

Captain Ziara held up two fingers. "The one the merchant governors operate and the one in the Moon Market."

Cassia pursed her lips. "I take it the governors don't let just anyone use theirs."

"There's a reason so many trade caravans travel here overland," Ziara said.

Huru wrinkled her nose. "Besides, goods are taxed going through official gates."

"What about an unofficial one?" Cassia asked.

Lio nodded. "May we take the Moon Gate, Captain? The less attention we attract from the merchant governors while searching for Solia, the better."

"To be sure. At the Moon Gate, with me vouching for you, they won't ask you any questions."

Lio gave a slight bow. "Thank you, Captain."

"My reputation can get you to the Sandira Court," Ziara said, "but after that, I'm afraid you'll be on your own."

Lio nodded. "We'll be cautious."

Cassia looked at Lio, her gaze full of questions, but it seemed she would leave most of them for later. "The night is passing quickly. Should we start tomorrow?"

"Let me check the time." He unfolded the robe he had left with her during his dive and retrieved the astrolabe he had cushioned inside. Consulting the instrument did not encourage him. "It's two hours till dawn here. The Sandira Kingdom is south of the equator, though. I would guess we'll have about an extra half hour of night when we arrive there. If we pack in a hurry, we should have just enough time to get through the gate and find accommodations before dawn."

Cassia's gaze flicked from him to Captain Ziara. "You think we should leave as soon as possible. The water mages may be a problem?"

"Two of them are still conscious, so perhaps," Lio answered.

Ziara smiled. "Gomba won't take kindly to their failure, considering how much he must have paid them, so they won't take kindly to the person who kept them from finishing the job. If you stay any longer on Marijani, you'd best keep an eye out for trouble."

"I can handle them," Lio said, "but I wouldn't want them to make me cause a scene."

Ziara's smile widened. "I can make sure no one asks any questions about that, either."

Lio could only imagine what connections and influence the captain, and her money, might have with the authorities. "As much as we appreciate that, I think avoiding a confrontation might be a wiser course. What do you think, Cassia?"

"The last time you had a mind magic duel was enough to last us an eternity. I think we should go."

"I agree, although these water mages aren't even worth mentioning compared to the necromancers."

Huru stoked the campfire. "A duel between a Hesperine mind mage and necromancers? It's a shame you're leaving. That must be a good tale."

"I'm sorry we have to leave so soon," Cassia said sincerely. "I hope we'll meet again."

"Thank you for everything," Lio told the privateers.

"Thank you." The vial of flametongue was in Ziara's hand, by no discernible magic. "Can you imagine how useful even one vial of this will be on my ship, my whole world made of wood and cloth? I'll have our crew's alchemist study its properties to see if she can replicate it using Imperial plants. If not...well, we shall use it where it counts."

"I'm sorry about your old ship and all she was carrying," Lio said.

Ziara tucked the flametongue in the document case. "It's all right. I owe Baharini, the ocean goddess. Letting her keep that load of treasures is the least I can do."

"Will it offend her that I brought these back to you?" Lio offered the jewelry purse.

Ziara's eyes gleamed with pleasure. "I think she'll understand."

She opened the bag. Lifting out a jeweled pendant, she stroked a loving hand over its heavy cabochon. "Twenty years."

Huru leaned against her with the smile of someone glad to see the one they love happy.

Ziara held a diamond bauble up to her lover's earlobe. "Almost fine enough for you."

After looking through the spoils, the captain lifted out a matched pair of gold rings set with quartz. She held them out to Lio and Cassia. "Gifts from the sea, that you might remember your adventures with us."

They both bowed. It was a remarkable gesture of generosity from the queen of privateers. But also a gesture of power, showing that she could afford to bestow such treasures. Lio slipped Cassia's ring on her index finger and his on his smallest finger. He held her hand in the firelight, and the matched rings gleamed on their hands.

Ziara ran her fingers through the purse once more and pulled out another treasure. This one was a delicate brooch of quartz and coral. She gave it a bemused smile, then nodded. "Give this to your aspiring privateer, Zoe, with my compliments."

"Oh, Captain," said Cassia, "she will be over the moons. That's incredibly kind of you."

Lio accepted the small, priceless trinket on his palm, grinning as he imagined the look on Zoe's face when she received this. "You have our gratitude, Captain."

"My pleasure." Captain Ziara tied the purse closed. "Meet me at the Moon Gate as soon as you're ready."

They took their leave of the privateers, and Lio stepped them back to their inn. Like the night they'd left Orthros, they packed in quick cooperation, this time adding the mementos of their visit to their trunks.

"I hope we did the right thing tonight," Cassia fretted. "I'm sorry Ziara put you in that position."

Lio shook his head. "Considering Gomba's character, I cannot imagine that Kassandra will be personally unhappy with the outcome."

"But officially, for Hesperines to rob a privateer of the letter the Empress awarded him is..." Dread coiled in her aura.

"Ziara won't advertise what we did for her tonight."

"Could there have been a better way to intervene? We've only just begun, and we're already courting the Empress's displeasure."

"I have no regrets, Cassia. Should Ziara apologize for courting the Empress's displeasure by smuggling an innocent shadowlander here? Should we apologize for depriving a less scrupulous member of her profession of his right to sail?"

Cassia sighed. "Good point."

"If I learned anything in Tenebra, it's that the spirit of what's right is more important than the letter."

"Even so, we should write an explanation to Kassandra as soon as we can, and let everyone at home know we're headed to the Sandira Court."

"That would be a good place for the Trial circle to meet us, if the vote is over."

"Poor Dakk," Cassia said. "I just realized I won't have a chance to take my leave of him. He'll wonder why I'm not at the Sun Market to mail our letters tomorrow."

"Did you find out where he's staying?" Lio asked. "We could send a note."

Cassia shook her head. "It hadn't come up in conversation yet."

"Well, we know so many students and alumni from Capital. Perhaps we have mutual friends who can help you get in touch with him later."

"I hope so. He's been so kind."

"I'm sorry I didn't get a chance to meet him."

"You and I were rather busy every night." Cassia rolled up her yellow dress with her secret smile. "It would be nice to come back to Marijani sometime, don't you think?"

He packed up the scrolls she had bought him. "Yes. We made some good memories here, didn't we? Let's plan to come back, after…"

"When we have more time."

"Yes."

Cassia tossed him the cassia butter. "We might need more of this later."

That brought a smile to his face as well.

"Now tell me why we have to be careful in the Sandira King-dom," she said.

"It is an influential state within the Empire. The Sandira King is pow-erful, and he expects everything and everyone who passes through his domain to do things the way he wants them done. It would be unwise to even give the appearance of bending the rules there. In fact, it would be wisest not to draw attention to ourselves at all."

"Lady Circumspect and a Hesperine mind mage can surely get in and out of his kingdom without ruffling his feathers."

Lio started laughing.

"Did I say something amusing?"

"Ruffling his feathers is an apt analogy. The king is an eagle shapeshifter."

Cassia's jaw was hanging open.

At her wonder, Lio smiled again. "The Sandira people have the ances-tral magical ability to transform into animals. Each bloodline is favored by a different creature and granted its spiritual gifts."

"Like the Changing Queen of Tenebran legend?"

"Yes. I'm not sure if Lustra changers draw their magic from the same sources as the Sandira's ancestral shifting power, but the results are comparable."

"Changers are so rare in Tenebra, some people doubt they still exist."

"The Blood Errant did battle with a changer once. He could command forest cats and transform into one himself. His kind are still there, although they keep to themselves."

"They would have to, since the Mage Orders consider them apostates."

"Here, the Sandira display their ancestral gifts with pride. Their magic and their architecture are widely respected. Their shifting abilities are so sophisticated that they can even transform only parts of their bodies at a time, to gain certain advantages of their animal form while remaining human."

"I can scarcely imagine."

When they were certain they hadn't forgotten anything, they made their excuses to their hosts, who were thankfully accustomed to Hesperine guests coming and going at all times of the night. Within the hour, Lio and Cassia were standing with Knight and their trunks before the Moon Gate.

It was in fact a collection of gates that opened to various locations throughout the Empire. Each one rippled with liquid magic, like small oceans hovering in the air in the center of the Moon Market.

Captain Ziara and First Mate Huru awaited them at a gate that ebbed and flowed blue-black. The gatekeepers didn't even glance at Lio and Cassia, much less ask them questions.

But Lio kept an eye out and an arm around Cassia. He wanted no obstacles to their departure, neither the port authorities nor pirate mages.

Knight positioned himself in front of Lio and Cassia. Lio reached down and scratched the dog's ears in silent agreement. They were allies in protecting her and getting her where she needed to go.

The hint of a familiar aura caught his attention.

They couldn't hide their auras on land as they had under the water. They weren't trying to. Two of the water mages loitered in a shadowed doorway nearby, the embers from their smokes bright pinpoints in the night.

Lio tightened his arm around Cassia.

"What's wrong?" she murmured.

Captain Ziara flicked a finger in the thugs' direction without looking their way. "A couple of the water mages are here to see you off."

Cassia stiffened, but didn't turn. "Well, they're even less of a match for Lio on land."

He rubbed her arm. "We are perfectly safe. They must know that."

"They do." Huru began idly tossing a very large knife.

The water mages didn't come closer. But they didn't leave, either.

Lio let them see him watching them. They made no move to attack, merely gazed back with a warning in their eyes. Their sneers looked like a challenge.

"Is there any water around the Sandira Court?" Cassia asked.

"Landlocked," Lio replied.

She straightened her shoulders. "Then we won't worry about them."

"They won't be anything to worry about." Huru's knife danced in the air.

Cassia's aura was a shifting sea of hesitation and determination as she faced Captain Ziara before the Moon Gate. "Words will never be enough to thank you for what you did for my sister. If there's a way I can honor our bond of gratitude, please let me know."

The queen of the seas gave a canny smile. "Spoken like a Hesperine. You're wise enough not to promise a favor to a privateer, and honorable enough to want to repay a debt. I do hope we meet again."

THE SANDIRA COURT

WALKING THROUGH THE SPIRIT gate only took an instant. But Cassia felt like she was there much longer, listening to the whispers.

Someone was pleased with her. She felt a sense of reassurance from the incomprehensible words. She was getting closer…no, *very* close to what she needed to find. To where she was meant to be.

She emerged on the other side into darkness, where the flares of torchlight seemed too bright and the quiet seemed heavy after the airy voices within the gate. Knight shook his head several times, then gave his ears a good scratch.

Cassia's eyes adjusted, and she saw they had arrived in a spacious courtyard, with a tall, curving wall made of smooth stone blocks. A few clouds studded the night sky overhead. She felt lighter here, somehow. The cool, dry air seemed to float into her lungs and rush to her head.

Lio steadied her with a hand at her elbow. "We just came from sea level to moderately high elevation. You'll want to move slowly until your blood adjusts to the change. It's drier here on the veld, too, so you'll need to drink plenty of water."

Several other people were nearby, presumably other new arrivals from the Moon Market. Tall, muscle-bound warriors ringed the area. They greeted the newcomers in courteous tones, but every guard held a long, sharp spear in his hand. The Sandira King definitely kept his might on display and wanted no trouble coming through his gates.

Lio approached the guard nearest them, who wore a shoulder cape and a cotton wrap that clothed him from waist to low thigh. Nearing the warrior, Cassia saw that the rest of his body was covered in a thin, rugged gray layer that seemed molded to him like a second skin. The armor stopped at his chin to reveal his face and his natural black skin tone. All the guards sported the same. It looked just like the skin of the rhinoceroses in Zoe's storybooks.

Lio and the guard exchanged words in Tradewinds. The warrior glanced at their Hesperine robes, then waved them and Knight graciously toward the doorway behind him without even asking for their papers. Cassia sighed with relief as Lio led her toward the exit, levitating their trunks behind them.

"You don't speak the language of the Sandira people, Sir Scholar?" she teased him.

He blushed. "I'm afraid I only know a handful of Imperial languages. I devoted the most study to Dynastic, Tradewinds, and the ancient language Annassa Soteira's mortal clan once spoke, as well as the tongue of the Azarqi nomads of the Maaqul desert."

"Aren't there dozens of languages in the Empire, Lio?"

"Hundreds. Thousands, if you count dialects."

"Of course you don't know every single one!"

"But I'm immortal. I have time to learn them all and no excuse not to."

The exit took them into a narrow passage between two thick walls, where they had to proceed single file. A very defensible arrangement, forcing newcomers into a tight space.

When they came out on the other side, torchlight revealed a crowd of round, wattle-and-daub buildings with thatched roofs. They went on for as far as Cassia could see. Her gaze traveled over the sea of moonlit rooftops, and she gaped.

Even in the darkness, she got a sense of how vast the city was. At various points among the humble dwellings, there rose the high walls of round stone enclosures, darker forms against the dark blue sky. They made the gate courtyard look tiny.

In the distance, a hill rose over the city. A stone complex perched atop the rise, the outlines of its walls marked by the fires burning atop them.

These were the most massive stone structures she had ever seen. They dwarfed Solorum Palace. They made a joke of the Temple of Anthros.

"Did humans build this?" she asked. "It looks like the work of a god."

Lio let their trunks come to rest on the grass next to them. "It is indeed the work of mortals who have been innovating new stone working methods for generations. Masons are highly honored here, and not likely to share their secrets."

"There must be thousands of people living here."

"Tens of thousands. It's one of the largest cities in the world."

The metropolis was quiet at this predawn hour. She could only imagine how it would teem with life as soon as the sun rose, while Lio would be dragged to sleep.

He pulled out his astrolabe again and aligned it with a bright star over the city. Cassia watched in tense silence as he adjusted the hand on the instrument's face and consulted the many tiny marks and measurements around its rim.

"We only have an hour and a half until dawn," he announced.

"We'd best hurry."

NO DIPLOMATS

AFTER THEY HAD LOST half their remaining time getting turned away from full inns, Lio began to doubt the wisdom of his decision.

"So many travelers here." Cassia shook her head as they left another lodging house with no rooms.

"Even worse, there's a festival." Lio sighed and pinched the bridge of his nose. "The city is packed with traders delivering the supplies. The Sandira King has ordered all kinds of banquets and ceremonies up on the hill. Something about his brother coming for a visit. 'Prince Tendeso' is all I overhear everyone talking about."

"No wonder there aren't any rooms left." Cassia sounded tired.

"You need sleep," he said.

"You're the one who will fall asleep first." There was an edge of panic in her laugh. "What am I to do, stranded in the middle of the road with a Slumbering Hesperine? You're too heavy to carry."

"I would never leave you stranded." He infused his voice with the calm she needed.

He still couldn't bring himself to mention his contingency plan. The king courted power. Hesperines were powerful. That was why they were welcomed on the hilltop as his guests.

But Orthros's Ambassador to the Sandira Court would recognize Lio, and he would have to introduce Cassia, and soon this would no longer be a personal visit at all.

They did not want the Sandira King taking an interest in why they were here.

He sighed. "Let's try one more place."

At the edge of the city of wattle houses was another city, this one of tents. The trading caravans' camps were just beginning to stir as they arrived. Nearby, a group of women were gathering around a fire, and the scents of breakfast were starting.

"Would you be comfortable on your own here during the day?" Lio hated the thought of leaving Cassia alone in a city she didn't know.

But her aura had already brightened. "I'll have so many chances to practice Tradewinds. Do you think they'll teach me new words if I offer to lend a hand with chores around the caravan?"

Lio smiled in relief. It was possible this would work. "I'm sure they would. Many of the caravans are owned by women, and they'll respect you for working hard and being willing to learn."

"Perhaps I can help their alchemists make tonics for common ills of the road."

"You aren't going to offer to assist with the sewing?"

She poked him in the side. "I don't want to get us thrown out on our ears when the caravan matriarchs discover I'm the worst seamstress in any hemisphere."

Despite the weight of the oncoming Slumber, his spirits lifted. "Let us find out who's willing to allow a Hesperine to take up space in the back of one of her tents."

"I'll earn your keep, not to worry."

"I would never be such a burden, my rose. They'll respect Blood Komnena's coin, too."

They approached the women around the nearest fire, who kindly suggested seeking accommodation with a friend of theirs. By the time Lio and Cassia crossed the camp to find her, his eyelids felt like adamas. They discovered that her caravan was waiting for the return of her daughter and son-in-law before heading out again, and that Lio and Cassia could use their tent for the time being. With his mind growing hazier and hazier with sleepiness, Lio was grateful when the caravan owner waved him into the tent without payment and told him they could agree on a price later.

Cassia breathed a sigh of relief. Lio had to admit, the basic accommodations looked like the lap of luxury to him after the long night. She gave him a little push, and he collapsed obediently onto the bedroll on his back.

"Come down here with me." He lifted a leaden hand toward her.

"I should—"

"You should sleep."

"If you insist."

"I insist. You need—" A mind-numbing yawn overtook him. "—rest as much as I do."

At last her soft body joined his on the bedroll. Finally he relaxed. He wrapped his arm around her, and she cuddled against his side with her head resting on his chest.

She shifted in his arms, and he felt her breath on his cheek. "You haven't had anything to drink since diving. You used a great deal of magic and physical strength down there. Can you stay awake long enough for at least a sip?"

He shook his head, his eyes already closed. "Sleep next to me. That's all I want right now."

"Will you be all right? I wish we'd found this place in time for me to feed you."

"Proper feast. After Slumber."

He thought he might have gotten a few more words out after that, but he wasn't sure which ones. His last thought was that this was much nicer than the Hesperine guest court, because there were no diplomats to bother him while he fell asleep with Cassia in his arms.

70

Nights Until

NOTIAN WINTER SOLSTICE

35 Annassa, 1597 IS

MONSOON

THE LIGHT CANVAS WALLS of the tent did little to keep the sunlight out. Cassia had kept Lio covered from head to toe in a dark blanket all day, but she wasn't sure how much it would help. As the daylight inside the tent turned orange with sunset, she burrowed under the blanket with him and waited to see how much longer than usual it would take him to awaken.

The sun went down, and she pulled the blanket away from their faces. But the twilight that usually roused Lio proved insufficient this time. It wasn't until full dark that his chest suddenly rose under her hand, and he gasped for his first breath of the night.

In this moment, when his body awoke and his mind could not protest, his fangs unsheathed, and his arm instinctively circled her, trapping her against him.

Her own lungs seemed to breathe for the first time in hours. Her yearning defied her reason. She wanted to lock her mouth to his and kiss him awake. At the barest touch from her, he would feast on her with the uninhibited, instinctive passion of his first waking moments.

But she couldn't trust herself. She braced her hands against him, pushing.

"Cassia?" The way he said her name was so tender, even when he was muddled. His arm loosened.

She scrambled out of the bedroll and put the length of the tent between them. Knight looked up from where he dozed at the foot of the bedroll and whined in concern.

She tucked her knees up under her chin and wrapped her arms around her legs. She should have known better than to test herself by lingering in his arms.

Lio lifted a lazy hand to his face and rubbed. Then blinked, then spotted her. He rolled up onto his elbow with sudden speed. "What's wrong?"

"I wanted to bite you in your sleep."

A smile broke across his face, and his pleasant laughter filled the tent.

"It isn't funny," she said, but she felt better already.

"I know. It's something we need to take very seriously." He was still smiling, though. "It's just that you're so adorable sitting there like that, talking about biting me."

A small smile came to her lips.

"For future reference," he said, "you are more than welcome to bite me in my sleep, as long as I don't miss out on anything *really* good."

Warmth spread across her cheeks, confirming once again that he could still make her blush. "When I'm a Hesperine, though, you'll be watching me sleep."

"It's true, since I'm slightly older than you, I will be able to stay awake longer."

"Yes, oh so slightly older by a mere century."

"So, also for future reference, what is your position on sleep biting?"

Her smile widened. "You are more than welcome, as long as it's right before I wake up, so I can start the night with your fangs in me."

"Duly noted." His fangs were showing off at the moment, and if he would only push the blanket off, she was sure she would see the rest of him showing off as well.

His nostrils flared slightly, and his eyes gleamed at her with hunger. She thought her heart would pound out of her chest. Her hands were wrapped tight around her ankles, his braid marking her palm.

"Cassia," he said gently, "you can come to bed now."

She flexed her tight hands on her ankles, hesitating.

"Are you all right?" he asked.

"Besides suffering a Craving I'm not allowed to act on yet, I'm fine."

"You're still leery after our close call. I know. But I'd say we did all right last time we feasted, don't you think?"

"All right is hardly sufficient to describe that."

"Come to bed, and let's see if we can find a better way to describe it. We can get creative, I'm sure."

Her resistance crumbled. She went into his waiting arms. They didn't find words to describe it all, for they were both speechless by the time they were finished with each other.

She was still catching her breath, spooned in his arms, when he found his voice. "What did you do today?"

"Slept, mostly. Took Knight out. The caravan leader was kind enough to provide food for him and me. I managed to arrange payment with her."

He ran his hand over her bare stomach. "I'm glad you waited to start searching for Ukocha. I know you're entirely capable on your own, but I still don't like the thought of you questioning a lot of mercenaries by yourself."

"Knight would defend me if I encountered any ruffians. But I don't speak Tradewinds well enough yet. I still need you for a translator."

"Is that all I am to you?" he asked woefully. "A tongue?"

"Your tongue is only one of your many assets, and what you were doing a few minutes ago was an even better use for it than translating."

He licked her shoulder, and she shivered.

"The truth is…" Her breath hitched as he teased the tip of his tongue where her shoulder and neck met. "…I barely left the tent. I needed to be near you."

He nuzzled her neck. "I'll be at your side every moment tonight."

With her Craving for him reassured, her mind cleared. She was finally able to consider the implications of what they had learned during the eventful night before.

"Solia needed a better plan," Cassia thought aloud. "What plan? And how could Ukocha help her with it?"

"Whatever her plan was," Lio said, "Ziara made it clear that Solia's goal was to get back to you."

She turned in Lio's arms and caressed his face. "You're right. They never said anything about her trying to get back to the throne. When we find her, I dare say she'll want nothing more to do with the king and the mages than I do."

"And we won't let anyone make her feel as if she should."

"We should write Mak and Lyros a summary of what we learned. And most importantly, a note wishing Zoe luck with her first lesson tonight."

Lio smiled fondly. "I can't believe she's starting courier training already. It seems like just yesternight she was asking to become a Hesperine."

"I'm glad sucklings don't grow up very fast. I'm not ready for Zoe to get much older."

"Me neither." Lio chuckled. "Let's write those letters and find a mail office before we start searching for Ukocha."

Dear Zoe,

We finally met the famous Captain Ziara. We cannot wait to tell you bedtime stories about her and the brave women of her crew. She sends her greetings and this brooch from her pirate treasure.

We learned that Solia had many adventures with the privateers. Then she stayed on land with a good friend of Ziara's named Ukocha. Now we're looking for her so we can ask her about Solia.

We've traveled to a place called the Sandira Court, where people can shapeshift. All the guards can turn into rhinos like the ones in your storybooks.

We're thinking of you and wishing you a wonderful first courier lesson. We're so proud of you, and we know you'll do well. You can tell us all about it soon.

Ask Mama and Papa to write to us so we can decide when and where to meet.

Love,
Lio and Cassia

"Shall we send Mak and Lyros the detailed version of Ziara's information?" Cassia suggested next.

"Yes, perhaps they know something about Ukocha, since she's such a famous warrior."

Cassia's shoulders slumped. "But what are we to tell Kassandra?"

"The truth of our actions, and that we stand by them."

When they left their tent, they asked their hostess for directions to the mail office, only for her to advise them that messengers were easy to come by in the traders' camps. The Sandira Court was a popular place for travelers to drop a letter home, but the city was large and tricky to navigate. Young Sandira citizens earned extra coin taking letters and packages between the tents and the mail office.

The matriarch of the caravan recommended a Sandira girl trusted for reliable and fast deliveries. Cassia made an effort not to stare at the feathers that grew amid her hair and covered her shoulders, left bare by her dress. Lio paid her, this time in gold coins stamped with an eagle's head, and she raced off into the city at a speed no child could achieve without magic.

"Now to inquire about Ukocha's whereabouts," said Lio. "Considering her fame, that shouldn't be too difficult."

"In such an enormous city, I'm sure rumors of her abound."

"I think we'll get the best results if we claim we're interested in hiring her."

"Good idea," Cassia agreed. "We're more likely to get her attention if she thinks it's worth her while."

There were warriors all over the traders' camps. Men and women alike were armed to the teeth and wore a wide array of armor, clearly from many different parts of the Empire, but all shared a certain hard eye and swagger in common. They patrolled the caravans, guarding those who had hired them or looking for work.

Lio gestured to a group of passing warriors. "See how they all wear knives on their right upper arms? Those are their fortune blades, issued by the Empress, or at least, her administration."

"Is that like a privateer's letter of marque?"

"Yes, it shows that a mercenary is professionally recognized and may fight for profit, and that they abide by the Empress's code of conduct."

"What are the rules?"

"Mercenaries are to fight only for the protection of the Empire and her citizens. They are not allowed to take contracts that would sow discord between sister states, and they must cooperate with the authorities when dealing with criminals."

"That's nothing like the mercenary armies the Cordian princes are always throwing at each other."

"In the Empire, mercenaries have a unique and valued role. They're fast, flexible, and politically neutral. They're able to lend their skills in situations where the Imperial army or the soldiers of a sister state couldn't. As long as they carry a fortune blade, you can rely on them to be professional."

"Is there a black market for mercenaries without fortune blades?"

"Yes, just like there's one for water mages."

"Let's hope we don't run into anyone like that."

"Their sort aren't tolerated in the bands of mercenaries like Ukocha."

A trio of warriors wearing shiny fortune blades welcomed Lio and Cassia around their campfire. They were battle-hardened men, but talkative, with the good cheer brought on by a few drinks. Their warm reception might also have had to do with the fact that everyone knew Orthros's reputation for deep pockets.

Between Cassia's slight grasp of Tradewinds and Lio's pauses to translate for her, she managed to follow the conversation.

"I'm surprised to see visitors from Orthros down here," said the warrior beside Lio, a burly man with a puffy scar cutting through the dark coils of his beard. "I'd expect your sort to be up on the hill, enjoying the king's hospitality and rubbing elbows with Prince Tendeso himself. To what do we owe the pleasure?"

"The festival isn't the reason we're passing through," Lio replied. "We're on a research expedition."

The warrior appeared pleased to hear that. "You two look like a couple of soft scholars. Veil spells are no help against booby traps in ancient ruins, and a tender heart is no good against vicious wildlife. Need someone strong to make sure you get where you're going in one piece?"

"We do," Lio answered. "We're hoping to hire Ukocha."

The big mercenary whistled. "She's the best."

"She won't take just any job," said the man across the fire. He was as thin and sharp as the spear he was polishing, his deep black skin decorated with pale tattoos. "She only hires out for special orders. If you just need skill, there's plenty of it to be had here, and we aren't picky."

"Thank you," Lio said graciously. "Under other circumstances, we would certainly take you up on your offer. But I'm afraid that for our particular task, we really do need Ukocha. Do you know her?"

"Everyone knows her by reputation," said the third mercenary, a short brown man with fists like anvils. "The mercs in her company *retire*."

"She must have been at this a long time," Lio said.

"She has been," the short mercenary replied, "and several of her comrades have left the company. In one piece."

"They *live* to retire," the burly man explained. "That's how good they are."

"Impressive," Lio agreed.

"Do you know why they're called the Ashes?" asked the spearman.

Lio and Cassia shook their heads.

The spearman leaned closer. "Because that's all that's left of their enemies when the job is done."

Well, that was suitably threatening. Cassia supposed bravado was an important professional asset for mercenaries, especially those with such a reputation to maintain. She had the feeling the Ashes backed up their bravado with results.

"What a woman." The burly mercenary shook his head. "There's not a man in the Empire who can best Ukocha with a sword. It's said she's wed to her blade, and the children they make together are the flames she conjures."

Cassia stifled a laugh, thinking of a certain axe in the Sun Market. She hoped she hadn't hurt Dakk's feelings by disappearing without a word.

"She has an affinity for fire?" Lio asked.

"They *are* called the Ashes," the warrior replied.

Cassia asked Lio in Divine, "She would be trained in the Imperial practice, then, like Xandra?"

"That's right," he answered, "although Xandra avoids battle applications. Ukocha would specialize in those, of course."

"I suddenly feel more reassured about Solia's safety."

Lio turned back to the warriors. "So where might we find Ukocha and her Ashes?"

The three mercenaries looked at each other, but shook their heads.

"They haven't been through here since we arrived," the burly man supplied. "We've been waiting on a job, and we haven't heard anything except the usual tales of their deeds."

"Tall tales," groused the short man. "I swear half of them are pure fancy."

"The Ashes have a legend." The spearman smacked him on the arm. "It doesn't matter if the stories really happened or not. They're true."

"Sorry," the big mercenary concluded. "They could be anywhere in the Empire."

The short warrior sighed. "Maybe someone who's been stuck here longer than us can tell you more."

"But probably not anyone in the camps," said the spearman. "The Ashes are on the gold roster. Mercenaries that famous don't waste their time down here."

"What is the gold roster?" Cassia asked Lio.

"A list maintained by the Empress's administrators of the mercenaries who have received the most gold in service to the Empire's interests. It's a measure of a mercenary's prowess, wealth, and how many contracts they've completed that benefit not only themselves, but the common good."

"It sounds like in the Empire, the common good pays well."

"Recognition on the gold roster is certainly a strong motivation to keep the code of conduct."

The burly man pointed away from the tents, into the city. "You'll find the gold roster blades in the Court of Claws, where they spar with the Sandira King's warriors. Invitation only."

"How does one procure an invitation?" Cassia asked.

Lio did not translate her question for the mercenaries. Instead, he turned to her with a frown. "We don't want an invitation to any place where we'll meet the royal guard."

"I know. That's precisely the kind of attention we wish to avoid. But we'll only be there to talk to the mercenaries, not the guards."

"The king's warriors will keep a close eye on every person who comes in and out. There's no sense in parading ourselves in front of them."

"If that's where we're likely to learn more about the Ashes, how can we avoid it?"

"There are still many people in the city we haven't spoken with yet. Let's keep trying."

Cassia relented, and they thanked the three mercenaries before continuing onward through the busy camps. Everywhere, traders were either packing or unpacking, haggling, or cooking. Lean spotted dogs with big, round ears ran freely between the tents. A few gave warning growls to any who passed too close to the caravans they guarded, but none dared pick a fight with Knight.

All the mercenaries they met told the same story. The great Ukocha and her deadly band hadn't been seen in months, although tales of their deeds were the talk of every caravan. Many confirmed what the three warriors had said: mercenaries of the Ashes' status spent their time in the Court of Claws.

At last Cassia and Lio joined a gathering at a campfire where a storyteller was spinning tales of the Ashes. Focused on their search, Cassia barely noticed the traders hawking hand foods to the audience, until Lio reminded her she needed to eat. He bought her peanuts and little sweet fruits called bird plums that actually reminded her of dates, as well as a roasted gourd that was halved and filled with seasoning and melted cheese.

The wizened, white-haired storyteller enraptured her audience with a grand recounting of the Ashes beheading a giant snake. Cassia had to admit, the tale captured her imagination. It did impart truth, whether or not it had actually taken place.

Perhaps such legendary warriors really could help Solia against the sort of monsters she had faced.

Unfortunately, the tale yielded no information that would help Lio and Cassia find Ukocha.

Once they moved on from the storyteller's campfire, they drifted to a halt.

"We're at a dead end," Cassia pointed out. "Everyone agrees there's only one place for us to go from here. The Court of Claws."

She didn't like the grim look on Lio's face, not one bit.

She touched his arm. "Surely the royal guard won't raise an eyebrow at a couple of scrollworms from Orthros passing through to hire mercenaries."

His jaw clenched, but his sigh sounded resigned. "It appears it's a necessary risk. If we run into any trouble, I'll step us to safety."

Now Cassia frowned. "You said there are restrictions on stepping, and the Sandira King doesn't tolerate anyone breaking the rules."

"Stepping reasonable distances in unrestricted areas is allowed, as long as I don't try to bypass guard checkpoints."

He seemed like he was about to say something more. When he didn't, Cassia said it for him. "And if one of his guards threatens us, it probably means we have already earned his disfavor and should leave the city as soon as possible."

"I'm afraid so."

As much as she trusted Lio to keep her safe, she also knew that if a scene with privateer water mages was bad, a scene with the king's guard would be infinitely worse.

"We'll just have to be on our best behavior," she said.

They returned to the three mercenaries who had first suggested they go to the Court of Claws and asked them for more information.

The burly warrior gestured to Lio's robes. "Orthros's wealth is likely all the ticket you'll need to get in. Gold roster blades will take an offer from any Hesperine seriously."

After he gave them directions, Lio and Cassia took their leave. They found their way out of the traders' camps and into the streets of the city proper. The neighborhoods of wattle and daub houses were quiet.

It was rather a long walk to the enclosure known as the Court of Claws, but its stone walls were visible long before Lio and Cassia drew near, making it easy to find. It was one of the smaller courts, but still intimidating in size.

Torches flanked the entrance, a gap leading into a narrow corridor like the one at the gate courtyard. A pair of warriors blocked the way. These must be the aforementioned royal guards. Their spears appeared exquisitely crafted. Like the spirit gate guards, they wore waist-wraps, but no armor covered their bodies.

Wings adorned their backs. Like living, feathered cloaks, they wore their power for all to see.

Lio bowed and addressed them in Tradewinds in a diplomatic tone. Knight showed the men his teeth.

"*Het baat,*" Cassia said sharply. What might the consequences be if her hound threatened one of the royal guard?

Knight dutifully went into a down-stay beside her, but he did not appear happy about it. She bowed to the warrior again by way of apology. Lio said something quickly in Tradewinds that she couldn't follow.

One guard disappeared through the entrance. The other stepped aside and motioned for Lio and Cassia to go ahead of him. Cassia doubted it was out of courtesy. In Lio's hesitation, she could see he also did not like the idea of being trapped between the guards in the narrow entryway.

He placed himself between Cassia and the warrior and let her go first, where she could see the guard ahead of her.

An instinctual frustration assailed her. That instinct didn't care that Lio was an immortal. It understood only that her Grace's back was to the man's spear.

Because she was human and needed protecting.

The guard watched them, stone-faced, waiting. Cassia bit her tongue and sent Knight in ahead of her, then continued inside.

Looking at the back of the warrior ahead of her, she could only marvel at the sight of wings on a human. She could only imagine him fighting from the air. Such mighty mage warriors were not to be trifled with.

Lio's hand on her back reassured her. His magic stirred around them, and he whispered to her in Divine, "I don't sense anyone with an ambush in mind."

"What do you sense?" Cassia asked.

"Someone powerful," he warned.

The guards escorting them, oblivious to their veiled conversation, allowed them to emerge from the entryway before returning to their posts. Lio kept his hand on Cassia's back, standing close at her side.

She looked around the Court of Claws, trying to spot the powerful person Lio meant. Torches ringed the perfectly curving enclosure, revealing two groups of spectators gathered around a fight.

On one side were the guards with their ceremonial spears. The vision before Cassia filled her with wonder. A whole gathering of men with wings and rhinoceros skin, all their rare and powerful magic resting easily upon them, part of their everyday lives.

The warriors for hire with fortune blades and motley armor watched from the other side. In the center, a gate guard in the mystical rhino armor faced off with one of the mercenaries.

Amid the cheers and raised fists, it was the mercenary's stillness that captured Cassia's attention. He stood with his fortune blade raised, poised and focused. His sleeveless tunic revealed muscled arms marked by scars, lighter striations on his deep brown skin that must be proud trophies of battles he had won. She was willing to bet he'd made many enemies. But it was he who had lived to show off the scars of their encounters.

His eyes blazed, his face a mask of pure concentration. The guard made a move with his spear. But the mercenary was twice as fast. He struck with far more ferocity.

He deflected the spear attack with his fortune blade, lunged under the soldier's defenses, and pressed the tip of his knife to the unarmored skin under the guard's chin.

The bigger, stronger man raised his hands. The fight was already over. The guard left the ring in defeat.

The mercenary stood, his face cold and his eyes hot, waiting for his next victim.

His skills had clearly earned him his place on the gold roster. It certainly hadn't been an award for his attitude.

"That's him," she guessed.

Lio's hand was tense on her back. "I can't identify his affinity, but whatever it is, his magic fills this place. It feels as if it could fill the whole city."

"Let's avoid him and ask the other mercenaries our questions."

"Most definitely."

Cassia observed the mercenaries, who were riveted to the scarred warrior's exploits. "I don't think we'll get very far by distracting them from the spectacle with annoying questions."

"Good point. We'd best show some enthusiasm for the fights."

"We'll just imitate the initiates who come to all of Mak and Lyros's matches, and we'll blend right in."

They joined in with the mercenary spectators, and their cheers loosened tongues much faster than questions. The scarred fighter defeated one guard after another, and in between each match, his fellow gold roster mercenaries talked. They asked Lio and Cassia about their journeys and told of their own.

These warriors were well traveled and world wise. Many of them had met the Ashes or even seen them in action. None of them knew where they were.

"Have you been talking to the off-roster rabble in the trading camps?" asked a lithe woman armed with leaf-shaped throwing knives. "They'd lie about the Ashes' whereabouts to get your contract for themselves. Those of us on the gold are above such tactics. We have our choice of work, and none of us would poach a contract from Ukocha."

"Of course," Lio said. "We would never doubt the word of a mercenary in the Court of Claws. We're grateful for your assistance."

She let out a whistle at the mercenary in the ring, who had just gifted the latest guard a new scar right under his eye. "I can tell you the Ashes didn't take their last contract here. The last time they were in the Sandira Court, they were between jobs. But the Ashes don't stay that way for long. They're on a contract all right, but whatever it is, they picked it up somewhere else."

"Do you have any idea who might have hired them, or where?" Lio asked.

The knife fighter shook her head. "But whatever the job is, it's a long one. The Ashes haven't been available in months."

So, Cassia thought, the Ashes could be anywhere in the Empire on a long contract doing anything. They felt farther away than ever.

"They don't keep a waiting list, either," the woman added. "Do you need them specifically?"

"Ukocha in particular," Lio answered.

"Then you're in for a long delay, I'm afraid. The best advice I can give you is to make a preliminary hire tonight, someone who can help you find the Ashes and get you to them safely. Then you'll be first in line to offer them your contract when they finish their current one."

"May we ask if you have any recommendations about who would be a good choice? We need someone who's available right away."

"I'm booked, and besides, I don't specialize in tracking." She gave them a rueful look. "Honestly, your best bet is Monsoon."

She pointed to the mercenary in the ring. He had his foot planted on a royal guard's back, right between his wings, which beat uselessly. Monsoon twirled the defeated man's spear in his hand.

"He can find anyone," the knife fighter said. "No one in the Empire can hide from that man."

Cassia had to wonder, did the vicious mercenary's expertise extend to bringing them back alive?

"Definitely the top choice for any kind of search contract," the knife fighter went on. "But his availability might be a problem. He's pickier than anyone about his contracts."

Lio didn't press the knife fighter for any more information. In fact, he changed the subject.

At her first opportunity, Cassia made an attempt in Tradewinds. She thought she asked something like, "Please more about Monsoon?"

She must have gotten her question across, for the knife fighter gave her an answer with a humorless smile, counting points off on her fingers.

Lio translated, reluctance in his tone. "These are the rules of dealing with Monsoon. Don't ask him to play nicely with others—he always works alone. Don't waste his time. Most importantly, don't get on his bad side."

Cassia lost count of how many guards Monsoon flattened. At last he left the ring by choice, as the victor. As silently as he had fought, he strolled over to the wall and propped himself against the smooth stones, crossing his arms over his chest. The spectators sent him off with deafening cheers, but no one approached him.

"Now is our chance," Cassia said to Lio.

He pulled her aside from the crowd of mercenaries. "We can't seriously consider hiring that man."

"I'm not fond of the idea either," she agreed, "but you heard the other mercenaries. None of them are experts in search contracts, and most of them are already booked."

"There must be other search contract specialists in the Empire. We'll find someone else."

"How many gold roster search contract specialists are there?"

"All we need is one to help us find Solia without endangering you."

Cassia looked sidelong at Monsoon. "He is obviously a dangerous man, but what evidence do we have that he's a danger to me?"

"I don't deem it wise to let a man with a big knife, a bad temper, and obscenely powerful magic of unknown affinity anywhere near my Grace."

Cassia swallowed a laugh. "I understand, my champion. But do you have any reason to believe the man's sour attitude is specifically directed toward us?"

Lio sighed, scowling. "Admittedly, I do not."

"Perhaps an interview," she suggested. "If anything he says confirms your concerns, we'll try a different plan."

Lio sighed. "That is entirely reasonable."

But Lio held Cassia so close to his side that a piece of paper wouldn't have fit between them. As they approached the man in the shadows, the spectators they passed let out a roar, making her jump.

She tried to gain more clues about Monsoon from his appearance, but what she saw was contradictory. She found his age difficult to judge; Imperial citizens, she had found, tended to look younger than Tenebrans of the same age due to the better living conditions here. But his manner—and his scars—suggested extensive life experience. He was twelve or so years older than her, if she had to guess.

She had only seen him fight with the long, wicked-looking fortune blade now strapped to his right bicep, but there was also a sword at his belt, fine in craftsmanship and elegant in its simplicity with a short, straight blade and no crossguard. He wore no armor over his plain, sleeveless cotton tunic and loose trousers. His sandaled feet were filthy, but he was otherwise well groomed. His beard and hair were carefully trimmed close to his head, except for one thick braid that ran from his forehead to his nape. He had a strong-jawed face that most would consider handsome, if his scowl did not ruin his looks.

Just outside his reach, Lio stopped her. At last Monsoon looked away from the fight and deigned to dignify them with his notice. He seemed to dismiss Lio with a glance.

But his attention fixed on Cassia with an intensity that burned. He studied her face, as if reading her soul from it. Then his gaze flicked to Knight.

Cassia put a hand on her hound's shoulder. His fur was standing on end.

Clearly Lio didn't like the way the man was assessing her, either, for his power rose, latent in the air, until goosebumps peppered Cassia's skin.

The mercenary snorted.

He was powerful enough not to fear a Hesperine. For the first time, Cassia wasn't sure she should have talked Lio into this.

Lio addressed the man in Tradewinds, his tone like silk over adamas.

It was as if he hadn't said a word. The man spoke directly to Cassia—in Vulgus. "Sneaking in on a Hesperine's arm doesn't change the fact that you're Tenebran. Tread carefully here."

The tongue of her old life hit her like a slap in the face. Cassia only spoke Divine at home with Lio anymore. It was a shock to hear the language of Tenebra at all, especially here in the Empire.

Where, why had this man learned Vulgus?

"I'm not Tenebran anymore," Cassia told him in Divine.

"Not everyone will make the distinction," the man continued in Vulgus.

"I will help them appreciate the distinction," Lio threatened, taking her side in the beautiful tongue of Orthros.

"What are you doing here?" the mercenary demanded of Cassia.

She laid a hand on Lio's arm. "I am Newgift Cassia—"

The man flinched.

"—of Orthros," she emphasized, no matter how it seemed to offend him that she distanced herself from her Tenebran origins. "This is Lio, my intended. We seek to hire you. Unless you aren't interested in what our bloodline's purse has to offer?"

"I can't help you."

"Your colleagues have assured us you are the best person for this contract. We're seeking Ukocha, but she isn't here, so we need someone to help us track down the Ashes."

"You're looking for the Ashes?"

The question was so hostile, she wasn't sure if it signified interest, but she continued anyway. Flattery and riches usually held universal appeal, so she stayed with that tactic. "We're told there is no one better than you at search contracts. As clients from Orthros, we're in a position to make an offer that is highly competitive, even by gold roster standards."

"You think I want your money? Do you know who I am?"

She cleared her throat. "Monsoon, I believe. Your fellow mercenaries speak very highly of your prowess."

He pushed away from the wall, and it took all her Will not to back away from him. Lio was suddenly in front of her with immortal alacrity, and for an instant, she feared they were going to make a scene after all.

Monsoon's gaze bored into Cassia's. "The best help I can give you is a warning. It's not safe for you here. Get out of the Empire. Now, or you'll regret it."

He narrowed his eyes at Lio. Then the man walked away.

Cassia stared in outrage at his retreating back. He didn't even look over his shoulder. She started forward to march after him.

But Lio didn't move, his arm still around her. "*Now* I have reason to believe he's a danger to you."

Cassia couldn't argue with that. She watched the man who had threatened her disappear into the passage leading out of the Court of Claws.

"Well, I'm not frightened of him, whoever he thinks he is. What did he expect to accomplish with such a theatrical threat?"

Lio's magic snapped in the air. "His goal was to frighten you, and you know how I feel about people who try that."

"If he imagines he can scare me off that easily, he will be as surprised as the king and the mages. We need to find out who he is and, more importantly, his price. Everyone has a price."

"If he wishes to draw attention to the fact that you're Tenebran, we need to avoid him like magefire. We can think of a different strategy for finding the Ashes. We don't need him."

"We can't afford to waste a single lead."

"He's not a lead. He's a threat." Lio met her gaze. "Cassia, I don't want that man anywhere near you. Please trust my senses about him."

She put a hand on his chest. "You really think it's too dangerous? Even after all the other threats we've faced together?"

"I believe him to be the greatest danger to you and our quest that we've yet encountered."

"Do you think he'll use his magic against us and risk a diplomatic incident with Orthros?"

"It's not just his magic." Lio glanced around the Court of Claws again. "It's his connections. He's a gold roster mercenary who fraternizes with the royal guard. What's more, he not only knows you were born in Tenebra—he cares."

"Sunbind him. You're right. Something about my origins gets under his skin."

"The guards respect him and probably owe him money or favors, after all the fights he's won. In his position, he could convince influential people they should care about your origins, too." Lio's gaze swept the shadows around them. "And if he didn't want to cause an incident, I suspect he could accomplish his ends quietly."

Cassia shivered. "He's not someone we should provoke thoughtlessly. I suppose even Lady Circumspect needs to be reminded to take the strategic approach sometimes. Thank you."

"I know you want to charge ahead and pursue every possible lead." He touched his lips to her hair. "But you will be of no help to Solia if you wind up in danger yourself. I promised to keep both of you safe."

"I'll do my best not to make that task more difficult for you."

They returned to their tent just before dawn. Lio fell onto their bedroll with obvious reluctance, muttering a curse at the sun. He didn't even take the time to undress, and neither did Cassia. She stretched out beside him, and Knight draped himself over their feet.

"Cassia, I want you to stay here beside me until sundown, all right?"

"Do you think Monsoon would actually turn up again and threaten me? He seemed in such a hurry to get away from us."

"I just think it would be wiser if you're here with me during daylight hours. I'm glad you have Knight with you."

"And all the women and children surrounding this tent, and the mercenaries protecting this trading caravan. I'm sure there won't really be any kind of scene, with Monsoon or anyone else."

"My veils will hide you," he mumbled. "Not me. Visible deterrent."

"I'll be fine, my love," she tried to reassure him.

"You're brave." His eyes slid shut. "But I know you don't like the idea any more than I do...of you being alone while I sleep..."

"I'm not alone." But she would feel so, as soon as his breathing stopped for the day.

He reached for her with his thelemancy and touched the ward upon her mind. When his magic faded from her thoughts, she knew he was asleep.

69

Nights Until

NOTIAN WINTER SOLSTICE

36 Annassa, 1597 IS

FRIENDS IN HIGH PLACES

MIDDAY LIGHT PULLED CASSIA out of a fitful doze. She fought off a yawn, but knew her thoughts wouldn't allow her to fall asleep again. As she lay beside Lio in the confines of the tent, her fears crept up on her.

What if Solia had met someone like Monsoon, who was hostile to Tenebrans?

Dakk had befriended Cassia. Ziara had not batted an eye at aiding shadowlanders. But the harsh mercenary reminded Cassia that there were those who would not be so generous.

What if someone had turned Solia in? What if she had been deported and was even now back in Cordium in the mages' clutches?

And now their search had reached a dead end.

Nike had returned to Orthros, Kalos had braved Cordium, Cassia and Lio had passed the privateers' challenges. For this. They had come so far, only to lose Solia's trail in a city full of people who knew all about Ukocha.

Unless they found a lead soon, it would take a Hesperine lifetime to search for Solia. What if she didn't have that much time? What if she needed Cassia this very moment?

Cassia shimmied out of the bedroll, then covered Lio carefully, as she had the previous day. Every Slumber he spent in the sunny tent, he would wake a little later. Each passing day eroded their nights together a little more. That was another reason they needed to move on from here as soon as possible, hopefully to a place where he would have proper shelter.

She lingered over him. As if an unseen vein ran between them, a powerful current seemed to pull her heart and mind toward him.

Vela Roth

Her need to be near him was natural. But she couldn't let it rule her every waking moment. She needed independence, too. Lio himself had fought so hard for her to have it.

She was free now. She must live like it.

With an act of Will, she moved away from Lio and got ready to leave. She secured her scarf around her hair and neck, then picked up her gardening satchel.

"Come along, Knight. Today we will make the most of our daylight hours."

He lifted his head from his paws, but didn't get up from the foot of the bedroll.

"I'm sorry, darling. No lazy day in the tent for us. We're going to keep searching for information."

He tensed, but still didn't get up.

"Don't look at me like that. I know Lio wants me to stay in the tent. But the worst threat right now is wasted time. *Dockk dockk.*"

At the ancient command in the liegehound training tongue, Knight no longer hesitated to rise to his feet and come to Cassia's side.

He sat down in the doorway, blocking the tent flap with his big, furry self.

Cassia felt a prickle of unease about her plan. She had always been glad when she trusted Knight's instincts—and usually regretted it when she didn't. The last time she had ignored his warning, Skleros had poisoned her.

But everything in the Empire was new to him. Since they had arrived here, he had growled at a woman shopping for scent, a jolly crowd of privateers, and very important royal guards. It was hard to read his instincts when he was adjusting to a new place, where both allies and threats were outside the realm of his Tenebran breeding and training.

She reached out with both hands and rubbed Knight's ears. "Is it really such a bad idea?"

He huffed and leaned down, nosing Lio's foot through the blanket.

Cassia smiled then. "I see how it is. Your protective instincts have expanded to cover my Hesperine. We've come a long way since the day you stood in the door of the shrine of Hespera and blocked my way, refusing to allow me to leave your presence in Lio's company. But it's all right now, darling. Lio will be perfectly safe here, and I'll be perfectly safe with you."

This time, when she told him to heel, he left the tent at her side.

Her first view of the city in daylight left her standing awestruck once again. The Sandira Court occupied a broad plain. Aside from scattered dots of green where trees grew, the work of humans covered the ground for as far as her eyes could see. The stone courts seemed to soak the sun into their proud, gray granite walls. At their feet, like supplicants, stood the little round buildings of mud and thatch, presumably the homes of the common people.

The city was so big, and it looked so different by day, that it took Cassia quite a while to find the Court of Claws again. By the time she approached its wall, she needed to stop. Lightheaded, she put a hand on the smooth stones to steady herself.

So this was the price of ignoring Lio's advice about moving slowly. Clearly her body wasn't accustomed to the elevation yet. The air was pleasant, though, cooler and drier than Marijani.

Once she had caught her breath, she approached the entrance to the Court of Claws, but Knight balked.

"I know. That's where the threatening man was last night. We'll just take a quick look to see if he's there, and if he is, we'll leave. If he isn't, it will be safe to ask the other mercenaries more questions."

She bowed to the guards on day watch and repeated some of the phrases Lio had said last night. She must not have botched it too badly, because after studying her silk robes from Orthros, they escorted her into the Court of Claws.

She lingered just inside, holding Knight back, and carefully studied the crowd. She didn't see Monsoon in the ring, among the spectators, or at his post by the wall. What she did see were many new faces who had not been present during the night. It should be safe to ask some questions, and useful, too.

Cassia waded into the mercenary side of the audience and struck up conversations as best she could with the day spectators. She was limited to simple phrases like, "Where Ukocha?" and "I hire Ashes." As frustrating as it was, a wasted day in the tent would have driven her mad much faster.

But the day crowd didn't tell her anything new. She learned the phrase "ask Monsoon" so well that she wanted to open her dictionary and scratch out the words with a sharp quill.

When she ran into the knife fighter from the night before, it was rather a relief. She was willing to speak more slowly, and kindly didn't laugh at Cassia's more creative ways of stringing words together.

"Any luck?" she asked.

Cassia shook her head. "Day people don't know."

"Sorry." The knife fighter looked sympathetic.

"More people tomorrow?" Cassia asked.

The mercenary shrugged. "Many mercenaries *something something* travel *something* Sandira Court *something*-roster rats."

Rats? Had Cassia understood that correctly? Was the knife fighter insulting the off-roster mercenaries again? Cassia wasn't sure whether she should be encouraged by that or not.

"More gold roster?" Cassia tried.

The knife fighter shook her head. "Don't know more. Ask Monsoon." Cassia sighed.

"Ask Monsoon where Ukocha *something*," the mercenary said slowly. "*Something* he knows."

Wait, could she mean he actually knew where Ukocha was, not just that he was capable of finding her? "Say again?"

"Ask Monsoon where Ukocha. *Something* he knows *something*."

"He knows where Ukocha?" Cassia repeated, just to make sure.

The mercenary nodded. "*Something*."

"Thank you, thank you!"

The knife fighter smiled.

Cassia offered her a gold coin.

The knife fighter appeared pleased, but refused and said the word "luck" again, then, "Monsoon bad. Careful."

At that sobering warning, Cassia winced and nodded. "Yes, know. Careful. Thank you thank you!"

The most dangerous threat to their quest was also the only person who had the information they needed to continue. Monsoon was no less a risk, but now he was a necessary one.

Lio was right. Hiring Monsoon was a very bad idea. His attitude toward shadowlanders was not only a threat to Cassia. She didn't dare lead a man like that closer to Solia.

All they needed was the information he had on Ukocha's whereabouts. She would negotiate a price for what he knew, then she and Lio could find her themselves.

"When Monsoon here?" Cassia asked the knife fighter.

She shrugged again. "Monsoon travel tonight. Contract."

Cup and thorns. That meant there wasn't much time. If Monsoon was leaving tonight for his next contract, Cassia had to find him today. Before sundown. Without Lio.

I'm sorry, my Grace. I know I promised I wouldn't. But I must.

Before taking a step further, she made sure her citizenship papers were within easy reach in her satchel. If Monsoon gave her a bit of trouble about her origins, she would brandish the Queens' protection that these documents represented before him or any Imperial authority.

"*Dockk,*" she murmured to Knight under the yells of the combatants. She led him to the wall where Monsoon had stood the night before. "*Seckkaa!*"

At the command to hunt, Knight put his nose to the ground and began a thorough investigation of the area.

Cassia waited in tense silence, hoping the guards wouldn't be suspicious of whatever she and her dog were up to. She counted the clangs of the fighters' swords. If only the fight would drag on and absorb everyone's attention.

When Knight's sniffing led him to the wall, he spent a considerable amount of time with his nose pressed to the stones where Monsoon had leaned his backside. Cassia wasn't sure if that was a compliment or an insult to the man.

Motion caught her eye, and she glanced up. No one was watching her except a large bird perched on the top of the wall above her head.

Was it foolish of her to wonder if it was a shapeshifter? Surely not every animal in the city was a person in disguise. She wished she knew how to tell the difference.

The big bird ruffled its feathers. It appeared to be an eagle of some kind, truly a magnificent creature with its brilliant red face and black plumage adorned with chestnut and gray markings.

She glanced at the royal guards. Their wings all had the same markings, but this eagle's didn't match theirs. This bird must not be one of them.

A cloud of dust puffed up from the fighting ring, and both sides of the crowd roared. The audience began to mill about as the two combatants left the ring limping. Cassia noticed some of the guards eying her. Uh oh.

"Dockk." She slipped out of the Court of Claws with Knight. Outside, she bowed and said thank you to the guards at the entrance, then rounded the curve of the stone wall until she was out of their sight.

She gave Knight a pat on the rump. *"Seckkaa!"*

At the tracking command, he bounded forward, and she had to run to catch up with him. She darted after him through the city.

Knight led her on a chase through dry, dusty lanes between mud huts. They wove in and out of the people, carts, and pack animals filling the streets. Fortunately, most traffic was headed in the same general direction, away from the trading camps. It seemed the entire city was on the move, getting the king's festival supplies from the caravans to wherever they needed to go.

Cassia called out an apology in Tradewinds at anyone who glared at her dog. Smoke of all different flavors wafted past her face from the midday cooking fires. She ran past the delicious smells of food and the not so lovely smells of many humans living too close together. Children laughed and pointed at Knight and chased him with her for a few minutes, before their mothers called them back. A couple of young men with dog ears offered to help her catch him, but she shook her head with a smile and followed Knight onward.

They wound through the city into ever cleaner and more spacious neighborhoods. She couldn't understand the conversations around her, but recognized the name Tendeso on everyone's lips. She wondered if they liked their royals that much. More likely they were simply looking forward to a day without labor, or whatever other benefits the king deigned to extend to his subjects during a festival.

When a broad, deep shadow fell over her, Cassia looked up. If possible, this stone court was even larger than the complex on the King's Hill. She didn't know its purpose, but there was no doubt it was of great importance to the Sandira.

As Knight led her closer and closer to the monumental structure, she began to worry. Going to the Court of Claws had been risky enough. She shouldn't approach an important court where surely only the privileged—and invited—were welcome.

This close, the great stone enclosure filled the sky. Cassia called for Knight to heel. He came back to her, and together they halted in the shadow of the walls. Her sweat cooled on her skin.

She thought she heard a strain of music from within, then the echo of feminine laughter. The Sandira people must have a Queen Mother, as did each sister state in the Empire. Could this court, even more marvelous than the king's, belong to her?

Cassia tilted her head back, trying to take in the sheer size of the structure, but it was too big to grasp. It made her feel tiny, almost anxiously dwarfed by the weight of all that stone. And yet, its vast expanse seemed to invite her spirit upward and send her aloft.

She couldn't fathom how the masons had gotten the granite blocks to fit together so perfectly. It didn't even look like there was any mortar holding them together. The wall ran in a smooth curve without a single edge or angle.

Humans had built this. The Sandira had demonstrated their greatness, stone by stone, generation by generation. She felt more moved by this than any imposing Tenebran palace or mage temple.

What must it feel like to be proud of your ancestors?

She thought back over the whispers she heard in the spirit gates, but came no closer to deciphering them.

When she'd caught her breath, she urged Knight onward. He sniffed around the perimeter of the great court, but to her relief, broke away from it and headed farther across the city.

Her relief was short-lived. An even greater sense of alarm came over her as she realized where Knight was leading her now.

They were headed right for the King's Hill.

She halted Knight at the edge of a stone mason's workshop. Keeping to the shade between the crafters' buildings, she glanced over her shoulder, afraid a royal guard might stop her at any moment and ask what a nobody like her was doing sneaking toward the royal complex.

But all she saw were citizens, traders, and mercenaries. On the crowded streets, it was not so difficult to go unnoticed.

Except by one of those eagles. There was another one perched atop the pole of an awning. Or perhaps the same one.

She looked away from it, her scalp prickling with the sensation of being watched. It might not be one of the guards, but could someone else be observing her activities?

First an innocent shopper in the Sun Market. Now a bird. Perhaps she was letting her suspicions make a fool of her. But just in case, she ducked out of sight under another awning so no one could watch her from the sky.

She gazed out across the bare grass between the king's subjects and the foot of his hill. It was more like a small mountain, a smooth head of granite rising from the plain. The perimeter around it made it appear as if even the citizens of the city didn't dare approach their sovereign too closely.

Some distance away, a broad stone boulevard led out of the city to the base of the mountain. She could imagine all manner of lavish royal or religious processions along that proud way.

But she couldn't see a way up to the mountain. There wasn't a stair or ladder in sight. If the only way up was in the company of people with wings, that was an effective deterrent indeed. But not to someone whom the royal guards owed a favor, it would seem.

"Curse that Monsoon. Of all places in the city for him to be. I trust your nose above all things, Knight. If you tracked him to the King's Hill, then that's where he is."

Cassia frowned, thinking back over every detail of their encounter. She recalled the dirt on his sandals and the dusty streets in the poorer neighborhoods she had passed through. In slums as in the halls of palaces, wherever there were humans, there were unsavory types.

"If Monsoon's friends in high places are that high, I'm not sure I want to know just how low his other friends are. He might be on the gold roster, but do you suppose he has contacts who don't carry fortune blades?"

Knight sniffed her pockets, searching for the treats he knew to expect after a successful hunt. She pulled out a nibble of dried meat for him.

"Monsoon must leave the hill eventually, since he plans to leave the city tonight for a contract. We'll catch him on his way down."

She glanced around again. No guards anywhere. She peered out from under the awning at the sky. The eagle was nowhere to be seen.

She settled onto a nearby barrel to wait, hoping whoever ran this masonry shop wouldn't come out and object to her loitering. She had a good view of the hill from here. Surely she would be able to spot anyone coming and going.

She even caught a glimpse of sun glinting off metal at the top of the hill. She had a perfect view of the guards who lined up at the edge of the bluff, spread their wings and glided down over the city.

Half of them landed on the road, while the rest began circling over the thatch roofs and stone walls as if hunting for prey.

Cassia's heart lurched, but she stayed where she was. There was no reason for them to come searching for her. Whomever they were after, it was surely someone who had committed a deed worse than sitting on a mason's barrel uninvited.

The guards on foot split up into groups of two and spread out. The citizens made way for them, stepping aside to clear a path through the streets. Cassia saw deference in the people's posture and caution on their faces, but no terror. These royal guards did not frighten this king's people, as Lucis's guards frightened Tenebrans.

Whatever their business in this part of the city, she and Knight should simply behave as if they weren't up to anything. She kept a hand on his ruff and murmured the command for silence.

When two of the guards turned toward the stonemason's shop, Cassia decided it would be better to leave voluntarily than be asked not to trespass. As the guards approached the mason's door in the bright sun a few paces away, she slipped through the shade under the awning and into the alley behind the shop. She would find a better place to sit and wait for Monsoon.

Footsteps behind her startled her. She glanced over her shoulder before she could stop herself.

Three of the king's guards had entered the lane.

Her gaze darted from side to side. The stone sides of the crafters' workshops ran in solid, curving lines, barring her escape. The eagle crouched on a nearby roof, its wings a taunt at her lack of freedom.

The guards in front of her crossed their spears and spread their wings, blocking the way forward.

She heard the three behind her draw closer.

Standing in a sun-baked alley in the Sandira Court, she saw around her the cold walls of Solorum Palace. Instead of the Imperial spearmen before her, she saw the hard, pale faces of Tenebran guards and their cruel swords. In that moment, she felt no fear of the Sandira King. It was the thought of another king that filled her with panic.

No clever words came to her mind. She didn't think of a diplomatic strategy. Her hands didn't reach for her papers.

They curled into fists, thumb on the outside. What ran through her mind were the sequences of moves she had practiced over and over in the training ring with Nike as she had tried and failed and tried again in one messy training session after another.

The instinct that had eluded her in the arena took over her body now.

When the guardsman reached for her, she started moving. She heard Nike's voice in her mind, reminding her of her targets.

Instep. Eyes. Groin.

The first guard staggered away from her, shouting. Another man closed in.

Use your smaller size to your advantage.

She darted under his defenses and bruised his ribs, sliding away before he could take hold of her.

The other two guards were waiting for her. But they didn't get near.

Knight didn't wait for a command to join her in the fight. His growl tore through the air. His fur blurred before Cassia's eyes. Then a spear was clattering on the ground with splashes of blood, and a guard was doubling over his mangled arm.

Oh Goddess. What have I done?

In the chaos Knight had created for her, she ran.

"*Dockk!*" she cried.

She pelted down the alley. She had to get to Lio. His veils. They would hide her from the guards.

Where was Knight?

An image flashed in her mind of him with a spear in his side, and she felt sick.

"Dockk!"

The alley ended at a busy street. Cassia pushed past startled citizens. She heard a few shouts.

"Dockk!"

She heard Knight panting, and then he drew alongside her. She heaved a breath. The crowd parted before his broad shoulders and snapping jaws, and they made it to an empty courtyard surrounded by more stone workshops.

A shadow passed over the ground in front of her. A shadow shaped like a man with wings.

Cassia darted for the nearest shelter, an awning attached to the side of a shop, which sheltered an empty cart. She crouched under the awning, holding onto Knight for dear life, and made sure their own shadows didn't extend outside the fabric covering.

She tried to catch her breath and think. With the guards searching the air, she would have to sneak back to Lio under shelter. Could she make it to the trading camps without getting caught?

When a man appeared directly in front of her, she scrambled to her feet, her back to the cart.

The elusive mercenary she had been hunting for all day had found her.

Monsoon seemed to have come out of nowhere. He presented a strange picture, shirtless, barefoot and unarmed. But the look in his eyes reminded her he was dangerous.

Knight faced the mercenary, his hackles up, his low growl rolling across the space between them.

Energy pounded through Cassia's limbs. *Instep. Eyes. Groin.*

Questions flitted through her mind with the fighting moves. What was Monsoon doing here? How had he gotten down from the King's Hill in the few moments she had been running from the guards?

"Just the man I was looking for," she bluffed in Divine. "I was hoping I could ask you a few questions."

"Any moment," he answered in Vulgus, "the king's guards will catch up to you, and you won't be the one asking the questions. You can stay here and get arrested, or you can come with me."

"The king will regret arresting a citizen of Orthros. I'm not going anywhere with you."

Monsoon took a step closer. "You think a piece of paper from Orthros matters? You can hide your hair and speak Divine, but they know what you are. A shadowlander in the Empire. Take your chances with me." He gave her a smile that sent a chill down her spine. "I guarantee I'm much friendlier than they are."

"I'm not leaving Lio."

"They won't touch the Hesperine. They wouldn't risk angering Orthros."

"Anyone who touches me will anger Orthros."

He huffed a breath, then looked from Knight to Cassia. He gave his head a shake. "It's a good thing I'm not scared of Hesperines."

He ducked under the awning so fast that she almost wasn't ready. She had barely enough reaction time to position her body.

When he grabbed for her, she slammed her foot down on his instep and drove her elbow into his ribs. His shocked grunt was immensely satisfying. She took advantage of his surprise and poked him in the eye.

She was just about to ram her knee into his groin when he blocked her, throwing her off balance.

She had spent the element of surprise. With two expert moves, he gained control and pinned her against him, her back to his chest and her arms trapped at her sides by his iron grip. She tried to kick, but he lifted her off her feet with disheartening ease and dragged her out from under the awning.

"Where did a Tenebran woman learn to fight like that?" he demanded.

"From the Stewards of Orthros, you bloodless vulture! I told you, I'm not a Tenebran!"

While he wasted his breath on a curse, she called out to Knight, *"Ckabaar!"*

The command that had inspired Knight to destroy a pack of heart hunters' mongrels now met with...silence.

"Knight?" she cried.

"He's fine. Mweya's Wings, I'm not here to kill your dog."

Knight backed under the cart, his tail between his legs.

"What did you do to him?" Cassia had never seen him respond that way to anyone except the Guardian of Orthros.

"The guards won't hurt the dog, either." He put his hand over her mouth.

She bit the inside of his hand, but he didn't let go, cutting off her chance to scream.

Their shadows struggled on the ground at her feet. An impact went through his body, and a rush of air swept from behind her. Then his shadow sprouted a pair of wings.

The shadow pinions spread, and she glimpsed the real feathers that cast them at the edges of her vision. They pumped, and the ground dropped away. They were airborne.

Cassia screamed uselessly into her captor's hand. This was nothing like levitating with Lio. The wind roared in her ears. Her eyes watered. And the man carrying her was never still. She felt the vibrations in his body of his wingbeats.

"If you scream again, I'll drop you," Monsoon said. "Do you promise not to scream?"

She gave a grudging nod.

He released her mouth and adjusted his grip on her. There came another rush of wind, the snap of wings, and suddenly they were carried smoothly aloft, soaring.

Her stomach felt like it was plummeting to earth. Her mind chose that moment to indulge in an unreasonable sense of wonder. She was flying.

They swept over the entirety of the city. The great courts looked huge even from up here. She glimpsed inside their guarded confines for the first time. Men in elaborate clothes displayed their wings proudly. Women sported leopard tails like luxurious trains. Girls with striped manes danced in what appeared to be a ritual of some kind.

They flew past the boundaries of the city. On the rolling green plains below, vast herds of cattle milled about like a child's toys. Then the pastures gave way to waving golden grass and trees clustered around brilliant blue watering holes that captured little pieces of the sky.

As Monsoon sped over the wilds, Cassia saw animals she had only heard of in Zoe's storybooks. Herds of giraffe seemed to race with them. Families of elephants lumbered along, their long noses swinging. Sunning on a rock was a golden lion like Apollon's familiar, surrounded by his lionesses and cubs tussling in the grass.

Monsoon carried her through moment after moment of fear and wonder, as the tent where Lio slept faded farther and farther behind them.

ENEMIES UNKNOWN

S HE WASN'T SURE HOW long they flew. It felt like hours. It had been easier to calm her panic when she had been buried in an avalanche for minutes.

Eventually she forced her mind into some semblance of order and began to strategize. She had gotten herself out of a number of dangerous situations, from talking her father out of executing her to escaping the clutches of one of the Old Masters. She had never had to persuade a man who was kidnapping her by air to put her down.

"What do you want?" she shouted over the wind.

"For you not to bother me."

"Kidnapping me is a strange way to remove me as an annoyance."

"This is the last thing I want to do today, I assure you. But I can't very well let the guards arrest you."

"You really expect me to believe you're helping me, after you tried to scare me yesterday?"

"If you'd listened to me, you wouldn't have stayed in the city long enough for the guards to come after you."

"What will stop them from coming after you? Flying off isn't very effective when the men chasing you have wings, too."

"That's true, if you aren't me." There was a smirk in his voice. "We weren't followed from the city. You're welcome."

Arrogant vulture. His shapeshifting abilities were powerful, but he would need to eat, drink, and rest, wouldn't he? Eventually his wings would tire, and he would have to land. That would be her opportunity to escape.

Unless he decided to drop her first.

Did he intend to kill her? If so, he could easily have done so already. He had only to let go.

Perhaps he wanted to make sure they were far enough from civilization not to draw attention.

She steeled herself against her fear. Her life had not ended in a snowy ravine in the mountains. She wouldn't let it end down there on a deserted stretch of wilderness.

She should keep him talking, keep trying to discover his intentions, and most of all, keep him interested in her continued survival.

"Whatever it is you want," she reasoned, "the money I can pay you is better."

He descended without warning. Wind roared in her ears, and her stomach dropped again.

"If you have to vomit," he shouted, "warn me first."

She contemplated aiming for him. But she would prefer not to give him the satisfaction of seeing her sick, so she didn't speak and kept swallowing.

His landing was surprisingly graceful. He set her on the ground without a jostle. But he didn't let her go.

His arms were like a vise. "It's not in your best interests to start running the moment I let you go. You would get lost, and then I would have to find you, and it would be a waste of time."

She recalled the knife fighter's warning. One of the rules of dealing with Monsoon: don't waste his time.

Well, she wasn't about to run off like a frightened rabbit the moment he released her, in any case. She would devise the perfect scheme to escape him at the most advantageous moment. "I won't run."

He hesitated, as if he doubted her. Finally he sighed and released her.

She staggered away from him, finding her balance. She had the urge to throw herself down and kiss the ground. It felt marvelously solid under her. But she stayed on her feet and kept alert.

She turned to get a look at her captor. She thought she knew what to expect, but she was wrong. At the sight of him this close, and she stared, awestruck.

His living wings flexed, as much a part of him as his arms and legs. His feathers gleamed in the sun, a deep, warm brown-black like his skin, with light tawny feathers on the undersides. He folded his pinions, and they lay smoothly against his back.

She shut her mouth and tried to draw useful conclusions. Lio had said each bloodline of the Sandira people had a different animal patron. Monsoon must come from a clan favored by eagles. So did the royal guard, although their patron seemed to be a different variety of eagle.

She didn't know how many ranks of warriors might serve the Sandira King, organized based on their shapeshifting abilities. Was Monsoon a former guard who had turned to the mercenary life?

Had he chosen to leave for his own reasons, or washed out? She should try to find out. Learning about his past and what motivated him could be useful against him.

She kept an eye on him while she straightened her robes and mustered as much dignity as she could. The scarf she'd been wearing was long gone, her hair a tangled mess. But the straps holding her gardening satchel closed had held.

When she opened the bag to check the contents, he made no move to stop her. But he did watch her.

Now she realized why his scrutiny had felt so uncanny when they had met. He watched her with the focus of a bird of prey, his gaze darting at her every minute move. She had little doubt he had the eyes of an eagle, as well as its wings.

She angled her back toward him, trying to make sure everything was there without putting her entire arsenal on display. The feeling of her spade in her hand and the sight of Solia's pendant reassured her.

When she turned back to him, he held out a paper. "Can you read?"

Standing at arm's length, she snatched it from his hand. "Of course I can." He didn't need to know how slow she was at it. She glanced over the tidy columns of letters, surely multiple Imperial languages written in parallel, and concentrated on the column in Divine.

She gathered that this was an arrest warrant issued by the Sandira King. There was no mistaking her own name written at the top of it.

Just to prove she could, she started to read the first sentence aloud. "'A shadowlander by the name of Cassia, traveling under the alias of Newgift Cassia of Orthros...' It isn't an alias! It's my legal name."

"How did you manage that?" Monsoon drawled.

She made herself work her way through the troubling words, although a headache quickly began behind her eyes, freezing in its intensity.

"'Traveling with false documents...bringing a dangerous animal into the realm...manipulating an honored Hesperine guest...! Stealing a letter of marque from one of the Empress's privateers...illicit gate travel... exploiting the hospitality of honest citizens...' Lies, all of it!"

"Just think how much more notorious you'll be once they add 'attacking and mutilating the king's guards' to the list of charges."

Shame crept over her. That was a charge she couldn't deny.

Monsoon crossed his arms over his chest. "According to what I've heard, the privateer has three witnesses from Marijani, one of whom is recovering from a serious brain injury."

She looked up from the paper, her fury making her hands clench. "These accusations, at least, are unjust. I thought better of the Empire."

"That's insulting, coming from a shadowlander."

She gathered her pride and her wits. She had more questions than answers at this moment, but one thing was clear.

She had made enemies in the Empire.

This wasn't an accident. It was a coordinated attack on her reputation and her safety. Whoever had concocted these charges, they knew exactly what she had done since the moment she'd arrived, and they had carefully cast each of her actions in a false light.

Who? Why? Gomba and his water mages hadn't known about her arrival, and they hadn't followed her to the Sandira Court. They were not the masterminds behind this, although they seemed all too glad to help whoever was. Whom had she offended, and why were they determined to get her arrested?

She would unmask her enemies and discover their purposes. But first, she had to escape the immediate threat before her.

Was Monsoon somehow connected to the conspirators? He seemed more like an opportunist who was taking advantage of the unfolding situation.

"Is it the reward money you want?" Cassia waved at the huge sum listed at the bottom of the page. "I will pay you twice that much."

"You expect me to believe you can afford that?"

"My bloodline has been amassing a treasury for sixteen hundred years. Of course I can afford it."

"Are you really worth that much to the Hesperines?"

"You don't understand. It's *my* bloodline's treasury. *I* can pay you."

"They let you into their coffers? I always did say Hesperines are too trusting."

She reached into her satchel and pulled out her coin purse, hefting it in her hand. "Here's a preview of my resources, but for you to get the full amount, I'll have to be alive to see to it you're paid. Do you want a reward from the authorities after going through a lot of paperwork, or do you want twice the reward from me, easy and quiet?"

"I want only one thing." He stalked closer to her, his wings spreading, casting a shadow over her.

She held her ground.

She was unprepared for the naked anger in his gaze. "I want to make it clear to you that you should get out of the Empire. Never set foot here again. You belong in Tenebra."

"Where I belong is Orthros. But I will not leave the Empire until I finish my quest."

She stared him down, giving him the look she had shown the king and the Collector, the one that revealed no hint of the fear tearing at her inside.

He held her gaze for a long moment. Then he gave a huff and turned away. His shoulders hunched. Was he going to fly away and leave her here?

He didn't. He disappeared before her eyes.

She scanned the skies above her. She didn't see a bird, much less a birdman. That vulture kept taking her by surprise.

Was this his plan, then? To leave her stranded in the wilderness? Oh, she was very safe from the guards all the way out here. Not so safe from the lions.

She observed her surroundings. He had dropped her near a skinny, twisted tree. She sought refuge in the spotty patch of shade offered by its branches. There she found a small campsite all but hidden in the grass. There was a tent large enough for one person, a stash of waterskins, and a wallet of dried meat.

She seriously considered taking the provisions and fleeing. But finding her way would be difficult, and she had no way of knowing if she would encounter a settlement before her food and water ran out. She knew nothing about the flora here, so foraging would be impossible.

She cursed. There were chapters on veld and savanna flora in the book on plants that Master Kona had given her. If only Cassia were a better reader, she might have made it that far into the text. She had stalled in the introduction.

She could remember every single one of the beautiful diagrams. But unable to read the captions, she didn't know which plants were medicine and which poison. She really should have offered to help the traders with their alchemy. She might have learned something.

Cassia dug in her satchel for the maps she had procured on Marijani. One showed the entire Empire. She spread it out on a patch of scrubby grass and knelt in front of it.

The Sandira Court was clearly indicated by a little drawing of a stone complex. The next nearest city marked on this map was another, smaller court. It appeared close, but given the scale of this map, it would be an impossible distance on foot.

But an easy distance with one Hesperine step. Lio could find her anywhere. All he had to do was focus on her blood, and he could come to her side no matter how far apart they were.

If nothing had happened to him.

Her anger felt vast enough to fill the wilderness. Fast and strong enough to carry her to Lio's side. If she had magic, she would never have been forced to leave him behind. She would protect her Grace as powerfully as he protected her.

Instead, she was stuck here, unable to lift a finger if someone back in the city threatened him. He lay defenseless in Slumber.

And yet his magic rested in her mind, whispering comfort to her. She drew a deep breath, closed her eyes, and turned within.

The distance between her and Lio seemed to disappear. She felt as if she could open her eyes and find him right next to her.

As long as the mind ward held strong, she knew he was well, and they would be together again soon.

A HINT OF A HEART

THE SUN SEEMED TO have barely lowered. Shouldn't it have moved more by now? It must have been nearly a human hour since Monsoon had dropped her here.

She was still on the alert, so when he appeared out of thin air before her, she leapt to her feet, her spade in her hand.

He lifted his palms, his mouth twisting with amusement. "A gardening spade? Really?"

She decided not to waste the advantage of surprise by telling him what a decent weapon it made, with a sharp, filed edge running along one side. Not to mention it had become a magical artifact after all the times she had used it in situations involving Hesperine blood magic.

Monsoon sighed. "I thought we established I'm not trying to kill you."

"The warrant doesn't specify if I'm wanted dead or alive. Since you seem determined to turn down my more lucrative offer, how do I know you don't want to collect a reward on my corpse?"

"Gods, sometimes I don't fully appreciate how barbaric Tenebra is. All arrest warrants in the Empire require the wanted person to be apprehended alive. The Empress doesn't allow guards to go around murdering people."

Hands on his hips, he turned away from her, then back again. The restless energy in him suggested he was frustrated, angry, even.

But when he spoke this time, his tone was actually gentle. "There are other things that Tenebran men do to women that you do not need to be afraid of here. It would never enter my mind, and if I met a man like that, I wouldn't wait for the guards to arrest him alive."

At least she didn't have to fear that. It was common knowledge in Orthros that rape was almost unheard of in the Empire. The culture here didn't give rise to that kind of behavior in men, and women's position in society didn't place them at men's mercy.

She lowered her spade. "I believe you."

He heaved a sigh and looked away again. "Good."

Now that her sense of self-defense had calmed, she noticed what he had brought with him. Lio's and her packs and trunks from the tent sat on the ground at Monsoon's feet.

Since he wasn't interested in her money or the reward for her capture, she could certainly rule out thievery as his motive. Was this a peace offering he thought to use to earn her trust for his own ends?

"You brought our belongings," she observed. "What a considerate kidnapper."

"You wouldn't believe what I went through to get these things back after the king had them confiscated. It's a good thing I have connections."

"What has he done to Lio?" she demanded.

"I told you not to worry about him."

"Is he all right?" Her voice rose.

Monsoon scowled. "Looks like the guards are taking pains not to involve him. The king likes Hesperines."

"If your connections can smuggle our trunks out of the city, can they do the same for an unconscious Hesperine? I could make it worth your while. Surely it would be possible, since you can traverse."

"Spirit walk," he corrected. "This is the land of my ancestors, where I can walk through the spirit phase without a gate. But I won't drag your Hesperine here. What possessed his goddess to make him so tall? And I'm not bringing your dog, either. I've had my wings bitten before, and I don't wish to repeat the experience, thank you. No reason to go to all that bother when he can just step to you as soon as the sun goes down. Let *him* bring the dog."

Despite his grousing, Monsoon didn't appear tired. He had flown for hours, then used magical travel twice in a single afternoon, all without breaking a sweat. Who was he?

Someone who could help her get Lio out of the city, but wouldn't.

"Allow me to make one thing very clear," Cassia said. "If something happens to him, I will make sure you regret it."

He gave his signature snort.

Fine. Let him dismiss her as a threat. He would be all the more surprised when she made her move.

He tossed a hand in the direction they had come. "It doesn't make any sense for you to show up here on the arm of a Hesperine. How did you manage to hitch a ride across the world with him in the first place?"

"Hitch a ride?" She took a step toward him.

His sneer didn't change.

"I never hitched a ride anywhere," she told him. "I made it every step of the way on my own strength. There was never anyone to carry me—except once, when Lio pulled me out of the snow and carried me over the border into Orthros, and I was safe for the first time in my life. Even then I had to fight the free lords of Tenebra, the Mage Orders of Cordium, and necromancers with power beyond your worst nightmares just for the privilege of never setting foot in Tenebra again."

She ripped the arrest warrant in half. "That pirate Gomba doesn't frighten me. The Sandira King and his guards don't frighten me. And there is certainly nothing frightening about you. Now tell me. Will you get out of my way, or must I knock you aside?"

He took a breath, his eyes widening. Then he started laughing.

He laughed long and hard. But she had to admit, it didn't sound unkind.

Finally he rubbed his face, shaking his head. "Mweya's Wings."

Cassia curled her fists around the pieces of the warrant, crumpling them. "You won't be so amused when Lio wakes up and finds me gone."

"I don't plan to be here when he comes for you. I would tell you to have him step you out of the Empire as soon as he gets here, but I can see now that you won't take my advice." He gave her one more long look, then lifted a hand. It almost looked like a salute. "There are forces in the Empire you *should* fear. If you don't want to become acquainted with them, be more careful from now on."

He turned his back to her, spreading his wings again.

Their only lead on Ukocha, their best chance of finding Solia, was about to literally fly away.

"Wait!" Cassia cried.

He sighed. "What?"

His role in all this was a mystery. Why save her from arrest, only to try to drive her out of the Empire? Why give up the reward and refuse a bribe from her?

"You know you have something I need," Cassia guessed. "You think to drive the price up with every step you take away from me. I admit, your bargaining tactics are impressive. What will it take? Shall I buy out whatever contract you planned to travel for tonight and pay for one of my own?"

"I told you, I don't want your money."

"There are many things more valuable than coin. So what's your price for telling me what you know about Ukocha's whereabouts?"

"She won't appreciate you dragging your troubles to her."

He didn't outright deny he knew something about her. "Surely you know a route to her that will ensure none of this trouble follows us."

"I won't lift a finger to help you," he said over his shoulder. "If you won't leave, you'll have to fend for yourself."

"I'm not here to harm the Empire."

"You couldn't if you tried, little shadowlander."

So much for an appeal to his Imperial citizenship. Would he believe her if she tried to explain how much she cared about this place? "I've done nothing but try to be a good guest. I'm supposed to come here as a diplomat after my Gifting."

He turned around, his eyes narrowed.

She dug her heel into the torn scraps of paper that threatened the future she wanted so much. How had she become a wanted criminal in the homeland of her mentor and one of her Queens?

"I'm almost a Hesperine," she insisted. "I was just hours away from my Gifting when we had to delay it."

He looked skeptical. "If you're so determined, why not go through with it?"

She should have. If they hadn't delayed her Gift Night, none of this would have happened. Instead, she was stuck with the liability of her humanity.

That was all she had to work with. Her humanity—and Monsoon's. He didn't seem to have much sympathy for her, but perhaps she could build some. As long as she didn't reveal they were looking for a shadowlander.

"We stopped because we learned that someone in the Empire needed our help." Cassia danced around lies of omission and gave Monsoon a version of the truth. "Fifteen years ago, a little girl of only seven lost her sister. She asked Hesperines for help saving her, but it was too late. Ever since, she believed her sister to be dead."

He drew in a sharp breath. There. A hint he had a heart somewhere under his temper.

She kept trying. "That night destroyed her. Nothing had the power to put her back together except the love Hesperines have shown her. She lives in Orthros now, where Lio's bloodline has welcomed her with open arms. But on her Gift Night, we learned that her sister is actually still alive."

"Bleeding hearts from Orthros," he muttered. But he didn't leave.

"We came to find her sister and bring her home to Orthros, where she can be part of our family, too." Cassia fingered the pendant inside her satchel. "If she could have her sister and her Hesperine family…it's a dream we won't give up on."

He grimaced and looked up at the sky.

"The Ashes can tell us what happened to her, perhaps even where she is now. That's why we need to find Ukocha."

He was silent for a long moment. Then he muttered something under his breath that might have been a curse or a prayer. "You're the greatest bother I've dealt with in years, you know that? And that's saying something."

She gritted her teeth. She didn't care if he insulted her, but for him to turn his sharp tongue at Solia's plight rankled her. "Well, then, why assign yourself the oh-so-unwanted task of bringing me out here?"

"I didn't volunteer myself for it."

"Then who had you do it?" Could she get him to reveal that?

There was a sardonic glint in his eyes. "You did."

"I beg your pardon?"

"You want to know who I work for? You."

She stared at him.

"You want to find Ukocha, correct?" he prompted.

"Of course."

"Consider me hired. I can take you to her."

"You know where she is?"

"I can hunt anything and anyone. Those who want someone found know to come to me."

She shook her head, hesitant to trust his sudden change of heart. "What made you decide to help me?"

Just as he had when they first met, he looked into her face as if he saw a great deal more there than just her freckles. But all he said was, "Clients from Orthros pay well."

She had to wonder if there was more to it. But at the end of the day, he was a mercenary, and she had money. In Cassia's experience, the most basic human motivations usually won out.

"Kidnapping your client is rather extreme, but I suppose you wouldn't want the guards to arrest your payday. Do you charge extra for personal delivery on wing?"

He let out a surprised laugh. "No. I'll throw that in for free."

"Well, I won't dock your pay for the discomfort of the ride. I agree that your company—unpleasant as it is—is preferable to the guards." She held out her coin purse.

"Hold on to that for now," he advised. "It's not enough to cover my fee, and you might need spending money where we're headed."

"Very well. We will negotiate a reward befitting your efforts once we've found Ukocha, and I will see to it you receive it from my bloodline's treasury."

"I don't think paying me is what that Hesperine of yours will have in mind when he wakes up. Best make myself scarce until you've explained matters. I'll give him till at least midnight to finish his temper tantrum."

His wings flexed, the muscles in his body bunched, and he launched himself from the ground.

Midair, he wrapped his wings around himself, until all she could see was a blur of feathers. When he spread them again, they were smaller, and there was no longer a man before her, only a large eagle with a red-brown mantle and gray markings.

The one who had been following her all over the city.

She watched him fly away and out of sight. He was no less a mystery, but at least she could cross him off the list of mysteries who were trying to harm her.

Her gaze landed on a packet of papers sitting on the top of one of the trunks. Her mail? She rifled through the letters, only to discover they had been opened. By the king's guards?

But Monsoon had somehow managed to bring them to her.

She curled up with her back to the trunks and opened Komnena's letter, a piece of home.

My dears,

We would be delighted to meet you at the Sandira Court. In fact, at any mention of this haven of masons, it is difficult to keep Apollon at home. He has many friends among the stoneworkers of the city.

Therein lies the problem. He is rather well known there, not only in the masonry workshops, but also in the Court of Claws, where the Blood Errant have been known to spar. I've accompanied him often enough that neither of us could visit without getting swept up in a warm welcome. Undoubtedly, word of an Elder Firstblood's family in the city would carry to the King's Hill.

Since you two want as little attention as possible, let us meet you at your next stop. As soon as you are ready to leave the Sandira Court, let us know, and we will join you in a less conspicuous place.

Love,
Mother

Cassia was the Grace-daughter of Elder Firstblood Apollon, she reminded herself. Surely there was a solution to this debacle with the Sandira King.

Next, she untied the purple ribbon from Zoe's latest note.

Dear Lio and Cassia,

I can't believe it!! You met Captain Ziara and she gave me a presant!!! It's the most prettiest brooch I ever saw and now I can wear a real pirate treasure in my hair when we play privateers and evryone will know it's from the real Captain Ziara!!! I can't wait for all the stories about her!!! Thank you so so so so much!!!

I wore it to my first courier lesson and I did better than I thought! Our teacher says I'm good at stepping! She asked me to help others!

Can people in the shaep shiftr city turn into goats? Can I can learn how? Will you ask them? Then I can talk to Moonbeam and Aurora!

I'll see you soon and you can tell Bosko and me all about Captain Ziara!!

Love love love,
Zoe

Cassia laughed, her heart aching. Zoe had clearly been too excited to seek assistance with her spelling. Cassia suspected there were no exclamation marks remaining in Orthros since Zoe had received her gift.

But apprehension came over her when she saw that the oracle had sent her and Lio a letter as well.

Dear Lio and Cassia,

It is true that my affinity brought me tidings of your encounter with Ziara long before your letter reached me. Even so, I enjoyed reading about it in your own words. Your honesty is commendable, although it comes as no surprise to me.

What was a surprise was your decision. In my visions, your free Will has always made it impossible to tell for certain whether you would agree to Ziara's favor.

I concur that discretion about the whole matter is the best course of action. The Empress would never tolerate one privateer stealing another's letter of marque or her Hesperine allies taking sides in such a feud. Officially.

Unofficially, Her Imperial Majesty does not regret Gomba's absence from her service. So if one of "Kassandra's boys" did an unofficial favor for the Empress's favorite privateer, let no more be said of it, except in the tall tales sure to circulate through the Moon Market.

I will enjoy hearing them next time Ziara and I have a drink. She is too clever to wager with an oracle, but if she had taken my bet that

Huru would get her pearl earrings back, she would owe me a bottle of Night Rose.

The wisdom of the oracle can only illuminate the possible consequences of your actions. It lies with you and your conscience to evaluate them. I can see that you are confident in your decision to perform the favor Ziara requested of you.

The Empress may laugh at the mischief known to occur under the acacia flag and the purple sail. I know I need not remind you that once you've left our protection, the alliance is no laughing matter.

Keep making independent decisions, my dears.

- Kassandra

Cassia's heart sank. Kassandra had faith in them. And yet Cassia's independent decisions today had left her stranded in the wilderness and their ally's guards bleeding.

TORN

L IO'S FIRST BREATH OF the night did not carry his Grace's scent. Mortal hearts beat nearby, but not Cassia's.

He reached for her place beside him, knowing already that he would find it empty. Alarm fueled his thoughts, and he forced his torpid body to sit up, wrenching his eyes open.

Knight lay at his feet, his ears drooping in misery.

Lio listened to the pulses of the humans outside the tent, searching among the traders' auras for his Grace.

She was gone.

She would never go far without Knight. She was missing, and her guardian was here, distraught.

Something had happened to her.

Lio's fangs unsheathed. His magic roared out for her.

His power swept the city, cascading past tens of thousands of minds, seeking the one bound to his own. His senses reached the edges of the metropolis and his magical range. She was nowhere to be found.

Then a thelemantic cord pulled him beyond his limits. Away, outside the city. Past the wild minds of animals.

He found her with a precision he had never expected. He could always take an arcane step to her side, regardless of the limitations of the physical world. But now he could sense her cardinal direction from him, the amount of distance between them, and the fact that there were no other auras around her.

She had transformed from auric focus to navigational star, defying the normal range for a mind mage, even one of his power.

The mind ward was his hand on her, always touching. He had felt it whenever they were in different parts of the city at home. Now he realized just what a long reach their new and deeper connection had.

She was hundreds of miles to the northwest of the Sandira Court, where the low veld gave way to empty savanna. There was nothing out there except Cassia—alone, angry, and frightened.

With a tide of magic at his fingertips, ready for any threat, he stepped himself and Knight to her side.

He found himself by a campfire. Cassia was a shadow at the edge of the flames. She leapt up and threw herself into his arms.

He held her so tightly that there was not a breath between their bodies. He needed to feel her heart beating against his. "Goddess. Just heartbeats. That's how long I didn't know where you were. But just heartbeats is too long."

"Thank Hespera you're all right."

"You suffered Goddess knows what while I slept, and you're worried about me? What happened to you? How did you get here?"

"Monsoon brought me."

Fury chilled Lio's veins, leaving his magic hard as ice. He spoke quietly, saving his rage for her captor and all the gentleness he possessed for the woman he loved. "Cassia, did he hurt you?"

"He did me no serious harm, although it was hardly a comfortable trip."

"Where is he?"

"He'll be back after midnight."

"I will take you to safety, and then *I will find him.*"

"No, wait! If we leave, we'll lose him."

"Oh, there will be nowhere he can hide from me."

"Don't step me away." Her hands tightened on his arms, as if a mortal could somehow hold him in place.

What did halt him was her adamant refusal.

"Let me explain," she insisted.

"What is there to explain? That man threatened you and took you from my side while I slept! How? What infernal power does he possess?"

"Wings," Cassia said. "He has wings."

"He's one of the shifters?" Lio tried to think of everything he knew about Sandira magic. Not enough. "It doesn't matter. I don't care who he is or how much power he has. I will teach him the consequences of threatening you."

"He's working for us now."

Lio took a step back to look at her, the fractures of anger in his thoughts giving way to understanding. "You went with him willingly?"

"Well, no."

"He kidnapped you."

"But in the end, I turned it to our advantage. I talked him into accepting a contract from us to find Ukocha."

"Bleeding thorns. The only pay he'll get from me is a lesson in how to treat my Grace."

Cassia wrapped one arm around Knight, who was making frantic attempts to insert his furry mass into their embrace. "He was not my chosen means of escape. But the fact remains that if he hadn't taken me, the guards would have."

Lio's pulse pounded. "The guards tried to—arrest you?"

"The charges are false!"

"What charges?"

She snatched a number of dusty, crumpled pieces of paper off the ground and held them out. "The ones on the warrant for my arrest."

Lio levitated the disjointed pieces so he could make out the whole. He read through a barrage of lies about his Grace. "How dare they make such accusations against you? How dare the king send his guards after you as if you were a criminal?"

She was supposed to be safe here. How could Lio have let this happen? "How did the guards get to you through my veils?"

"Your veils didn't fail, my love. Everything would have been fine if not for that godsforsaken warrant. I had a plan."

He knew that tone. She was negotiating. "Cassia, the veils over our tent were tailor made to hide you. How did anyone find you?"

"I was extremely careful. I only failed to predict the warrant."

He realized there was only one explanation. The simplest one, the one he hadn't wanted it to be. "You left the tent."

She took a step back, her hand in Knight's ruff. "I had Knight with me. I made sure Monsoon was *not* in the Court of Claws before I entered."

"You went to the Court of Claws—where the royal guards are."

Her face was composed, her tone matter-of-fact. "I didn't know about the warrant yet, and neither did they. They let me in without any trouble."

Lio dug a hand through his hair. "Cassia—!"

She squared her shoulders. "The day audience was different from the night spectators. There were mercenaries there we hadn't interviewed yet. I found out something important. Monsoon isn't just good at finding people. He knows where Ukocha is."

"Oh, Goddess. You went looking for him."

"I wanted to wait for you, of course. But I also learned he was due to leave tonight for another contract, so I had no choice. If I had waited, he would have gotten away."

"You sought him out after he threatened you?"

"I was very careful while Knight and I tracked him through the city. When I realized he was on the King's Hill, I couldn't follow him. So I decided to wait until he came back down. Unfortunately, the guards came down from the hill first."

She had been right there, easy prey for them. How could she sound so calm, so reasonable as she described it? "You were almost arrested!"

"I was on my way back to the tent," she said, as if that made it better somehow. "I tried to get back under your veils. Monsoon got to me before the guards did."

"Anything could have happened to you!" Lio's magic howled within him.

Knight laid his ears flat on his head and whined.

"Lio, I'm all right."

"Cassia, you promised you would stay safe."

"I made every effort to keep that promise."

"You left the tent!"

"I had to!"

There she was. The lady of ice, shattering like a blizzard over Orthros, rattling the foundations of everything immortal power could build.

"I could have lost you," he said.

Her eyes gleamed with sudden tears, thawing. "I'm not that foolish. I'm not useless, Lio."

"What? Cassia—you are precious beyond words. You are my everything. You can't take risks like that."

"When have I not taken risks?" she cried. "That's all I've done since we met!"

"You weren't supposed to have to do that here."

"I had to do something. I couldn't sit in that tent another moment, wondering if Solia has already been deported back to Cordium."

"I thought I persuaded you long ago that trusting my magic is the best course of action. On a night when a war mage in disguise almost caught us together in the woods."

"You know it's not a question of trust. You also helped me find the courage not to let fear rule my life. I've faced the king and the war mages and the necromancers. I didn't think a stroll through an Imperial city would end like this."

"Ever since Monsoon threatened you, we knew the Sandira Court might be dangerous for you. I thought you weren't going to take any chances."

"What happened to my champion in the woods who told me to take chances with everything?"

"Everything was different then."

"Nothing was different. I was still your Grace. You just didn't know it yet."

"But I knew you were important. More than anyone I had ever met. I was just foolish enough to believe—"

He caught himself before the monumental admission came out of his mouth.

Goddess, he couldn't say that to her. He must never admit such a failure to her. She needed to be able to have absolute faith in him.

She searched his gaze, her own full of hurt. "What, then? What did you say to me then that you do not believe in any more?"

Oh, no. "No, Cassia, that's not what I meant. Our Oath is sacred. Surely you know that."

"What about those first nights of our love seem foolish to you now?"

"Me. I was the fool. Because I thought…"

His uncle's words came back to him…*you hide your wounds to project an image of strength, because you want to make those around you feel safe.* He had been right.

But this time, Lio had only succeeded in wounding Cassia.

It would take their Oath to reassure her. Nothing but the truth would be enough. And he would rather expose his weaknesses than cause her a shred of doubt about their love.

"I was overconfident that I could protect you," he said.

Her aura softened, and she gave her head a shake. "Lio, you did. You always do."

"I beheld the king and thought I understood the monster we were facing. We hadn't realized he had another one behind him."

"There are no Old Masters in the Empire."

"There are still so many reasons you need to be careful. Please, Cassia. Just take some reasonable precautions, as long as you're still human."

Her anger sharpened, shredding through their Union. He hadn't seen her like this since the night he had first asked her to do something dangerous, and she had refused.

All of that was turned on its head. How had they gotten here?

"I won't be helpless," she shot back. "I know I'm just a human. This cage of flesh is all I have to work with. But I made what I could of my own two feet and my ill-formed questions today. I won't sit and be helpless until my Gifting."

"Being a Hesperine doesn't make you all-powerful, Cassia. There are times when immortals feel helpless, too."

That was exactly how he had felt just now. Helpless.

Just like her.

The sun and her mortality had been pulling them apart. But in this moment, they added a powerful current to his empathy with her.

He looked at her, so ferocious and beautiful in her anger. Anger was always her defense of choice. Tonight it was armor against her own humanity.

"I understand, Cassia." He reached into their Union.

She gasped, taking a step toward him.

He let his emotions flow toward her, as he would if she were Hesperine and he wanted to communicate what was in his heart. He felt the mind ward light up in response.

Her eyes widened, and she came forward another step, as if pulled on that tide of emotion. "You can't get all sweet like that in our Union when I—I…"

"When you still want to be angry?" He lowered more of his own inner defenses. He let her feel his fear, his need, and how much he cherished her.

Her eyes slid halfway shut, and her lips parted with a moan. He needed to kiss her.

"You need me," he said.

She crossed her arms, all prickles inside. "It's not fair. Your temper always cools before mine does."

"On the contrary, my rose, your temper is as cold as ice and just as beautiful."

"You can't tell me things like that when I'm trying to stay angry." Her heart pounded, and furious tears hovered on her lashes.

He let her anger wash over him and his love wash into her, the two mingling.

She closed the distance between them and pulled his mouth to hers.

He caught her tightly, molding her to him, and put a hand behind her head to hold her to their kiss. He couldn't erase this day. He couldn't fight day itself. But by night, right now, he could reaffirm their vows with touch.

She gave herself over to their kiss completely. As she sagged against him, she opened her mouth to him, offering up her tongue. His fangs, already unsheathed in defense of her, now lengthened with eagerness to sate her.

But instead of flushing with arousal, her skin was clammy. He pulled back. "Have you eaten anything?"

"I finished the food and water we had left in our packs." Her hands roamed over him.

"Do you feel ill?"

"No." She licked her lips, her eyes dilated.

No human ailment then. "Your Craving symptoms are worse. It's never made you feverish before."

"I've never been torn away from you like this."

Heart hunters had tried. The Collector had tried. A sunbound mercenary with bad manners and a pair of wings had succeeded.

"That will never happen again," Lio vowed against her mouth.

In this kiss, he felt how frightened she had been, how angry she still was. He tasted a deeper fear—the instinctual one that came over them both whenever they were forced apart, even for a matter of hours.

He held her and let her devour his mouth until she drew back to breathe.

"Don't be afraid, even when I'm far from you." He allowed his magic to permeate his words so she would know them in her mind, feel them in the Union. "I could tell exactly where you were, thanks to the mind ward. It doesn't matter how far apart we are. I can pinpoint you like my very own truth star."

"I felt you with me," she gasped. "I knew I wasn't alone."

He slipped his magic along the paths of the ward. Her mind pulled at his power. Goddess, it was intoxicating, as if she were dragging his very essence to her and begging to have it inside her.

"I need you." Her hands fisted in his robe.

"This is no place to care for you, my Grace. Let me take you somewhere safe."

She shook her head. "Here. Now."

The simple demand made Lio's blood pound. The blood he could not let her have. But his magic, his fangs, his body all demanded that he give her everything he had.

He had thought nothing was more powerful than his Craving. But this was—his instinct to sate hers.

With his riled magic, he slammed veil after veil over the campsite. "Forget everything that happened today. Let me hold you and show you that I am here now, and I always will be."

Then her mouth was on his throat, her kisses rough yet so soft, more and more urgent. He took a Hesperine step that placed him behind her. She gasped at the deepening touch of his magic in her mind. Attuning to her inner thoughts, Lio became less and less aware of the fire burning down nearby and Knight posting himself at the edge of camp.

"Forget where we are," he told her. "Forget everything but me."

She let him strip her to her freckled skin there under the moons. He urged her toward the nearby tree until she put her hands out to catch herself on its narrow trunk. Taking her tousled hair in his hand, he draped it over her shoulder to expose the column of her neck.

He ran his hand along her throat, then down her spine. She arched into his touch. Her Craving pulsed out of her, a music he heard in her veins, an intoxicating musk in her scent. More than that, a hunger in her aura that seemed already to be feeding on him, drawing his magic out of his chest and over her skin.

He didn't need to slide his fingers between her legs to know she was ready. With Hesperine speed, he yanked off his robe and unfastened his trousers. When he took her buttocks in both hands, she rolled her hips up in his hold, seeking his body.

He levitated her to meet him and filled her demand in one motion, burying his rhabdos deep in her while he listened to her cry out his name.

She was streaming wet and impossibly tight. Her Craving had primed her for what she needed. Him.

He held her on his rhabdos. "Is that what you wanted, my Grace?"

Her nails scraped into the tree's bark as she panted. "More."

"Always more." He massaged her buttocks, parting her, and adjusted the angle of his hips until he felt her pleasure flare in their Union.

"Yes," she cried. "Goddess, I need you so much."

"I'm here."

Bearing her up on his magic, the pace was his to set. Fast. Hard. He gave her a feast, filling her again and again with his magic and his rhabdos.

Is this what you need? he asked, deep within her mind.

You. Always you. Only you.

I'm here.

She climaxed then. But he didn't release into the silken grip of her krana. He kept pumping into her and watched the shudders moving through her. He held her buttocks as she rocked and rubbed against him.

There was a force greater than her Craving. His power to banish it.

He bent over her and braced one hand over hers against the tree. Her skin was hot against his now.

"Is this what you hunger for?" he asked around his unsheathed fangs. Her hand tangled in his hair, pulling him to her vein.

He sank his fangs into her with the same force as he had joined their bodies. She threw her head back, arching back into him.

He tasted wild excitement in her blood. He too forgot where they were and why. He knew only that she had been taken from him, and now she was here. All his vast magic concentrated on her with the precision of a fang tapping a vein.

They climaxed hard, grinding together on waves of his magic. Her breath came in harsh gasps, as if she sought to drag his power into her lungs. Shocking pleasure crashed through him with every wave of magic she devoured.

As she quieted under him at last, he didn't want to release her. He levitated her more firmly against him, wrapping an arm around her to hold her. He drew long draughts from her vein.

"I'm here," she sighed.

When his own blood hunger cleared from his senses at last, he stood there joined with her, hanging onto the deep Union between them.

"Let me take you home," he said.

"Oh. Don't tempt me, especially when you're holding me like this."

He ran his tongue over the smear of blood on her shoulder. That was precisely why he was asking her now.

"Before we decide anything...I need to tell you what else happened today."

The words rose out of her from a deep well of shame. Taken aback, Lio straightened and gently withdrew from inside her.

She said nothing else while he worked a cleaning spell and retrieved his cloak from their trunks. He recognized her stiff, prideful silence. She was trying to get the words out, but dreaded speaking them.

He wrapped the cloak around them both and settled with her near the fire, holding her close to the warmth of his body. He had no intention of letting her out of arm's reach anytime soon. "Cassia, what happened today?"

"One thing I did was my mistake, Lio. A terrible mistake."

After her impassioned defense of the rest of her actions, he couldn't imagine what would burden her with such guilt. "What can you mean?"

"When the guards surrounded me…" Her breath hitched.

He gentled his hold on her, his power ready to shake out of him again. "Hespera's Mercy, did they hurt you?"

"No. I hurt them."

She described her encounter with the guards as if pulling glass out of herself with every word. "I don't think any of the Stewards would be proud of how I used their training."

"You were outnumbered by armed, trained opponents, and you managed to escape. In a real moment of fear, you succeeded at exactly what you and Nike practiced."

"That's just it. The fear."

His Grace had been afraid, and he had been unable to lift a finger to help her feel safe. He tried to give her the comfort she needed now. "It's always worse in reality. Training can't fully prepare you for making decisions in a crisis. But you excel at handling such situations."

"Not this time. I didn't think, Lio. I didn't strategize. I lashed out to get away. All I could think about was…the king's guards, and how many times they had threatened me…what happens to the people they drag into his solar, who don't come out again…"

"Oh, Cassia. I'm so sorry."

"That isn't how I'm supposed to use my training. Nike taught me to protect myself and others, to act justly. Not to attack our allies. Even though they were trying to arrest me, they're not the enemy. They're the Sandira King's guards, acting according to the law. The king himself is probably acting in good faith, believing that he must protect his people from me, because someone has convinced him I'm a dangerous shadowlander."

Lio was unable to muster any charity for the Sandira King at the moment, but the voice of reason in his mind wouldn't let him ignore the fact that Cassia was correct.

"I should have let them arrest me," said Cassia. "If I had gone with them peacefully, we could have sorted all this out—"

"—with you in the Sandira King's prison?" Lio protested. "Goddess, no."

"The worst thing is, I can't bring myself to regret running away. It doesn't matter how much better prisons are in the Empire. It would still remind me of the king's dungeon. All I can think of is how glad I am that I'm not in a cell."

"Think how glad I am that you're in my arms right now instead."

"But I didn't react as a diplomat should. I didn't even comport myself as a Steward should. What does that make me? Not Hesperine."

"My Grace, you are one of Orthros's truest hearts."

"Not today." She hung her head, her chin trembling. "My Hesperines have given me everything. Life. Love. My very self. And I have failed you all. I'm so ashamed."

He lifted her face. "Whatever the consequences of your actions today, you mustn't blame yourself for how you reacted when the guards cornered you. That shame belongs to the people who hurt you in the past, not to you."

He felt her rapid breathing slow down. "Oh."

"I'm so sorry you had to endure this today. The last thing you needed after surviving Tenebra was to be threatened in a place you felt safe. You are still healing."

He watched the understanding dawn in her gaze and felt the guilt in her aura begin to ease. She leaned into him. "Thank you for reminding me."

"None of this is your fault."

"You're right," she said slowly. "It's not. And my fears haven't been entirely misguided, either. Someone has targeted me. Someone was following me on Marijani."

"What? When?"

"During the day, when I was alone at the Sun Market."

"Why didn't you tell me?"

"I decided it was just my imagination. I'm so suspicious after my life in Tenebra. I thought I was seeing a threat where there was none. Now I believe I was right."

"Tell me everything."

He listened carefully to all the details she could give him about the woman who had followed her through the market. The thought that someone might have been using magic on her while she was out of his reach was unbearable.

Here in the Empire, where she had expected to be free from danger, there were still threats that brought back her darkest memories.

Lio held her and enfolded her in his mind magic, but it didn't feel like enough. He could not change anything that had happened to her today or in her old life.

The best he could give her was their Union, a way for her inner burdens to become his own in truth. But even that was only partial for the time being, the mind ward a bridge to make up for what they couldn't have until her Gifting.

He felt her mind pulling at his magic, as if holding it to her. "None of this would be a problem if I were a Hesperine. I'm so sorry, Lio."

"You've done enough apologizing already tonight."

"I will not heap blame upon myself, but I must take responsibility for my actions. The fact remains that I caused a diplomatic incident. I may have driven a wedge between Orthros and the Empire."

"Your anonymous enemy is the one with the wedge, and the merchant governors and the Sandira King are driving it. The Queens will not tolerate such treatment of any of their people."

"But my reaction cost us the moral high ground in that debate. Tell me truly, Lio. Do you think I have lost my chance at my medallion?"

"Uncle Argyros would never hold any of this against you."

"It is the Queens' final decision whether to approve the candidates he recommends for the diplomatic service."

"When have you ever known the Queens to be harsh in their judgments?"

"Never." She swallowed.

"Annassa Soteira is a mind healer. She will understand what you experienced today better than anyone."

"But knowing I am still so vulnerable to reminders of my past...am I even fit to be a diplomat?"

"Cassia, you have earned the right to any future you want among our people—over and over again, risking your life each time."

"I don't know if the Empire will be impressed with those deeds. Are they likely to accept me as a diplomat from Orthros, after a false warrant and a very real fight with the guards?"

"They should count themselves lucky you still want to come here," Lio growled.

Orthros and the Empire had developed sixteen hundred years' worth of complex diplomacy, and what good had it done Cassia today?

She shook her head. "They can have their choice of qualified Hesperine ambassadors. Why would they open their lands to one they may not trust?"

Lio was all too aware of how fragile an ambassador's medallion could be. There were always positions in the home office, but at the moment, he didn't even find that thought particularly comforting. What comforted him was just the thought of home.

But Cassia had looked forward to serving here, and he could not bear the notion that his Grace might have to do without anything she had dreamed of. "There will be time to decide all of that later, and whatever happens, Orthros will always advocate for you."

"How soon do you think this news will reach home?"

"That's a good question." Lio rubbed his beard. "I'm surprised I didn't wake up to a visit from the Hesperine ambassador. If he knew about this, he would certainly have involved me."

"Do you think Marijani and the Sandira King are trying to keep it quiet?"

"Where was this warrant posted today?"

"I never saw it posted. The guards weren't even showing it around the streets when they were looking for me. I didn't know a thing about it until Monsoon gave me this copy. I think he has contacts from the King's Hill to the back alleys where bladeless mercenaries lurk."

"This is even more unacceptable. Not only have they branded a citizen of Orthros a criminal, they haven't approached the proper Hesperine channels to mediate about the matter."

"What are we going to do?"

"I want to take you home right now, where no one will threaten you."

Cassia twisted her hands together. "I would like to explain everything to the Queens and Uncle Argyros in person. At least we'd have the chance to tell them our side of the story first. I'd much rather them hear about it from us than the Empire's ambassadors."

"I can step you back to House Annassa right now, my Grace." He caressed her face and asked again, "Won't you let me take you home?"

She rested her cheek against his palm. "If we left, would they let me back into the Empire?"

Lio sighed.

"That's what I thought," she said. "I can't travel as a mere visitor anymore, and I'm not sure they'll accept me as a diplomat. That leaves sneaking back into the Empire illegally, in which case, it is wiser not to sneak out in the first place. I can't believe I'm suggesting I stay here as a fugitive. This is a disaster."

"We will have the opportunity to sort it all out, but I want you to be behind the safety of the Queens' ward while we do it."

"You could go home, Lio. You can travel freely. If you gated back to Orthros, you could explain to everyone what happened and decide what to do, then come back for me."

He was shaking his head long before she finished speaking. "Out of the question. I won't leave you here."

"We cannot both leave. Monsoon will not be waiting for us when we return, and we'll lose our only lead on Ukocha."

"We can't trust him to help us find Ukocha. He could betray us."

"I've tried to think through all his possible motivations and what he might have to gain by taking our contract and stabbing us in the back later. But none of it makes sense. If he knows someone who will pay a greater reward for a shadowlander than the king's guards, he would have just taken me to them before you awoke. I'm forced to conclude he really does want our money."

"There must be a better way to find Ukocha." If he had any way to achieve focus on her, he would step past any number of border checkpoints, and to Hypnos with the consequences. But he couldn't pinpoint the aura of a woman he had never met, somewhere in the vast Empire.

"I don't see another way," Cassia said, "not with my diplomatic pass in doubt. We will have to evade my mystery enemy without the benefit of official channels—even though official channels are their weapon of choice."

The only solution available was the mercenary who had threatened and kidnapped his Grace. Lio bared his fangs at the deserted landscape.

Cassia touched his arm. "Can you reconcile yourself to working with him?"

"He could still have ulterior motives we haven't predicted."

Cassia nodded. "We'll have to keep a close eye on him."

"I will keep a Hesperine eye on him."

"One thing that's not in doubt is his skill. He is on the gold roster. And considering his wings, I suppose he was a royal guard before that. Would they have given him permission to become a mercenary?"

"He was probably expelled from their ranks."

"Is that an educated guess, or an accusation from my protective champion?"

"Both. I'm sorry I don't understand the inner workings of the Sandira Court better. It was outside my area of study."

"Oh my. How could you, as a diplomacy student, not consider that you and your Grace might one night be fugitives in the wilderness, with our fate hinging on an oversight in your schoolwork?"

Lio huffed a laugh. "I do know that certain shapeshifting abilities accompany status. The royal guard are all from influential clans who can take the form of birds of prey. So Monsoon has fallen from a lofty nest."

"Whatever we do, we cannot let him find out we're looking for a shadowlander. I led him to believe we're searching for an Imperial human related to a member of our bloodline."

"That was clever. Hiding the truth in plain sight."

"Exactly. So if he passes any information to old comrades of his on the royal guard, they'll still only know about one shadowlander in the Empire. We cannot lead the authorities who are chasing me to Solia as well." Her gaze dropped. "Well, I suppose I am a wanted woman again. I find I don't enjoy it as much this time around."

"Hesperines extricated you from the king and the mages. We are not about to allow the Empire to brand you a criminal."

She patted his chest. "Well, whatever Uncle Argyros hears about this, he will have faith in you, my love."

"You're right." Why did his uncle's trust in him, in that moment, make the situation feel more painful rather than less so? "Do you know you give me courage, Brave Gardener?"

"When we tell Zoe this story, perhaps we should skip the more anxious parts."

"Agreed."

They shared a silent jolt of longing.

"She'll worry when she doesn't get her nightly letter," Cassia said. "We have to send word to the family."

Lio winced. "I'm afraid meeting for a cozy midnight meal is not in our future."

Cassia looked up at him. "We could have been enjoying a trip to goat country with Zoe right now."

"Yes. But Solia is the missing piece of our family. Until we restore her to her place among us, we are not complete."

There came a sudden sheen of tears in her eyes. "Is that really how you feel?"

"Of course." He rested his hand over her heart. "Your pain is my pain. Your love is my love. I will not rest until we find her."

"Thank you, Lio."

THE PLAN

WHEN THE PUMP OF wingbeats reached Lio's hearing, he leapt up and stood between Cassia and the sound. "Someone is flying toward us."

She scrambled to her feet and stood at his side. "Monsoon? Or a guard?"

He recognized the aura on the wind. "The mercenary."

Lio altered his veils, making the area detectable only to Monsoon. The shifter descended from the night sky and landed a few paces away. The campfire wavered as if the air flocked to him, depriving the flames.

Monsoon strolled toward them, folding his wings behind him. Knight cowered. Lio was the only one feeling predatory at the moment, his fangs lengthening with every step Monsoon took nearer to Cassia. The man was favoring one foot. Lio took some undiplomatic satisfaction in the knowledge that the mercenary was still sore from Cassia's attempt to escape him.

Monsoon halted on the other side of the fire. "Happy reunion over? Good. I'll tell you the plan."

Lio stalked forward, letting his magic go ahead of him to fill the space between him and Monsoon. "Before you say another word, I will make a few things clear to you. If you do not understand and agree, the only plan I advise you to make is to get as far away from me as possible."

Monsoon crossed his arms. "You should be thanking me."

"Since we met you, you have insulted Cassia, attempted to frighten her, and hunted her. Then *you took her from my side*. I will not thank you, and you will not do any of those things again."

"Would you rather she be sitting in the Sandira King's prison right now?"

"I would rather you show her consideration and respect."

"Your woman isn't that fragile, silkfoot."

"She is the strongest person I know. All the more reason to treat her well, as she deserves."

Lio thought he sensed a tiny sliver of grudging respect in the man's aura, but it was too fleeting to be sure.

Monsoon quirked a brow at Cassia. "Doesn't seem like you to stand there and let him speak for you."

"I had my say all the way here," she replied. "After what Lio and I went through over the past day and night, I know he needs to have his say, too."

And he was far from finished. He took another step closer to the mercenary. "I will tell you the plan. When I must sleep, Cassia will remain within arm's reach under my veil spells for the duration of my Slumber. If I wake and find that something has happened to her, you will answer to me. If I wake and find a tiny bruise anywhere on her or the smallest cloud over her good mood, you will answer to me!"

"Not worried I'll make sure you don't wake?"

Lio gave him a cold smile. "No. Because you would answer to Orthros, and you know it. No Hesperine has ever been murdered within the Empress's lands. I sincerely doubt you want to make me the first."

Monsoon laughed. He simply wasn't afraid of Lio.

Lio wasn't afraid of Monsoon, either. But he was afraid of what could happen to Cassia.

That gave Lio the advantage. He knew that in diplomacy as in war, it wasn't fearlessness that made you the likely victor. It was having something to lose—someone to fight for.

"Monsoon." Lio let his thelemancy infuse his tone with danger. "Are you familiar with the bond between two Hesperines who are committed to one another for eternity?"

Monsoon shifted on his feet. "It's no secret here in the Empire."

"Then you'll understand the significance when I tell you my life depends on Cassia, and hers on mine."

Shock flashed in Monsoon's eyes, so clearly it took Lio aback. He had hoped to get a reaction out of the man, but that was not the one he had expected.

"You have the Craving for her?" Monsoon demanded.

"As we told you," Lio answered, "she is my intended. She has chosen to stay with me for eternity."

The mercenary gave his head a shake. "There must be some mistake."

"Imperials are usually accepting of human and Hesperine pairings," said Lio. "What do you have against Cassia's and my bond?"

Monsoon rubbed his hands over his face, but the only explanation he offered was a vivid curse.

Cassia put her arm around Lio's waist. "Like the author of my arrest warrant, I think Monsoon is under the impression that I am some sort of master manipulator. He believes I have made you my plaything in order to secure transport from Tenebra to the Empire."

Lio bared his fangs at Monsoon. "Do these look like toys to you?"

"Oh, there's no doubt *you're* playing for keeps," Monsoon said.

"I told you not to insult Cassia again."

Cassia raised her chin. "I don't care what he thinks, any more than I cared what the pontificators in Tenebra believed about me. I have demonstrated my love to you, Lio. Our people know the truth. I have nothing more to prove."

Monsoon flared his wings, and if looks could kill, Lio would be flat on the ground in the Court of Claws with a sword at his throat.

But the man's glare had no such power, and his mortal protests would go unheard against the eternal decree in Lio and Cassia's veins. They were Graced.

"I don't care who you are to her," Monsoon said. "I'm not doing this for your sake, silkfoot."

"Of course not," Lio said. "You're doing it for our bloodline's riches."

Monsoon snapped his wings in an unmistakable gesture of displeasure. "See there, no reason to doubt you're safe with me. Dead customers don't pay."

Lio nodded, satisfied. "As long as you remember that, we will all get along perfectly."

Monsoon crossed his scarred arms over his chest. "Now, do you want me to do the job you hired me for?"

"We need to strategize," Cassia said.

"You should consider yourselves lucky I'm bothering to help you," Monsoon replied. "I can find and retrieve anyone—alive. Sometimes that means search and rescue from the air. Other times, it means knowing whom to ask. Where to apply pressure."

"How do you intend to find Ukocha?" Lio asked.

"I have a contact," Monsoon answered, "but we'll have to travel to get to them, and cross a border on the way."

"Where are we headed?" Lio returned.

"Somewhere you'll never find without my help."

They were about to go blind into unknown territory. Their only guide was a man who despised Cassia's origins. Her only recourse were her documents, now as useless as the medallion Lio had left in the ashes of Rose House.

But she didn't need a piece of paper, and she didn't need a diplomat.

She had her Grace, one of the most powerful immortal mages on any side of the world.

Lio was not afraid to use his power. He would keep Cassia safe at any cost, and they would put their family back together again until everyone they loved was safe as well.

"Let's get moving," Monsoon said.

Lio looked down at the man from his bloodborn height. "We are ready."

Lio and Cassia's story continues in
Blood Grace Book 6, *Blood Union Part Two.*
Learn more at
vroth.co/union2

GLOSSARY

Abroad: Hesperine term for lands outside of Orthros where Hesperines errant roam, meaning Tenebra and Cordium. See **Orthros Abroad**

adamas: strongest metal in the world, so heavy only Hesperines can wield it. Invented in secret by Nike.

affinity: the type of magic for which a person has an aptitude, such as light magic, warding, or healing.

affinity reading: magical test to determine a person's affinity.

Akron's Torch: an artifact of the Order of Anthros, which holds great magical power and symbolizes their authority. Prometheus stole it from the Hagion of Anthros, enraging the Aithourian Circle. It is now in the possession of his mother, Kassandra.

Alea: one of the two Queens of Orthros, who has ruled the Hesperines for nearly sixteen hundred years with her Grace, Queen Soteira. A mage of Hespera in her mortal life, she is the only Prisma of a temple of Hespera who survived the Ordering.

Alexandra: royal firstblood and Eighth Princess of Orthros, the youngest of the Queens' family. Solaced from Tenebra as a child. She raises silkworms for her craft. Lio's childhood sweetheart.

Alkaios: one of the three Hesperines errant who saved Cassia as a child. He retrieved the ivy pendant from Solia's body for her. He and his Grace, Nephalea, recently settled in Orthros after years as Hesperines errant with his Gifter, Nike.

Anastasios: Ritual Firstblood who Gifted Apollon, founder of Lio's bloodline. He was a powerful healer and Prismos of Hagia Boreia, who sacrificed his life to help Alea protect their Great Temple from the Order of Anthros's onslaught.

Annassa: honorific for the Queens of Orthros.

Anthros: god of war, order, and fire. Supreme deity of the Tenebran and Cordian pantheon and ruler of summer. The sun is said to be Anthros riding his chariot across the sky. According to myth, he is the husband of Kyria and brother of Hypnos and Hespera.

Apollon: Lio's father, an elder firstblood and founder of Orthros. In his mortal life before the Ordering, he was a mage of Demergos. Transformed by Anastasios, he was the first Hesperine ever to receive the Gift from one of the Ritual firstbloods. Renowned for his powerful stone magic and prowess in battle, he once roamed Abroad as one of the Blood Errant. Known as the Lion of Orthros. Now retired to live peacefully in Orthros with his Grace, Komnena.

apostate: rogue mage who illegally practices magic outside of the Orders.

Archipelagos: land to the west of the Empire comprising a series of islands, which maintains strict isolation from the rest of the world. See **Nodora**

Argyros: Lio's uncle and mentor in diplomacy and mind magic. Elder firstblood and founder of Orthros from Hagia Anatela, Gifted by Eidon. Graced to Lyta, father of Nike, Kadi, and Mak. An elder firstblood and founder of Orthros like Apollon, his brother by mortal birth. Attended the first Equinox Summit and every one since as the Queens' Master Ambassador. One of the most powerful thelemancers in history, known as Silvertongue for his legendary abilities as a negotiator.

Ashes: band of mercenaries renowned for their great deeds in the Empire. See **Ukocha**

Atalanta: bloodborn Master Steward of the Stand who used her running skills to rescue humans from heart hunter territory. Martyred when their liege-hounds hunted her down.

Athena: two-year-old Eriphite child Solaced by Javed and Kadi. Younger sister of Boskos by birth and blood. The severe case of frost fever she suffered as a mortal damaged her brain. While the Gift has healed her, she is still recovering lost development.

avowal: Hesperine ceremony in which Graces profess their bond before their people; legally binding and an occasion of great celebration.

Baharini: an ocean goddess in the Imperial pantheon, worshiped in the Kwatzi City-States, especially by privateers.

Baruti *or* **Baru:** Hesperine scholar and Fortress Master in the Prince's Charge; a theramancer and the librarian of Castra Justa, responsible for dangerous magical tomes and artifacts Chargers discover in the field. Began his mortal life in the Empire and chose to become a Hesperine at the First Prince's invitation; alumnus of Capital University.

Basir: Hesperine thelemancer and one of the two spymasters of Orthros, alongside his Grace, Kumeta. From the Empire in his mortal life. His official title is "Queens' Master Envoy" to conceal the nature of their work.

Bellator: Tenebran free lord who kidnapped Solia and held her for ransom inside Castra Roborra. Led the short-lived rebellion that ended there with the Siege of Sovereigns.

Benedict: First Knight of Segetia, Flavian's best friend, who harbors unrequited love for Genie. Cassia trusts him and considers him a friend. Traveled to Orthros as Lord Titus's representative during the Solstice Summit.

Blood Errant: group of four ancient and powerful Hesperine warriors who went errant together for eight centuries: Apollon, Nike, Rudhira, and Methu. The only Hesperines errant who have ever carried weapons, they performed legendary but controversial deeds in Hespera's name.

blood magic: type of magic practiced by worshipers of Hespera, from which the power of the Gift stems. All Hesperines possess innate blood magic.

Blood Moon: Hesperine name for one of the two moons, which appears red with a liquid texture to the naked eye. Believed to be an eye of the Goddess Hespera, potent with her blood magic.

Blood Union: magical empathic connection that allows Hesperines to sense the emotions of any living thing that has blood.

Blood-Red Prince: see **Ioustinianos**

bloodborn: Hesperine born with the Gift because their mother was transformed during pregnancy.

Bosko *or* **Boskos:** ten-year-old Eriphite child Solaced by Javed and Kadi. Elder brother of Athena by birth and blood. Zoe's best friend. Harbors anger over what the children suffered and is struggling to adjust to life in Orthros.

Callen: Perita's loving husband, who served as Cassia's bodyguard in the royal household and accompanied her to the Solstice Summit. Has since returned to Tenebra.

Capital University: university located in the capital city of the Empire, open to all Imperial citizens of any social class; known for egalitarianism and cutting-edge research.

Cassia: newgift awaiting her transformation into a Hesperine so she can spend eternity with Lio, her Grace. Once a Tenebran lady who secretly aided the Hesperines and helped Lio secure peace during the Solstice Summit. Born the illegitimate daughter of King Lucis and his concubine, Thalia.

Castra Justa: the stronghold of the First Prince and base of operations for the Prince's Charge.

Castra Roborra: fortress in Tenebra belonging to Lord Bellator, where he held Solia captive. Site of the Siege of Sovereigns.

Chalice of Stars: Nike's legendary round shield, which she uses along with the Stand's hand-to-hand combat techniques.

changer: practitioner of Lustra magic with the power to take on animal form.

Changing Queen: Queen Hedera of Tenebra, the Mage King's wife and co-ruler during the Last War. As a Silvicultrix, she was a powerful mage in her own right. Her own people knew her as Ebah. Also known as the Hawk of the Lustra and associated with her plant symbol, ivy.

the Charge: see **Prince's Charge**

Charge Law: legal code of Orthros Abroad, named for the Prince's Charge. An evolving body of laws established and enforced by the First Prince, based on the Equinox Oath and Hespera's sacred tenets.

charm: physical object imbued with a mage's spell, usually crafted of botanicals or other materials with their own magical properties. Offers a mild beneficial effect to an area or the holder of the charm, even if that person is not a mage.

Chera: goddess of rain and spinning in the Tenebran and Cordian pantheon, known as the Mourning Goddess and the Widow. According to myth, she was the Bride of Spring before Anthros destroyed her god-husband, Demergos, for disobedience.

Chrysanthos: war mage from Cordium with an affinity for fire. As the Dexion of the Aithourian Circle, he is one of the elites in the Order of Anthros. During the Solstice Summit, he tried to sabotage peace talks with hostage negotiations.

the Collector: one of the Old Masters, both a necromancer and mage of dreams, who uses his power to possess his victims and force them to do his bidding. He has used essential displacement to amass unnatural amounts of magic of various affinities. The Gift Collectors are his willing servants, helping him carry out a far-reaching conspiracy to achieve his mysterious ends in alliance with King Lucis. With the help of Skleros and by exploiting Eudias, he entered Orthros during the Solstice Summit and would have caused terrible suffering and destruction if Lio and Cassia had not stopped him.

Cordium: land to the south of Tenebra where the Mage Orders hold sway. Its once-mighty principalities and city-states have now lost power to the magical and religious authorities. Wealthy and cultured, but prone to deadly politics. Also known as the Magelands.

Council of Free Lords: a body of Tenebran lords who have the hereditary authority to convey or revoke the nobility's mandate upon a reigning monarch. Their rights and privileges were established in the Free Charter.

Court of Claws: exclusive sparring area at the Sandira Court where gold roster mercenaries and royal guards challenge each other.

the Craving: a Hesperine's addiction to their Grace's blood. When deprived of each other, Graces suffer agonizing withdrawal symptoms and fatal illness.

Dakk: student from Capital University who befriends Cassia in the Sun Market on the island of Marijani.

Dawn Slumber: deep sleep Hesperines fall into when the sun rises. Although the sunlight causes them no harm, they're unable to awaken until nightfall, leaving them vulnerable during daylight hours.

Demergos: formerly the god of agriculture, now stricken from the Tenebran and Cordian pantheon. His worshipers were disbanded in ancient times when the mages of Anthros seized power. According to myth, he was the husband of Chera, but disobeyed Anthros and brought on his own death and her grief.

Departure: contingency plan that dates from the founding of Orthros, when Hesperines feared the Last War might break out again at any time. If the Queens invoked the Departure, all Hesperines errant would return home, and the border between Orthros and Tenebra would be closed forever.

Deukalion: bloodborn firstgift of Apollon and Komnena, Ambassador in Orthros's diplomatic service who has devoted his career to improving relations between Orthros and Tenebra. Since he and Cassia, his Grace, succeeded in securing peace during the Solstice Summit, he has taken a leave of absence for her Gifting.

Dexion: second highest ranking mage in the Aithourian Circle.

Discourses on Love: Orthros's canon of erotic texts.

displacement gate: destructive portal that can be opened by necromancers skilled in essential displacement.

Divine Tongue: language spoken by Hesperines and mages, used for spells, rituals, and magical texts. The common tongue of Orthros, spoken freely by all Hesperines. In Tenebra and Cordium, the mages keep it a secret and disallow non-mages from learning it.

diviner: Imperial theramancer trained in ancient traditions who protects their people from necromancy and communicates with the ancestors. Their ancestral magic enables them to open passages through the spirit phase.

dream ward: specialized spell used by Gift Collectors to shield their minds from Hesperine thelemancers.

Dynastic: mother tongue of the Owia dynasty used for all political discourse in the multilingual Empire.

Eidon: Prismos of Hagia Anatela. Ritual firstblood and Gifter of Argyros.

Eighth Circle: Lio and Cassia's Trial circle. See **Alexandra, Eudokia, Lysandros, Menodora, Telemakhos**

elder firstbloods: the ancient Hesperine founders of Orthros. Gifted by the Ritual firstbloods. See **Apollon, Argyros, Hypatia, Kassandra, Kitharos, Timarete**

the Empire: vast and prosperous human lands located far to the west, across an ocean from Tenebra. Comprises many different languages and cultures united under the Empress. Allied with Orthros and welcoming to Hesperines, many of whom began their mortal lives as Imperial citizens. Maintains a strict policy of isolation toward Tenebra and Cordium to guard against the Mage Orders.

the Empress: the ruler of the Empire, admired by her citizens. The Imperial throne has passed down through the female line for many generations.

the Empress's privateers: pirates who sail with the sanction of the Empress, granted by a letter of marque, which authorizes them to rob her enemies. They make voyages to Cordium to secretly pillage the Mage Orders' ships.

enchantment: a spell anchored to a power source, which can last indefinitely without a mage's attention.

envoy: according to common knowledge, a messenger attached to the Hesperine diplomatic service. In fact, envoys are the Queens' spies who gather information from the mortal world to protect Orthros and Hesperines errant. See **Basir, Kumeta**

Equinox Oath: ancient treaty between Orthros and Tenebra, which prescribes the conduct of Hesperines errant and grants them protection from humans.

Equinox Summit: peace talks in which the Hesperines send ambassadors from Orthros to meet with the King of Tenebra and renew the Equinox Oath. Each mortal king is expected to convene it once upon his accession to the throne.

Eriphites: worshipers of the pastoral god Eriphon, branded heretics by the Order of Anthros. The last surviving members of their cult are twenty-four orphaned children recently brought to safety in Orthros thanks to Cassia and Lio. See **Zosime, Boskos, Athena**

errant: a Hesperine who has left Orthros to travel through Tenebra doing good deeds for mortals

essential displacement: process by which necromancers can transfer the magic of one person, the source, into another person, the vessel, through a third person called the channel. The vessel must die for the source to reclaim their power.

Eudias: young war mage from Cordium with an affinity for weather, including lightning. Compelled to join the Aithourian circle due to his magic, he defected during the Solstice Summit, aiding the Hesperines and the Tenebran embassy against Chrysanthos and Skleros. He and Lio faced the Collector in a mage duel, in which Lio helped him free himself from the Old Master's possession.

Eudokia: Hesperine youngblood, one of Lio's Trial sisters in Orthros. Solaced from Tenebra as a child. An initiate mathematician, calligrapher, and accomplished scholar. Daughter of Hypatia.

Eugenia: young Tenebran lady, believed to be Flavian's cousin and daughter of his late uncle, Lord Eugenius. In fact she is his sister, the daughter of Titus and his concubine Risara.

Evander: see **Evandrus the Younger**

Evandrus the Elder: Tenebran free lord who assisted Lord Bellator in Solia's kidnapping and joined forces with him inside Castra Roborra during their rebellion.

Evandrus the Younger: son and heir of Evandrus the Elder, who was with him at Castra Roborra during the Siege of Sovereigns.

familiar: the animal companion of a Hesperine, bound to them by blood.

the Fangs: Prometheus's famous twin swords.

the Feast: Hesperine term for drinking blood while making love.

fire charm: a charm created by a fire mage that those without the affinity for fire can use to light a flame.

First Circle: Rudhira, Nike, and Methu's Trial circle. They were the first Hesperines to go through the Trial of Initiation together and founded the tradition of Trial circles.

Firstblood Circle: the governing body of Orthros. Every firstblood has a vote on behalf of their bloodline, while non-voting Hesperines can attempt to influence policy by displays of partisanship. The Queens retain veto power, but use it sparingly.

firstgift: the eldest child of a Hesperine bloodline, first to receive the gift from their parents.

flametongue: rare herb whose oil can be used to fireproof armor or clothing against mundane flame. Offers no protection against magefire, but still prized by the few royals and nobles who can afford it. The Order of Anthros forbids anyone but their mages to grow and prepare it.

Flavian: young Tenebran lord, son of Free Lord Titus and heir to Segetia's seat on the Council. Despite his family's feud with Hadria, he is admired by both sides of the conflict and is a unifying figure for the fractured nobility. Cassia has prepared the way for him to take the throne from Lucis in a peaceful transfer of power.

Florian: see **Chrysanthos**

Font of the Changing Queen: stone fountain on the grounds of Solorum Palace that dates from the time of the Changing Queen. This historical monument is a subject of legends, which say it ran with blood the day the Mage King died. Lio and Cassia first met here in a forbidden nocturnal encounter.

fortune blade: dagger issued to mercenaries by the Empress's administration, which shows they are professionally recognized and may fight for profit, and that they abide by the Empress's code of conduct.

gargoyles: mythological creatures with fangs, horns, and wings, said to be Hespera's familiars, created from her blood. Hesperines believe they guard the gates of her divine Sanctuary to protect it from Anthros and the other gods.

Genie: see **Eugenia**

geomagus: mage with an affinity for geological forces, who can use their magic to conjure heat from the ground or create artifacts like warming plates for heating food and drink.

the Gift: Hesperines' immortality and magical abilities, which they regard as a blessing from the goddess Hespera. The practice of offering the Gift to all is a Hesperine sacred tenet.

Gift Collector: mage-assassin and bounty hunter who hunts down Hesperines for the Order of Hypnos using necromancy, alchemy, and fighting tactics. Known for adapting common items into weapons to skirt the Orders' religious laws against mages arming themselves.

Gift Night: the night of a person's transformation into a Hesperine, usually marked by great celebration.

Gifting: the transformation from human into Hesperine.

Glasstongue: see **Deukalion**

glyph stone: the capstone of the doorway of a shrine, inscribed with the glyph of the deity worshiped there, where any spells over the structure are usually seated.

the Goddess's Eyes: the two moons, the red Blood Moon and the white Light Moon; associated with Hespera and regarded as her gaze by Hesperines.

gold roster: list maintained by the Empress's administrators of the mercenaries who have received the most gold in service to the Empire's interests. A measure of a mercenary's prowess, wealth, and how many contracts they have completed to benefit the common good.

Gomba: unscrupulous former privateer, Ziara's nemesis.

Grace: Hesperine sacred tenet, a magical bond between two Hesperine lovers. Frees them from the need for human blood and enables them to sustain each other, but comes at the cost of the Craving. A fated bond that happens when their love is true. It is believed every Hesperine has a Grace just waiting to be found. See **Craving**

Grace braids: thin braids of one another's hair that Graces exchange. They may wear them privately after professing their bond to one another, then exchange them publicly at their avowal and thereafter wear them for all to see to signify their commitment.

Grace-family (Grace-son, Grace-father, Grace-sister, etc.): the family members of a Hesperine's Grace; compare with human in-laws.

Grace Union: the particularly powerful and intimate Blood Union between two Hesperines who are Graced; enables them to communicate telepathically and empathically.

Great Temple Epoch: the historical period when the Great Temples of every cult flourished across Tenebra and Cordium, and all mages cooperated. Came to a cataclysmic end due to the Ordering and the Last War.

Great Temples of Hespera: powerful, thriving temples where mages of Hespera worshiped and worked their magic in peace, before they were branded heretics. Razed during the Last War.

Guardian of Orthros: see **Hippolyta**

Hagia Anatela: one of the four Great Temples of Hespera that flourished during the Great Temple Epoch, located in eastern Tenebra. See **Eidon**

Hagia Boreia: one of the four Great Temples of Hespera that flourished during the Great Temple Epoch, located in northern Tenebra. See **Alea**, **Anastatios**

Haima: capital city of Orthros Notou.

Hammer of the Sun: Apollon's famous battle hammer, which he wielded while Abroad with the Blood Errant. He left it in Tenebra when he brought Komnena to Orthros.

Harbor: bay in Orthros around which Selas was built. The founders landed here when they first escaped Tenebra and found refuge in the unsettled north.

Harkhuf Addaya Khemkare: Imperial human guest visiting Orthros to study theramancy, a cousin of the Empress. Xandra's share.

Healing Sanctuary: infirmary in Orthros founded and run by Queen Soteira, where humans are given care and Hesperines are trained in the healing arts.

heart hunters: warbands of Tenebrans who hunt down Hesperines, regarded by their countrymen as protectors of humanity. They patrol the northern borders of Tenebra with packs of liegehounds, waiting to attack Hesperines who leave Orthros.

Hedon: god of pleasure and chance in the Tenebran and Cordian pantheon, patron of sexual acts and gambling. Styled as the god of fertility and prosperity by the Order of Anthros in their attempts to promote morality.

Hespera: goddess of night cast from the Tenebran and Cordian pantheon. The Mage Orders have declared her worship heresy punishable by death. Hesperines keep her cult alive and continue to revere her as the goddess of the moons, Sanctuary, and Mercy. Associated with roses, thorns, and fanged creatures. According to myth, she is the sister of Anthros and Hypnos.

Hespera's Rose: the most sacred symbol of the Hesperines, a rose with five petals and five thorns representing Hespera's sacred tenets. Frequently embroidered on clothing or represented in stained glass windows. Based on real roses, which are the Goddess's sacred flower and beloved by Hesperines. The mages uproot them wherever they're found in Tenebra or Cordium and punish those who grow them for heresy.

Hesperine: nocturnal immortal being with fangs who gains nourishment from drinking blood. Tenebrans and Cordians believe them to be monsters bent on humanity's destruction. In truth, they follow a strict moral code in the name of their goddess, Hespera, and wish only to ease humankind's suffering.

Hesperite: human worshiper of Hespera, persecuted as a heretic by the Orders.

Hesperite settlement: community of Hesperites living in secret in the wilds of Tenebra. Reliant on the Prince's Charge to help them survive the hostile territory.

hex: a circle of six necromancers who exchange magical secrets and punish any who betray them.

High Court: council of diviners who attend the Empress during audiences. Their role is to ensure no petitioners or advisors use illicit spells to influence her decisions.

Hippolyta: Lio's aunt, Graced to Argyros, mother of Nike, Kadi, and Mak. Greatest and most ancient Hesperine warrior, a founder of Orthros. Known as the Guardian of Orthros for her deeds in Tenebra during the Last War and for establishing the Stand.

Hippolyta's Stand: Orthros's standing army, founded by Hippolyta. Under her leadership, they patrol the border with Tenebra as Stewards of the Queens' ward. So few of the peaceful Hesperines take up the battle arts that Nike, Kadi, Mak, and Lyros are the only Stewards.

Huru: Ziara's first mate and lover, a knife expert and theramancer.

Hypatia: an elder firstblood and founder of Orthros from Hagia Anatela, mother of Kia. Orthros's greatest astronomer, who invented the Hesperine calendar.

Hypatia's Observatory: tower in Orthros established by Hypatia, where Hesperine astronomers study the heavens and teach their students. Every Autumn Equinox, Orthros's diplomats watch for the Summit Beacon from here.

Hypnos: god of death and dreams in the Tenebran and Cordian pantheon. Winter is considered his season. Humans unworthy of going to Anthros's Hall are believed to spend the afterlife in Hypnos's realm of the dead. According to myth, he is the brother of Anthros and Hespera.

Imperial University: illustrious university in the Empire. Only students with wealth and the best references gain entry, usually those of noble or royal blood. Known for traditionalism and conservative approaches to research.

Ioustin *or* **Ioustinianos:** First Prince of the Hesperines, eldest child of the Queens of Orthros. Lio's Ritual father. Solaced from Tenebra as a child. Once a warrior in the Blood Errant known as the Blood-Red Prince, he now leads the Charge. Young Hesperines call him Rudhira, an affectionate name given to him by Methu.

Iris: Tenebran lady, Solia's handmaiden and closest companion, who was with her at the Siege of Sovereigns.

Iskhyra: name used by Nike to conceal her identity Abroad.

ivy pendant: wooden pendant carved with a triquetra of ivy. Secretly passed down from one Tenebran queen to another and finally, from Solia to Cassia. Imbued with Lustra magic and connected to the Changing Queen in some way.

Javed: Lio's Grace-cousin, avowed to Kadi, father of Bosko and Thenie. From the Empire in his mortal life. Has an affinity for healing and now serves in Orthros's Healing Sanctuary.

Jaya: Hesperine warrior and Fortress Master in the Prince's Charge. Warder and siege expert, responsible for the magical defenses of Castra Justa.

Jua: patron goddess of the Sun Market and commerce, worshiped on the island of Marijani.

Kadi: see **Arkadia**

kaetlii: word in the tongue used by Tenebrans to train liegehounds, meaning the person the dog is bonded to and will protect until death.

Kalos: the Charge's best scout, who uses his tracking skills to find Hesperines errant who are missing in action.

kalux: Hesperine word in the Divine Tongue for clitoris.

Kassandra: Lio's Ritual mother, an elder firstblood and founder of Orthros. Ritual sister to the Queens, who Gifted her, and mother of Prometheus. A princess in her mortal life, she became the first Hesperine from the Empire and secured her homeland's alliance with Orthros. Now the Queens' Master Economist who oversees Orthros's trade. Has the gift of foresight and as Orthros's oracle, guides the Hesperines with her prophecies.

Kia: see **Eudokia**

King of Tenebra: see **Lucis**

Kitharos: an elder firstblood and founder of Orthros, father to Nodora. One of the Hesperines' greatest musicians.

Knight: Cassia's beloved liegehound. Solia gave him to Cassia as a puppy so Cassia would have protection and companionship.

Komnena: Lio's mother, still rather young by Hesperines standards. Fled a life of squalor as a Tenebran farmwife and ran away to Orthros with Apollon, who Gifted her while she was pregnant and raised her son as his own. Now a respected mind healer. As the Queens' Chamberlain, she is responsible for helping newcomers to Orthros settle and adjust.

Konstantina *or* **Kona:** royal firstblood, Second Princess of Orthros, the second child and eldest daughter of the Queens. From the Empire in her mortal life. As the Royal Master Magistrate, she is the author of Orthros's legal code and an influential politician who oversees the proceedings of the First-blood Circle.

krana: Hesperine term in the Divine Tongue for vagina.

Kumeta: Hesperine light mage and one of the two spymasters of Orthros, alongside her Grace, Basir. From the Empire in her mortal life. Her official title is "Queens' Master Envoy" to conceal the nature of their work.

Kwatzi City-States: forty islands off the eastern coast of the Empire, which dominate ocean commerce. See **Marijani**

the Last War: the cataclysmic violence sparked by the Ordering sixteen hundred years ago. When the Order of Anthros sought to suppress all resistance to their authority, magical and armed conflict ravaged Tenebra and Cordium, destroying the civilization of the Great Temple Epoch. Peace came at the cost of the Hesperines' exile and the Order of Anthros's victory, while the Mage King secured his rule in Tenebra.

liegehound: war dogs bred and trained by Tenebrans to track, hunt, and slay Hesperines. Veil spells do not throw them off the scent, and they can leap high enough to pull a levitating Hesperine from the air. The only animals that do not trust Hesperines. They live longer than other canines and can withstand poison and disease.

Light Moon: Hesperine name for one of the two moons, which appears white with a smooth texture. Believed to be an eye of the Goddess Hespera, shining with her light.

Lio: see **Deukalion**

Lion of Orthros: see **Apollon**

lithomagus: a mage with an affinity for stone. Can manipulate stone with magic for architectural, agricultural, or battle purposes.

Lustra magic: Tenebran name referring to old nature magic. Practiced in ancient times by the Changing Queen. The Orders have never been able to understand or control it, and most knowledge of it is now lost.

Lysandros *or* **Lyros:** Lio's Trial brother and Grace-cousin, avowed to Mak, Solaced as a child from Tenebra. Also a warder and warrior serving in the Stand.

Lyta: see **Hippolyta**

Mage King: King Lucian of Tenebra, who reigned sixteen hundred years ago, widely considered by Hesperines and mortals alike to have been a great monarch. He and his wife, the Changing Queen, made the original Equinox Oath with the Queens of Orthros. A fire mage and warrior, he ruled before the Mage Orders mandated that men must choose between wielding spells or weapons.

mage of dreams: mage of Hypnos with an affinity for thelemancy.

Mage Orders: the magical and religious authorities in Cordium, which also dictate sacred law to Tenebran temples. Responsible for training and governing mages and punishing heretics.

Magelands: see **Cordium**

Mak: see **Telemakhos**

Marijani: the largest, wealthiest, and most powerful of the Kwatzi City-States, this island is an important port of call for Imperial merchants, privateers, and Hesperines. See **Sun Market** and **Moon Market**

Martyrs' Pass: the only known passage to Orthros through the Umbral Mountains. When an army of heart hunters possessed by the Collector ambushed the Tenebran embassy here, Lio defeated them with his mind magic and rescued Cassia.

Menodora: Hesperine youngblood, one of Lio's Trial sisters. Daughter of Kitharos and Dakarai. An initiate musician, admired vocalist, and crafter of musical instruments. She is one of only two Hesperines from the Archipelagos and the immortal expert on the music of her mortal homeland.

Mercy: Hesperine sacred tenet, the practice of caring for dead or dying humans.

Methu: see **Prometheus**

Migration Night: event twice a year when Hesperines travel between hemispheres to avoid longer hours of daylight. The night after Spring Equinox, they vacate Orthros Boreou in the northern hemisphere and migrate to Orthros Notou in the southern hemisphere. The night before Autumn Equinox, they change residence again, leaving Orthros Notou and returning to Orthros Boreou.

mind healer: see **theramancer**

mind mage: see **thelemancer**

mind ward: mental defense cast by a thelemancer, which protects a person's mind from mages seeking to invade their thoughts or subdue their Will.

Monsoon: gold roster mercenary who defeats all challengers in the Blood Court. Known for his bad temper, he always fights alone and is said to be dangerous.

moon hours: by the Hesperine clock, the hours corresponding to night, when Hesperines pursue public activities.

Moon Market: hidden bazaar on the island of Marijani, where the Empress's privateers sell their spoils.

moskos: Hesperine term in the Divine Tongue meaning testicles.

Mweya: winged Sandira deity.

Namatsi: one of the Empress's privateers who supplies information to the Hesperine envoys.

natural phase: the physical world where living creatures exist, as opposed to the afterlife. See **spirit phase**

Nephalea: one of the three Hesperines errant who saved Cassia as a child. She and her Grace, Alkaios, recently settled in Orthros after years as Hesperines errant with his Gifter, Nike.

newgift: a newly transformed Hesperine, or a person who has decided to become immortal and awaits their Gifting.

Nike: see **Pherenike**

Nodora: see **Menodora**

northwestern Empire: remote area on the fringes of the Empress's jurisdiction, where some people are born without citizenship.

Obruza: major port city on the southern coast of Cordium.

the Old Masters: the oldest known hex of necromancers in Tenebran and Cordian record. Little is known about them from legends and surviving ancient texts, but their influence is linked to catastrophic events and suffering throughout history. They extend their lives and hoard power using abusive magic such as essential displacement. See **the Collector**

Order of Anthros: Mage Order dedicated to the god Anthros, which holds the ultimate religious and magical authority over all other Orders and temples. Bent on destroying Hesperines. War mages, light mages, and warders serve in this Order, as do agricultural and stone mages.

the Ordering: historical event over sixteen hundred years ago, when the Order of Anthros came to prominence and enforced its doctrines upon all other cults, who had previously worshiped and practiced magic freely. New mandates forbade warriors from practicing magic and required all mages to enter temples and remain celibate. The war mages also branded all Hespera worshipers heretics and destroyed their temples. The Ordering caused the Last War and the end of the Great Temple Epoch.

Orthros: homeland of the Hesperines, ruled by the Queens. The Mage Orders describe it as a horrific place where no human can survive, but in reality, it is a land of peace, prosperity, and culture.

Orthros Abroad: the population of Hesperines who are errant in Tenebra at any given time. Under the jurisdiction of the First Prince, who is the Queens' regent outside their ward.

Orthros Boreou: Hesperine homeland in the northern hemisphere, located north of and sharing a border with Tenebra.

Orthros Notou: Hesperine homeland in the southern hemisphere, located across the sea to the southeast of the Empire.

Owia: the dynasty that currently holds the throne of the Empire.

Perita: Cassia's handmaiden and dearest friend who accompanied her to Orthros for the Solstice Summit and assisted with all her schemes. Has now returned to Tenebra with her husband, Callen.

Phaedros: mage of Hespera and brilliant scholar from ancient times. The only survivor of his Great Temple's destruction by the Aithourian Circle. After he took revenge against the mortals, he lost his status as an elder firstblood. Now lives in eternal exile under the midnight sun.

Pherenike: Lio's cousin, a warder and warrior second only to her mother Lyta in strength, a thelemancer second only to her father Argyros in power. Solaced from Tenebra as a child. Known as the Victory Star, one of the Blood Errant alongside her uncle, Apollon, and her Trial brothers Rudhira and Methu. After the surviving Blood Errant's campaign to avenge Methu, she remained Abroad alone, missing in action for over ninety years.

Prince's Charge: the force of Hesperines errant who serve under the First Prince.

Prismos: highest ranking male mage in a temple.

privateers: see **Empress's Privateers**

Prometheus: legendary Hesperine warrior and martyr. Bloodborn to Kassandra and descendant of Imperial royalty. Known as the Midnight Champion, he was a member of the Blood Errant with his comrades Nike, Rudhira, and Apollon. Captured by the Aithourian Circle before Lio's birth. Orthros still mourns his death.

Queen Mothers: matriarchs from each sister state within the Empire who possess the sacred artifacts that symbolize power to their particular people. Each Imperial dynasty must secure their blessings in order to reign.

the Queens: the Hesperine monarchs of Orthros. See **Alea**, **Soteira**

the Queens' Couriers: young Hesperines who serve Orthros as messengers, delivering correspondence and packages throughout Selas.

the Queens' ward: the powerful Sanctuary ward cast by the Queens, which spans the borders of Orthros, protecting Hesperines from human threats.

rhabdos: Hesperine term in the Divine Tongue meaning penis.

rimelace: flowering herb that requires extremely cold conditions. Difficult to grow in Tenebra, even with the aid of magic, but thrives in Orthros. The only known treatment for frost fever.

Ritual: Hesperine sacred tenet. A ceremony in which Hesperines share blood, but in a broader sense, the whole of their religious beliefs.

Ritual circle: area where Hesperines gather to perform Ritual, usually marked with sacred symbols on the floor.

Ritual Drink: the Drink given by one Hesperine to another for healing or sustenance, without intimacy or invoking a family bond.

Ritual firstbloods: the eight blood mages who performed the Ritual that created Hesperines. As the leaders of the Great Temples of Hespera, all except Alea were martyred during the Ordering. See **Alea, Anastasios, Eidon**

Ritual hall: central chamber in Hesperine homes where the bloodline's Ritual circle is located.

Ritual parents: Hesperines who attend a new suckling's first Ritual or who give the Gift to a mortal becoming a Hesperine as an adult. They remain mentors and trusted guides for eternity. Comparable to Tenebran temple parents.

Ritual tributary: Hesperine who establishes their own bloodline rather than joining their Gifter's family.

Rose House: the guest house on the docks of Selas where Cassia stayed during the Tenebran embassy's visit to Orthros for the Solstice Summit. Site of her and Lio's battle with the Collector.

royal firstbloods: the Queens' children, who are to establish their own bloodlines in order to share the Annassa's power with their people.

Rudhira: see **Ioustinianos**

Sanctuary: Hesperine sacred tenet, the practice of offering refuge to anyone in need. *Or* Hesperine refuge in hostile territory, concealed and protected from humans by Sanctuary magic.

Sanctuary mage: a mage with a rare dual affinity for warding and light magic, who can create powerful protections that also conceal. Queen Alea of Orthros is the only mage with this affinity who survived the Orders' persecution of Hespera worshipers.

Sanctuary Rose: a variety of white rose that originated in the Great Temples of Hespera. The only vine that survived the Last War now grows in Princess Konstantina's greenhouse, and she has propagated it throughout Orthros. Traditionally, each person who requests Sanctuary is given one of these blooms in welcome.

Sanctuary ward: ward created by a Sanctuary mage, which can both protect and hide those within it. Strong Sanctuary wards require the caster to remain inside the boundaries of the spell. Should the mage die there, their sacrifice will increase the ward's power and sustain it indefinitely.

Sandira Court: capital city and royal seat of the Sandira Kingdom, one of the most populous cities in the world. Known for its magnificent stone architecture. Mercenaries congregate in this metropolis seeking contracts with trade caravans in need of protection.

Sandira King: eagle shifter and monarch of the Sandira Kingdom known for showing no leniency. He rules with a strong hand to meet the challenges faced by his rapidly expanding people.

Sandira Kingdom: powerful sister state that controls the flow of gold, ivory, and copper between the Kwatzi City-States and the Empire's interior. Ruled by hereditary shifters whose animal forms signify their status within the hierarchy of warriors, nobility, or royalty.

Selas: capital city of Orthros Boreou.

shadowlands: Imperial term for Tenebra and Cordium, sometimes used with pity or disdain.

shadowlander: Imperial term for a person from Tenebra or Cordium

share: human or immortal with whom a Hesperine is romantically involved, sharing blood and intimacy.

shifter: a person of Sandira descent who is blessed by their ancestors with the ability to shapeshift. Sandira shifters take on the form of a particular animal with which their clan has cultivated a sacred bond over many generations.

Silklands: see **Vardara**

Silvertongue: see **Argyros**

sister states: independent lands within the Empire ruled by their own monarchs, all owing allegiance to the Empress. She is seen as their eldest sister, and they are symbolically members of her clan.

Sisters' Port: harbor in Orthros Notou that is the hub of sea traffic between the Empire and Orthros.

Skleros: master necromancer and Gift Collector who holds the Order of Hypnos's record for completing the most bounties on Hesperines. Expert in essential displacement. Helped the Old Master known as the Collector cause devastation during the Solstice Summit.

Slumber: see **Dawn Slumber**

Solace: Hesperine sacred tenet, the practice of rescuing and Gifting abandoned children.

Solia: Princess of Tenebra, King Lucis's legitimate daughter and heir before the birth of his son. When she was seventeen, rebel lords kidnapped her. Lucis refused to ransom her and ensured all witnesses perished in the ensuing Siege of Sovereigns. Nobles and commoners alike still mourn her.

Solstice Oath: new treaty between Orthros and the Tenebran nobility, secured thanks to Lio and Cassia's efforts during the Solstice Summit.

Solstice Summit: diplomatic negotiations between Tenebra and Orthros that marked the first time a mortal embassy from Tenebra ever entered Hesperine lands. An unprecedented event proposed by Lio in an effort to prevent war and make it possible for Cassia to stay with him.

Soteira: one of the two Queens of Orthros, who has ruled the Hesperines for nearly sixteen hundred years with her Grace, Alea. Originally from the Empire, she was a powerful mortal mage with an affinity for healing before leaving to found Orthros alongside Alea.

speires: symbolic hair ties Lyta gives to trainees when they begin learning the battle arts. Stewards wear them as part of their Stand regalia.

spirit gate: a portal that allows magical travel by opening a passage through the spirit phase. Imperial diviners maintain regulated spirit gates throughout the Empire and Orthros Notou.

spirit phase: the spiritual plane of existence where the ancestors dwell, where living souls originate and to which they return in the afterlife.

spirit walk: ability of Imperial mages, who can walk through the spirit phase to travel between locations in the natural phase. Spirit walking is only possible in the territory of their own ancestors, and they must use spirit gates in other regions.

starflake: evergreen tree that thrives in Orthros's climate. Its fruit, which it bears in winter, is sweet with a tart aftertaste, a beloved Hesperine delicacy.

stepping: innate Hesperine ability to teleport instantly from one place to another with little magical effort.

Steward: see **Hippolyta's Stand**

suckling: Hesperine child.

Sun Market: bazaar on Marijani renowned for its wonders.

Telemakhos: Lio's cousin and best friend. Exposed as a child in Tenebra due to his club foot, Solaced by Argyros and Lyta. A warrior by profession and warder by affinity, he serves in the Stand. He and his Grace, Lyros, are newly avowed.

Temple of Kyria at Solorum: most influential and respected temple of Kyria in Tenebra, located near the royal palace. The Prisma was a friend and ally of Cassia's when she was in Tenebra.

Tenebra: human kingdom south of Orthros and north of Cordium. Agrarian, feudal society ruled by a king, prone to instability due to rivalries between lords. Land of the Hesperines' origin, where they are now persecuted.

Tendeso: prince of the Sandira Court, brother of the king.

Thalia: Cassia's mother, King Lucis's concubine. Murdered the day Cassia was born by an apostate fire mage attempting to assassinate Lucis.

thelemancer: a mage with an affinity for thelemancy, or mind magic, which gives them the power to manipulate others' thoughts and control their Wills.

Thenie: see **Athena**

theramancer: a person with an affinity for theramancy, or mind healing, who can use magic to treat mental illness.

Thorn: Rudhira's two-handed sword, which he carried as one of the Blood Errant and now wields as he leads the Charge.

Timarete: an elder firstblood and founder of Orthros, mother of Lyros. One of the Hesperines' greatest painters.

Tradewinds: mother tongue of the Kwatzi City-States, which is used to conduct all commerce across the multilingual Empire.

traversal: teleportation ability of Tenebran and Cordian mages; requires a great expense of magic and usually leaves the mortal mage seriously ill.

Trial circle: age set of Hesperines who go through the Trial of Initiation together. They consider each other Trial sisters and brothers for the rest of their immortal lives. Although not related by birth or blood, they maintain strong bonds of loyalty and friendship for eternity.

Trial of Initiation *or* **Trial:** Hesperine rite of passage marking an immortal's transition into adulthood.

Ukocha: leader of the Ashes, a swordswoman and fire mage who inspires awe among mercenaries.

Union: Hesperine sacred tenet, the principle of living with empathy and compassion for all. See **Blood Union**

Vardara: now one of the mightiest sister states, once a sovereign land that fought wars with the Empire throughout history. The conflict ended sixteen hundred years ago when the Empress and a royal from the Silklands had a child together, Kassandra. Their union joined Vardara to the Empire.

veil hours: by the Hesperine clock, the hours corresponding to day, when Hesperines Slumber or devote their private time to friends, family, and lovers.

veil spell: innate Hesperine ability to cast magical concealments that hide their presence and activities from humans or fellow immortals.

veiled blood seal: Hesperine spell for securing confidential correspondence.

Victory Star: see **Pherenike**

Vigil of Thorns: five nights of meditation during the Hesperine Winter Solstice observances. Each vigil is dedicated to a thorn of Hespera's Rose, representing the Hesperines' sacred duties. See **Gift**, **Mercy, Solace, Union**, **Will**

Vulgus *or* **the vulgar tongue:** common language of all non-mages in Tenebra and Cordium.

warder: mage with an affinity for warding, the power to create magical protections that block spells or physical attacks.

Waystar: Hesperine fortress, Orthros's first refuge for those crossing the border from Tenebra. Hesperines errant who use weapons must leave their armaments here before crossing the Sea of Komne to Selas.

Will: free will, willpower. *Or* Hesperine sacred tenet, the principle of guarding the sanctity of each person's freedom of choice.

Xandra: see **Alexandra**

Yasamin: ancient Hesperine of Imperial origin who established the architectural style of Haima.

youngblood: young adult Hesperine who has recently reached their majority by passing the Trial of Initiation.

Zalele: supreme goddess of the Imperial pantheon, the deity of the sun and sky who is revered as the maker and nurturer of all creation. Believed to be too great and powerful to trouble herself with day-to-day mortal affairs, which she leaves to lesser deities and the ancestors.

Ziara: one of the most accomplished of the Empress's Privateers, famed for her powerful wind magic and daring voyages to Cordium. Captain of the *Wanted*, which she sails with Huru and their all-woman crew.

Zoe *or* **Zosime:** Lio's little sister, a seven-year-old Eriphite child Solaced by Apollon and Komnena. Loves her new family and idolizes her brother for his role in saving her from Tenebra. Has yet to heal from the emotional wounds she suffered as a mortal.

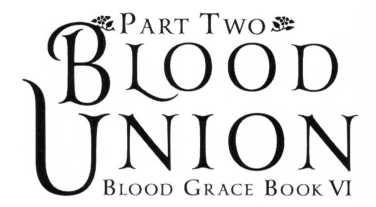

PART TWO
BLOOD UNION
BLOOD GRACE BOOK VI

An ancient magic will put their love to the ultimate test.

When Lio brought Cassia to the land of their allies, he believed his mortal love would be safe. But a nameless enemy has ensnared her in a conspiracy reaching as high as the Imperial Court. With the Empress out for Cassia's blood, will Lio abandon his path as a diplomat and unleash his fangs?

Although Cassia is now a fugitive, she can't flee to safety until they uncover the secret that could change the fate of two continents. Their path leads into a treacherous desert where long-forgotten magic threatens to tear her apart from Lio forever. Can she, a mere mortal, find the hidden power within herself to survive?

Steamy romance meets classic fantasy worldbuilding in Blood Grace. Follow fated mates Lio and Cassia through their epic love story for a guaranteed series HEA..

Learn more:
vroth.co/union2

BLOOD DREAM

A BLOOD GRACE STORY

The nightmare is over, but can they live their dream come true?

Cassia is finally free to stay with Lio. Safe in Orthros and done with human politics, she's ready to celebrate with him and her immortal family. And yet she feels uneasy in her new home.

Lio wants the start of their life together to be everything Cassia dreamed. But he can tell something is wrong, and she's trying to hide it. Now there's nothing to keep them apart. So why is she pulling away?

They've defeated necromancers, war mages, and the tyrant king so they can be together. Can they win against the personal specters that threaten their happily ever after?

This touching and steamy Blood Grace bonus novelette is set after the events of Blood Sanctuary Part Two.

Get Blood Grace 4.5 for free!

vroth.co/dream

ACKNOWLEDGEMENTS

THIS BOOK would not have been possible without my amazing friend Dani Morrison. Thank you for reading Union with your skill as a fantasy romance author, your passion for the history and beliefs of many cultures, and your personal experience as a Black creative. Your feedback has been invaluable both on story craft as well as how to practice respect in my wordlbuilding.

Thank you also to Tiara Hendricks for reading the original draft with your knowledge as an English major and your insights as a reader of Black literature.

Thank you to MJ Faraldo for being a true friend in so many ways, including sharing your insights on my LGBT+ characters from your perspective as a bisexual author. You're the only fan who has dibs on both Rudhira and his moms, ha!

Gratitude to all the gorgeous, gifted, BIPOC and LGBT+ creatives in the FaRo Authors group for being in our community and shining your light. I learn so much from you every day. I'm grateful for the opportunities you give us to listen and deepen our empathy as we share our creative journeys.

To Harriet, thank you for building the foundation of so many wonderful friendships and projects in our community. Colleen, Elsie, Steph, Lisette, and Erin, thank you for helping me keep my sanity on my quest to write these ridiculously big books. You always know how to pull me out doom spirals and make me laugh. I will die on a hill for all of you (preferably in a billowing coat and wielding a cactus for a weapon after eating tacos for my last meal).

I also have to gush thanks to Patcas for the beautiful art on the front of this book! I say this every time, but this one is my new favorite.

So much gratitude to Brittany Cicirello for being my editor and research ambassador. The research for this book was a massive undertaking, and I could never have done it alone. I'm thankful that you find it fun to go digging for pre-colonial Shona fashion trends in between all those legal documents from your day job.

Kai, I want to officially state for the record that I had you first and I will fight anyone who says otherwise. Thank you for amazing loyalty and generosity to all of us who are "your" authors.

And finally, heartfelt thanks to my Ko-Fi donors and my amazing reader team, the Ambassadors for Orthros!

ABOUT THE AUTHOR

Vela Roth grew up with female-driven fantasy books and classic epics, then grew into romance novels. She set out to write stories that blend the rich worlds of fantasy with the passion of romance.

She has pursued a career in academia, worked as a web designer and book formatter, and stayed home as a full-time caregiver for her loved ones with severe illnesses. Writing through her own grief and trauma, she created the Blood Grace series, which now offers comfort to readers around the world.

She lives in a solar-powered writer's garret in the Southwestern United States, finding inspiration in the mountains and growing roses in the desert. Her feline familiar is a rescue cat named Milly with a missing fang and a big heart.

Vela loves hearing from readers and hopes you'll visit her at velaroth.com.